The Shadow of
THE EAGLE

Pete Davie

For my family

First Published 2024
Copyright © Pete Davie 2024

Cover Design Copyright © Nick Buchanan 2024

Interior layout and design by Nick Buchanan.
Email: n.buchanan@hotmail.co.uk

A CIP record of this book is available from the British Library.

ISBN: 9798398987096

Acknowledgements

Thanks to my wife Dawn for her support, patience and understanding.

Thanks to my brother, Keith for his proof reading, encouragement, and advice.

Thanks to my editor Nick Buchanan for his editing skills,
creative cover design and constant encouragement.

Important note

While some of the events and characters are based on historical
incidents and figures, this novel is entirely a work of fiction.

1

Cairo, Egypt, 1798

The perspiring kadi nervously shuffled into the shaded gardens of the sumptuous palace set resplendently on the banks of the Nile. He removed his tarboosh in deference to the man he had come to meet. He was accompanied by a dishevelled, exhausted, dust covered and equally anxious figure, a courier. Copious amounts of moisture, beads of sweat, trickled down the emissary's forehead, a cruel parody of the liquid he craved to quench his parched throat. Several fierce looking bodyguards were scattered around the grounds like sculpted statues. They were protecting the formidable Murad Bey, the joint Mameluke ruler of Egypt, who idled languidly on a chaise longue. He was surrounded by several attractive, young female concubines from his harem. He beckoned the obsequious official over with a calloused finger. The kadi charily took a few faltering steps towards the reposed figure.

"M-m-my Lord," he stammered, "another messenger has arrived from Alexandria bearing a despatch from governor El-Koraïm. He says the French army are now massing at the gates of Alexandria like a swarm of locusts. He has requested that you urgently send reinforcements. El-Koraïm warns that the French have arrived to seek justice and reparation for the French merchants whom, they allege, have been intimidated by the beys."

Murad Bey remained impassive. After a moment of silence, he slowly raised his head on which sat a jewel embossed turban, to reveal a face festooned with a glut of scars cascading down his countenance like tributaries of the mighty Nile that meandered close by, the welts souvenirs of his violent, warrior past, permanent badges of honour. Each one a gruesome reminder of a former victory on the battlefield that had propelled him inexorably towards his current, previously unopposed exalted position. He stared unerringly at the trembling kadi and fearful herald, unsettling them. He caressed his elongated mustachios and stroked his long, bushy beard then rose slowly and spoke in a low, guttural growl.

"Rest assured, we will exterminate the infidels. We will drive the French pigs back into the sea from whence they came."

He seized the gold, diamond-encrusted hilt of his scimitar, unsheathed the magnificent weapon and held it aloft. It glinted and glistened in the early evening rays of sunlight.

He brought the sword down in a sudden swift motion and sliced through a watermelon that sat amidst other fruit displayed on a large ceramic plate placed on an adjacent side table. The plate shattered into numerous fragments scattering the fruit and his favoured wives and concubines in the process, their kohl-darkened darting eyes, registering fear from the aperture of their niqabs. The Mameluke leader dismissed his startled female company with a flourish of his hand. They fled like a spooked flock of disturbed Egyptian geese. Menacingly he strode forward and thrust his intimidating face into the stricken official's countenance. "I will personally look forward to slicing open the infidels' heads, like watermelons!" he growled, emitting a garlic-laced breath from within the confines of his jungle-entwined, twisted mouth.

The stricken kadi shrewdly chose not to wipe his spittle-flecked features. He stuttered into a reply. "M-m-my lord, El-Koraïm has also sent you a gift."

The cowed emissary stepped forward, bowed then presented a small wooden box to a Mameluke bodyguard. Murad Bey gestured to his guard and the squat, muscle-bound soldier lifted the lid off the box. His head jerked back prompted by a foul stench before he unflinchingly pulled out the severed head of a French soldier.

Murad Bey laughed raucously and grasped the severed head. He too reacted to the putrid smell by screwing up his face in disgust and holding it at arm's length. Nevertheless, he continued to roar with laughter. Everyone else felt compelled to join in.

"Do you see? The watermelons are ripe. Extremely ripe! We shall gorge on them! The harvest shall begin! Hahahahaha! Every single Mameluke warrior will bring me back a hundred infidel watermelons! Hahahahaha!"

Murad Bey's demeanour suddenly changed from mirth to menace unsettling those around him. He snatched the missive from the trembling hand of the official, read it and then threw it violently to the ground, his fierce red eyes burning into the souls of those who stood before him.

"Ali, fetch my horse! I must go to Ibrahim Bey. We shall call a divan. Send word to Pasha Abu Bakr. Send word to every other bey, every emir, sheik and kadi along the Nile delta. And to the ulema. Let the ulema gather at the El-Azhar mosque and pray each day to Allah. Tell them to read each day from the Holy Book."

His fearsome eyes then rested on the courier. The frightened man trembled as the Mameluke leader loomed over him.

"M-m-my lord..."

"Silence! I do not like harbingers of bad news. Do you think you brought me good news, herald?"

The messenger, cowering even more from the imposing figure before him, tentatively nodded his agreement, his body shaking.

"Perhaps it is good news that we can again ride into battle and defeat a cursed enemy. Is the threat from these infidels merely another opportunity for us to demonstrate our God given potency and supremacy? Alas, do I welcome this incursion into our lands? Or do I believe it to be the work of Allah? A punishment perhaps?"

Murad Bey walked away from the envoy, who momentarily relaxed a little, then suddenly, without so much of a warning, the scar-faced Mameluke leader spun around and with one swish of his scimitar savagely decapitated his victim. The headless corpse sank to the floor. The severed head rolled and stopped in front of the cruel, heartless perpetrator. He looked down upon it with contempt. The kadi stood shaking, mouth agape, his blood-spattered face creased in terror. A pool of urine developed around his sandaled feet like floodwater seeping through floorboards and a wet patch was visible on his robes.

"Hahahahaha!" Murad Bey laughed heartily and jabbed a finger at the unfortunate, embarrassed official, this being the cue for his underlings to join in.

"Go, kadi! Spread the word that Murad Bey is fearless and that men piss themselves in his formidable presence. Hahahahaha! Death to the infidels! Hahahahaha!"

2

Liverpool, England. Present day.

Dr Jules Pollyanna Johnson stepped out of the University of Liverpool premises on Abercromby Square. The ornate Georgian square's gardens set before her, sandwiched by Oxford Street to the north and Cambridge Street to the south, had been constructed as a communal garden in the early 1800s for the surrounding townhouses and was named after General Sir Ralph Abercromby, a Scot who commanded the British forces in the Battle of Alexandria, Egypt in 1801 and who subsequently died due to wounds inflicted on the battlefield. Jules Johnson was all too aware of the name of the square's link to Egypt, being a Doctor of Egyptology at the University of Liverpool department of Archaeology, Classics and Egyptology, specialising in ancient texts. She was held in high esteem in the international world of Egyptology having achieved her PhD in the subject and having led teams in Egypt on digs to Saqqara and Thebes and other ancient sites along the banks of the Nile and beyond. She was also a bona fide trustee of the Egyptian Exploration Society based in London. She was just one of several fellow alumni who had studied at the University of Liverpool gaining BAs, MAs and PhDs who were trustee members of the Society. Indeed, the University of Liverpool Department of Archaeology, Classics and Egyptology held its own in the world of academia. Jules knew all about the history of Abercromby Square and its former residents, like the Gladstones, relatives of Prime Minister William Ewart Gladstone, who was born in Rodney Street a few streets away. Some of these relatives were active in the pernicious slave trade, like William's Scottish father and invested some of their wealth, like others, in the Liverpool to Manchester railway, the first inter-city railway in the world. Other former residents of the square played a role in the American Civil War in support of the Confederate South. History was her thing.

It was lunchtime and Jules was heading over to an express mini-market on Brownlow Hill, to grab a sandwich and coffee but first she had to retrieve a file from her car which was in a university car park on Mount Pleasant nearby. She skirted the square admiring its floral spring blooms, wrapping her university scarf tighter around her neck for there was still a significant chill to the air, despite it almost being the month of May. She paused at the Liverpool Heroes Memorial, a bronze statue depicting Captain Noel Godfrey Chavasse attending to a wounded soldier accompanied by a stretcher bearer from the Liverpool Scottish regiment. Chavasse was the only man to be awarded the Victoria Cross twice in World War I. She read the names of the other fifteen Liverpool-born recipients of the Victoria Cross

4

displayed on the memorial and made a mental note to research their feats of courage. It was fitting, she thought, that the Chavasse Statue should be situated at Abercromby Square because the Chavasse family had also resided there, in number 19.

Jules strolled down Oxford Street and stopped at the lights by the Medical Institution on the corner of Hope Street, a thoroughfare which symbolically linked Liverpool's two main Christian faiths by virtue of the city's two imposing cathedrals standing at either end as beacons of hope in a city now, thankfully, largely cleansed of its historic sectarian divisions. The Medical Institution, behind her, had existed on that site since 1779, and the structure, in its current form, housing a library, lecture hall and historic exhibits had stood since 1837. It was established on what was the former birthplace of William Roscoe, the slavery abolitionist and writer, one of the leading lights of Liverpool's colourful and at times, painful history. She crossed the junction along with other pedestrians and looked up at the towering iconic Metropolitan Catholic Cathedral Of Christ The King, or 'Paddy's Wigwam' as it was affectionately known. Built on the site of a former workhouse that gave refuge to up to five thousand destitute inmates, the spiritual rotunda shrouding them perhaps now gave succour to their tortured souls. Jules walked along Mount Pleasant to the car park and retrieved her file. Then she walked up to the junction with Brownlow Hill and crossed the road again checking the time on the clock tower of the red brick Victoria Building on the opposite side of the road. She paused on the other side to briefly chat to a student of hers and then continued to the convenience store situated just before the entrance to the vast Edward Lutyens designed cathedral crypt.

She was about to step over the threshold of the shop when her leisurely stroll in the midday sunshine was disturbed by a sudden screech of brakes behind her, followed by an audible, sickening thump, and screams. She turned around, horrified to see someone sprawled on the road in front of a black cab taxi. Everyone around had frozen momentarily in shock, then passers-by rushed to attend to the victim. Jules ran too, thinking it could be one of her students. This was a busy stretch of road with the university campus spread across several streets. Two or three people were attending to the victim already. One was on the phone to the emergency services whilst two others were directing traffic at the junction. Another attempted to console the distraught driver who had leapt out of the cab and was now pacing around with his head in his hands.

Jules was relieved to see that the victim was not a student, but she was still concerned to see that it was a homeless man she knew by sight who frequented the area. She had often bought him food, a coffee, or other things from the express supermarket. Practical items like a toothbrush and toothpaste or deodorant. She had also seen him in Abercromby Square Gardens, sitting on a bench by himself or standing, gazing forlornly at the Chavasse Memorial.

Jules crouched down beside him, her lanyard swinging annoyingly from her neck. She removed this over her tousled long red curls and placed it in her jacket pocket. The man was moaning in agony, barely conscious. He managed to half-open one eye

5

and caught a glimpse of someone with beautiful large, lustrous eyes and ethereal beauty hovering over him. An angel perhaps? Then he slipped into unconsciousness. His left leg looked fractured. There were abrasions on his bloodied face. His arm twisted beneath him. His scuffed and tattered trainers lay ten foot in front of him having been jettisoned by the impact. Jules had undertaken first aid training years ago when an accident had occurred involving one of her colleagues on an archaeological dig in Egypt. She had looked on helpless when the assistant had broken her arm in the middle of nowhere in the desert. From that moment on she had decided to get some sort of medical training. She immediately responded to the homeless man's unconscious state, checking his airway was not blocked, then rolling him carefully over onto his side into the recovery position with the help of another woman. She gently placed a coat donated by someone under the unkempt bearded man's head and then covered him with her own, despite the man's musty smell. The ambulance, which seemed to take an eternity, arrived within fifteen minutes followed by a police car. The injured man was finally despatched to A&E.

3

Jules managed to retrieve her coat. She shook it and, still trembling, returned to the shop. Her appetite had diminished and so she only bought an americano to go. Grasping it with two hands she tried to get some warmth back into her chilled body. On her return, she crossed the junctions more cautiously than before and proceeded to the Garstang Museum of Archaeology, the entrance to which was located around the back of Abercromby Square. She was to carry out research for a talk she was due to give at the Athenaeum Club in the city in a few days' time. She sat in reception and drank her coffee trying to compose herself. The image of the homeless man's injuries popped up in her thoughts. She shuddered. The pattern of events played over in her mind anew. The ominous screech of brakes followed immediately by the sickening thump of the impact. Another frisson rippled down her spine.

She was no stranger to pain herself though, being the victim of her current partner Richard. Her previous marriage to David had failed, their split due in part to her frequent trips abroad. The organisers of these field trips and conferences insisted on her attendance owing to her knowledge, highly valued opinion and professional expertise. The other reason was her husband's infidelities. Being a handsome lecturer of History, or 'lecherer' of History, as she dubbed him, David, with time on his hands, had little difficulty attracting the attention of young female undergraduates. She had loved her husband, who had now emigrated to Australia with his younger girlfriend. Fortunately, Jules and David did not have any children. She ended up on the rebound with the 'charming' Richard Reeves whom she had met at a cheese and wine party charity fundraiser. Her best friend Penny Carter, Managing Director at the World Museum in Liverpool had dragged her over to meet this suave, debonair, handsome, brown-eyed, black-haired, well groomed 'dish', as Penny called him, after she had noticed him eyeing up Jules. Penny, no great admirer of David because of his womanising, thought the sun shone out of Richard's backside feeling a warmth for him as if she were back in the Caribbean, home of her antecedents, sunning herself.

At first, Richard had treated Jules like a princess, lavishing gifts on her; flowers, perfume and jewellery. She fell for him but then, gradually, he turned, into a monster. He became abusive, controlling, coercive. He had alienated her family and become jealous of her friends. He began to hit her. Punching her on her thighs or arms or other parts of the body that she could conceal. Torturing her with needles or cigarette burns. She was under his spell. He was a Svengali. Yet, disturbingly, she remained with him, for some perverse reason. He could still, on occasions, show the good side of his character. Be loving and gentle and romantic but then something innocuous, trivial, would occur which would make him flip and he would display the depraved characteristics of a sadist, his nasty alter ego emerging from some dark place in his soul. He always convinced her that she was in the wrong, citing her failed marriage to David as her fault and her fault only. This she believed in earnest. Everything was her fault. But being a professional woman, a respected woman whom others aspired to be like, she was reluctant to reveal, in her own eyes, this weak, feckless side of her character. Someone who could not stand up to a bully and who cowered from his punches and rages and insults, all designed to control her and demean her. She had well and truly been gaslighted. Her one saving grace was her job. Richard wanted her to quit so he could break that strong bond she had with her fellow university colleagues. He wanted to isolate her even more. But she loved her job more than anything else. She was hanging in there by the skin of her teeth. Her colleagues and friends had started to notice though, changes in her demeanour but none of them would guess it was to do with her relationship to Richard who superficially seemed perfect. Young, handsome, reasonably wealthy, caring and loving. Often creating public displays of affection by presenting floral bouquets or expensive looking trinkets to her in front of her friends. She was the woman who seemed to have everything. Attractive, highly intelligent, fantastic career, good looking partner. However, with regard to Richard, it was all a charade.

Jules was snapped out of her trance by someone standing over her. She looked up sharply from her coffee cup and found herself staring at a rotund potbelly. She could see a navel protruding out of a gap between the straining buttons of a white shirt. The paunch belonged to Jimmy the security guard.

"Are you alright luv?" Jimmy asked, scratching his bald pate.

"Oh, hi Jimmy. Just about. There was an accident on the road. A homeless guy got knocked down by a taxi. I attended to him and I'm just a little shaken up. He looked in a bad way. Poor fella."

"I wondered why you looked a bit pasty faced."

Jules raised herself up slowly, with Jimmy uncomfortably invading her personal space. The security guard shuffled back a few paces. She placed her empty cup in a bin.

"Oh, I'm alright Jimmy. Now, you'll have to excuse me I've some research to do."

She stepped towards the doors of the museum entrance, but Jimmy blocked her path.

"Sorry Dr Johnson. You're not allowed in."

The erudite Doctor of Egyptology looked perplexed.

"You've got no I.D."

"Oh!" Jules reacted reaching into her jacket pocket. "I put my pass in my pocket when I was assisting the homeless guy."

"I'm just joshing with you," the security guard laughed. He moved aside.

"What are you like Jimmy?" she said giving him a mock smile. She whacked him with her folder in the midriff. The security guard flinched and grunted, not expecting it. Recovering his composure, he flashed a grin at Jules, and then held the door open for her, taking the opportunity to admire her curves as she entered the room.

"Right!" she said emphatically. "Let's get to it. Focus."

Jimmy could be a pain, but he always made her laugh. He cheered up her day. He was a typical Scouser. He'd call her a 'woolyback' because she was from Irby on the Wirral. Anyone not from Liverpool was a 'wool', despite her telling him that both her parents were Scouse. Dad from Anfield, mother from Childwall. Her mother and father now ran a *gîte* in the Charentes in France. She loved to visit when she could. She longed to be there, sat under the shade of the mimosa tree having *petit-déjeuner*; *croissants, pains aux raisins, café au lait* in the spacious grounds amongst the people she loved and the people who loved her. It was especially fun when her sister Jane turned up from Brussels with her husband Marc and their two young children.

4

Qasr Ibrim, an Egyptian archaeological site in Lower Nubia, was the focus for the academic's talk for the Athenaeum. She had worked on the site six months ago for the University and the Egyptian Exploration Society using her epigraphical skills to read inscriptions on stone stelae located there. Being university open day, a small group of people emerged from a research room she was heading for. Mums and dads or guardians accompanying teenagers, all interested in what the faculty had to offer. Guiding the party was Randip Singh Sohal, her colleague and friend from the Faculty of Archaeology. Randip's expertise lay in Ancient Indian History and Oriental Studies. Randip or Randy as she called him, was a tall, handsome Sikh but he preferred not to wear a turban and he was clean shaven. He wore his jet-black hair in a ponytail. The last time he wore a turban was on his wedding day when he had married his beautiful Hindu wife Salena. His side of the family failed to turn up for the wedding ceremony and the subsequent celebrations because they did not approve of him marrying a Hindu woman. His only contact with his family was with his maternal grandmother and an uncle. He had not seen his brothers and sisters for years and only on his father's death bed did his father meet his grandson, little Vihan. But still, his father refused to see Salena, his wife. He did not relent, sadly. He did not know what he had missed for Salena was a vivacious, bubbly and warm, caring woman and a loving mother.

"Hi Jules," he called.

"Hello Randy, are these fine young men and women some of our potential future undergraduates?" Jules said addressing the gathering.

"And not so young," a middle-aged man shouted out from the rear of the group. Everyone laughed.

"Well, I hope you've all been impressed so far by the campus facilities."

They all nodded. "Have you all seen the Garstang Mummy?" Jules continued.

"Yes. Amazing. Incredible," were the utterances of the group.

"Well, enjoy the rest of your day."

"Only two more tours to do," Randy whispered to Jules. "Thank God."

The procession made its way to the exit. Jules entered the research facility and settled down to her task of sourcing artefacts for her talk.

5

After a day of research, lectures and seminars Jules rushed back to the apartment she shared with Richard. The spring sunshine had dissipated, and it was now overcast and there was a chill wind blowing in from the Mersey. Her apartment block, Wapping Quay, stood close to the banks of the river. It was a former 19th century dock warehouse.

Sometimes she walked to and from the university. She particularly enjoyed strolling through the sunken St. James's Cemetery Gardens amidst the flowers, shrubs and headstones where she was able to view the sealed entrances of the catacombs hewn out of the sandstone. The cemetery, a former quarry, thought to be based on the famous Père-Lachaise cemetery in Paris, sat in a hollow, under the shadow of the looming Anglican Cathedral impressively perched on St James' Mount. She would then emerge from the Gardens by the Cathedral entrance and proceed along Hope Street oft times remembering the song lyrics, 'If you want a cathedral, we've got one to spare, in my Liverpool home' as she looked down along the thoroughfare towards Paddy's Wigwam at the far end. Sometimes, if she had time, she would saunter along historic Rodney Street adorned with impressive Georgian terraces, once home to several notable residents like Nicholas Monsarrat, author of 'The Cruel Sea', Brian Epstein, a familiar name for Beatles aficionados and William Ewart Gladstone, Prime Minister of Great Britain in the 19th century, on four separate occasions. This time however, she had taken her Range Rover Evoque mindful of her need to transport the artefacts and documents she needed for her talk that evening at the Athenaeum Club. 'What mood would Richard be in?' she thought. Sometimes he was kind, calm and reasonable. Other times he would be angry and aggressive. It was this unpredictability that made her anxious. Never knowing what she was coming home to. It was all part of his strategy to control and subdue her. To strike fear into her. If he was continually violent, then the decision to leave him would be easier. She was confused. As it happened, she arrived home first. It was going to be a quick ready meal out of the freezer for both of them that evening due to her commitments. She placed her frozen meal in the microwave and ten minutes later it pinged. At the same time a key turned in the lock. 'Richard's back.' He entered. He had been drinking. She tried to be nice to him kissing him on the lips.

"Have you had a nice day?" she asked. No response. She smiled hesitantly, took the steaming meal out of the microwave with a tea towel and placed it on a tray. Richard just stared. Cold, icy, vacant. He looked at the ping meal. Then he stared at Jules contemptuously. 'It's coming...'

"Give me that!" he snarled. Richard snatched the meal from the tray burning his hands in the process.

11

"Shit!" he cursed. He dropped it back on the tray, his mood darkening even more. "I don't want this crap! I want proper food!"

Suddenly, and without warning, he slammed the hot carton of food and all its contents onto Jules's head.

"No!" she screamed in vain, as she put her hand up to protect herself.

The burning pain shot through her scalp, the hot pot contents and gravy transforming her beautiful red hair into a dark, slimy, brown mess. She staggered back a few paces, humiliated. She turned away from him sobbing. He laughed.

"Why?" she uttered, between sobs. "Why?"

Before she could say anything more, he punched her violently in the back of the head twice and punched her in the kidneys for good measure. Jules collapsed to the floor. Richard then staggered over to the settee and reaching for the remote control, put the TV on and started watching a film in silence. Jules fled to the bedroom. She locked the door, wincing at the excruciating pain in her back and head. She undressed gingerly and stepped into the shower in the en suite bathroom, her scalded scalp stinging from the burns, the warm water and fragrant shampoo though washing away the odour and remains of the wasted meal, and her tears. Hopefully, she prayed, no visible sign would remain of the assault, and she could still manage her presentation at the Athenaeum. After showering, she crept furtively out of the bedroom wrapped in a towel, to retrieve the lipstick in her bag, still shaking. Richard had fallen asleep on the settee and was snoring heavily. She was safe, for now. She returned to the bedroom and dropped the wet towel to the floor and stood in front of her mirror. She half-turned her lithe, naked body to examine the purply red bruise on her back and cringed again when she saw it. She sat on a chair and gently brushed her hair back, lowering her head to verify that the swelling caused by the punches and burns on her stinging scalp were not discernible. She gazed at the forlorn image sat in front of her, with tears welling up. Jules recalled a story that her grandmother Evelyn had told her, about her maternal great-grandmother Molly when she was a child in Victorian Liverpool. Molly's mother would take her and the rest of her siblings out before their father was due to return home from the pub, for their own safety. The young child was pushed in her pram around the streets of Anfield, the family biding their time, giving their father time to fall into a drunken slumber on his return. Only then would they creep home. Never did Jules imagine that she would be a victim of domestic violence too. How much longer, she thought, could she put up with this coercive relationship, the intimidation, the brutality, the humiliation?

6

Jules reached the Athenaeum by 7.30pm, thirty minutes before her talk was to take place. The private members club was founded in 1797 by slavery abolitionists, professionals, merchants and political radicals. Men who were at the forefront of Liverpool society of the time and within its library there was amassed an abundance of valuable books, reference works, maps and navigation charts including the collection from one of its founding fathers, abolitionist William Roscoe. The current premises, located near to the Blue Coat Chambers, one of Liverpool's oldest buildings, had housed the club since the 1920s. Jules was a member of the club and so she was able to get access to one of the world's finest private literary collections. She was greeted by the chairman and led into the Committee Room. It was packed to the rafters. She busied herself organising her presentation whilst the audience chatted. She unconsciously fingered the burn on her head from time to time. She recognised many of the faces. When she was ready, she delivered an interesting professional lecture on Qasr Ibrim and her experiences in Egypt, making full use of her resources, a video screen and artefacts, to enhance the experience.

The talk, ending with a Q and A, drew generous applause and after packing up her items she joined others at the bar where she encountered an acquaintance, Ibrahim Shaqtar, who worked for the Abdullah Quilliam Society. The society was named after a Victorian white English convert to Islam, William Henry Quilliam, who had opened Britain's first ever mosque in Liverpool in 1887.

"Good evening, Jules. What a fabulous talk. I enjoyed it immensely."

"Thank you, Ibrahim. It's nice to have some feedback. Not too boring?"

"Not at all. Hey, let me introduce you to someone."

As Ibrahim made his way through the scrum to the bar, Jules took the opportunity of snatching a champagne flute from a tray held by a waitress. Someone in a rush carelessly brushed past her banging into her bruised kidney. She nearly dropped her drink. She winced in pain but quickly gathered her composure. Ibrahim returned dragging someone through the throng.

"May I introduce you to Mr Edwin Calder. Edwin, meet Dr Julia 'Jules' Johnson B.A., M.A., PhD, blah, blah, blah."

Jules held out her hand and the grey-haired gentleman, in his early fifties, took it gently and kissed it.

"Ah, old school I see," Jules said.

Jules did not mind the over familiar show of affection after what she had experienced earlier.

"*Enchanté,*" he replied.

"Edwin is from the Society of Antiquaries," Ibrahim said. "I take it you two have never met?"

13

"No, but I've heard so much about you Dr Johnson from some of my colleagues in the Egypt Exploration Society and the Society of Antiquaries."

"Oh, I'm a member of both but I haven't seen you there at any of their functions."

"No, but there's a good reason for that because I only recently joined, a few months ago. I've been living in Aigues-Mortes, in the south of France, running an antiques business there for the last twenty years."

"Aigues-Mortes? I love that place! I've been there many times. The family used to holiday in France every year. Mum and dad still live there. They own a *gîte*. Have you ever been to Aigues-Mortes, Ibrahim?"

"No, what's so special about it? Edwin, you tell me."

"It's a medieval walled town, in the Camargue, south of Nîmes, on the coast."

"Similar to Carcassonne but smaller," Jules added.

"Oh, right, of course, I know of Carcassonne, but I've never been there either."

"Do you know what my favourite place is in Aigues-Mortes?" Jules said excitedly. "*La Cure Gourmande*."

"Hey! Mine too Dr Johnson!"

"Er, what exactly is *La Cure Gourmande*?"

"It's a *confiserie*, Ibrahim. A sweet shop," Edwin replied.

"A sweet shop? Hold on, you two aficionados of history go to an ancient medieval walled town and your favourite place is a sweet shop?"

The three of them laughed.

"It's a special sweet shop though," Jules continued. "It's like an old-fashioned sweet shop crammed with a wonderful array of ostentatiously displayed confectionery of all flavours, colours and shapes."

"Shame on you two! Especially you Julia Johnson, being an archaeologist."

They laughed again until they were interrupted by Penny, Julia's friend.

"Hello, how are we all?"

"Oh, hi Penny. This is my friend Penny Carter, Managing Director at Liverpool Museum, and fellow archaeologist. Penny, meet Ibrahim Shaqtar from the Quilliam Society."

"We've met before. Hello again Penny."

"Hi Ibrahim."

"And this is Mr Edwin Calder, he's an antiques dealer and fellow of the Society of Antiquaries in London."

"*Enchanté* Ms Carter."

Again, Edwin held Penny's outstretched hand and kissed it. Penny chuckled.

"What soft hands you've got Ms Carter."

"Are you kidding? These are archaeologist's hands! Rough as a bear's a-"

"That's enough Penny," Jules interjected, laughing.

Penny guffawed and slapped Jules on the back, right on her bruised kidney.

"Ouch!" Jules cried.

"Oh, what's up Jules? Sorry, did I hurt you?"

"I have a bruise on my back. I slipped over in the shower this evening."

"Sorry hun. Mr Calder, what brings you all the way up to Liverpool?"

14

"I deal mainly in religious artefacts, so I'm interested in anything ecclesiastical, from any religion, but of course, I sell any sort of antiques on my premises in Aigues-Mortes."

"Aigues-Mortes? The south of France. I'm impressed. Love it," Penny said.

"I read somewhere about Liverpool having the first mosque in Britain which was very intriguing and so I contacted the Quilliam Society and Ibrahim kindly invited me up to Liverpool."

"I did indeed. You're very welcome, Edwin."

"Ibrahim has been my guide for a few days, not only telling me about Liverpool's Islamic cultural origins, but he's also taken me to see the Princes Road Synagogue and the magnificent Greek Orthodox Church opposite it. Wonderful!"

"Well, there certainly is plenty of religious history on Merseyside to discover. Some good, some bad. But if you want to see something spectacular come to my church, Christchurch in Toxteth Park for a little bit of gospel inspiration."

"Ah, thanks for the invite, Ms Carter but I'm back down to London tomorrow morning."

"Well, nice to meet you. Jules, everyone wants to have a chat with you so I'm afraid I'll have to whisk you away from these gentlemen and we'll continue mingling."

Penny dragged Jules away, the latter mouthing apologies as she went. It was going to be a busy evening, but Jules relished every minute of it. She was amongst like-minded friends.

7

A few months later, mid-July, it was university graduation day. Graduation ceremonies had been taking place at the Philharmonic Hall, and the University campus and surrounding areas were awash with ecstatic graduates and their loved ones. They watched as mortarboards were gleefully launched into the air with reckless abandon by the fully fledged alumni. Jules, who was present, bizarrely imagined herself producing a shotgun from her robes and blasting away at the square caps as if on an academic clay pigeon shoot. Young men and women were hugging each other, draped in their academic subfusc of black gowns with silk sashes and hoods of various colours. Jules and her colleagues were happy to see their former students reaping the rewards of their studies in Egyptology, Archaeology, the Classics, Ancient History, Anthropology, and other disciplines. It was a special day for all. The Philharmonic Dining Rooms, the popular ornate Victorian pub adorned with impressive carvings and mosaics opposite the venue, was rammed with celebrating families. Once they had socialised with the graduates and their families outside the hall Jules and her colleagues had arranged to meet in Peter Kavanagh's pub tucked away on the fringe of the Georgian Quarter. Peter Kavanagh's, built in 1844 was full of peculiar curiosities and was a hidden gem. She stayed there until 7pm, when most of her friends decided to leave. She strolled along Catharine Street with Randy in the warm evening sunshine both admiring St Brides Church and the elegant Georgian terraces that gracefully defined the area. Liverpool had 1,150 listed buildings, 28 of which were Grade I. A fact Jules had regurgitated many a time whenever she saw the need to defend or promote the city from the negative stereotypical point of view espoused by certain elements of the national press and in her role as a 'Stop the Rot' campaigner. They paused further along the road and bade farewell to each other since Randy lived nearby in an elegant Georgian terraced house in Falkner Street. The street was now a regular location for international and domestic TV and film crews filming period pieces. Jules headed towards Abercromby Square to retrieve the bag she had left at the faculty. She'd arranged to meet Richard for a lift home since she'd had a couple of glasses of rosé. She turned into the square and was surprised and overjoyed to see the homeless man who had been in the road accident sitting on a bench in the square. She approached him.

"Hi! I'm so glad to see that you're ok after your accident. I hadn't heard anything."

The man looked up and smiled. He looked years younger. It surprised Jules how young he was. About early to mid-30s she reckoned. His brown hair had been cut in a short to medium pompadour style and his blue laughing eyes twinkled. His unkempt beard and straggly moustache were gone, replaced by a five o'clock shadow that complemented his swarthy, masculine complexion. Jules thought, in fact, that he was strikingly handsome, so much that her heart missed a beat.

"I was there when you got knocked over. I came to help you, but I couldn't do much," she rasped, slightly flushed.

The man had a flashback to that terrible day. He remembered the face. The beautiful, angelic countenance. It belonged to her. The stunning woman who now stood in front of him. Although he had seen her often before and been a recipient of her generosity, at the time, he couldn't quite figure out whose face he had seen. He thought he had been hallucinating but this confirmed that it was not just a dream. She really had come to his assistance and comforted him.

"I'm Jules Johnson, by the way. What's your name?"

"Paul," the man said quietly. "Paul De Vere."

"That's sounds like a French name to me. You're not from France, are you?"

"No, born and bred in Liverpool."

He smiled again. It was rather a melancholic smile this time. This man, she thought, had a lot to hide. Something searingly painful ached deep within in.

"How's the leg?"

"It's fine now. Thanks. I was in hospital for seven weeks. I had a fractured elbow as well. Thanks a lot for coming to my assistance and for the numerous occasions you've bought me a sandwich and coffee."

Jules sat down on the bench next to him, her feet aching from her kitten heels.

"I'm indebted to people like you who've helped me. I feel the need to pay that debt back now. Curiously that accident was a turning point. An epiphany of sorts. I couldn't go on like I was."

"Are you still homeless?"

"I'm in a hostel at the moment, but I'm not keen. It's full of drunks and druggies some of whom can be violent at times."

Jules was surprised about the way he distanced himself from the alcoholics and drug addicts and was about to ask him more about how he came to be on the streets when a car screeched to the halt outside the faculty. She looked behind her anxiously. It was Richard. She instinctively got up.

"Nice to meet you Paul. Take care. My lift is here."

She rose from the bench. Paul observed the look of concern etched on Jules' face. She traipsed over to the car, her heels in her hand. The driver had already got out and was ringing the bell on the faculty. He had not noticed her sitting in the gardens. Richard looked around after getting no answer and spotted Jules approaching. He strode towards her, looking angry and grabbed her forcefully by the wrist, squeezing it tightly to inflict pain.

"Ouch," she whimpered in pain.

"Get in the damned car," he seethed between gritted teeth.

"No, wait, I have to get my bag. It's in the faculty."

"Go on then. Quick! I'm meeting the lads for a pint in half an hour."

Jules rushed to the door, opened it up and went inside to fetch her bag. She came out immediately. She looked fearful and embarrassed, head down. She got in the car, and it sped off immediately. Richard glanced towards Paul giving him a look of real contempt as if he were shit on his shoe. Paul stared back, vexed by the manner in which the pleasant, engaging, beautiful redhead had been treated.

Over the last few months Jules had spent some time away from Richard. She had been away on a field trip for three weeks, working at the ancient site of Göbekli Tepe. She'd also had a week's holiday in France at the *gîte* alone with her parents whilst Richard was on a business trip to Canada. Jules's mother had taken an instinctive instant dislike to Richard when they first met. There was something about him, Diana had said to her daughter. But her father Geoff had rejected this insinuation out of hand and on the contrary found him to be a decent chap. At that stage, the dark side of his character had not emerged. Diana had detected something was not right with her daughter during that week of repose, but she could not extract anything out of Jules. Fortunately, Richard was in such a hurry to meet his friends that she escaped any more punishment until later that evening, when, on his return, he turned violent attacking her without warning, punching her in the eye and smashing her head against the bedside cabinet, then drunkenly raping her before falling asleep leaving her sobbing and in pain. On this occasion though, his normally carefully planned strategy of concealing his dirty work had been compromised by his inebriated state. A crucial error.

8

Egypt, 1798

N apoleon Bonaparte and his entourage swept into a room in the house the diminutive general had requisitioned for his temporary headquarters. Sergeant Pierre Cousseau of the Grenadier Guards, 61st*Demi-Brigade*, stood to attention and saluted.

"*Mon général*, permission to speak sir," Cousseau said. "All thirteen soldiers captured by the Bedouin have been rescued. We have one of them with us."

"Bring him in," ordered the charismatic Corsican.

The French soldier was helped into the room, supported by two of his comrades. He was dishevelled, covered in dust, his uniform in tatters.

"*Asseyez vous. Prenez une verre.*" The private sat down and took a much-needed gulp of water.

"Tell me, citizen soldier, how did the Bedouin treat you?"

"Like animals, *mon général. Non*, they are the animals. They beat us and tortured us. And, and…"

"Spit it out man," one of Napoleon's *aides-de-camp* growled.

"*On…On…On m'a violé! On m'a violé!*" The distraught private burst into tears.

"*Vous êtes un nigaud, citoyen!* A blockhead!" Napoleon shouted unsympathetically. "Don't you realise this was the least offensive thing that could have happened to you? You could have had an iron rod inserted up your *cul* and be left stranded in the sweltering heat of the desert to die or had your neck sliced from ear to ear and been left to bleed to death at the mercy of the jackals. It was your own fault for being a straggler and not keeping up with the main column. Be grateful it was only *un zizi* up your backside and not that iron rod!"

Napoleon's whole entourage laughed. The private whimpered.

"Get some rest soldier," the general advised. "Take him away."

The humiliated, sobbing victim was escorted out. Sergeant Cousseau led the way leaving the French leader to address his commanders.

"Generals, you have your orders. I reiterate, increase the patrols out of Alexandria, reconnoitre as far as Rosetta and Damanhur. Keep probing. Once we've extended our influence in the vicinity, we can then concentrate on advancing towards Cairo."

9

Sergeant Cousseau, of the *Armée de l'Orient* was a veteran, like many in his division, of the Italian campaign. On arrival in Egypt the tall chestnut-haired, handsome grenadier had followed orders like the good soldier he was, encouraging and urging his comrades on through the desert heat to carry out their operations. Privately though, now a week into the campaign, he was cursing Napoleon under his breath, having brought them to such an infernal and medieval place. He was as bewildered as anyone with the customs and practices of the people of this unfamiliar and contrasting land having witnessed one strange and shocking event. On departing Alexandria, Cousseau and his company had been advancing towards Cairo with the bulk of the land forces when a commotion erupted in a small, isolated village. A woman suffering from the plague, holding a baby in her arms, was seen being dragged to a cemetery by a baying mob. The enraged French soldiers watched on in horror and astonishment as she and her baby were buried alive. The angry sergeant and others felt the urge to intervene, but they were constrained by the orders of their superiors who were following Napoleon's instruction that the local inhabitants' mores should not be interfered with. A few days later, with the main body of troops bivouacked, Cousseau was leading his platoon on a reconnaissance patrol. Approaching another village, they came across another wailing woman also carrying a baby, alone, in the blistering heat of the barren desert. Her face was smeared in blood. She stumbled towards the soldiers.

"Help me! Help me!" she implored. "Help my baby. Save him. Please! I beg you!" The distraught mother sank to her knees.

Sergeant Cousseau ordered his subordinates to give the exhausted woman food and water.

"Here take this," private Givray said, offering his canteen to the woman. She slaked her thirst then held the bottle to her bawling baby's mouth.

"What's happened woman?" Cousseau asked. "Who's done this to you?"

A solitary figure appeared from the direction of the village walking hurriedly towards them. The terrified look on the mother's face provided the sergeant with his answer. The man approached in an agitated manner, remonstrating with and berating the troops for caring for the woman.

"Ashraf, what's he saying?"

The Arab interpreter embedded with the patrol began to translate. "He claims to be the woman's husband, sir. But he's saying that he is not the father of the baby and therefore the reason for his ire is apparent.

"Givray, try and calm him down, man!"

"I'm trying Sergeant. Only the butt of my musket will suffice, I reckon."

The screaming woman cowered behind Givray and Ashraf. The soldier raised his gun in a threatening manner to discourage the animated man who babbled incoherently, throwing his arms up wildly in gesture. His wife continued to shriek. The sweat poured from Givray's streaked face. The burning sun unrelenting. He wiped his brow with his sleeve. The irate husband suddenly side-stepped Givray, unexpectedly whipping out a concealed dagger. He lunged at the terrified woman plunging the knife into her jugular twice over with frightening speed. She screamed anew, a blood curdling, constant screech this time. The blood spurted from her wounds. It drenched the wailing baby clutched in her arms. Her legs buckled. Givray raised his musket, aiming it at the attacker's back. He dithered, compromised by the proximity of the woman and her baby. Ashraf, rooted to the spot, was aghast. Undeterred, the slaughter continued, the husband frenziedly stabbing the victim in her chest. Cousseau and others surged towards the killer but were unable to prevent him ripping the crying child from her mother's grasp and throwing it violently to the stony ground, killing it instantly. Givray's rifle butt crashed down on the murderer's skull. The man fell to the ground.

"Seize him!" the shocked sergeant bellowed. Givray and Clement, another private, grabbed the child killer and wrenched him to his feet. The demented peasant moaned but jabbered on incessantly. The anxious sergeant smoothed his sand-flecked moustache down.

"What's he saying now? Tell me man!" he said to the interpreter.

Ashraf translated the diatribe.

"He's saying that he cannot be considered evil for his actions. He feels the only thing he has done wrong is to thwart the will of Allah."

"But he has just callously murdered his wife and a baby!" Cousseau responded, incredulously. "That, in my eyes, is an evil act, would you not agree?"

"Let me explain, effendi," Ashraf said. "If the woman had survived alone with the baby for forty days and forty nights in the wilderness, she would perhaps have been taken in by someone charitable and looked after. That would have been Allah's will, but the husband did not allow for that scenario to happen. He did not allow her this period of grace. He only regrets this, disrespecting Allah, not the slaughter of his wife and the baby."

"*Mon Dieu!* What vile and bewildering logic exists in this land! This coward has perpetrated a malevolent act in front of my very own eyes that deserves swift justice and retribution. To hell with Napoleon's orders. Givray, run him through."

Givray did not hesitate. He skewered the murderer with his bayonet through the heart and then between the eyes, ignoring the screams. The patrol buried the woman and baby but left the husband's corpse to the vultures, then moved on. The platoon pressed on, reconnoitring the villages in the area in the searing, literally blinding heat, returning later to the main camp. The horrific events of the morning playing on the men's minds.

Over the coming days of the army's advance south, the harsh climate began to take its toll on the invaders. Some soldiers were afflicted by an eye infection, diagnosed subsequently as ophthalmia, and could barely see. Others overcome by heat and exhaustion, weighed down by their heavy kit and unsuitable uniforms and fuelled by the relentless march through the oppressive heat of the desert, collapsed, and were left where they fell. Cousseau continued to give assistance and encouragement to his men where he could but was suffering just as much. His men were staggering over the unforgiving terrain largely in silence, many praying for deliverance. A soldier cried out.

"*Regardez la rivière Nil!*" Lousson croaked, through his sore, cracked lips.

The young private and some of the other troopers broke ranks and ran, several falling, their weak legs unable to hold them up. Cousseau and the others decided to run too. Stumbling towards the water course, jettisoning their knapsacks and weapons, cheering wildly, they suddenly all stopped further on. The mighty river had disappeared before their disbelieving eyes. It was their first experience of a mirage. The deception was too much for some of the delirious, dehydrated men who took their own lives, amongst them Lousson who snatched a pistol from Lieutenant Cros's belt and blew his brains out. Cousseau and the rest of the disorientated, bedraggled French column eventually reached their destination, streaming into the town of El Rahmaniyah situated on the banks of the Nile. As soon as the exhausted, dehydrated and sunburnt sergeant reached the river, he, like most of his companions, plunged into the reviving waters to refresh himself. He lay there on his back amidst the hordes of ecstatic, relieved soldiers and watched as feluccas, crewed by bemused and frightened Egyptians, glided up and down the waterway. Indignant cranes took to the skies and river buffalo fled for their lives on the opposite bank. As the day wore on, the scene was repeated several times over when other divisions arrived. Cousseau and his subordinates gorged on melons and other abundant fruit growing in the vicinity whilst others could think of nothing but sleep. Those who gorged on the fruit soon regretted it, clutching their bellies and suffering the effects of diarrhoea. Just two days later some of those afflicted soldiers found themselves facing the enemy at Shubra Khit, a village a few miles to the south. In the skirmish that took place, a vanguard of Mameluke cavalry was repulsed by a formation of *tirailleur* squares. Fortunately for Cousseau and his unit, they were held in reserve and so the only battle he experienced that day was with his bowels.

Napoleon's Army of the Orient, 25,000 strong, continued their push to the capital. After an arduous slog in the scorching heat more men were carelessly lost through suicide, illness, and heatstroke before the battalions arrived at Embaba. The parched, starving, exhausted troops repeated the process of bathing in the river and foraging for food, some risking the debilitating effects of diarrhoea again by gorging on fruit. Cousseau, this time, was careful what he ate. It was not long before the call to arms was made, and the sergeant lined up with thousands of other combatants in defensive squares and marched towards Cairo. He could see in the distance, across the Nile, the walled fortifications of the city built by the great Saladin. Domes and mosques and even church spires loomed above the snarl of streets. Then, in the lung-busting, furnace-like heat Pierre set eyes on the shimmering distant pyramids of Giza rising out of the flat, arid plain to the east, the Great Pyramid of Khufu dominating. Then his eyes focused on another curious spectacle. Something gleaming and glittering amidst the haze. Another mirage? As his square marched forward, the sergeant's heart started to beat faster, the sweat poured down his streaked and sand-covered, sunburnt face. He suddenly realised what the cause of the glinting effect was. Adrenalin surged through his aching body as if he had been bitten by a venomous desert horned viper. It was an arc of steel he could see, stretching from the pyramids to the river, consisting of Murad Bey's massive Mameluke led army of mounted warriors, foot soldiers and *fellahin*, peasants. Finally, the French army was about to confront the enemy in earnest. A wave of relief and optimism surged through the ranks and the French soldiers cheered heartily.

"*Les ânes, au milieu!*" came the cry from a captain.

The fusiliers and grenadiers making up the bulk of the square laughed wholeheartedly. *Les ânes*, the 'donkeys', were Napoleon's '*savants*'. Highly intelligent men, scholars, educated in a variety of disciplines. There were artists, scientists, botanists, engineers, astronomers and the like amidst their ranks. Amongst these scholars stood the bespectacled slight, sandy-haired figure of Antoine Demeraux. He grimaced on hearing the insulting remark, as did the other affronted *savants*, who were then subjected to the sounds of braying by the phalanx of soldiers surrounding them. He begged to differ about who exactly were the donkeys. Antoine and his fellow learned colleagues positioned themselves in the middle of the formidable square ironically with the pack animals. They held pistols and other weapons to protect themselves from the enemy in case the square was overrun. Antoine was praying that he would not have to use his weapon in anger. Pierre Cousseau let a smile ripple across his face when he heard his fellow soldiers ribbing the intellectuals. He and Antoine were old friends having been brought up in the same town in the Languedoc. They had been reacquainted on the long voyage from France when in the citadel of Valletta. The French had invaded Malta en route to Egypt and the rulers of that isle, the Knights Of Malta, descendants of the Crusaders, were captured and imprisoned. The fleet transporting the army had docked in Valletta and although they had arrived on separate ships the two old friends had met at the port by chance.

"*Regardez!*" went up a cry.

Movement was spotted amongst the vast ranks of the enemy eliciting a wave of euphoria and a sense of anticipation through the squares. Murad Bey and some of his officers galloped wildly along the broad dazzling array of Mameluke cavalry who bristled with weapons - scimitars, daggers, pistols, carbines and *djerids*, their short spears. They were whipping up their fighters in a frenzy of emotion. At the rear of this line thousands upon thousands of foot soldiers and attendants, emirs and beys and the local *fellahin*, pressed into service, whooped and chanted. Swords and spears rapped out a deafening rhythm on shields whilst gaping onlookers looked on in anticipation of a murderous, blood-letting spectacle.

It wasn't long before the 'Battle of The Pyramids' began. A cohort of Mameluke cavalry courageously charged at the squares probing for weaknesses and assessing the enemy's strength. They were easily repulsed by the power of the French musketry. The next assault began soon after. Hordes of mounted Mameluke warriors, screaming insults and yelling battle cries descended upon the invaders.

Pierre and his comrades raised their muskets and waited for the order. The shrieking mass of cavalrymen bore down on them. The drumming and pounding of horses' hooves seemed to shake the earth beneath them, becoming louder and louder with every surge forward. Pierre waited and waited, until the enemy were almost upon them. He took a deep breath. Anxiety devoured the ranks. A recruit in the line fainted. Another wet his pants nearby. Cousseau picked out a target like every other trooper. Then the order was given.

"*Tirez!*"

A salvo of hot lead ripped into the Mameluke horsemen and their chargers sending many sprawling. Some of those behind the first stricken wave tried to swerve past the fallen riders and beasts, to avoid the carnage but only served to barge into other horses or were brought down themselves by flailing legs or equine torsos. Pierre knelt to reload his musket. He inhaled some warm air to offset the effects of the rising smoke above him and the smell of poisoning sulphur, whilst the middle row of soldiers stood and fired. The noise of battle was deafening. Around him some of his companions were falling, screaming in pain and bloodied, hit by the enemy's carbines and pistols. A fierce looking Mameluke on his steed charged into the square thrashing about with his razor-sharp scimitar but his horse's front legs suddenly collapsed, a lieutenant's slashing sabre disembowelling the poor, terrified beast. It bowled over crushing some of the French soldiers hurling it's Mameluke master straight onto the spear-like tip of the *porte-drapeau*'s fluttering *guidon*, raising a cheer from the ranks.

Cousseau waited, crouched on his haunches whilst the fusiliers in the rear line of the square discharged their weapons. He encouraged another frightened new recruit next to him with comforting words, then stood up when ordered to do so, took aim and discharged his weapon into the melee. Riders were hit and flung off their steeds then trampled by the surging cavalry behind. The bold Mamelukes though continued their attack breaching the defensive formation again and Pierre and his comrades fought for their lives firing their muskets and carbines at close range. Cousseau brought down another sword-wielding screaming cavalryman with his pistol, the warrior crashing down on him revealing a gaping hole in his skull but not before his opponent had slashed at him with his sword, effecting a gash on his shoulder. He winced in pain, then happened to glance to his right. The new recruit, St Clair, was pinned under the wounded horse. He was calling out for his mother, a Mameluke lance through his chest. The enemy continued to attack the square almost penetrating into the middle of the defensive formation on occasions, as it began to disintegrate. Antoine and the other savants braced themselves. Suddenly a horse appeared, galloping out of the acrid smoke directly towards him. It was like a vision from hell. On its back was another scimitar-wielding rider screaming like a banshee, engulfed in flames, like one of the horsemen of the Apocalypse. Antoine stood there, transfixed, frozen in fear and awe amidst the cacophony of battle. The warrior was almost upon him when a lance thrust by a fellow savant pierced the breast of the four-legged beast. The injured steed reared up and Antoine, snapping out of his trance just in time, raised the pistol grasped in his violently shaking hand

and shot the enemy cavalryman through the neck. The horse collapsed onto its knees spilling its master out of his saddle. The mortally wounded warrior somehow managed to raise himself despite the flames consuming him, and in spite of the hole in his neck. He staggered around swiping at anything in his path. The blade of the sword caught Antoine on his temple, but there was little force, its momentum slowed by the weakened, dying Mameluke who crumpled to the ground. Nevertheless, Antoine was knocked to the ground with the impact and his head bled liberally. He lay there momentarily staring at the dead Mameluke lying beside him convinced that he too was mortally wounded until the smell of burning flesh stung his nostrils bringing him to his senses. He dragged himself up and gingerly felt his wound. Blood trickled through his fingers. His head throbbed. Around him the battle raged on. He was pushed to the back of the square as the void was filled by other soldiers.

Pierre Cousseau and his brave companions fought valiantly side by side, bayoneting the sword-slashing Mamelukes and side stepping wild-eyed frantic steeds. Gradually, they repulsed the attack earning themselves a brief respite during which the injured were attended to, Antoine amongst them. Canteens were hurriedly raised to parched lips, muskets were reloaded, bodies removed, and the severed heads of comrades kicked out of the square. Then they closed ranks again. They re-established their shape and equanimity and continued to thwart the enemy repeatedly as Murad Bey sent in wave after wave of his mounted warriors. With each attack the Mameluke cavalry's formidable arsenal was deployed to its full effect. Carbines were drawn first, then pistols, then *djerids*, the small spears were launched, all whilst the riders simultaneously and dexterously wielded their scimitars or daggers and all whilst still in complete control of their mounts. The warriors on horseback were bizarrely followed by their attendants on foot who tried to recover the spent weapons that their masters had flung to the ground, compelled through fear of retribution to carry out this suicidal task by their cruel and sadistic overlords. The cavalry assaults continued unabated, the fearsome riders wreaking terror by charging into the French ranks repeatedly, emitting blood-curdling screams and curses, causing chaos and carnage. *Sergent* Cousseau was in the thick of the action. He parried a blow from a scimitar with the butt of his musket which he then used to jab at his opponent. The butt crunched into the cheekbone of the frenzied warrior whose silk attire was burning from the wad of a musket, then he swiftly and adroitly passed his Charleville through his hands and bayoneted the dazed rider in the heart. The terrified horse, sensing the grip of the reins had loosened, ploughed through the ranks, sending men sprawling. The dead Mameluke was catapulted from his mount. On impact, his brightly coloured turban dislodged, and several gold sovereign coins spilled from its interior to the utmost surprise and jubilation of the ranks.

"Leave them!" Captain Dugard yelled. "Focus on the barbarians! Damn it! I will shoot any man who picks up a coin!"

Suddenly a cannonball smashed through the ranks detaching Captain Dugard's head from his epaulette-embellished shoulders as easy as cheese wire slicing effortlessly through a truckle of Roquefort. Behind him, Lesoux, the *porte-drapeau* was also decapitated. Corporal Beaune, reacting the quickest of the stunned troops, wrestled the *guidon* from the dead standard bearer's grasp and thrust it into the air waving it proudly in defiance of the enemy. In that instant the Colours had taken on greater significance with the scattered brains and blood of Frenchmen smeared onto its fabric, symbolic of the sacrifice. Some of the fusiliers dived to the ground in an unseemly scramble for the gold sovereigns prompting Cousseau and Lieutenant Cros to restore order. The sergeant dug his musket butt into the backs of two or three scrummaging troopers then the furious lieutenant dragged them to their feet and confiscated the coins much to their chagrin. However, the sight of the booty encouraged the ranks immensely and they doubled their efforts, euphoric in their knowledge that their sacrifices and hardships might not be in vain. The squares held firm as the onslaught continued. Napoleon's artillery and sharpshooters began to make a difference. Lead and shot ripped into the charging chaotic, feverish mass of Mamelukes who were still displaying heroic acts of courage but little tactical nous. Eventually, the repeated assaults faltered, and the vanquished foe retreated.

The cry, *"En avant!"* suddenly came and the French infantry, flanked by the French cavalry went on the attack, their battle cries piercing the caustic air. Cousseau, his own battle cry erupting from his dry throat, surged forward, exhorting his subordinates to follow. He leapt over numerous burning human corpses and dead and maimed horses, blood oozing from their innocent mangled bodies. The crimson tide from beast and man seeped into the arid Egyptian soil over which the sergeant and his men charged, towards the lines of enemy Janissary foot soldiers who were dug in around the village of Embaba. The French forces reached the enemy's lines of defence; a rout ensued. Cousseau thrust his bayonet into the bodies of his terrified opponents time and again in an orgy of violence. The Janissary infantry were pushed back towards the river in disarray and found that their only course of action was to plunge into the Nile which they did in their thousands, amidst them fleeing cavalrymen and horses also. The gawping spectators watching on from the opposite bank of the river panicked and fled hindering the troops of Egypt's co-leader, Ibrahim Bey. They had been standing in reserve and now attempted to help their brethren by crossing the river in boats. They all somehow contrived to converge in the middle of the river, a confluence of confusion and mayhem. Cousseau and his comrades fired volley after volley into the chaos. A violent wind blew up churning up the reddening waters of the Nile and causing sand to blow into the grim and terrified faces of the enemy to compound their already perilous situation. The other disparate elements of the defeated enemy tried to escape the carnage over land, amongst them Murad and Ibrahim Bey, who fled into the Egyptian hinterland and desert, leaving the scarlet Nile behind, awash with corpses. That evening another shade of red manifested itself, the red band of the French *tricolore* flying triumphantly over the minarets of Cairo.

10

That evening Pierre and his victorious comrades enjoyed the spoils of war by plundering the treasure found on the dead Mamelukes who had sewed gold coins or jewels into their turbans and tunics, and by recovering jewel-encrusted scimitars strewn about the battlefield. Others fished for dead bodies with their bayonets from the blood-soaked river or ransacked the remnants of the hastily abandoned enemy encampment. Meanwhile Napoleon and his entourage had taken up residence in an opulent palace deserted by another prominent Egyptian leader, Elfi Bey. Most of the savants chose to tour Cairo, having been seduced by its architectural charms rather than those of the female variety which many of the French troops had sought out. Antoine, the polymath, was amongst them. He was in high spirits, elated to have survived the conflict, and had joined his fellow scholars proudly displaying a blood-soaked bandage on his aching head as if he were a lauded 'sans-culottes' revolutionary from the barricades of Paris. They toured the city discovering grandiose Islamic mosques and minarets, marvelling at Coptic Christian chapels and churches and ancient Egyptian ruins amidst its myriad narrow, dusty, garbage-strewn streets. At times being harried by packs of roaming feral, mangy-looking canines or stalked by legions of anguished denizens and chapfallen beggars emerging from Hadean-like shanties and hovels, displaying a witches brew of afflictions.

Napoleon's reaction to the medieval conditions was swift; hospitals were set up to deal with the diseased, the practice of dumping refuse in the Nile was forbidden, street-cleansing was introduced and cemeteries were established outside of the city. The disease-spreading scavenging dogs that feasted on the newly interred, buried indiscriminately around the capital, were killed en masse, poisoned.

Pierre Cousseau's company had been billeted in tents in the courtyard of one of the Mameluke palaces. He awoke one morning, his face reddened by bites from countless mosquitoes. He itched from head to toe. He stank of sweat. His head was banging, due to the local grog he had imbibed the night before in the ongoing celebration of the French victory. The troops had been given time to recuperate. The women of the city of all colour and creed had begun to fraternise with the invaders. Prostitutes, female slaves, and local Egyptian women were all in demand, some having gifts lavished on them, much to the bewilderment of the older Egyptian males who preferred young men and boys for their extra-marital stimulation, a practice common for generations in the land. Pierre had taken a young Nubian slave girl as his spoil, originally a gift to the platoon from Mehmet Ali, a larger than life Turkish 'doctor' who had ingratiated himself with the French occupiers. Pierre had made love to the attractive Nubian and had caressed her sleek ebony body affectionately with fascination whilst others slept with prostitutes or the broader-hipped locals that most Egyptians favoured. Mehmet Ali mystified the men when he

27

told them that the locals' compliment for a woman was 'she was so beautiful she couldn't fit through the door'.

11

Liverpool. Present day.

University for the students in Liverpool would begin again in the autumn. For the time being, Jules still had plenty of work to do, not only in her capacity as an academic but also as a trustee of the Egyptian Exploration Society. She had scholarly papers to prepare, reports to submit and was also due to lead an archaeological dig locally with a charitable organisation. A few days after Richard's latest attack she returned to the faculty. A sun hat was pulled down over her face in an attempt to hide her black eye and bruised forehead. It was a warm breezy day. Paul was seated in the gardens with his sleeping bag and haversack. She saw him but felt compelled to ignore him this time, embarrassed by her injuries. Paul had been hoping to see her and when she walked by without any acknowledgement, he felt slighted by her indifference. He had felt a strong desire to engage in conversation with this alluring lady again. He liked her immensely. 'Too good to be true', he thought, after being ignored. 'I'm just a vagrant. Some people do nice things for us but at a distance. They don't want to commit. But who could blame them? We are weak-minded, feckless people. We are given opportunities by good-hearted people but throw them back in their faces. We let people down. Time and time again. We promise not to start drinking again. We promise no more drugs. We promise to sort ourselves out.'

He recalled a benevolent woman paying the rent on a flat for six months for two homeless guys, only to find them on the streets again after a few months. They had spent the rent on booze and drugs and got kicked out by the landlord.

Earlier that week, Paul had been given the opportunity of a job interview for a hotel position during his rehabilitation. It was on the Friday. After an hour or so he got up off the bench. He wanted to go to the library to gen up on the company and the role of night porter. He was determined to get back into mainstream society. People were sunbathing in the Square's gardens and others were sitting and chatting in small groups. He looked across to the faculty. The woman who had helped him happened to step out at the same time as he was about to leave. Her sun hat suddenly flew off her head. It sailed over the railings blown by the zephyr. Paul chased it. It eluded him. He ran in and out of couples and groups and leapt over individuals to catch it. This amused Jules. It blew straight into the face of a little girl who was covered in chocolate ice cream. Paul politely asked for the hat back. The child's indignant mother passed the hat to him then took the toddler's arm and led her away. He apologised on behalf of Jules and took the recovered item back over to her. She was laughing. He drew closer and Jules noticed his laughing eyes had a certain radiance to them. Suddenly she remembered her injuries and snatched the hat from him and covered her eyes with it.

"Oh, thanks Paul."

"You're very welcome."

It was too late though, Paul had seen the marks on her forehead and her black eye despite the make-up she had applied to mask her appearance.

"What happened to your eye?"

"Oh that," she replied airily. "Richard was painting the lounge and he was on a ladder. I was holding it and he slipped and the tin of paint which was full whacked me in the eye, then the ladder and him came crashing down on me as well".

"Wow!" Paul said, staring at her, not believing a word.

"What a palaver!" she laughed, trying to make light of it. Encouraged by her glib rejoinder, she felt more relaxed in his company.

"That was hilarious," she sniggered. "Seeing you chasing after the hat, leaping over everyone and tripping over prone bodies."

"Not as funny as you though," he retorted.

"What do you mean?"

"Look inside your hat."

Jules took off her hat and Paul belly laughed. Her hair was matted with chocolate ice cream and a brown line creased her forehead.

"Ugh! What's that?" she recoiled in horror.

"It's chocolate ice cream. The little girl was eating an ice cream cone when the hat blew into her face. It's all over your hair."

"Yuk! Wait there I'm going to nip back into the faculty and wash it off."

"Oh shit! I've left my backpack on the bench."

Paul turned and noticed, to his alarm, the bag was not there. He looked to his right and saw a scrawny figure making off with it.

"Hey! You! Come back!"

The gaunt faced individual glanced back and then broke into a run. Paul sprinted after him with Jules running hesitantly behind. The backpack's contents were spilling out of the open top of the haversack unknown to the thief. Paul gained on him and grabbed him by the scruff of the neck. The thief dropped the bag in panic and fear. Paul spun him around. He recognised him. From Lambert House, a homeless hostel. He was a smack head. The sallow looking junkie cowered.

"Don't hit me, lah."

Paul's fist was clenched, ready to hit him. He then let go of the guy who scarpered.

Paul searched the bag frantically. 'What's he searching for?' thought Jules. 'Drugs? Pills? Booze?' The academic then set eyes on a discarded photograph that was held in a transparent plastic holder which had fallen into a flower bed, unseen by Paul. She retrieved it from a display of pink camellias and then spotted a paperback book amidst them also. She looked at the photograph. There was an attractive young woman and a smiling beautiful little boy in it, a toddler. She then glanced at the book she had recovered entitled *'Napoleon in Egypt'*.

Paul saw her standing there focused intently on the picture. He gently removed it from her grasp.

"Thanks. Oh, thank God, it's there."

"Did you get everything back?"

"Yeah. What little I have. This is the most important thing I have. I wasn't bothered about the rest."

"Listen, I'd like to buy you a cup of coffee and a sandwich. Just let me rinse this ice cream out of my hair."

Paul did not object to the generous proposition. He was hungry. He sat on the bench again and waited for Jules who had nipped back to the faculty to freshen up. He stared at the photograph, tears welling up in his eyes. A little later Jules appeared in front of him. He thought she looked stunning with her red tousled hair covering part of her face.

"Come on," she urged. "Let's go."

They arrived at a diner and ordered sandwiches and coffee. They sat at a table, attracting a few stares. Jules fortunately had applied a strong perfume to her body that morning which masked most of Paul's B.O.

"May I ask you who's in the picture?"

Paul hesitated for one moment. He fidgeted uneasily for a few seconds. Then reached into his pocket and passed the photo to Jules.

He spoke forlornly. "It's my wife and child."

"Oh, they're beautiful. Your wife looks amazing. The baby is so cute, now I can see it, he looks like you." Jules blushed realising what she'd said. "Why aren't you with them?"

"B-Because they're dead."

A pained expression appeared on Paul's face. He sat back. Tears again forming in his eyes.

"Oh, I'm so sorry Paul. I didn't mean to intrude."

"It's ok. I don't often talk about them. Maybe I should... Remember the tsunami? In 2004? I was on leave from the British Army at the time. I'd been in Iraq and Afghanistan. I'd joined up when I was eighteen in the officer corps. I was a lieutenant at the time. An Intelligence Officer. I spoke fluent French. My father was French. A French teacher. My mother was a teacher also. She was from Liverpool."

"Hence the surname," Jules contributed.

"Anyway, I had two weeks leave. My wife Andrea and baby Thomas and I went to Sri Lanka. It's a beautiful place."

"I've been there a few times. I agree, an incredible place."

"We'd had a fantastic time. The day of the tsunami we were on the beach. I'd gone to get some drinks from a bar. Suddenly, people were gesticulating. People were standing up chattering wildly. Then someone shouted 'run'. All hell broke loose. There was screaming and shouting. People panicking. I thought it was a terrorist attack. Then I saw what they were pointing at. The ocean had disappeared. I dropped the drinks and searched in the fleeing crowd for Andrea and Thomas. Then suddenly the tsunami loomed up out of nowhere and hit. I was swept back into a

31

bar. It was like being in a washing machine. I was thrown around. I managed to hold onto a beam on the ceiling and find a pocket of air. Then just as the water started to recede, I was knocked unconscious by a piece of debris. I never saw Andrea and Thomas again. They were swept out to sea. We never recovered their bodies…"

"Oh, I'm so sorry Paul. I wish I'd never asked. That's horrendous. Forcing you to relive it all again."

Paul put his hands over his anguished face and wept.

"Do you have any other family?"

Paul took a moment to compose himself before answering.

"I have a brother in Australia and a sister in Canada, but my parents are both dead. I've lost touch with my siblings. I don't see any of Andrea's family either because her parents made it known that I was responsible for the death of their daughter and grandson. The last time I saw them was at the funeral service."

Seeing how painful this was for Paul to open up, Jules decided to change the subject and lighten the conversation.

"Hey, this book, 'Napoleon in Egypt'. I've not read it. Is it interesting?"

"Fascinating. It tells the story of Napoleon's invasion of Egypt in 1798 and the subsequent campaign. There's some amazing characters in the book."

"So, you're a history buff like me."

"Anything to do with Napoleon fascinates me."

"You're obviously a Francophile as well. Having a French father."

"I love France. I have fond memories of holidaying there with my parents. We used to go to different places each year when Mum and Dad had their long summer break. We used to visit my French *grands-parents* as well. Sadly, no longer with us."

"I love France too. My parents have a *gîte* in France, south of Poitiers. They live there."

"Do you speak any other languages other than French?"

"Yep, Spanish. I learnt it at school to A level then continued studying it as part of my army training. I also studied Arabic in my role as an Intelligence Officer."

"Wow! Don't forget Scouse."

"Of course. And Scouse," Paul laughed. "What do you do for a living?"

"I'm an academic. A Doctor of Archaeology."

"Gosh! So, you must speak a few languages."

"French, Spanish, Arabic, like you. Some German. I can also read Ancient Greek and Latin, Sumerian, Akkadian, Ancient Egyptian and Coptic."

"That's amazing. You're a polyglot. What's Akkadian, by the way?"

"It's an extinct language that was spoken in ancient Mesopotamia. In my role as an Archaeologist and Egyptologist, I specialise in hieroglyphic texts, demotic and hieratic script."

"That's incredible. It mentions those types of ancient scripts in this book. Once I've read it you can have it."

"Thanks. I've read other books on Napoleon. In fact, the French created Egyptology, as a field of study, so I'm indebted to him. *Merci beaucoup Monsieur Bonaparte!* Do you know, you should put your language skills to good use."

"I did do at one stage. After the death of Andrea and Thomas I threw myself into my work as an Intelligence Officer. I did several tours of Iraq and Afghanistan. I stayed in the military for ten years becoming a captain. I left, physically exhausted and emotionally drained. I took some time off and then did my PGCE and then applied for a post as a modern language's teacher at a school in Manchester."

"A teacher?"

"I stuck at it for two years, but a combination of emotional turmoil and PTSD dragged me down and I grabbed an unruly pupil, a bully, by the scruff of the neck and threatened to kill him. They sacked me of course. I went into a deep depression. Got hooked on stimulants and anti-depressants. I lost my apartment, everything, and as a result ended up on the streets. I decided to come back to Liverpool and here I am."

"Are you still on stimulants and anti-depressants?"

"I managed to get off the stimulants a while ago, thankfully. I was still dependent on anti-depressants until recently. The accident. It was beneficial in a way. It helped me break the routine and dependency. I was in a coma for a few weeks. I'll have to find the taxi driver who knocked me down and thank him. And do you know what? The first thing I thought of when I came out of the coma was you."

Jules blushed.

"You were the last thing I saw. It was like a celestial vision. I didn't know if you were an angel, and I was in Heaven."

Jules was about to respond when suddenly she heard her name being called. She looked up to see one of Richard's co-workers Frank.

"Hi Jules. What's going on?"

He stood there looking at Jules and then Paul and then at Jules again, implying something.

"Oh, hi Frank. What are you doing up this end of town?"

"I've just been to the Philharmonic to pick some tickets up for a gig. Just grabbing a spot of lunch before I return to the office. Everything alright?" He glanced at Paul again, disdainfully.

"Yeah, fine. I've just had some lunch myself and I'm off to the uni library to do some research. This is Paul. I've just bought him some lunch as a thank you. Some low life tried to pinch my bag and he stopped him," she lied.

"Oh, right," Frank said. "Nice to see you then."

Frank returned to his seat and Jules got up to leave immediately and left Paul sitting there.

"Nice to meet you, Paul. And thanks again for helping me," she said curtly. "Bye Frank."

She left the café promptly and headed towards the university's Sidney Jones library, leaving Paul in her wake. 'She must be embarrassed to be seen with me,' Paul thought.

After Frank had departed, Paul left. He ambled back to the Gardens and sat on the grass. Moments later Jules reappeared.

"Sorry, I left so abruptly. It's nothing to do with you. Listen, I've booked you a hotel for the night. Bed, evening meal and breakfast. At the Feathers Hotel. Down the road. Here's some smellies as well. Don't be offended. You do reek a bit. You can get in there after two pm. It's all paid for. Just quote my name - Dr Julia Johnson. They know me. Here's a booking ref."

She passed him a chit of paper. "Here's £50. Go and buy yourself some new clothes."

"That's very kind of you, Jules," Paul said humbly, astonished by her generosity. "Thank you."

"Hey, would you be interested in coming along to an archaeological dig with me on Saturday?"

"Er-yeah. I suppose. That would be interesting. Egypt, by any chance?"

"Ha! Ha! No. Local. Good, I'll meet you here in Abercromby Gardens and fill you in on the details. About noon tomorrow. I've some research to do, in the library, so I'll speak to you tomorrow."

Jules spun away turning once to smile and walked off in the distance. Paul reciprocated the smile in appreciation of the academic's kind act and sat there staring at the money.

12

Egypt, 1798

O nce the French forces were deemed to have recuperated from 'the Battle of the Pyramids', Pierre's regiment was ordered to fan out into the hinterland of Egypt to spread the word of Napoleon's edict that he was in Egypt as a friend of the people rather than as a conquering tyrant. They were to establish outposts and reconnoitre villages and oases, whilst being on the look-out for Murad and Ibrahim Bey or hostile Bedouins. Pierre, donned in full dress uniform, marched proudly out of the city at the head of his company of grenadiers, accompanied to the outskirts by the sound of the drums and flutes of the military band. Antoine Demeraux was part of the throng that waved them off. It would be a while before he was re-acquainted with his friend Pierre Cousseau.

That same day Antoine and some of the other 165 savants who had been commissioned for the Egyptian campaign were invited to tour the Pyramids with several of Napoleon's entourage. Antoine and his fellow scholars arrived, their backsides aching from their journey on the backs of donkeys, their throats parched, and their faces plastered in dust. Antoine and his colleagues toured the ancient site and were in awe of the immense stone structures.

"Everyone will have a race to the top of the Great Pyramid," Napoleon declared.

Antoine gaped in awe at the massive structure in front of him as the pronouncement was made. Others were simply amused. The savants and officers of the entourage began to scramble up the huge blocks of limestone and granite. Antoine hauled himself up layer by layer, gasping for breath and sweating profusely whilst Napoleon, guffawing, watched the competition from below. To his surprise, due to his slight frame, Antoine was beating some of the military men who he deemed to be fitter, although many were older than his twenty-two years. He was well beaten by others and to his astonishment, by another savant Gaspard Monge, a brilliant mathematician, who won the race, beating all of the soldiers. Antoine, exhausted, slumped besides the winner and congratulated him on his victory.

"Here, have a swig of this." Monge passed a gourd to the rasping Antoine as they sat atop the huge structure. A vessel he presumed contained water. Antoine glugged down the liquid. A warm sensation flowed down through his body and then crept back up to his throat. He almost gagged and felt like vomiting. Monge laughed.

"So, my young friend, you can't stomach *eau de vie*. Hahaha!"

35

13

General Louis-Charles Desaix was given the task of pursuing the outlawed Murad Bey through Upper Egypt. The column of soldiers that included Pierre Cousseau's company passed through many villages during their ongoing expedition. Some villages welcomed the arrival of the French and benefited by selling their produce. Others were hostile culminating in the French forces razing certain villages to the ground and putting the inhabitants to the sword, a reprisal for attacks made on them. Although the French deemed themselves civilised and compassionate, from time to time, some were guilty of awful atrocities and sometimes plunder was the only way of surviving in the harsh, barren desert. Pierre often had grave doubts about this aspect of the mission, but Captain Allier was a disciplinarian and would not tolerate gratuitous violence from his men. The sergeant, therefore, had seen the good, the bad and the ugly. But this was the world he lived in, he mused. A savage, brutal, unpredictable one. A godless world where death was omnipresent. He had witnessed terrible things. Cruelty beyond measure and people mentally and physically scarred by devastating diseases like the plague and leprosy. As a soldier of the Revolution, however, he felt it was his duty to spread the revolutionary zeal and ideals of the new republic far and wide. He denounced religion and royalist sentiments. He was a citizen soldier, obliged to fulfil his destiny of emancipating the downtrodden masses. Emancipated men alone could only guide others to greater, more worthier realms, he believed. Not a belief system in a higher entity.

Yet, his perceptions began to change one day when the column rounded a mountain and came across the awe-inspiring sight of the magnificent ruins of Thebes. The soldiers all burst into spontaneous applause on seeing this spectacular panorama of ancient temples and stone carvings. They formed up and presented arms in honour of the immensity of the experience without prompt from their superiors. Across the Nile loomed the fantastic temple of Luxor replete with towering stone obelisks adorned with curious pictograms. Further north was the Temple of Karnak. Awe-struck soldiers wandered around the stunning ancient ruins.

"Who built these structures?" Corporal Massy asked. "How could it be the ancestors of the Egyptians when even the sight of a wheelbarrow amazes them?"

"Perhaps, these ancient constructions are the work of some higher, unknown power, not of this world?" Vivant Denon, a savant, suggested.

"They truly are mysterious," Cousseau replied. He was shadowing Vivant Denon, on a tour around the ancient ruins as his protective guard. Denon was tasked with sketching everything he could. As he sat there with pencil and paper drawing, Cousseau, fascinated by the ubiquitous, elaborate symbols and characters adorning the huge structures wanted to know more.

"Citizen Denon, these carvings inscribed on the stone, do you know what they mean?"

"They're called hieroglyphs, sergeant. It is a form of ancient language. I will ask *Monsieur* Jacob our interpreter if they bear any resemblance to Arabic or Coptic because I have no idea, at present, what they reveal."

He called over a tall, thin, bearded man dressed in the traditional garb of a local. Jacob was an Egyptian Copt. The Copts being the original Christians of Egypt.

"Jacob, do you understand these symbols and icons?" Denon inquired.

"*Non, Monsieur* Denon. The knowledge and ability required to interpret the hieroglyphic language has been lost to us Egyptians for more than 1500 years unfortunately. We are as puzzled as you French. Maybe one day someone will be able to translate the pictograms. Perhaps a Frenchman. Perhaps you, *Monsieur* Denon since Napoleon deems the French to be superior."

The granite obelisk they were staring at was destined to be relocated to La Place de la Concorde in Paris, thirty years later. A gift from an Egyptian ruler, in exchange, for a faulty clock.

General Desaix's pursuit of Murad Bey led his French forces to other ancient sites and sacred temples, one of which led to the discovery of the famous circular Zodiac of Dendera inscribed on the ceiling of a temple chapel. A revelation that would subsequently cast doubt on the timespan of the world's origins. The expedition force also re-discovered the ancient rock tombs of the Necropolis of Thebes and the Valley of the Kings where Denon and Desaix almost became the latest to be buried there after having to flee for their lives from the ferocious troglodytes that lived amongst the ruins. It was at this juncture that Cousseau was sent back to Cairo as an envoy. Whilst swimming in the Nile someone screamed, "*Crocodile!*" In the scramble to get out of the river Cousseau twisted an ankle badly on some rocks. He considered himself fortunate as a private was dragged under the water by the giant beast, never to be seen again. Despite the rigours of the campaign, Cousseau had relished discovering the ancient sites of Egypt with his compatriots and enjoyed the company of erudite savant Vivant Denon who knew his friend Antoine Demeraux. He therefore had mixed feelings about leaving the expedition. He was given a horse and despatches and instructed to return to Cairo to provide an update for Napoleon on General Desaix's progress along with a few other troopers and injured and sick men. The plan was to return via the outposts that Desaix had established along the route, but the return journey was hindered by the fierce *khamsin*, the 'poison' wind of Egypt, resulting in the troop losing their way in the desert. The small cohort managed to get back on track several days later but ten stricken soldiers never survived the prolonged journey. Some fell victim to dysentery and heatstroke. Others to the effects of their wounds, or maladies like typhus and venereal disease. The survivors eventually found refuge at the first of the garrisons the French had built along the Nile. In the meantime, Desaix's three thousand plus column continued onto Aswan and the Nile cataracts, still in pursuit of the elusive Murad Bey.

14

Pierre Cousseau had just finished cleaning his musket, removing the fouling from the barrel and applying its lubrication when his platoon was chosen to carry out a recce. A couple of months had passed since his arrival in Cairo with the despatches from Desaix. Shortly after his return to duty, having recovered from his badly twisted ankle, Cousseau was back on the move again. Bonaparte had launched a fresh, bold campaign. Despite the success of Desaix's forays into Upper Egypt expanding Napoleon's sphere of influence and despite the *tricolore* flying over most of Egypt, a calamity had occurred when Rear Admiral Horatio Nelson obliterated the French fleet at the Battle Of The Nile in August of 1798. The French invaders now felt isolated, cut off from Europe, but Napoleon turned the defeat into a positive by focusing on his ambition to conquer India by way of the Levant or to at least forge a possible escape route back to France overland. His megalomania had led him to believe that he could follow in the footsteps of his hero Alexander the Great.

Cousseau shivered. He was reluctant to move away from the crackling campfire. The harsh winter conditions of the Levant had taken everyone by surprise and the invading force found itself ill-prepared for the incursion into Syria, lacking food, water and other provisions, along with warm clothing. After crossing the Sinai Desert, Napoleon's invasion force had arrived starving at the gates of the fortress of El-Arish on the Mediterranean Coast. The French troops had besieged the town resulting in the farcical situation whereby the starving besiegers faced the equally hungry Islamic defenders of the garrison who were observing the fast of Ramadan until sunset. The French had been reduced to eating their own camels and donkeys. The smell of food wafting over the walls of the citadel at dusk was driving Cousseau and his compatriots almost crazy. Huddled over the licking flames, two of Cousseau's fellow grenadiers, privates Jendin and Figot felt impelled to act to relieve the hunger in the platoon.

"Permission to hunt for food, sergeant, whilst we're out on patrol."

Cousseau just laughed but he could not ignore the rumbling inside his stomach.

"Private Figot, you can bring me back an *entrecôte* with onions and *petits-pois*. In fact, take everyone's order before you leave."

"Sergeant Cousseau, you punish us with those words. I am salivating at the prospect. How cruel of you," Corporal Beaune, who was at his side, sighed.

The platoon's operation began as soon as the men were mustered. Figot and Jendin stole away once it was dark carrying jute sacks. The patrol returned to base after completing their recce and shortly after Jendin and Figot reappeared miraculously lugging two sacksful of meat which were eagerly cooked and devoured by the men and their followers. No questions asked. They slept content with full bellies. At reveille next morning, a furious major from the Dragoons appeared, searching in vain for his horse that had simply disappeared into thin air. He questioned random units whether they had seen a stray steed. He paused close to where Jendin and Figot were sitting and scanned the bank of resting troops. Jendin and Figot both avoided eye contact with the officer. Cousseau scrutinized the two rogues. He could not believe they had been instrumental in the requisitioning of an officer's horse for food. The apoplectic dragoon stumbled on to the next group of men cussing and slapping his redundant riding crop into the palm of his hand as he went. Cousseau shook his head in dismay at his two subordinates but gave them a wry smile. He and the others were grateful for the unexpected feast the poor beast had provided them with.

After several days of siege, the garrison capitulated after a breach was achieved by the French artillery and then Gaza, further up the coast, was taken without a fight, the defenders having fled in fear of the invaders. The column then moved on to Jaffa.

"Come on you lazy bastards. Move!" Cousseau growled. "Jendin! Don't forget your bayonet, soldier. You will be needing that soon. We are in the first wave of attack. The regiment will have the honour of taking Jaffa. Hey, Figot! No more hooch! Smarten up, the rest of you drunken imbeciles! I'll be back in ten minutes. I want everyone out in five, standing to attention. General Bon will inspect the troop forthwith."

Grenadier Maurice Jendin had not long since recovered from the bubonic plague. He was one of the fortunate ones. Hundreds of his comrades had died from the disease during the march into Syria.

It was hitherto unknown that infected fleas from rats transmitted the disease which had caused much fear amongst the ranks. Jendin's compatriot, Millet, had contracted the plague in Damietta but had survived the ordeal by cutting an incision into the pus-filled bubo afflicting his groin. As a result of his advice Jendin too, had survived by applying this method of DIY surgery to his suppurating sores.

Napoleon's artillery was in the process of bombarding the besieged city of Jaffa which was offering stubborn resistance. The weather was foul, the French invaders were stricken by illness and exhaustion and the morose Napoleon's patience was sorely tested since he was keen to overcome this final, important strategic impediment before his advance on Acre. The regiment lined up ready for inspection and General Bon rode slowly past, issuing threats to some of the more slovenly and indolent infantrymen and encouragement to others. Sergeant Cousseau was summoned after the inspection. He was requested to find an emissary to take a message from Napoleon to the Turkish commander in the fort.

"Figot!" he called. Jean Figot came over, stood to attention and saluted his superior.

"I have a task for you. You have been selected to convey a despatch to the enemy at the citadel. This despatch is from General Bonaparte himself. You must ensure it is passed *only* to the commander of the Syrian forces. Our regiment has been honoured with this mission. Do not fail General Bonaparte or your regiment."

"Yes, sergeant."

"Make haste, Private Figot. The artillery has finally made a breach in the wall. Your safe passage to the citadel will be guaranteed."

Figot saluted then took the message.

An hour later Sergeant Cousseau and the others were still waiting for Figot to return. His comrades were becoming anxious. A few more hours passed. Figot must have been taken prisoner they assumed. The Turkish commander had not responded to Napoleon's terms. It was time to act.

"Soldiers!" Cousseau barked. "Our regiment has been given the honour to lead the attack. We will advance to the forward trenches and prepare ourselves for an assault on the enemy through the breach."

The grenadiers moved forward under the withering fire of the garrison and achieved their first objective, arriving in the trenches dug by sappers.

Peering over the rudimentary earthworks, Jendin cried in horror, "*Mon Dieu! Sergent* Cousseau, *regardez!*" He pointed towards the fortress.

Cousseau looked. Up on the tower ramparts Figot's decapitated head with its mutilated face appeared on the end of a lance. It was lolling like a macabre dancing marionette being manoeuvred up and down and sideways. The 'puppet master', spurred on by the mass of taunting defenders strewn along the parapet, pranced around like a court jester. Cousseau and his comrades, bursting with rage, charged the breach yelling their battle cries and oaths at the enemy, amidst a hail of deadly fire, their courage in the main fuelled by alcohol. Men were soon dropping all around Cousseau, agonising screams emanating from their throats, their bodies mutilated by cannon and musket fire. But a good many still managed to break through the breach, engaging the enemy ferociously. Cousseau, bristling with anger, bayoneted a tarboosh-headed Turk who came at him brandishing a sabre. A mace-wielding Mameluke was his next victim. Cousseau thrust his bayonet into his opponent's gullet before he could swing the weapon, the wound disgorging copious amounts of Caucasus blood onto his tunic. He was then set upon by a ferocious looking Nubian, whose ebony muscles rippled from his sleeveless garb. The giant glabrous Nubian thrust a djerid towards Cousseau's midriff. He parried it with his bayonet but a dagger in the assailant's other hand tore through his lightweight uniform and pierced his forearm, making a deep gouge, from which French blood seeped. The pain was immense. A musket ball fired indiscriminately into the melee from the tower creased his forehead knocking him over. The musket ball continued on hitting Jendin, exploding into his jaw. Teeth, blood and gums flew everywhere. Just as the bald, fierce-looking Nubian raised his spear, to go in for the kill on the disorientated French sergeant, Cousseau's superior Lieutenant Niort blasted his pistol at close range through the side of the giant's head, scattering his brains. Niort suddenly arced up in pain, cut down by a scimitar thrust into the small of his back by another Syrian fighter. The one-eyed Syrian slit the young lieutenant's throat with a dagger as the supine Cousseau, with the slain giant Nubian prostrate over him, watched his officer helplessly, Niort's eyes almost popping out of their sockets as the crimson sluice gurgled from the aperture in his throat. The Syrian was then, in turn, despatched by a bayonet from another French grenadier from the second wave that

40

had swarmed through the breach in support of the survivors of the initial assault. These fearless soldiers from the same regiment, motivated to avenge the deaths of their fallen comrades, bayoneted the enemy combatants at close quarters and lobbed grenades into the baying hordes. They gradually pushed the defenders back and then set about remorselessly killing anyone they could find in a frenzy of blood-letting; men, women, and children unflinchingly hacked to death, the foot soldiers fortified by a potent, toxic combination of alcohol, revenge and rage. Rampaging through the streets they slaughtered everyone in their path, slitting the throats of Muslims, Christians and Jews alike. Long into the night the rape and pillage and massacre ensued in a drunken orgy of violence despite the pleas of clemency from the enemy.

15

Cousseau was ferried to the field hospital where his wounds were treated and, exhausted, he fell into a deep sleep. In the meantime, the rest of the garrison, holed up in a tower had surrendered to some of Napoleon's aides-de-camp. The following day Cousseau, having woken stiff and sore from his wounds, was able to leave the casualty station. He went outside of the marquee just in time to witness masses of prisoners being led away from the encampment, arms tied behind their backs. Among them were Egyptians, Turks and Moroccans. He wondered where they were being taken so he decided to follow the abject line of wretches. The ragged procession of the vanquished was forced to a halt at the shore. He watched, perplexed, as the ill at ease Moroccan fighters were separated from the others and lined up along the beach. Cousseau was shocked to see a detail of fusiliers march in front of them. An officer ordered them to take aim. The men at first seemed hesitant until their superior reissued the order emphatically. The Moroccans fled in terror towards the open sea, but many were shot, and the others chased and bayoneted or drowned. A French general arriving at the beach witnessed the end of the slaughter and called a halt to it. Cousseau stood motionless. He stared at the mass of dead bodies sprawled on the beach and then at the line of corpses bobbing in the red, foaming surf. The fusiliers, their body language betraying their shame, lowered their weapons. The wails of the dying and the crash of the waves replaced the sound of gunfire. The ghastly puppet-like image of Figot's disfigured face with its gouged eyes and severed lips suddenly burst into Cousseau's mind, a stark, vivid reminder of the cruelty of war. He calmly walked away.

The terrified Egyptians and Turkish captives were forced to dispose of the corpses in the sea and feared the worst but were unexpectedly returned to camp. The following morning the Egyptians were fortunate to be sent back to their country, but the fearful Turks were shown no mercy. They were marched again to the beach to be reminded of their fate by the bloated corpses of the Moroccans still pitching in the surf by their dozens. The same process was repeated by another company of fusiliers who sent a volley into the ranks of prisoners, dispersing them in every direction. Then the bayonet hunt commenced, accompanied this time by dragoons and cuirassiers on horseback who slashed at the wretches or forced them into the sea to drown. No one was spared, not even terrified children who clung to their fathers' sides.

This time it was Demeraux who happened to witness the carnage. Sickened by this horrific spectacle unfolding before his eyes, he vomited. He turned away from the slaughter. The shrieking, wailing and screams of the victims filled the poisoned air and tortured his ears.

'Why?' he thought. 'Why was Napoleon, a man of supposed culture, a man who espoused the virtues and values of the Enlightenment, allowing this to happen?'

He ran, stumbling over rocks, back to the encampment. The environs were littered with the wounded and the detritus of battle. He sought out Berthollet, a savant who he knew was close to Napoleon. Many of the savants had accompanied Napoleon to Syria with the intention of enlightening the local populace with their knowledge and with the intention of finding more discoveries in the fields of botany, archaeology, and science. Demeraux had been assigned a role as a cartographer and been tasked with others to map Syria. He found Berthollet with Monge in their billet. They ushered the distraught, young scholar into their tent.

"Antoine, my God, what's happened?"

"*Qu'est-ce qui s'est passé, messieurs?* I should ask you the same thing. This is not enlightenment. That, which is happening right now on the shore, is nothing but murder. The captives are being slaughtered. Innocent children are being slain also. The sea has turned red! God forgive us! I thought we were men of culture and respect. Here to educate and be educated. Not to commit brutal, witless savagery!"

"I am sorry you've had to witness something like that citizen Demeraux," Berthollet answered. "We all are. It is horrific. Unedifying, shameful. But listen, Napoleon had the right to do this because of the terms of surrender. Blame the commander-in-chief of the citadel if you must. Napoleon had breached their defences and gave them the opportunity to surrender as per the protocols of war. If they refused to surrender, which they did, then they could expect no mercy. He had every right to massacre its occupants."

"Surely we are above the status of a heathen or barbarian army. In victory we should be magnanimous and show mercy to the vanquished. We should disregard these perverse, archaic martial rules. Are we not here to spread our revolutionary ideals amongst these people? One cannot educate a corpse!"

"War is war, my friend and art is art," Monge replied. "Literature is literature. Science is science. And science and art and literature are what we savants know. There are different rules. Different strategies. Let those who know better about the art of warfare deal with those matters."

"The *art* of warfare? How can we define slaughter as art? Art is about creativity, expression, ideas, imagination, beauty and emotion. Murder and carnage cannot be defined by any of those concepts!"

"Tell me," Monge snapped, "what would you do with these thousands of prisoners? Take them with us?"

"I would. I would take them."

"Are you hungry Demeraux?" Monge asked.

"Yes, but..."

"We are all hungry. We are starving. The soldiers are starving. The camp followers are starving. There's almost mutiny amongst the ranks. How are you going to feed these extra thousands of people? We've been eating our camels and donkeys and horses already!"

"Well, we-we should let them go then, send them into the desert. At least they'd have a chance of surviving. Show them mercy, don't you think?"

43

"What? And let them flee to Acre to strengthen Djezzar the Butcher's army?" Berthollet said. "There are already Albanians amongst those prisoners, Mamelukes, that we captured at El-Arish and set free to go back to Egypt and others who were given the opportunity to march with us but deserted. What folly is this that we set free those we have defeated only for them to confront us again?"

Monge elaborated more. "General Bonaparte is also sending a message to Djezzar. If he doesn't bow to the power of the revolutionary army Acre will experience the same fate as Jaffa. Also count yourself fortunate Demeraux that you wear the uniform of a savant and not that of a grenadier like your friend Cousseau. I saw him at the field hospital lying on a stretcher, wounded and bloodied."

"Or indeed that you were in the shoes of wretched private Figot," Berthollet added. "No mercy was shown to that unfortunate man. I understand your anguish Demeraux, but it would be wise not to lose your head in earshot of any of Napoleon's *aide-de-camp* or you might be chosen to be the next envoy for Acre. Djezzar, the Butcher, lives up to his name, you know. His victims, those who have survived, it is said, bear the scars of their torture; ears sliced off, eyes gouged out, noses and feet hacked off. And other unfortunates have had their feet shod with horseshoes!"

"And they were just his servants," Monge said grimly. "What would he do to his enemies? We know all too well."

Demeraux stood in silence for a while reflecting on what he had just heard before turning on his heels and departing in some distress.

16

Atop the battlements of Acre, stood British naval commander Captain Sir Sidney Smith, proud and fearless, the famed 'Swedish Knight', as he was disparagingly known. With one eye closed and the other pressed to his spyglass he peered at the enemy. His focus was on the approaching French troops encircling the citadel. At his side was Colonel Louis-Edmond Phélippeaux, a French royalist who had escaped the French Revolution of 1789 on the night he was due to be guillotined. Sidney Smith had reason to thank his French colleague for it was he who, with a few other Royalists, had released Smith, in an audacious plot, from the notorious Paris Temple prison where the former had been languishing as a prisoner. Phélippeaux, who went to military school with Napoleon and knew him well, was now an officer in the British Army and had accompanied Sidney Smith on his battleship the *Tigre*. Their mission was to persuade Djezzar to hold out against Napoleon at Acre. For Napoleon, Acre was strategically important. He could not bypass it because his supply lines would be cut off as he progressed towards his ultimate goal of India. Phélippeaux had improved the defensive installations at the fortress and Djezzar had been informed that naval squadrons from Britain and Turkey were racing to his aid. The fleet arrived soon after, bringing artillery, ammunition, food and water supplies and reinforcements of hundreds of British marines.

Napoleon's troops arrived at Acre exhausted and hungry but buoyed by the support given them by the local Druze population who feared Djezzar. Here, food was in abundance. Napoleon stood on the heights overlooking the citadel, peering through his monocular whilst simultaneously barking out incessant orders to his staff. After a courteous exchange of letters from Smith to his adversary, requesting an exchange of prisoners, which was granted, the battle commenced in earnest with the French artillery sending up a barrage. The British and Turkish fleets responded, as did the guns of Acre.

Sergeant Pierre Cousseau, having recovered from his injuries, found himself once again at the forefront of the battle. Being a grenadier was an honour. They were the vanguard of the army and a prestigious fighting unit. The grenadiers launched themselves out of their sapper made trenches, charging a breach in the walls. Once again deadly fire rained down on them. Cousseau led his platoon forward but stopped abruptly, thwarted by an unseen moat stretched before them.

"Mon Dieu! We need more ladders! Lautruc! Return to the trench! Get them to bring more ladders, *vite!"*

Before Lautruc could respond a cannonball smashed through his body and obliterated, in an instant, the head of the next man, Corporal Veray. Cousseau, splattered in blood, told his men to take cover. Some had already leapt into the moat and were trying to climb up the other side and scale the walls but were being picked off one by one by the foe. Cousseau, wild with fury, threw himself into the moat.

"*Attaquez! En avant, grenadiers!*"

The brave grenadiers leapt into the void and tried in vain to haul themselves the ten feet or so up to the breach. A block of tarred flaming wood sailed past Cousseau's head and smashed into the face of young Malpas. He screamed in agony, his tunic and hair ablaze. Grenades were tossed exploding and ripping the legs off soldiers Givray and Manait. On the ramparts the cruel and oppressive Djezzar, white beard flowing, his jewel-embossed scimitar in one hand and pistol in his other, had emerged from his lair to urge his men on who were taken aback by the courage of the grenadiers. He callously shot two of his own men he considered 'cowards', as a warning to the others. This was a man who had killed several women of his own harem with his bare hands.

Cousseau, amidst the turmoil, was making progress in his ascent towards the breach when suddenly he was flung backwards, pole-axed by a rock thrown from the ramparts. It crashed on to his head and he fell back into the moat landing on Malpas who lay on his back, his face charred and blackened. He moaned as Cousseau fell on him. Cousseau, lay dazed and bleeding, his vision momentarily blurred. He listened, barely conscious, to the cacophony around him. The bugler's call of retreat. Cannons booming, muskets flashing and cracking, grenades exploding, the shouting of orders, battle cries, men screaming and crying out in pain, some calling out for their mothers.

"*Mamam! Maman!*" Others crying out for help. "*Aidez-moi!*"

And still more, muttering desperate prayers as they lay dying with their ghastly open wounds, their faint utterings soon fading from their parched lips and dry throats as they succumbed to their injuries. And then, he heard the strains of ululating women emanating from somewhere in the citadel.

"Retreat! Back to the trenches, *mes braves!*" Captain Allier cried.

Cousseau, still confused and bleeding from his head wound, was shaken by the captain.

"Cousseau! Cousseau! Can you stand?"

This brought him to his senses, and he scrambled up the bank with the assistance of his captain and was dragged away under the enemy's withering fire. Men all around him were being cut down in flight by musket balls. Others were disappearing instantly in the flash of an explosive blast then reappearing as crimson-coloured chunks of flesh and guts spread over the fleeing troops. The sergeant glanced back to see the Turks leaping from the breach into the moat and then climbing back up the ladders cheering and holding the severed heads of the butchered wounded and fallen. Amongst them was the burnt, smoking, blackened head of young Malpas being swung like a ghoulish Hallowe'en lantern, the choking tar in the dead private's mouth having been re-lit by the gloating Turk who held it.

That evening the heads of Malpas, Givray and Manait and other fallen comrades were displayed on spikes along the walls of the fortress, a bounty having been paid for each infidel head. The entrenched French troops watching on, vowed to avenge the deaths of their brothers in arms.

Pierre Cousseau sat outside the medical tent once more gingerly fingering an enormous bump and gash on his forehead. He carefully placed a compress to the purple mound matted with blood. He was suffering from concussion and was ordered to rest a while. The siege continued, the enemy making a surprising, bold foray into the French trenches to counter it. They were repulsed and a contingent of wounded Englishmen were taken prisoner but were looked after courteously within the camp as if they were fellow Frenchmen, in contrast to Djezzar's brutality.

17

Rumours spread throughout the encampment that a vast army of more than 30,000 combatants from Damascus was on the march coming to the aid of Djezzar so Napoleon despatched columns of cavalry and infantry towards Nazareth and Galilee. Cousseau watched as Napoleon's dashing generals Junot, Murat and Kléber and their *aides-de-camp* directed their Arabian steeds out of the camp followed by a column of soldiers marching to the beat of the drummer boys and the high-pitched shrill of the flautists. Each of the generals subsequently located advanced units of the approaching army and defeated them. However, the main bulk of the new threat was encamped near Mount Tabor so General Kléber decided on a surprise attack but unfortunately mistimed it arriving too late to effect it. Instead, his army of 5,000 men found itself confronted by 35,000 enemy combatants. They repulsed the attacks time and again having formed two defensive squares, but things were getting desperate. One last charge by the enemy would finish them off but to Kleber's astonishment Napoleon, with amazing prescience came to the rescue himself commanding a division of men which attacked the supplies of the enemy and panicked the foe encouraging Kleber's forces to go on the attack. They pursued the enemy and forced them into a lake and the river Jordan whereupon thousands were slain or drowned, and the rest put to flight in disarray.

18

On his return to Acre, '*le petit caporal*', as Napoleon's soldiers called him, stood and surveyed the war-torn landscape from a hill which would one day be known as 'Napoleon's Hill'. The diminutive general also scanned the sea. He was expecting more artillery from his small but still active flotilla commanded by Admiral Perrée, the remnants of the fleet which had been destroyed by Nelson at the Battle of the Nile. The siege had continued in Napoleon's absence, his sappers attempting to mine the keep. Finally, they succeeded in creating another breach which became the catalyst for another grenadier led charge.

Sergeant Pierre Cousseau stood amongst his men once more, ready to fight. He was in the second wave and considered himself fortunate because the vanguard had fared badly. The vanguard had been repulsed by barrels of gunpowder launched at them from above, then ignited by gunfire, setting everything ablaze, burning and suffocating their victims. Cousseau and his attacking comrades were met by a blazing cauldron of fire which blocked their path to the breach. The sergeant's nostrils flared as he was engulfed in a miasma of burning flesh and he could only watch in horror as some of his companions flailed around before him, screaming, flames engulfing their bodies. They were forced to retreat almost immediately. Pierre's face and hands stung, as did those of his men, scorched by the intense heat of the flames.

The siege was nevertheless having an effect. The artillery bombardment continued relentlessly, resulting in mounting casualties in the stronghold, yet Sir Sidney Smith was still influencing events, with fearless determination, however Phélippeaux had succumbed to a fever. Smith, an extraordinary character, who had thwarted Napoleon before at the siege of Toulon in 1793, and was renowned for his reckless courage, went to confer with Djezzar. Smith, a one-time spy, chief adviser to the Swedish navy, and veteran of the Swedish-Russian war, once rescued the Swedish King and was knighted for his deeds. He seemed to have no fear of the Butcher of Acre and appeared to be equally respected by the Mameluke since Smith's reputation and status earned as a Turkish navy volunteer and subsequent leader of the Turkish Porte land and naval rescue forces held him in good stead with the Bosnian-born Djezzar. Sidney Smith, British sea captain, intelligence officer and former prisoner of the French; a man who had clashed with Nelson over rank and who was considered a corsair by the French, entered the daunting, intimidating surroundings of Djezzar's court.

"Ah, Sir Sidney, welcome. Please come, repose here." Djezzar indicated to a sofa. The English commander sat down. "What news do you have for me?" Djezzar asked sullenly.

"We are losing casualties at a considerable rate, my lord. Our supplies are running low. Water is scarce and our ammunition is rationed. We are using rocks and spears and anything we can find to repel the invaders, but I promise you we will be able to hold out."

"How can you tell me that when those French dogs are blasting my citadel to bits? Are you a mystic? A sorcerer? How can you be so optimistic? Guard! Bring my astrologer to me immediately."

The guard exited at once. Several minutes later, a one-eyed obsequious individual shuffled into the room.

"Astrologer, read me Napoleon's mind. Tell me his next stratagem. Do it, now!" he snapped.

The shaking humble astrologer pulled out a leather purse from inside his garb and extracted chicken bones from it. He began to mutter indecipherable incantations and then tossed the bones dramatically into the air. They landed, scattering across the blue and white tiled mosaic floor. He stood and stared at the dispersed bones in a trance-like state.

"Tell me now!" Djezzar ordered. "What news do they foretell? The bones!"

"Sire, the-the enemy will try and weaken the tower. They will aim their infernal weaponry at the tower and blast it away, piece by piece, until they achieve an enormous breach."

The Butcher, Djezzar reflected in silence... "Go, now. Retrieve your magic bones and leave! I had come to the same conclusion. Once the tower is down, the walls will crumble around it and there will be no stopping Napoleon."

"Have faith in Allah, Pasha Djezzar. The Porte will come to our aid," Smith vowed.

Djezzar remained silent for a moment before he spoke again. "Leave. Leave me in peace, Sir Sidney. I have much to ponder."

"Yes, my lord."

19

Five days later Napoleon had mounted most of his guns, facing the tower. It looked as if the astrologer's interpretations would come true. Demeraux was assisting at the field hospital that day when he heard a commotion outside. He was getting used to the sight of blood due to the constant flow of injured personnel in and out of the large canopy. He even administered aid to the superficial burns of his friend Pierre's face and hands. When the chattering outside exploded into cheering, the bespectacled savant rushed outside with chief surgeon Larrey and some of the women who were acting as volunteers.

"*Qu'est-ce qui se passe?* What's happening?" Antoine asked a passing *tirailleur* who hobbled on a makeshift crutch, one leg a mashed-up stump.

"Reinforcements. From France."

But soon the excitement evaporated. The fleet approaching the harbour came into view flying British and Turkish flags. It was the turn of the occupants of the beleaguered garrison to explode into euphoria. However, this became the cue for Napoleon to re-double his efforts. His batteries pounded the fortification incessantly and gradually parts of the tower crashed into the moat. Sir Sidney Smith, during a lull, peered down from the battlements at the mounds of earth and sandbags which the French sappers had built up and fortified with the dead of each side. The engineers' efforts with their explosive charges had already resulted in the undermining of the towers leading to their partial collapse. The next assault, he determined, was imminent and potentially decisive. He gathered his marines in anticipation.

The grenadiers once more rushed forward supported by sharpshooters, their battle cries piercing the acrid air. Pierre was leading his section in the vanguard. He was fatalistic. He had survived the brutal attrition so far, but he felt that the inevitable was drawing near. However, the enemy's lack of ammunition and resources had lessened the threat. He scrambled over the earthworks and corpses of his former comrades which acted as a bridge across the moat and used the broken rocks of the tower as stepping-stones, surging towards the breach. The grisly, sickening sight of cadavers sticking out of the earth like scorched demons rising from the depths of Hell did not help his fatalistic mindset but regardless, he and his fellow grenadiers pressed forward, fuelled by an unrivalled esprit de corps and infiltrated the breach.

"Kill the barbarians! Revenge your dead comrades!" Cros bawled, now a captain.

Up on the ramparts, Smith waited with his men. This was do or die time. "Follow me my brave men! To the breach! Fight to the last! For king and country!"

His contingent of marines and sailors flooded down into the breach and engaged the enemy. Smith's men fired their muskets and pistols at point-blank range and resorted to hand-to-hand combat. Smith cut down a grenadier with a thrust of his sabre and took out another with his pistol. The grenadiers responded by bayoneting the British fighters. Amidst the rubble and enveloped in a deadly pall of smoke from musket and cannon, carnage ensued once more. Cousseau fired his weapon bringing down a mulatto marine and followed up by bayoneting him savagely.

"Onwards!" he roared, adrenalin coursing through his veins. A dagger wielding sailor jumped towards him sending him sprawling on the rocks. The snarling, tooth-blackened Englishman leapt at him bringing a knife swiftly down to Cousseau's face, a fraction from his cheekbone, still sore and red from his burns. The skin on his burnt, bandaged hand chafed and peeled away agonisingly as the two struggled. His musket hand was pinned back. He couldn't adjust his grip enough to take advantage of his bayonet, but he just managed to bring his knee sharply up into his enemy's abdomen. The winded Englishmen grunted, and they both tumbled off the block of stone. They crashed to the ground entwined, the grip of the mariner loosening with the impact. The Englishman's head suffered a glancing blow from a spent stationary cannonball, disorientating him momentarily. The Frenchman's musket spilled out of his hand after the jarring fall but remained tantalisingly beyond his grasp. His opponent, regaining his senses, still clutched his knife but Cousseau reacted quickest. He saw a bayonet protruding from the earthworks still in the charred fist of a headless cadaver. He ripped the weapon from its gnarled grip just as his bloodied opponent bore down on him with his dagger. He sank the bayonet into the sailor's chest and rolled him away. Cousseau lay exhausted, trying to catch his breath. He stared at the charred bayonet, noticing the name Malpas, scratched roughly into the hilt.

"*Merci, mon jeune compagnon,*" he muttered.

Cousseau was jolted abruptly by a musket ball flying past his head. Shards of rock shattered over him, some penetrating his face. He grimaced, rolling instinctively onto his back ready to defend himself with Malpas's bayonet. Poised on a large block of kurkar stone above him, stood an English officer, brandishing a sabre in one hand and a smoking pistol in the other, peering down at him. He braced himself expecting the enemy combatant to instantly leap upon him. Then he heard drums, British drums, emanating from the ramparts, sounding the retreat. The Englishman glanced over his shoulder and then turned to Cousseau and spoke to him in perfect French.

"*Aujourd'hui, vous avez de la chance, citoyen. Retournez au petit caporal avec mes salutations les plus cordiales. Sir Sidney Smith à votre service.*"

The dark-haired Englishman smiled and then took his leave. The French sergeant's heart pounded in his chest. He had been lucky. He exhaled, his tense shoulders relaxing. Cousseau looked up into the breach to catch a glimpse of another animated figure exhorting the British fighters back from their foray. It was Djezzar again, fierce eyes blazing with demented fury, scimitar glinting in the sun. The French attack had run its course, stopped in its tracks by the courageous English detachment. The French drummer boys struck up, battering their drums to order the retreat too. The attackers pulled back leaving the breach to be reinforced by Djezzar's fresh turbaned troops, disembarked from the newly arrived fleet.

20

Smith used the lull to supervise the offload of supplies from the fleet before returning to the crumbling ramparts. The English commander extended his spyglass and scanned the vicinity. He could clearly see Bonaparte on 'Napoleon's Hill' with his entourage. The French general was again gesticulating incessantly. Smith again assumed rightly that another attack was imminent. He went immediately to confer with Djezzar who gave him strict instructions to follow. The tactics for the besieged, this time, were to allow some of the attackers into the grounds of the fortress, then surround, trap and annihilate them, a common Turkish stratagem. Cousseau and his unit, fortunately, were not called up for this attack. They were allowed to stand down.

Cousseau staggered into his tent and collapsed. After a couple of hours of deep sleep, a hand on his shoulder startled him. He grabbed instinctively for Malpas's bayonet which he had taken from the battlefield, only relinquishing it from his manic grip when he had crashed out. He relaxed when he saw the hand belonged to his Nubian 'princess', Chione. She had accompanied the army into Syria with the other camp followers and wives. She caressed his scalded, battle-scarred, grimy face gently with the back of her slender black fingers. He winced. He seized her bangled wrist gently. She understood. She beckoned him to follow her back to her quarters in the middle of the sprawling camp. She had been fortunate to find Cousseau. She was a slave destined to become a prostitute, to be shared by the sergeant and his coterie of subordinates who had pooled their resources for her upkeep. However, Cousseau had pulled rank on his brethren, claiming her first. He subsequently fell for her and could not bear the prospect of her being passed around, so he bought her out, returning the monies to the others with interest. He had also managed to protect her from a purge of prostitutes back in Cairo by hiding her in a coffin. Her fellow *'filles de joie'* had not been so lucky. A local sheik had been instructed by the French authorities to remove all sex workers from the barracks and camps because venereal diseases were ravaging the troops, however Napoleon was incensed when he discovered that the official had decapitated over four hundred women, sewn their headless corpses into sacks and thrown them into the Nile. Chione had scared the wits out of several fusiliers when she had rapped on the coffin lid to be released.

"What devilment is this!" shrieked one when the ebony figure emerged from the wooden casket in the evening and flung herself into the arms of her awaiting lover.

His Nubian concubine pulled him into her tent. First, she tended to his wounds by dabbing his face softly and soothingly with a cloth dipped in linseed oil. Then she kissed him passionately and let her gown slip to the floor. She started to undress the weary soldier, his loins stirring as he contemplated the sensual pleasures to come. Her smooth, glistening naked body pressed into his bare torso, her nipples brushing his hairy chest. The sensation sending him into ecstasy. Her full lips exploded again on to his mouth, and he slowly guided her to the floor and made passionate love to her.

21

The new assault had begun, led by General Lannes. The troopers poured through the breach and made their way into Djezzar's palace gardens whereupon the vanguard was set upon by Djezzar's warriors and fresh Albanian troops from the flotilla. Soon after, a slew of headless corpses were strewn around the gardens as if some overzealous horticulturalists had taken to their secateurs and shears in an orgy of ruthless dead-heading. Some desperate French survivors, who were now cut off, began to fight their way into the narrow streets. Others tried to retreat through the breach to escape the trap, but their numbers gradually diminished, fusillade after fusillade cutting them down, the raking enfilading coming from the surrounding defensive positions. The screams and the cracking of muskets were punctuated only by the sounds of ululating Moslem women. The survivors sought refuge in a mosque and were prepared to defend their position to the last with swathes of Turks and Albanians massing ready to butcher every single one of them. However, remarkably Sidney Smith intervened, and a detachment of his marines gave two hundred of their fellow Europeans a safe passage out and into his protection as prisoners of war.

22

By now Napoleon was desperate. He decided, after another lull, to resume the attack. This time General Kléber's troops were to be the vanguard buoyed by their recent victory at the Battle of Mount Tabor. They had enjoyed the spoils of war pillaging the tented camp of the fleeing rag tag Army of Damascus and were keen for more. The newly arrived troops of Hassan Bey's Turkish reinforcements counter-attacked though from a different breach, surprising the French. Mortal combat ensued in the forward trenches. The French regrouped and Kléber valiantly led his men again, only to be discouraged by mines laid in the moat and by the potentially lethal flammable conditions therein, and also by the stench and sight of the avalanche of dead bodies that lay piled up on the approaches to the breach. No corpse had been removed for days. Ten days later, after a constant barrage, the siege ended.

23

Liverpool. Present day.

At 2pm prompt, Paul entered the Feathers Hotel. Some guests and hotel staff looked at him sniffily. He gave his name and quoted the reference number and was passed a key card. He found his room, opened the door, saw the welcoming bed and jumped on it. He could hardly believe his luck. A beautiful and kind woman had taken an interest in his plight. He removed his clothes giving his arm pits a sniff, made a face and then headed for the shower. After his refreshing ablutions he applied his deodorant then shaved his stubble awkwardly with a cheap razor and shaving foam he found in the bag of smellies and popped his clothes back on, lamenting the fact that they smelt musty. Then he went shopping for clothes. He was on a bargain hunt. He purchased some cheap trainers, jeans and chinos, t-shirts, underwear, a cap and a hoody. Every penny well spent. Then he returned to the hotel to make the most of his stay and read his book, looking forward to his evening meal. When Paul went for breakfast in the morning, he checked at reception for the time he had to vacate his room. He was surprised and delighted to find that he had been booked in for another night. At 11.45am he strolled up Mount Pleasant to meet Jules at noon.

He sat on the bench and waited. Jules came into the gardens and promptly walked past him. "Hey, Jules I'm here."

She turned. "Oh, my goodness! I didn't recognise you!"

He looked even more handsome dressed in a long-sleeved white cotton top and beige chinos, with his slicked-back shining mane, giving him the air of a caparisoned thoroughbred stallion. She looked stunning in her tight top and blue jeans which highlighted the contours of her body. She still wore her sun hat. Her beautiful auburn tresses flowing like a cascading waterfall around her pretty face. As she sat beside him, she let out an unintended groan and held the lower half of her back.

"What's up?" Paul inquired with concern.

"I must have twisted something when that ladder fell on top of me the other day. Hopefully, it will clear up before the weekend."

Paul gave her a meaningful stare, but she averted her eyes. There was a moment of silence.

"I thank you for your generosity by the way. You shouldn't have paid for -"

"It's no problem. All I ask is for you to do someone else a favour in return. Now, about this dig. I belong to a charitable organisation, the Merseyside Archaeological Society. We've got a dig lined up at Irby Hall, on the Wirral. The Hall was built on the site of an 11th century medieval manor and courthouse."

"Sounds interesting."

"We're allowed to camp on site so we can spend as much time as possible there. You don't have to bring anything with you. We've got tents, equipment, food, the lot. I'll get one of my friends to pick you up at 7am tomorrow. His name is Randy. Ok?"

"Great!"

"I'm going to meet Randy now to sort out some of the equipment and provisions. I just need to collect a few items from the faculty. The clothes look great by the way. One other thing. Go to the Central Library and do some research on the site. I'm going to test you on it tomorrow. Here. Take this tenner for your lunch."

And with that Jules slowly raised herself up, forced a smile, then left.

The next morning Paul was waiting in reception. He sat in contemplation, wondering about the outcome of his interview. At 7.15am a tall, lean Asian guy with a ponytail came in and went straight over to the receptionist and spoke. She pointed across to Paul. The man came over to Paul and introduced himself.

"Paul? Hello, I'm Randip. Nice to meet you."

They shook hands.

"Likewise."

"Have you been on a dig before?"

"Not really. I used to have a metal detector though."

"Oh, find anything interesting?"

"Just some IED's, mines and shells."

"Ah! I see, you're in the military."

"Used to be."

"Come on, we'd best go. You can tell me about it in the car. My grandfather was in the army in WWII. Sikh regiment."

"Oh, yeah? Interesting. You'll have to tell me more."

Paul picked his haversack up and followed Randy out of the hotel.

At the dig site, they met up with Jules, her friend Penny Carter and about twelve others. After introductions they had a brief meeting detailing the day's procedures and set about the first task which was to organise the sleeping arrangements. A few, like Paul were given their own single tent and others had doubles. Paul helped set up the tents and a larger marquee which was to be used as a 'finds' centre in case anything interesting was unearthed. They then concentrated on the dig, with Jules, Penny and Randy, the professionals, lending their experience to the amateurs. The day turned out to be quite successful with some 'finds'; some bits of pottery dating back, the experts reckoned, to the 11th century and some fragments of old farming tools dating back to the 16th century. Dinner was arranged at the nearby Anchor pub for 7.30pm. Everyone was waiting for Penny and Jules who were sharing a tent together. Randy sent Paul over to see what they were doing. Paul was just heading over there when Penny came out and approached him.

"Hi Penny. Is Jules ready?"

"She's just putting her face on. Just go straight in and give her a shout."

Penny carried on walking, chuckling to herself. Paul walked into the tent. "Hey, Jules."

He stopped suddenly and gawped. She was still in her bra and panties. She yelped and scrambled for her dressing gown. His look was one of astonishment and his mouth opened as if he were about to speak. He turned his head away, diverting his eyes, not before registering the array of bruises on her back and legs. She had wrapped herself in her dressing gown and waited until Penny had left before dressing.

"You should have knocked!" she said flustered.

"Bit hard to on a tent. I'm sorry. Penny told me to go straight in."

"Did she now?"

"Everyone's ready to go."

"Ok. Let me get dressed and I'll be straight there."

Paul departed, his blood boiling. 'How could anybody treat a woman like that? One so sweet, kind and beautiful'.

He re-joined the group, keeping his observations and opinions to himself. They all had a great evening in the pub. Jules slipped Paul some money to buy a round of drinks and to pay for his meal. He would pay her in kind. He promised himself. He was embarrassed.

On the Sunday they excavated, measured, and recorded other minor finds until 6pm. They packed up, had dinner in the pub again and all left at 9pm. Randy gave a lift to Jules this time. Penny had changed her plans and was going to stay on the Wirral at her parents' home in nearby Pensby overnight. Jules was dropped off first at Wapping Quay, so Paul got an idea of where she lived. Jules had paid for him to stay one more night in the Feathers hotel and had promised she would help him find somewhere more permanent in the coming week. Randy dropped Paul off at the Feathers. The ex-military man went to his room, deposited his bag and went straight out again. He headed back down to the Strand. He grabbed a pint at the Baltic Fleet pub and sat looking across at the large, Jesse Hartley designed building where he had seen Jules head for. He watched carefully for any activity. The lights went on and off in the different apartments of the brick-built four-storey rectangular edifice. He was not sure if Jules's apartment lay on his side of the building or the other, then suddenly another light came on. His question was answered. He saw Jules. She seemed to be remonstrating with someone. Richard came into view. He grabbed Jules by the hair violently. Paul seethed with anger. The couple moved out of view and never returned. Paul finished his drink and left.

24

The next evening Paul, who was back on the streets again, returned to Wapping Quay. He had left his rucksack at the left luggage facility in Lime Street Station using the last of the money that Jules had given him. He had kept just enough for a beer. He approached the entrance to the apartments pretending to take an interest in the nearby listed Gate Keeper's Lodge and Hydraulic Tower and noticed that Richard's car was not in the parking lot. Then he went across to the Baltic Fleet for a pint and sat and waited until it was dark. He crossed the road and hid in the shadows, waiting for thirty minutes. Eventually a vehicle appeared at the gated entrance. It was Richard's car. The electronic gates opened, and Paul slipped through unnoticed at the side of the silver BMW. He waited for Richard to park up the car. Paul, hoodie on and scarf over his face, slipped out of the shadows and landed a blow to the back of Richard's head, poleaxing him. He picked him up and started to kidney punch him. He left him in a heap on the floor and used his victim's fob to re-open the gates and casually melted away in the darkness. Richard didn't see a thing.

A few days passed and Paul hadn't seen Jules around. He sat in the Square. He hovered around outside the two university libraries and walked around to the Garstang Museum. He went down to the Strand. He was concerned. But her white Range Rover Evoque wasn't there. He went to the World Museum to see Penny. He waited in the foyer and eventually saw her by the reception desk. He approached her.

"Excuse me Penny, sorry to bother you. Have you seen Jules at all?"

"No, because she's away at a conference in Berlin for the rest of the week. She phoned me."

"Oh, she didn't tell me."

"Well, I'm sure Paul you're way down on her list of people she'd notify."

Paul was momentarily offended by the acerbic comment. 'She's probably right. Who am I? A nobody.' He could see that Penny was preoccupied.

"Listen Penny. I know you're busy and you don't want to talk to nobodies like me, but I'm concerned for Jules. This is very important if you value your friendship with her."

Penny glanced around. No one was in earshot.

"You've got two minutes."

"I think Richard is attacking her."

Penny laughed. Disbelieving. "What? Don't be ridiculous! He wouldn't harm a flea. Not even yours! Where did you get that idea from?"

Paul ignored the jibe.

"I've seen the evidence, Penny. The bruises. All over her body."

"Bruises?"

"Paul, have you been popping pills again or something? You must be hallucinating. Richard's a lovely man."

"Remember at the dig when you told me to fetch her out of her tent? She was half-naked when I went in."

Penny guffawed. "Gotcha Jules! I bet you got an eyeful then Paul."

"I certainly did. She's beautiful but I'm telling you she was covered in bruises."

"No way, Paul!"

"Did you see her thighs, the top of her arms or her back?"

"Not really. She had that dressing gown on all the time."

"Well, exactly. Who takes a dressing gown with them when they're camping?"

Penny paused for thought.

"I'm telling you Richard is an abuser. A violent man."

"Well poor Richard was violently attacked himself."

"I know."

"You know? How? You haven't seen Jules. She's not back until Mon-"

Penny stopped mid-sentence. Sickened, she stared at Paul contemptuously.

"It was you, wasn't it? You attacked him! Get out of here before I call the police."

A security guard approached them. Paul hesitated, wanting to clarify things but decided to leave immediately. 'Damn', he thought. 'That didn't go to plan. Why did I tell her that?'

Jules had attended the conference on anthropology and human evolution at short notice since she felt the need to get away from Richard again. She had nursed him after his mugging for a day or two. He stayed off work to recuperate from his injuries. Richard's mate Frank had called and told him about seeing Jules and some 'tramp' having a coffee. Richard quizzed Jules about 'this dirty tramp'. He was looking to take his anger out on something or someone after his beating. Despite the care and attention that he received from Jules she became the easy target again.

"What the fuck are you doing with a tramp? Who the fuck is he? Are you fucking stupid or something, you daft fucking bitch! Spending money on a fuckin' waster!"

He slapped her hard knocking her over a coffee table. He yanked her up and grabbed her by her hair and frog marched her into the bedroom. He threw her on the bed, slapping her and then ripped off her casual joggers. He forced her face down on the bed and taking the cigarette from his mouth he burnt her numerous times with it stubbing it on her buttocks. Then he raped her again, strangling her until she almost passed out.

25

The plane landed smoothly on the runway at John Lennon Airport on the Monday morning. Penny was unexpectedly waiting in the arrivals terminal for Jules to give her a lift. She wanted to forewarn her friend about Paul. Tell her that he had mugged Richard. That he was dangerous. They got in the car.

"I just want to buy some plants from Dobbies, the garden centre," Penny said. "We'll have some lunch as well. I've got the day off."

They perused the plants. Penny bought some dahlias and an agapanthus. Jules, who was subdued, which she insincerely blamed on a late night, began to look through the summer collection of dresses in the store.

"That one's nice Jules. That'll suit you. Go on, try it on, there's a cubicle over there. Take that one also. I'll go and grab us a table at the café."

'Right', Penny thought, 'after this we'll have a bite to eat, and I'll tell her about Paul. I'll give her the option of notifying the police. I'm sure they'll want her to press charges'. Jules took the pretty floral-patterned dresses off the rail and entered the cubicle but Penny, instead of heading for the café, paused, spying another summer dress on the rail that might suit Jules. She took it over to the cubicle and popped her head around the curtain. Jules was in a state of undress. She was down to her undergarments.

"What the -" Penny cried, in horror.

Jules had spun around and was now holding the dress up to her body. Penny stared at her. She saw the burn marks and bruises on her friend's back and buttocks. She then realised that Paul had been telling the truth. Richard was the real twat. Her shock turned to rage.

"Who the hell has done that to you, Jules? Richard?"

Jules broke down and wept. "Yes," she said quietly between sobs.

"The bastard! I don't believe it! Why has he done this to you? How long has it been going on?"

Penny had a million questions. But it was not the time or place.

"Come on, get dressed. Leave the dresses there. You're coming back to mine. You're going to stay with me."

They got in the car and drove to Penny's house in Woolton, not too far away. The house was empty, her husband Ian was at work and her teenage kids out with their friends. Penny had a tête-à-tête with her distraught friend. All that angst and pain and the awful memories that she had bottled up flowed from her like a waterfall of emotions.

"Listen Jules. I need to pop out for a while to pick up my son. I want you to stay here, do you understand? When I come back, we'll figure out what to do next."

Penny left Jules resting on the settee. She jumped in her car but instead of picking her son up, which was a ruse, she drove to Abercromby Square to find Paul. He was there, in the gardens. She approached him.

"Paul!" she called. Paul looked up, saw Penny, and ignored her. She sat beside him.

"Listen, Paul. I owe you an apology. You were right about that horrible get, Richard. I've just seen the burns and bruises. They're horrific! Sickening! She's just opened up to me. I can't believe the punishment that poor woman has taken off that horrible prick. I'm going to inform the police."

At that moment she received a text. It was from Jules. She had left the house in a taxi and was heading home to grab some things whilst Richard was at work. Penny tried to call Jules back.

"She's going to the apartment! I told her to wait at my house. Shit! She's not picking up."

Just then Penny's mobile rang.

"Hello, Max. What's up?...You've fallen off your bike...Your knee? Oh, great! Great timing you big oaf...Right, I'll come and get you now. Where are you? Calderstones Park?"

Penny stood up and ended the call.

"Hey!" she suddenly shouted. A traffic warden was taking an interest in her 4x4. She'd not bought a parking ticket.

"I don't believe this! Paul, here, take these keys. They're the spare keys to Jules's apartment. She's no.10, second floor up. Can you go and help her whilst I sort my son out?"

Penny rushed out of the gardens to save herself from getting a ticket. Paul placed the keys in his pocket, picked up his backpack and started to jog down the road, weaving in and out of pedestrians and dodging cars. Meanwhile Jules had reached the apartments. She paid the taxi driver and then surveyed the car park for Richard's car. 'Good,' she thought, 'it's not there. He's at work'. She entered the building swiftly and took the lift. She got to her apartment door, turned the key and went in. Suddenly a blow caught her across the head. She fell to the floor in agony.

"Argh!" she cried.

Richard stood there; fists clenched. He had parked away from the car park and was waiting for her. He wrenched her up by the hair.

"Come here you little bitch! What's this?"

He thrust a bank statement into her face.

"Feathers Hotel. £180 quid. £50 quid here. Another £50 there. What the fuck have you been up to? You dirty fucking whore! Are you shagging someone?"

She smelt the alcohol on his breath. He grabbed her aggressively and snarled, pushing his hate-filled face intimidatingly into hers.

"No! Richard! Please! Let go! You're really hurting me!"

"You're fucking lying, you bitch!"

He punched her in the head. She wailed in pain and crashed to the floor.

"I swear I'm going to do you good and proper. You fucking tart!"

Richard grabbed a knife and held it to her throat. "Who is he?"

63

"No-no-no! Richard don't! I promise there's no one else. The hotel was for the homeless guy. I-I felt sorry for him. I paid for his lodgings for a few days. That's all. Please stop!"

She could feel the blade pressing further into her skin. "I don't believe you. You horrible slag! You're shaggin' a dirty fuckin' meff, aren't you? Is that your sordid little way of getting kicks? Your little fetish? Your fuckin' little secret! It takes a tramp to know one, doesn't it? What is he? An alky? A junkie? A weak little shithouse who probably gets a good kicking every night but couldn't be arsed as long as he's high!"

Richard punched her again, this time landing a heavy blow on her lip that spurted blood. He was as mad as she had ever seen him. She feared for her life. This time he couldn't care less what he did or where he hit her.

"What's his name? Come on! Tell me, what's his fucking name?"

He raised his fist again to hit her when suddenly from behind someone grabbed his wrist tightly.

"Paul, my name's Paul."

Richard froze in shock. He turned to see who it was.

"Paul De Vere."

Paul smashed him in the face with a left. Richard fell backwards, hit the table, and landed heavily on the floor. He dragged himself up, wiped the blood from his mouth and charged at Paul with the knife. Paul evaded him, grabbed his knife-wielding wrist, and broke it, disarming him. Richard let out a piercing scream.

"Who's the weak little shithouse now?"

Paul punched him again, flooring him a second time, then jumped on top of him smashing him in the face.

"Don't ever go near her again! Don't ever hit a woman again, you little turd!" he spat as he continuously punished him.

Paul picked him up one more time and flung him over the table. He then strode over to the whimpering Richard, picked up a chair and smashed it down on his legs so forcefully it broke Richard's kneecaps. He roared with pain. At this moment, the police, alerted by neighbours, burst in and tasered Paul. He fell to the ground.

"You've got the wrong one!" Jules screamed. "He's the wrong one!"

Another police officer looked at her perplexed.

"He saved me! He saved me!"

She burst into tears. With her head in her hands, sobbing and trembling she collapsed down onto her knees and buried her head in a settee cushion.

26

Acre, 1799

At the onset of dawn on the 21st day of May 1799, a jaded, bleary-eyed Sidney Smith was at his station on the ramparts. He brought his spyglass up to his eye again and scanned the battlefield. As the gloom lifted, he noted no movement behind the earthworks nor amidst the detritus of war scattered across the churned-up, battle-scarred landscape. He allowed himself a wry smile. Napoleon and his troops had disappeared. The dispirited enemy had slunk away covertly during the night. Cheers rang out from the defenders who had guarded the city throughout the night alerting the rest of the weary besieged denizens and evoking widespread jubilation. The siege had been lifted. They had survived. The triumphant Smith had not only out-thought the formidable Bonaparte, but he had also won the psychological battle by dint of his written communiqués to Napoleon and by his practice of printing leaflets in French, sending them fluttering down from the ramparts to the Gallic rank and file below. Their propaganda content playing heavily on the enemies' minds, undermining their morale.

The French column was snaking its way through the Levant back towards Egypt. The wounded and sick were carried on horseback, donkeys, and stretchers. Equipment was abandoned to lighten the load; mainly ordnance and tools belonging to the artillery. The cavalry guarded the rear. Pierre Cousseau marched near the front of the column. Chione and Demeraux were in the middle with the sick and wounded. Pierre had asked Antoine to look out for Chione. The retreating army was joined by scores of Christians fleeing Djezzar knowing he would seek revenge, taking his anger and brutality out on them. The column hugged the coastline. As the days wore on, they were harassed by Bedouin tribesmen. Pierre trudged on relentlessly with his comrades when suddenly they heard the boom of cannons. It came from Sir Sidney Smith's vessel the *Tigre* and the other ships in the enemy squadron shadowing the retreating column like a pack of hungry wolves. A cannonball smashed into the ranks behind the sergeant. A *tirailleur* was cut in two, another had his arm taken cleanly off. The screams echoed along the line. Medics attended to the injured, but the order came to keep marching. Again, in the rear, Pierre heard more screams. Another cannonball had buried itself somewhere into the legion of the vanquished. He could only hope that Chione and Antoine were safe.

27

On arrival at Jaffa the column was ordered to halt. Pierre, who had arrived the day before, waited eagerly for the rest of the column to arrive. All day he waited anxiously. It was now the evening. Throughout the day sections of the ragged column had entered the city gates. Then the wives, savants and sick and injured began to arrive. He dragged himself down the snaking, chaotic column, scouring the wretched line of humanity desperately for Chione.

"Chione!" he called. "Chione! Demeraux! Antoine Demeraux!"

He stopped some exhausted women whom he vaguely knew. "*Avez-vous vu* Chione? *La nubienne.*"

The weary women shook their heads. He continued his search. He came across some other savants distinctive by their grey uniforms.

"*Excusez-moi. Où est citoyen* Demeraux?"

"*Il est malade. Il arrive avec les malades. Derrière nous,*" answered one of the fatigued, shuffling savants.

Pierre increased his pace, passing the donkeys, mules and horses transporting the wounded, interspersed with stretcher bearers, soldiers or prisoners, struggling with their abject human loads. Occasional moans emanated from these unfortunates, some of whom were in a state of delirium, others with their faces carpeted in flies. He frantically swiped away at the swarms of winged creatures in his desperate desire to scrutinise each passing pallid, dirty face, but to no avail. There was a delay before the next meandering collective of miserable souls arrived, so he sat and waited under the shade of a palm tree. He shared the shade with others and drank the tepid, brackish water from his canteen. The plague of persistent flies fought for access to the moisture around his cracked lips. He swotted them away irritably, spitting more than one out from his parched mouth. He offered his canteen generously to the bombardier sitting next to him. There was no response. He was dead. Cousseau rested his head on the tree and peered up into the azure blue skies and watched as several white scavenger vultures, 'pharaoh's chickens', circled on the hot thermals. One landed on the stony ground beyond him and pecked at some human faeces. Hors d'oeuvres before its main course. A banquet of human flesh, bones and entrails that would be shared with roaming jackals and others of that ilk. Gradually, more prisoners, faces contorted in agony, staggered past with their stretcher loads of human misery, accompanied by guards. Cousseau rose to his aching feet and stood wearily, ready to inspect them. Clusters of camp followers were scattered amongst the retreating rank and file. Victuallers too, constantly prodding and thwacking forlorn, overloaded beasts of burden with sticks. Other poor beasts transported human cargo more dead than alive. He maintained his vigil, glancing down at each stretcher observing stricken, anguished faces or examining those individuals slung over animals. Some were already dead, the trance-like stretcher bearers or animal guides too exhausted or traumatised to notice. Then suddenly he stiffened with fear as his eyes focused on the unmistakable sign of buboes bulging from the armpit of a prostrate soldier. He frantically ran along the line of casualties checking each disease-ridden victim, disregarding his own safety until, further down the line, he could just make out the ebony features and jet black closely cropped hair of a woman sprawled on an ass, her hands tied around its neck. He dashed up close.

"Chione! Oh no! Chione."

Her eyelids flickered. She was still alive. Cousseau angrily dispersed the mass of flies tormenting her. She raised her head with difficulty, half-opened her eyes and smiled weakly, uttering his name. "Pierre, Pierre, *mon amour...*,"

He stared in horror at the pus-filled bubo bulging from her delicate neck. She always wore a choker, but she had discarded it. The last time that they had made love she had worn it and he was not aware that she had contracted the disease. Tears filled her eyes. Insects congregated again, swarming to slake their thirst from the moist droplets on her fevered brow. Cousseau futilely swotted them away once more, then he took the reins of the ass and relieved the Bedouin prisoner of his duties. He veered out of the column and increased his pace, heading towards the town. He stopped at a square where a field hospital had been set up. He untied the rope binding Chione to the animal, and she slid into his arms. Laying her down carefully on a sheet on the ground, he covered her with the blanket from the ass. He took out his water bottle and held it to her cracked lips and she weakly sipped at the tepid but thirst-quenching contents.

"*Merci,*" she whispered.

Pierre held her hand softly in his palm. The bubonic plague was feared by all, since very little was known about it; how it was spread or if it was contagious, but, at that very moment, Cousseau could not care less if he succumbed to it. All he wanted was to be by her side. He remained there for some time. More and more plague victims were brought into the square. Then Cousseau spotted the grey uniform of a savant amongst the new arrivals.

"*Un moment,*" he whispered to Chione. "I will return."

He skirted around the stretchers of moaning and wailing victims and came to the stretcher the savant was laid upon. It was Demeraux. Cousseau froze in horror. The putrid stench was unbearable around the stricken savant. Cousseau baulked. Some of the wretched victims had dysentery as well and lay in their own faeces. He pressed his hand over his nose and mouth then spoke.

"Antoine! Antoine! *C'est moi,* Pierre!"

Demeraux opened his eyes slowly and focused on his friend. A faint smile crossed his lips. He too had all the dreaded symptoms of the bubonic plague. He was febrile yet shivering and bruised. Inflamed lymph nodes were clearly visible, protruding from under the skin of his neck. Cousseau removed his tunic and draped it over the sick young man.

"Chione," Demeraux uttered. "She has succumbed to the disease also."

"I know," Cousseau replied, tearfully. He held his canteen up to his friend's mouth. "I have found her. She is here."

"Go back to her," Demeraux croaked.

Cousseau firmly grasped his friend's hand and said a few words of comfort to him, then returned to Chione. He took her palm and caressed it delicately. She opened her eyes and gently smiled.

"I have something to tell you. Come closer," she said softly. Cousseau bent over her. His ear close to her lips.

"I am with child."

Cousseau's face crumpled. His tears flowed down his rough, unshaven cheeks and he laid his head on her bosom, sobbing. His shaking hand moved to her abdomen, and he felt a slight curve there which he had not noticed when he last slept with her. He pushed up her robe to place a kiss on her stomach but momentarily hesitated, alarmed, his eyes transfixed on more buboes; red-purplish sores around her crotch.

On an adjacent stretcher lay a dragoon, sweating profusely, shouting out in delirium. His boots had been removed, presumably stolen. His toes were green, a gangrenous green and decomposing, the stench from his lesions, almost making Cousseau retch. The delirious cavalryman kicked off his blanket to reveal his naked groin pockmarked by several swollen, festering, pus-seeping mounds. He coughed. Sputum and blood spurted from his mouth. His eyes opened wide, and he stared manically as if he had seen an apparition above him, then his body stiffened. The seizure ending his suffering.

The overworked surgeon, Larrey came along accompanied by his attendants. The medic ordered the two prisoners to remove the corpse, its blood shot eyes still bulging in a death stare. He turned to Cousseau.

"Sergeant, come. We have a job to do here. Please, return to your unit. We shall do our best for her."

"*Je t'aime toujours*, Pierre," Chione said in hushed tones.

"*Je t'adore, ma princesse*," he blurted out, crying. He let go of her hand and swiped away the flies in anger then gently kissed her on the lips. She vomited almost straight after, retching violently. A look of terror crossed his countenance, and he staggered back aghast. The flies swooped again, feasting on the chunks of puke.

"I'll take care of that," Larrey said positioning himself between the stricken Chione and the soldier she loved. "Go now. That's an order."

Cousseau returned solemnly to his unit, a broken man.

28

Cousseau could not sleep that night. At dawn, he crawled out of his tent careful not to wake any of the other sergeants who were entitled to a tent over their heads, his boots in his hands. He pulled them on and proceeded to the square. The sun was beginning to rise over the city of Jaffa. The call to prayers competed with crowing cocks to disturb everyone's slumber. He arrived just as an orderly was covering Chione's face with a pall. He rushed over and dragged back the shroud, cursing the attendant.

"Non, ne faites pas ça!" The orderly glared at him indignantly. Cousseau looked at his lover's face. It was serene and despite the buboes scarring her smooth face, still beautiful.

"Elle dort!" he blubbed. *"Le bébé dort, aussi."*

The medic simply stared at Cousseau, believing him to be deranged. His indignation turned to sympathy. But Cousseau knew deep down she was lost as was the child he would never know. The orderly moved away, and Cousseau sank to his knees, head bowed, weeping. He then peered up at the cloudless blue skies and cursed the God that had forsaken the one he loved.

A friend of Chione's, Jemila, approached him. She wept also when she saw her deceased friend.

"Come, Pierre, we have to bury her," she said softly pulling Cousseau up from his knees. "We shall not let her be dumped in a pit like the others."

Cousseau looked around the square. He sniffled and wiped his reddened eyes with his sleeve. The attendants were taking away the cadavers of those that had died during the night leaving dozens of empty spaces that were previously occupied by the sick. He peered towards the spot where Demeraux had lain. He was no longer there. Cousseau put his hand to his face and cursed.

"Putain! Mon ami aussi! Pourquoi? Pourquoi?" he raged.

Jemila hugged him before kneeling and praying.

"Verily we belong to Allah, and truly to Him shall we return."

She then placed the shroud over Chione's beautiful but now pallid visage and beckoned to some prisoners. They placed Chione's body on a stretcher and Jemila cajoled Cousseau into following them, pulling at his sleeve. They followed the stretcher-bearers out beyond the city walls and Jemila told them to halt at a stable. The pallbearers laid the stretcher down. Cousseau just stood in a state of shock, overwhelmed with grief. Jemila disappeared but came back ten minutes later escorted by an imam. She held a jug of water and a white cloth. The men waited outside the stables whilst Jemila washed Chione's body as best she could. She invited the imam in, and they gently rolled the Nubian's body onto the cloth and wrapped it securely. The attendants took Chione over to a barren patch of land.

69

Cousseau followed lamely behind. Jemila looked on from a distance. They placed the stretcher down and started to dig a grave. Once ready, Cousseau and one of the prisoners slowly lowered the body into the grave ensuring that Chione was facing towards Mecca. They covered the shroud with bits of wood from an abandoned old cart. The kadi uttered prayers for the deceased then nodded to the men who responded by tipping spadefuls of earth and lime into the pit in which Chione rested until it was filled in. Another prayer was said on completion of the task. Jemila approached the grave and placed a flower on it, then she, the kadi and the others melted away leaving Cousseau alone with his thoughts.

After several minutes of contemplation, he wiped the tears from his eyes and left. Now he wanted to find out where the body of his friend, Demeraux, lay. Heading towards a mound of earth that he could see a quarter of a mile away, he presumed rightly that this was a mass burial pit for the other deceased, those who had died of the plague, dysentery and a multitude of other diseases, ailments and wounds received on the battlefield. He approached two *chasseurs à pied* whom he knew, no doubt on fatigues as a punishment for some misdemeanour. Both skirmishers were unsavoury characters that he had no time for.

"Private Roucard, tell me. Have you buried Demeraux, the savant here?"

Roucard scratched the prominent side burn on his right cheek before answering. "What's that sergeant, a donkey? No, we haven't buried a donkey today, have we Minardi?"

Roucard smelt of alcohol. The other rogue shook his head.

"We could do with one though, we need its *merde* to shovel on these smelly bastards. They smell of even worse shit." Minardi guffawed after his crass comments. "Not to mention the stinking vomit and putrid pus!" he added.

"So, who've you been burying over there?" Roucard asked. "I thought it was your donkey friend. Whoever it is must fucking stink even more because you've buried them away from the other smelly fuckers."

Minardi tittered away again. Cousseau grabbed Roucard by the throat and punched him on his stubbly chin sending him sprawling into the lime-filled burial pit. He lay there concussed amidst the ripe and rotting corpses. Minardi, who had stopped laughing, tried to run for it but Cousseau ran after him and caught him easily and whacked him over the head with the shovel the skirmisher had slung to the floor. The irate sergeant dragged him back to the edge of the pit and launched him into the foul-smelling morass of bodies. Then he went in search of the medical officer in charge, finding him in a bivouac, near the square.

"Excuse me, sir. Do you have the names of the French deceased? I need to know if my friend is amongst them so I can write to his family."

"What's his name?" said the officer tersely.

"Demeraux, Antoine Demeraux. He is a savant."

The medic scanned the list of names.

"No one of that name."

"Are you sure?"

"Of course, I'm sure. Now leave me be, I'm very busy. Try the hospital."

29

Cousseau, hopes raised, rushed to the marquee which served as a hospital. Inside, it was crammed with more plague and dysentery victims and the wounded. The stench again was overwhelming, nearly choking him. He covered his nose with his tunic and frantically scanned the rows of sick and injured for Demeraux but he couldn't see him. He began to think the officer had made an error. His head dropped, his heart sank and dejectedly he turned and headed towards the exit then suddenly he noticed a stretcher half-hidden under a sagging part of the canvas to his left. He walked over to it and as the canvas billowed, he saw that there was someone on it. His heart leapt. It was Demeraux! To his great surprise, he was still alive, just. The rash of buboes had spread to his neck and underneath his armpits. His face was gaunt and wan. Beads of perspiration cascaded down his face.

"Antoine, Antoine. It's Pierre!"

Demeraux struggled to open his eyes to acknowledge his friend. Cousseau withdrew a blade from the scabbard tucked in his belt. Demeraux looked fearful. He stared at Cousseau perplexed. 'My old friend is going to finish me off as an act of mercy'.

"Trust me, *mon ami*."

Demeraux braced himself and swallowed hard but instead of plunging the dagger into his heart, Cousseau used the knife to make a small incision in a bubo. Demeraux flinched, his eyes were bulging now. Foul-smelling, yellow pus oozed out from the suppurating sore.

"Remember Jendin. I told you about him. How he miraculously survived the plague. This is how he did it. Maybe it will work for you."

Demeraux sighed with relief. He winced as Cousseau lanced all the buboes he could find. Removing the sheet covering the savant's midriff, Cousseau discovered more sores, around the groin. He was gently prodding the knife into these when a physician approached flanked by two orderlies and a lieutenant.

"Hey!" the rotund physician called. "What are doing, man? Get out of here!"

One of the orderlies manhandled the sergeant and escorted him to the entrance. Cousseau looked back to see the physician and the other orderly transferring Demeraux to a vacant camp bed. Then he witnessed the medic administering something to Demeraux in the form of a reddish-brown liquid.

"What's that, sir?" he asked the lieutenant before he was bundled out.

"A tincture containing laudanum," he replied morosely.

"Laudanum? Opium! But how will that help?"

Then he suddenly realised. The plague victims were being euthanised.

"*Mon Dieu!* You're killing them all!"

"Go back to your unit. That is an order sergeant! Would you rather have the sick left to the mercy of Djezzar's barbarian hordes who will inflict torture on those they find alive? Or would you prefer to see these unfortunates expire in the compassionate arms of their brethren?"

Cousseau stood there feeling helpless. He understood the sentiments having witnessed the barbarity that existed in these cruel, unforgiving lands. His last sight of Demeraux was of him jerking up, vomiting and falling back onto his camp bed, awaiting death. Cousseau left crestfallen. He paused outside and gulped in some fresh air. Then he exhaled deeply. The day ahead looked so grim and unforgiving. He was to mourn the woman he loved and his unborn child as well as his close friend, Antoine Demeraux. The cocks crowed louder. The call to morning prayers grew more vociferous. There was a distant boom of a cannon. He covered his ears with his hands and ran.

30

The following morning, after having volunteered for a night shift supervising pickets on duty knowing that he would not sleep a wink, a weary Cousseau set off for the burial pit to pay his respects to Demeraux. He trudged solemnly along the street. He paused and pressed his fatigued body against a stone wall to allow a cart pulled by a mule to trundle past in the narrow, otherwise deserted street. He watched the cart draw to a halt further along. Two men leapt from the carriage. One kicked out at a bundle of rags lying across the way. The other clung to the side of the cart and manoeuvered himself slowly along to its rear and unlatched the back of the cart. On the instructions of his colleague, the blind man then took a few tentative steps towards his reassuring co-worker and located the body by touch. Then the two men lifted the body of the beggar and heaved it on to the cart; the dawn-breaking ritual, the cleansing of the wretched dead, had begun. Observing this served only to savagely crush the doleful French soldier's spirits even more. His melancholic thoughts refocused on his friend as the cart rumbled off into the distance. He continued on. As he passed the hospital marquee and happened to glance inside, he froze on the spot. There, sitting up on his camp bed was Demeraux. Cousseau rushed in.

"Antoine! Antoine! You're still alive! I can't believe it! How?"

"I-I don't know but I'm feeling better. They gave me laudanum but apparently, I vomited. I slept through the night, and I woke up feeling better. Look! The swelling has gone down on the buboes."

He displayed his neck and groin.

"It's a miracle!" Cousseau clamoured, his spirits lifted. "I lanced your boils, maybe that helped as well."

"Perhaps! I don't know. Some of the other plague victims have also been revived, but as you can see, others weren't so lucky." He gestured to the shroud-covered corpses around him.

"They're moving me to another hospital so that I can fully recuperate."

"Make sure you do. We are leaving Jaffa tomorrow for Gaza." Cousseau placed his hand firmly on his friend's shoulder.

"Chione, did she...?"

Cousseau shook his head. Demeraux grasped his friend's hand.

"Get some rest. You'll need all your strength for the rest of the journey to Cairo."

31

Liverpool. Present day.

Jules thanked the doctors and nurses at the Spire private hospital for her treatment. They had kept her in overnight giving her a thorough examination and noting all the injuries she had sustained. The police confirmed that Richard had been detained, arrested for domestic abuse and GBH, and that he would be remanded in custody once he was out of surgery at the Royal Hospital. Her ordeal, much to her relief, seemed to be over. Penny came to pick her up. She was to stay at Penny's. A female detective was to interview Jules. She had been advised that it was better to undertake the interview in less intimidating surroundings than in her apartment.

"Where's Paul?" asked Jules, as she stepped into the 4x4.

"He's at the flat. I took the liberty of telling him he could remain there for the time being, save being on the streets. He was in hospital, Aintree, for a few hours, for observation."

"Thanks, Penny. I was going to suggest that. I owe him my life. I-I think Richard was going to kill me this time."

"Don't even think about that lowlife. He had me fooled. I'm sorry I ever dragged you over to meet him in the first place."

"It's not your fault. I had many opportunities to expose him, but I was a coward."

"On the contrary, Jules, you were exceptionally brave. How did you put up with all that abuse and violence for so long? But let's not talk about that little shit now."

"How is Paul?"

"He's ok. He was still a bit dazed and in pain. I called Aintree early this morning to check on his welfare. He got tasered, in the gonads."

Penny gave her friend a look. They both shrieked with laughter.

"Ouch!" Jules winced in pain. "It hurts to laugh! Oh! I shouldn't. Poor Paul!" Jules blurted.

"You're right, Jules. He probably saved your life. A sobering thought."

Penny switched on Radio Merseyside for the 11am news as they made their way to Woolton. The bulletin made mention of a man being arrested on a charge of domestic violence. They glanced at each other in satisfaction. Another item of news immediately caught their attention. Scrolled correspondence had been found in three leather document holders, dating back to the early 1800s, in a hitherto unknown secret compartment in an item of furniture at The Lady Lever Art Gallery in Port Sunlight. The art gallery and museum, built by philanthropist William Hesketh

Lever, the 1st Viscount Leverhulme, housed a superb, world class collection of paintings and antiquities. A cleaner had been cleaning the exhibit which was on display when she discovered the items. The artefact in question dated back to the Napoleonic era and was in the Napoleonic collection at the museum. The news report said that the discovered cylindrical tubes contained an assortment of anonymous letters, rubbings of hieroglyphic logograms and illustrations on separate sheets of paper depicting two different animals. The correspondence had an address written on it. The recipient had been a one 'Cardinal Fesch'. Gallery sources confirmed that he was an uncle of Napoleon Bonaparte, a member of the Roman Catholic clergy and a French statesman and it was also relayed that the sofa in the Museum had once belonged to him. The content of the letters was being kept secret for the time being until they were authenticated, and expert advice was being sought on the translation of the Ancient Egyptian script to see if that too was authentic.

"No way!" Penny shrieked. "What a find! A secret compartment! Hieroglyphs!"

Penny's phone rang. It was on hands free. It was Randy.

"Hi Penny. Hey, have you seen Jules? I've phoned her mobile and she's not answering."

"She's with me, Randy. We're in the car. She hasn't got her mobile with her."

"Hi Randy," Jules replied. "What's up?"

"Hi Jules. The Lady Lever have been after you about a hieroglyphic print or something. They want you to decipher it."

"We've just heard about it on the news. It sounds interesting, if it's genuine. Can you call them back and tell them I will definitely contact them today?"

"Sure. By the way, where've you been? What have you been up to?"

"Er, I'll tell you later. Thanks Randy. Bye!"

Penny and Jules arrived at the detached house in the leafy suburb of Woolton village. Penny had recovered Jules's mobile and bag from the apartment but had forgotten to take them with her to the hospital and so Jules sat on the settee scrolling through her phone messages whilst Penny put the kettle on. Penny's own mobile rang. It was the police. A Detective Armitage was coming to the house to interview Jules. Meanwhile Jules rang the Lady Lever to arrange an appointment whilst she waited for the police officer to arrive. She was keen to throw herself back into her work and therefore arranged to pop over to Port Sunlight as soon as possible with Penny, her curiosity piqued by the unusual event. Within thirty minutes DI Armitage accompanied by DS Noades came to take statements. They stayed for a while listening to Jules's ordeal. Once the two female detectives had taken their leave, Penny and Jules left immediately for Port Sunlight, once built to house the Victorian workers of the Lever Brothers soap factory. They went through the old Kingsway tunnel emerging on the Wirral side of the river Mersey. They passed Birkenhead Priory, classed as a Scheduled Ancient Monument, purported to be the oldest building on Merseyside, dating back to 1150, and then drove past the famous Cammell Laird's shipyard, birthplace of *HMS Ark Royal* and the *Mauretania*. They both laughed when they saw *Boaty McBoatface*, the miniature submarine attached to the *Sir David Attenborough* research ship which was in dock undergoing repairs. The vessel had also been constructed in the yards. Jules winced again as she continued to giggle with Penny. They arrived shortly afterwards at Port Sunlight after a dash up the New Ferry by-pass glimpsing en route the near hidden Victorian villas of the Rock Park conservation area which had been unfortunately bisected by the dual carriageway. They entered the domed neo-classical Lady Lever and sought out the head curator. Penny, being a director of the affiliated World Museum in Liverpool knew Tom Yates well. The forty-five-year-old squat bearded man led them first into an exhibition room.

"This is it ladies. The Napoleonic Room, where the items were found."

The small gallery held a collection of antique furniture and ornaments. Lord Leverhulme had been fascinated with Napoleon Bonaparte and the Napoleonic era and had purchased items from France, some of which were reputed to have been from Malmaison, Bonaparte's Palace in Paris. However, subsequent research had deemed some of the artefacts to more likely be from a later period, the 1840s perhaps. The guests surveyed the items. There were various exotic pieces of furniture; elaborately patterned commodes and chiffoniers; a decorative bureau, an attractive armoire, an exquisite chaise longue, an elegant four-poster bed, and fine, sleek upholstered chairs all ornately carved and all of the highest craftsmanship.

"Which commode or bureau had the items in?" Jules asked.

"None of them," replied the middle-aged curator.

Penny, puzzled, sought clarification. "But I thought you said that they were found in a hidden compartment."

"They were. The radio researcher just assumed it was in some sort of bureau or chest of drawers. We were moving the display around to see if we could accommodate a couch in here. One that is normally in the main hall that belonged to Cardinal Fesch, Napoleon's uncle. It's quite a long thing but it wouldn't quite fit."

"I know the one. With the griffin-like design on the arm rests."

"That's right Penny, you've seen it before."

"As some of the staff manoeuvred the piece one of them tripped on the stairs leading up to the display and dropped it. It tumbled over, and a leg was damaged unfortunately. The tenon had come loose from the mortise. I told the staff not to touch it until we had someone look at it to assess the damage. We just laid the sofa on its back and left it there."

"Oh dear," Jules said.

Penny was not too pleased; she sat back, arms folded, her top lip curled. Tom frowned and shifted his feet uncomfortably, then continued.

"Well, Janet, our cleaner was dusting the other items on display in the gallery when she noticed something protruding slightly from the hollow space of the mortise joint of the loose leg. She examined the material and saw that it resembled leather. She informed me so I had a look."

"Good old Janet," Penny chirped.

"She was right. There *was* something leather-like in there. I couldn't believe it. On further scrutiny, I found the leg to be hollow. I put my fingers in and managed to extract the item. It was a bit of a struggle to release it because I didn't want to do any more damage to the leg. I was staring at a cylindrical leather tube. A document holder. I shone the torch into the hollow of the lower part of the leg and found two other leather tubes in there."

"Two more, eh? How interesting!"

"Yes, two more Jules! I managed to get the other one out with the help of Simon and other members of staff. They lifted the settee at an angle while I carefully slid them out. I opened all three. Two of the document holders contained a scrolled letter and one lithograph print of hieroglyphs in each whilst the other also had in it a letter, another hieroglyphic print plus some scrolled illustrations. Fascinating!"

"Where are the items and sofa now?" Penny inquired.

"The sofa's in the workshop and the document tubes are in my office."

"Have you checked the other legs yet to see if there are any more compartments?" Jules asked enthusiastically.

"Not yet forensically, but we will, in due course. We were just in the process of examining the leg in question when you arrived. Come on, we'll go and see it now."

They followed Tom into the basement. He opened a door and ushered them in. The sofa was in the process of being examined by Clive Hamley, the museum's antique furniture expert, and another employee.

Clive greeted them. "Hi all."

"Hi Clive," Penny replied.

"Found anything else of interest Clive?"

"As a matter of fact, Tom, I have. A closer inspection of the mortise and tenon joint undertaken by my good self has revealed a wooden release lever which serves to separate the arm from the leg which, of course, no one had noticed earlier."

"Interesting and impressive Clive. That's what we pay you for. Your expertise," Penny said smiling.

"We've examined the other arm and leg and ran a brief check on the other sofas and chairs in the collection and this seems to be the only one with this type of mechanism."

"Ok, thanks Clive," Penny said.

Penny and Jules were allowed to see for themselves the hidden compartment and release mechanism.

"Are you going to repair it straight away?" Jules asked.

"I'm in two minds," Tom said. "The Wirral Globe and the Liverpool Echo have already been on to us. They want to have a look at it before we repair it. I'm wondering if we should leave it as it is so customers can have a gander at it. The story has generated a lot of interest already and we've had to close the gallery for today until we decide what to do with it."

"Hmm. Food for thought. Can we see the documents now Tom?"

"Sure Penny. Let's go."

Tom took his visitors to his office, donned a pair of white gloves, unlocked a safe and produced the items of interest. He first showed them the two illustrations. He unrolled them and anchored them down carefully with cut-glass paperweights.

"Please don't touch ladies."

Penny gave him a dirty look. Tom grinned, then Jules and Penny pored over the illustrations.

"Wow! They're good, aren't they?" Penny drooled.

"Whoever drew them was very talented. Look at the details in those feathers," Jules added.

"And this one. The head and face. Very convincing. Really, really good," Penny said impressed.

Then Tom produced the letters. Three in total. He laid the first one on his table according to their chronological order and secured it with more paperweights borrowed from the gallery shop. The first letter was dated 29th January 1811. The second one in May 1812.

They both read the first one with difficulty, grappling with the quill-scribed cursive script of the writer, picking out letters and words. When they finished reading it, they looked at each other and at Tom in amazement. Then he laid out the second and third one, which was dated 22nd August 1812 and they followed the same process, the transcribing becoming easier as they familiarized themselves with the handwriting. Their reactions were the same, utter shock. Finally, Tom presented the prints of the hieroglyphs which Jules had been keen to see. The first was placed and secured on the table again. There were only three lines of hieroglyphs. She took out her notebook and pencil from a shoulder bag and started to translate the script. Then she stopped halfway through a line. Something astonished her. She drew back and looked at Tom.

"What it is?" he asked excitedly.

"I'm not sure yet."

She continued and read to the end of the third line. She paused, slowly raising her head, a look of bewilderment on her face. She rubbed her forehead with her hands and then rubbed each side of her face, bringing her hands down, to rest together on her chin as if she were offering up a prayer to the Heavens.

"Come on, Jules. What does it say?" Tom implored. "Penny?"

"She's better than me. That's why I'm a director of a museum and not a professional archaeologist."

"It-it says, *this fiat* or *decree is a warning for future generations that...* Jules paused again.

"Go on, spit it out girl!" Penny urged.

"*This decree is a warning for future generations that your star, or let's say planet, will witness the return of the Elohim. They will return to your planet in the year inscribed below, or earlier, if prompted by cataclysmic events caused by man alone or by natural forces that threaten the very existence of your world.*"

"The Elohim? Cataclysmic events?" Tom queried.

"The Elohim!" Penny reiterated.

"Yes, the Elohim. Another Hebrew word for God, like Yahweh," Jules confirmed.

"I know that," Penny said, pulling a face. "So, it's another proclamation about a Second Coming of sorts."

"Yes, but not one specifically related to Jesus Christ. In reference to this particular Second Coming, it just says 'they' will return. Not 'he'. Elohim can be singular or plural in the Hebrew language."

"They, will return?" Tom said, seeking clarification.

"Yes, they."

"Whoever wrote this could have written Eloah instead of Elohim to identify 'God', but this definitely implies 'gods'. I've seen it crop up in the Hebrew Bible. Psalm 82, comes to mind, referring to Elohim, meaning 'gods', not God. Off the top of my head, God or Elohim as it's written, 'stands in the divine assembly. He administers judgement in the midst of the Elohim', i.e. *gods*."

"Christ," Tom uttered.

"May I have a butcher's at the second print please, Tom?"

Tom laid out the other lithographic print. All the items were in relatively good condition considering they were over two hundred years old. Jules began to translate again. She paused anew in the middle of her transcription and glanced up at the other two.

"What now?" Penny drawled. "God's persona on Earth is Jurgen Klopp. Well, that's false. We all know it's Robbie Fowler," she continued, Jules aware of her being an avid Reds fan much like herself. The transcriber finished translating and scribbling. She picked up her notebook and read.

"This proclamation was written by the hand of Eloah himself and conveyed to your planet after the ice age –"

She paused to swallow.

"by our heavenly vessel under the guardianship of the Elohim."

She paused again to look at the other two.

"It serves to forewarn you of the dire consequences of not treating your world with the respect it requires."

"Eloah? Heavenly vessel? Dire consequences! What the-" Tom remarked incredulously.

"Eloah, as I've explained, is another Hebrew word for God. And yes, there's a reference to an extra-terrestrial spacecraft!"

"This has got to be some sort of hoax!" Penny clamoured derisorily. "Tom - is this one of your ideas to drum up interest in the Lady Lever?"

"No! Of course not Penny. I'm a professional, like you."

"Maybe it's one of your employees then. Simon? Clive? The cleaner?"

"Don't be absurd," Tom laughed. "You've seen the letters. Who would go to such lengths?"

"Well then it's the anonymous writer who's playing the hoax."

"Hold on Penny. He's got a great imagination mentioning a spaceship for someone in the early 1800s if he's just fabricated this," Jules countered.

"Maybe he was an aficionado of Da Vinci then."

"Point taken. On the other hand, no one knew how to decipher hieroglyphs until Jean-Francois Champollion, the French orientalist, building on the work of Brit Thomas Young, cracked the code in 1822. But these letters are dated 1811 and 1812.

All I know folks, is that's what it says."

"So, whoever's written these letters has genuinely copied something off an authentic Egyptian hieroglyphic stele."

"Correct Tom. And it mentions there are twenty more lines of hieroglyphs on the tablet and, according to our anonym, it's somewhere here in Britain."

"Bah! It all sounds too far-fetched to me, Jules. It's got to be an elaborate hoax from someone present day then."

"What does the third one reveal?" Tom said laying out the print.

"Ok, let's see."

A few minutes passed and the outcome was the same. Jules's expression was one of consternation. She gazed at the others. She began to translate.

"*In the beginning, you became our Experiment, to see if we could transform sub-human species found on your planet into intelligent human entities who could sustain and preserve their world for generations. We inseminated some of these sub-human creatures with our seed and departed. We returned, in later times, to discover, to our surprise, that these creatures had not only survived but evolved into what you are today.*"

They looked at each other in astonishment.

"Experiment. Sub-human species. Insemination?" Tom reiterated robotically.

"I would say the latter definitely refers then to the Second Coming. Don't you think Jules?

"Oh Penny! Trust you!"

The museums' director ripped the notepad from her friend's grasp.

"No way!" Penny remarked in wonder, reading. "Is this for real? Surely not!"

"Well, Penny," Jules said, addressing her friend, after a moment of silence. Penny remained open mouthed, awe struck, dazed by the revelation that had been exposed in the transcription scrawled on the lined page of the pad. "Penny!" The director jumped. "The first thing we need to do then is carbon date the items back at the university lab if we can take them."

"Oh, sure Jules. Whatever. Go ahead. Yeah, do it. Go for it" Penny babbled.

"Er, that's fine, ladies," Tom said emerging from his own trance. "I'll leave them in your capable hands. I won't tell the Press anything yet except how and where we found them. They'll probably assume it's just some sort of hoax too."

"We'll take good care of them," Penny reassured her colleague. "We'll grab a coffee whilst you make the preparations for them Tom."

The two women went to the café for refreshments and then went up into the galleries and strolled around the exhibits since Tom was taking a while to prepare the items. They gazed glossy eyed at the impressive Wedgwood collection and Chinese Ceramics on display, failing to register the facts about the valuable artefacts or appreciate their aesthetic qualities. Instead, they were mulling over the astonishing information and the implications revealed by Jules's decipherment. There was minimal conversation between the two friends as they wandered around. Fifteen minutes later Tom appeared.

"Ah, sorry ladies. I had to field a few phone enquiries about the items. Looks like

I'll have a busy day. Here's the letters et al. Just imagine if this isn't a fake. Gods and spaceships, hey. It'll have all the alien freaks frothing at the mouth."

"Hey, watch what you're saying Tom Yates!" Penny said, making a face.

"Don't tell me you're one. I thought you just dismissed this as a hoax."

"I did but it still doesn't mean I don't believe there's a link between extra-terrestrials and ancient history. God, I love Ancient Aliens on TV. So does Jules!"

"Right, I have to go and arrange some visits. Speak to you soon. Let me know asap about your findings."

"Will do! TTFN!" Jules shouted as she left.

32

The Levant, 1799

Throughout the next day the column moved off into the pulsating heat of the desert. The surgeons were overwhelmed by the dying and the dead as the order to evacuate was issued. The dying were abandoned and the dead who could not be buried in time were dumped unceremoniously upon the decaying corpses of those the French invaders had slaughtered earlier during the bloody conquest of Jaffa. Sir Sidney Smith disembarked after the withdrawal. Those still alive were taken into his care. On the long journey back to Cairo, the French troops, exhausted, ravenous and thirsty, began to mutiny. More of the wounded were callously jettisoned, the victims of a desperate every-man-for-himself mindset that rooted itself in the psyche of the retreating French. Others succumbed to heat stroke and died amidst the sand dunes. Napoleon, on his eventual arrival in Cairo however, insisted that his Army of the Orient adopted the stance of heroic, conquering heroes. He issued orders ensuring that his army was welcomed by the denizens of the city on their arrival with all the pomp of a victory parade. Cousseau and his comrades donned new uniforms which had been rushed out from the city to the column and they marched through the gates of the city, the cheers of the crowds resonating in their ears. Cousseau listened to the ululating women and applause amidst the sounds of the drums and flutes, but he and many of his fellow soldiers felt like frauds and knew it was fake enthusiasm and false approbation emanating from the local populace. In fact, everything was based on the Corsican's deception. The wounded and sick were hidden from view having been despatched to other towns around Lower Egypt along with the Christian refugees before the staged procession.

Demeraux survived the exodus as did Monge and Berthollet who had also been struck down by illness. All three had sufficiently recovered by the time the column arrived in Cairo and there Demeraux remained. After a period of recuperation, Demeraux and the other savants continued with their tasks. Demeraux assisted in the topographical mapping of Cairo and beyond, whilst other savant-engineers manufactured bullets, weapons, and tools under the supervision of another genius, Conté. Large scale public works had been authorised by Napoleon, keen to demonstrate his benevolent side, so bridges were built across the Nile and grand sweeping boulevards were constructed under the supervision of the savants whilst naturalists like Geoffroy Saint-Hilaire made advances in scientific studies of creatures.

Demeraux was then despatched to Alexandria to collate the maps of Lower Egypt and to carry out more public works with a group of savant-engineers. The savants went there under the protection of a contingent of soldiers, amongst them his friend Sergeant Cousseau. There had been a number of recent insurrections and uprisings in the area. Demeraux and some of the savants were soon relocated to the town of Rashid or Rosetta, as it was also known, along the coast from Alexandria, to assist in the strengthening of Fort Julien, named in honour of General Julien, a young aide-de-camp of Napoleon's who had been a victim of a massacre. After some rest and recuperation, the detachment was sent to the old Mameluke fortification, a rectangular structure built originally in 1470 overlooking the Nile, a few miles outside the town, and the men were to report to Lieutenant Pierre François Bouchard, a savant-engineer in charge of the construction.

The lieutenant commanding the newly arrived squadron located Bouchard and they were set to work with the sappers, the savants using their mathematical and engineering skills to advise on the construction and the soldiers helping to dig the foundations for the extension or shore up the crumbling stonework of the dilapidated fort. Pierre was handed a pick. He took off his tunic and began to toil in the relentless heat with his comrades. It was July. Demeraux went off with Lieutenants' Durand and Bouchard to discuss the design of the extension. Demeraux knew Bouchard who had studied under Conté, Monge and Berthollet and was a former member of the *Commission des Sciences et des Arts* back in Paris.

"Those donkeys always get the easy jobs," private Duvalier, a fellow soldier, complained.

"Duvalier, if you were as intelligent as those donkeys, you'd be with them now, but you can't even write your own name properly! I'd wager that real donkeys are cleverer than you," Cousseau replied. "These fellows have helped us more than you know," he continued.

"Like when?" Duvalier responded. He dropped his shovel and galloped around braying like an ass.

The other members of the working party laughed.

"They've built roads and pontoons, made tools and weapons and bullets and identified new species of creatures and animals like, you, the Rosetta ass."

They all laughed again.

"Back to work my four-legged friend."

The party toiled away in the fierce sun, digging out the foundations. Cousseau momentarily paused and wiped his brow. Duvalier continued planting his shovel in the earth when he struck something solid. Another rock he assumed to be tossed onto the mound of spoil and debris to the side. He tried to lift the obstruction out, but it was too heavy. He called to Cousseau for assistance. The sergeant obliged and hacked along the edge of the object and discovered that it was not a rock. It seemed to be some sort of slab, greyish black in colour. He took a spade and scraped away the soil and stone around it. He then brushed and carefully swept away the dirt on top of it and to his surprise some of the same pictograms that he had seen at Thebes came into view.

83

"Hey! Look at this, there are carvings on this stone!" he called out.

The other men stopped working and formed a circle around the stone.

"The pictures and symbols on it are called hieroglyphs. Ancient Egyptian writing, that is. See, even the savants have been educating me."

He scraped away the soil around the edges to reveal more of the slab and brushed away the detritus to reveal the script inscribed on the stone.

"That's different writing to that above," Duvalier said. "Even I can see that although I can't read."

"You're right. It's got different letters on it," Cousseau confirmed.

The two men dug into the earth further, then scraped away more soil to reveal a third script on the same basalt slab.

"Oh! Another language which is written in a different form as well. Duvalier, get Lieutenant Bouchard, I think this might be of some significance."

Lieutenant Bouchard arrived in a state of flux and grievance ten minutes later.

"What's all this fuss about? I was in the middle of a meeting."

Duvalier made a rude gesture behind him simulating intercourse. The others tried to hide their amusement.

"We've found something, sir, that might be of interest to you. Here, take a look," Cousseau said.

Bouchard climbed over a mound of earth and set eyes on the granodiorite stele.

"My, what have we here?" he said with a sudden change of tone. He brushed away some dust that had already reclaimed the stone. "Hieroglyphs! And what's that below it?"

"Another language sir," Cousseau replied.

"Yes sergeant, I can see that, but which? I can't identify it."

Duvalier brushed away more sand and soil.

"*Mon Dieu!* There's another different script below that as well! Is that Ancient Greek? Yes, I think it is! Oh, my word! This carving, alas, could be very significant, having three different forms of writing on it. If they all mean the same thing, we can perhaps crack the code of the hieroglyphs! Right, men, get that cart off those sappers over there. I want you to load this stele onto the cart and bring it to my quarters."

"Some of it looks like it's missing sir, at the top. Shall we carry on digging to see if we can find it?"

"Good idea Duvalier. And if you find any more fragments you will all receive a flagon extra of ale tonight on top of the additional one that you'll receive for your find."

"Hurrah!" went up the cheer.

Duvalier and Fourier, another private, went to fetch the cart whilst Cousseau and the others started to dig away at the base of the granite slab to loosen the soil and dirt.

Duvalier and Fourier returned with the cart attached to a braying donkey.

"There's donkeys everywhere," Cousseau joked which was the cue for Duvalier to start braying also.

The men managed to manoeuvre the huge slab away from the rest of the earthworks. It took about ten of them to carry and heave the 750 kilos stone onto the wagon once they had got some purchase on it. They dragged it onto a mound of soil and rubble and backed the donkey and cart towards it, then slid the slab down the pile of spoil. Cousseau and Duvalier pushed and pulled the reluctant donkey to the lieutenant's quarters and tethered it outside. Bouchard sent word to the other savants to meet him there. Cousseau and Duvalier remained with the donkey guarding the 'find'. Demeraux, accompanied by the other savants arrived for the meeting. They gathered outside Bouchard's quarters in the fort, then the officer addressed the small group.

"*Citoyens*, I have something in my possession that may be of great interest to the scholar and may have great significance for the understanding of the ancient world. We are surrounded by the artefacts of antiquity. We are surrounded by temples and walls and pyramids adorned with symbols that we do not comprehend but now we have discovered something that may help us unravel the mysteries of time. Gentlemen, I give you - *La Pierre de Rosette!*"

Bouchard then revealed the slab to the group by theatrically pulling off a sheet covering the stone. The savants crowded around the stele, jockeying for a better position, some climbing up on the sides of the cart for a better view.

"*Mon Dieu, qu'est-ce que c'est?*" a young savant asked.

"Hieroglyphs, and two other scripts," Demeraux said curiously.

"The bottom one looks like Ancient Greek," added a third.

"I think you're right, Greek. My sentiments entirely," Bouchard replied.

"What's the other language?" Demeraux enquired. Has anyone got any ideas?"

The savants examined the script and conjectured.

"Amharic?"

"Coptic?"

Bouchard interjected. "I'm not sure, but, if this is definitely Ancient Greek then we might be able to understand the other two languages if the Ancient Greek is a translation of the above two scripts."

A moment of silence occurred whilst the savants computed that scenario.

"So, we French will have the honour of unlocking the mysteries of Ancient Egypt by deciphering the code of the hieroglyphs," Demeraux remarked cautiously.

"That's it! This stone, therefore, is priceless!" roared the lieutenant.

Duvalier and Cousseau exchanged glances whilst the savants showered Bouchard with compliments and congratulations. "*Bravo* Bouchard!"

"Gentleman, please excuse me, I have to inform Colonel D'Hautpol of my discovery."

Bouchard returned to his quarters. The animated savants babbled amongst themselves excitedly discussing the Implications of such a discovery. Demeraux left the group and went over to Cousseau and Duvalier.

"Pierre, did you hear that?"

"What? Bouchard saying, '*my* discovery' when Duvalier found it."

"Well, no, about its value."

"It's always the case isn't it. Officers taking the credit," Duvalier sighed. "We found it whilst digging the foundations."

"I thought it might be of importance when I saw the hieroglyphs and other languages on it. We told Bouchard about it," Cousseau said.

"So, Bouchard reckons it's priceless, eh?"

"Yes, Duvalier. Priceless indeed!" Demeraux confirmed.

"What? An ancient stone slab is worth a fortune!" a dubious Duvalier blurted out.

"In scholarly terms, yes it is. Not so much in pecuniary terms perhaps, but, then again, on reflection, it could be worth a substantial sum. Hey, Pierre do you think there might be more slabs like that buried in the earth nearby?"

"It's possible. Bouchard has ordered the men to continuing digging. Some of the slab is missing. The boys are at it now."

"It's just that I'm thinking if we find something similar then it might be of considered value when we return to France, if we keep it to ourselves. At least we'll have something to show for our travails in this cursed country."

"You're right," Duvalier agreed, his eyes lighting up, "because, we're still owed back pay and if they haven't got money to pay us, were going to have nothing to show for this whole damned catastrophe they've dragged us into. Maybe we'll just have to look out for ourselves."

"Duvalier, you've got something there. We can perhaps return tonight, all three of us, whilst the lads are in Rosetta, getting laid and drunk," Cousseau replied. "We can start digging around the environs of the fort. We'll meet, let's say, 9.30pm at my bivouac. If we leave some picks and shovels underneath the pile of spoil outside, we won't attract any undue attention when we're leaving. We'll just be carrying our lanterns and some sacks."

86

33

Cousseau and Duvalier were ordered back to their detachment whilst the cart was moved to a secure place in the fort and placed under guard. Demeraux continued with his topographical assignment and the working party returned to their excavating and wall strengthening duties. Nothing else of merit was found.

That evening, Duvalier and Demeraux made their excuses and left their respective company. They met up with Cousseau at the rendezvous at 9.30pm precise and, with lanterns and sacks, set off into the night looking like they were off on a nocturnal hunt for rodents or other creatures to eat or to capture for the benefit of Geoffroy St. Hilaire's naturalist study. They arrived at the deserted site and recovered the tools from the slag heap and proceeded to dig. They toiled for a good few hours more without success around the same area where they discovered the stele. Then they rested a while, dozing before resuming again. They were beginning to lose heart. The first light of dawn broke. A red hue streaked the skies. They decided to call it a day at 0600 hours. The hour approached. Cousseau, digging half-heartedly, was fleetingly immersed in shadow. Hearing a squawk, he looked skywards and saw a large bird of prey, a majestic white-tailed sea eagle. It soared above him on the warming thermals. He watched as it circled around, its screeching becoming more and more vociferous. Then he returned to his digging again. Suddenly he was eclipsed by the shadow of the eagle once more. The bird of prey had unexpectedly swooped down at great speed, hovering over him, with its sharp talons inches away from his scalp. Unnerved, to the amusement of Duvalier, he launched himself into a pit and as his shovel hit the earth, he struck something hard, jarring his arms. He let out a cry dropping the shovel. He stood up and brushed himself down, the laughter of his companions ringing in his ears. The sea eagle was several feet away rising from the ground, its outstretched wingspan fanning the dust underneath it, a fat, wriggling sand rat clutched in its talons. Cousseau cussed, picked up his shovel and drove it into the earth where he had felt something hard.

"Hey! Stop laughing. I might have something!"

Duvalier jumped into the pit still chuckling. He thrust his shovel into the dirt, and he too registered something solid. Demeraux joined them. The three of them looked at each other then started to dig faster. As something rectangular-shaped came into view, they eased off.

"It looks like another slab of granite!" Demeraux cried.

They doubled their efforts to free the stone. It was buried at least four feet down. Gradually they loosened the debris around the artefact and managed to extract it from the earth. The three of them frantically started to dust away the years of dirt and grime accumulated on the object. Then they realised it was not stone.

"It's ivory! And look! Hieroglyphs!" Demeraux gasped. "There are hieroglyphs on it! We found something, boys. We found something! *Mon Dieu!* Incredible!"

They slapped each other's aching backs triumphantly, then they swept away the rest of the dirt and a rectangular slab of ivory two foot by one was revealed containing lines and lines of hieroglyphic pictograms, but their initial enthusiasm was tempered slightly when they realised there were no other languages on it like the previously excavated 'Rosetta' Stone.

The ivory slab was manoeuvred carefully into the coarse muslin sack and then they continued to dig for fifteen more minutes until, having found nothing else of interest, they abandoned their search, exhausted and parched. The three agreed to bury the artefact under a solitary palm tree on their return back to their encampment noting its location, still undecided about their next step.

34

In the ensuing days, Cousseau and Duvalier were assigned to the same working party. They continued to assist in the preparation to extend and strengthen the fort. One day, at mid-day, when the men had paused for lunch, Demeraux showed up. He had been away for a few days on cartography duty along the coast. One of the labourers had caught some fish from the Nile so they sat down to a meal of catfish and lentils followed by dates. The savant joined them and was offered some of the fare. The men chatted, bantering between themselves. Afterwards, Cousseau went to clean his utensils in the nearby waters of the Nile and Demeraux took the opportunity to go with him.

"I have to leave, Pierre," he whispered to Cousseau. "I am to return to Cairo with some of the other savants."

"On whose orders?"

"General Menou's. He has been visiting Rosetta and he and Colonel D'Hautpol have decided that the Stone must be sent forthwith to Cairo to be examined by the Institute and we are to return prior to this with a report on the artefact drawn up by Lancret, another savant. We have to ensure that preparations are made for the Stone to arrive safely in the hands of Monge and Berthollet."

"That's a shame."

"It's fine. I believe Denon is to return from his adventures in Upper Egypt and will undoubtedly lecture us on his findings and I most certainly want to be present when he does so."

"What do we do then about our discovery?" Cousseau mumbled as he was joined by others washing their implements.

"I should take it with me to Cairo. There are more places to hide it. Some of the more gifted savants might be able to decipher the hieroglyphs on the Rosetta Stone and that will, in turn, give me some ideas on deciphering our own stele."

"Alright. I'll let Duvalier know the plan. When are you leaving?"

"At 3pm today."

"I'll get Duvalier to retrieve the item. He can meet you at your quarters. How will you transport it?"

"I'll keep it in the sack and attach it to a donkey. I'll fill the sack with flora cuttings and rock samples and the like which I'll say I'm bringing back for the Institute to catalogue. Tell him to meet me at 2pm. *Adieu, mon ami.* I promise to keep the tablet safe."

Demeraux departed and Cousseau immediately informed Duvalier of the plan, reassuring him that the artefact would be in safe hands. Their own situation could change at a moment's notice and the carving could be lost again for, who knows how long, centuries perhaps?

35

A murmur of excitement and anticipation rippled around the walls of the chamber in the occupied Mameluke palace that had been sequestered to house the *Institut d'Égypte*. Demeraux was present. He had hidden the ivory relic securely beneath the floorboards of his lodgings in Cairo without anyone seeing him on his return from Rosetta. He now sat amongst the audience in eager anticipation of the meeting. The murmur faded as Gaspard Monge took to the floor and presented the agenda to those present. Papers were subsequently read on scientific and botanical findings and then the discovery of the Rosetta Stone was announced. Lancret's report was read to a hushed audience, the real value of the Stone becoming apparent when the report divulged the fact that a hieroglyphic script and an unknown, demotic language were carved into the same granite slab along with a written script identified as Ancient Greek which could possibly mean that all three scripts were translations of the same message. On this basis, the report concluded, the mysterious code of the hieroglyphs could now be deciphered. This revelation sparked uproar and pandemonium amongst the members of the Institute. The attendees around Demeraux went wild with joy. He stood there and simply smiled. A debate ensued and a flurry of questions were hurled at Monge and Berthollet who did their utmost to respond. The Institute had been set up by Napoleon and run by the savants he considered his friends, notably Gaspard Monge and Claude-Louis Berthollet, two men of prestigious intellectual talent. Demonstrations, meetings and talks on a wide range of academic subjects had taken place there on physics, music, art, sculpture, literature, science, engineering and many other disciplines. Napoleon even attended some himself. Demeraux contributed too, delivering a session on cartography explaining the mapping of Cairo that he had undertaken with other scholars.

Afterwards, Demeraux and his savant friends filed out into the splendid gardens of the palace. The atmosphere was tempered somewhat by the news that a large Turkish invasion force had landed at Aboukir Bay, north-east of Alexandria under the auspices of that 'lunatic', as Napoleon referred to him, Sir Sidney Smith. Napoleon had ordered his army consequently to march northwards. Demeraux's thoughts were with his friend Cousseau who would almost certainly be involved in the forthcoming battle.

36

In the following weeks, the Rosetta Stone was examined by the learned and gifted members of the Institute with great interest. They discerned that the translation of the Ancient Greek Inscribed on the stele was a decree issued by King Ptolemy V in Memphis, Egypt in 196BC but attempts to decipher the hieroglyphs and the other ancient script proved frustrating. Lithographic copies of the scripts were therefore made available by the savants to be despatched to eminent scholars throughout Europe. Demeraux had helped in this task, keen to understand the copying process for his own ends. He continued to attend the regular meetings and debates at the *Institut d'Égypte* and found himself one evening waiting impatiently with the rest of the audience in eager anticipation for Vivant Denon to commence his talk on his findings in Upper Egypt. The euphoria and almost obsessive interest created in the discovery of the Rosetta Stone had persisted, exponentially increasing by the time Denon returned from his adventures.

Demeraux had already heard the layman's tales of the adventure from his friend Cousseau and how he was enthused about ancient Upper Egypt, which, paradoxically, was southern Egypt. He had also heard astonishing reports from a fellow savant returning from the expedition of ferocious troglodyte inhabitants on the island of Philae, on which the Temple of Isis stood, who had drowned their own children whilst others had sewn up their young daughters' genitals, fearing their violation by the French invaders. But now Demeraux yearned to hear the intellectual and scientific accounts of Denon's explorations, that were more in line with his thinking.

Denon was formally introduced, and a presentation of his findings was made to the enthral of his audience, followed by a debate. It caused much excitement and interest. Denon's sketches of the magnificent ancient ruins were made available for everyone to peruse and Demeraux took great interest In the copies of the hieroglyphics Denon had produced. The discovery of the Rosetta Stone was truly significant, but Denon's findings were the icing on the Egyptian cake, he thought. Truly spectacular. Everyone concurred that a new science had, in effect, been born - 'Egyptology', and Denon, in Demeraux's estimation, could quite possibly be considered one of the founding fathers of that new discipline.

37

Liverpool. Present day.

enny and Jules returned to Liverpool via the Wallasey tunnel under the River Mersey. Penny drove along the Strand and past Jules's apartment to avoid roadworks up Islington. Jules looked up forlornly at her residence. She was not quite ready to return home there just yet. Penny drove up Upper Parliament Street and took a left along Hope Street, past the Georgian era Gambier Terrace to her right and St James's sunken cemetery to her left with the huge Anglican Cathedral perched above it. She was diverted into Rodney Street, as the other section of Hope Street was undergoing roadworks too. Penny always liked to see Mackenzie's tomb also, in the small cemetery of the former St Andrews Church and imagined his skeleton, seated in an upright position as per the apocryphal story she heard on a ghost tour. Legend has it that Mackenzie, a railway merchant sold his soul to the devil but by being placed above the ground in his pyramid shaped tomb, he hoped to avoid being claimed. The traffic was slow, so they had time to gaze at it. They took a right out of Rodney Street and parked up in a university car park on the campus. Barely had Penny set foot out of the vehicle when her phone rang. It was the manager of the church holiday club. Her youngest son had been involved in an altercation and had to be collected immediately. So, Jules went alone to carry on her investigations into the items. Before she began the examination, she contacted the hospital to try and speak with Paul, but he had already been discharged. She did not want to return to the apartment and had no other means of contacting him since there was no landline there and Paul didn't own a mobile. She decided to ask Penny later if she would check on his well-being the following day. In the meantime, she concentrated on organising the carbon-dating of the letters, prints and drawings, still believing that it was probably a hoax as Penny and Tom had predicted.

The following day Jules was dropped off at the University by Penny who continued on to work. Jules's car was still in the apartment block's car park. At lunchtime, Penny nipped out to go to the apartment. She was glad of some fresh air after a morning of meetings about future exhibitions at the World Museum. She parked up in a visitor bay in the car park and took the lift to the second floor. She located the apartment and knocked but there was no answer. She took the key that Jules had passed to her and opened the door. She opened it partially and called out for Paul. There was no answer again, so she entered. She suddenly stopped and stood there in shock, gawping. The apartment was trashed. Furniture was wrecked, drawers and their contents strewn everywhere. Glasses and crockery smashed. Then suddenly the door was brutally kicked open. Penny screamed in fright and saw

Paul standing there in an aggressive stance. His threatening mien instantly vanished.

"Penny! Oh, sorry I didn't realise..."

His eyes fell upon the trashed rooms.

"Paul! My God! You scared me to death! Just what, just what have you done to Jules's apartment? You've trashed it!"

"Penny, you've got to believe me. It wasn't me! This is the first time I've been here since the fight. I stayed at Lambert House last night. I wasn't too sure about coming back."

"Are you trying to tell me this is how it was left after the fight?"

"No! It wasn't like this. There was some damage but not like this."

Penny looked around the room, then at Paul.

"I don't believe one word of it, Paul. You probably got drunk and trashed it for some perverse reason!

"But, but -"

"You don't deserve to live anywhere nice! Jules allowed you stay here in good faith and this is how you repay her. Give me that key!" Penny snatched the key from his grasp. She then bundled him out.

"Get out! You're not fit to live in a nice place. Wait till Jules hears of this. My God!"

She locked the door. "Go back to Lambert House if you haven't already wrecked it!"

Penny strode off, brushing past him. Paul was stunned, hurt and bemused. She would not listen. He had stayed at the council's homeless facility.

38

Richard sat propped up in his bed. He had been transferred to Murrayfield, a private hospital on the Wirral at his own behest. His face was a mass of bruises and cuts. His broken wrist and kneecaps had been operated on. He seethed and fumed. He was the one to be charged.

"I'm telling you Frank. He's a dead man when I get out of here!"

"You take it easy, mate. You look half-dead yourself."

"That bitch was having it off with a tramp! I'm not going to let her get away with that either!"

"Calm down, Ritchie. You're already in trouble. Don't make any more threats to her. That's just playing into her hands."

"Frank, I really need your help on this one. You owe me big time. I brought you in on that insurance scam, remember. That tramp. I want him gone. Can you and the boys set him up? An overdose or something? Throw him in the Mersey? No one's going to miss him, are they? As if. A fucking tramp?"

"Alright, I'll speak to the boys Ritchie."

"It's about time you paid off that debt, mate."

"Here's the nurse and doc. I'd best go."

"Remember Frank. I want that debt paid because if I go down and they investigate my business dealings I'm going to take you with me. My jacket's over there. It's got my keys in. Take them. If he's in there with her, do him good and proper. Save her for me. She's not getting away with this."

39

"He did what?"

"He trashed the place! Wrecked it, Jules! All of it! Every single room!"

"Oh, my God, Penny! Are you sure it was him?"

"Well, it wasn't me. Who else has got a key? Soft lad in hospital who's incapacitated. And Paul! I'm telling you, steer clear of that one! You've got a knack for choosing the wrong fella!"

"Excuse me, Penny Carter. Who thought the sun shone out of Richard's arse? Who dragged me over to talk to him?"

Penny took a deep breath then sighed. "Hmm, you've got me on that one, girl. But this other friendship has got to stop. It's causing you no end of problems."

"But, if it hadn't been for Paul, I'd still be getting attacked by Richard. So, he's solved one very big problem for me."

"Ok, I'll give you that, but don't give yourself another problem. Out of the frying pan into the fire!"

"Ah, an idiom first recorded by general and poet Germanicus Caesar in the Greek Anthology."

"Don't go all academic on me Jules! We're talking serious shit here. Let's not change the subject. How do you know that anyway, freak?"

"Alright, is he still at the flat?"

"No way! I kicked him out."

"You kicked him out?"

"Of course. You didn't think I'd let him stay there. After what he did?"

"Listen, after work tomorrow. Will you come with me to the apartment and show me the damage? I don't want to go there on my own."

"No, I can't tomorrow. I've got Jake's disciplinary at the holiday club. Should be fun. The parents of the other boy involved in the fracas are going to be there. It'll have to be Friday."

"Ok, Friday it is."

There was a pause. Penny put her head down for a moment then Jules changed the subject.

"Any news of the carbon-dating?"

"I'll get the results back on Friday. I'm awaiting a second opinion. A colleague is doing a few more rigorous tests on the items. I'll let you know."

40

That same Wednesday evening Frank Baines was sat in the mid-19th century built Baltic Fleet pub, facing Jules's apartment block, the name of the hostelry deriving from the sailors that used to frequent it from Siberian whaling ships. Two other associates accompanied him. They were all peering up at the apartment which was in darkness.

"You got the syringe Mick?" Frank asked.

"I've got everything you asked for Frank. Joy flakes, tablets, the lot."

"Shh, keep your voice down Mick, yer knob!" Robbo cautioned, surveying the pub's clientele carefully. "We've got to make sure it looks like an accident or suicide. That's what Ritchie wants."

"Look Frank. I still think it's better if we get inside there now, rather than wait for him to come back," Mick whispered. "He won't suspect anything."

"I agree, Frank. It's getting late. Let's get in there," Robbo added.

"Alright, boys. We'll do it your way. I'll bow to your better judgement. Finish your pints, I'm going for a piss."

"We'll be outside Frank, having a smoke."

"Ok Mick, see you in a mo."

Minutes later Frank stepped out into the mid-summer air. The tables outside were crammed with punters enjoying the rare opportunity to sit outdoors on a warm evening and enjoy drinks. Mick and Robbo stubbed out their cigarettes, or rather spliffs and followed Frank across the road, the waft of the weed poisoning the air around them. They strolled along to the gated entrance, gained access with a fob and took the stairs to the second floor. Arriving at the apartment Frank took out the key and unlocked the door. They had noticed the apartment was still bathed in darkness, from the pavement outside the property. They entered in silence. Frank took out a torch and the others used their mobiles.

"What the fuck!" Frank whispered. "The place has been trashed. Probably that dirty bastard."

Frank closed the curtains. The others checked the bathroom and bedrooms. It was all clear, so they sat and waited, sharing some sausage rolls and a few beers that they found in the fridge but keeping the noise down to a minimum. Thirty minutes later they heard a faint sound at the door. They extinguished the torch and the mobiles and lay in wait. Someone entered. Frank took out a hunting knife from within his jacket. Robbo held a handgun and Mick grasped a cosh and wore a knuckle-duster. They could just make out each other's silhouette, owing to a chink in the curtains that let in the light of a streetlamp. Suddenly, all three heard a singular clicking noise then, almost instantaneously, Frank saw Robbo's head thrown backwards. He crashed to the floor. He had been peering over the back of the settee.

Then it was Mick's turn. He tried to crawl in vain to a safer place, but a noise suppressed bullet coursed through his neck, killing him instantly. He collapsed to the floor. Frank looked on in horror and in fear of his life. He scrambled into a bedroom away from the killer. His bowels opened. The assassin glided through the beam of light permeating the gap in the drapes, providing Frank with the briefest of glimpses of him before he closed the door. Frank tried desperately to barricade the door but the assassin, clad in black, night vision goggles on, fired his .44 magnum twice through the thin white panelled, moulded door, the sound again muffled by the silencer. The deadly intruder heard someone cry out. He kicked open the door. Frank was spread-eagled over the bottom edge of the bed, whimpering and wild-eyed, his chest pumping copious amounts of blood. The assassin smiled and finished him off, a bullet between the eyes. Frank's body slid to the floor leaving blood and excrement stains on the duvet and the carpet. Then his killer turned and left.

41

On Friday, midday, Jules received the news she was waiting for. The samples were carbon-dated to the early 1800s as she had claimed. They were genuine. She went to tell Randy whom she had already briefed, trusting him to keep schtum about the prints. They sat in his office pondering the ramifications, both in shock, but equally excited by the discovery. Up to that point she had not told anyone else what the prints revealed and had deliberately chosen a colleague who was an expert in carbon-dating, but unable to translate the hieroglyphic script, to confirm her initial findings.

"Randy, I still can't believe it. The prints, letters and illustrations are one hundred percent authentic. So, there's a stele somewhere in Britain, from ancient Egypt, forewarning us about a Second Coming, involving an extra-terrestrial visitation by, gods! Can you believe that?"

"The cataclysmic events alluded to could have already happened, Jules. World War I and II were pretty cataclysmic, don't you think? And so was the Great Plague. So maybe they're not coming back for whatever reason."

"True. But what if they are? What a remarkable story!"

"Well, I'm hoping the cataclysmic events have been and gone for our sake and everyone else's. But that's wishful thinking, I suppose, with international relations deteriorating between the superpowers and the destruction of the rain forests. Anyway, remind me what the declaration said."

Jules picked up her notebook and read.

"This decree is a warning for future generations that your planet will witness the return of the Elohim. They will return to your planet in the year inscribed below, or earlier, if prompted by cataclysmic events caused by man alone or by natural forces that threaten the very existence of your world.

This proclamation was written by the hand of Eloah himself and conveyed to your planet after the ice age by our heavenly vessel under the guardianship of the Elohim. It serves to forewarn you of the dire consequences of not treating your world with the respect it requires.

In the beginning, you became our Experiment, to see if we could transform sub-human species we found on your planet, into intelligent human entities who could sustain and preserve their world for generations. We inseminated some of these sub-human creatures with our seed and departed. We returned, in later times, to discover, to our surprise, that these creatures had not only survived but evolved into what you are today."

"We have to find the stele. To discover the date. Simple as. At least we know it's somewhere in Britain. Thank God it's not in Egypt!"

"Well, you don't know that Jules. It's more than two hundred years since those letters were written. It could be anywhere if someone has already located it. Did you say the anonymous letters were sent to Cardinal Fesch?"

"That's right."

"Then maybe he found the artefact and it's been hidden away in the private vaults of the Vatican or the Catholic Church in France."

"That is a possibility, Randy."

He continued.

"Religious zealots would probably have looked upon it as something threatening, to their way of life, as something inherently heretical."

"They still might Randy, if it's still lying somewhere waiting to be discovered."

"It might even open up a Pandora's Box."

"Well, the cat's already out of the bag. I've already had dozens of calls from news channels around the world and different organizations. So has Tom Yates at the Lady Lever. It's gone viral."

"So, what are you going to tell them?"

"I'm not going to tell them anything. Tom is. I've already sent the results off to him. He's going to confirm the items' authenticity. Radio Merseyside, the Wirral Globe and the Liverpool Echo are all going to have a worldwide scoop today. He's going to put it out there that the hieroglyphs convey an enlightening though disturbing message without revealing the gist of the glyphs. That'll cause a stir!"

"Wow! So, we'll just sit back and gauge the impact."

"No, Randy. On the weekend, me and you are going in search of the Holy Grail."

"Hey, maybe that is the Holy Grail!"

"Who knows? I'll give you a call later. I've got some work to do. Isn't it exciting?"

Randy nodded his assent. "Oh Jules -"

Jules was already out the door. "Speak to you later, Randy," she called back. "Got to go."

That afternoon, Tom Yates informed a small retinue of local journalists about the authenticity of the letters, illustrations, and prints. Within a matter of hours, the phone lines went ballistic at the university and at the Lady Lever. Their websites crashed too. The world's Press demanded more information. Tom arranged a news conference for Monday, to be fronted by him, Jules and other senior members of the University of Liverpool's Archaeology and History departments.

After work, Penny picked up Jules outside the Garstang Museum and drove her to her Wapping Quay residence. Jules was slightly apprehensive, this being her first time at the apartment since Richard's brutal attack. The two of them waited for the lift. It was currently on the top floor, then it paused at the second floor before arriving at the ground floor. The doors opened and Marsha Evans, Jules's next door neighbour, stepped out.

"Jules! Hi, I'm so glad your back."

"Hi, Marsha, everything alright?" Jules responded.

Penny stepped into the lift to hold it.

"Not really. I've been away, as you know. I got back today. There's a strange smell on the floor. The other residents have been complaining. They thought the smell was coming from my flat, but I let them in. It was fine. Nothing. It might then be coming from your apartment. Perhaps you could check?"

"Oh! Well, that's where I'm off to now."

"Jeez, I don't believe it! Paul must have got a copy of the key. I bet he's moved back in with some of his homeless mates!"

"Penny!" Jules said reprovingly. "Thanks Marsha, I'll check it out."

The lift doors opened on the second floor, and they walked along the passageway. As they were fifteen feet away from the flat a foul odour stung their nostrils.

"Ugh! It stinks!" Penny wailed.

She put the key in the lock and turned, then covered her nose with her hand. They pushed the door open. The baffling, obnoxious smell hit them full on. The place was in darkness with the curtains still drawn.

"Ugh My God! What a stink! Paul! Are you in here?" Penny bawled.

Jules was almost gagging, pulling her top over her nose.

"What have I left myself in for!" she half-laughed. "Jeepers!"

Jules switched on the light then the two of them suddenly screamed. Their eyes were focused on two corpses lying amidst the carnage of the ransacked room, flies swarming all over their blood-soaked bodies, a window having been left ajar. In the bedroom they could see a third stiff slumped on the floor. They ran out as fast as they could screaming for help. A resident came out of his apartment to see what all the fuss was about. Penny and Jules rushed to the man imploring him to call the police. He made towards Jules's apartment and was taken aback by the stench. He entered and then seconds later shot out immediately, retching, feeling nauseous. He returned to the two women who were shaking uncontrollably and called the police.

42

Egypt, 1799

Cousseau was already at the town of Damanhur when the main body of Napoleon's Army of the Orient arrived. He re-joined his regiment and then the army was deployed en masse to Aboukir Peninsula in preparation for the 'Battle of Aboukir'.

Duvalier, Cousseau and their comrades had one last draw on their clay pipes before being called to arms. The sun was up and at six am the attack began. Cousseau's division under the command of General Lanusse charged the Turks who were dug in, but unprepared for the encounter.

Cousseau urged his fellow grenadiers on, the objective being the fort on the peninsula, and they dashed forward with their customary elan serenaded by the deafening noise of the cannons. The sergeant fired his .69 calibre Charleville musket from one hundred yards out at a Turk who was wildly goading the French fighters and brandishing a scimitar on the redoubt. The musket ball impacted on the Turkish officer's chest, and he fell backwards. Unrelenting missiles hurtled over the heads of the assault troops smashing everything in their paths, but Cousseau and his unit were still receiving their share of ordnance and small arms fire with soldiers falling as they advanced.

"Up and at them lads!" he yelled. He leapt into the trenches, bayonet glistening in the morning sun and thrust the steel blade at an enemy combatant. The swarthy, squat Turk parried his lurch with his carbine and jabbed the butt of his weapon at Cousseau's head. It connected, a glancing blow, knocking the grenadier slightly off balance. His musket clattered to the ground and blood trickled from the wound down his face. He was slightly dazed but managed to right himself, regaining his balance with the aid of the trench wall ready for the Turk's inevitable assault. The fierce Turk, now on the offensive, sprang at Cousseau with a serried dagger. Cousseau managed to grasp the Turk's wrist with one hand whilst fending off punches with the other. The cold steel inched towards his eye. He was surprised by the strength of his diminutive opponent. The Turk's cold stare transformed into a toothless grin as he grew confident in their deadly struggle, the dagger edging closer towards his French opponent's eyeball. Cousseau fought with all the might that his six-foot frame could muster. He swiftly brought his other hand to bear on the dagger's hilt clutched firmly in the assailant's grip, despite being punched repeatedly in the face, but just enough to guide the blade away from his terrified, sweat-streaked face. He managed to wrap his right leg behind the Turk's leg, tripping him.

The Turk lost balance, then stumbled over the body of the officer that Cousseau had previously downed giving the French grenadier the upper hand in their fight to the death. Cousseau quickly reached for his own knife, withdrew it from his belt and plunged it into the head of the Ottoman soldier whose smile instantly dissipated, exchanged for a grimace. He cried out and slumped to the ground. All about Cousseau there was pandemonium. The French were gaining the initiative. Cousseau, shaking, took a few seconds to steady himself and regain his breath. He wiped some blood from his temple, grabbed his musket and immediately impaled another onrushing Turk on its bayonet. Then he saw Duvalier struggling with another opponent and promptly assisted him by driving his bayonet into the small of the Ottoman's back. Duvalier finished him off with his own bayonet, acknowledging his sergeant's timely intervention with a cursory nod. The Turks, alarmed by the sight of another French division trying to encircle them, were now fleeing their trenches in droves. They panicked and fled into the sea to try and escape, many drowning, and if not, bayoneted by the spirited, pursuing French soldiers.

The French regrouped and attacked a second trench in front of the fort but here they came up against fiercer resistance. Cousseau and his fellow combatants hurled themselves to the ground as the musket balls flew at them, their advance checked but nevertheless some troops bravely pressed on amidst the onslaught. Duvalier was one of those. His blood was up. Cousseau watched from a prone position as the stocky Duvalier charged on. Seconds later a shell propelled from the fortress exploded, tearing up the earth around the rampaging private. The sergeant saw poor Duvalier thrown up into the air amidst a spray of dirt and stones. Cursing, Cousseau managed to scramble forward to him under continuing, withering fire. Duvalier's body was clothed only by the shredded remnants of his uniform. His left leg jutted out at an improbable angle. His right leg had vanished, torn off with the blast. Cousseau looked around and gasped in horror. To the left of Duvalier lay the body of a *chasseur à cheval*, another casualty of the bombardment, draped across the mangled corpse of his steed as if he were lounging casually on a chaise longue. His face had been ripped away by the blast and in the hole that appeared there, bizarrely and grotesquely, Duvalier's shattered leg protruded, conjuring up the surreal image of Hieronymus Bosch's character 'the Prince of Hell', in his painting the Garden of Earthly Delights, a sketched copy of which the sergeant had once seen in a publication.

Cousseau turned Duvalier over. Duvalier opened his parched maw as if to speak. More blood trickled down his chin. Cousseau cradled him but before Duvalier could say anything his eyes rolled, and his last breath left his crushed body. The drummers sounded the retreat. Cousseau took shelter by crawling behind the dead horse then made his way to the safety of his own lines at the first trench. The Turks ventured out from their trench in triumph. Cousseau and the remnants of his division watched as the Ottoman's combed the battlefield chopping off the heads of any dead or dying French soldiers. Cousseau seethed with anger when he saw one Turk holding up Duvalier's severed head. Another held up the head of the *chasseur à cheval* with

Duvalier's severed leg thrust through the gaping hole, much to the goading Turks' amusement.

Suddenly all hell broke loose as General Murat led his cavalry on a swift and unexpected charge scattering the foe asunder. A hussar caught up with the Turk who brandished the head of the dead cavalryman and lanced him through the face much to the pleasure of the foot soldiers. The other Turk who brandished Duvalier's head was scythed down by a *chasseur à cheval* seeking retribution for his fallen companion severing his opponent's neck with one blow. The Turk's head rolled along the battlefield as if a polo match were being played by the riders, knocked inadvertently from one to another under the hooves of the galloping steeds.

The cavalry, led by Murat, penetrated deep into enemy territory tearing into the chaotic foe ferociously. Cousseau and his comrades, their blood up and their spirits revived, chased down the thousands of Turks fleeing in terror. The dispirited rabble's escape towards the sea was again futile. The carnage was repeated. Many drowned, others shot or bayoneted; another famous Gallic victory had occurred.

43

The campfires burned brightly. The faces of the victors glowed in the light from the incandescent flames. Some of the men chatted loudly and excitedly above the din of the constant beat meted out by the drummer boys on their snares and by the cacophony of musical instruments; fifes, trumpets, and horns being played incoherently and erratically by their inebriated possessors in celebration of the victory. In the distance the boom of cannon fire could still be heard. Napoleon's artillery was laying siege to the fort that still contained a trapped garrison and those that had sought refuge from the onslaught outside its walls. Those French troopers still with the energy or encouraged by drink, danced or cavorted with the female camp-followers. Others sat and gorged on the bounty of sweets and other delicacies purloined from the tents of the vanquished Turks who, it seemed had transported the whole of the edible produce of the Grand Bazaar to Egypt. Many others sat around exhausted by their endeavours that day smoking their long clay pipes. Cousseau sat solemnly amongst them reflecting on the day's events and on the fact that he had lost more comrades, not least, the larger-than-life Duvalier. The fallen soldier would not now share in the potential spoils of the ancient relic that they had unearthed. Cousseau, however, vowed that Duvalier's family would still get a share of any monies received. He yearned to be back in his homeland. Back in the beautiful, idyllic landscapes of the Languedoc. Amongst the vineyards and hilly terrain of the province where his family had a smallholding, consisting of sheep and goats, producing wool, meat and cheese. Having seen his father suffer at the hands of a brutal landowner he had decided to join the Revolution swearing allegiance to Revolutionary France. He had personally run through the landowner with a pitchfork when he was fourteen years of age and tossed his body into a well. This strapping man from the foothills of the Hérault valley was a veteran of Napoleon's Italian campaign, which culminated in the defeat of the Austrians and its allies. Cousseau had, at first, been a *tirailleur*, being a crack shot, having honed his skills hunting in the forests and mountains of the Languedoc for *sangliers*, the wild boar, and for wolves and deer. Although the Charleville musket was wildly inaccurate, he always seemed to find his target. He was promoted from private to sergeant after the Battle of Arcole where his heroic deeds in sharpshooting and skirmishing brought him to the attention of his *chef de brigade*. He was presented with a sword on his swift promotion to sergeant, but he always preferred to use his musket as a weapon of choice but still kept the sabre amongst his meagre belongings.

Cousseau puffed on his pipe, content to listen to the men around the campfires bragging of their derring-do and bravery during the battle. They all guffawed and shook their heads in dismay after one soldier told the tale of the gallant Murat who was observed returning from the onslaught, cantering on his mount, with blood smeared down his jaw and neck. Murat's decisive attack had penetrated so far deep behind the enemy lines that he had entered the tent of the surprised Turkish commander who had, at once, confronted the French general and shot him in the jaw with a pistol. Murat had responded by putting the Turkish officer to the sword after apparently saying that his wound would not affect his chances with the ladies of Paris. This had sent everyone into raptures. "*Quelle légende!*" they cried.

The siege continued for eight more days, the constant artillery bombardment eventually forcing the garrison into submission. Some of the occupants, amongst them a contingent of British marines, were able to escape to Sidney Smith's ship, *Le Tigre* offshore but most staggered out half-starved and half-crazed imploring the French to send them into the arms of Allah. The French fed and watered the wretched survivors, though many died through their intake of too much food too soon.

44

A few days later, Cousseau's regiment found itself in Alexandria. The men were settled down in their billets when the sergeant's superior requested him and a fellow sergeant, Rochard, to accompany an officer, Descorches in negotiations with the British for an exchange of prisoners. The three of them boarded the battleship *Le Tigre* anchored in the bay, under a flag of truce. Stood before them was the commander of the British naval forces, Sidney Smith and his entourage. Smith exchanged pleasantries with Descorches and then gave a perfunctory nod to each of his aides. The naval officer met the gaze of Cousseau and stood momentarily transfixed recognising him as the combatant he had shown mercy to, at Acre. Cousseau also recognized the English fighter who had once stood on a rock above him, bloodied sabre in his hand, the man who had spoken to him in French and spared his life by disappearing back through the breach of the fortress walls. A knowing smile spread across the Englishman's countenance. Cousseau returned the gesture by giving him a cursory nod in recognition that the Englishman's inaction had saved his life. Smith reflected momentarily on the encounter too. He respected his opponent as a survivor who had fought at Acre, endured the retreat across the desert and no doubt participated in the Battle of Aboukir. In fact, he admired the courage, tenacity, and endurance of the French forces in general. At the side of Smith stood an Ottoman officer, a grim stare emanating from his steely eyes in contrast to the relaxed demeanour of the Englishman. This Albanian soldier, Muhammed Ali by name, was destined to become a future leader of Egypt.

Descorches conducted the meeting in private with Smith and his aides. The exchange of prisoners having been agreed, Descorches reappeared with Smith and his entourage.

"Take the French envoy to see the prisoners," came the order from Smith.

The French officer beckoned to Cousseau and Rochard. They followed their officer and some British sailors along the deck and progressed down steps to the bowels of the ship. Then they followed the sailors who had equipped themselves with lanterns into a dark foul-smelling, dingy brig where the clinking of chains could be heard. The three of them gagged on entering. Descorches spoke to the prisoners.

"I am an officer of the Imperial French Army. Follow me, you are free men."

Murmurs and cheers of relief filled the putrid, confined space.

"*Allons-y!* Let's go!" Cousseau shouted.

"*Vite! Vite!*" Rochard added.

The men struggled to their feet and were led up to the top deck of the impressive ship of the line. The bright sun exploded into their faces, and they were forced to shield their eyes. Most of them were in good shape, despite their smell and ramshackle appearance, thanks to the benevolence of Smith. They lined up and one by one they were freed from their shackles, assisted by British marines and placed into the smaller craft.

"By the way, sir," Smith addressed the French officer. "Have you heard any news from back home?"

"*Rien,*" Descorches replied.

"Ah, that's indeed interesting. Then I must give you these recent periodicals. Please ensure that '*le petit caporal*' receives them post-haste. I am sure he would take great interest in reading about the events taking place at home. I believe also that the Directory has requested that his presence is required back in his homeland henceforth."

Descorches looked hard at the English commander, then took possession of the newspapers before taking his leave, Cousseau and Rochard in attendance. Their vessel pulled away from the side of the English man-of-war, that had once flown the red, blue and white of the French *tricolore*. Sidney Smith peered down at the departing French launch from his poop deck. He smiled mischievously when he saw Descorches perusing a journal and talking animatedly to his fellow Frenchmen who were hanging on his every word.

45

Cousseau marched back into Cairo with the triumphant Army of the Orient, Napoleon at their head, again receiving the adulation of some and the fake obeisance of others in the mass turnout. The Corsican general had read the papers revealing the perilous situation back home with great interest. A tri-partite alliance between Britain, Russia and Austria had come into effect threatening France. At home, the French army had lost the gains he had personally made in Italy. France was politically, socially and militarily in turmoil. His ambitions of emulating Alexander the Great and conquering India and vast swathes of the Middle East had been thwarted. However, he had recognised that his destiny lay elsewhere; the time was ripe for him to seize power in his homeland. He was to return to France without delay. And so it was, late in August 1799 that Napoleon and his select, small retinue stole away from Cairo.

"I don't believe it," Cousseau said. "*Le petit caporal* has just upped and left. He's abandoned us! After all we've done for him! All our sacrifices here."

"Denon, Monge and Berthollet have departed as well, as part of his little clique," Demeraux added. "Who's in charge now?"

"General Kléber. Rumour has it he is furious with Bonaparte."

"I fear it's the beginning of the end of our adventures in Egypt."

"I believe so Antoine. Well, I'm all for returning to France. I've had enough of this God forsaken place."

"I hope to see the Valley of The Kings and Thebes before we leave. An expedition of savants is to be sent to Upper Egypt to build on Denon's good work and I hope to be chosen."

"If you do get selected, my friend, you should be able to conduct your business in less hostile conditions because Desaix has apparently pacified the region. Kléber is also suing for peace. He's had enough as well."

46

Several months passed. Cousseau was fortunate to stay in and around Cairo whilst Demeraux was indeed selected for the Egyptology trip to catalogue and map all of Denon's finds.

One day, Cousseau was indulging in the calming vapours of a nargile at a café on the streets of Cairo, when a furore took place across the square. He got up from his table and went over with some friends curious to see what the fuss was about. Barthelemy, the city's chief of police was addressing the crowd. Cousseau listened but he could not understand the Greek language that the Copt was spouting effusively. Someone shouted, "In French! *Parlez français!*"

Barthelemy obliged, telling the crowds that the peace negotiations had been rejected and a vast army of Turks had arrived on the border with Syria again having already slaughtered the French garrison at El-Arish. The putrefying heads of the French soldiers had once again been displayed on spikes around the encampment. Cousseau and the other soldiers present were incensed. It was not long before Cousseau was called to arms again and was part of the ten thousand strong French army sent to confront the forty thousand strong enemy led by the Grand Vizier. Kléber attacked the numerically superior enemy at Heliopolis, just outside of the capital, routing the multi-ethnic warriors who turned out to be nothing more than a disorganised rabble. Cousseau relished the encounter, and no quarter was given to avenge the deaths of their comrades. Some of the enemy managed to escape into Cairo though causing anarchy and mayhem. Subsequent negotiations resulting in a parley.

Months later the hero of Heliopolis, General Kléber was stabbed to death in the grounds of his palace by a young Arab. Cousseau and Demeraux, having returned from his mission, witnessed the funeral and the subsequent execution of the assassin. The multitude avidly gathered around to watch. First, the hand that the condemned man used to plunge the dagger into its victim, was burnt. Then, a lance was inserted up a widened hole into the Arab assassin's anus which had been carved by the executioner's knife. A mallet then pounded the spike to his torso. He was then raised in the air, hands tied behind his back and left to die. Cousseau admired the Arab's sang-froid and courage. He never once cried out in pain. Demeraux was appalled at the savagery and vomited the contents of his guts on the ground.

Demeraux and Cousseau left the execution site and picked their way through the capital's maze of streets. They strolled past the souks and bazaars, redolent with all manner of items; cookware, confectionary, food, spices, knives, and weapons of every description where customers were haggling animatedly over the wares.

French boutiques had also been established. Milliners, haberdasheries, *boulangeries*, *couturiers* and many others. They passed dozens of restaurants which had sprung up in the city since the occupation - Greek, Maltese, Moroccan, French and other nationalities and a multitude of other cafés, the smells of the Mediterranean and the Orient wafting out into the narrow streets and mercifully diluting the vile stench of human and animal waste. Napoleon had done much to alleviate the city's foul unsanitary conditions, but the malodorous vapours still pervaded the densely populated quarters. Clients sat outside the eateries, puffing on hookahs and watching the amorphous mass of humanity drift by like the ubiquitous flotsam on the Nile. Beggars of every description lined the thoroughfares. Legless ones pulled themselves along on their arms. Blind ones stumbled around, hats held out in desperation, imploring passers-by for alms. Armless wretches created street art with a paint brush thrust out of their mouths or held between their toes whilst prostitutes milled around on every street corner, attracting the attention of interested soldiers who were debating in groups or having wagers to discover who their next conquest was to be. The prostitutes, some of whom were male but mostly female, ranged from early teens to what seemed like haggard sexagenarians but were more likely women in their forties, life having not been too kind to them. Carts clattered by laden with fruit, spices and vegetables pulled by slaves or donkeys and carriages trundled by carrying officer's and their splendid looking wives attired in their regalia in contrast to the ragged and pitiful dregs of humanity who struggled to remove themselves from the danger of being trampled or beaten by impatient drivers or their exalted customers. Cousseau had taken a *coup d'oeil* at the eye-catching pulchritude of Pauline Fourès, Napoleon's former paramour, passing in one carriage with her ladies in waiting, all looking resplendent in their finery. Josephine, Napoleon's wife had refused to accompany him on his expedition to Egypt, preferring to continue her tryst with an officer of the realm and had remained in Paris in the arms of her lover much to the commander-in-chief's fury. Napoleon had denounced her infidelities but had no qualms about courting the wife of one of his own officers nor about abandoning his concubine to her fates, leaving her behind in Egypt.

47

Cousseau and Demeraux arrived at their eatery of preference, Café Languedoc, situated on a square. Across from it was an old Coptic church and more bars and cafés. They took a seat at a table outdoors and waited to be served by a waitress. Jemila, the Nubian friend of Chione approached them. Demeraux had managed to find her employment in the café having known the owner of the café, Malachy, another fellow Occitan, a Jewish food merchant, who had been imprisoned by the Knights of Malta on some frivolous misdemeanour. He had been granted his freedom when Napoleon had captured the island en route to Cairo.

"*Bon après-midi messieurs Pierre et Antoine. Vous désirez?*" she asked in near perfect French.

"*Du thé s'il te plaît,*" Antoine replied.

Antoine smiled at the woman who had become his love interest. She had taken on the arduous task of caring for Antoine on the retreat from Syria. This had saved both their lives. Jemila had access to the small amounts of food and water available to Antoine on the journey home, which he had kindly shared with her to keep both their strength up. By the time they had arrived in Cairo they had become enamoured with each other. Demeraux's first sexual encounter was fraught with embarrassment. He had stood there in awe of Jemila as she performed the dance of the seven veils in front of him. She was sprawled naked on his bed, and he just gawped at her glistening, ebony body and large, full breasts, cap in hand as if he were in front of his former headmaster. Although he was twenty-two, he was still a virgin. His 'sex' had been the excitement that knowledge gave him. Being a polymath, his head had been buried in books rather than in the bosom of a woman, but the broad-hipped, buxom Jemila had changed his perceptions. She had chased him around his room laughing, trying to remove his clothes and then she finally cornered him, stripping him naked and pinning him against a table. A table on which he realised you could do more on than just dine or spread study books or maps on. His lust for a knowledge of a different kind instilled by his first love-making experience, carnal knowledge, knew no bounds after this, although he remained loyal to his partner and sexual guru.

"*Du thé pour moi aussi,*" Cousseau responded. "*Ça va*, Jemila?" he then asked.

"*Ça va bien,*" the black, broad-hipped woman confirmed with a smile.

Jemila returned to the café with the order. The two friends took out their clay pipes, lit them and puffed on them, the smoke rising up and away to the azure blue African sky.

"I believe General Menou has been installed as the new general in chief and is taking up residence in Elfi Bey's palace."

"Indeed Pierre. Word has it he wants to keep the Rosetta Stone under his bed!

He's treating it as if it were his own personal property!"

"Well, I suppose, he's right to protect it, such is the interest in the Stone. That might be the safest place. That's where our artefact is. Under the floorboards of your bed, Antoine!"

"The *Institut d'Égypte* has taken prints of the text on the Rosetta Stone anyway. They will work on them once Menou has taken ownership of it. I'm afraid they haven't made much progress. The mathematicians and orientalists have been driven to despair. Each one in competition with the other hoping to be the first scholar to break the hieroglyphic code. Denon, Monge and Berthollet have taken copies with them back to France as well. They intend to distribute them to scholars around Europe. I'm surprised they didn't take the original with them."

"So, I suppose it will be a while before we know our tablet's real value."

"*Exactement*. I'm hoping someone has the ability to decipher it. I'm trying desperately myself."

Jemila returned with the tea.

"*Merci* Jemila. I will see you later on this evening," Antoine cooed.

"*À tout à l'heure*, Antoine," she replied seductively. She giggled and then spun away dramatically to wait on other customers.

"I too have made a lithographic copy of our text," Antoine continued. "I watched Conté perfect the technique and I surreptitiously copied the process when you were away on duty at Heliopolis. I will give you the copy just in case the tablet is found."

"Bravo, you are a genius, Antoine. At least then we'll still be able to discover what the script says."

"I will also show you the location because I am due to go on an expedition to the Coptic monastery of Saint Antoine Le Grand in a few weeks' time to map the area. You may even want to conceal it elsewhere, just in case I have the misfortune not to return."

"Ah, so, the powers that be have seen fit to ordain you with the title of 'saint'. *Saint Antoine Le Grand,* eh? I have heard of St. Antoine de Padua, the patron saint of lost things but not St. Anthony the Great. Perhaps you should be the next St. Anthony of Padua in light of our discovery of a tablet that has been lost for thousands of years, it would seem. Hold on, I seem to have mislaid my purse."

Cousseau genuflected and placed his hands together. "St Anthony, grant that I may find that which has been lost. My purse. But let me only find it after St. Antoine here has paid for our mint tea."

The two laughed.

"Alright Antoine, I'll take a look at the hiding place. If I feel it's already in a safe place, then I will leave things be." Cousseau lowered his voice. "Have you told Jemila about the artefact?"

"*Non*. I think it's best for it to remain our secret."

The two sipped their tea and sucked on their pipes then proceeded to the savant's lodgings.

48

They arrived at the two-storey dwelling. Demeraux shared the ramshackle abode with a few other savants. He turned the key in the lock of an old, weathered door that creaked open and went into the sparsely furnished house. No one else was at home. The light through the window shone weakly but it was enough to partially bathe the room in sunlight. Demeraux went up the rickety staircase and entered the bedroom. He dragged his wooden framed bed to one side and removed a small woven rug. He took a dagger from the drawer of a dressing table and manoeuvred it into the side of a large stone floor tile giving himself and Cousseau enough leverage to get their fingers underneath it and prise it away. They slid the stone away and there in the hole below was the sack containing the artefact. Demeraux reached in and wrenched the bag up with the help of his friend. He set it on the floor and extracted a lithographic print of the script and then the heavier object. Cousseau brushed away some dust and gazed at the ivory slab. He ran his eyes across the tablet adorned with symbols and figures, birds, creatures and humans depicted in some task or other. He pointed out a horizontal oval shaped carving containing more symbols and animals.

"Any idea what this is Antoine?"

"No idea, but it must be of some significance because of its distinctiveness compared to the other symbols. Maybe it's the name of a place or person."

"We saw these on the ruins and monuments in Thebes and other places. The men called them 'cartouches' because they look like powder cartridges."

"That's what the savants now call them. Whoever first thought of it has invented a new word for the lexicon."

Down below, the door creaked open and was slammed shut and laughter and loud banter could be heard. The other savants had returned. Demeraux quickly held out the sack and Cousseau shoved the artefact into it. Then they carefully placed it back into its hiding hole. Cousseau lifted the stone tile and inserted it back into position, Demeraux making slight adjustments to make it sit perfectly in place. They heard footsteps trudging up the steps and hurriedly placed the mat back into position and lifted the bed, gently laying it down completing the task. There was a rap on the door and Rabat, one of Demeraux's housemates, entered.

"Ah, Demeraux, you have company."

"Yes, this is my old friend Sergeant Pierre Cousseau. We grew up together in Mourèze, Languedoc. I'm just showing him around our humble quarters," Demeraux replied, deftly taking one step to his left to conceal the print which he forgot still laid on the bed.

"*Enchanté!*" Rabat and the sergeant said simultaneously, holding out a hand each. The two of them smiled. Rabat was slightly intoxicated. "Well," he continued, "I have just come back to freshen up and then I'm off back out again with Florent and Debussy. We have been invited to a recital by Madame Belliac and I must look my best. She has some very attractive maids of honour who are in desperate need of some gentlemanly company. I must powder my private parts!"

Rabat tottered over to the water bowl, poured some water from a jug into it, and began to splash his face. Demeraux grabbed the print whilst he was otherwise occupied and handed it over to Cousseau who immediately folded it and shoved it inside his shirt.

"Right, I must be away, back to the barracks. *Adieu*, gentlemen."

Rabat reached for a towel and dabbed his face dry. He waved flamboyantly and saluted the departing soldier then returned to his ablutions, stripping off his clothes, leaving Demeraux to continue with his studies.

49

After a few hours of study on cartography, Demeraux washed and then prepared supper. He was ravenous. Jemila was due at any moment. He laid the table with two plates with a hunk of bread on each and two knives, an extra lit candle and holder since it was now dark outside and a plate of goat's cheese. He also placed a dish of figs down and covered the plates with cloth to prevent the ubiquitous flies from crawling over the food. He waited. It was past 9.30pm. Normally Jemila would be back by now. She would be escorted back to Demeraux's house by Malachy. If not, by one of the other waiters or porters. It was one of Malachy's favourite chores, being a bit of an opportunist with the ladies. Sometimes he got lucky, but not with Jemila. As time ticked on, Demeraux surmised that she must be doing an extra shift as sometimes occurred and so, being famished, he could no longer wait. He removed the cloth from his bread and lavished it with an abundant smear of soft goat's cheese, savouring every moment. He waited an hour or so more. By this time, he was becoming anxious, so he left the house and decided to walk the half mile to the café. He passed Rabat, Florent and their friend Debussy on the way back, worse for wear, singing merry ditties. Few of his fellow savants could hold their liquor, just like him. He asked them if they had seen Jemila. They had not. He pressed on and arrived at the café to be greeted by Malachy who looked at him solicitously.

"My friend. What are you doing here?"

"Is Jemila here?"

"Jemila? No. She left on time."

Concern was etched on Malachy's face.

"She's not returned home. I thought she was doing another extra shift."

"No, Antoine, she left just after her normal time at 9.15pm. We were terribly busy, and I could not afford to accompany her, nor could I afford anyone else because a waiter had fallen sick. She was not feeling too good herself. She complained of feeling nauseous and so she did not want to work longer so she left on her own."

"Maybe she's gone to her friend's house."

"I will come with you to look for her. It's quieter now. My son can take charge."

The two men left.

"Where does her friend live?"

"Not far from here."

Malachy and Demeraux pushed their way through the throng of revellers in the streets and disappeared down some narrow back streets to a 'massage parlour'. They inquired if they had seen Jemila, but no one had. They retraced her journey back from Malachy's *Café Jardin d'Eden*, now accompanied by Malachy's muscular son David in his pony and trap. They skirted a patch of scrubland and called out into

115

the cooling night air and then suddenly Demeraux stopped and held his hand aloft. A whimper emanated from somewhere close by: "*Au secours. Aidez-moi!*"

They rushed in the direction of the weak cry, stumbling over a mixture of waste and vegetation and located its source. It came from Jemila, lying amidst the thorny undergrowth of an acacia bush, weeping, barely alive. They extracted her gingerly from the thorny shrub and laid her down on the ground. She was naked and bloodied not only from the lacerations of the thorns but also from cuts to her bruised and battered face. David ran back for the pony and trap.

"Jemila, my love, who has inflicted this pain on you?" Demeraux screamed.

"By the love of God, what have they done to you?" Malachy cried angrily.

Jemila could barely talk. Each utterance an enormous effort.

"A-a-a soldier. A-a-attacked me. De-filed m-e," she managed to divulge before lapsing into unconsciousness.

Demeraux removed his jacket and wrapped it as best he could around Jemila. David then returned bringing with him a blanket from the trap which he used to cover Jemila's bare body. He gently swooped her up and carried her to the carriage placing her in the back. Demeraux climbed in next to Jemila and Malachy jumped up next to his son. They headed back to the savant's lodgings with an anguished Demeraux cursing and threatening revenge between bouts of weeping. On arrival, they carried Jemila upstairs and placed her down on the bed then Malachy's son went in search of a physician. He returned not long after with a Jewish doctor who examined the motionless Nubian diagnosing a fractured cheekbone, two broken ribs and trauma to her vagina amongst the other many contusions she had scattered throughout her body.

The physician sedated her with a small dose of laudanum and Malachy, David and he departed, leaving the distraught Demeraux to watch over her.

116

50

The following morning Cousseau arrived at the *Café Jardin d'Eden* for his breakfast whereupon Malachy informed him of the attack on Jemila. He purchased some bread and cheese and rushed away to see Antoine. When he arrived at Demeraux's lodgings he was let in by Florent. He ran upstairs and found his friend by Jemila's bedside. Demeraux looked drawn and tired. He smiled perfunctorily.

"My God! I've just heard the terrible news from Malachy. How is she?"

"Very weak. She's in a lot of pain. She's suffered a vile and vicious attack."

"Malachy informed me as to the injuries she suffered. She looks in a bad way."

"She's slightly better than last night when I thought I might lose her. She opened her eyes and smiled at me before. It was a very special moment."

Tears welled in the savant's eyes. Cousseau placed his arm around his friend and comforted him.

"Here, I brought some bread and cheese for you and Jemila. Are you going to be alright Antoine?"

"I'm just tired but burning inside with anguish. I want to find out who did this to her and kill them!"

"Have you any inkling about who would have perpetrated this crime?"

"Only that she said it was a soldier."

"Well, that narrows it down a bit. Leave it with me. If it's someone from the military that's my jurisdiction. I'm going to make inquiries. I will ask Malachy to inform Barthelemy also. Malachy has told me where the rape took place so I'm going there now to look for some clues. Take care and give my love to Jemila when she awakes."

Cousseau raced down the stairs and exited the building. He went to the wasteland and started to search near to the thicket that Malachy had indicated. The area was awash with the detritus of Cairo despite Napoleon's best efforts to sanitize the city. He picked up a palm frond and snapped off the palm and poked about amidst the thorns with the stick. His eyes focused on something red with a dash of green on it. He leant into the bush and scraped the item towards him. He recognised it instantly as an epaulette from a *chasseurs à pied* tunic. Jemila must have torn it off in her struggle. He picked it up in the hope that the perpetrator had not realized the significance of it and replaced it already. He continued to search in and around the bush. He spotted something else. Something that provoked a wave of euphoria and hope within him. He frantically clawed at it with his improvised utensil until it was in range. He manoeuvred his hand gingerly into the tangle of vicious thorns. He grimaced as the fleshy web between his thumb and forefinger was penetrated. He grasped the item and slowly withdrew his stinging hand incurring more painful scratches as he did so. Once clear from the bush he unfurled his bleeding fingers to reveal a green pompon, which he assumed had come from the same *chasseur's* bicorne. This was all the incriminating evidence he needed.

He immediately sought out Malachy who arranged for him to meet Barthelemy, the notorious, baggy-trousered Cairo chief of police of Greek persuasion whose tendency was to scour the streets of the capital, scimitar in hand, singling out rogues and malcontents who were subsequently beheaded or guillotined, five or six daily, whether guilty or not. Malachy, a friend of Barthelemy's, enjoyed his patronage. Malachy found him pacifying some Muslims who were airing a grievance about the French. Simmering tensions remained in the city due to some of the practices of the French occupants, like converting mosques into coffee shops, which offended the local Muslim population. Barthelemy headed straight for a military encampment, the bivouac of a *demi-brigade* of light infantry accompanied by Cousseau and two other constables. He informed an officer of the crime and the officer called for a company of *chasseurs à pied* to stand to immediately. Cousseau could not be certain that the perpetrator was from this particular body of men, but at least he had the cooperation of the colonel. The colonel requested a lieutenant to peruse the lines of soldiers armed with the information about the evidence. He rode along the ranks of men and paused in front of a soldier with an epaulette missing but with a pompon on his bicorne. He scrutinized him hard then continued along the ranks and then halted in front of a *chasseur* on the last row.

"Roucard! One step forward!"

Cousseau, standing with the colonel and Barthelemy's retinue, instantly recognized the name. A slovenly soldier, a look of surprise on his face cautiously stepped forward.

"Right turn! March!" came the order.

The lieutenant led the soldier towards his commanding officer. Cousseau glared. He felt the ire welling up inside him. It was the drunken gravedigger he had punched into the burial pit. His reputation as an obnoxious troublemaker was known throughout the brigade and beyond.

"Halt! Stand to attention, man!"

Colonel Dumas ordered a sergeant major to remove the musket from Roucard's grip, but he tried to object.

"Quiet, man!" the sergeant major roared.

The colonel requested the epaulette and pompon from Cousseau. He approached the private and revealed them to him. Roucard instantly glanced at his shoulder nervously.

"Stand still *chasseur!*" the burly SGM bawled.

"Remove your hat soldier!" the colonel ordered.

Roucard took off his bicorne and presented it to the officer. The hat was missing its green pompon. He suddenly realised it was clenched in the stern looking colonel's grasp much to his consternation.

"Soldier, what's your name and rank?"

"Roucard. Private Émile Roucard, sir!"

"Roucard, you are missing an epaulette on your tunic and a pompon on your headdress. This is unacceptable private! Can you ascertain how and where you lost them?"

Roucard, who was still under the influence of intoxication stammered his way through an unintelligible response. The colonel ordered him to stop, took a step closer to him and examined scratches amidst each sideburn that stretched down each side of Roucard's dirt-streaked face. The *chef de brigade* could smell the alcohol on his noxious breath. He noticed too, more lacerations to his neck and other scratch marks and red gouges on his forehead where Jemila's fingernails had penetrated the skin underneath his greasy, dark hair. He also observed dried blood stains on his uniform and grabbing the drunken soldier's hands one by one, examined the bruised knuckles and specks of dried blood under his filthy nails. This was enough to convict Roucard as far as Colonel Dumas was concerned. He ordered his arrest. Barthelemy's associates shackled the hands and feet of the remonstrating soldier and dragged him over to a tethered mule. The two men threw him onto the mule, but he slipped off on the other side much to the amusement of the other ranks. They yanked him up and this time placed him on it securely. Barthelemy and Cousseau thanked the colonel. Before leaving he spoke to them earnestly and privately.

"I've put up with that *imbécile* Roucard for longer than I can remember. Beastings and incarceration have failed to curb his wrongdoings. If he's overstepped the line this time, he deserves punishment. As you are aware, corporal punishment is not permitted in the French army, so I have no objections if you exact retribution on him. As far as I am concerned, it was a civil matter and therefore in your jurisdiction. Maybe a good thrashing will set him right. Good day gentlemen."

The accused soldier, protesting his innocence vehemently, was taken to police HQ, dragged from his mule, blind-folded and tied to a post. Citizens gathered round in expectation. Barthelemy disappeared inside the building briefly then reappeared with a cat o' nine tails which he promptly passed to Cousseau.

"You have the honour of being the scourger, sergeant. Ten lashes and make them count!"

Cousseau seized the whip with relish and strode menacingly towards the bound and blind-folded coward Roucard, who quivered like a bowstring in anticipation of his punishment. Cousseau knew Demeraux would not be able to mete out his own punishment. Demeraux was not a man of violence. He was five foot nothing and puny and could hardly lift his own pencil.

"This one's for Jemila," he growled venomously. Then he lashed him. Roucard's screams pierced the air.

"That one's from Demeraux," he spat, as the flails gouged skin from the inebriated rogue's bare back.

"And this one is for the wretched mother who brought you into this world!"

The hard knots of cord bit deep into Roucard's skin. He cried out again.

"The next is for the father whose poisoned sperm created a monster! You!"

The scourger savoured every thrash of the flail. Cousseau threw the lash to the stony ground satisfied with his retribution. Roucard's limp, scarred body lay slumped

119

against the t-post, his legs having buckled beneath him. The sated crowd of onlookers, gradually drifted away. Cousseau felt no sympathy for Roucard, nonetheless his forlorn expression, on completion of his task, seemed to convey a scintilla of regret. Cousseau himself had once been the unfortunate recipient of the lash when he was a young recruit meted out on the orders of a brutal, sadistic maverick captain whose whims and frivolous compulsions had seen many a man flogged for the most spurious of reasons. Each welt on his own back was testimony to that, and each of his own scars seemed to emit a tingling sensation as if it were secreting its own trickle of blood every time the cat o' nine tails had gouged out another strip of Roucard's flesh.

The semi-conscious Roucard was released from the wooden post and carried into the gaol by two of the constabulary. A contented Barthelemy informed Cousseau that the perpetrator would remain fettered in a cell to await trial. The prognosis was grim for the villain since anyone in Napoleon's army previously convicted of rape had been decapitated.

51

Cousseau was too fatigued to trudge back to Demeraux's lodgings to notify him of what had occurred, so he returned to his bivouac. He had been on duty all night supervising the pickets who were stationed around the camp to prevent the theft of horses, camels, valuables, weapons, provisions and anything else the urchins and vagabonds took a fancy to. Anyone caught in the act of pilfering was shot on sight. Instead, Cousseau requested a quill and paper from a clerk and despatched a note to Demeraux, delivered by one of the young trustworthy camp followers who ran all manner of errands for the soldiers for food, drink or other items in return for renumeration. The note read:

'Antoine,

We have identified the assailant and detained him.

I have personally taken the whip to him and flogged him to within an inch   of his pathetic life. Justice will follow.

I hope Jemila's God is watching over her.

Concentrate all your energy into facilitating her speedy recovery and I will take care of the rest.

Your dearest friend,

Pierre.'

52

Liverpool. Present day.

DCI Armitage confirmed that none of the deceased was Paul. She had met Paul in hospital when she went to interview him. Two of the victims she knew, low level drug dealers, Mick Kerslake and Liam McAteer. The other she could not identify. His face had been blasted away. She immediately put out an arrest warrant for Paul De Vere. Penny and Jules were escorted home, suffering from shock. They had informed the police where they might find the suspect.

Paul was sat in the Abercromby Square gardens, on his usual bench, reading a book, *Sniper One*. He had hoped to see Jules. He had not seen her since her ordeal with Richard and assumed that she was convalescing, taking time off to recuperate. The next minute he was surrounded by armed police officers, the muzzles of their weapons staring him in the face. DCI Armitage appeared, read him his rights, and arrested him for the murders of the three men. He was handcuffed and frog-marched away before he could object. Twenty-four hours later he was released without charge. When Jules had called Randy to tell him what had happened, her colleague informed her that Paul had slept on his sofa on the Wednesday night. He had encountered him in the Abercromby Square Gardens and told him he could kip down at his for the night. Randy's wife, Salena, was not too impressed with his impromptu arrangements since she had invited friends over for dinner, something which her husband had completely forgotten about. Nevertheless, Paul was kindly asked if he would like to join them for dinner which he readily accepted being ravenous and having smelt the spices of the curry dishes being prepared in the kitchen. After a quick shower and shave he joined the others at the table and regaled them with stories of army life impressing Randy with his knowledge of the Sikh, Hindu, and Muslim military associations with the British Army. Paul was amazed when Randy told him that one of his ancestors had been in Egypt in 1801 as a young sepoy, as part of the Indian contingent of the British invasion forces that ousted the French. Randy had meant to tell Jules that morning that Paul had stayed but she was too absorbed in her nascent quest for the stele. Furthermore, the bar staff at the Baltic Fleet had confirmed three men were in the pub on Tuesday night, two of whom fitted the descriptions of two of the victims and a resident at Wapping Quay had seen three characters loitering outside the block the same evening. Forensics also confirmed that it was likely the three died the same night, given the corpses' state of decomposition and that it appeared to be a 'hit', possibly involving drugs. The following day Frank's girlfriend contacted the police to say he was missing. In response to the question, 'did he have any distinguishing features on his body', she said he only had one testicle. Frank was subsequently identified. His face was missing but his one gonad was still intact. DCI Armitage, however, still regarded Paul as a suspect given his army background.

53

Jules's mobile rang. It was DCI Armitage. She took the call in private in the kitchen, listening intently.

"Frank? Frank Baines? You're kidding. Are you sure? His girlfriend's identified him. No, I don't know why he was in the flat. He's a business associate of Richard's. Maybe he gave him his key. Right, ok. Thanks for letting me know. That's shocking. Frank! Dead!"

Penny, draped on a settee in the living room, still in her dressing gown, waited in anticipation for her friend to emerge.

"Well?"

"The other guy, in the bedroom. It was Richard's mate. Frank Baines. I can't believe it. He must have got the key from Richard. The detective said they were tooled up. One of them even had a gun," Jules revealed, in shock.

"Jesus, who were they waiting for?"

"Me? Paul? The both of us? I don't know."

"Bloody hell! I was there only the other day, with Paul. They could have shot me, thinking it was you! But who killed them and why? If it wasn't Paul."

"DCI Armitage is keeping an open mind on it. She says she's not ruling out Paul because of his military background. They reckon it was a professional job but if they want to stitch someone up for it, Paul's DNA is everywhere."

"God, you're right."

"They reckon the assassin used a silencer and possibly night vision goggles. Whoever killed them must have trashed the place the other day as well. They must have been searching for something. Or maybe it was Frank and his cronies."

"And there's me blaming Paul for wrecking the joint!"

"And for stinking it out! What are you going to tell him next, that he smells like a two-day old corpse! Charming!"

"Well, he does whiff a bit."

"So would you if you were homeless! I need to go and see him. I think we both need apologize to him, again!"

"Listen Jules, someone is out to get either you or Paul or even Richard. Maybe he's mixed up in something. Someone is prepared to kill. Now, what would anyone want from you?"

"I don't know."

"The tablet, of course! The stele!"

"Well, I haven't got it! I'm just the messenger! But I hadn't even considered that. Oh, there's been so much going on of late!"

"True, you haven't got it. They're jumping the gun a bit. No pun intended. Maybe they think you know more than you've already revealed and wanted to extract every teeny-weeny bit of information from you, before, before killing you!"

"Shut the front door!" Jules said, a frisson of trepidation shooting down her spine.

"They could have waited for the flipping news conference tomorrow! But who are 'they'?"

"Well, it could be, let's see, anyone. Anyone whose interest lies in wanting to keep the proclamation a secret. Or any person or organisation that sees great monetary value in finding it. It could even be the aliens trying to get it back!"

"As if...Shut up!"

"Well, from now on I think you need some sort of protection, be it from the police or the university."

"You're right. I'm seeing the principal tomorrow at the conference. I'm going to insist on it."

"Can I sleep in your bed tonight?"

"Er, no. Three's a crowd. Ian's back tonight. Hey, look what's on the telly. Indiana Jones And the Last Crusade! Have it!"

54

The nurse scurried away from Richard's bedside, tears in her eyes, after listening to his foul-mouthed rant about the quality of the food. He was showing his true colours. His demeanour suddenly changed though when DCI Armitage and DS Noades came calling. He feigned his reaction to the news that Frank had been murdered swooning in mock shock and horror. He had seen the TV footage about three male bodies found in an apartment. He had assumed that this was De Vere and maybe some other homeless non-entities, buddies of his. He was privately cursing Frank because of the mess he had left. The plan was to make it look like a drug overdose and then dispose of the body in the Mersey, not to involve others. He had rung around some other pals to ask if anyone had seen Frank. He thought it unusual that he had not been in touch with him and assumed he was lying low after the debacle. Someone subsequently confirmed that Frank was dead. He could not believe it. He was raging. Frank had screwed up and so another grilling by the plod was inevitable.

"Ah, DCI Armitage, have you come to give me some good news? Is that piece of scum De Vere being charged for attempted murder?"

"I'm afraid not Mr Reeves. I presume you've heard the news about the murders of three males that took place in your apartment."

"I have. It was shocking. Appalling. I have no idea who these people were and how they got into my apartment. Did they break in?"

"Not exactly, Mr Reeves. There was no sign of forced entry to the apartment. They were all shot. Have you got any enemies Mr Reeves?"

"Well, only that scumbag De Vere. It was probably him! Looking for me again. Or maybe they were druggy mates of his and he just took it out on them in some blind fury fuelled by booze and drugs."

"I don't think that particular theory holds water since one of the victims, I believe, is a work colleague of yours. Frank Baines," DS Noades said, in her strong Glaswegian accent.

"Frank? Frank Baines? Oh, God. No! Not poor Frank!"

"Yes, I'm afraid so. I'm sorry but what would Frank Baines be doing in your flat with two drug dealers, known thugs with previous, Mick Kerslake and Liam McAteer?"

"Drug dealers? No idea."

"So, you don't know them?"

"No. Of course not. Maybe the pushers were mates of De Vere's."

"No, we have evidence to suggest that they were associates of Frank Baines. They were seen at a pub enjoying drinks together that evening," Armitage confirmed.

"Did Mr Baines have a key to the apartment?" Noades enquired.

"Not that I know of."

"Where's your key then?" she queried.

"In my jacket pocket over there. It's hanging up."

Noades fetched the jacket and checked in the pockets. She pulled out his wallet and a condom. No keys.

"Maybe they're in my trousers. Over there."

Armitage checked them.

"Nothing."

"We found a set of keys on Frank's body," Noades then confirmed.

"Frank was here. A few days ago. Maybe he took them. I never said he could take them! The little shit! Maybe he was setting up a drugs den in my apartment without me knowing! Or maybe he was hoping to get off with Jules! The slimy rat!"

"So, you're sure you didn't give him the keys?" Armitage asked.

"No chance!"

"Ok, thank you for your time, Mr Reeves. We'll be in touch," Armitage replied.

Noades threw the condom on the bed.

"You won't be needing that where you're going."

55

On the morning of the conference, Jules received a phone call to tell her that Richard had also been charged with conspiracy to commit murder. DCI Armitage and her colleague had seen through Richard's deceit and crocodile tears and had returned that morning to Murrayfield Hospital to charge him.

The conference was to take place at the nearby Catholic Cathedral at 2pm prompt. The venue had been hastily commissioned when the University realised no other campus space would accommodate the hordes of hacks and camera crews from the world's media and other interested parties descending on Liverpool. It was considered an ironic choice of venue since the revelation of the tablet was expected to have significant repercussions for the world of religion, but 'Paddy's Wigwam' needed the funds and could not let slip the opportunity of hosting the event.

The panel of experts chosen to front the news conference filed into the impressive rotunda led by the tall, thick set, bearded figure of the Chancellor of the University, Dr Edmund Parkes. Jules took her place on the dais between him and Tom Yates. The others took their seats. In front of them were rows and rows of journalists representing every sector of the world's media; news organisations, TV, radio, internet websites, newspapers and journals et al. Also present were representatives from the Church and every faith, government representatives, politicians, historical organisations and societies, linguists, orientalists and distinguished academics from other universities and institutions renowned for their archaeological expertise. All from every corner of the world. Merseyside's hotels had been awash with news crews and other guests from far and wide.

Dr Parkes began by welcoming everyone to Liverpool. He introduced the panel and thanked the Catholic Bishop of Liverpool for the use of the cathedral at such short notice. After explaining the procedures of the meeting and asking attendees to only ask questions during Q&A after the presentations, Tom Yates was invited to take the floor. With the aid of the giant screens erected all around the venue, he explained the sequence of events, showing the Lady Lever, the Napoleonic artefacts and the Cardinal Fesch embroidered sofa together with a picture of Janet who discovered the first leather document holder. Her face went crimson when she was spotted in the audience. She slumped in her chair, embarrassed by the attention. Then the Chancellor, in his address, revealed the contents of the letters in a brief resumé.

"The first letter is dated 29th January 1811 and was anonymously written in cursive English. It explains that an ivory stele transported from Egypt had come into the possession of the anonym, the mystery letter writer. The tablet, it says, like the Rosetta Stone, had hieroglyphics carved into it. The only difference being that hieroglyphic pictograms were the only script on the tablet. The letter then goes on to say that the artefact may be of interest and value to the Catholic Church if it conveys a biblical or religious message and that Cardinal Fesch, being an intermediary in his role of ambassador between Napoleon and the Vatican, was deemed the right person to approach, given Fesch's family links to Napoleon Bonaparte himself. He was Napoleon's uncle, of course and was resident in Rome from 1803-1806 and subsequently retired to Rome after his nephew's second abdication in 1815. Furthermore, the Cardinal, it reveals, was also chosen as the recipient of the correspondence because of his penchant for collecting valued works of art and other collectables."

A few murmurs rippled around the auditorium.

"Fesch," Dr Parkes continued, "like many around the world, had taken interest in the discoveries made by Napoleon's troops and savants during the Egyptian campaign of 1798-1801. He had taken advantage of his eminent position in the Napoleonic and ecclesiastical hierarchy amassing valuable works of art from all corners of Napoleon's Empire and was perhaps the right person to approach in this case, given his mediation role between Napoleon and The Vatican."

More murmurs ensued.

"The second letter dated 2nd May 1812 refers to someone's death allegedly at the hands of the Catholic Church, thus proving the value of the artefact, according to our mystery correspondent."

A more audible reaction permeated the venue, in response to the alleged fatality at the hands of the Catholic Church. All eyes were on the podium where Bishop McRae sat. He fidgeted uncomfortably, looking embarrassed.

"And a third letter dated 22nd August 1812 has a sarcastic, goading tone to it and referred to even more deaths and claims of torture and espionage! The stakes, it seems, had evidently been upped in the pursuit of the artefact. The anonym bizarrely challenging Cardinal Fesch to play some sort of game!"

The noise levels rose considerably, leading to incredulity, debate, laughter and consternation. Dr Parkes took a moment and waited for the clamour to subside. He was particularly peeved and irritated by someone in one of the rows of seats constantly trying to gain his attention by calling out, "Dr Parkes! Dr Parkes!" Despite his insistence that no questions would be answered until the Q&A session. He decided to confront the irritating heckler once and for all. He addressed a cock-sure, blond-haired young man amongst the press pack.

"Excuse me, sir. Yes, you, sir. I thought I made it clear to everyone that we would answer all questions after the presentations so I would kindly ask you to stop interrupting and refrain from asking your questions until the end. By the way, who are you representing?"

The hack brandished his press pass, attached to his lanyard, in an arrogant manner. Dr Parkes was close enough to recognize the distinct logo. He immediately called for security. Two burly security guards moved along the row to remove the protesting journalist. A brief scuffle ensued before the aggrieved journo was frog-marched to the exit, leaving the other bewildered delegates looking on in surprise at the commotion.

"This newspaper is not welcome in Liverpool," he explained, sparking some jeering and cheering and several pockets of applause.

Penny, in the front row next to Randy, sat with a broad smile on her face. Although Dr Parkes was a big Everton FC fan, where the Hillsborough tragedy was concerned, there was nothing but solidarity amongst the Blues and Reds' fans. The Egyptian Minister of Antiquities, sat to her immediate right, reciprocated her smile and softly sang to her, "Mo Salah, Mo Salah, running down the wing... ." Penny burst out laughing, the gentleman amused, joined in, guffawing loudly, holding his ample waistline.

Once order was restored, Dr Parkes continued.

"Back to the rules of this 'game'. The rules were: To locate seven more clues. Each clue discovered will lead to another clue being recovered. The clues, it states, in the third letter, are all illustrations of creatures, animals. So, there are nine illustrations in total. The first two we have courtesy of the anonym, to start the game off and the discovery of the last one will lead to the location of the ivory tablet in question. The letter writer also discloses that each clue or drawing is related to the previous illustration in some way. So, there you have it, in a nutshell, seven more linked clues to find in total that I presume would lead to a place associated with the final creature where the coveted artefact could be found."

Again, the audience erupted. Shouts emanated from the crowd. Everyone was eager to know what the first two animals were. After a delay of five minutes or so, the enthralled delegates settled down. Only then did Dr Parkes proceed.

"I will reveal the said animals in due course, once Dr Julia Johnson has briefed you on the transcription of the hieroglyphs."

A collective groan echoed around the Cathedral.

"Believe me, Dr Johnson's address is worth listening to. *Really*, worth listening to. Dr Johnson, it's all yours."

Jules rose on cue and straightened her tight-fitting red dress, courting admiring looks from many in the audience. Despite the terrifying and draining tribulations of the previous few days, she calmly and coherently addressed the audience delivering a short speech with her customary fluency and professionalism. She pointed out another member of the panel, her colleague Dr Fatima Marsh, fresh from a trip back from Egypt, who had confirmed that her carbon-dating analysis was precise and that her transliteration was accurate, give or take a few minor disagreements on semantics. Both esteemed academics exchanged smiles. She then referred to the giant screens which projected the first lines of hieroglyphs and started to translate them verbatim, exhaling deeply before commencing.

"*This decree is a warning for future generations that...*" She paused for dramatic effect. "*...your planet, will witness the return of the Elohim. They will return to your planet in the year inscribed below, or earlier, if prompted by cataclysmic events caused by man alone or by natural forces that threaten the very existence of your world.*"

A volcanic eruption of noise exploded. Gestures were being made amidst animated discussions propagating a fusion of laughter, shock, offence and disbelief.

Others, not comprehending the significance of the word 'Elohim', sought clarification from those around them.

"Fraud! Fraud!" hecklers were calling out.

Dr Parkes called for order and Jules resumed only after it was secured. The next few lines of script appeared. Some, who were experts in the study of hieroglyphs themselves, gasped before Jules could even translate them.

"This proclamation was written by the hand of Eloah himself and conveyed to your planet after the ice age by our heavenly vessel under the guardianship of the Elohim. It serves to forewarn you of the dire consequences of not treating your world with the respect it requires."

Outside, just as she conveyed this message, the billowing grey clouds momentarily dispersed causing shafts of iridescent light to permeate the stained-glass windows, atop the Cathedral lantern tower bathing the podium and Jules, in particular, in brilliant rays of glorious sunlight. On hearing her words, those present reacted again. The same animated responses, negative and positive, emanated from the delegates and some representing various religious factions or theocracies, walked out in disgust.

"Beam me up Scotty!" shouted some, including Penny who was loving the chaotic reaction whilst Randy hummed the Star Trek theme amidst the tumult.

The rumpus died down to a manageable degree, enough for Jules to clarify the salient point that Eloah, in this instance, meant God whilst Elohim referred to 'gods'. Others sat silently trying to configure in their minds the implications of it all.

The Chancellor called again for complete silence and order. After achieving this with some difficulty, he simply said, "There's more," then nodded to Jules. She took another deep breath before delivering the final paragraph, translated from the third hieroglyphic print.

"In the beginning, you became our Experiment, to see if we could transform sub-human species we found on your planet, into intelligent human entities who could sustain and preserve their world for generations. We inseminated some of these sub-human creatures with our seed and departed. We returned, in later times, to discover, to our surprise, that these creatures had not only survived but evolved into what you are today."

More dissent and derision was directed at the rostrum as delegates howled, hooted and laughed whilst others remained silent. More delegations quit their seats in disgust and left, babbling and gesticulating furiously. Edmund, drowned out by the clamour, seemed to wait an eternity before managing to quieten everyone down by announcing that it was time for the Q&A session.

Dr Parkes scrutinized the banks of reporters and randomly jabbed his finger at one of the hacks who had his hand aloft.

"Dick Jones, Daily Express," the journalist said. "Surely this has to be some sort of hoax."

"How did I guess that was going to be the first question?"

A ripple of laughter manifested itself in the auditorium.

"Well, you can make your own minds up. We're just presenting you with the facts.

The hieroglyphs have been translated by, as mentioned in my address, two erudite experts. Dr Fatima Marsh is one of our esteemed professors. She has a PhD in Egyptology and Assyriology from Cambridge and liaises with the Egyptian Museum of Antiquities sitting on its board as an honorary director. She is a renowned expert in philological research of Ptolemaic hieroglyphic texts and highly respected amongst the academic fraternity. Dr Julia Johnson has a PhD in Egyptology and Archaeology and has led many archaeological expeditions to Egypt and other sites worldwide and is a renowned linguist, specialising in ancient texts. She is also a trustee, as is Dr Marsh, of the Egyptian Exploration Society and a member of a plethora of other archaeological and historic societies. We will permit any bona fide news organisation to come to our facility to inspect and validate the carbon-dating process, but, it will cost you! Other venerated academics from any renowned institution are welcome to conduct their own research, gratis. Next question, you, madam."

"Also, if I may jump in, Dr Parkes," Jules said. "The print copies were dated to the early 1800s just like the letters and illustrations, but the decipherment of hieroglyphics only occurred in 1822 principally through the efforts of French savant, Jean-François Champollion and before him the English polymath, Thomas Young, so, unless the anonymous writer of the letters knew how to translate hieroglyphs before Young and Champollion then it can't be a hoax."

There was a hum of consensus on this point.

"Jane Naughton, Sky News. Can you just explain the Elohim-Eloah connection, and can you confirm when those words came into existence?"

"I will pass that on to our eminent sage of Judaism, Rabbi Mirsch of the Princes Road Synagogue. Rabbi Mirsch, please."

"Thank you, Dr Johnson."

Rabbi Mirsch rose from his chair and reiterated in simple layman's terms that Elohim was the generic word for God in the Hebrew language but in some cases referred to gods or deities. He explained that Eloah also meant God, as did Yahweh, but not in the plural sense, only in the singular. Elohim could also refer to kings or angels and even the Messiah, and furthermore he added that the Hebrew Bible, theologians and other experts in the scriptures reckoned, dated back to the 6th century BCE when Hebrew writing developed but linguistically its roots stretched back to 1,200 BCE or even earlier to the era of Moses.

Suddenly a disturbance erupted on one side of the Cathedral. Four or five delegates were involved in a fracas. It seemed to be a confrontation between Muslim and Hindu groups trading insults. Security intervened and separated the quarrelling factions, order was restored, and the questions continued.

"Max Wheatley, BBC News. How old do you think the alleged tablet is?"

"Dr Marsh," Dr Parkes said.

"Well, the last Ice Age ended about 11,700 years ago and the Early Dynastic Period in Egypt was about 3,100 BCE when the era of the Pharaohs commenced. The Predynastic Period pre-dated this, lasting from 6,000 BCE to the Naqada III period circa 3,000 BCE when hieroglyphs, it is thought, came into existence about 3,200

BCE, so the stele could be anything up to 5,000 years old."

"You, next sir."

"Ray Peters, *Liverpool Echo*. What do you think the consequences of such a revelation will have on the world of religion?"

"Well, we've already seen the impact it has had," Dr Parkes replied, referring to the scuffle.

He was interrupted by laughter.

"Some people felt it necessary to leave, no doubt upset that their orthodox views are being challenged. It has opened a Pandora's Box as to our faiths and existence. Welcome or not. For good or for bad. The only way mankind can mentally prepare itself for what trials and tribulations lie ahead, or put itself at ease, is to find the bloody thing! Oops! Apologies Bishop! What do you think Dr Johnson?"

"Well, there needs to be a period of reflection on this. The script referred to so-called 'cataclysmic events' but as one of my colleagues remarked those events may have been and gone. The two world wars, the Black Death, the Spanish Flu, who knows?"

"Man United being relegated!" a wag shouted out soliciting more laughter.

"On the other hand, those cataclysmic events referred to might only occur hundreds of years from now in the future when we are long gone. Many faiths believe in a Second Coming so the message appears to confirm what these faiths have been predicting all along, albeit in a different way to what was previously envisaged. So, I suppose the only issue is with the extra-terrestrial heavenly vessel reference, viz. a spaceship. If, and when the tablet is located, only then will we be able to ascertain the truth."

"You, sir. Yes, in the front row."

"Dr Razek, Egyptian Minister of Antiquities. Will the stele be returned to Egypt once it has been located?"

"I'm afraid I can't answer that one, Dr Razek. It depends where it is. If it's on someone's land, or actually in someone's possession already and they don't realise what it is then there could be an issue. After two hundred years it could be anywhere. It could be back in Egypt! If it is located in Britain, you'll have to take that up with our government and if it's elsewhere, with the appropriate authorities."

"One more thing, do you believe it to be in Liverpool?"

"It could well be," Jules answered. "But as Dr Parkes explained, it could be anywhere. Liverpool at the time was a thriving port with many migrants settling in the area in addition to mariners, soldiers and merchants coming and going. Maybe the stele has been found already and been secreted away from this area. All we know is that the return address given by the anonymous writer was Ye Hole In Ye Wall, Hackins Hey, Liverpool, a public house that still exists today. They do a nice pint of beer there but don't all rush at once, it's not an excessively big pub."

"How do we get there?" a delegate shouted.

"Follow the signs for the Gay Quarter," Dr Parkes interrupted. "And if a bloke dressed as Cinderfella kisses you on the cheek, you'll know that you've arrived."

Laughter reverberated around the auditorium, then subsided.

133

"Ruby Slater, CNN News. You still haven't revealed what the first two clues are. Can you do that now?"

Dr Parkes momentarily consulted with the other members of the panel and then after a brief private discussion, gave his response.

"On reflection, given the outpouring of emotions we have witnessed already today we have decided to postpone the unveiling of the images until a later date."

Moans and groans and hoots of derision filled the air. Dr Parkes raised his voice above the din.

"We need a short period of deliberation! A cooling off period. We have much to contemplate already. As stated previously, mankind has to mentally prepare itself for what lies ahead!"

The delegates remained unconvinced.

"Who knows? That time might have already passed."

The dissatisfaction spread like wildfire.

"Look. I know you are all disappointed, but we think it's the correct course of action, to initiate a moratorium on the process, so I am calling a one week recess. The details of an additional press conference will be given in due course. Those of you who want to scrutinize the letters and prints, you can arrange to see them at the university!"

Some delegates tried to raise more questions amidst the outpourings of emotion.

"I understand your frustration and recognize the fact that we must ascertain the date of the proposed extra-terrestrial return visit! Please bear with us!"

The cacophony of noise and dissent grew louder causing Bishop McRae to react. He rose from his chair and signalled to an aide who subsequently took to his walkie-talkie. Moments later the bells of the Metropolitan Cathedral Of Christ the King rang, tolling a monotonous, deafening chime which had the effect of subduing the tumult.

The Bishop strode to the lectern.

"Ladies and gentlemen, now that I have your undivided attention, I'm afraid we have to conclude today's conference as the Cathedral has a service due shortly that you are all welcome to attend. Thank you for your attendance today. Please also make a donation to the Cathedral on your way out if you can. Refreshments are available in the Cathedral crypt below us. Thank you and safe journey home."

Reluctantly people began to leave. Jules shook hands with the other panellists and chatted to them as she gathered her belongings. She caught Penny's eye.

"See you in Peter Kavanagh's," she mouthed and then turned and left with Randy joining the flow of delegates into the cathedral foyer. Penny inadvertently bumped into Ibrahim Shaqtar, from the Abdullah Quilliam Mosque, apologising to him before exchanging pleasantries. No one paid any attention to the two men of Middle Eastern origin at the back of the cathedral. They watched Penny and Randy leave, then waited until Jules and the other dignitaries had made their way to the exit. Once there, Jules and the others all paused above the flight of stone steps leading down to the concourse and said their goodbyes before dispersing in different directions, some to the crypt, others to the underground car park. The two men followed Jules and Dr Parkes out, without them noticing.

56

Cairo, Egypt, 1800

It took Jemila three months to recover from her ordeal and to regain her health. She was able to resume her post at the café. Demeraux had lovingly nursed her back to health, maintaining a constant vigil by her bedside during the critical period. He had forsaken his trip to the Red Sea mountains but was due to leave on another expedition to Upper Egypt to study the various ancient nilometers located at various points along the Nile, their purpose to measure the levels of the great river to determine harvests and subsequent levels of taxation.

On the day of the trial, Cousseau, Demeraux and Jemila arrived together to give evidence against Roucard who sneered menacingly as soon as he caught sight of them. Roucard was subsequently found guilty of rape and attempted murder but, miraculously, escaped the guillotine through the intervention of General Menou who stated that he could not afford to lose any more soldiers, even scoundrels like Roucard and since the Nubian had made a full recovery the perpetrator's incarceration for four months and his flogging was deemed punishment enough. The trio had no obligation but to reluctantly accept the verdict. Jemila was devastated.

A few days after the trial Cousseau, Demeraux and Jemila were passing the Garden of Eden café when they spotted Roucard and his cronies celebrating his release in the *Taverne Oasis* on the other side of the square. The three friends walked by. Demeraux happened to glance over to the gang of reprobates who had stopped conversing. Roucard stared down the savant and drew an imaginary blade across his neck threateningly. Cousseau saw his gesture and stopped dead and turned towards the group. He told Antoine and Jemila to walk on and then he approached the gang. Roucard had no intention of making the same grim gesture to his nemesis by dint of his fearless reputation amongst the ranks knowing that the tall, thickset sergeant could probably take the lot of them. Cousseau, wary of being placed on a charge himself, just stood in silence staring out one to the next. He then turned and left. Roucard smirked.

Demeraux subsequently left on his voyage down the Nile with Florent, Debussy and Rabat. Jemila had been allowed to stay at the lodgings with her friends to keep her company and to look after the savants' meagre possessions.

57

Cousseau, in the meantime, kept his eye on Jemila and the others. Jemila's friends, Elpis, a Copt and Sanura, a Muslim of Egyptian extraction, liked the French sergeant, but he was not keen on starting a new relationship. His heart still belonged to Chione. That had not prevented him though from employing the services of a prostitute from time to time, particularly after the stresses and anxieties of combat. At the first opportunity he would make for the massage parlour to wind down and would not be averse to the extras on offer as he sunk into a deep state of relaxation, his nostrils inhaling the sweet fragrances of lavender, patchouli and vetiver; his glistening muscular frame anointed with a potent mix of aromatherapy and aphrodisiac scents. The experience had, on one occasion, left him with a bout of 'clapier bubo'. The physician's treatment consisted of the injection of sandalwood oil directly into his phallus and the ingestion of 'blue mass' which made him vomit.

One day Cousseau's unit was sent on patrol to a desert caravanserai five miles out of the capital to hunt down some Bedouin marauders who had been harassing travellers. Life in Cairo had been quiet recently, however Roucard had been waiting for his chance to revenge his flogging. He had been informed by Minardi, one of his few companions, that Cousseau was out of Cairo. That evening, when Jemila finished her work at the café, Roucard followed Malachy and the Nubian woman to Demeraux's lodgings. He hid in the shadows and waited for Malachy to leave. Jemila was alone. Her friends were still at their places of work in different cafés or taverns. He waited a while more after observing a candle or lantern being extinguished in the bedroom above. Roucard reached into a small pouch and recovered a tinderbox. Slyly he glanced around. It was quiet in the neighbourhood. He took the cotton char cloth out of the box and placed it with some kindling on the doorstep of the house and attempted to light it with a fire striker and a piece of flint. He looked around anxiously as he tried two or three times to create a spark. On the fourth attempt he succeeded. The fire took hold and devoured the char and set alight the kindling. Flames leapt from the brushwood transferring themselves to the wooden door. Smoke was billowing as the fire crackled into life spreading to the ground floor wooden window and then it leapt like an agile cat burglar on to the window above where Jemila slept. Roucard, with a vile, toothless grin, disappeared into the darkness.

Cousseau's patrol was on its way back to Cairo having dealt with the marauding Bedouin. They caught them unawares in an oasis and slaughtered most of them, freeing some slaves in the process. The rest had fled in terror on their steeds into the depths of the desert. In the distance they could see the glow of a fire as they neared their base on the city perimeter. Cousseau's senses were pricked when someone in the cohort reckoned the fire was in Old Cairo. Demeraux's lodgings were in that vicinity. As soon as they arrived at their camp Cousseau deposited his knapsack and musket in his tent and took his sword and pistol with him. He and a few others proceeded into town. They drew closer to the scene of the fire and Cousseau, realising that it *was* near Demeraux's home, started to run ahead. He reached the corner of the street. It was shrouded in acrid smoke. He frantically pushed through the gawping crowds seeing, to his horror and confirming his worst fears, that it was Demeraux's lodgings engulfed in flames. It was a raging inferno.

"Jemila!" he cried. He looked around the onlookers in desperation, grabbing hold of anyone whose head was swathed in a shawl much to their indignation. He called out. "Elpis! Sanura!"

He grabbed a firefighter who was futilely throwing buckets of water onto the conflagration.

"Do you know if anyone is inside?"

"There was someone. Some of the neighbours heard screams. But it's no good now. They'll be dead by now. No one would survive that."

Cousseau grimaced. He turned despondently and pushed through the throng but stopped when he thought he heard someone calling his name. He looked around the sea of faces. Suddenly the building collapsed, the roof caving in sending a wall of heat pulsating out of the debris and scorching some of the firefighters and onlookers.

"Get back!" came a cry.

It was too late for some. The injured fell about with blistered faces and hands, screaming in pain. Others cried for help. Cousseau struggled through the swarm of panicking spectators some of whom were stumbling to get away from the furnace and others who were pressing forward trying to get to the injured. Then he distinctly heard someone call his name.

"Pierre! Cousseau! Over here!"

He set eyes on a figure beckoning him from atop a cart. It was Sanura.

"Sanura! Have you seen Jemila?"

"No. Her shift finished before mine. Elpis is somewhere in the crowd trying to find you. We saw one of the men from your company and he said you were here somewhere."

Cousseau was relieved that the two women were safe, but he stared at the ground dejectedly. Deep down, he knew Jemila had gone. His heart ached for her and for Antoine. Cousseau had promised him he would look after Jemila and now he had failed. Furthermore, he had failed in his duty to protect the ivory tablet.

The fire was gradually extinguished and Cousseau, Sanura and Elpis could only wait, huddled together until the early hours of the morning. The warmth of the embers a source of ironic comfort owing to the cool night air. As dawn broke, scavengers descended on the burnt-out shell, poring over the ashes and scorched remnants of the building hoping to find something of value. Cousseau, bristling with anger approached one of them, a scrawny one-eyed beggar and grabbed him by the scruff of the neck. He yanked his sabre from his belt and held it closely to the scavenger's Adam's apple. Close enough for the razor-like blade to draw blood.

"If anyone should dare touch anything whatsoever from this site I will decapitate them, so I will! Away with you dregs of humanity!"

He pushed the vagabond to the ground and saw him immediately scramble away. The others scattered like disturbed flies. Cousseau returned to Elpis and Sanura.

"If the scavengers ventured onto the charred remains of the house then it must be cool enough to walk on. Come on," he said.

Sanura, Elpis and Cousseau began to sift through the blackened debris, removing bits of scorched wood, the remnants of furniture and broken stone slabs from the site. Certain parts of it were still smouldering so they picked their way through it cautiously. Cousseau found a large piece of charred wood that could possibly have been part of a bed. He lifted it carefully and there, underneath, was a burnt almost skeletal corpse laying twisted in the detritus face down its arms tucked under the body, its blackened, distorted legs at impossible angles astride the torso, its toes deformed grotesquely. It was Jemila.

"Oh my God!" shrieked Elpis, bursting into tears.

"Jemila! Poor Jemila! May Allah take her into his care!" Sanura added, distraught.

Cousseau pulled the two of them to his breast and hugged them tightly. After a moment of silence only disturbed by the sobs of the women, he spoke.

"Elpis, can you find a shroud?"

The Copt nodded and wiped a tear from her eye.

"I hope to God she was suffocated by the smoke before the flames got to her," he said softly.

Elpis departed returning soon after with a white shroud. Cousseau attempted to gently lift up the charred, reddened, contorted cadaver but its arms seemed to be stuck under something. He struggled to get Jemila's right arm free and then he noticed a soot-covered slab was trapping it. He tried to manoeuvre it and then froze. He realized it was the tablet. 'She must have known about it and tried to protect it,' thought Cousseau. 'She must have been clutching it prior to her succumbing to the smoke or fire. She must have crawled under the bed.' He carefully managed to get her right arm free and then stepped over her body to free the left arm. Elpis and Sanura were momentarily occupied, the former genuflecting reciting a Coptic prayer and the latter kneeling, head bowed in reverence towards Mecca, responding to the calls of 'Allahu Akbar' echoing from the surrounding minarets, it being Salat al-Fajr. Cousseau took the opportunity to assess the possible damage to the tablet. He did his best to brush off the soot and debris. Then he examined it scrupulously. It was charred on the back, but the reverse seemed fine, the hieroglyphs' yellowish patina only blackened by more soot and particles. Both right hand corners of the oblong had been slightly damaged, the pieces having sheared off by the impact when the top floor collapsed, but this had not affected the script in any way. It was intact, much to his relief. Cousseau remembered there were gunny sacks on the back of the cart. First, he took possession of the shroud and spread it out on the ground. He then scooped up Jemila's remains and laid them carefully on the sheet of cotton.

138

Having finished their dawn prayers Jamila's friends wept over her unrecognisable body and paid their last respects to her. Their trilling, ululating tongues expressing their grief for her. Whilst they were preoccupied with this, Cousseau went over to the cart, leapt up on the back of it and removed a gunny sack. He returned to the fire-ravaged site and retrieved the slab surreptitiously and deposited it in the bag. He then carried it over to the cart and placed it under several more of the jute bags before returning to the charred remains of the dwelling to search for other salvageable items. He discovered a partly burned Bible and some blackened metal pots, pans and cutlery, and some tools but not much else. He placed the items in the same sack as the tablet.

By this time, the owner of the cart had arrived with his forlorn looking donkey to reclaim his cart for another day's work. Cousseau asked if he could loan the wain to take Jemila's corpse to the burial grounds outside the city walls. The owner consented and a fee of brass buttons was arranged. Cousseau had stripped them from a dead French artilleryman's tunic on the battlefield of Heliopolis knowing their value as a local currency. Sanura helped Cousseau load the body into the cart whilst the Egyptian owner harnessed the donkey to the ramshackle transport. Elpis climbed in the back whilst Sanura and Cousseau rode up front.

58

They buried Jemila facing Mecca, Cousseau now all too familiar with the proceedings. Afterwards he took the women to their respective places of work and returned cart and beast to its owner. The Frenchman heaved the sack over his shoulder and went in search of the fire officer. He found him at the fire brigade headquarters, which was no more than a shack which housed a few tethered donkeys, carts and battered metal buckets, and questioned him about the blaze. The fire chief told him that he thought the blaze was suspicious and started deliberately because his men had arrived in time to see the door had been burnt off its hinges and the flames had leapt up the façade of the house first. He explained that they could not gain entry to the inside of the premises because the fire had spread through the downstairs rooms and could not be stopped. This information was enough to convince Cousseau that he knew exactly who the perpetrator was.

"Roucard!" he growled.

He stormed out of the fire station and headed back to his camp seething with rage. Once there, he concealed the sack in his tent. He decided to rest having had little or no sleep after the trek back from the oasis and the vigil during the night. He conjured up a plan to exact revenge on Roucard. That evening he spied on Roucard, knowing exactly where he would be - at the *Taverne* Oasis with his coterie of rapscallions. He disguised himself as a local in a keffiyeh headdress and a long flowing burnous and waited until the group were all paralytic on date alcohol and high on hashish. He watched them, one by one or in twos stagger away from the venue. Roucard finally left with two others. Cousseau followed them at a distance. He was in the donkey cart, having hired it anew. They staggered up a dark narrow street. Cousseau looked around. It was deserted. He then jabbed his sabre into the animal's hind quarters forcing the beast to bolt. The three inebriated soldiers were totally oblivious to the approaching imminent threat and were only aware of it when the frightened beast and cart ploughed into them, mowing them down. Cousseau managed to restrain the donkey. He leapt from the cart and sought out Roucard. The three drunken soldiers were sprawled on the ground. Roucard's companions had been knocked unconscious with the impact. One of them, Minardi seemed to have broken a leg. The wheel of the cart having crushed his calf. As for Roucard himself, he was barely conscious. He lay groaning, blood seeping from a wound on his temple. Cousseau grabbed Roucard roughly and bundled him into the back of the cart. He jumped back into the driving seat and was about to trot up the narrow thoroughfare when he noticed a crumpled figure sitting in the shadows of a doorway. He raised a lantern from his side. The dim light revealed a solitary hooded beggar who had almost certainly witnessed the altercation. Cousseau paused fleetingly in front of him and put his fingers to his lips. He then flipped him a couple of brass buttons to buy his silence. The milky-eyed vagrant nodded his assent and scrambled for the currency. Cousseau drew back with a start when he saw the beggar's gnarled leprous stubs pawing frantically for the buttons. He immediately prodded the donkey with his boot and headed off in the direction of the Nile. Soon after, he pulled on the donkey's rudimentary harness and stopped the cart on some wasteland adjacent to the great river. The orb in the cold, clear night sky shed its pale light on the riverbank scrubland. Cousseau yanked the dazed Roucard out of the cart by his legs and the drunk fell to the stony ground with a thump. He moaned again. Cousseau dragged him to his feet and punched him to the ground again. Blood spurted from his split lip. Cousseau repeated the assault. This time breaking his nose and splattering the blood over Roucard's face. Roucard lay on the floor choking from his own blood. The aggressor then brought his boot down on the victim's genitals. He writhed in pain. Cousseau dragged him over the stony scrub, then paused and proceeded to rip the tunic and shirt from the drunk's back followed by his gaiters and pantaloons. He then stood him up and with a fierce drop kick launched him into a thicket of Egyptian thorn. Roucard cried out. The sharp firethorns had made their mark, gouging the flesh from his naked body. The irony was not lost on Cousseau. In fact, he had deliberately chosen the site. Roucard lay there, his arms splayed either side of his body, his forehead crowned by a knot of vicious thorns. Cousseau pulled back the hood of his burnous and removed his keffiyeh and Roucard's bloodied gob opened as his barely open blinking eyes fell upon his assailant.

"Cousseau! *Putain de merde!*" was all he could utter before the enraged sergeant reached into the thicket, lacerating his own arms in the process, to seize him by the throat. The last thing that the terrified rapist saw was the blade of Cousseau's razor sharp sabre gleaming in the luminescence of the full moon before it crashed down on his neck severing his head from his torso.

Cousseau stood motionless for a moment, his gaze transfixed on the decapitated head of his vile adversary, eyes bulging from its sockets. He dragged the corpse over to the river and rolled it down the bank. It splashed into the flowing waters and the current carried it away. He went back for the severed head. He dug his sword into it, and it squelched. Brain tissue, blood and other cerebral matter oozed out. He carried it perched on the point of his sabre and retraced his footsteps to the watercourse and flung the head into the maelstrom much like a clay wanger he used as a child to target rats with on a river island on the Hérault. He sucked in a few deep breaths of cool air and calmly walked back to the thorn bush. He picked up the dead man's bicorne, gaiters and other clothes and also tossed them contemptuously into the Nile then he jumped up into the seat of the cart, cajoled the grazing donkey and departed.

59

No one knew what had happened to Roucard. Minardi and Trussot, the other *chasseurs* injured in the assault, could not remember a thing about the 'accident', except for the initial impact. Suspicions did arise about Cousseau but Sanura, who was informed about the incident by the Frenchman concocted an alibi for him. He was at the massage parlour enjoying a 'massage' with a friend of Sanura's, Aaliyah. Barthelemy made formal enquiries at the brothel. Aaliyah saw to it that the Greek chief of police soon forgot about the real purpose of his visit. Truth be told, even though General Menou had asked him to investigate, he was not remotely interested in the disappearance of a low-life rapist.

60

Liverpool. Present day.

Paul De Vere watched the rush of people cascading down the numerous steps of Christ the King from outside the Medical Institution. He observed TV crews replete with camera operators and sound engineers rushing around, falling over each other, trying to find adequate space for their reporters to submit their reports to their waiting audiences. The swarm of humanity fanned out. Some went along Hope Street to the pubs and bars, to the Everyman bistro and La Casa and to Ye Cracke just around the corner in Rice street. Others surged down Mount Pleasant, past the dilapidated Wellington Rooms, the Regency building, built to house grand assembly rooms in 1816, a derelict, forlorn parody of itself awaiting a benefactor to restore it to its former glory. A group of Japanese delegates stopped on the corner of Mount Pleasant opposite to where Paul was standing, perusing a map of Liverpool, gesturing extravagantly and arguing amongst themselves. All Paul could make out were the words 'Hole In The Wall! Hole In The Wall! Hackins Hey!' A homeless man shuffling past, who Paul knew from the shelter, named Tommy, intervened. He seized the map and pointed the way, then he held out his hand expectantly. He was rewarded with a one pound coin and off the group went along Hope Street thanking Tommy, but Tommy had sent them the wrong way not out of spite or malicious intent but because he had mental health issues. Paul's attention was focused on the group, and he did not notice the attractive auburn haired woman who was turning other people's heads coming down the Cathedral steps with her colleague pursued by the press pack. The academics were politely declining their offers and ignoring their calls for an interview. Paul followed the Japanese who were conversing rapidly in their native tongue. He stopped them by the Philharmonic pub and set them right. He didn't ask for any succour through pride. That was not his style. He did not beg. They thanked him. One of the Japanese delegates dashed into the opulently styled pub to use the loo whilst the others waited. Shortly, he returned, animated. Paul assumed that he was telling the rest about the lavishly patterned urinals. They all disappeared inside emerging a few minutes later checking the photos on their mobiles, the two women with them giggling. Paul presumed they had gone into the gents whilst someone was urinating, a common occurrence or hazard of sight-seeing at the listed premises. The Japanese contingent turned right into Hardman Street whilst Paul continued across to the other side of Hope Street in the direction of the Anglican Cathedral this time, which loomed into view. Penny had left a note at Lambert House for Paul. He had picked it up and read it. In it, Penny had apologized profusely for accusing him of trashing

143

the apartment. As a gesture of reconciliation, she had invited him to the pub, Peter Kavanagh's, telling him that Jules would be there too. Paul desperately wanted to accept the invitation so he could see Jules, but he thought he would be a fish out of water with all of her academic circle in attendance. Nevertheless, he felt compelled to head in that direction, drawn by her allure but then having second thoughts, he went and sat in nearby Falkner Square Gardens, which was set amongst the impressive array of Georgian built terraces that adorned Liverpool's Canning Georgian Quarter. It was a warm afternoon and people were taking advantage of the humid conditions picnicking and sun-bathing in the former enclosed private gardens. Another excuse for him not to go to the pub emerged from his stomach which rumbled. He was starving, not having had anything to eat since breakfast at the hostel but help was at hand close by in Percy Street. St. Bride's, a listed, neoclassical Anglican Church with a progressive congregation was hosting an 'everyone welcome' LGBTQ event with refreshments. He joined the mix of individuals for a short early evening service and then partook of the food on offer. He was ravenous. A female folk singer took to the altar, guitar in hand, whilst he tucked into a bowl of scouse and soda bread with other unfortunates and members of St. Brides. On Egerton Street, hidden away, Peter Kavanagh's pub, festooned with antiques and oddities, was rammed with Jules and her colleagues. The wine, beer and prosecco flowed. The atmosphere convivial. Gradually, as the evening wore on, the group reduced in size. Penny, Randy, and Jules were the last to leave. Randy walked the short distance to his house on Falkner Street, but the ladies, craving a kebab, headed towards Hardman Street. They started to walk down Catherine Street. It was getting dark. Paul had finally summoned up the courage to make an appearance. He had returned to Falkner Square Gardens and waited, deducing rightly that there would be fewer of Jules's retinue in the pub by now, but he had misjudged how long they would actually remain. Approaching Catherine Street, he heard the screech of a vehicle, then screams. He ran round the corner concerned, thinking there had been an accident when he saw two men in hoodies grappling with Penny and Jules. He saw Penny punch one of the assailant's before she in turn was smashed in the face. She collapsed. The other assailant was trying to drag Jules to a nearby 4x4. She was struggling to free herself, kicking out at him. Paul dropped his haversack and leapt into action. Like a shot he was across the road. He floored Penny's attacker with a flying punch which the assailant didn't see coming. He turned his attention to the other man, who'd managed to open the door of the BMW and was trying to bundle in a screaming and terrified Jules. Paul sprinted and went for him. The swarthy abductor shoved Jules hard against the car and tried to reach into his pocket to retrieve his gun, but he was a fraction too late as Paul dived and caught him around the neck with his forearm, both men clattering to the ground. Paul, who was quicker to react stood up and aimed a kick at the would-be kidnapper. He connected. The assailant cried out, blood from his nose smearing his face. He punched him three or four times before he could react. Paul grabbed Jules. She stumbled over her attacker's legs and both she and her rescuer ran back towards St Brides.

"Penny! Penny!" she cried.

Paul was in two minds about what to do. He saw the first aggressor had picked himself up. Suddenly, the decision was made for him. The welcome sound of the blues and twos sang out. The two thugs came to their senses and scrambled into the black BMW and took off with the police vehicle in pursuit. Jules, hysterical, rushed back to Penny's side, followed by Paul. Penny coughed, spitting out some blood as other police vehicles arrived, followed by an ambulance. The residents who had called the police emerged from their home across the road as did others.

"Oh God! Paul!"

Jules thrust herself into the arms of Paul and sobbed.

61

Slumped in a chair, Jules awoke. She opened one eye, uncertain of her surroundings. She saw Penny's husband Ian sitting in a chair next to Penny's bedside and then, realising where she was, sat bolt upright.

"Ian! Is Penny alright?"

"She's going to be fine Jules. She has some nasty bruises and concussion and a slight fracture to the cheekbone, but the doctor assures me it won't need surgery. How are you?"

"I got a few bumps and scrapes, otherwise I'm fine," she said, recalling the incident, a shiver creeping down her spine. "Sorry, I must have had a nap."

"More than a nap, Jules. It's past seven in the morning. You must have been exhausted."

"Seven am! What? I've been here all night?"

"Yep, and by the way, you snore worse than Penny. But you don't fart as much."

"Oh, Ian!"

Ian guffawed.

"Where's Paul?"

"Who?"

"The guy who came to our rescue."

"Oh, him. He went to help the police with their enquiries. The police said they'd come back to interview you this morning. They posted a guard outside. Listen, you go back to the house later, Jules. I'll wait here. I've sent the kids to their grandmother's."

"I-I'd rather not on my own, Ian. To be honest, I'm running out of options. I'll stay here, if you don't mind and wait to see what the police say. I'll just freshen up. Would you like a coffee?"

"Tea please, one sugar. That'll be great."

Jules had just finished her coffee when DC Noades appeared.

"Good morning, Dr Johnson, this is becoming a habit."

Even though Jules looked as if she had been dragged through a hedge backwards, Noades still felt she looked like eye candy. DCI Armitage arrived shortly after. DC Noades popped out to grab some coffees and then they began questioning Jules about her attempted abduction. Jules's explanation tallied up with Paul's story.

"Where is Paul?"

"He's at the police station," Armitage confirmed.

"Oh, did you detain him?"

"No, we gave him a free cell for the night. To sleep. He's having breakfast there as well."

"Did you get the assailants?"

"No, they got away unfortunately. The pursuing police car had a prang. The officers are ok, just a bit shook up. Mr De Vere reckoned both suspects were of Middle Eastern appearance, one with a short black beard and the other with a black moustache and a small scar under his mouth. Have you seen these men before?"

"No, but I agree they looked Middle Eastern. One did have a beard. The other still had his hood up so I couldn't give you his description. Maybe Penny got a better look at him."

"We'll check with her later when she wakes up. She's sedated at the moment," Noades rejoined.

"Well Dr Johnson," said Armitage, "we'll keep you posted. We'll post a guard at Penny's house for 24 hours but after that I recommend you get yourself some sort of protection."

"Someone's out to spoil that pretty face of yours," Noades added before both detectives left.

Jules turned towards Ian open mouthed. Ian's raised eyebrows and knowing expression left little else to be said.

Jules was dropped off by a police vehicle in Woolton. The police protection was already in situ. The officers went in with her and searched the house, which calmed Jules's fears. Then they returned to their posts outside. Jules made a coffee, running to her phone when it rang. She detached it from the charging lead and answered. It was Dr Parkes.

"Jules, thank God, you're alright. Randy spoke to Ian since he couldn't get hold of Penny. He told me she's awake now and doing ok. Still got her sense of humour which is a good sign. Listen Jules, do you think your attempted kidnap was something to do with the stele?"

"I'm beginning to think it's *all* to do with that. With the murders in the apartment and now this. I'm scared Edmund."

"Well, in that case we'd better release the information about the drawings asap. Whoever's desperate for the information is prepared to kill for it."

"The police recommend I get some sort of protection. Can the University help me out?"

"Of course, it's University business. How about Jimmy? Over at the Garstang."

"You're kidding me Edmund! Jimmy? He couldn't run five paces without being out of breath and doing his groin."

"What about someone from security from the student's disco?"

"What! You're having me on! A student?"

"Well-"

"I know someone who could do the job. Paul. Paul De Vere."

"Isn't he the homeless guy you were talking about?"

"Yes. He's saved my ass twice now. He's ex-military. He needs a job. He'd be perfect."

"Well, if you're sure about that we can employ him I suppose as a personal bodyguard. Who knows? We might *all* need his services. Yes, ok, I'll draw up a contract and we'll arrange an informal interview for tomorrow, say 10am, my office.

147

We'll also discuss bringing the news conference forward to Tuesday. At least with the information out in the public domain, whoever is prepared to kill for it might leave you alone, I hope."

"Oh! Edmund. Just one more thing. Paul is homeless. Can we put him up somewhere?"

"Er, I suppose for now we can put him in the halls of residence down at Mossley Hill, rent free. There's only a few foreign students there at the moment until the new term begins in October."

"That's great! Thanks. Oh, and what about me? I'm definitely not going back to the apartment. In fact, I've notified the estate agent already to rent it out and I don't think it's appropriate for me to stay with Penny and Ian anymore, given the situation."

"Of course, if you need to stay close to your bodyguard, why don't you take the warden's cottage on site? He's not due back until October either. Security at the halls have got the key. I'll call them."

"That sounds great Edmund. I'll make sure I keep a low profile for now. See you tomorrow."

As soon as she had finished her conversation with Dr Parkes, she rang the police HQ to find Paul. She was notified he had already left the custody suite so Jules rang Randy and asked if he could try and locate him to tell him to meet her at Abercromby Square tomorrow at 9am.

62

Paul was bang on time for their rendezvous having slept rough on a bench in the Square. Randy couldn't accommodate him this time since it was his daughter's birthday and she had invited her friends over for a sleepover. His belly growled with hunger. At 9am prompt, a police car drew up and out stepped Jules, looking tired. A look of concern on her face. She smiled though when she saw Paul. As she drew near Paul noticed a few scratches on her face and a bruise on her neck. Paul smiled back.

Jules felt obliged to thank Paul again for saving her even though she had already done that countless times on the evening of the assault.

"Paul," she said excitedly, "I needed to see you. I've got a proposition to make to you."

Paul smiled warily.

"Go on. I'm all ears."

"The police said I need some sort of protection so, would you be my bodyguard? It's a temporary salaried position, paid for by the University. Dr Parkes has agreed to it. He wants to meet you this morning to confirm it. You can start right away."

Paul hesitated a moment.

"So, you mean I'm not going to be paid for protecting you during your last two scrapes?"

"I'll get him to back date it," she fired back before adding, "or maybe this will suffice."

Jules pulled out a MacDonald's sausage and egg muffin and a coffee from a plastic bag she was holding.

"Woh! We'll call it quits then. You must have read my mind. I'm famished."

"Get that down your neck and you can take a shower in the faculty, but you've got to be quick, the interview's at ten. It's just a formality. By the way, the job comes with temporary accommodation. You've got a room in a hall of residence in Mossley Hill just around the corner from me. I'm in the warden's cottage on site."

"Gosh!" he said between munches. "Seriously, thanks. That's amazing."

"Say it. Don't spray it!" Jules laughed as Paul tried to talk and eat at the same time. "Come on, get your backpack. Let's go!"

The informal interview went to plan. A scrubbed-up Paul impressed Dr Parkes with his knowledge of self-defence and his armed forces experience. He agreed a salary, albeit modest but Paul was happy to accept the short-term package which provided a roof over his head and a bonus on conclusion, providing Jules was kept safe. Something he vowed to do and would gladly do with or without remuneration. The post began with immediate effect and so Jules, armed with a modest budget to purchase essentials for the role and an advance from the university's coffers for Paul, dragged her new bodyguard shopping to Liverpool One, as if he were an embarrassed kid off to buy a school uniform. They purchased a mobile, a computer, a watch, and some clothes, including a couple of cheap off-the-rail suits, trainers, and shoes. They took a taxi to Mossley Hill, received the keys for their respective new abodes, inspected each other's places, dumped their purchases, and ventured out again for a food shop. Later, they met up in the university refectory for a quick evening meal before Paul accompanied Jules to see Penny who had been released from hospital. At Penny's house Jules took a call from Dr Parkes. He had made the decision to move the next news conference to Tuesday.

Once the news broke about the decision to move the conference at short notice to the Tuesday local hotels were deluged with calls from frantic TV stations and other media outlets and interested parties desperate to re-book rooms. Some news crews from far off locations, however, had sagely remained in Liverpool for the week rather than return home. The mayor of Liverpool revelled in his home city being in the world's spotlight and was delighted with the boon to the region's economy. He was amazed that the world's media and other interested parties wanted to descend again on Merseyside for the unveiling of the clues when it would, more than likely, be a brief undertaking. The grand revealing of the clues was the hottest ticket in town. Many of those present at the first conference had left Liverpool with great memories and sore heads the day after, having experienced the delights of the city's famed nightlife. With the Metropolitan Cathedral unable to hold the meet at short notice, the conference was to be held at the Arena on Liverpool's waterfront. Luckily, there had been a vacant slot between shows mounted at the events centre and the management were pleased to take advantage of the huge financial windfall for the business.

On the day of the unveiling, the same panellists took their seats on the stage watched by thousands of excited, expectant and raucous delegates. The experts were all invited back, out of courtesy, although their attendance was not deemed necessary. Paul surveyed the audience from the wings and other security personnel ringed the stage. Dr Parkes rose from his seat and addressed the huge audience surrounding the rostrum.

"Welcome back to Liverpool, everybody! I apologise for the short notice. There were unfortunate circumstances that made us evaluate our previous decision to postpone the unveiling to a later date. You've no doubt read about them in the press or heard the story on the news. In light of those events, we decided it would be in everyone's best interests to reveal the illustrations to you as soon as possible. You all know the back story by now so we will just concentrate on the clues provided by the anonymous letter writer. The third letter, you will remember, referred to the proposal of a game. A hunt for clues. The clues being images of animals. So, we have two illustrations to show you which, combined, act as the first clue. These clues, according to the letter, lead to a location where the next clue will be revealed."

A buzz of anticipation arose in the arena and questions were shouted out from all points. Once the noise was suppressed Dr Parkes continued.

"Any questions can be raised after the presentation. Without further ado, Martin, please display the first image on to the screens."

150

Dr Parkes gestured to the screen operator. A ripple of excitement coursed through the arena as the delegates waited impatiently for the first image to appear. Then suddenly a swan flashed up on the giant screens, and then what seemed to be, a monster of some kind.

A huge din erupted as individuals turned to their neighbour or group to discuss their implications. Others just stared at the images, perplexed. After several minutes, Dr Parkes intervened and with some difficulty quelled the mayhem in the arena. Then the Q&A session began. Dr Parkes, Jules, and Tom Yates fielded a plethora of questions, some sensible and others impossible to answer or just plain dumb.

"Do these clues relate to somewhere in Liverpool?"

"We're not sure ourselves but it's a strong possibility," Jules replied.

"On the other hand, they could refer to anywhere in the British Isles. They're so vague," Tom Yates added.

After thirty minutes the questions dried up and the chancellor brought the conference to a conclusion.

"There are hand-outs in the foyer detailing the prints, letters and images and a map of Liverpool. All I ask of you is to make sure you respect other people and their property if you're going to charge around Indiana Jones style in search of the artefact. The British government have confirmed that whoever finds the tablet will be obliged to hand it in to the nearest authorities. In addition, the police informed me that anyone acting in a reckless, anti-social or aggressive manner or found trespassing on private property, will be arrested on the spot and detained. So, good afternoon and farewell everyone. Keep safe! And in the best traditions of the hunting fraternity. Tallyho!"

Throngs of people rushed for the exits in a disorderly fashion. The hunt for the stele was on.

63

Dr Parkes had booked a couple of tables for lunch for his coterie at Lunyalita, a Catalan and Spanish eatery at the Royal Albert Dock, a favourite of his. He had a holiday home at Tarragona, Costa Dorada and loved the Iberian way of life. He was a historian and authority on the Spanish Civil War. As the group piled in, Paul, who was invited, ended up on a separate table to Jules. She sat with Penny, who had led Jules by the arm to her seat. Dr Parkes and Tom's colleague Simon, assistant curator at the Lady Lever filled the other two seats on the table. Paul had waited until he was invited to sit down. He sat with Tom, Dr Fatima Marsh and Randy. Dr Parkes conversed in faltering Spanish with a waiter, Pablo, ordering a carafe of *vino tinto* and water for each table. After giving the diners time to peruse the menus, a petite, jet-black haired waitress approached Dr Parkes' table and spoke with him in Spanish, taking the orders. Then she went over to Paul's table. Paul surprised everyone by also speaking to her in fluent Spanish, impressing all on his table and especially Esther, the waitress. Jules felt a pang of jealousy as Paul, looking clean and smart in his dark suit laughed and joked with the attractive young server. Jules made a point of chatting to the handsome Simon over the course of the lunch, ignoring Paul and only now and again glancing casually over to see if Paul was watching her flirting. She continued to take a sneaky peek at Paul's table whenever the waitress appeared. Simon and Jules discussed the tablet and several other matters, and she shared a *crema catalana* with him for dessert after her *tortilla and alioli* sandwich, occasionally glancing over to Paul's table to gauge his reaction. She saw Paul make his way to the bar and decided to join him. Standing next to him, she ordered a glass of *sangría*, and he ordered a Voll Damm.

"Your Spanish is very impressive," she said.

"Thanks. It's a bit rusty."

"The waitress seems rather impressed with you, too."

"Oh, do you mean Esther? We were just having a bit of banter. It's just an opportunity for me to practice my Spanish, nothing more. It's been a while since I spoke the language. You seem to be having a good time as well. Did you enjoy your *crema catalana* with Simon?"

"Oh, it was *fabulosa! Deliciosa!* Just like Simon himself."

Paul took receipt of his bottle of beer and with a broad grin on his face, whispered in Jules's ear.

"Good luck with that one. He made a pass at me in the gents earlier."

He left Jules at the bar stunned. She stood there for a moment fuming. She was skilled at reading ancient hieroglyphic texts and other languages but not so great when it came to reading people. Her 'gaydar' was way off. She returned to her seat with her *sangría*, feeling stung but trying hard to conceal it.

Dr Parkes tapped his spoon on his plate and asked for silence.

"In order to establish a team to hunt for the tablet I've decided that the University will pool its resources with the Council and National Museums Liverpool. Rather than compete against each other and waste resources, the Mayor, the NML and other stakeholders have agreed to this. So, Jules you will head up the team that will consist of Randy, Fatima, Tom, and Simon. Penny has reluctantly had to bow out due to other commitments and pressure from her husband Ian, which is understandable after her assault the other day. However, she will lend her support and attend meetings when she can. In her place I'm drafting in Lydia Longfellow."

"Who's Lydia?" Paul whispered to Randy.

"She's Laurel to Penny's Hardy," Randy answered. "She's highly intelligent but not exactly streetwise. She works at the Liverpool Record Office in the Central Library."

Jules nudged Dr Parkes in the ribs and gestured towards Paul with her eyes.

"Oh, and Paul is our security manager. He's shadowing Jules but I'm sure he'll be looking out for all of you. Vis-à-vis security, what he says, goes. Jules oversees the rest. Ok? The team's inaugural meeting is scheduled for tomorrow at 1pm. My office. I think we should call ourselves Team Quest. It will be prestigious for the City Region if we locate the tablet first, so here's to our good hunting!"

The group cheered wildly and raised their glasses in honour of the newly formed team.

A few hours later Paul, Penny and Jules jumped a cab. Both Penny and Jules were a bit worse for wear, having mixed their drinks. Penny was dropped off on her doorstep in Woolton and the taxi continued to the halls of residence. Paul helped Jules out of the taxi. She pushed him away as the taxi driver drove off. She stumbled and one of her kitten heels fell off in the process. Paul found it amusing, Jules less so. He held his hands up.

"Ok, you just carry on."

He watched as she staggered over to the shoe and tried to put it back on her foot, hopping around then sitting on the pavement, showing her knickers. Then she vomited onto her shoe. Paul made a face in disgust. He picked up the vomit-filled shoe and threw it into the campus bushes intending to retrieve it in the morning. Scooping her up gently in his arms, Paul carried Jules towards the warden's cottage. She tried to fight him, drunkenly lashing out but gave up her struggle and placed her head on his chest, snuggling into him. She babbled on incoherently.

"Who's better looking, me or that Esther? Go on, tell me! It's me, isn't it? You fancy me, don't you Paul? Go on, tell me!" she ranted, nuzzling further into him.

Paul sat her on a bench whilst he searched for her key. He opened the door and picking her up again, took her over the threshold. He told her to stand there whilst he security-scanned the rooms. Everything was ok. Then he carried her straight to her bed. He laid her down and she tried to kiss him, but he resisted, partly due to his chivalrous nature and partly due to the trickle of vomit protruding from the corner of her mouth. He removed her other blue shoe and pulled the duvet over her fully clothed curvaceous, slender figure and placed a wastepaper bin by her bedside, just in time. She turned her head and retched. She followed this with a prolonged, rasping fart. Paul just grimaced and laughed. He fetched a bottle of water from the fridge and placed it on the bedside table then left for his room in the hall of residence, with a wry smile.

64

The mobile in her handbag rang repeatedly, and Jules awoke just as it tailed off. She crawled, blurry eyed out of bed in search of it. She was surprised that she was fully clothed. She felt dehydrated and nauseous in the pit of her stomach. Her head throbbed. She sniffed the air and it reeked of vomit. It was on her blue Laura Ashley tea dress. She baulked. She looked down and noticed her foot seemed yellow and crusty. An expression of disgust transformed the perplexed look on her face as she vaguely recalled getting up in the night to urinate and putting her foot in the sick bucket, but she was too inebriated and knackered to care. She had managed to gulp down some water from the bottle Paul had left her saving her from an even worse hangover. Suddenly the doorbell rang startling her. She looked out of the window. It was Paul accompanied by two cleaners. She popped her head around the door trying to remain calm and composed but her unkempt auburn hair told another story, one which entailed being dragged through a hedge backwards.

"Hi," she said. "What's up?"

"Your shoe Cinderella," Paul retorted. "I've cleaned out the vomit."

"What? Oh! Ugh! Did I puke in it?"

"You did indeed." The two cleaners could not hide their laughter. "These two ladies have kindly responded to my request for help. They're going to clean the cottage for you."

"But, but…"

"Listen, it's 11am. You're due at the meeting at 1pm."

"What? 11am? Why didn't you wake me before?"

"Believe me. I've been trying. Check your phone! Right Jules, you get in the shower, I'll go and get a breakfast bap and coffee for us, and the ladies can get on with cleaning up your mess."

"But…"

"Now!"

Jules relented and let the cleaners in. One of them opened a window straight away letting in some fresh air to dispel the stale smell of vomit and garlic. Jules was embarrassed and went straight to the bathroom. The cleaners did not bat an eyelid when they saw the sick bucket. They were used to it, cleaning students' rooms in the halls of residence. One hour later, Jules, was looking and feeling human once again, after her shower, coffee and bacon and egg panini. She then left with Paul for the meeting at the University. They arrived promptly and settled down with the others for a brain-storming session and to set out a strategy. They were equipped with the information sheets that Dr Parkes had issued to the delegates at the news brief.

"Right," Jules said, now feeling more like herself. "We've got a picture of a swan and a monster of some sort. Let's start with the swan."

"The local link," Lydia began, "of course is Old Swan, in Liverpool."

"Why is the district so called?" Tom Yates asked.

"It's named after an 18th century inn called the Three Swans which lay on the pack-horse route along Prescot Road."

"You're right Lydia," Simon agreed, looking at his mobile. "It says here on Wikipedia that the moniker was taken from the Walton family's coat of arms, who were the local landowners."

"The inn stood on the junction between Prescot Lane or Road as it is now called and Pettycoat Lane which is now Broadgreen Road. Prescot Road was a turnpike," Fatima continued reading from her tablet. "Two more inns were established on the same junction at a later date, the Swan Vaults which is now renamed The Old Swan and the Cygnet."

"Wow!" Randy said. "It must have been thirsty work for the pack-horse handlers."

"And the carters, waggoners and coachmen," Fatima added. "The first pub, the Three Swans was replaced by another and renamed the Red House, but that is now closed."

"Sign of the times, I'm afraid," Tom remarked lamentably.

Jules spoke next. "Hmm, that's interesting, plenty to look at there. We've got three pubs with names linked to a swan and the Walton family coat of arms. The original Three Swans pub fits in to the timeline of that era. I think we need to go and recce the area. We should also look into the Walton family."

"Good night, John Boy," Randy quipped.

"Good night, Mary Ellen", Simon replied camply.

"Funny!" Jules responded.

"I can check into that," Lydia volunteered.

Paul, who had sat quietly away from the group, spoke up.

"You need to find a link to a monster, don't forget."

"You're right Paul," Jules responded, mindful of not wanting him to feel out of the process. "That's probably the hard bit. Anyone aware of tales of monsters in Liverpool or properties in the Old Swan area linked to a monster?"

"It could be something to do with an old sea-farers tale. Or maybe another pub," Tom reckoned.

"Yeah, we'll have to do some research," Simon agreed.

"Not that research Simon. It's not a pub crawl," he laughed.

"Hey, it says here," Randy interjected, "on the BBC news website, that people are flocking to Loch Ness. They're arriving in droves. News crews too".

"It's trending on Twitter as well," Fatima confirmed. "Old Swan is trending too."

"Well, they're two obvious places to start swanning around."

Lydia tittered. The others groaned. Fatima chided him.

"Don't encourage him Lydia. Randy, not funny!"

"Well, I suppose it's obvious people are heading to Scotland," Simon stated. "Given the monster clue. Maybe Loch Ness or Urquhart Castle has a link to a swan in Scottish folklore."

"I think we need to split up and cover each potential site then. Who wants a trip to Loch Ness?"

"Jules, I think Simon and I would prefer to stay local," Tom announced.

"So would I," Fatima added. "My recent trip to Egypt drained me."

"That's fine by me. Then you three go to Old Swan and Randy and I, with Paul, of course, will have a mooch around Loch Ness and Lydia, can you be our researcher and stay in house?"

"No problem, Jules. That's my forte."

"Right ladies and gentlemen, I'll leave it to you to organise your own trip to stunning Old Swan and we'll sort out our trip to lousy Loch Ness. Randy, Paul, we got the short straw don't you think? By the way, the University and NML will cover your expenses and ours. Any questions? No? Let's get to it then. Make sure we all stay in touch with each other and with Lydia in the command centre. Gosh, by the sounds of it we're already playing catch up."

65

Egypt, 1801

The tragic news reached Demeraux about four or five weeks later in the form of a letter. After reading the fateful news he sank to his knees in despair and wept uncontrollably. Jemila was the first woman he had ever loved. The other savants tried to comfort him, but he was inconsolable for several days. The expedition was drawing to a close and it was not long before they were making their way from the Temple of Kom Ombo. They had studied the nilometers as far south as Elephantine Island at Aswan. These units of measure had been used for five thousand years to determine the water levels of the river.

It was February 1801 by the time Demeraux and the other savants reached Cairo. Florent had been killed by a marauding band of brigands consisting of Mamelukes, Bedouins and Turkish army deserters. Eventually the accompanying bodyguard of cavalry and camel corps had gained the upper hand in these sporadic skirmishes. Cousseau had found new lodgings for Sanura and Elpis and for the returning savants although the place was shabbier than the previous residence. Arriving on the doorstep of the dilapidated property, Demeraux felt as if he was at death's door. When he knocked, Cousseau opened it and Demeraux virtually fell through the aperture, with Rabat and Debussy trying to assist him. Cousseau reached for his friend. "Antoine! *Mon Dieu!*"

All three carried the stricken Demeraux upstairs to a bedroom and laid him on a bed. Demeraux groaned.

"He has some sort of malaise, I know not of," Debussy said.

"Ever since he received your letter, he has not been himself. He has not eaten much. His heart is truly broken, I suspect," Rabat lamented.

"Alright, thanks. I will show you to your room. Let him rest a while and I'll take care of him."

Cousseau returned to Demeraux's bedside. The savant was feverish and had lapsed into delirium. Cousseau started to remove his friend's clothing. He unbuttoned his *chemise* and withdrew each arm from the sleeves and lifted him gently to drag the shirt from under him. He was surprised by how emaciated his frame looked. He noticed a rash on his hands. Next, he removed his boots and stockings which revealed another rash on the soles of his feet. Then he took off his friend's breeches. As soon as he removed these he caught sight of more sores around his groin which went so far as to confirm Cousseau's suspicions that he had

158

contracted the 'malady of Venus', venereal disease, probably syphilis in his estimation, although he was no surgeon. He remembered observing a small chancre on Demeraux's lip on the day he left for Upper Egypt. He had seen many gruesome looking chancres on the lips and tongues and genitalia of his fellow soldiers. Unfortunately, in the rush to depart, Cousseau did not have a chance to warn his friend that he should get the lesion checked out by a doctor. Besides, Jemila was present, and he did not want to embarrass her in front of everyone in case she was the source of the infection. It suddenly dawned on him that Roucard had most probably infected Jemila. Cousseau recalled seeing a scab on the rapist's penis when he had stripped him naked. Jemila had more likely recognized her own symptoms, being more sexually savvy, and had probably had them treated at once. She would have become a pariah with accusers unsympathetic to her plight and uninterested in how she contracted the infection if she had not sought immediate treatment. However, Cousseau thought she was lucky to be living in an age of 'enlightenment'. In the old days, if she were in France, she might have had her nose and ears slit.

Rabat was asked to tend to Demeraux whilst Cousseau fetched a physician. The only one he could find was Mehmet Ali, the rotund, jovial Turk, more mountebank than doctor. A flimflammer extraordinaire.

"Now, let me see," Mehmet said as he examined Demeraux. He inspected his hand first. "Ah, yes, a rash "

"There's one on the other hand also," Rabat added.

"Let me check the feet. Ah, yes. More papules on the soles." Mehmet whipped the sheet off Demeraux unceremoniously.

"Oh dear! More pustules around and on his manhood." He then yanked Demeraux's jaw down indelicately. "Warts on the tongue! Fevered brow. Emaciated body. Yes, my diagnosis therefore, is 'morbus gallicus.'"

"*Pardon?*" Cousseau said.

"French disease," Rabat interjected.

"*Non, non, non*. We French call it Neapolitan disease," Cousseau asserted.

Mehmet spoke. "I don't care what you call it gentlemen. *La grande verole* or great pox, the French pox, the Spanish disease. Who cares? Yes, this man has syphilis! It looks like second stage. Has no one treated him for the first stage?"

"I don't think so," Rabat said. "He's been on an expedition to Upper Egypt. We did have a surgeon accompany us, but he was killed early on during the expedition by brigands. They attacked the column, but they were repulsed. Surgeon-General Dupont took sympathy on a young Arab who had been hit with a musket ball. He went to his aid, but the Arab cried, 'Alluha Akbar!', then slid a concealed dagger out of his thobe and slit the doctor's throat."

Mehmet winced.

"We were then without a physician for months."

"Anyway, back to this fellow," Mehmet said. "The victim of too much congress methinks. You know what they say, a night with Venus and a lifetime with mercury! Ha! Ha! Ha! I have just the thing for him."

Mehmet withdrew a bottle from his medicine bag.

"This vessel contains my magic mercury potion enriched with my secret ingredients. This remedy will cure his pox without doubt. He can either imbibe it, apply it through inunction or through suffumigation. Twice a day."

"What about the toxicity levels in the mercury?" Cousseau asked.

"Don't worry. There's not too much mercury in there but when it reacts with my secret concoction, that is what will cure him. It's not known as 'The Elixir of Life' for nothing, you know. I will send you a receipt for your purchase. Good day gentlemen."

The chuckling quack waddled out.

Rabat administered the first dose of 'The Elixir of Life' orally to his feverish fellow scholar. They left him to sleep. In the following days Demeraux's condition, to the surprise of his friends, improved considerably. Cousseau visited one morning and to his joy and amazement also he discovered Demeraux sitting up in bed eager to engage with him.

"Pierre, I would like to visit Jemila's place of rest. Thank you for everything you've done. Did you find out how the fire started?"

Cousseau had not divulged in his letter that Roucard was the perpetrator and that he had taken care of him, just in case anyone else read the missive.

"Come on, I'll tell you everything on the way."

By the time they arrived at the burial site, the savant was in a state of anxiety and apoplectic with rage, cursing through his flowing tears. His grief all too raw. Cousseau led him to Jemila's final resting place marked with a small headstone fashioned from granite with her name inscribed on it, donated by Malachy. He gave his friend some time alone to mourn his loss. A distraught Demeraux threw himself on the stony grave uttering his undying love for Jemila.

On the return solemn journey, the silence was punctuated by Demeraux.

"The tablet. I presume it got burnt in the conflagration."

"No, my friend. Miraculously, it survived!"

The savant's jaw dropped.

"I was going to tell you at an opportune moment."

"My God! I can't believe it survived. How did you find it?"

"Jemila, she seemed to be protecting it. I found it underneath her body. She seemed to be clutching it. She must have known about it. When the building collapsed, she must have been holding it. It got slightly damaged, but the script is intact. The back of it was charred but otherwise still in good condition."

"Where is it now?"

"I took the liberty of concealing it, in Jemila's grave. I sincerely hope you do not think ill of me. I didn't know where to hide it at the time."

After a moment of reflection, Demeraux responded.

"That's fine, Pierre. She is protecting it in death, as she did in life. At least no one will find it there. You did well. At least we've salvaged something from our sorrow and misfortune."

160

66

Menou's administration of Egypt had been, by and large, successful and peaceful although provisions were becoming scarcer by the day for the Army of the Orient. Demeraux managed to overcome his grief to some extent, enough for him to busy himself with the works of the Institute. Cousseau welcomed a period of inactivity. However, this lull came to an abrupt halt in March of 1801 when the news reached Cairo of a new peril. A British force, 17,000 strong under the command of General Sir Ralph Abercromby had landed near Alexandria backed up by Turkish allies who had landed further down the coast. The British wanted to eliminate the threat once and for all of French desires to seize Britain's prize possession, India. Yet another army of British and Indian forces had arrived at a port on the Red Sea.

General Menou, however, instead of following the lead of Napoleon and Kléber in moving at the earliest opportunity to confront the enemy, delayed his response thus allowing the British to gain a foothold. So, Pierre Cousseau found himself on the battlefield once more situated at Canopus, northeast of Alexandria, as part of the opposing 12,000 strong French army.

The square advanced to the beat of the drums and the shrill tones of the fifes. In the distance, Cousseau and his compatriots could barely see the perfectly formed red counter squares of the enemy as dawn was yet to break. They were only illumined by the enemy campfires in the rear and the discharge of canons attempting to find their lethal range.

Then the conflict began in all earnest. The French attacked with all the elan and esprit de corps for which they were now renowned. The first wave was repulsed, the British line holding firm but then a column of infantry managed to outflank the enemy and there ensued a bitter and grim struggle amongst the ruins of Nicopolis. The strange and unsettling sound of wailing bagpipes could be heard somewhere in the darkness as the French confronted a regiment of mostly kilted, ferocious Scots who gained the initiative in the confused scenario, killing and capturing many of the Gallic soldiers.

Cousseau's *demi-brigade* was on standby as the first attack faltered. The cavalry was thrust forward somewhat avenging their comrades' sacrifice by inflicting heavy casualties on the Scots. Then the infantry followed up in support of the mounted charge. Cousseau and his division launched into the fray. They fired into the red masses, re-loaded and discharged their weapons again and again. Cousseau aimed at a cavalryman involved in a confrontation with two French dragoons one of whom toppled from his steed, transfixed by the steel of a sabre. The foot soldier pulled the trigger of his musket and the ball whipped through the air with a flash and penetrated the leg of the enemy horseman forcing his dismount. Before the second dragoon had a chance to finish off the wounded British soldier, he was bayoneted by a British grenadier. Several foot soldiers closed ranks around the fallen British rider and managed to spirit him away out of the melee. Cousseau thought he might have bagged an important general. The French sergeant waded into the foe, his bayonet searching out British flesh. He set about the grenadier that had felled the dragoon. Their steel bayonets clashed. They glared at each other, both struggling to gain an advantage, his British opponent snarling and uttering English oaths. Around them the battle raged. Missiles launched from gunboats offshore rained down behind Cousseau, lifting earth and stones high into the acrid air, scattering men and horses, and separating skin from bone. Cousseau's personal battle seemed to be enacted in slow motion. He parried the thrusts of his enemy and responded in kind, the two of them enthralled in a macabre dance of death, encircling each other, then lunging, swapping places like two revellers in a bizarre, fatal Morris dance. Suddenly, they were both on the ground propelled there by the haunches of a charging French steed. The slow-motion bubble burst and the two entwined combatants grappled hand to hand, in mortal combat. Cousseau had landed more favourably on top of his opponent, and he swiftly managed to pull a small dagger from his boot. His opponent struggled in vain to wrest the blade from the French grenadier's grip, but the latter's strength and experience told, and he plunged it into the Briton's windpipe. The blood gurgled from the infantryman's gullet. There was no time for the French sergeant to take stock. Motivated by the adrenalin surging through his Gallic veins, he unleashed his pent-up emotions in a frenzy, the scent of blood in his nostrils fuelling his euphoria. He recovered his musket and charged again but suddenly his body was flung back. He landed with a crash. Another combatant thumped to the floor beside him spewing the contents of his brains over Cousseau's face, a victim of the murderous volleys that the skilled British fusiliers were drilling into the ranks of the French now that the morning light had exposed them. Cousseau tried to raise himself, but a searing pain shot through his shoulder, his scapula crushed by the impact of the lead ball rendering his right arm useless. His blue tunic turned crimson. He felt nauseous. He tried to elevate himself using his good arm as a lever, then suddenly he looked up to see a mad-eyed riderless horse bolting from the battlefield towards him. The last sensation he felt was a blunt, excruciatingly painful trauma to his head as the terrified animal gave him a glancing blow on the temple with its hoof. Then everything went black.

67

Cousseau awoke in a supine position. His vision blurred. He could barely make out the canvas above him. His shoulder ached with pain, and he had a thumping headache. He could hear French voices mainly spouting unfathomable gibberish. He heard moans and groans. At least he was amongst friends. Outside he could hear drums, fifes and cornets playing in celebration, he assumed, of victory. He ran his tongue around his gums. His mouth was dry, his lips cracked. The lads were in triumphant mood, he thought. And then the sound of swirling bagpipes oddly filled the air. Maybe it was a Breton contingent he was with, he mused. He tried to stretch his legs wide, but something restricted his movement. Metal clanked. He realised he was in shackles. Instinctively he tried to free his legs, but they rattled louder.

"Calm down Frenchie, you're nae goin' anywhere," a Scottish voice, he could barely understand, called. Then the sergeant realized he was a prisoner of war. He tried to raise his head but the stab of pain emanating from his shoulder forced him to cede. He slumped back.

"Here, ha' some of this."

A hand cradled his head, and he felt a water bottle touch his lips. He managed a few sips before spluttering.

"*Merci,*" he gasped.

Gradually his vision returned. He glanced around and saw that the canopy covered fifty or so of his brethren in various stages of distress. Some with limbs or arms amputated. Some with both, waiting for death to claim them. Others with heads or chests swathed in bandages. The majority of them crying out in pain or delirious. Cousseau glanced rapidly down to check if he had both arms still attached. He was relieved to see that he had. A surgeon placed a sheet over the body of the French carabineer lying next to him and directed two orderlies to remove the corpse. A priest had already issued his last rites. Cousseau was at least thankful that he was in the care of the British. If he had been captured by Turks, he would have been butchered. The medic turned his attention to Cousseau. He checked his bandaged shoulder. The bandage was saturated in blood.

"Orderly, please change this dressing."

"Yes sir."

The doctor then spoke in French to Cousseau. "You're one of the lucky ones. The wound will heal in time as long as it doesn't become infected. The musket ball went straight through. You have a broken scapula. General Mcnou has fled with the remainder of your forces to Alexandria. Your future is uncertain, but you are safe here for the time being."

Cousseau nodded. The medic went off on his rounds whilst the orderly changed the dressing. He winced as the blood-soaked bandage was replaced. He reflected on what captivity might mean for him. Incarceration in some grim, dark, foreboding prison somewhere, wallowing in excrement and urine, half-starved, being fed on scraps for years on end, resulting in insanity or a long painful death through disease. His fate was now out of his hands. Ever since Nelson had decimated the French fleet at the Battle of the Nile, he had felt like a prisoner trapped in a nightmare in the unforgiving and alien world that was Egypt. His thoughts turned to his home region of Languedoc, to the lines of bee laden purple lavender wafting its delicious scent over the landscape, and to the rows upon rows of grapevines stretching over the hills bejewelled with clusters of bloom-covered plump grapes; to the welcoming shade of the olive trees and to the majesty of the yellow petaled mimosa trees; to *les fêtes,* to the abundant rivers he swam in and the gorges he loved to explore; to the hunt for wild boar, deer and wolves; to the warm summer evenings and the clear night skies, redolent with shooting stars. These images soothed away his concerns and he drifted into a deep slumber.

68

"Rosetta and Damietta have fallen to the British and Turks!" Debussy blurted out to Demeraux. "Menou is holed up in Alexandria besieged by the enemy and the British Army are now headed here, to Cairo. What a disaster! They say that we suffered four thousand casualties at Canopus, more than half their number. The British commander in chief, General Abercromby is dead. Apparently shot through the leg, he died of his wounds."

"Another army has landed at Kosseir on the Red Sea," Rabat added. "They say there are Indian troops amongst the invaders and the Mamelukes have switched their allegiance to the British because Murad Bey has died unexpectedly."

Debussy continued. "General Belliard has requested that every available man is to prepare himself to defend the city. He has 12,000 soldiers at his disposal but a call to arms has been made to Egyptians, Turks, Greeks, *savants*, slaves, and men of every nationality."

"We will lose everything that we have worked hard for, if we are defeated," Demeraux said. "All our academic findings. I hope the British understand the importance of our work and if they overcome us, they will at least preserve what we have discovered."

"If the Turkish hordes arrive first, they will butcher us and destroy everything in their path. God help us," Rabat sighed.

Demeraux rose gingerly from his seat. For the last few weeks, his health had taken a turn for the worse. His rashes and other ailments had miraculously disappeared after applying Mehmet Ali's magic potion to his weak frame via inhalation, ingestion, and anointment. He had been in fine fettle but now he hobbled over to the table in some pain to retrieve his spectacles.

"Are you alright, Antoine?" Rabat asked solicitously.

"I'm fine. Just a bit of indigestion. Don't you worry I will be able to defend the honour of France and rally to our leader Napoleon's cause. No, I meant Kléber's. Or is it Menou's? No, it's now Belliard's cause," he said sardonically. "Maybe one of us savants should take control next. What a mess we find ourselves in! Abandoned to our fate by *le petit caporal!* Where are the reinforcements that we were promised from France? Listen, I am going to pay my respects to Jemila. This might be the last opportunity I may have to be with her. Please excuse me. Thank you, gentlemen, for warning me of our imminent peril. I will see you later."

"We'll meet you at the Institute," Debussy said. "All the *savants* have been requested to assemble there to secure the artefacts, papers, books and samples from the library and laboratories. Conté reckons we may have a chance of concealing them or spiriting them away in containers."

69

Demeraux hired a cart for his journey to the cemetery. Already, activity was taking place on the fortifications. A swarm of men were bolstering the defences, hoisting more canons onto the walls and filling sandbags. The savant thought about his friend Pierre. He had received no news of his whereabouts or whether he had survived the battle. Demeraux, after a thirty minute cart ride, pulled sharply on the reins of the donkey, bringing the cart to a halt. An acute pain instantly scythed through his abdomen. He groaned and exhaled deeply. It was becoming more frequent now. He tentatively climbed down and stood by the grave. After solemnly placing a blue lotus flower that he had purchased off a small child at the cemetery entrance in front of the stone, he stood for a while in silent contemplation. He returned to the cart and retrieved a spade. He started to dig at the end of the grave near to where Jemila's feet would be and recovered the sack containing the artefact, ensuring that no one was around to see him. He heaved it onto the cart and covered it with other sacks. Then he returned to the grave, smoothed over the disturbed earth, and sank down on his knees beside it. A tear rolled down his cheek. "Forgive me for disturbing you," he said with a lump in his throat. "Farewell my love." A solitary gust of wind blew sand and earth into his eyes. He raised his head, rubbed his eyes, and bewildered, looked around. He half smiled, kissed the headstone, and returning to the cart, departed. Arriving back at his lodgings he carried the burlap sack to his room, dug a hole under a stone slab and deposited it there whilst his savant friends were out at the Institute.

Two weeks later, with morale at an all-time low and Cairo surrounded by the enemy's armies, Belliard capitulated and negotiated a surrender much to the relief of Demeraux and the other inhabitants of Cairo who feared annihilation.

Savant Joseph Fourier dashed into the crowded auditorium at the *Institut d'Égypte*. "Silence!" he called.

"Good news abounds! The British, as part of the peace negotiations, have gratefully allowed us to retain our research."

The gathering of *savants* acknowledged this by bursting into a round of applause and cheers.

"We are permitted to retain our geological, botanic and taxidermy samples but, alas, there is some bad news. Despite our vigorous protestations we are not allowed to keep possession of the Rosetta Stone."

Uproar engulfed the chamber.

"*Silence! S'il vous plaît!* We are still, however, able to keep our prints and copies of the Stone. We have one week to organise our affairs and then we will leave for a designated port on the Nile whereupon we will be transferred by barge to Rosetta.

The British have guaranteed our safe passage back to France and have arranged for a flotilla of ships to transport us there."

Cheers of joy ricocheted around the walls of the auditorium. The savants hugged each other. At last, they were going home.

A week later the mass exodus commenced. The French divisions started to move out, proudly sallying forth. They were accorded full military honours by their victors. The bands struck up. The French ceremoniously carried the coffin of slain General Kléber. The evacuation continued over the following two weeks laying bare the true extent of the condition of the vanquished. Many were in a wretched state, ill with dysentery and afflicted by syphilis and a multitude of other diseases. Most evacuees, be it from the ranks of the military, savants, tradesmen, victuallers, engineers, administrators, wives and camp followers displayed signs of malnutrition, amongst them Demeraux. He was accompanied on the journey north by Rabat and Sanura and by Debussy and Elpis who had formally married in a Coptic ceremony. France beckoned.

70

Liverpool. Present day.

B y 4pm Randy, Paul and Jules were heading north in a hired Vauxhall Zafira Tourer with Randy at the wheel. They planned to stay at Fort William for the night and so they settled in for a six hour plus journey. As it happened the traffic was down to a crawl on the M6, severely hampering their progress. They decided to find a hotel in Glasgow for the night and continue on in the morning. They were up and out early after breakfast hoping to still stay at the hotel in Fort William, which they had booked originally for two nights. A few hours later they arrived at Drumnadrochit at 12.30pm, having enjoyed the fantastic views of the Trossachs, Loch Lomond and the peaks of Glencoe Valley en route. The place was heaving with tourists, camera crews, reporters and other interested parties. Individuals of different nationalities were all drawn to the magnificent freshwater lake in the Scottish Highlands having drawn the same conclusions. Randy, Paul and Jules had briefly stopped at Fort Augustus at the southern tip of Loch Ness for a coffee and toilet break. Similar conditions prevailed. They were lucky to find a parking space. They had stretched their legs with a short preamble to the banks of the loch and around the village. This time, in Drumnadrochit, they were not so fortunate. Paul, who was now driving, struggled to find a parking space. He dropped Randy and Jules off at the medieval ruins of Urquhart Castle and drove off to find somewhere to park. He caught up with them in the long queue for the castle, perched on the banks of Loch Ness after having abandoned the car along the road where other vehicles had been parked up illegally, barely allowing the traffic to squeeze past in both directions. The line was swollen by legions of opportunist relic hunters amidst the bemused tourists. Overnight, someone had been digging in and around the ruined remnants of the castle, causing damage to the historic site. The castle authorities had drafted in more security and threatened anyone with arrest if they tried to remove or excavate anything. The tour guides were ran off their feet and were fed up with people asking them if the castle or loch had any links to a swan. The local council were, however, overjoyed with the number of visitors to the area. Jules was recognised by one local councillor after seeing her appearance on TV and so he arranged for her, Paul and Randy to skip the queue and gain immediate access to the ruins. He personally took them on a tour of the castle. The three visitors scoured the site for clues and viable hiding places as they listened to their tour guide. Despite wishing to invent an apocryphal tale of a swan, councillor McKay reluctantly told them that he did not know of any such connection, anecdote, or myth other than the obvious fact that the long stretch of water attracted such creatures. He suggested a trip to the Loch Ness Centre and Exhibition in nearby Drumnadrochit to obtain another opinion. The team accepted the inevitable parking ticket sealed on the windscreen with good grace. On the short journey to Drumnadrochit Jules took a call from Tom. He told her the same thing, that visitors and news crews were flocking en masse to Old Swan mithering the locals, asking if anyone knew anything about tales of mythical monsters in folklore. They had been to the Old Swan pub, which was rammed, looking for anything remotely related to the hunt after scouring the area for clues. They had been swept up in the convivial atmosphere and, tempted by the local brew, partook of a few scoops. Simon had found a new 'friend' and so they had not made much progress, like everyone else it seemed. Back at the Loch Ness Museum, where Jules and her party again received priority access, ignoring the groans of those queuing, they were met with the same response. Yes, definite links to a monster, no, to a fabled swan. So, they drove up to Inverness for a late lunch, enjoying the stunning vista from along the loch banks of pine-clad woods and foreboding mountain crags. They managed to squeeze in a world wind visit to both Inverness Cathedral and the museum and art gallery before, finally exhausted, they accepted defeat. They decided to delay their journey back to Fort William to let the traffic on the A82 subside and found succour in a traditional Scottish hostelry. Paul had a pint whilst Randy tried out a few whiskies. Jules restricted herself sensibly to a solitary white wine and soda, having learnt her lesson. Lydia called making reference to the Walton family. She had sent a picture of the Walton family coat of arms displaying two swans to each team member's phone but, other than that, had not really discovered anything of significance. She also referred to the existence of a Swan Hill Farm, now long gone, that once stood in the Liverpool suburb of Wavertree. The revellers left a couple of hours later as it was getting dark, not intending to stay that late. Randy immersed himself in the local culture by joining in some ceilidh dancing and it was hard to drag him away. Despite drawing a blank they were in good spirits on the return journey. A mist had formed over Loch Ness and Randy swore he saw Nessie. They laughed and accused him of having too many drams of Scotch.

"You probably saw a swan, not Nessie!" Paul quipped. They all laughed. Then, a moment later, out of the gloom, car lights appeared behind them. The vehicle approached rapidly, drawing up uncomfortably close to the back of the Zafira. Paul glanced anxiously in his rear-view mirror.

"Here's someone else that's had too much of the good stuff."

"What's he playing at?" Randy said turning to view the driver.

"Slow down a bit Paul, just let him pass," Jules said.

Paul reduced his speed, but the vehicle just stayed unnervingly close behind without attempting to pass. It was misty but this particular stretch of road was relatively straight and there were no signs of oncoming lights. Paul became unsettled. "This is deliberate. Something's not right."

Paul applied pressure to the accelerator and surged away but the car behind him responded and crept up behind them again. Then suddenly the vehicle shunted the Zafira.

"Bloody hell! What's going on?" Randy cried.

"They're trying to force us off the road!" Jules screeched, looking just to her left towards the glistening dark waters of Scotland's deepest loch.

"Hold on tight!" Paul shouted. He pressed hard again on the accelerator and sped away, but their pursuer easily gained on them and rammed them more forcibly. Jules screamed. So did Randy.

"The bastard!" Paul cursed, gritting his teeth.

"Randy! Phone the police!" Paul snapped.

The pursuing vehicle suddenly shot out of the Zafira's slipstream and came alongside it. Paul increased his speed again, but the other vehicle which Paul had now identified as a black 4x4 seemed to cruise effortlessly alongside him again. This time he glanced over and saw two men in the front seats. They were the same thugs who had attacked Penny and Jules in Liverpool.

"It's them again! The ones that jumped you by St Brides."

"Oh God!" Jules cried.

In the next instance the sneering driver turned his steering wheel sharply left and the BMW careered into the Zafira.

"Shit!" Paul growled as he struggled to stay on the road. "They mean business!"

The Zafira was at top speed. Again, the aggressor launched his vehicle into the side of the people carrier forcing it off the road into the verdant terrain astride the loch. The car just avoided smashing into a tree due to Paul's handling of the vehicle. Paul only just managed to steer it back on to the road, more by luck than skill. He desperately flashed his lights at an oncoming vehicle, but it continued on into the gloom in the other direction. The dark silhouette of the pursuing BMW had momentarily been forced to tuck in behind the Zafira then once again it ominously appeared to his right. Randy was screaming down the phone at the police. This time Paul noticed that the dark bearded figure in the passenger seat was holding a pistol.

"Randy!" he screamed to his rear-view mirror. "Pass me those bottles of whisky, pronto!"

Randy had purchased three different bottles of vintage malt. He reluctantly handed them to Jules who was in the passenger seat. She grasped them and looked nervously across to the other car and despairingly realised the extent of the threat they were facing.

"He's got a gun!" she screamed.

Paul pressed his window button, then seized a bottle of whisky from Jules and placed it out of view on his lap. The cool Highland air surged into the vehicle and Jules's auburn locks swirled wildly around her contorted face, her eyes widening in terror, giving her the appearance of one of Macbeth's Highland witches. As the 4x4 moved alongside, Paul acted first by slamming the Zafira into it, causing the driver to grip the steering wheel harder and jolting the passenger. The 4x4s passenger window slid down. A grinning thug raised his gun.

"Get down Jules!" Paul warned.

Suddenly Paul hurled the bottle of whisky at him. The armed thug fired his pistol simultaneously, but the unexpected projectile put him off and he fired into the bottle. The glass exploded into his face. Paul instinctively ducked, his vehicle lurching to the left to almost hurtle down an embankment. The would-be assassin screamed in pain and then the 4x4 suddenly careered out of control, the driver slumped over the wheel. The bullet had ricocheted off the Zafira's bodywork above the window and had penetrated the driver's temple. The 4x4 veered to the right, scraping its side against a low stone wall on the other side of the road, sparks flying everywhere. Then it clipped a post sending it up into the air, somersaulting. Paul slammed on the brakes as the BMW tumbled in front of him, its momentum propelling it down an embankment. It plunged into the water and then sank into the dark depths of Loch Ness. Paul screeched to a halt. Silence pervaded only punctuated by the whimpering of a distraught Jules and the puffing and panting of Randy. Paul placed his arms around her, comforting her.

"The Loch has two more monsters," he said laconically.

"Hey, maybe that's what you call a Highland fling!" joked an adrenalin and alcohol fused Randy. "Thank God, I've still got two bottles left."

He grabbed a bottle of single malt Macallan that was wedged between the two front seats, opened it and glugged some, forcing him to cough.

"Give me that!" Jules snapped. She snatched it from Randy's grasp and downed two gulps without any reaction whatsoever. Randy and Paul gawped in surprise. She offered some to Paul who refused. He drank from his bottled water instead. He drove on. Soon after, a light appeared in the mist before them, and Paul spotted a man by the roadside gesticulating for him to pull over. Paul snatched up the other bottle of malt that lay in the footwell and held it by its neck. As he slowed, he realised it was a break down recovery truck with a car in tow and the occupants of the car, a family with two small children in the passenger seats. Paul heaved a sigh of relief. He pulled in after the emergency vehicle. The mechanic had heard what sounded like a crash from the direction they were coming from and wanted to know the cause of it. Shortly after, a police vehicle arrived followed ten minutes later by an ambulance. Randy hid his bottles of whisky whilst the police conducted their enquiries.

It was midnight by the time they returned to the hotel in Fort William after being questioned in the town's police station. Exhausted, they returned to their respective rooms and each one, famished, raided the mini bar. Paul lay on his bed. Despite being tired he couldn't sleep, continuously going over the night's events in his head. An hour later he heard a knock on his door. He cautiously crept out of bed and peered through the door's spy hole. It was Jules in her PJ's. He opened the door, and she entered sobbing.

"I'm scared Paul."

He wrapped his arms around her, and she felt instantly comforted by his muscular frame. As her eyes closed her lips were drawn to his mouth and she successfully and sensually located his.

71

Jules awoke about 6am. She slipped naked from the white sheets, removing Paul's arm gently from across her breasts. She put on her PJs, found her room key card, and left quietly. They met for breakfast at 8am. Jules was glowing, and Paul was feeling a tad embarrassed. Randy was none the wiser about their nocturnal liaison. They were due at the police station for more questioning at 9am. A body had been reported washed up on the banks of the loch in the early morning. Paul subsequently identified it as the would-be assassin, whose pallid face was still embedded with shards of glass. The task of locating the submerged vehicle was ongoing and a witness, a GP driving the vehicle that was flashed at by the Zafira, confirmed that the BMW looked as if it was tailgating and harassing the car in front. He had also notified the police. The Zafira had been examined and the bullet hole, along with the dents to the rear and side of the vehicle were consistent with the story that each had told under questioning. The three were released at midday pending further investigations. The news had broken about the rescue effort to locate a vehicle that had crashed into Loch Ness. Seven hours later they were back in Liverpool. On the return journey they had tried to make sense of the previous day's events but generally they were all too traumatized and fatigued to be able to think dispassionately. They dropped Randy off at his home and Paul returned to Mossley Hill with Jules. On arrival Paul cautiously entered the cottage first and did a routine security sweep of the premises. He brought in their luggage and deposited it on the floor. Jules grabbed him by the arm and led him straight to the bedroom. An exhausted Paul, only too happy to submit to her beguiling charms.

Twelve hours later, the phone rang. Drowsily, Jules clawed for her mobile on the bedside cabinet. She located it and answered. It was Tom reminding her that they had a meeting arranged over at Port Sunlight. There was another university open day on and so it was deemed more appropriate to hold the meeting over at the Lady Lever gallery. After ending the conversation, she turned her head to the left, but Paul was not there. He entered the bedroom holding a tray with a cup and saucer, a jug of milk and a pot of tea. He placed the tray on the bedside table and kissed her on the lips. Before it got too passionate, she, reluctantly, pushed him gently away.

"We've got a meeting Paul, over at Port Sunlight, this morning at 10.30am. That was Tom. I'd forgotten. We must have slept for twelve hours or more."

"Well, not exactly."

He slithered under the bed sheets beside her.

"Oh, don't remind me Paul."

She kissed him. Then pushed him away again.

"No, much as I'd like to, we've got to get ready and have breakfast. I'm famished."

"Ok," Paul said. "I'll jump in the shower. You enjoy your tea."

Jules smiled and sat up in bed and sipped her hot drink whilst Paul threw back the sheets and walked naked to the bathroom. She liked what she saw. After a hearty breakfast at the refectory, they left at 9.30am for the Lady Lever on the Wirral. Their passionate night of lovemaking had gone some way to making Jules forget about her latest ordeal. They arrived in Port Sunlight, turning left at the impressive Grade I cenotaph, centrally located in the 'model' village. The sculpture had been erected by William Hesketh Lever in memory of his workers lost in the Great War. It had been a while since Paul had been there and he was happy to be reacquainted with the grandiose monolith. They drove down the boulevard, Queen Mary's Drive, towards the Lady Lever Gallery. As they drew to a stop beyond the fountain in front of the domed neoclassical edifice, Jules noticed Penny's car. They entered the building and stood in the foyer whilst they were security checked. Jules glimpsed Penny walking past the doors of the main gallery with someone.

"Penny!" Jules called out.

Penny and her companion walked past the double doors. Then they re-appeared. Jules and Paul were allowed through into the gallery.

"Jules! Welcome back. You know Ibrahim."

"Yes, of course Penny! Ibrahim, you were at the first conference weren't you? In the Cathedral. I saw you in the audience."

"That's right. I also attended the second meet at the Arena. I'm fascinated by all this mystery of the stele. It's created turmoil in the Muslim world, you know? And I daresay with all religions."

Someone else strolled into the gallery and joined them.

"And do you remember Edwin? Edwin Calder," Penny said.

"That's right. We first met the other month at the Athenaeum."

"Delighted to meet you again Dr Johnson. Yes, we discussed our favourite confiserie, La Cure Gourmande. Ha! Ha!"

Edwin gently took her hand and kissed it again.

"Quite the gentleman! Oh, this is Paul. Jules's bodyguard," Penny added.

Paul nodded to Edwin and Ibrahim.

"Ibrahim was just showing him around the gallery."

"Yes, it's very impressive," Ibrahim responded. "We've come to see the Fesch furniture in particular. Fascinating stuff."

"It is indeed," Edwin agreed.

"Edwin contacted me with a view to visiting Port Sunlight. He couldn't get hold of Ibrahim at the time, nor you Jules. I was only too happy to oblige. Ibrahim was initially away on business and only got back yesterday. We've just had a private tour of the Fesch suites and the other furniture in the Napoleonic room. He's off to Chester shortly for an auction. Ibrahim is going to take him."

"Have you any Napoleonic furniture amongst your collection, Edwin?" Jules asked.

"I most certainly do."

"You should check it to see if you can find any more secret compartments."

"I already have!" laughed the antiques dealer. "Over and over!" he chuckled.

173

"Well, we must dash. Penny, thanks for offering to drop us off at the station but we want to stroll through this splendid village before boarding the train. It's a real pleasure to see you again Dr Johnson, and Penny. Paul."

Edwin and Ibrahim left.

"Are you coming into the meeting Penny?"

"Sure. I want to hear all about your trip to Scotland. I hope it wasn't too eventful for you guys," Penny said, unaware of their death-defying ordeal.

Paul and Jules smiled knowingly.

Fatima, and Simon were already sat with Tom in his office. Jules, Paul, and Penny were, soon after, joined by Randy. Simon offered to start off the meeting. He talked about his trip to Old Swan with Tom but seemed more interested in talking about his new French 'ami', Tufiq, rather than any leads to the next clue. Paul and Jules exchanged glances. Tom jumped in and steered the conversation back towards the tablet. Lydia, who had phoned saying she would be late, crept into the room, mouthing apologies. Simon, now concentrating on the job in hand, spoke again.

"I am certain that the next clue will be found somewhere on the premises of the Old Swan pub, formerly known as the Swan Vaults. Tom, however, reckons it may be at the location of the other pub The Three Swans, where the Red House used to be."

"Or maybe on the site of the Cygnet on the other side of the junction," Tom proposed.

Lydia speculated that the clue might be linked to the site of the former Swan Hill Farm and therefore would, sadly, be impossible to find. Finally, Fatima informed everyone that a tomb depicting a swan feeding three cygnets which was located in the churchyard of St. Oswald's Church in Old Swan had been smashed to bits during the night and the skeletal remains of the tomb disinterred and left strewn across the church grounds. Simon looked particularly disturbed by this revelation. That was exactly the spot where he and Tufiq had lustily become more than just friends that very same night, unbeknown to the others.

"Whoever smashed it might have been searching for something. The next clue obviously. That could be it! Our chance gone. No one's going to own up to the desecration of a grave," Tom said in a defeatist tone.

"Not necessarily Tom. We just don't know. Besides, what link is there to a monster?" Penny chimed. "Probably just some dickhead vandals."

"What about St. Oswald? Who was he? Any links to a monster there?" Fatima said.

"He was an ancient Northumbrian King. Seventh century. No links to any monsters as far as I can see," Lydia confirmed, reading from her laptop.

"Hmm," Tom grunted. "Anyway, what about your trip to Scotland, Jules? Anything interesting to tell us?"

Randy burst out laughing and Paul, sitting away from the table, smiled quietly to himself. He excused himself, needing the gents. Jules then told the others at length what had occurred with Randy chipping in with other details. Their colleagues sat open mouthed, jaws dropping to the floor in disbelief. Finally, they concluded the meeting and decided that they were to concentrate their efforts on Old Swan. They were to approach the proprietor of the Old Swan pub for permission to conduct a professional, archaeological survey of the premises whilst researching the two other potential sites further. The Loch Ness monster was, to all intents and purposes, they suspected, a red herring.

"A ginormous herring," suggested Randy. "Or rather a damp squid. A rather large one."

Everyone groaned.

"Squib," Lydia said. "A damp squib."

"Lydia, I do know that," Randy responded. "It's a joke."

Lydia stared at him vacantly.

Paul had been gone for twenty minutes so Jules went in search of him. The others remained chatting amongst themselves. Members of the public were streaming into the gallery, their interest piqued by the whole saga, which was great for business. She found him in one of the exhibition halls upstairs. He had mentioned on the way that he would like to look around the displays, especially the Napoleonic room, not having visited the gallery before. She found him staring at a portrait of a pretty young lady with long, flowing chestnut hair down her back, dressed in the garb of a Roman goddess, holding a tambourine as a volcano erupted in the background. Jules sidled up to him grabbing his arm. He smiled and she reciprocated.

"That's our clue, perhaps," he said nonchalantly.

"What?" Jules scrutinized the painting. She had seen the painting somewhere before, but her memory failed her as to who it was. She looked at the volcano and tambourine as if they were the clue.

"It's Emma Hamilton, Horatio Nelson's mistress," Paul stated.

"That's right," Jules replied suddenly remembering who it was.

"Read that," Paul said pointing to the information plaque displayed on the wall beside the picture.

Jules started to read aloud. "Lady Hamilton as a Bacchante, probably painted in 1792 by Elizabeth Vigee-Lebrun (1755-1842) Oil Paint on Canvas. Emma Hamilton was born Amy Lyon, in Ness, Wirral..."

She stopped abruptly and stared at Paul. "Ness," she hissed. "Of course. Maybe it's a play on words. Something metaphorical, figurative. I didn't think of that at all. Gosh! I wonder if there's a connection with a swan."

"Here." Paul shoved his mobile in her face.

Jules started to read an online page about Lady Hamilton. "Early Life - she was born Amy Lyon, in *Swan* Cottage, in Ness, Wirral!"

She looked at Paul, mouth agape. "That's it! Paul! For goodness sake! You're the only one of us employed for brawn rather than brains and you've solved the clue!"

"I thought you being a mastermind would figure that one out," he teased.

"Come on, I am good, but it's impossible to know everything! Well, I did know she was born in Ness, and I hadn't made the connection. But I didn't know she was born in a *Swan* Cottage. Why didn't you come and tell us all?"

"I wanted your judicious opinion on it first. I've been waiting for you to come and

175

find me for ten minutes. I was checking on my mobile though and other sources say that they don't reckon she was born at Swan Cottage because she was born into poverty."

"Does the cottage still exist?"

"It seems so."

"Come on, we'll have to check it out. Let's tell the others."

She planted a kiss on his cheek and dragged him off hurriedly by the arm. Paul almost tripped.

When Jules and Paul returned to the office the others were still there with Randy holding court regaling them with the dramatic events of the previous evening in detail, embellishing his own role in the incident. However, everyone's admiration was reserved for Paul only, especially Simon's, and even Lydia, the geeky bookworm, felt something stirring in her cobwebbed loins for the hero of the hour. Paul was also growing on Penny. She had given him down the banks without remorse, but he had saved her and now saved Jules on more than one occasion.

"Hey guys, Paul's got something to tell you."

Paul hesitated.

"Go on Paul. Spit it out!" Penny yelled.

"Who's that?" Paul said holding up his mobile to show them a photograph.

"It's Lady Hamilton. Emma Hamilton. Nelson's other half," Tom replied instantaneously.

"Does that make her a half-Nelson?" Penny quipped, guffawing. No one else laughed, except for Lydia who giggled incessantly.

"Don't encourage her Lydia," Fatima warned, shaking her head.

"You've just taken it in our gallery," continued Tom. "And?"

"Where's she from?" Paul stated.

"The Wirral," Simon responded.

"But where, specifically?"

"Oh, come on Paul, enough of your games," Penny protested impatiently.

"Ness," Tom responded.

"Allegedly born in *Swan* Cottage, Ness," Paul stressed.

The room fell silent for a moment.

"I see where you're coming from, Paul," Fatima said, "A swan and then Ness, alluding to a monster, perhaps? You clever boy! That's better than what we've got with the Old Swan link."

"Swan Cottage, Ness. Hold on a minute," Penny said. "Why didn't you think of this link, Tom, or Simon? It was staring you both in the face! That's what we pay you for. Your knowledge!"

"Well, management skills as well. But I-" Tom tried to explain but Penny cut him off.

"You two see that bloody portrait every day. You two probably both stand there ogling her every morning. Er, well, you Tom. Maybe not Simon. And you didn't think once about that connection! I think we'll employ Paul instead."

She winked in his direction. Tom then replied.

176

"The link is tenuous only because it may be a myth that she was actually born in that cottage."

"That's right," Paul responded. "But who knows?"

"She was born into poverty. Allegedly the daughter of a blacksmith and a maid," Lydia confirmed.

"Have you seen the cottage?" Simon asked.

"You mean it still exists?" Fatima said, surprised.

"Absolutely," Simon replied. "And I would suggest no poverty-stricken child was ever born there."

"Well, we don't know that," Jules cautioned.

"You're right Jules," Fatima added. "Who knows what went on in those days? She could have been the offspring of the houseowner or occupier and her mother. Maybe the blacksmith was not the father. Maybe she was the product of a scandal. An illegitimate child."

"Or, the mother's waters may have broken in the vicinity of the cottage, and she could have been taken into the house by the benevolent owners or residents and the child born there as a result," Jules surmised. "I know we're just speculating but it's all plausible, I suppose. What we need to do then is check it out immediately. But how?"

"That's easy," Randy interjected. "The property is owned by Leahurst, the University of Liverpool Veterinary School. It belongs to us, Jules! I've got a friend who lives there as well. Viren. He's a lecturer at Leahurst. He shares the cottage with a couple of other undergraduate vets. We can get as much access as we want, presumably."

"That's fantastic!" Jules said enthused. "I'll call Dr Parkes. Maybe we can carry out a dig there as well. Can we go and see it now?"

"Sure, I'll give Viren a call. He might be busy lecturing, but we can at least go and locate the place. There's a pub directly opposite, the Wheatsheaf. Maybe we can park up and have a spot of lunch."

"Sounds good, Randy. This bird is feeling peckish, so we'll kill two birds with one stone, as it were. Get it Lydia? Me, swan, bird?" Penny flung her arm around her friend. Lydia remained unimpressed this time.

"Paul, you're not just a pretty face after all are you?" Simon called. Jules stifled a laugh registering the look of concern on Paul's face. Tom and Simon elected to remain at the Lady Lever due to work commitments. The others decided to leave at different intervals and took different routes so as not to bring attention to themselves. Penny and Lydia, then Fatima and Randy and finally Paul and Jules. They all met up again in the car park of the Wheatsheaf.

"There it is," Randy said, pointing to an elegant detached, white-washed cottage on the bend of the main road into Ness. With the cars parked up the group negotiated the bend and paused at the entrance to the Georgian era cottage.

"See," Paul uttered. "The date on the plaque. 1724. That fits in with the historic timeline."

They remained at the gates out of courtesy, whilst Randy knocked. There was no answer. Randy tried to contact Viren by phone again but to no avail. He was not responding to his messages. The group momentarily surveyed the cobble-stoned drive from the entrance, but with nothing piquing anyone's interest, they all returned to the pub for lunch in high spirits, Randy being confident they could get permission from Dr Parkes to conduct a dig in the rear garden and examine the interior of the house.

72

Dr Parkes gave Jules permission to search Swan Cottage after agreeing it was a more than plausible possible location. He immediately contacted Leahurst whereupon those in authority agreed to sanction the search with the full backing of the occupants. Viren and the other tenants were to be present when the team carried out their inspection. An archaeological dig was authorised for the rear garden. Randy was nominated to supervise the dig. He had plenty of experience of digs on the Wirral having been part of a team that unearthed Roman artefacts and evidence of the existence of a Viking settlement in Irby. More recently, in Bromborough, he had been engaged in the quest for the location of the highly significant Battle of Brunanburh that occurred in 937AD. The battle was instrumental in uniting Wessex and Mercia, thus creating one single and united entity – the nation of England.

Two days later a university archaeological team headed by Randy turned up in Ness and started to excavate the grounds whilst Jules and Paul were given access to the house with Tom. Fatima, Simon and Lydia had been despatched to the pub, the Old Swan, with another dig team, the proprietor, having given permission, for a fee, to search the premises. Dr Parkes had publicised this visit but not the Swan Cottage dig, to ensure the focus from the media and the general public remained on the Liverpool site. A comprehensive search of the house had not revealed anything of interest, so the focus switched to the grounds of the cottage, Jules lending her expertise. It was on the second day of the dig that Peter Banks, an archaeology undergraduate struck something with his trowel in the rear garden, two feet underground. He carefully sifted away the soil to reveal a small, weathered brown leather scroll case. He shouted for Randy, who in turn called Jules and the others who were inside the house. Everyone gathered around excitedly. Randy gave Peter the honour of excavating the rest of the cylinder tube out of the soil and he presented it to Randy triumphantly to applause from the rest of the team. Randy carefully cleaned the dirt off and then held the 'find' out to Jules who indicated for him to open it. Time was of the essence. He put on some white latex gloves, removed the worn leather top, and held it upside down. Nothing. He then peered down the tube.

"There's definitely something inside it."

He wriggled two fingers into it and felt paper or parchment inside, but he could not extract it. He banged the tube gently on the palm of his hand and gradually and painstakingly out slid the top edge of the scrolled paper. He deftly pulled the contents of the cylinder out which consisted of one sheet of paper. He passed it to Jules. It was tied like a scroll with a red ribbon. She untied the worn ribbon and looked around the excited group. Taking a deep breath, she unfurled the scrolled sheet to reveal a moisture damaged, slightly impaired image, of a lion. They could not believe their luck. They had solved the first clue. They all cheered and high-fived each other. The dig was immediately curtailed, the garden made good, and the rearranged furniture and carpets in the cottage all returned to normal. They all marched over to the Wheatsheaf to celebrate their success. Jules had rung Dr Parkes Immediately whilst Tom had rung Simon to tell him the good news and to stop their search in Old Swan. They scheduled a meeting in the morning at the University. Everyone was sworn to secrecy until such time that they would announce the discovery to the media the following day. Later, Viren and his two housemates joined them in the pub to celebrate.

73

Egypt, 1801

A few weeks later, the itinerant rabble from Cairo arrived at Rosetta in dribs and drabs. Menou was still holed up in Alexandria hoping for reinforcements from France to lift the siege, but he was bemused like everyone else when a ship purported to be bringing those reinforcements docked and humiliatingly offloaded a troupe of entertainers instead of the required soldiers. One of those British soldiers who laughed wholeheartedly on hearing of this episode was Seamus Michael O'Rourke, a sergeant in Dillon's Regiment. The corps consisting of French royalist émigrés and other nationalities was part of the British invasion force. It was given the task of searching the baggage and bodies of the rag-tag defeated French before they boarded the flotilla of boats awaiting them. O'Rourke and his regiment had fought well at the Battle of Canopus and during the engagements prior to the main battle. The regiment had distinguished itself on the battlefield, an assault being made on French units to repulse them from their positions at a strategic canal, enabling the British forces to maintain their momentum. The Dillon's sergeant had been in the vanguard of the attack, leading his platoon of men with aplomb and courage into the affray, despatching several of the foe in hand-to-hand combat. The red-headed soldier, son of an Irish Jacobite exiled father and an Irish mother was selected, like several more of his multi-national regiment for the task of searching the departees, on account of his fluent French. This was a lucrative business for O'Rourke and his comrades who amassed a great amount of contraband not only for the British and Turkish authorities, but also for himself. He knew that most of his own booty might be confiscated by his superiors and that, owing to the speed of the operation, he could not search everyone. He had to get the vast numbers of sick and diseased French on board the frigates and schooners and away from Rosetta.

"*Arrêtez!*" O'Rourke ordered, standing on the quayside. A French hussar stopped. He was about to climb the gangway. The British sergeant took him to one side and searched his baggage. The cavalryman tried to object, cursing the British soldier, in French, only to be shocked when the British soldier in front of him responded with even stronger oaths in French. Then O'Rourke discovered a jewel-encrusted dagger wrapped in an undergarment in the hussar's trunk and swooned at the beauty of the prize.

"*Oh là, là! Je suis désolé, mon ami. C'est à moi maintenant. Vous pouvez garder les pantalons!*" And with that he threw the breeches into the face of the cavalryman who bristled with anger. O'Rourke's pals on guard duty laughed. The Irishman deposited the knife inside his already bulging tunic.

"*Allons-y,*" he said, dismissing the remonstrations of the French cavalryman. "Next! *Suivant!*"

A handsomely dressed turbaned Mameluke robed in a vibrant red silk waistcoat, silk green sashes and fine blue silk pantaloons strutted forward like a peacock accompanied by his wife and two children. O'Rourke was well aware of the Mameluke's propensity for concealing jewels and gold and silver coins in their garb. He admired these warriors of the Caucasus. He had marvelled at their horsemanship on the battlefield. The Irish sergeant patted the proud Circassian down, receiving a contemptuous look. He ordered him to remove his turban. He checked inside the layers of silk and felt something solid. He prised out a purse. The Mameluke objected but a guard stepped menacingly forward and forced him to back down. The sergeant opened the purse to reveal a stash of gold sovereigns. O'Rourke could not believe his luck. He and the guard laughed. O'Rourke spirited it away inside his tunic leaving the Mameluke seething and cursing. He then emptied the evacuee's bags on the ground. There was some food, garments, and children's wooden toys but nothing else of value. O'Rourke reckoned that the Mameluke had most likely concealed more treasure on his wife or children. The children were already crying hysterically. The sobbing mother tried to calm them. Reluctantly, he let them pass since they needed to embark the passengers swiftly. O'Rourke glanced down at the long queue of people waiting to board the ships. He could see more Mamelukes in line and rubbed his hands in anticipation. Some of the Mamelukes had been serving with the French in a cavalry unit and had remained loyal, electing to escape to France to avoid being at the mercy of the Turks who would have butchered them at the first opportunity. Likewise, there were Copts and Syrian Janissaries amongst the multitudes at the port who had served in French units who also thought it would be more prudent to leave with the French. O'Rourke had already searched a few of these and confiscated daggers, pendants, jewellery and other items of interest.

The Irishman held up his hand and beckoned to the next contingent. They shuffled forward. O'Rourke surveyed them. Amongst them stood Debussy and Rabat dressed in their grey, tattered savant uniforms accompanied by Elpis and Sanura. O'Rourke started to search their baggage pulling out papers, maps, books, stuffed animals, botanic samples, and other strange specimens in jars. All were of no interest to the Irishman, and he allowed them to retrieve them having been ordered not to confiscate any papers or samples from the scholars.

"You two can go aboard," O'Rourke indicated to the men.

"Hey, what about the women? That's my wife!" Debussy protested, pointing at Elpis.

"Can you prove it?" the soldier asked.

"Yes, most certainly," Debussy replied.

He dived into his bag and recovered a scroll tied with a silk yellow ribbon. He unfurled the scroll and showed it to O'Rourke.

"I take it you can read," the savant quipped in a patronising manner.

O'Rourke glared at the Frenchman forcing Debussy to lower his eyes. The

182

Irishman perused the document which was written in Coptic and French. He then read out aloud in French the confirmation of marriage between Elpis and Debussy. He paused, looking disdainfully at the stunned savant.

"Take her," he ordered. He thrust the licence into the savant's chest. Elpis moved swiftly to Debussy's side. "What about this one?"

Rabat intervened. "This is my wife also."

"Prove it. Where's your wedding certificate?"

"We-we had to leave it. We could not go back to her town, where her family live, to fetch it. They kept it for us," he lied.

"I'm sorry, she can't embark. I need evidence. I have strict orders. Only men with legally married wives and family are to be repatriated."

"What?" Rabat objected. "But that's preposterous! She's my wife!"

"No licence, no voyage. And that's final."

"But I can't just leave her!" Rabat responded aggressively.

The looming figure of the guard brandishing a musket and bayonet intervened. He laid the weapon across Rabat's chest.

"Any problems, sir?"

"No, private. Get one of the men to accompany this woman to the market. She should fetch more than a few pennies."

O'Rourke motioned to an animated crowd of British soldiers on the dockside who were bidding for women paraded before them.

"No!" Sanura screamed when she set eyes on the unseemly scrimmage of the 'cattle market'. She cried out. "Jean-Claude! Help me!"

Two more British soldiers grabbed her by the arms and frogmarched her away. Sanura burst into tears. Rabat could only watch in horror, his way still barred by the weapon thrust in front of him.

"Sanura! No!"

"Have faith," O'Rourke said, "she will be safe. Better to be the concubine of a British soldier than be left to the barbarity of the fiendish Turks. They've threatened to mercilessly put to death any Arab woman who has had liaisons with a Christian."

"Get them on board now, private."

The private started shoving the group forcefully up the gangway with his weapon. Rabat glanced back. Although he was not in love with Sanura as much as his friend François was in love with Elpis, he still cared enough for her and had vowed to protect her by taking her to France with him. Dejectedly and in shock, the remaining three boarded the corvette. The trio remained on the deck and watched as Sanura was dragged to the scrum of soldiers and civilians on the quayside. The raucous, bawdy servicemen were bidding for each woman that was stood before them. Once a bid had been accepted an officer called the winner over to claim his 'prize.' The women had no choice but to leave with their new partner. Some struggled and beat the men they were partnered with to the amusement of the throng. Others acquiesced and left of their own accord submissively. It was Sanura's turn. Elpis wept. There was a flurry of bets for her, and the victor emerged, a small dark-haired man of Mediterranean appearance. He led Sanura away from the auction by the

183

hand. She stared at the ground only looking up to the ship wistfully before disappearing into the morass of bodies coming and going on the waterfront. Rabat, Debussy and Elpis were forced into the hold of the vessel.

Next in line were some more savants, amongst them Demeraux who was trying to remain inconspicuous at the back of the group. O'Rourke searched the bags of each one finding the same journals and samples as before which were of no interest to him. He waved them forward to board the ship. He watched as the last grey-uniformed scholar of this contingent approached, a frail looking bespectacled man struggling to carry his bags. He had noticed him being defensive about his personal effects, not letting his companions assist him. The feeble looking, emaciated individual stumbled forward, head down. O'Rourke barred his path.

"*Attention! Mon ami. Attendez, monsieur.*"

Demeraux looked up anxiously and frowned. O'Rourke wrenched a bag from the savant's puny grasp. He was surprised by the heavy weight of it. "*Mais, mais…,*" he tried to object but the curious Irishman emptied the contents of the bag on the quayside. Books, journals, clothes and samples all tumbled out and then he came across something well-wrapped, concealed in rags and clothing. He opened it up and saw an ancient looking tablet that looked like ivory displaying strange symbols ornately carved into it.

"*Non, s'il vous plaît, pas ça*" Demeraux whined. "It is a sample of my work. I am allowed to keep it as part of the accord."

He observed the Frenchman's angst as he delved into the bag further and recovered a lithographic print of the same strange, illegible text.

"Here," he said to Demeraux. "You can keep this. You'll do yourself a permanent injury trying to lug this heavy thing about." He bundled the item into a different sack belonging to himself and thrust the print into Demeraux's hands. "Pick up your effects and get on the ship. Come on! Move!" O'Rourke shouted aggressively.

Demeraux continued to argue his case. The butt of a musket ploughed painfully into his back.

"Argh!" he cried. He collapsed to the ground. The threatening guard stood over him.

"You heard the sergeant! Get your things and get on the bloody boat!" the soldier ordered.

Demeraux gingerly climbed to his feet and started to retrieve his papers and other paraphernalia some of which was being blown about in the sea breeze. He mewled querulously like a new-born baby. He managed to recover it all. Then he snarled at O'Rourke, holding his stare, before hurrying aboard evading the guard who tried to administer another blow to his slight frame.

74

Several hours later, the frigate set sail with its multifarious aggregate of human cargo. Some passengers cheered. Others sat broodily in fear of the unknown. The voyage across the Mediterranean was not going to be a gentle, pleasant cruise, although many on board knew what to expect. The first British frigates, corvettes and schooners of the fleet tacked out of the port and headed north up the Nile with other ships of the line providing an armed escort. Once out in the open sea the British sailors allowed those prisoners who had been captured at Canopus and the other earlier battles to emerge from the bowels of the ship. Their manacled feet were unshackled. They had been warned that any mutiny would be dealt with severely and the ship would be blown to smithereens by the escorting battleships, however, most were in no shape physically or mentally to resume hostilities and the majority were, in fact, elated to be going home. Amongst the weary, chastened men emerging from the hold was Pierre Cousseau. He was weak, his shoulder still not fully healed and his features sallow and drawn. He had not by and large been ill-treated but his meagre diet, lack of exercise and the cramped, unhygienic conditions he had experienced had rendered him virtually incapacitated. He staggered out into the dazzling sunshine and gulped in the salty sea air thankful that he had escaped from the fetid environment of the sweltering brig.

It wasn't until one week later that he realized that Antoine Demeraux was on the same ship. Space was at a premium and most people had claimed an area on deck or elsewhere, where permitted, and had stayed put, protecting their luggage and not venturing too far. Cousseau had no belongings with him. No money. Nothing. Just the shirt on his back, his pantaloons and his tunic. His boots, acquired from a dead Mameluke warrior at the Battle of the Pyramids, had been pulled from his feet when he was wounded, and he never saw them again. No doubt a British soldier was now the proud owner of them. After gaining some of his strength, he began to take strolls where he could, to get the blood circulating in his legs. The problem of the lack of space was eased gradually since those who expired during the voyage were despatched overboard. Anyone suspected of the plague was also unceremoniously and callously bundled over the edge into the heaving sea. On one of his walks, to his surprise, he bumped into Rabat. It was he who informed him that Demeraux was on board. Cousseau was delighted to hear that, but Rabat warned him that his friend was poorly again. Rabat led him down to the sick bay. Rows of people were laid out on the floor, some laying in their own excrement and vomit. Orderlies were struggling to cope amidst the foul deleterious mess triggered by the lurching and pitching of the ship in the swell. Rabat and Cousseau pressed their sleeves to their noses. The savant picked his way carefully over the feet of the prone and the supine, followed by Cousseau. He paused at a shrunken stricken figure who Cousseau barely recognized as his friend. Demeraux's complexion was pallid. His cheeks hollow. He seemed to have aged considerably. He was asleep, snoring. Cousseau could see gaps in Demeraux's blackened teeth whenever his friend's ulcerated mouth opened and shut. Rabat gently shook him awake. Demeraux weakly opened his eyes. They opened wider as his vision focused on Cousseau. He too looked older and thinner. Demeraux smiled faintly.

"*Mon ami*, you're alive! Thank God!" he rasped.

Rabat excused himself and went to do his business over the side of the ship.

"And so are you my friend."

"Alas, not for long I fear."

"I think Mehmet's magic potion has worn off. My teeth are rotting and ulcers fester in my mouth. I can hardly talk."

"I will get the surgeon. He will administer more mercury to you."

"No, Pierre, that's what's killing me, I suspect. Mehmet's elixir must have been ninety per cent mercury and ten percent of his secret ingredients which was probably more mercury."

Cousseau forced a laugh and his sick friend responded with a weak smile, then continued.

"I'm afraid I lost the tablet. I brought it with me, hidden in my baggage. I was about to step on to the gangway when this red-haired clod of a British soldier stopped me, and I was astounded when he spoke perfect French to me. He emptied the bag and confiscated the tablet. I-I tried to stop him. I was so close to secreting it onto the ship. So close!"

Cousseau remained silent for a moment. "Never mind," he sighed. "Your health is more important."

"I have something for you, Pierre. Take my pack from behind my head."

Cousseau carefully removed the satchel from behind Demeraux's head and replaced it with his own tunic. He looked inside the bag and pulled out the print of the hieroglyphs.

"You keep it," Demeraux uttered.

Suddenly the stricken savant unleashed a cry of anguish. His back arched and his bony hand extended to his rear flank. A spasm of pain engulfed his scrawny frame.

"Antoine! Antoine! What's happening? Antoine!"

Cousseau stuffed the print in his shirt and sought to help his friend.

"Argh! my kidneys," he gasped. "The pain flares up, now and again."

"I'll get you some water."

"I'm alright for now. It's sporadic. Listen, before you go there's something else in the satchel for you. In the pouch."

Cousseau fished about in the bag and extracted a journal.

"This, you want me to have your journal. No, when you feel better, you'll need it," Cousseau said in a dissembling manner, knowing full well that his friend was dying.

"Not the journal. Inside, look inside it."

Cousseau thumbed through the pages, then a loose leaf protruded out. He pulled

186

it out and stared in wonderment at an illustration. A familiar beautiful face stared back at him. It was unmistakably Chione. A brilliant, sketched portrait of the woman he loved.

"Your own face is a picture," Demeraux spluttered.

Cousseau's jaw had dropped in amazement.

"Did you draw this Antoine?"

"No. No way I could do that. I commissioned it from one of my savant companions, an artist named Baudelon. I was waiting to present it to you on your birthday in August."

"It's amazing. He's captured her perfectly. But how did he do that? Had she sat for him when she was alive?"

"No, he just has the ability to recollect. He has a powerful memory. He knows beauty when he sees it. He saw her with you of course and he remembered her."

"He's captured every minor detail of her features. That's amazing! He is a genius! Is he onboard so I can thank him?"

"No, I was told he's on another ship."

"I'll find him or write to him when we return to France and thank him."

Rabat returned with water for Demeraux and helped him drink some. A surgeon then intervened.

"The patient needs to rest. Enough now."

"Keep the satchel," Demeraux whispered "for the drawing and the print."

Cousseau lent down and kissed his friend on the forehead. He clasped Demeraux's hand within his own and held it fleetingly.

"*Merci bien,*" he said softly with a tear in his eye, then he took his leave with Rabat.

75

The following morning Cousseau was picking his way through the clusters of people on the deck, when he saw Rabat, Debussy and Elpis approach him. He smiled as he moved towards them, but they did not return his smile. Their forlorn look said it all, and he knew at once that Antoine, his boyhood friend, was dead.

Cousseau held his head in his hands and wept. Together the four of them hugged each other.

"I'm afraid the priest can't wait," Debussy said. "We have to despatch his body to the sea at once. The surgeon reckons it was kidney failure brought on by mercury poisoning. Antoine had informed him that he had been stricken with syphilis and had taken the medication."

It was four weeks later, in the autumn of 1801, when Cousseau set foot on French soil again, the British vessel having reached Toulon. Cousseau had thankfully survived the journey. Many others had not. He had survived the expedition of the Army of the Orient. He had survived Napoleon's megalomaniacal folly in attempting to follow in the footsteps of Alexander the Great only to be immersed once more into the turmoil of post-revolutionary France, a maelstrom perpetuated by Napoleon's political and militaristic ambitions. The Corsican was bent on conquering Europe, like his other great hero, Julius Caesar. Cousseau, now physically and mentally scarred, a war-weary soldier, bade farewell to Rabat, Debussy and Elpis on the quayside and departed for Languedoc with some other soldiers of the region, penniless and downtrodden. Through the assistance and kindness of sympathetic strangers he arrived there one week later to be greeted by his mother and younger siblings. His family had barely survived the lean years of war. The farm's produce was appropriated to feed France's armies, the family somehow managing to maintain production. Cousseau was welcomed back home with open arms into the comforting bosom of his loved ones.

76

General Menou, marooned in Egypt, had finally come to his senses after several weeks of siege by the British and had negotiated a peace to avoid a bloodbath. Sergeant Seamus O'Rourke was chosen to accompany Colonel Turner and his retinue on a mission to find 'the Rosetta Stone' and other artefacts that the British deemed valuable. The stele was in the possession of General Menou. The French general had negotiated long and hard the terms on which the Alexandria garrison could surrender with his counterpart General John Hely-Hutchinson. With the British having the upper hand, it was finally agreed that the remaining savants could keep their papers and samples as per the current agreement. The scholars had protested that they would rather be slaughtered and have their findings destroyed than hand them over to their conquerors. Such was the strength of their feelings. However, an English scholar had empathised with them and persuaded the commander of the British forces to meet them halfway. They were to retain their collections, but the larger artefacts were to be turned over to the British. O'Rourke had been chosen to be part of Colonel Turner's detail to identify, catalogue and sequester the artefacts, on account of his linguistic skills.

The party arrived at Menou's palatial home and began a search of the premises. The British soldiers were still being harangued by the savants who were furious that their 'Rosetta Stone' was to be confiscated by the British. O'Rourke, however, was more interested in finding jewellery, precious stones, silver and gold. The detachment of artillery personnel accompanying O'Rourke shared the same sentiments. They were ordered to transport the artefact back, once located, to General Hely-Hutchinson in a devil cart. O'Rourke assisted in translating the Colonel's demands. When the party was finally presented with the stone slab, wrapped in carpets and secured in a wooden case, Colonel Turner instructed his men to open the case so that he could examine it. He perused the Stone with the others but, apart from an accompanying British scholar, Colonel Turner and another French speaking British officer, the other men were indifferent to the pictograms and text on the granite slab and could not understand the fuss over the relic. O'Rourke, however, on the other hand, was startled to see the same strange symbols on the slab that were on the confiscated ivory tablet. He registered the interest shown in the artefact and listened to the passionate arguments of the French scholars and concluded that there was maybe some sort of value in the tablet he had hidden amongst his possessions at the bivouac. O'Rourke tried to pacify the savants but their fervent objections and animated remonstrations about the value of the 'hieroglyphs' as they called them continued unabated. Notwithstanding, the artillery men were instructed to load the heavy granite relic onto the cart. The British search party then scoured the palace for other artefacts. Some had been concealed from them. It was a bit like cat and mouse. Finally, they were satisfied that all the major artefacts had been located, catalogued, and ready to be spirited away. O'Rourke and the artillerymen steered the devil cart heaped with the surrendered artefacts through the narrow streets of Alexandria, running the gauntlet of the jeering French garrison. Ultimately, the savants and the two opposing commanders in chief arrived at the same conclusion that if the ancient stone slab was abandoned in Egypt it would be considered of no value whatsoever. The Egyptians, Turks and Mamelukes were not interested in antiquity and the relic in question would end up being re-used for building projects in time, once again.

77

Some days later O'Rourke's linguistic skills were required again. A sacred religious sarcophagus taken from a mosque that had been destroyed by the French was carried off by the Ottomans as a prize without consulting their British counterparts in the aftermath of the capitulation of Alexandria. The British wanted it returned to the locals who were upset, in order to maintain good relations. An armed party was sent to recover the artefact. It had been moved to the captured French ship, the privateer *Corse*, which had been given to the Ottomans. The sarcophagus was considered by Egyptian Muslims to be a special antidote to all diseases and particularly to the plague. People used to pay the imam a fee to touch it with their tongue to obtain a cure. O'Rourke and the others in the British squadron took back control of the relic after a confrontation during which the Turks backed down. The commander of the Turkish fleet was admonished. Again, the sergeant noticed the hieroglyphic carvings on the recovered sarcophagus, giving credence to his belief that they added to the value of the relic.

O'Rourke then accompanied some officers on a trip to Cairo and the Giza Pyramids as an interpreter. The British, like the French, had been smitten with ancient Egypt. The party arrived at the huge bivouac outside of Cairo that contained the British forces. Not far away the Turks were also encamped. The officers decided to visit the Turks to secure the services of a body of Mamelukes who would accompany them to the pyramids, given their knowledge of the terrain and to protect them from marauding Bedouins on the way. The detachment watched on with interest and awe as the Mamelukes entertained the massed ranks of Turks with a breathless, audacious display of horsemanship, charging at each other with djerids, avoiding these lances with dexterous movements, as they clung to the side of their galloping steeds. O'Rourke enjoyed this spectacle immensely and marvelled at the array of fierce looking warriors in the vast camp, of all colours and creeds. There were Turks from mainland Turkey, Albanians, known as Arnauts, and considered to be the finest of fighters, Circassians and Georgians from the Caucasus. Then there were the Deli's, a shock troop of Ottoman cavalry and the Janissaries, elite troops who acted as bodyguards drawn from Bosnia, Bulgaria, and other Balkan regions. However, the visiting party of British were unsettled by the ghastly vision of rows of putrefying severed French heads located in the camp. They were appalled to see the Ottomans kicking and spitting at the heads and cleaving them with their scimitars. The victims were former prisoners of garrisons and patrols captured as the Grand Vizier, the Ottoman commanding officer, and his army had moved towards Cairo in the Delta and down the banks of the Nile. The British had also heard of ugly incidents of murder, rape and plunder occurring in the local populace as well with the Turks failing to respect the people who they had come to liberate. O'Rourke and his party left soon after.

Once at the Pyramids, O'Rourke and the others were astonished by the immense size of these extraordinary edifices. The visit stimulated the Irishman's interest in antiquity even more. The party then headed into Cairo itself. O'Rourke and the others had viewed from afar the diverse panorama of hazy, shimmering minarets and spires dotted across the city. As they drew nearer, a smog enveloped them, and a malodorous stench assaulted their noses, caused by the raw sewage and by the dried dung fuel the inhabitants used for cooking. O'Rourke was shocked to find a war-torn city, the result not of the British army's own doing, but due to a French bombardment to pacify a revolt there during their occupation. The narrow streets were choked with fumes and dust, and were crammed with carts, carriages and animals; dogs, mules, asses, and camels. Ragged beggars and half-starved, half-naked citizens mingled with inebriated British troops, some kilted, pushing and barging their way boisterously through the crowds. O'Rourke also observed sepoys from the Indian army chattering away incessantly in their native tongues outside the souks and cafés. The homogenous mass seemed to move as one, as people or beasts were carried away with the throng like jetsam floating down the Nile. The group decided to pause for lunch. They stepped over several comatose Turks and entered a café. The prostrate Turks had overindulged in the opium that they had added to the tobacco in their pipes and hookahs, alcohol being forbidden. It was bedlam everywhere. After refreshments and a meal consisting of a dish of *ful medames*, they continued their tour of the sights taking in the Citadel of Cairo, Roman ruins, mausoleums, palaces and bazaars, churches, and mosques and by nightfall they were relieved and happy to get back to their bivouac, exhausted by their itinerary.

78

O'Rourke and the others in the touring party returned to Aboukir Bay after a day of rest. The Dillon's sergeant was then ordered to accompany the commanders of the Mamelukes, the Beys, to negotiate with the Turks on board the flagship of the Turkish navy. Feuds had arisen between the two factions. The Beys had requested a British escort, being wary of the Ottomans. However, the detachment of guards, including O'Rourke, was refused entry to the boats by the Ottoman sailors, despite the vigorous objections of the British officer in charge of the bodyguard. The sailors were to ferry the Mameluke leaders out into the harbour. O'Rourke sensed unease. His suspicions were confirmed when shortly after setting sail for the Turkish flagship, the sailors abandoned the launches allowing Ottoman gunboats to suddenly turn their fire on the vessels, killing most of the Mamelukes and taking some prisoner. O'Rourke and the others were horrified at the treachery and devious tactics of the Turks but were relieved all the same not to have set foot in the launches. Hely-Hutchinson was enraged at the deception and responded by mustering a force to confront the Turks. He vented his spleen at the Captain Pasha of the Ottoman Navy and tensions rose as he subsequently threatened the Grand Vizier with war. The Turkish leader had also duplicitously imprisoned another contingent of Mamelukes at Cairo as part of the ongoing struggle for power created by the vacuum after the French withdrawal. O'Rourke returned to his Dillon's regiment after the debacle, the Turks fortunately heeding the warning. Nevertheless, the uneasy alliance produced conflict on a daily basis.

One day O'Rourke and some men of his platoon were approaching a village outside of Damietta on patrol in search of two missing soldiers, Hortz and Caselli, who had vanished during a search for food supplies the day previously. A contingent of Turkish cavalry arrived at the same time. The Irish sergeant was wary of the mounted troop after the slaughter in the bay. He had also witnessed the Turk's deceptions and cruelty first hand in the aftermath of the Battle of Alexandria when some of the Ottoman foot soldiers combed the battlefield seeking out wounded French combatants, slitting their throats and beheading them. Captain Deloitte of the Dillon's had shot two Turks on the spot for their unacceptable transgressions. O'Rourke and his squad, on Deloitte's orders, had run some more Turks through with bayonets after they had refused to cease their unnecessary vicious conduct.

From a distance, O'Rourke and his comrades, watched some of the riders dismount. The Ottoman's rounded up a few locals, shouting at them, pushing some aggressively to the ground and corralling and buffeting others with their steeds. Although the British ranks, like their French predecessors were no angels and harboured some criminals and rogues, the onlookers were shocked when the leader of the band of Turks drew his scimitar out of the silk sash wrapped around his waist and administered a blow to an Egyptian elder's neck, almost severing his head. Others laughed and followed suit attacking the villagers, stabbing some of them with their daggers and decapitating others. O'Rourke, followed by his men, rushed up to the Turks shouting angrily.

"Hey! You! Stop! Stop this outrage! What's happening? Why are you slaughtering these people?"

The commander of the Turks, who was about to bring his sword down on an innocent child, paused and turned towards O'Rourke. Contempt for the British soldier was written all over his grimy, blood-spattered features. The other Turks halted their murderous pursuit of the villagers, leaving several victims, men, women and children, dead on the ground.

The Turkish officer spoke in English. "They refused us food! And yet we are their liberators! And we are their masters now! The people of this God forsaken land must obey us! They should be happy to serve us!"

"You cannot treat them like this! Leave them alone, I say!"

"And who are you to give me orders, you infidel! You are a mere sergeant. I am an officer of the Sultan's Army! You cannot give me orders, you English pig! Take your men and leave the village now! We were here first. It is no concern of yours."

"No! By the will of God, we will not leave and let you slaughter these wretched people."

At that moment, one of O'Rourke's men, a Swiss soldier, private Freudel, spoke to O'Rourke in French prompting the surprised Turkish officer to respond.

"You speak French? Then you must be French deserters masquerading as British! You are defeated, your army has left you to rot. You are at the mercy of my warriors now!

The officer, turned to his men, some of whom were still on horseback, and said something in Turkish that made the others laugh. Some of the riders rode out of the cohort of cavalrymen gruesomely holding up the heads of victims that had been slung over and attached to the backs of their saddles.

O'Rourke and his men suddenly froze in horror. Facing them were two blood-smeared and scarred countenances familiar to the men. One belonged to the German, Hortz, and the other to the Italian, Caselli, the soldiers in Dillon's regiment they were searching for.

The men's horror turned to disgust and then rage.

"They're our men!" O'Hanlon, another Irish private screamed.

"They're British soldiers, you bastards!" O'Rourke snarled.

"You lie, you dog! Your fate awaits you! My men will have more heads to exchange for rewards! Soldiers of the great Sultan's Army, kill them all!"

The foraging party were already on a war footing. The Turkish foot soldiers launched themselves suddenly at the twelve strong detachment, wielding scimitars and daggers and screaming oaths to Allah. They were swiftly despatched by British musket fire and finished off by the cold steel of bayonets. The enraged Turkish officer then steered his steed into the band of men slashing with his sword cutting

194

down the Swiss private. O'Rourke deftly manoeuvred himself to one side and aimed his pistol at the Turk and fired. The Ottoman's jaw was taken off with the impact and he fell to the side of his horse which bolted away, dragging the screaming cavalryman with it, his leg caught in a stirrup.

The other Ottomans on horseback shrieked cries of revenge and galloped into the fray forcing the British soldiers to defend themselves stoutly. They took refuge where they could, priming their Baker rifles rapidly and firing another volley into the charging body of riders, bringing at least five down. The attack never stalled though. The remaining horsemen were upon them, slashing wildly with sabre and scimitar. A Turk bore down on Private O'Hanlon lancing him through the chest, leaving him mortally wounded. He sank to the earth unleashing a torrent of expletives at his slayer. Blood spluttered out of his mouth and trickled down his beard before he managed to issue his last words. "You bastards!"

O'Rourke took on another cavalryman whilst around him others from his platoon were cut down. He deflected a blow from a lance with his sabre. The sabre was knocked to the ground with the impact, but he managed to drag his attacker from his horse. He plunged the dagger, swiftly wrenched from his belt, into the unseated rider's heart, a dagger acquired from a dead Mameluke at Canopus. Suddenly, a ball from a carbine tore through his trousers and creased his calf. He grunted and cursed between gritted teeth. He felt a trickle of blood run down his leg and into his boot. The mounted Turk who had shot him came in for the kill, his scimitar held high in one hand and his spent carbine in the other. The Irishman tried to backpedal but lost his balance. He fell backwards but managed to unleash his dagger and in the same movement skewered the rider's throat causing him to arch back and fall from his beast before he had a chance to bring his sword down.

Suddenly, the remaining British soldiers heard more carbine fire coming from behind them. They feared the worst believing themselves to be surrounded, waiting to be butchered, however it was the Ottomans who were falling to the ground. The soldiers spun around and saw a squadron of Hompesch's Horse coming to their aid. The cavalrymen set about the Turks with gusto, slaughtering all but one of them who cowered in a doorway pleading for his life. Suddenly his mouth opened, and his eyes widened in terror. He fell face down in the dirt, a knife protruding from between his shoulder blades. The avenger, an Egyptian child, not more than twelve, stood, mouth agape, in the doorway.

"Damnation, what's happened here?" asked the captain of the Horse.

"The Turks, sir. They were slaughtering the villagers. We just happened to be here on patrol. They turned on us when we told them to stop," Corporal Schultz, a German Jager, replied.

"I see. Not a pretty sight. Men, see to the wounded. Bury those soldiers. Lieutenant Shields, take some men with you and round up the horses," Captain Ormrod ordered.

The traumatised villagers had now emerged from their hiding places. Some of the women were screaming and wailing or ululating at the side of their deceased brethren. Others had descended on the corpses of the Turks like pharaoh's chickens,

195

scavenging feverishly for loot. They ripped off the boots and clothes of the dead and emptied their pockets, leaving naked carcasses abandoned in the dirt. A village elder approached the captain.

"Thank you for your assistance, master. How can we repay you?"

"Feed my men and horses. We'll take what provisions you can spare and pay you for them. We need a cart to ferry the wounded back to Aboukir. But first we need to dispose of the Ottoman bodies. If you help us get the dead in your carts, we'll dump them in the Nile. You must not speak about this to anyone. Tell your people they can keep their booty, but they must hide it somewhere securely - everything, because the Turks may come searching for their men. Tell them the Bedouin may have taken them. Clean up the blood."

"We will do everything you have commanded, sir. Allah be with you."

79

The rickety cart bumped and rattled over the stony, sandy dirt tracks, the forlorn ass labouring in the sweltering late afternoon sun. Every jarring movement was felt by O'Rourke. The pain shot up his injured leg, but the discomfort was dulled somewhat by a flagon of henqet, which the villagers had produced as a parting gift. He shared the cart with two other injured comrades, one Italian and the other, Swiss. Torricelli, the Italian was in a bad way. He had been lanced in the side and was delirious with fever. The three casualties sweated profusely. O'Rourke swatted at the cloud of flies relentlessly swarming around them. The winged creatures were gorging themselves on the soldiers' makeshift bloody bandages, attempting to lay eggs in the festering wounds. It was late by the time they arrived at the hospital in Aboukir. The oppressive heat of the day had transformed into the chill of the night. O'Rourke and Helder were helped from the cart. Helder had suffered a bad concussion having received a blow to the head with a carbine, his head swathed in crimson bandages. They were all placed on stretchers. Torricelli, though, was dead on arrival unbeknown to the others. The two remaining casualties were transported to the marquee and were delivered into the care of the medics. O'Rourke was placed on a grimy straw mattress. Groans emanated out of the gloom. A doctor arrived to examine his leg, a female orderly in attendance. He did a double take as he recognised the attendant. It was the girl he had prevented from embarking on the boat to France. It was Sanura. He felt a pang of guilt and regret but felt relieved that she had been delivered into safe hands by the looks of things, for now. She recognized him, too. The doctor ordered her to remove the patient's pants. She held a knife in her hand and glared at O'Rourke. He gulped. His throat was dry. Then she grabbed O'Rourke's worn boot roughly. He yelped as the pain seared through his shin and calf.

"Easy, woman!" the surgeon growled.

She gave O'Rourke another dirty look and then proceeded to rip the fabric of his trousers exposing his dirt encrusted scarlet bandage. She was ordered to cut through the dressing. O'Rourke stiffened slightly but this time Sanura cut carefully through it. The surgeon examined the wound.

"The ball has gone clean through your gastrocnemius muscle, in other words, your calf, but fortunately missed your tibia and fibula. Hopefully, in time it should heal. No need to amputate at this stage. We're going to clean the wound and apply a new dressing. Here, have a swig of grog."

The surgeon passed a bottle of whisky to O'Rourke and then a small block of wood.

"Put that in your gob. This'll hurt."

The physician poured alcohol on to the wound making the patient stiffen. Then he started to clean the wound as carefully as he could. O'Rourke felt nauseous due more to the effects of the Egyptian beer he had gulped down on the journey than the pain in his leg. He spat out the wooden block and threw up on the blanket. The doctor ordered Sanura to clean it up, then O'Rourke passed out.

80

It was midday by the time the Irishman awoke. He had been in a deep sleep, exhausted by the previous day's events. The pain was still coursing through his limb, although it had lessened compared to the day before. He reflected on the unfortunate skirmish between two supposed allies. He thought about O'Hanlon, one of the few actual Irishman left in the brigade, one of his pals. Two orderlies passed carrying a stretcher with a legless corpse on it. He instinctively and tentatively reached down and touched his injured leg, relieved that it was still there. An orderly came over and placed a bottle to his lips. His swollen tongue cleaved to the roof of his dry mouth. The water was brackish, but it slaked his thirst, and he gulped it down.

"Are you hungry? Can you eat something?" the orderly asked.

The patient nodded his head. He was ravenous. The orderly returned with some sort of insipid goat stew that was more like a broth. The flies were swarming all over O'Rourke. The wounded sergeant spooned a mouthful of stew into his mouth. He was about to repeat this but first spat out a fly that had crawled inside his mouth. He nearly choked on another. He coughed it up with some bile. Despite the best efforts of the young Egyptian boys with feathers and palm fronds hired to flap away the ubiquitous insects, the flies incessantly congregated around the injured serviceman. He cupped the bowl of soup to his mouth and drank, chewing on pieces of fat and gristle and bits of vegetables whilst trying to prevent the creatures from crawling in the bowl again.

"Helder, the Swiss soldier, who came in with me, is he…"

"He lives. He had a nasty trauma to the head. He awoke this morning with a bad headache, nothing more."

"The other soldier, Torricelli…"

"I'm afraid he was dead on arrival. My woman Sanura briefed me this morning when she came off duty."

"Sanura, is your woman? You have me to thank for that. I wouldn't let her embark on the ship to France. I feel bad. She has attended to me."

"Do not feel bad, my friend. I will take better care of her. She has a job here. She is safe. I will take her back to Malta with me when we leave Egypt."

"Make sure you take her hand in marriage before the evacuation otherwise I might have to stop her again."

The orderly laughed. "I, Gabriel Zammit, former inmate of the Valletta Slave Prison, do hereby swear that this woman, Sanura will become my wife. Thanks for the advice. Get some rest now."

"Can you do me a favour and scratch my foot? The one with the wound on. It's itching like hell. So is my face."

"Ah, mosquito bites. I'll apply some citrus lotion then I'll put your sock back on.

I'll put some on your face as well. You look as if you have the measles."

A surgeon called for the orderly.

"I have to go now. I'll be back shortly. We have a plague victim that we have to remove to another tent. I believe November is the start of the plague season. This land is cursed. Nothing but blains and boils and buboes."

"And frogs and flies and fleas," O'Rourke added, scratching his groin. "Damned lice, damned mosquitoes, damned gnats, locusts and even crocodiles!"

"Damn all these diverse murrains of biblical proportions. That's it! The book of Exodus, you see. God inflicted Egypt with all these calamities to coerce the Pharaoh to release the Israelites from servitude!"

"Orderly, now!"

"Yes sir!"

"Don't worry about the plague victim. More people die of dysentery here, or amputations. How is your leg, by the way?"

"Thanks for the vote of confidence, my friend!"

81

Over the next few days O'Rourke's fears were realised and Gabriel's jocular remark backfired as the wound became infected. He was feverish. His leg became swollen through inflammation. The pain was unbearable. He feared for his leg and his life. Despite the best efforts of Sanura, Gabriel and the surgeons, the wound was exposed time and again to greenbottle blowflies laying maggots. Miraculously, the swelling subsided over the next week and the lesion began to heal. His joy was tempered somewhat by the news that Helder had been stricken with dysentery and had died. He himself had now been afflicted by ophthalmia that made him febrile again. His eyelids were now swollen, and his vision was impaired. The bacterial conjunctivitis made his sockets explode with pain as if someone had thrown scalding water in his pus-secreting eyes. He could barely open them. The first time he had been able to exit the tent on crutches he was driven back by the sunlight stinging his milky eyeballs. He had begun to hate his sojourn in Egypt. However, as luck would have it, the opportunity arose to leave North Africa for good. It came from a surgeon who came to see him one day.

"Sergeant, I have secured a berth for you on one of the navy's ships returning to England. We have begun the evacuation of our own troops now that the French have all left. Anyone incapacitated but otherwise healthy can leave. This will alleviate our beleaguered hospitals here and elsewhere. You must collect your effects and report to the dockside at Alexandria, Tuesday of next week. You are to sail on the frigate *L'Égyptienne*. We will arrange for transportation to your bivouac. From there you have to make your own arrangements to get to the port."

O'Rourke's spirits rose. Gabriel was in attendance. He was visibly pleased for the soldier.

"Sergeant O'Rourke, can you take a letter to my parents in Valletta? The fleet will, I assume, berth there en route to England for a few days, to take on supplies, weather permitting."

"Of course, I will. Wherever we dock, Malta, Sicily, Menorca, I will ensure that your letter will reach home. It's the least I can do my friend, since you and Sanura nursed me back to health."

"Come, I will seek out your transport. Take this eye-patch. You might need it if the sun still harms your eyes."

"My vision is better in my right eye but alas, with the left one, it is still blurred to the point that I am virtually blind."

"I have known patients whose vision has been restored months later, so have faith, sir. By the way, make sure you tell everyone you do not have the measles, just mosquito bites on your face, otherwise the authorities might send you back here and you'll miss your departure!"

201

"To be sure, I'll tell them!"

Gabriel helped his patient out. O'Rourke limped out with his crutch and recoiled at the dazzling sunlight. Gabriel placed the patch over the Irishman's milky eye. A trap drew up. The driver, a corporal, jumped down.

"Orderlies!" shouted the man. "At the double!" The corporal unlocked the cart flap revealing two injured soldiers, covered in blood and flies. One was unconscious. The other was a walking wounded case, an arm suspended in a rudimentary sling, a bloodied rag held to the spot where his ear had been. The unconscious casualty had reddened bandages wrapped around each stump of his fingerless hands. Two assistants arrived with a stretcher and ferried the casualty inside the marquee. Gabriel assisted the other.

"Bedouin buggers!" the corporal spat. "They captured five stragglers. Tortured them all. A Hussar patrol came across them by chance and managed to save these two. They slaughtered the Arabs, good and proper."

Gabriel returned with some Egyptian boys and ordered them to swill the interior of the cart down with sea water.

"Your transport awaits you, sir. Driver, can you take sergeant O'Rourke back to his camp?"

"Thirty minutes, my good man. I need some refreshments and a shit."

O'Rourke took the opportunity to bid farewell to the surgeons, orderlies and his fellow invalids, conscious of the fact that this would be the last time he would see most of those maimed, given the mortality rate of the sick or injured. He embraced Gabriel and took possession of the letter.

"Send my regards to Sanura."

"I will. I don't think it will be long before the main body of troops are withdrawn. Perhaps we will meet up some time in Malta."

"Maybe. I have not decided where to convalesce yet. I will consider it on the voyage home. I can't return to France, they'd guillotine me! Perhaps Malta, Gibraltar or maybe England. Or perhaps I'll go back to Ireland. That's if I survive the voyage!"

He struggled into the back of the cart and the driver, having been 'refreshed', returned. He carried a wooden crate of supplies to be transported to the hospital in Rosetta. He loaded it on to the cart, jumped into the driver's seat and cracked the whip and urged the ass on its way.

82

They arrived at the base a few days after, having been diverted to Rosetta's hospital to deliver the medical supplies. Their course ran parallel to the great river along the verdant banks of the Nile. They fed on figs, bananas, olives, dates, and oranges and passed fields of rice, barley, and wheat.

O'Rourke was welcomed back with open arms. His commanding officer checked regularly on his well-being when he was in a febrile state and reckoned he wouldn't pull through. He was delighted to see him. He was also aware of the fate of Helder and Torricelli. He told O'Rourke that the regiment would be leaving a few months later in his estimation, if not sooner.

Early the following morning, O'Rourke hired a cart and set off towards Tell Mutubis to recover his booty which he had hidden near a limestone block amidst the ruins of the ancient settlement. He returned to the camp with a goat, having exchanged it for a Mameluke dagger with a fellahin, providing him with an excuse for his unannounced disappearance after the lads had poked mullock at a previous effort to forage for food. After enjoying a last supper with his comrades, he set off to Alexandria accompanied by the same corporal he arrived with, Corporal Burke. The regiment's good wishes were ringing in his ears and his booty was concealed in a sack with his meagre belongings. Two bits of human cargo made up the load. Two soldiers, one, a Corsican Ranger suffering from heatstroke and dehydration diagnosed with rat-bite fever, the other, a sepoy on secondment with suspected typhus. Both to be delivered to the hospital in Rosetta.

83

Liverpool. Present day.

R andy was shaving, slurping a cup of coffee and checking his mobile, when it rang. He was due to rush out for a waiting taxi to recover his car which he had left at the Wheatsheaf. It was Edmund Parkes. Leahurst had been on the line asking if anyone knew where Viren was as he was due to take a seminar with his class of students. They could not contact him. Nor could anyone contact his housemates. The Principal thought maybe Viren, and the others had stayed overnight at Randy's if they were out celebrating their discovery somewhere late in Liverpool. Viren had called his boss, Joan Muir, to let her know of the find and told her that they were having a jar or two to celebrate, in contravention of the agreement not to advertise the team's success. Randy confirmed that they had stayed put in the Wirral pub and he had left all three housemates in the Wheatsheaf when he left at 10pm in a taxi. The others returned to Liverpool at various stages of the evening. Dr Parkes called Joan Muir to relay this information. She assured him she would send a member of the Leahurst staff, a friend of Viren's, who lived nearby and who had a spare key, to the house in Ness, to inquire about their whereabouts. However, Randy arrived there first. The taxi dropped him off in the pub car park. He nipped over to the cottage and hammered on the door. The curtains were still drawn, and the house was in darkness. He rang the bell. There was no answer. He laughed, assuming that Viren and Stuart and his girlfriend Clare had taken the celebrations too far and had ended up comatose. He felt slightly guilty as he knew Viren was in for a reprimand. Randy returned to his car and jumped in as he was late for the meeting already. Thirty minutes later, en route to the meeting at the university, he took a call. It was Dr Parkes again.

"Randy, I've got terrible news...the..."

The phone cut off as Randy was swallowed up by the Kingsway Mersey Tunnel. The traffic was particularly slow that morning rush hour as it crawled through the tunnel, adding to Randy's frustration. He wondered what the hell Edmund had been talking about. Was he going to be sacked for being a bad influence on Viren or for some other unknown misdemeanour, or made redundant? Or was it something related to the discovery? As soon as his car emerged from the tunnel, he phoned Edmund. It was engaged. More frustration. Then a moment after, it rang again. It was Dr Parkes. Randy responded on the hands-free.

"Edmund, I got cut off. I was just entering the Mersey tunnel. I didn't hear a word. What's happened?"

"It's terrible news Randy. It's Viren!" He paused. "He's been murdered!"

204

"He's what? Murdered? My God!" Randy pulled over in a lay-by.

"He was killed sometime last night, they reckon. So were his housemates."

"Oh, my God! No!! What the -"

"Joan Muir sent Dave Trellis over to Swan Cottage earlier to find out where he was. He knocked but there was no answer. Dave had a key and tried it in the lock but there was something blocking the door. The curtains were drawn but there was a slight gap at the top. He had the shed key with the front door key, so he opened the shed and found a ladder in there and used that to peer through the gap. Then he saw an arm draped in blood. He called the police straight away. They broke in and found Viren, Stuart and Clare tied to chairs, dead, their throats cut. They had been badly beaten."

"Jeez! I can scarcely believe it. It's obviously something to do with the find. We are going to tell the world this morning about it. Why couldn't they have just waited?"

"I know. It's dreadful. I'm beginning to wonder what we have got ourselves involved in. I'll see you at the meeting. I just wanted to forewarn you. Expect a visit from the police when you arrive, as you were one of the last people to see them alive. Once again, my condolences. I know you and Viren were good friends. I'll let the others know."

Randy stared out of the windscreen, dazed. The rush hour traffic snaked past. He wiped away tears. The euphoria and excitement of revealing the lion clue had instantly dissipated, replaced by feelings of fear and despair. He eventually turned the key in the ignition and sped away.

The group sat in silence punctuated only by sobs and sniffles. Jules consoled Randy while Fatima comforted the sobbing Lydia. Dr Parkes arrived. He asked if Team Quest wanted to disband. Despite the horror and heartache everyone felt, they decided to carry on. Dr Parkes vowed to increase security around the group before he left for Leahurst. He had failed thus far to employ anyone else to protect the team other than Paul, for Jules. Penny arrived soon after, having heard the awful news. She gave Randy a big hug. They all sat in silence for a while. Gradually, the conversation turned towards the lion image as the quest to find the tablet now seemed more important than ever.

"So," Jules said sniffling, dabbing her eyes. "What links do we have with a lion?"

"Well, there's four big hulking ones outside St George's Hall. They're the ones that come to mind immediately," Penny tendered.

"Lydia, when exactly was St Georges Hall built?" Jules asked.

"Er, just a moment." She blew her nose gently, then tapped on her PC. "The foundation stone was laid in 1838 to commemorate the coronation of Queen Victoria," she confirmed reading from her PC. "Then there was a competition for a design of the Hall in 1839 won by Harvey Lonsdale Elmes. Construction began in 1841 and lasted until 1854. Gosh!"

"Anything about the lions?" Tom asked.

Lydia scrolled down. "Two of the four lions designed by architect Charles

Cockerell were sculpted in 1856 by W.G. Nichol and moved to their present position in 1864. I'm not sure about the other two."

"It's immaterial anyway because the timeline doesn't fit in with when the first letters were sent to Fesch. We're way out," Fatima said, eliciting a response from Tom.

"I was just wondering if the lions came from somewhere else, sculpted at an earlier date and placed there."

"Fatima's right," Randy said. "The first letter was dated 1811 and the second and third ones 1812, so we can most probably rule out St George's Hall. We're not thinking properly, obviously, given the circumstances."

"Any links to zoos?" Paul enquired.

"Well, there were always plenty of exotic animals arriving in Liverpool brought in by captains and ships' crews during those years but again, I think it was later, yes," Lydia replied, checking her laptop, "in 1833, Liverpool Zoological Gardens were established on West Derby Road."

"How about pubs?"

"What is it with you and pubs Simon? Have you given your new boyf, Tufiq, the elbow already? You hoping to meet someone else?" Tom joshed.

The others laughed bringing a moment of light relief to an otherwise sombre and downbeat ambience.

"That's not such a bad idea. There's the Lion Tavern, opposite the old Exchange Station on Moorfields," Paul chipped in, feeling more confident around the group."

"Let me have a look," Lydia said. "Hmm, I can't find a date for it but it's something to look into. Yes, I know the one, next door to the Railway. It's probably maybe a bit after the time period again."

"I seem to recall there was also a Golden Lion Tavern somewhere in Liverpool from that era. I remember a reference to it in an article," Penny recalled.

"There's one in Ormskirk. I used to hang out there as a student," Simon added.

"Here we go again!" Tom quipped.

"Ok, I'll check it out," Lydia responded. "I think we're all of the same opinion that the clues are most likely hidden around Merseyside."

"Damn," Tom said. "No more exotic trips. I was looking forward to our turn to go somewhere other than Old Swan."

"Well, you can check out the Ormskirk pub if it's the right era. Ormskirk's exotic," Jules said.

"Thanks, Jules," Tom said, feigning indignance.

"Penny's right, there was a Golden Lion Tavern, in Dale Street but I can't recall it being there now," Lydia said.

"Definitely not," Paul confirmed. "But that's a point we have to consider. If the clue was hidden somewhere in a building and it's already been demolished then we may not get any further than we have now."

"I think we need to draft in a Liverpool Blue Badge Guide. Those guys know their stuff, so we can pinpoint exactly where this tavern stood," Jules announced.

"Good idea. The council will recommend one," Penny added.

"If anything else comes to mind regarding lions, let me know," Jules said. "Fatima, will you contact the press to reveal the lion image asap? Tom and Simon, you check out Ormskirk. Lydia you do your thing. Penny, can you chase up the tour guide then and make arrangements for us to meet up later? Paul, Randy and I, we'll have to wait for the police to show up."

"Dr Parkes has asked me to follow him over to Leahurst, to liaise with Viren's folks and Stuart and Clare's next of kin. Shit! I'll be otherwise engaged with that," a subdued and disinterested Randy sullenly pronounced.

"That's fine, Randy. Take as much time as you need. No probs. Leave the rest to us, but the sooner we find the clues, the better, I think everyone would agree."

"You're right Jules. Just one more thing though," Penny said. "I'm confused. Didn't the letter state that each illustration would be linked to the last one? If so, where's the link between a swan, monster and lion? Jules? Anyone?"

"Well, the swan related to Swan Cottage as you know and the monster to Ness and...you're right Penny. Where does the lion fit in?"

"I think I know Jules," Paul volunteered. "On the information plaque in the Lady Lever, next to the painting of Lady Hamilton, it mentioned her birth name, Amy Lyon, of Ness."

"You're absolutely right Paul. Lyon with a y. It's a play on words. And of course, the drawing is of a lioness, to be precise," Tom confirmed.

"Good job, Paul!"

"Thanks Penny."

207

84

Armitage and Noades were the officers who came to interview Jules, Paul and Randy. They took statements. Whilst there, they paused as they watched the BBC Northwest News breaking the story about the lion image and the death of three individuals at Ness. The detectives also confirmed that their counterparts in Scotland had managed to dredge up the vehicle from the depths of the loch along with the remaining body. They had now identified the men as Magdy Habib and Adel Kemal, Egyptian nationals. They belonged to an obscure fanatical Coptic religious sect, the Sahidic Sons of St. Mark, an increasingly militant group, espousing violence to protect their religion from persecution and to preserve it from all threats. They were also awaiting the results of a ballistics test to check whether any of their weapons matched the one used to murder Frank and his cronies. Enquiries were ongoing with the Egyptian authorities as to whether the mysterious organisation had sanctioned their mission or whether they had been acting alone and whether any other hit squads had been commissioned to attack targets, with the Swan Cottage murders in mind. DCI Armitage also confirmed that Richard had been given bail but was the subject of a court order forbidding him to make any contact with Jules or approach her. All this was too much for Jules. After the detectives and Randy had left, she felt drained, so Paul took her home. Penny phoned to say that she had arranged a meeting with Blue Badger tour guide, Miles Rowson, the following day in the Liverpool Central Library at 10am. Jules, head pounding, took some paracetamol and had a long soak in the bath, soothed by aromatherapy oils. Then she put on her PJs and snuggled up to Paul on the sofa to watch a film, comforted by a tub of salted caramel ice cream. She awoke some hours later next to Paul, the two of them having dozed off on the sofa. Paul stirred, and feeling frisky, moved his hand to her leg. She placed her hand on his.

"Not tonight," she whispered. He understood. They ordered an Indian takeaway instead and were in bed asleep by 9.00pm.

85

The next morning Jules and Paul met Miles Rowson in the foyer of Liverpool Central Library. Paul recognized him straight away. He had seen Miles conducting private tours around Liverpool's historic Georgian Quarter and other places of interest and had sometimes earwigged as he shuffled around the city. He hoped and prayed that those down and out days were past. He had always been impressed by Miles's knowledge of Liverpool and his endless anecdotes. The thirty-something, balding tour guide exuded confidence and enjoyed impressing the ladies on his tours, but Paul sometimes found his manner arrogant and dismissive.

"Hi, Miles? I'm Julia Johnson. Jules."

"Ah! Hello! Jules! Nice to meet you. You're just as Penny described. Voluptuous!"

Jules blushed with embarrassment.

"Oh, thanks. I'll have to thank Penny for that description. This is Paul by the way."

"Hi. Hey, don't I know you? You look familiar. Maybe you've been on one of my famous Liverpool tours."

"Probably more than one."

"He's my other half," Jules said, smiling at Paul, nipping in the bud any unwanted attention from the geeky and slightly creepy Miles. Paul reciprocated the smile. He was not just a bodyguard. He was Jules's partner. That meant a lot to him, although she hadn't told anyone else.

"Right, I believe you wanted to know about the Golden Lion. Come on then, I want to show you something."

Miles strode away and led them into the beautiful rotunda that was the Picton Reading Room. A student on a table nearby coughed and the echo of the cough reverberated around the splendid cupola crowned library. Peering over his glasses, he surveyed the room, conscious that he had broken the near-perfect silence. Satisfied that no accusing eyes were focused on him, he returned to his studies. Paul was very familiar with the place. He used to spend hours in the warmth of the building reading newspapers, journals and books. Miles paused at one of the several cast iron spiral staircases gracing the library that led to the next level of bookcases which swept all around the reading room.

"After you," he said to Jules quietly.

"Thank you," she whispered.

Before Paul could move, thinking the act of kindness was for his benefit as well, Miles positioned himself between the two of them keeping his face uncomfortably close to Jules's pert backside clothed in figure hugging black slacks as they scaled the spiral steps. He ushered her along the narrow balcony to a section of 'local history' with Paul in their wake. Miles scanned a bookshelf and picked out a green weathered book. '*Liverpool*', by George Chandler. He checked the index, then

209

thumbed through the pages stopping at a coloured print of a painting.

"There we are. A reference to the *Golden Lion Inn*, Dale Street. Dated 1790. There were several taverns and inns on Dale Street probably catering for passengers awaiting or alighting from the stagecoaches. That's where they picked up or dropped off customers in Liverpool at that time."

"Do you know where it stood exactly on Dale Street?" Jules whispered.

"Oh, of course!" he said confidently. "Let's go."

He shoved the book back on the shelf and squeezed past Paul and Jules, too close to comfort, brushing her nipples.

"Oh! Apologies! It's a tight squeeze up here, is it not?" Miles said slavering.

Jules gave him a perfunctory smile and then rolled her eyes at Paul.

Miles went along the passageway and started down the spiral iron staircase. He turned around to talk to Jules and as he did, he tripped which sent him clattering down the steps. Jules burst out laughing. The acoustics of her laughter rippled round the quiet room. She started to mouth apologies to people who, disrupted by the noise, had glanced up and frowned, then buried their heads in their books and news journals. Paul managed to stifle his laughter until he got out of the reading room and then he let rip. Both of them were in stitches and had to apologize to the bemused and indignant tour guide. Miles, with a face like thunder, strode purposefully out of the library down past the World Museum and across to Dale Street with Paul and Jules in his wake. They were still trying to stifle their laughter but could not rid their minds of Miles making a complete tit of himself. Dale Street was one of Paul's favourite streets, not because it was gilded with several listed buildings like the Municipal Buildings and the Prudential Assurance Building, but because he had slept in most of the doorways. He could finally appreciate the architectural gems lining the street once more, seeing them from an aesthetical as opposed to a practical viewpoint. When he was down on his luck and, homeless, nothing mattered. Beauty did not exist. Colours were immaterial, except for one, grey. All he thought about was where his next meal was coming from and where he could bed down or take refuge for the night without threat of violence or abuse. The only other thing that troubled him was where to defecate. Miles paused theatrically, hand up in the air, in front of the Queens Insurance Building.

"Here we are folks. This is where the Golden Lion Inn was. I believe it was so named after a ship of the same name, that had originally been a French warship captured during the Seven Years War in the year 1749 by a Liverpool privateer. It was converted to a whaler."

"Wow! How do you know all this Miles?" Paul asked.

"It's in that book," he said phlegmatically. "Personally, I don't think you'll find what you're looking for here."

He glanced up at the elegant edifice now adorning the site.

"Built circa 1837. The six Corinthian columns are surmounted by a lion and a unicorn. Best seen from the other side of the road."

Paul and Jules looked at each other. They stepped across to the other side of Dale Street to peruse the lion. "Maybe we can get access to the roof," Paul said.

Miles joined them. "I don't know if the lion is an acknowledgement of the fact that the Golden Lion once stood on the same spot. It's Grade II. I can't see you getting permission to dig that up. Well, I have my own ideas as to where the next clue might be and yes, like many others, I'm out to find it myself."

"Happy hunting then," Jules said.

"Listen, I must shoot off. I've got a Confederate War Tour to do. There's a bunch of Yanks coming off a cruise ship in thirty minutes."

He held out his palm expectantly.

"Penny said you'd remunerate me."

"Oh, yes, of course."

Jules pulled a tenner from her purse and handed it over.

"Much obliged! See you soon. By the way, there was also a *Red Lion* inn on Dale Street once as well but I'm not sure where that was located."

Miles hurried off to the cruise terminal without so much of an acknowledgment of Paul.

"Easy money, eh?" Paul said.

"Hey," Jules responded. "That could be a good line of business for you. You know your way around Liverpool, and you speak French, Spanish and Arabic. Perfect for all the tourists."

"Would I have to be an arrogant know-all prat as well?"

"Probably. Miles could teach you."

"Over my dead body!"

"Probably not the best phrase to use in the current circumstances. Come on, let's see if we can gain access to the building."

211

86

Alexandria, Egypt, 1801

The Irishman watched from the deck of *L'Égyptienne* as a carriage drew up on the quayside at Alexandria. Out stepped Colonel Tomkyns Hilgrove Turner. O'Rourke observed the officer barking orders at some of his men who were in his wake in two other carts pulled by draught animals. They were joined by a few sailors from the ship. Then they manoeuvred something large and heavy out of a devil cart and onto the dockside, something wrapped in carpets. O'Rourke saw the captain of the captured French frigate descend the gangplank and greet the colonel. He overheard them say the large item was the Rosetta Stone, the granite slab he had helped secure in Alexandria alongside Turner. The master mariner shouted orders to the motley crew assembled on the quayside. There was a flurry of activity. The slab was bound and secured with ropes and winched on deck. Colonel Turner supervised the freight movement with the captain, then followed him aboard. Egyptian baggage handlers took up the rear with the officer's personal effects. The same baggage handlers who had assisted O'Rourke with his accoutrements. No one had paid much attention to *his* load. He was just another casualty being evacuated, one of many with various ailments and diseases from which most of the lumpers tried to steer clear.

As the frigate tacked out of the bay, Pompey's Pillar faded from view. The long voyage home was arduous and many of the diseased and infirm perished in the crowded and unsanitary conditions. The water was foul, and the salt pork and ship's biscuits were riddled with worms. O'Rourke, like many, could only eat them in the dark. He survived a bout of dysentery. The ship finally reached Portsmouth, England in the month of February 1802. Undernourished, with a patch over his milky and blurred eye, gums swollen and bleeding from the onset of scurvy, a picture of poor health, O'Rourke lethargically staggered down the gang plank, his knapsack on his back and the sack bearing his mementoes slung over his shoulder. He stood swaying on the quayside; the sensation triggered by *mal de débarquement*. He exhaled a fetid breath and walked away unsteadily, stumbling through the gathered throng.

87

It took six months of convalescing before O'Rourke fully recuperated from his leg wound. His eye though, was a different matter. The ophthalmia militaris had left the vision in his left eye permanently impaired. He chose to wear an eye patch. His right eye, although also being afflicted by the conjunctivitis, had fortunately been saved.

With the Treaty of Amiens ending the conflict between Britain and France, O'Rourke considered his options. He could return to his regiment in Malta or Menorca. However, his allegiance to his regiment had waned. The Dillons regiment had taken on a more cosmopolitan appearance with new recruits accepted from diverse countries and the Irish influence and camaraderie he had felt previously had gradually diminished. He could return to Ireland where he had family but the situation there was unpredictable and chaotic due to political unrest. On the other hand, unemployment loomed if he stayed in England with regiments returning from Egypt being disbanded. Some of the military had been employed to quell social unrest and disturbances caused by the Stale Bread Act which had forced up the price of bread. He had been fortunate to secure work for several months as a labourer on the construction of the Portsmouth Block Mills. However, his decisions were ultimately influenced by a woman he met in Portsmouth one day. Kitty Steers had travelled from Liverpool, where she lived, to Portsmouth to visit the grave of her deceased husband John Steers, a sailor who had fought at the Battle of the Nile with Nelson. Steers was one of the casualties, wounded on board Nelson's flagship, *HMS Vanguard*, during the naval engagement which decimated the French flotilla, isolating Napoleon in Egypt and securing the Royal Navy's dominance of the seas for years to come. Kitty was at the graveside of her late husband who had succumbed to his injuries. He had returned from Sicily where he had been convalescing but fell ill on the *Vanguard's* journey to Portsmouth and subsequently died on the day of arrival. Kitty, in the two years since, had never been able to journey south to pay her respects to her deceased husband, through lack of funds until her new employer offered to pay her expenses. She was in the Naval Cemetery in Gosport when she was set upon by footpads as she was leaving. O'Rourke had come to her rescue with the aid of some other Irish recruits from the Ancient Irish Fencibles Regiment, friends of O'Rourke whom he befriended in Egypt. The group had seen the footpads off, killing one, and returning a purse to the stricken widow. She had been knocked off her feet in the fracas. Kitty's striking green eyes proved to be a magnet for O'Rourke. Even with his eye-patch his handsome rugged features still attracted the ladies, and the feelings were mutual when this chance encounter presented itself. O'Rourke escorted Kitty to the inn where she was staying. She was fatigued, shaken by her experience and sore from her superficial injuries and emotionally exhausted after her trip to the cemetery to see John's resting place. She thanked O'Rourke and he departed. The following day, after O'Rourke had a sleepless night, caused by thoughts of this captivating woman, he got up early and went to check on her well-being. Five minutes later and he would have missed her. She had checked out and was about to leave to catch the coach back to Liverpool. The coach was delayed in any case since a wheel had to be replaced so she had time to kill before its departure. Consequently, she agreed to take tea with her rescuer. It was the least she could do. He discovered that she had Irish and Scottish connections and he spoke freely about his career in the military. He told her about his family's Jacobite past. She was astonished that he had fought for both sides of the Franco-British conflicts. He, in turn, was enraptured by the tales of her gallant husband who had fought side by side with Nelson at the Battle of the Nile and other naval conflicts. He also expressed interest in her upbringing, in Scotland and Ireland, the daughter of a soldier like himself who had settled in Liverpool and worked as a lumper on the docks until his death. She told him she was a seamstress. They both paused and reflected after a while. Both feeling that, with hindsight, it was perhaps inappropriate to have divulged too much information about their private lives to a complete stranger. Her recollections about her husband stimulated her emotions and she felt compelled to return to Haslar Cemetery, Gosport. O'Rourke arranged for a pony and trap to take them there. She located the grave again and O'Rourke remained with the driver whilst she stood alone in contemplation buffeted by a warm sea breeze. Having returned to Portsmouth, when the time came to separate, she felt a hint of regret that she had to leave, and he felt his heart miss a beat. She took a quill from the office of the coach company and scrawled an address on a piece of paper, and he likewise wrote down the address of his lodgings. He accompanied her to her coach departure point carrying her bag. Then helping her climb aboard, he bade her farewell. Her eyes locked onto his one good eye, and he held her gaze until a pang of guilt forced her to avert her eyes. The coachman cracked the whip and the horses responded, the carriage wheels crunching over the stones and spraying muddied rainwater onto the boots of the Irishman. He continued to wave until the coach disappeared around a corner.

214

88

As the months rolled by, there was a flow of correspondence between Seamus and Kitty. As predicted there had been a spike in unemployment in the country due to the returning soldiers from the Egyptian campaign and O'Rourke's finances were now dwindling since the work at the docks had ended. He had sold some trinkets and rings he had acquired in Egypt to maintain a decent standard of living but now needed to earn a wage, so he decided to head for Liverpool. The town was an obvious choice. He was eager to see Kitty again and he hoped to gain employment there. The town's prospects were on the rise. Before he left though he had one more thing to do. It was evening by the time he reached the cemetery. With his lantern he located John Steers grave and began to dig. The ground was freezing over on the surface but not enough to prevent him from penetrating the earth below with his spade. He dug at the foot of the grave to a depth of half a metre and extracted a sack that contained the relic, some other trinkets and jewellery and a few Mameluke weapons that he had confiscated. The light of the lantern captured his frosty breath as he exhaled. He spoke softly.

"My apologies for disturbing you, John Steers. I will take care of Kitty for you. You were a good man. She will not live a life of destitution. I give you my word."

He took out the last of the jewellery, trinkets and weapons and returned the sack containing the artefact to the disturbed grave. He made good the soil and crept away in the cool night air, knowing he would be Liverpool bound the next day. Until he could identify a safe place in Liverpool to stash the relic he was reluctant to take it with him. His plan was to return sometime in the near future.

It was April 1803, when Seamus O'Rourke first set foot in Liverpool. He climbed down from the coach, his backside and limbs still aching from the cramped conditions he'd endured. His boots were squelching in the muddy slush. It was cold and sleeting. He stretched his frame and then patted the snorting horses as he waited for his luggage to be offloaded. He pulled up his greatcoat collar and fastened every button to keep out the chill. An icy wind was whipping off the river Mersey causing a frisson down his spine. A phalanx of ragged, scarecrow-like urchins loomed out of the sleet like deathly apparitions and surrounded the carriage hounding the new arrivals, jostling with each other, imploring the newcomers to choose them to assist in transporting their baggage.

"Hey lad," O'Rourke addressed a small, emaciated urchin who had been crowded out by the older ragamuffins. "Can you show me the way to Hackins Hey?"

He flipped a coin to the shivering lad.

"This way, sir!"

O'Rourke's jute sack had just been passed down to him from the top of the carriage. The young boy, feet wrapped in rags, motioned to take it off him.

"It's alright, lad. I'll take that. Just show me the way."

O'Rourke heaved his knapsack onto his shoulders and followed the child. The lad trudged through the slush and sleet. He took his customer along the length of Dale Street and paused at a narrow thoroughfare.

"Hackins Hey, sir!" he said, shaking with cold.

"Thank you boy!" The Irishman reached into his knapsack and pulled out a hunk of bread and piece of cheese and handed it to the waif. "Here."

"God bless you, sir!" the lad said, tucking the bread into the inside of his shirt. He walked away taking only a few steps before savouring the irresistible lump of cheese. He devoured it in an instant. O'Rourke walked up the street and stopped outside a public house, reading its name, Ye Hole In Ye Wall. He had arranged to meet a friend, Frederick, inside. They had met at Aboukir Bay. Frederick Kennedy had served with the 8th (Kings) Regiment of Foot and now worked for his uncle who was the proprietor of the establishment. He had told O'Rourke to look him up if he was ever in Liverpool. The Irishman entered. The smoke from dozens of clay pipes invaded his lungs, causing him to cough. A welcome roaring fire was emitting a furnace of heat. He peered around in the dim, smoky gloom. Some of the patrons glanced up from their ale. There was a raucous atmosphere. The patrons were a mixed bunch of mostly mariners and merchants grouped around tables. Prostitutes sat on the knees of some of the sailors, from time to time wrestling themselves out of the grip of a potential punter only to fling themselves at another. O'Rourke spotted Frederick pouring ale into tankards at the bar and passing instructions to serving maids. He approached him.

"Now, then, sir, I'll partake of a tankard of your finest Liverpool ale!" shouted O'Rourke through the din. Frederick did not look up at first since he was busy pouring beer from a keg. O'Rourke raised his voice. "Sir, I said I'll partake of…"

Frederick cut him short. "I heard you the first time, sir." He then looked up and saw his friend in front of him beaming, his grin as wide as the Mersey.

"Seamus O'Rourke! Ha! Ha! My God! I didn't recognise you with your eye patch. My good fellow! It's great to see you!"

"And you my friend. I'm making good my promise to come up to Liverpool!"

Frederick poured him a flagon and escorted him to the snug where it was quieter. A few merchants were in discussion, seated in a corner.

"I've not been here that long myself. The regiment was posted to Gibraltar after Egypt, and I've just recently returned. There's rumour of war again. Old Boney's been ranting on about those caricatures in the English press. Ha! Ha!"

"I know. The whiff of invasion is in the air. Everyone's paranoid down south. Talk of conspiracies abound. It won't be long before the regiments are mobilised again. I may have to take the King's shilling anew!"

"There's turmoil and upheaval throughout the land. The riots in Wiltshire and Yorkshire have prompted fears of a Jacobin revolution in England. Those gentlemen there have been debating the current status quo daily for the last few weeks. Although we are laughing about it now, Napoleon could launch another invasion of

216

Ireland and then Liverpool's commercial activities would be vulnerable so they're taking measures to protect their interests. They're very serious about this. Anyway, enough of this pessimism. What brings you to Liverpool?"

"I'm looking to stay here for the foreseeable future. I need to find some work. I've got some private affairs to attend to also."

"Hmm, jobs are scarce here as well. There's plenty of unemployed mariners at the moment, as you can see. Listen, you can take a room upstairs for the time being. I'll arrange it with my uncle, the landlord. Wait here."

Frederick disappeared but returned five minutes later.

"All arranged. Drink your ale and I'll show you to your quarters."

89

The next morning O'Rourke awoke with a pounding headache. Frederick had been able to spend the evening with his friend and introduced him to some acquaintances. A raucous, ale infused night was had by all. After a hearty breakfast and some strong coffee, O'Rourke felt reasonable, although a bit weary. He took the piece of paper with Kitty's address on it out of his coat pocket and left. He returned to the coach terminus and looked around. It was a cold crisp morning. The overnight snowfall had stopped. He exhaled and the water vapour in his breath condensed into a cloud in front of his face. There were no coaches departing or arriving. He walked down towards the Mersey cautiously. The broad river was crammed with marine craft of all types, tacking up and down the watercourse and George's Dock was a forest of swaying masts. He found the person he was looking for sitting, curled up in a doorway, knees drawn to his chest, wrapped in a ragged blanket. He tapped him with his boot.

"Hey, lad. Wake up."

The lad jumped up with a start, thinking it was the shopkeeper come to open his premises. He would normally be woken with an unwelcome and unwarranted beating about the head.

"Oh, it's you, sir." O'Rourke read the address to him.

"Do you know where that is, boy?"

"Quite, sir. Would you need me to guide you there?"

"Indeed so. Here, take this." O'Rourke handed him another chunk of bread and a piece of salted pork.

The child thanked him and ate ravenously. Then they set off for their destination. They trudged back up Water Street and onto Dale Street. The boy led, stamping his feet to get his circulation going. It was a good start to the day for him. He had temporarily suppressed the constant, gnawing hunger in his belly. He had not been beaten about the head by an irate shopkeeper or kicked by a constable. He did sport a black eye though that he'd received from another urchin, a brute, a bully who had seen him place the bread he had received from O'Rourke in his shirt the evening before and had violently wrenched it off him. He hopped and sprang about frivolously like a playful kitten in front of O'Rourke, trying to get warm.

"What's your name, lad?"

"Francis, sir," he said, rubbing his icy bare hands together.

"Don't you have any family to look after you?"

"No, sir. My father died in the West Indies of yellow fever. He was in the marines. My mother passed away in the workhouse not two months ago, of consumption. I prefer it on the streets, although it's extremely dangerous, as you can see, sir." He pointed to his bruised eye socket. "Are you a soldier, sir?"

"Yes, I am or was a soldier."

They walked up together to the verdant pastures of Islington now carpeted in a thin layer of snow, passing drovers, farmers and pedlars taking their beasts, produce and wares to the various town markets.

"That's the site of the Gallows Mill, sir, where the Jacobites were hung."

O'Rourke laughed. "What do you know about Jacobites, boy?"

"They were Papists, sir. They wanted to restore the House of Stuart to the throne."

"Ah, that's where you're wrong, Francis. There were Protestants involved in the movement as well. One day I'll give you a history lesson on it."

"Are you one of them, sir?"

The Irishman's set expression provided the answer for Francis.

"Do tell me more, sir."

"Another time, perhaps. What's that over yonder, lad? Those arches," O'Rourke said, changing the subject.

"That's the Fall Well, sir. The stream we've just crossed feeds into it. It's the main water supply for the town, sir. And further yonder is Mosslake Fields. It's a marshy area that they want to drain to construct more dwellings. More elegant houses, like on Rodney Street, sir. It's all part of the Great Heath. That's what we're going to cross now, but it's smaller now compared to what it was a few years back."

"And what's that place on the ridge?"

"Everton village, sir. Nice view from the top. Nice place to go and visit."

The two reached their destination forty minutes later after a walk uphill that was quite a struggle, the icy conditions causing them to slip and slide.

"Here's the street, sir. Shall I wait for you, sir?"

"No, that's ok. Here Francis. Thanks again for your help."

O'Rourke placed a coin in the child's palm and bade farewell to him. Francis smiled then turned and slid along an icy stretch of the cobbles, grinning to himself as he tried to negotiate it.

O'Rourke stood outside the residence for a minute to regain his composure. He was apprehensive. He did not know what to expect. He had not even told Kitty he was coming to Liverpool. Perhaps, he wouldn't be welcome. Maybe she had another suitor. He knocked on the door and a maid answered soon after. It was Kitty. She stood there astonished. He gawped at her unable to think of anything to say. She appeared more beautiful to him than he had originally perceived. She had told him previously she was a seamstress by trade, and it just took him aback momentarily to see her dressed in a parlour maid's outfit.

"Good morning, Kitty Steers," he finally said as he swallowed hard.

"Mr O'Rourke! Ye god's! It's you! What are you doing here, in Liverpool?"

"I'm seeking work up here."

"You mean, you're staying, here, in Liverpool?"

She could not contain her excitement. She lunged towards him from the step, slipping on an icy patch. He just managed to catch her. They both wobbled, struggling to stay upright. They held on to each other trying to find their footing again. They both laughed once they managed to secure themselves. She hugged him and then suddenly remembering her decorum, straightened her outfit and blushed. All his nagging doubts about whether she might have found someone else dissipated in that special moment.

"Kitty, who's at the door?" someone barked. "No hawkers today. Tell them straight."

"Who's that?" O'Rourke whispered.

"That's Mrs Wylie, the housekeeper."

"I thought you were a seamstress. I didn't expect you to answer the door dressed as a maid."

"I still do some work as a seamstress, but it was not enough to pay the rent after John died. The kind gentleman who owns the house offered me a position here in service to commence on my return from Portsmouth. He was my benefactor. His wife told him about my dilemma, and it was he who paid for my trip. John knew him when he was a mariner, before he enlisted in the navy. The gentleman of the house has many business interests and shipping is one of them. John worked on a vessel he owned. We used to rent a two-roomed basement in one of his properties. Listen, I can't talk now. I get an afternoon off tomorrow. I can meet you then."

"For sure. Where shall we meet?"

"Outside St Nicholas's Church. Down by the quay. One o'clock. Don't be late."

She stepped back into the house at the reproach of her superior and waved him away with a smile. He reciprocated then slipped on a patch of ice, causing her to double up in fits of laughter. He got up gingerly, embarrassed but amused all the same, pleased he had not injured himself and happy that he had brought so much joy into the life of the widow. He struggled to gain his footing, hearing more laughter behind him. A child's tittering.

"Ha! ha! Are you alright, sir? I thought I'd wait a while to see that things were fine with you. The lady, she's beautiful, sir. I'll show you around town, sir. I'll show you St Nicholas's Church where you have to meet at one o'clock on the dot tomorrow, sir."

"What? You cheeky imp Francis! You've been eavesdropping as well!"

The Irishman picked up some snow, moulded it into a ball and hurled it at the youngster who tried to dodge it with some nifty footwork, but Francis's legs buckled as he stepped on a sheet of ice. He was sent sprawling in the crusty snow, his cap dislodging from his black, lank-haired head. The two of them laughed until they ached, then together, they set off back to the town centre carefully negotiating the carpet of snow and sporadic patches of ice.

90

A brisk icy wind whipped off the Mersey. O'Rourke waited, huddled in his greatcoat, standing in the grounds of St Nicholas's church sheltering behind the walls from the cold that had seeped into the marrow of his bones. The wind rattled noisily through the forest of sails in St. George's Basin. Carts laden with barrels and crates ploughed along the Goree Causeway and up Chapel Street. Beasts of burden were urged on by the whip. O'Rourke stamped his freezing feet. He was about to see if he could seek refuge in the church when he felt a tap on his right shoulder. He turned and there was Kitty, her green smiling eyes shining bright, wrapped in her overcoat, her dark locks tucked under the bonnet that was tightly secured around her elfin-like, ruddy face.

"Ah, there you are!" O'Rourke cried.

"Good afternoon, Mr O'Rourke. I hope you've not been waiting too long. I had to run an errand for the good lady of the house. I'm sorry I'm a bit late."

"It's no problem. I took the opportunity to stroll along the docks asking the foremen for work. They said there's no chance unfortunately. I'm at the back of the queue with the other ex-redcoats. Sailors and locals are chosen first. Never mind. I'll worry about that another day. Where shall we go?"

"The Folly Fair is on today, being Easter. It'll be on for the next few hours. We need to walk up to Islington. It's a tad warmer up there, away from the waterfront."

Kitty linked arms with her escort. They both smiled at each other and set off. Kitty led him through the grounds of the church into Water Street, past the Tower Gaol, ignoring the cries and howls of inmates emanating from deep within its dark and dank recesses. Then they headed along Dale Street, chatting the length of it. They passed St. John's Church behind the Infirmary on Shaw's Brow. Beyond were limekilns, and in the distance, several mills and the pleasant patchwork of fields and gardens of Islington, with its paucity of dwellings.

The Folly Fair was heaving. Amassed around an ad hoc cockpit was a raucous crowd of cheering people eagerly watching the outcome of a fight between two fighting cocks. Laughter, encouragement and curses, could be heard from the punters, the dénouement of the fight, by the sounds of it, in the balance. Others were crowded around the bear-garden arena absorbed in the bear-baiting contest that was taking place, roaring on Old English bulldogs as they ferociously attacked the poor, trapped, chained bear which was tethered to a stake. They paused briefly to witness the sad spectacle of the bear being prodded by a sharp stick to goad it into some form of retaliation. Neither of them classed this as entertainment. They walked away appalled and instead ordered a drink each from a stall. O'Rourke chose a flagon of braggart and Kitty, a lemonade. He was about to quaff some braggart when he was barged into by a drunken lout, one of several obnoxious characters

221

staggering around, three sheets to the wind. The ale spilt over his greatcoat. He frowned but kept his calm in the presence of the lady he was escorting. This cadre of uncouth oafs was oblivious to the attentions of another group of men who were following them from a distance. One he thought had the semblance of a rat, with his thin face and narrow eyes. This rodent-like character nudged one of his companions and indicated over to the Irishman. The other man shook his head, and they focused again on the group of boisterous boors pushing and elbowing their way through the crowd. O'Rourke perceived them to be members of a press gang biding their time. He determined to keep abreast of their movements since the rat-faced one had targeted him without him being aware that O'Rourke had noticed. He guided Kitty over to some booths to watch children trying to win prizes. They then watched a game of bowls and had a game of skittles in the skittle-alley. Due to the many leary characters roaming around, they decided to leave before things inevitably got out of control. Kitty took O'Rourke by the hand and pointed up the hill.

"Come on, Seamus. Do you like toffee and a nice view?"

"I do."

"Then let's go. In Everton village, on the heights, there's a shop that sells delicious toffees. They're my favourites."

They trudged up the hill and paused to take in the vista on Everton Brow. It was a clear day. The chill wind buffeted their ruddy complexions, and they gasped as they gulped in the icy fresh air. Dozens of foaming white wakes criss-crossed the river below them as ships of every description ploughed through the choppy waters of the Mersey. They could see Birkenhead Priory, the oldest standing building in the area, situated to their left on the banks of the waterway, on the Wirral side. The new windmill, its sails churning, sat atop Bidston Hill also located across the Mersey and down below, on their side of the river, was the burgeoning sprawl of Liverpool. The church spires of St Nicholas and St Peters and the dome of the Town Hall with Minerva resplendently poised on its summit, all prominent landmarks, could be easily picked out. More churning windmills stretched across the fields of Islington and beyond to the Great Heath in the distance, where new dwellings encroached. The snow-capped peaks of North Wales formed a backdrop to the panorama. Kitty and Seamus only stood there for a few moments for fear of turning into frozen statues. They headed for Molly Bushell's toffee shop. After gorging on Everton toffees, they went to a tea garden for refreshments and to take shelter from the elements. The skies darkened so O'Rourke escorted Kitty home. He wished her a pleasant evening, placed his hand softly against her rouged cheek and drew her body gently into his giving her a long, lingering kiss that stirred Kitty's senses. She pressed her body into his. O'Rourke held her firmly and whispered.

"Time to go in Kitty. You're freezing, my dear. The night is drawing in. I'd best get back before the footpads and scoundrels start crawling out from beneath the stones."

Kitty smiled and kissed him on the cheek, looking lovingly at him. He watched her disappear through the tradesman's entrance to make her way to the small attic

222

room she shared with another maid. The Irishman felt a strong desire in his heart and in his loins. He pulled the collar up on his greatcoat and disappeared into the fading light.

91

A week later, on Kitty's afternoon off, they met on the quayside. Their mutual sexual attraction was so great and irresistible that he whisked her back to Ye Hole In Ye Wall and spirited her up to his room, to cheers and catcalls from the punters. Although embarrassed, Kitty giggled. They made passionate love all afternoon, their groans of ecstasy drowned out by the lively ambience and music from below. Afterwards, they lay in bed reflecting. Kitty suddenly remembered something. Her new love interest had mentioned that he would have to leave the tavern soon. His money was running out and his friend could not engineer anymore free board for him. She sat upright, holding the sheet to her naked bosom.

"Seamus, I know the captain of a brig, the *Mary Lou*. She's a privateer. John sailed with her before he joined the marines. I can ask the captain, Bram Moorcroft, if he needs any additional hands. The ship, I believe, is at sea at the moment but on its return I will seek him out."

"That could be very helpful Kitty, thank you. Although I'm not much of a *matelot*."

"You'll learn quick."

"No doubt. It's not a slave ship, is it? Because I don't agree with that heinous barbarity. Besides, the sailors are treated worse than the cargo, I've heard!"

"What do you mean?"

"The value of a sailor is less than the value of a slave, I was told."

"My love, no one is treated worse than those savages. The conditions they have to endure. The *Mary Lou* was a former slave ship. A French ship. *L'Oiseau de Paradis*, the *Bird-of-Paradise*, captured in the Caribbean and renamed. John sailed to Africa on two occasions to fetch slaves. He said the conditions on board were horrendous. Men, women and children lying in their own excrement and vomit, chained together like fish laid out on a market stall, squashed together, side by side. What could be worse than that?"

"They're considered cargo. A precious commodity, like timber or spices. 'Tis indeed a wicked metaphor, I know. But that's why they're more important than your average hand. They represent money. A sailor is an expense, a cost to the merchant, easily replaced, dispensable, whereas a slave is an investment."

"These slaves are human beings just like us and should be treated like anyone else. They should have the right to live a life of dignity and respect like the people of these shores and the citizens of all countries."

"What? Like, the respect and dignity shown to starving beggars and waifs, young children I see every day eking out an existence on the frozen streets of Liverpool. Like the respect and dignity given to women in Cairo who were beheaded and thrown into the Nile for having a liaison with a Christian."

"Oh Lord! I must agree, *that* is uncivilized. Utterly shocking! You are right Seamus, absolutely right, we are blind to the needs of our very own."

"No one has any dignity and respect for these people. Dignity and respect only exist within the upper echelons of society. The only reciprocated dignity and respect are between one master and another, one rich merchant to another, one landowner to another, one gentleman to another. The rest of us are shit on the shoes of those who govern us."

"Language now, Seamus."

"Wherever people of low status reside, in a mud hut in the African jungle, in a workhouse in Lancashire, in a peasant's croft in Ireland, the difference in quality of life and existence is comparatively negligible."

"I imagine so."

"You do what you must to feed yourself and your family, to escape from poverty and its consequent depredations of disease. So, in Africa, for example, to survive, one village attacks the occupants of another village and sells those survivors they have not slaughtered into slavery. Elsewhere, one country invades another country and rapes it, plundering its riches, resources and produce, subjugating and impoverishing its people, causing untold misery and famine. Look no further than west of here to see the evidence."

"The country of your birth."

"War, pestilence, and famine is all the down trodden of this world have ever known. If you don't starve to death, you will die of a multitude of diseases like yellow fever, malaria, plague, consumption, syphilis and all manner of afflictions yet to be identified. Take your choice. If you survive pestilence and famine, there's always good old war to finish you off. This is the life the oppressed face on this earth today. Have always faced."

He paused.

"Seamus…"

He turned towards her and kissed her.

"We have fleeting moments of happiness, like this beautiful moment I've shared with you. But for the most part life is like a living hell. Our children die young, our women die in childbirth. Our backs are broken with the burden of work. Life is harsh for the underprivileged of this earth wherever they may be."

"I have to agree Seamus, life is harsh everywhere. But compassion for everyone and everything must start with us. It's our generation that must see what is just and what is evil. Slavery in whatever form is evil. Black slaves from deepest Africa, slaves from the Caucasus who have served the Porte for hundreds of years. Even the Cornish plundered and enslaved by the Barbary Pirates. If we accept slavery, then we in turn might be enslaved. This generation, our generation, has to break the chains as it were, once and for all."

"I understand your sentiments. The world is slowly evolving. More peasants have been rioting. People are demanding change, standing up for their rights. They want to see improvements in their daily lives. The authorities fear revolutionary ideals. The government has watched the turmoil in France with some trepidation. If they're not careful, the revolution will spread to England."

A moment of silence and reflection was shared between the two lovers.

"My dear Seamus. Have we just had our first argument as a couple?"

Seamus laughed and rolled on top of her naked body, kissing her gently.

Several days later Kitty took Seamus to the Golden Lion on Dale Street. The privateer had returned. She knew that John's friends gathered there. She asked Seamus to wait outside whilst she went in. She waded through the smoke-choked saloon and greeted a grey-bearded fellow, the bosun of the *Mary Lou*, Jock McGinty. She chatted to him, raising her voice amidst the din. She gestured over to the entrance and handed over a letter addressed to Captain Moorcroft. McGinty stood up and followed her outside where he met O'Rourke. They conversed. Jock invited him in for an ale whilst Kitty nipped to the White Cross market off Tithebarn Street for some victuals.

92

After another week and not before time, for he was about to leave the premises for good, a letter arrived at Ye Hole In Ye Wall for Seamus. He had paid for his room himself for several weeks so as not to take advantage of the generosity and good will of Frederick, but now he was down to his last few shillings. He opened the letter tentatively and to his delight and relief, Captain Moorcroft had invited him for a meeting with a view to joining the crew of the *Mary Lou*. When Kitty found out, she inevitably had mixed feelings. She had lost one husband, killed by the rigours of seafaring and did not want to lose another potential husband so soon after becoming his lover, but needs must. A job offer, however unappealing it might seem, could never be declined. It was a life-or-death choice.

O'Rourke went to meet the captain who was suitably impressed with him. The other hands had vouched for him, enjoying his company at the tavern. He was taken on and told that the brig would set sail one week hence. Captain Moorcroft graciously gave him an advanced wage to tide him over until departure, trusting Kitty's judgement that her new love interest was bona fide.

When the day came, Kitty stood at the Salthouse Dock. She was sad to see her Seamus go. They hugged and kissed and said their goodbyes just like all the other women bidding farewell to their loved ones, not knowing whether they would return. Although a tear rolled down Kitty's cheek, O'Rourke noticed a gleam in her eyes. She looked at him and spoke softly and nervously.

"I think...I think I am with child."

Seamus stood speechless. His mouth agape.

"Bosun!" he called. "What time do we sail?"

"On the next tide. Two hours' time."

O'Rourke approached the captain discreetly and spoke quietly to him.

"Captain Moorcroft, sir. Permission to get married, sir. Err, Kitty, she is with child."

Captain Moorcroft removed his cap and dusted a speck of dirt off it.

"Permission granted Mr O'Rourke. Be back within the hour."

O'Rourke thanked him, grabbed Kitty's hand, and started to drag her to a church, the Catholic Church of St Peter which was on Seel Street.

"Hold on," she said. "We need to marry in an Anglican church. Otherwise, our child will be considered a bastard and our marriage will be deemed illegal remember. We don't have time to marry in both a Catholic and Protestant church."

"We'll be lucky to get married at all at this rate. To Our Lady and St Nicholas then. Back to the port!"

The over-excited couple raced back to the dock and burst into the church and stopped suddenly. They had arrived in the middle of a funeral. The mournful congregation glowered in disgust. The couple made their apologies and backed out sheepishly. They waited impatiently outside. Luckily, the funeral ceremony ended soon after. A tearful widow drenched in black, accompanied by her family, filed out. Kitty and Seamus lowered their eyes. The other mourners cast scornful glances at them. Once the path was clear they ran into the church to accost the reverend and implored him to marry them on the spot. He told them he could not because he was about to administer the graveside blessing in the church grounds. Kitty unexpectedly produced a purse of money given to her by the kind lady of the house in the hope that she could get wed before the father of her expected child left Liverpool. The reverend's eyes opened wide when he saw the lucre. His green orbs spun around rapidly, chameleon-like, and satisfied no one else was present, he stuffed the purse inside his cassock. Then he ushered them up to the altar. He read them their vows in record time finishing breathlessly by saying, "I now pronounce you man and wife. You may kiss the bride."

Kitty and Seamus embraced gleefully. They were still embracing when the anxious clergyman unceremoniously bundled them out of the chapel and left hurriedly for the burial plot around the side of the church, blowing profusely.

93

The *Mary Lou* sailed on the tide waved off by the privateers' tearful women and children. They were heading out into the Atlantic and sailing to the West Indies. Captain Moorcroft ventured west in anticipation of the resumption of hostilities between Britain and France which everyone thought was inevitable. A letter of marque had already been drafted and submitted to the government by the ships' sponsors and the shipowner. The captain wanted to be in a position to claim prizes immediately, so he headed for Martinique. It was not long before Britain declared war on France in May 1803, fuelled by suspicions that Napoleon was still intent on invading England or Ireland. This news reached the *Mary Lou* when in port in Antigua. The vessel departed soon after, lying in wait for any French ship plying its trade. Two days later they managed to attack a French merchant sloop. They gave chase, firing cannonade, splitting masts and ripping gaping holes in its sails, scattering the French matelots who were trying in vain to retaliate with their own broadsides. The British privateer came alongside the commercial vessel and boarded it. O'Rourke and the others swung over on ropes, swords or pistols at the ready and overpowered the French crew with minimal casualties. Those put to the sword were tossed overboard, manna to the sharks. The sloop was found to have a valuable cargo of coffee and molasses and had set sail from Martinique. They imprisoned the crew in the hold and took the ship in tow back to the Leeward Islands. The *Mary Lou* participated in several attacks on the enemy in the ensuing months.

It was November 1803 by the time the *Mary Lou* returned to the Mersey, accompanied by the captured French sloop crewed by the privateers, both vessels laden with precious and valuable cargo that also included sugar cane destined for Liverpool's burgeoning sugar refinery businesses and palm oil for lubrication of the machinery of the Industrial Revolution. The purloined goods were offloaded on the docks and the manacled prisoners were escorted to the Tower Prison close to the dockside. O'Rourke received his pay and parted company with his crewmates after a flagon in the Golden Lion to celebrate their success. Then he headed for Kitty's place of work in a hired pony and trap. He was eager to see his wife and his baby. All he knew was that Kitty was due in November. He had prayed to God that mother and baby had survived the birth.

He reached the elegant mansion house and rapped anxiously on the door. He exhaled deeply. A maid came to the front door and smiled broadly as she recognised him. His one good eye lit up in response. He knew in that moment, that mother and baby were well. He thanked God that the maid, Elspeth, had not averted her eyes. She indicated for him to go around to the tradesman's entrance. He dashed around and waited for what seemed an eternity. The door eventually creaked open and there, stood on the threshold was Kitty overcome with joy, holding a little bundle that swaddled a tiny ginger-haired boy. Kitty wrapped her arm around her husband and smothered him in kisses.

"Seamus, thank God you've returned home safe! My love, meet your son, Patrick Seamus O'Rourke."

She passed the baby to Seamus. He held it up awkwardly in front of him. He stared at his baby son in disbelief and shock. His eyes became moist.

"My life has just changed!" he roared, gawping at his son and then his wife in turn.

"Look at that red hair!" he remarked. "Look, he's smiling at me."

The baby broke wind and they both laughed.

Kitty arranged with her employer for a lease on a cottage on lands he owned nearby. They spent the winter months there, happy in the knowledge that it was affordable owing to Seamus's earnings. It was the most fulfilling time of Kitty's life. Seamus had located Francis one morning huddled next to a young friend who had frozen to death during the night, unknown to the young waif. Francis was in a bad way too. Seamus had carried him to a cart and the carter transported them back to the cottage. Ever since, Francis, who was nursed back to health, after almost succumbing to the elements, had become a part of the household.

In the spring of 1804, O'Rourke returned to his duties on board the privateer. Kitty, Francis, and baby Patrick waved him off at Salthouse docks. The Caribbean beckoned once more.

94

Liverpool. Present day.

Paul and Jules spent the next thirty minutes on an impromptu tour of the Queen Insurance Buildings, accompanied by a manager who was only too happy to help. He recognized Jules from the TV. But they came away with no real encouragement that they could get permission to carry out any excavations in the basement. However, they did get the opportunity to inspect the lion and the unicorn at close quarters from the flat roof but there appeared to be nothing of interest. In the meantime, Tom and Simon had reported that the Golden Lion in Ormskirk didn't throw up anything of interest either.

"Hey, let's have an early lunch," Jules said. "Come on, one of my favourite restaurants Viva Brazil is in Castle Street. We'll dine al fresco. It's warm enough to sit outside. Watch your step," she warned as she held Paul's hand and dragged him across the junction. This sent her in raptures again as the memory of Miles falling down the spiral staircase came to mind. Paul laughed because she laughed. Despite everything that had happened Jules could still find time to feel happy, a result of Paul's positive influence. They were shown to a table outside the restaurant. They ordered coffee then selected their lunch of several different cuts of BBQ meat and salads. Paul sat so he could see both ends of Castle Street. The Town Hall to his left and to his right the law courts near to the Queen Victoria monument. He was in alert mode surveying the people nearby clustered around tables and scanning rooftops and possible points of attack. His military training was kicking in. It had served him well on tours to Iraq and Afghanistan. The trail of recent horrific events had heightened his senses making him aware that an attempt on their lives could be imminent and could come from anywhere. As he looked up, a *passador* arrived laden with succulent cuts of meat and salad dishes.

"When in Liverpool, always look up. That's what they say," Jules said, skewering a piece of lamb.

"Pardon?"

"Which building are you admiring? That's what tourists are told to do when they come to Liverpool. Look up. Look up at the marvellous detail on some of the buildings."

"Oh, yeah, some of them are spectacular on this street."

"I like that one over there, with the green onion-like dome on the roof. It reminds me of Egypt with all its minarets."

"Yeah, I suppose so. It reminds me of Iraq or Afghanistan. That building used to be a bank, the Adelphi Bank, I believe. If I'm not mistaken."

"How do you know that?"

"Oh, it's just something you pick up or hear other people mention when you're on the street."

"You're right, it says here on a website," she said, looking at her mobile, "that it was absorbed into Martin's Bank. Wow! Now Martin's Bank. Have you ever seen the interior of that place?"

"I've just seen a glimpse of it from outside. I've not been in it."

"It's a shame it's closed at the moment. You can see the interior in Fantastic Beasts and Where to Find Them."

"What?"

"It's a film. Lots of buildings in Liverpool appear in films because of the architecture. The film, have you not seen it? Oh, I don't suppose you have."

They both sat for a moment in silence enjoying their platters.

"Have you been inside the Town Hall?"

"No," Paul responded. "Never."

"Oh, I'll have to take you. They do tours. And tea dances and weddings. Maybe we can do that!"

Paul almost choked on his *frango com pimenta*.

"Do what?" he spluttered.

"A tea dance!"

"Oh, yeah. Sure. Sounds great."

"It's very grand in there. And there's a war memorial in there. You'd like that. With the names of the fallen of the Great War on it."

"Yes, that would be nice to see. The façade of the building is impressive too."

Jules gestured to Paul to take a look. He raised his head and peered to his left.

"The Queen's stood on that balcony, as well as our own royalty, the Beatles," she said.

"They have indeed," Paul replied. One of my favourite buildings. Lots of ornate stone carvings of figures and - animals!...Hey, I wonder if there's any lions up there? There are! There's one on top by the clock on the dome. Come on!"

He stood up.

"Hey, wait! Slow down a minute, Paul. Let's finish our lunch first. There's more delicious meats to come."

They finished their lunch, paid and walked towards the Town Hall, scrutinising the stone carvings on the exterior high relief friezes adorning what seemed like every niche of the Georgian façade.

"There's an elephant," Paul said as he strained his neck upwards.

"And a crocodile," Jules added as they turned around the right-hand corner of the building.

They moved back a few steps to study the stone sculptures on the roof, craning their necks. "There's more than one lion up there!" Paul shouted. They looked at each other. "When was the Town Hall built? Any ideas?"

"Off the top of my head I think late1700s or early 1800s," Jules replied. "I know there's been a few on this site. It burnt down once." She pointed. "Here's another lion in the frieze."

They moved slowly around the side of the Grade I listed building into Exchange Flags Square then Paul suddenly stopped dead.

"What's up?"

"I'd forgotten all about the detail on the Nelson Monument. Look!"

Jules peered at the large bronze statue dominating the central space of the square depicting a naked Nelson, one foot on an enemy corpse and the other on a cannon, surrounded by the figures of Victory, Death, a British seaman, and Britannia. Below him, encircling the stone base were four bronze statuettes of manacled prisoners of war, representing Nelson's great victories; the battles of the Nile, Copenhagen, St Vincent, and Trafalgar. The chains of the forlorn prisoners were held in place and secured above them by rings held in the mouths, of lions.

"More lions!" Jules blurted.

"It was erected circa 1812 or 1813. That fits our time scale as well."

"Now, how do you know that?"

"I remember Miles doing a tour here. I earwigged. He mentioned it. And it fits in of course with a Nelson link. First Lady Hamilton, then this. Come on, let's take a closer look."

They both started studying the bronze lion heads, disrupting, dodging and apologising to tourists who were taking photos of the listed monument. They were circling around the statue when Jules glimpsed something in the narrow gap between a lion's head and the granite plinth it was attached to, that was not apparent on the others. She ran round each one double-checking, cocking her head, courting strange looks and glares from by-standers and tourists as if she were demented. Paul laughed. She approached him excited by something.

"There's something behind one of the heads," she whispered.

"Don't be daft. You can't fit a leather tube behind there. It's minute."

"No, it's not a tube. It looks something like a thin leather wallet."

"Are you sure?"

"Yeah, have a butcher's yourself. It's barely visible. You need to get really close to see it."

Paul followed Jules to one of the lions' heads and, making sure no one was watching him, leapt onto the granite base and scrutinized the narrow aperture between the bronze and stone. Then he spotted the item in question. He jumped down immediately. Two female tourists frowned after catching him on the plinth. He ignored their indignant stares.

"You're right!" he whispered. "You could be on to something here. But how can we get access to it?"

"We'd have to contact the council or Historic England. On the other hand, it might be just something shoved in there by someone, like a bit of litter."

"There's no time to wait. If we let it be known that something's there, someone might grab it before we do, if there's a delay granting access to it. I'm coming back tonight, to get it."

"What are you going to do?"

"Prise the lion's head off or hammer it off, if I have to."

"Paul! You can't do that. That's vandalism."

"Well, if it saves lives then it's the right thing to do. Don't worry, I won't damage it too much. They can easily repair it. I'm not going to smash it to bits."

"Well, ok then. We won't tell anyone about this until we've got our hands on it, in case it turns out to be nothing. In the meantime, I'll get Lydia to check out the lions on the Town Hall and get Penny to ask her contact in the council for any possible access to the rooftop."

Jules rang Lydia first but there was no response. Next, she phoned Penny. Again, no response. Then suddenly she heard a ping. A text message appeared on her mobile. 'Soz. In a meeting. Talk later'. Jules texted back 'Soz. Is Lydia with you?' The response was monosyllabic. 'Library'.

"I might have guessed. Lydia's in the library. She lives in that place. She loves it. Penny's in a meet. Come on, we'll go back to the library. She's probably in the archive section."

The two of them made their way back along Dale Street. Ye Hole In Ye Wall, tucked away in Hackins Hey, just off the main thoroughfare, had a queue of people snaking around the corner waiting to go inside, who were being entertained by drag artists. They paused for a moment watching their antics and listening to their uproarious Scouse banter. Jules and Paul continued up the street.

"I used to study a lot in that library myself," Jules reminisced. "I loved it in there when it had the International Library. They had all the history and language books displayed along the shelves in a circular auditorium with a study desk running the full length of it."

"I used to study there, as well," Paul said. "It was nice and quiet. It was like a lecture theatre in there. Rows upon rows of seats all the way around it. It's the children's library now. I used to study up on the balcony as well, overlooking the central part of the library. It's a shame they did away with that part. They had solid, wooden bookcases all along that balcony, not the cheap looking flimsy plastic ones they have now. And they did away with the cast iron spiral staircases. Shame."

Jules laughed. "Don't mention those. You'll start me off again."

They arrived at the Central Library.

"Listen Paul, why don't you go and have a look in the archive section upstairs? I'll take a look in the Picton, otherwise if we both go in there, one look at you and I'll be in pleats. They'll throw me out."

Paul smiled. "Ok," he said. "See you in a minute. If I find her, I'll phone you."

Paul stepped onto the escalator in the atrium and was transported up craning his neck for any sign of Lydia as he went. Jules scanned the Reading Room through the window of the double doors at the entrance. Then she saw Lydia at one of the large communal desks. She turned to call Paul, but he had already disappeared. She went in. The officious female librarian seated at the desk by the door peered over her spectacles and gave Jules a dirty look, remembering the disturbance she and her friends had caused earlier. Jules looked towards her and placed her finger to her

234

mouth to acknowledge she understood the need to be quiet. She took one step forward. It was like treading on eggshells with every sound acoustically accentuated and feeling as if all eyes were on her. She reached the table. Lydia had her head buried in a book and didn't notice her at first. There were three others sharing her table. Two students of seemingly Middle Eastern descent, typing on their laptops and one black gentleman dressed in a suit reading a newspaper.

"Lydia," she whispered, conscious of her voice still echoing.

The black gentleman looked up from his journal and smiled as she spoke.

"Oh, hi Jules," Lydia whispered back.

"Is that your bodyguard?"

Lydia peered over her book and smiled at the black man.

"No," she whispered. "He's just gone for some lunch. He's a bit of a pain. He keeps wanting to chat. He keeps disturbing me. What's up?"

People sat on other tables started to look across to them as the whispered conversation began to echo around the rotunda. The two students were distracted from their studies also. They glanced up and frowned at Jules.

"I need you to check something for me."

Jules was conscious of everyone now staring at her. She developed a tickle in her throat, causing her to wheeze, making her as popular as halitosis in a Hazmat suit. Then her phone rang. She'd forgotten to set it to silent mode. She rummaged around for it in her bag and switched it off, mouthing an apology to the librarian whose mouth was twisted in disapproval and whose squinting eyes burnt into her from over the top of her spectacles. Jules took a pen out of her handbag and scribbled on a sheet of paper while Lydia watched in anticipation.

'Confidential. Can you check out the lions on the roof and exterior frieze of the Town Hall for me? Thanks'.

Lydia read it, folded it and placed it in her satchel nodding. Jules waved to Lydia and held her hand up to the others on the table to express her apologies. The black man glanced up from his paper and smiled again but the students, ignoring her attempted gesture of conciliation, just buried their heads in their books. She held an imaginary mobile to her ear as she left. She left the Reading Room and exhaled deeply. Paul was there.

"You found her then."

"Did you just ring me on purpose?"

Paul laughed. She hit him playfully on the chest. "Trying to get me in trouble, eh? Come on let's go home. We need to do a shop on the way. Hey, there's Jimmy."

"Who's he?"

"He's a security guard at the university. Oh, no. Don't tell me he's Lydia's bodyguard! I thought Edmund would get in some professionals. Quick, don't let him see us, he'll have us chatting for ages."

Jules and Paul sneaked out of the library. Jimmy, sitting at the café, stretched and yawned and as he did so his belly button protruded from his tight-fitting shirt looking as if it would burst open at any second. Then he downed the last dregs of coffee in his cup, got up, burped, ignored the glares and returned to the Picton.

235

"My turn now Jimmy," Lydia whispered when he arrived at the table.

The two students glanced up and frowned again.

"Oh, alright luv, do you want me to come with you?" Jimmy's baritone voice echoed around the room. He didn't care if he upset anyone. He found the Picton's echoing acoustics a novelty.

"No Jimmy, I'll be fine. Just watch my laptop and papers. Thanks."

"Going the loo, are we?" he said in a puerile manner, so everyone in the place could hear.

Lydia glared at him, yearning desperately to scold the grinning security guard. She rose from her seat and left, feeling more than a tad embarrassed. As soon as she went into the atrium she vented her spleen.

"I don't know why they've sent me that tool! I'm safe here!" she muttered to herself, fuming.

Lydia spent a good half hour away from her work and from Jimmy. She was writing up a time-sensitive report for the Library in addition to the tasks presented to her by Team Quest. On her return she whispered to Jimmy that she had to go to the archive section, but she was going to return to the Reading Room, so she collected her things, smiled at the suited African gentlemen and the two morose students and started to leave but Jimmy insisted he went with her. He was on duty until 8.00pm and he was under strict orders from Dr Parkes to stay close to her. Lydia relented because Jimmy's voice was again reverberating around the chamber in protest. Miriam, the librarian who knew Lydia, locked eyes with her. Lydia mouthed the word sorry to her and shook her head, the grimace on her own face said it all. She spent a good few hours in the archives room. Jimmy became interested in some old maps of Liverpool pinpointing where every Luftwaffe bomb was dropped in WWII, so she was left to her own devices for quite some time. Then Jimmy felt peckish. Food was always on his agenda, and nothing would stop him scratching that itch. It was, after all, 5.30pm.

"Chlamydia," he whispered in her ear. "I mean Lydia. I'm going for a break. Teatime. You going to be ok for a while? There's other people in here and a couple of librarians."

Lydia just shook her head at his tasteless retort and Jimmy left but not before farting. He was getting bored of his new post. Lydia screwed up her nose and put her hands over her face. 'Why did I draw the short straw?' she thought. 'Jules has got the ravishing Paul and I've got soft lad'. She spent one more hour in there before they closed the archive. Jimmy had still not returned. Lydia made her way to the Picton Reading Room again. She wanted to get another hour's work in before the library closed. There were fewer people in the rotunda than before. She sat at the same desk which was now vacated by the two students and the black gentleman. Whilst she was having a coffee break earlier in the day Lydia had eavesdropped on a conversation between the two Middle Eastern students and the African who were sat behind her on another table in the café. The former two were from Beirut studying medicine at Liverpool University and the latter was on a research trip to the Quilliam Mosque in Liverpool funded by the Quilliam think-tank in London. They spoke mainly in French but sometimes in Arabic, two languages that Lydia was fluent in, having studied them, the Arabic from ab initio level, as part of her degree course in Archaeology, Classics and Ancient History at Birmingham University. Lydia was reluctant to engage in or gate-crash their conflab. She learned that the Lebanese men were named Abbas and Fadi and the African, having also divulged his name, was of Algerian descent but now lived in Montpellier, France.

Eventually Jimmy came back smelling of beer and making excuses that he had ordered a meal in a pub, and it had taken ages to come. Lydia couldn't care less. She was glad he had disappeared for a while. He soon got bored again and wandered off, climbing up the spiral staircases at an effort and wobbling along the narrow passageways to peruse some books. By the time he came down again, Lydia and Miriam the librarian were the only ones left in the room. Jimmy let one drop again and was highly amused by his acoustic fart.

"Apologies ladies. I need the bog. See you in a bit."

An announcement was made over the public-address system informing everyone that the library was closing in fifteen minutes. Lydia spent another five minutes on her laptop then started to pack up. She heard a noise over at the librarian's desk and glanced over, ready to jokingly chastise Miriam about her making a racket this time but she couldn't see her. She had only been there a minute ago. She assumed she was in the office. Then suddenly the library was plunged into darkness.

"Miriam! I'm still here, don't forget!" Lydia sang out. Her voice resonating around the Picton.

Then there was silence.

"Or is that you Jimmy? Being a dick!" she called out in exasperation. The echo swept around the domed ceiling and oak-panelled bookcases. The silence returned. Then she heard a faint noise behind her. 'He's going to jump out and scare me now, the divvy,' she thought. 'I'll kick him in the balls and say I didn't know it was him'. Then suddenly a piano wire was thrust over her head. She screamed, the cry reverberating around the deserted rotunda. The ligature tightened around her throat, cutting into her flesh, stifling her ever diminishing cry until it was nothing but a weak utterance. She struggled frantically as the assassin's grip grew stronger. Her bloodshot eyes bulged and her face flushed red. The swollen veins in her neck becoming more palpable as the wire cut into her trachea and her nose and ears bled. Lydia fainted, barely alive. Then suddenly the assassin swore under his breath as he was disturbed by someone at the door calling for Miriam.

"Putain de merde!"

The lights went up and so he hid behind a nearby bookcase. He listened as someone's footsteps echoed around the empty cupola-crowned room. They belonged to another female librarian who entered the librarian's office and found Miriam dead on the floor, her skull caved in, bludgeoned by a fire extinguisher. The terrified librarian let out a piercing scream. As she stood over her colleague's body, horrified, momentarily transfixed, the crouching hitman seized Lydia's satchel and laptop, and furtively sneaked out of the Reading Room joining the other library visitors filing out of the building onto William Brown Street. He heard a commotion

237

behind him. The traumatized librarian had staggered into the atrium to raise the alarm. A security guard accompanied by a male librarian, ran into the Picton. The librarian went straight to the office, but the security guard noticed Lydia's prostrate body lying on the carpet across the Room. He thrust his head back out of the doors and screamed for a doctor, then rushed over to Lydia. He checked her weak pulse. She partially opened her eyes, a reservoir of blood filled each of her ducts. She tried to talk. He cradled her in his arms. She uttered one word to him before suspiring. It was her last breath.

Over at the gent's toilets Jimmy's body was found not soon after by a freaked-out cleaner. The door to his trap had been kicked open. A porno mag lay on the floor. Jimmy with his kecks still down by his ankles, had been garrotted also, found head slumped back with a broken, bloodied nose, still perched on the lavatory, with piano wire wrapped around his throat, the killer having repositioned him there to avoid detection.

95

Jules had just left the shower when the phone rang. Paul was still lying in the bath they had just shared. It was 10pm. It was Penny. The shocking news did not register at first, Lydia had been murdered. Except for Penny's sobbing down the phone, there was a moment of silence between the two. Jules stared into space, speechless, struck by the stark reality of the dangerous and deadly journey they had embarked upon.

"I've had it with this hunt. It's cursed. I'm out," Penny finally said before ending the conversation abruptly.

Paul was now showering. Jules sat motionless on the settee. Her wet, auburn locks dangling on her shoulders. Paul came into the living room towelling himself. He noticed Jules sat, clutching her mobile in silence.

"What's up?"

"It-it's Lydia," she sobbed. "She's dead. Murdered."

"What? Jeez. No, not Lydia."

"I can't believe it. Penny's had enough. So, have I. I think we need to disband. Poor, poor Lydia."

Paul sat on the sofa and comforted Jules. She wept uncontrollably. After an hour of near silent contemplation, Paul asked the question that was playing in his mind like a stuck record, not having had the audacity to broach the subject, nor wanting to sound callous.

"What shall we do about the Nelson Monument?"

"Forget it! Leave it well alone."

"The problem with that Jules," Paul said cautiously "is that it doesn't give us any more protection than we have now. I'm assuming poor Lydia has been killed for the information she was privy to."

"Oh, rub it in Paul, why don't you? Thanks for making me feel worse than I already am now!" she shouted.

"Jules, I'm sorry. I'm not having a go at you. Of course, I'm not. We're in this together. It isn't your fault. We all knew the risks involved but I'm trying to explain that we'll still be at risk even if we don't find the clue. Once the next clue is found, we can announce it and then tell the world we are disbanding the team forthwith. Then it's up to others to locate the tablet. Otherwise, we're still going to be a target."

After a moment of thought, Jules responded. "Maybe you're right, Paul. Sorry for snapping at you. Maybe we should get it as planned tonight. We'll wait to see if it's anything of significance before we tell anyone."

"I reckon we should go for it about 2 am."

"Ok, I'll drive you there. You take care of the rest."

239

96

At 1.30am the car left for the city. The roads were quiet. A fox running across its path from Sefton Park startled a nervous Jules who was driving. They proceeded along Princes Road and then down Upper Parliament Street. As they penetrated more into the city the roads were busier. They saw one police car and assumed correctly that others would be present at the Library. They had heard the news en route that three fatalities had occurred there.

"Jimmy!" Jules blurted out. "Oh no, Jimmy! What's happened to him?"

They parked up in Bixteth Street adjacent to the former Exchange Station, opposite Exchange Flags. No one was around. Paul took a crowbar and hammer out of the boot and placed them inside his jacket. He told Jules to lock the doors. He nipped across the road and into Exchange Flags Square. The monument stood before him. He was about to act when he was disturbed by a couple appearing on the concourse, a bit worse for wear, barely registering him. In any event Paul had on his hoodie, so he could not be identified too readily. He stepped around the side of the monument to avoid them. He looked around again once the inebriated couple had staggered out of the plaza. It was clear. He scrambled up onto the stone plinth and located the lion's head under the cannon to the left of a bronze statue of a chained prisoner and took out the crowbar and wedged it between the granite and the bronze head of the lion and put his weight into it. It moved slightly so he gave it a couple more wrenches then the head broke off and it clattered onto the knee of the crouching figure, still dangling on its chain. He smiled. He put the crowbar down. Seizing the lion's head, he manoeuvred a wobbly metal plate inside the hollow back and forwards. The thin metal plate he assumed had worked loose over time exposing the item of interest that had been concealed there for all these years. He still couldn't extract it though, so he took the hammer out of his inner pocket, held the lion's head firmly on the granite slab adjacent to the seated bronze statue of the French prisoner and brought the hammer down swiftly and accurately on the edge of the metal plate. The plate bent back a little. He smashed the hammer down again, bending it more, just enough for him to fish out a small, weathered leather wallet. He scanned the immediate vicinity. No one was around. He picked up the crowbar and placed it and the hammer back in his jacket. He then opened up the wallet, extracted a tattered folded piece of paper out of it, unfolded it carefully, perused it and then placed it back in the wallet which he stuffed in the inside pocket of his jacket. He leapt down. He walked swiftly through the short underpass to the road and heard a noise to his left. He looked instantly. Further down Chapel Street a refuse wagon was slowly sucking up litter and cleansing the gutters. He checked the other way then casually jogged across the road and around the corner to where the car was stationary. He rapped on the passenger window startling Jules. She unlocked the door. Paul deposited the tools in the boot and got in the passenger seat.

"Did you find something?" she said excitedly.

"I did. Let's get out of here."

Jules started the engine and did a U-turn. At the junction she paused to allow the refuse wagon to sweep slowly by. Then she pulled out and overtook it taking a left onto Pall Mall, then left again to drive along the Strand back home. She halted on red at the traffic lights, in the shadow of the Tower building.

"Show me then!" Jules said impatiently.

Paul reached into his bomber jacket pocket. He cursed.

"Shit! It's not there!"

"What?" she exclaimed.

He frantically checked his other pockets. The lights turned to green.

"You'd best move. There's a cop car behind us. I must have dropped it when I was running back to the car! You'll have to go back! Take a right here!"

Jules, indicating, veered to the right and turned in front of the Three Graces and headed back up the Strand. They followed the road around to the Old Hall Street junction and took a right.

"Stop here," Paul said as they got to the end of Old Hall Street. He leapt out and ran into Exchange Flags Square. Then he came out and scoured the pavement and road, tracing his footsteps. He crossed Tithebarn Street and disappeared into Bixteth Street where they had originally parked. He was back shortly. He jumped in the car.

"I can't find it! The road sweeper. It must have sucked it up."

"Oh! Paul! I don't believe it!"

"I'm sorry Jules. I screwed up. It's fallen out my pocket as I jogged back."

"What was it?"

"A small, brown leather wallet. There was a tiny rectangular shaped piece of tattered paper in it, folded at least five times."

"Did you open it up and see what it was?"

"No, because the edges had worn and split, and the paper was fragile. I didn't want it to disintegrate. I thought it best if you opened it up since you're more skilled at these things."

"What? At opening up bits of paper. Don't be absurd."

"Besides, I thought it best to get away from there as quick as possible."

"And now we're back here. None the wiser. That went well didn't it?"

"Maybe someone found it and picked it up."

"Hopefully, we'll just have to wait and see. If someone found it though, would they realise what it was?"

"Come on, let's get out of here, Jules. Drive along Tithebarn Street we might see someone."

Jules drove off but the area was deserted. They returned home. Jules was not too impressed.

241

97

They had only had a few hours' sleep when Jules's mobile began to vibrate and buzz beside her head. Drowsily, she answered. It was Dr Parkes, confirming that Jimmy was one of the other victims. She leapt out of bed and threw her hair back over her head, cursing. Tears welling. Dr Parkes wanted to see them both at 9am for a meeting. They arrived to find Fatima, Penny and Tom all consoling each other but no Simon or Randy. Randy was preparing for Viren's cremation at Landican on the Wirral. His ashes were to be spread on the Mersey. Tom couldn't locate Simon although he had granted him a day off.

Emotions were raw and running high and Penny accused Jules of putting Lydia at risk. Jules left the meeting in tears. When Penny was made aware that Jimmy, whom she knew from the Garstang Museum and could not so much as punch his way out of a paper bag, had been posted as Lydia's security guard, she turned her wrath on Edmund accusing him of being a cheapskate. She also stated that any other security guard of the calibre of Jimmy was pointless. Although she was officially not part of the search team, just offering her advice and expertise when called upon, she left them all in no doubt that she would not have anything to do with them going forward. She was just about to storm out when DCI Armitage and DC Noades turned up. They quizzed the group and asked for motives for Lydia's murder. Jules confessed that she had passed a note to Lydia earlier on that day about the lions on the Town Hall, but the police officers confirmed that there was no memo fitting that description amongst those left in her file on the table. They were still looking at CCTV images.

"There's one more thing which may or may not be an important lead," Armitage said. "The man, the librarian who reached Lydia before she died told us she uttered one word, a name, we presume - Tufiq."

"Tufiq?" Fatima and Tom uttered simultaneously.

"Yes, we don't know if she knew anyone with this name or if she knew any of the others who sat on her table at the Picton. We've been checking the CCTV as I say. It's a bit grainy but we're aware that Tufiq is an Arabic name and there are some people on her table who may fit that description."

Fatima and Tom looked at each other in consternation.

"Anything the matter?" DCI Armitage asked.

"One of our team, Simon, is friends with a guy called Tufiq. He's of Algerian descent. He's just recently met him. Simon's not here today. He's having a day off, with Tufiq," Tom said warily. "They're...they're in a relationship."

"Can you get hold of Simon?" DS Noades inquired.

"No, I've tried. But I suppose it doesn't mean anything. I'm sure there's plenty of Tufiqs around."

"Can you come, sorry, what's your name?" Armitage said.

"Tom, Tom Yates."

"Mr Yates, can you come down to police HQ to view this footage to try and identify if this is one and the same person at Lydia's desk? And keep calling Simon for us, will you? But don't tell him anything."

"Sure. No probs."

"Does anyone know anything else in the meantime?"

Jules put her hand up. "I saw three men on her table in the afternoon. Two were of Middle Eastern origin by the look of them and the other one, who was sat apart from the other two, I would say, was, of North African appearance."

"Can you come to HQ as well Dr Johnson?"

"Yes, fine."

"By the way, Dr Johnson, our ballistics counterparts in Scotland confirmed that the weapons used by the Egyptian fanatics to attack you did not match the weapon used to kill Frank Baines and his friends."

Penny and the Team Quest members all remained silent each one mulling over the consequences of Armitage's statement that seemed to confirm that more than one organisation or individual was prepared to kill to obtain the artefact.

"Can you give us five minutes, detectives?" Dr Parkes requested.

Armitage nodded her assent and the two officers left.

"I think we have to disband the team. Out of respect to Lydia. At least until her funeral is over."

"I think we should stop immediately," Penny growled. "For good. I'm not going to put my family in jeopardy over this. I've already been attacked once. In any case, the next clue has already been found."

"What? Are you sure?" Dr Parkes exclaimed.

"Yep. I heard it on the radio whilst I was on my way here."

"I didn't hear anything on the radio."

"That's because you listen to boring Radio Four, Edmund. It was on Radio City. Someone anonymously rang in with it."

"It'll be a hoax. They've had loads," Fatima retorted. "Every day, dozens."

"This news bulletin also gave a place where the clue was possibly located. The Nelson Monument at the back of the Town Hall. Exchange Flags Square. Someone from the council confirmed that one of the lion's heads on the monument had been found vandalised."

Paul and Jules exchanged furtive glances.

"They reckon the clue was under a lion's head but the guy who rang in just said he had found a leather wallet in the vicinity of Moorfields Station, which, of course, is nearby Exchange Flags."

"Under one of the lion's heads?" Tom mused. "Of course! That's plausible. None of us thought of that. Personally, I was going to mention the Liverpool Eye and Ear Infirmary building up Myrtle Street, around the corner from the Phil, with its two lion statues above the entrance."

"I must admit, I didn't even think of that one," Edmund said.

243

"Perhaps whoever found it was reluctant to reveal that he had damaged a Grade II listed monument for fear of prosecution," Jules chimed, glaring at a sheepish looking Paul.

"Go on then Penny. Put us out of our misery. What's the clue?" Fatima urged.

"A bear," Penny declared.

"A bear eh? Linked to a lion?" Edmund pondered the conundrum.

A murmur went round the group. Again, Paul and Jules glanced at each other. They all sat puzzled ruminating on this fresh revelation. However, they all decided on a moratorium, Fatima agreeing to inform BBC Radio Merseyside and the *Liverpool Echo* that the University of Liverpool search team, Team Quest, was disbanding owing to the murder of one of their colleagues.

98

Jules and Paul left with Tom for the Police headquarters to try and identify the individuals who had been at the Picton. They were shown grainy CCTV footage of Lydia's table at the time Jules arrived. She saw herself on the video. It seemed surreal to her to think that Lydia, a few hours from then, would be dead. Jules felt sick to her stomach.

"That's the two students there and the other guy on the opposite end of the table sitting to Lydia's right."

"Can you zoom in on that individual?" Armitage asked the technician.

As the technician enlarged the image, Tom froze in horror.

"That's him! Tufiq! Simon's new boyfriend! Shit!"

"Right, we need to try and get hold of Simon. He could be in real danger. Did Lydia know Simon?"

"Yes, she knew him but only through the search team," Jules answered.

"Did Lydia know Tufiq?" Noades probed. "She mentioned the name of Tufiq before she died."

"Not that I know of," Tom replied.

"Have you any idea where they've gone?" Armitage added.

"He didn't say. But -"

"Go on," Noades said.

"I heard them talking in the Old Swan pub before I left them to it the other day. Simon is from New Brighton, so he was telling Tufiq that New Brighton used to have a tower bigger than Blackpool's and being a huge fan of 'Strictly' Simon wanted to go to Blackpool some time to see the ballroom in the Tower. I remember Tufiq saying he'd like to see it also. It stuck in my mind because Simon then asked Tufiq if he liked, 'big erections'. When Tufiq said 'most definitely', that's when they hit it off."

Jules squirmed. "Ooh, too much information," she said, screwing up her face.

Silence momentarily pervaded the room.

"Right, Blackpool it is then," Armitage declared. "We'll sweep New Brighton as well. We'll keep an open mind as to the motive. We're not sure at this stage whether Lydia's death and Jimmy and Miriam's, the librarian, are the result of a terrorist threat, an act of random gratuitous violence or whether it is linked to the search for the relic."

Paul ran his fingers through his hair. Jules exhaled deeply. Armitage continued.

"We reckon it's to do with the latter but were going to get the CTFSO, the armed police unit deployed anyway. Tufiq could be innocent in all this. Lydia might have just mentioned his name as someone who might have information on the killer. We don't want to racially profile him, but all the same we've got to be prepared."

"Is there any other information you'd like to solicit?" Noades said.

Tom spoke up. "Just something Simon told me. He said Tufiq had been on a secondment to the Quilliam Mosque here in Liverpool."

"Ibrahim Shaqtar is the man you want to speak to then, at the mosque," Jules added, "but I'd be surprised if he had anything to do with this."

"Thanks. We'll call him," Noades responded.

99

Jules, Paul and Tom left the Police HQ. Tom was picked up by his wife and taken home to Spital. The other two headed to the Royal Albert Dock, for a bite to eat and a coffee. They then went to the Pier Head and watched the Dazzle Ship, the Mersey ferry *Snowdrop* leave its moorings at Woodside and glide towards the mouth of the river knowing that Randy was on it along with Viren's close family, other friends and relatives, the vibrant colours of the vessel contrasting with the no doubt sombre, reflective mood aboard. Whilst lunching, Jules and Paul sat in silence for quite a while. Finally, Paul broke the silence.

"What are you thinking about?"

"Everything really. Lydia, Simon, poor Jimmy. Us, Randy, Viren. I feel guilty that innocent people have been dragged into this and are now dead."

"You can't blame yourself Jules. That's ridiculous. You were brought in to do a job because of your expertise. The others as well. We're all adults. We made our choices."

"Ok, but none of us realised that our lives would be at risk."

"Unfortunately, Tom's discovery has thrown the world into turmoil. You've seen the news. Riots, churches and mosques being burnt, countries governed by theocracies on the verge of revolution. This has upset the status quo. There's a lot of people out there with agendas that either want to bury the truth or expose it and are prepared to kill to succeed in their objectives."

"I suppose it's a good time for us to get out then."

"The new clue though. The bear. I still can't get it out of my head. It's as if we're inexorably drawn to it. Maybe Providence has chosen us to locate the tablet."

"Well, it wasn't us who disclosed it, was it Paul? Maybe it's the other guy's destiny to find the tablet, the one who found the wallet. At least we know it didn't get sucked up by the road sweeper wagon. That's one positive. The other thing is, at least we know it's not a hoax."

"Aye, that we do."

"Do you think we should tell the others that we know that?"

"Not yet."

"I have to admit, Paul, I keep thinking about it as well. It's like an addiction. Oh, sorry Paul. That's a poor analogy to use."

"It's fine. No offence taken. You're right. We're obsessed by it. Like a lot of people. I just feel that it's our destiny to find this thing."

"Well, we'll just have to take some time out to consider whether the both of us want to get involved again."

They left the eatery and stretched their legs along the waterfront. As Paul paid homage to Captain Frederick 'Johnny' Walker, pausing at the statue of the illustrious anti-submarine warfare commander, a hero of the Battle of the Atlantic in WWII, Jules took the time to check her Twitter feed.

"Paul!" she called. "Reports coming in that New Brighton is awash with armed police. Roadblocks are going up."

At that very moment Tufiq Ben Hassan was staring out at the panoramic view of the vast expanse of the Irish Sea atop the Blackpool Tower, encased within the glass observation platform called the Eye. Simon was next to him, droning on about some little known 'celebs' as he called them, prancing around on his favourite TV show. Simon had picked his new love interest up from his rented Wavertree flat early that morning at 7am to beat the traffic. Simon had gone to bed early the night before, at ten o'clock in preparation for their trip. He had not heard his mobile buzzing under his pillow. He had left it on silent mode by mistake. Then he managed to oversleep resulting in him dashing out without checking his phone. Tufiq was ready for him as agreed. He jumped in the car and congratulated Simon on the music he was playing. A CD of Kylie's greatest hits. Tufiq did not want Simon to tune in to the radio, so Simon kept playing the same songs over and over making him feel chuffed that Tufiq was enjoying his personal selection of music. The story had broken about the slaughter in the library. The Algerian was surprised when Simon didn't bring up the subject. Simon hadn't seen or heard any news and was just happy thinking about later when he would seduce Tufiq in the privacy of their hotel room.

On arrival at the tacky three-star hotel, they had dumped their bags in the room and left more or less straight away with Simon, eager to show Tufiq the delights of Blackpool. Simon had inadvertently rushed out without his mobile, not realising that Tufiq had shoved it under the bed after checking it for messages whilst Simon was occupied in the bathroom. He had memorized the password when they first met in the pub when Simon was showing him pictures of Blackpool. He saw that Tom had tried to call Simon several times. Simon, realising sometime after that he had left his mobile in the hotel room, intended to pick it up after breakfast but Tufiq had kept him busy all day. They hadn't returned to the hotel, so Tom's multiple messages went unanswered. By now, Tufiq was fed up with the gushing, tiresome, self-obsessed flirt that was Simon who was trying to impress at every opportunity. He had bored him silly when they had toured the Tower ballroom. Tufiq wished it were Simon whom he had garrotted, not the bespectacled bookworm or the fat security guard. Suddenly, down below at street level, he spotted police cars speeding along the front and screeching to a stop outside the Tower, armed police spilling from the vehicles. His heart missed a beat. 'Shit! How did they get on to me so fast?' he thought. The answer was that the hotel receptionist recognised him from a TV bulletin and had notified the police. Simon had told her they had tickets for the Tower. Tufiq immediately scanned the enclosed area. There was another family there, a mother, father and two toddlers. Another family had just left the deck. There were three more levels above, accessible from the outside but escape was impossible from those narrow areas. The only way to escape was down. He thought about grabbing one of the kids to take as a hostage, but on hearing the sirens, the

248

father had ushered his family quickly off the platform concerned that there was an emergency, maybe a fire at the Tower. There was only Simon left. He would have to be the hostage. Tufiq silently cursed Simon for allowing him to take him somewhere where he was trapped. If he fled now, he knew he would run straight into the armed police officers. There was no choice. Tufiq placed his hand on the knife concealed in the inside of his bomber jacket and waited. Simon was still rabbiting on inanely, Tufiq not listening to any of it. Instead, he was listening acutely for any sound of movement at the door. On hearing something he suddenly grabbed Simon roughly around the neck just as three armed officers burst through the doors, each holding a Glock pistol.

"Get back!" Tufiq yelled. "Fuck you! *Putain de flics!* Away you bastards!"

The officers hesitated and then stepped back, their weapons still trained on the North African. Simon screamed in terror, his numb brain trying to comprehend what had just occurred. He glanced down in horror at the blade held across his neck. He instinctively struggled.

"Tufiq! What are you doing?"

"Shut your ugly face," he sneered as he held the blade closer to Simon's neck, nicking his skin and drawing blood.

"Ouch, you're hurting me, Tufiq," he squealed.

Tufiq ignored him this time and manoeuvred him around the edge of the glass deck.

"Move! Fucking move!" he shouted to the Kevlar-armoured officers.

They remained static.

"Drop the knife Tufiq! You've got no chance of getting out of here. Let Simon go," pleaded the officer in charge.

Tufiq took a moment to weigh up his options. He could hear Simon's snivelling and the sound of more blues and twos wailing below. "Fuck you!" he finally said. He smirked as he pressed the sharp blade firmer into his hostage's neck. The blood spurted from his victim's throat as he slowly moved the knife across the flesh, the gurgling Simon's legs buckled from under him as he slipped in the pool of piss that had trickled down his leg, inadvertently revealing more of the police target's torso. At the same instance, several shots rang out, the impact propelling Tufiq back against the glass window that had been weakened by bullets passing through him resulting in the fractured glass exploding and Tufiq's body being launched through the gaping hole. The killer had still clung on to Simon's neck in a forlorn attempt to protect himself, dragging him backwards as the bullets impacted on his chest, leaving Simon's crumpled body dangling over the broken window frame. Before the police officers could react, his legs slipped out of the aperture and the corpse followed the same grim trajectory as Tufiq's body, crashing into the exterior steel frame of the Tower before landing with a grisly and audible thump on the roof of the main structure of the building below.

100

As Paul and Jules walked back through the Albert Dock to recover her car parked at the University, Paul noticed through a bar window an image of Blackpool Tower being displayed live on TV. They dashed in. The reporter was stating that two bodies had fallen from the shattered window pane of the deck of the Eye and the image was being constantly replayed. Jules placed her hands over her face in shock. They watched for a minute or two before Paul put his arm around her and encouraged her to go outside. They reached the car. Paul drove whilst Jules searched her phone for any confirmation of the deceased. The police had confirmed that two people were dead, but no more information was forthcoming about the dramatic and tragic events.

It was Tom who delivered the awful news to Jules. Simon had been murdered by Tufiq. A police press conference was to take place in the next forty-five minutes. This had been pre-empted by a news agency drone shot of the two bodies. Simon's broken body lay between Tufiq's mangled legs, face down on the assassin's crotch.

It was Randy's third funeral in a matter of weeks, the second time he had been to Landican Cemetery. The remaining members of the team were traumatized. It was ironic that Simon had refused a bodyguard stating that the tall, muscular but wiry Tufiq was all the protection he needed. The team were shocked to subsequently find out that a gun, found in the Algerian's holdall in the hotel, matched the bullets from the murders of Frank Baines and his cronies in Jules' apartment. Ibrahim Shaqtar had been taken in for more questioning after initially being approached by the police. He denied all knowledge about any of the horrific murders. After further enquiries abroad, police henceforth discovered that the name Tufiq was an alias, Rachid Omar being his real name, and that he was in fact a French-born Christian of Algerian descent, from Montpellier masquerading as a Muslim, his parents having emigrated to France from the Kabylie region of the north African country. What concerned each remaining disbanded group member most was that this meant that it would appear that there were definitely two confirmed violent and murderous parties, acting independently of each other who would stop at nothing to discover the stele, and no doubt even more.

101

The Caribbean Sea, 1804

Off the coast of Saint-Domingue Captain Moorcroft's brig, the *Mary Lou* intercepted a barque bound for France. They met little resistance from the crew and the traumatised passengers on board who were French survivors of massacres that were taking place in the newly proclaimed Republic of Haiti. Black slaves had revolted and sought out the white population on the island slaughtering most of them. Some of the devastated survivors on board were infected by yellow fever betrayed by their hollow, jaundiced faces and the blood that gradually oozed from their eyes, mouth, and nostrils. Others were torpefied by the terror they had witnessed on the streets. One white woman told of her husband being stripped naked in the street by a mob and then a resident she knew only as Jean Zombi, with the look of a possessed man, had plunged a dagger into her partner's heart. Amongst the prisoners were soldiers of the garrisons. O'Rourke listened to their stories about the carnage from which they had fled. The soldiers were arguing amongst themselves and with a captured black seaman, named Verzon, who spoke passionately claiming he was a 'free' man.

"The French Revolution has inspired people around the world to seek emancipation. However, when it is black slaves who, after years of subjugation, seek freedom from oppression, it's a different matter. Are they not the same revolutionaries, the same downtrodden citizens fighting against their masters?"

Another prisoner, Lescard, a plantation overseer, growled in response.

"They are just savages. Sub-human savages. They have no morals. No feelings. They raped and slaughtered our people because they were white. That's all that mattered to them. The colour of their skin. They were blind to everything else. Kind citizens who were white, like Madame Cartier's husband who had helped them, were executed and mutilated!"

"I personally do not condone the violence, but they were just responding to years of vile oppression," Verzon argued. "Their European masters may have had white faces, but their hands were red, permanently stained from the blood of black Africans and those born into captivity on the island. The whites have committed many atrocities. Let me tell you what, I, Patrice Verzon, have seen with my very own eyes."

Verzon was distracted for a moment as orders were barked to a member of the crew.

"Mr O'Rourke, trim the jib."

"Aye, aye, Bosun McGinty."

Verzon wiped the sweat from his brow with his fettered hand, swallowed and then resumed.

"I've seen black slaves tied in sacks and drowned on the whim of white overseers, like you. Black slaves crucified or hung by their feet, by white people. Black slaves buried alive by white people, on ants' nests or tethered to stakes in the swamps and eaten alive by mosquitoes. Black slaves thrown into boiling cauldrons of cane syrup, by white people. Blacks set upon by packs of dogs or rolled down hills in barrels pierced with spikes, by white people. Is it no wonder these people have revolted?"

"This mulatto exaggerates. I've never seen or heard of these calumnies," Lescard sneered.

"I myself have the scars of bondage on my back, wrists and ankles and see, here, around my neck, the burns from a hangman's noose. I was reprieved at the last moment by Toussaint L'Ouverture himself who sacked the town and saved me during a slave revolt. Believe me, I speak the truth!"

"Do you trust the word of a black man, or has he just created these far-fetched tales to deflect attention away from the hate filled crimes of his people?" the overseer spat.

"I do not lie, sir! So, tell me, my learned friend, are all these punishments and tortures representative of a civilized people, of a cultured society? Just who are the 'savages' if one is capable of inflicting this manner of violence and cruelty on another human being? It's no wonder that years of suppression and brutality has led to these vicious reprisals and vengeance."

"Mulatto, you say you are a free man. How did you win your freedom?" a French soldier asked after a moment of reflection and silence.

"My white master fell into Lake Saumâtre when out hunting. He was drowning. His people feared the crocodiles. They hesitated. I did not. I dived in and saved him. That's how I won my freedom. He, the white master, was my biological father."

O'Rourke was momentarily called away after listening awhile to the sobering testimony of the black man. The Irishman had been conveniently placed on duty close to the French prisoners to listen out for potential mutiny. The British privateers had relieved the French of their possessions. Most were too weak to resist. They were all half-starved and many of them were suffering from illness. But Lescard, driven by hatred, summoned up the strength to attack the freed slave. He slyly withdrew a knife concealed in his boot and flew at the black man unexpectedly shocking everyone. The wary Verzon saw him out the corner of his eye and managed to grab his wrist just before the blade was plunged into the flesh of his neck. Both fighters quivered with the strain of the contest. The muscular Verzon forced his opponent back with a kick, which gave him time to stand. The others nearby recoiled in fear, too weak to intervene either way. Lescard rose to his feet, wild-eyed and frothing at the mouth, snarling his vitriol.

"I seek revenge for all those slaughtered by you black savages, you dark heathen!"

O'Rourke, busying himself with the rigging, heard the commotion. Peering over, he witnessed the struggle. He leapt on to the gunwale, grabbed a rope and swung

252

out over the side of the ship. His momentum brought him back into the vessel in a sweeping arc. The other captives were barely cognizant of the swooping silhouette above them, until the Irishman spectacularly caught Lescard in the temple with both feet, sending him sprawling. O'Rourke landed on deck but slipped and crashed into some wooden crates injuring himself. This allowed the bitter Frenchman to haul himself back to his feet and recover the knife, ready to throw himself upon the supine Irishman. Suddenly Bosun McGinty's blunderbuss thundered its lethal shot propelling the Frenchman back with deadly consequences.

"You'll all be getting some of that if you don't behave!" the gnarled mariner roared, adding to the anxiety of the other captives who were huddled together, cowering.

McGinty helped O'Rourke to his feet. Verzon acknowledged O'Rourke's selfless act of courage and unexpected intervention with a cursory nod. The peppered body of Lescard was tossed overboard and calm prevailed once more. The only audible sounds, the rattling of the lines and the flapping of sails, and the snivelling of a young child clasped in the bosom of his mother.

The captured barque had a cargo of cotton, coffee and raw sugar and so Captain Moorcroft decided that the *Mary Lou* should return to Liverpool with her prize. The privateer, followed by the barque, sailed into her home port in July 1804. An unexpected bonus for O'Rourke and the other sailors. They were paid their dues and celebrated their success in the Golden Lion tavern. One of the other sailors, Welshman Henry Roberts told O'Rourke where to hide his booty, if he felt it was vulnerable back at home.

"Over the water, in Liscard, there's an inn, Mother Redcaps. Poll Jones, the proprietor, can be trusted. She hides our booty, our money. No one knows where. Except for her. But whenever we call upon her to get some of our funds, she always delivers without fail."

"Does she take a cut?"

"Of course, she takes a percentage. She keeps a record in her ledger. Besides, the ale is good too and the fare. She gets rewarded that way, too! Seamus, I'm off there now. Come with me if you want. There's an anchorage, Red Bets, right outside the tavern."

Seamus checked a silver pocket watch, one of his 'prizes', and agreed to sail across the Mersey to Mother Redcaps. He, Roberts and Fairbairn, another of the crew, paid for a passage across in a fishing smack. The boat ferried them across and moored at a small wooden jetty. The three men jumped down onto the rust-coloured sand of the shore and walked the short distance to the inn. The tavern was packed with revellers; smugglers, seamen, local farm workers and others. Poll Jones, distinguishable in her red head dress, greeted them and explained the process to Seamus. They deposited most of their earnings and kept sufficient funds for their own and their families' needs. They enjoyed another few flagons of ale and some pies having arranged to meet the fishing smack, two hours after they had arrived. They left Mother Redcaps finding that a mist had descended. Fairburn assured

O'Rourke that the fishing smack would return. He stayed put, close to Mother Redcaps on the watch for their passage. Roberts took O'Rourke along the shoreline to show him where two other inns stood; the Magazine Hotel and the Pilot Boathouse and to check to see if the smack had moored there as it sometimes did. The *Mary Lou* had docked there with a skeleton crew earlier to deposit its supply of gunpowder at the coastal army depot as all ships entering the port of Liverpool were required to. Work at the depot had ceased for the day, the raucous noise from the taverns confirming this and any ships arriving in the Mersey late were forced to anchor mid-channel and wait until morning before docking. O'Rourke and Roberts waited for a few more minutes. There was no sign of the craft, so they decided to head back to Fairbairn. They were on their way back to Mother Redcaps when they heard someone whistling, which they presumed rightly was Fairburn warning them of the approaching smack. They jogged back to where he was and peered into the gloom. A faint light approached from the river. The vessel drifted closer. Suddenly Fairburn seized O'Rourke by the arm. The perplexed Irishman looked at him, then out to the Mersey. The flag of the Royal Navy fluttered from the gaff.

"It's not the smack! It's the impressment! Run!" Fairburn yelled.

Fairburn ran back to Mother Redcaps. O'Rourke followed Roberts in the other direction. The navy launch offloaded five or six men who chased them. Others went in pursuit of Fairburn. He dived into the tavern shouting, "Press!" Several mariners immediately let go of their whores or abandoned their tankards of ale and ran to an exit at the back of the inn from where Mother Redcap was beckoning. Fairbairn joined them. The press-gang entered the premises and scanned the clientele for potential mariners. The locals carried on regardless, familiar with the procedure of Mother Redcap and her staff hiding the men in caves and other concealed bolt holes within and around the tavern. However, an impulsive midshipman, cudgel in hand, approached a young male, sat at a table, and seized him. The place erupted.

"Hey! What do you think you're doing? That's Little Lionel!" an older man roared. "He's only twelve. He's a child."

"He's no child!" the midshipman scoffed. "Look at the bloody size of him!"

"He's big for his age because he's Giant Reginald's son, the blacksmith. You'd better beware! He's just relieving himself," warned a whore who stood defiantly in front of the ratings to protect the youngster.

The midshipman ignored her, shoving her out of the way and ordered his men to haul their target off his chair. Two sailors roughly dragged him to his feet. The boy stood six feet, towering above the squat seamen.

"He ain't half big!" gasped another member of the press gang.

"Not as big as me!" boomed a voice behind the pressmen.

They turned to see Giant Reginald, all six foot four of him, a corpulent man-mountain, fuming, fists like lumps of granite. He charged at the navy ratings like a snorting bull, sending them flying in every direction. The midshipman hit him with a blow of his cudgel, but the huge blacksmith barely felt it. He picked the officer up and threw him across two tables. The two men who had hold of Little Lionel released him and scarpered. They were followed swiftly by the other three members of the

254

press-gang, all nursing cuts and bruises, especially the midshipman who limped away in fear of his life.

In the meantime, O'Rourke had followed Roberts along the waterfront. Suddenly, the Welshman stopped. Five other press-gang ratings emerged from the mist having been disembarked from another vessel at the Magazine berth.

"Oh Lord! This way!" Roberts shouted.

O'Rourke followed his companion up a track to try and find a place to hide amongst the sparse homesteads of Magazine village. O'Rourke found himself at a crossroads not knowing which way Roberts had run. The mist was swirling around him. He could hear the voices of the press-gang.

"In here, quick boyo!" Roberts whispered. The privateer's Welsh accent unmistakable.

It came from a cottage garden to the left of the crossroads. O'Rourke leapt over the sandstone wall and lay flat and silent next to Roberts. The pressmen paused at the crossroads not knowing which path to take. They split up. Two took the route in front of them and two to the right. The other one remained at the intersection, on alert, slapping a staff made of baleen and metal into his hand. The noise of the slap was the only indication for the pursued that someone was still there. Then there was silence. Roberts whispered to O'Rourke. "They've gone." Roberts carefully climbed over the wall. A candle flickered in the dimly lit window of the cottage shedding its light on an old couple enjoying a meal oblivious to the intruders in their garden. He stepped on to the stony track. "This way. Run!"

O'Rourke scrambled over the wall. He saw Roberts break into a run and disappear into the mist then suddenly he heard a thud and a groan, and the Welshman flew back. He lay on the floor, winded. Out of the gloom, a figure emerged holding a staff. Roberts was rolling on the floor holding his abdomen. O'Rourke instantly recognized the rating. It was the rat-faced individual he had seen at the Folly Fair. The press man sneered as he saw O'Rourke.

"There's some for you as well." He smacked the weapon he held into his hand three times.

He bawled at the top of his lungs for the rest of the gang. A few moments later two individuals armed with marlin spikes were there at the side of the rat-faced character.

"Look who George has found," cackled a toothless matelot. "Got the King's Shilling ready, have we, for these two?"

"Well done Sewell," said the other. "A nice little earner you've got us."

Roberts tried to stand but he was struck again on his back by the baton-wielding thug who seemed to take pleasure in his brutal approach. The three naval ratings surrounded O'Rourke. He pulled a knife from his boot. It was the only weapon he had, since they had left their pistols and swords in the tavern, as Mother Redcap insisted until their departure. They were to retrieve them when the fishing smack had docked. The press men backed off. He thrust it towards them. Roberts, partially recovered from the blow to his stomach and seething with rage suddenly attacked one of the men whose focus was on O'Rourke and not him. He bludgeoned one with a stone, knocking him unconscious. The others turned to see what was happening. O'Rourke took his chance. He leapt at the rating, avoiding the thrust of his marlin spike, bringing the knife hilt down on the bridge of his nose which exploded. He veered away in agony. In the same movement he tilted the blade towards the sailor, he now knew as Sewell, and ran it down his cheek before he could react with his bludgeon. Sewell raised his staff threateningly, not realising he had been cut. He then felt blood trickling down his face, the pain suddenly hitting him and the next minute he was pole-axed by a punch thrown by Roberts. O'Rourke sheathed his dagger and knocked out the other seaman who was nursing his broken nose, with one punch and he and Roberts fled up the path.

"This way! I know a farmstead we can hide out at," Roberts said, stooping to seize the cudgel. "Across Bidston salt marshes. We can get back across the river tomorrow. They'll be looking for us. Keep that knife handy. We might need it if we run into the others."

"What about our other weapons? They're back in Mother Redcaps."

"Fairburn will recover them if he's escaped the press himself. He'll remain there for the night now if he's been lucky. If not, we'll have to get them another time. Mother Redcap knows me well. She'll keep them safe."

The two men scrambled over some scrubland and into a wood and followed a track with which Roberts was familiar. Ten minutes later George Sewell was shaken out of his unconscious state by the naval officer in charge of the press. The three injured ratings were helped to their feet with Sewell cussing and raging, vowing revenge on the person who scarred him.

102

Later the following day, O'Rourke finally returned home having recovered his personal belongings from Fairbairn who had indeed escaped the clutches of the press-gang and lodged overnight at Mother Redcaps. O'Rourke spent precious time with Kitty and the baby whenever her work allowed her to, and they enjoyed an enhanced standard of living for the next few months. The surviving remnants of the captured French soldiers, civilians and mariners from the vessel secured by the *Mary Lou* had been incarcerated in the Tower Gaol. Some were destined to perish shortly after arriving in Liverpool or on the long voyage home from their various ailments. Non-combatants and survivors of different nationalities, together with women and children were to be repatriated to their respective countries. The *Mary Lou* was commissioned to effect the repatriation and set sail again in August 1804 to Gibraltar, with a reluctant O'Rourke onboard. He had said his goodbyes to Kitty, Francis and his young son Patrick on the Gorce with a heavy heart waving farewell from the decks of the privateer alongside his fellow crewmen. Before the ship had departed, however, Kitty had sprung another surprise. She was pregnant with their second child.

The brig set sail, heading for the open waters of the Mersey estuary and the choppy Irish Sea and headed on down past the rugged coast of Wales, Henry Roberts pointing proudly to his hometown of Llandudno and the promontory of the Great Orme. The vessel docked at Fishguard to take on more supplies before venturing south, alert to the threat of enemy shipping but protected in the main by the British navy's dominance of the high seas. Tragedy struck however, in the Bay of Biscay, in the form of a tempest. The *Mary Lou* survived a severe buffeting in the storm, but two hands and two passengers were lost overboard, one of them being Fairbairn who tried to rescue a mother and baby who were swept off the ship by a rogue wave. O'Rourke railed against the vicissitudes and unpredictability of life. One minute he had been sharing a tankard with his companion in Mother Redcaps, the next he was gone. The death of the mother and baby also struck him hard. He thought of home and his own dear family. The brig continued on its journey, with all on board, hoping for a less eventful journey.

After passing south of Cadiz, one breezy morning, the look-out spotted two vessels approaching fast.

"Gunboats astern!"

Captain Moorcroft, at the helm, reached for his monocular. He peered at the craft making headway towards the *Mary Lou*. The surf crashed around the two marauding vessels he identified as xebecs.

"Battle stations!" he yelled.

Swiftly the vessels drew nearer. The captain's steely gaze focused on a blood red flag adorned with skulls and crossed swords.

"Damn it! Picaroons! Barbary Pirates!" he cursed.

Before he knew it and before the men had time to man the guns properly the swift pirate ships were upon them. Cannon fire erupted from the two xebecs across the bows of the *Mary Lou*. The motley crew of ferocious looking buccaneers held grappling hooks and were armed with cutlasses and pistols. One vessel collided with the brig and the other came around the bow to the port side. Bosun McGinty aided by Roberts smashed glass bottles on the decks as a deterrent to the marauders, but to no avail. The corsairs fired their pistols and launched their grappling irons into the rigging. The crew of the *Mary Lou* engaged them. A bullet from O'Rourke's carbine crashed into the tattooed face of a bald-headed pirate. The dagger held firmly in the buccaneer's blackened teeth exploded into smithereens like his face. O'Rourke then took aim at another attacker who had managed to swing across the swell between the vessels and stood on the rails of the brig slashing with his cutlass at the morass of frantic humanity below him. Henry Roberts' eyes bulged, and he hit the deck with a thump, a gaping fissure in his cleaved head. O'Rourke, horrified, was momentarily stunned. He suddenly came to his senses and pulled the trigger of his pistol. The metal ball flew out of the barrel into the pirate's torso with a flash and a bang. The Barbary pirate screamed in pain and fell backwards into the churning sea. In the next instance a mace exploded into O'Rourke's back. The pain seared through his flesh, his skin ripped away by the blow from the shark teeth embedded in the head of the vicious weapon. He screamed. He half-turned to confront his assailant, sabre in hand and saw the black-bearded Muslim twirling the mace above his head. The picaroon moved in mercilessly for the kill but trod on a shard of glass. It pierced the sole of his bare foot, and he yelled out in pain, hopping about the deck. This gave O'Rourke his chance to run the corsair through with his sword. Out of the corner of his eye he saw Bosun McGinty struggling with two other pirates and Verzon the mulatto despatching another with a cutlass. The freed slave had been taken on as an extra hand due to his physique, strength and experience as a mariner. Suddenly O'Rourke's swashbuckling defence came to an abrupt and painful end. He was flung to the deck with a crash and blacked out. The mast of the gaff-rigged spanker shattered by cannon fire came crashing down delivering a glancing blow to his head. His last audible memory was the sound of screams from the women and children cowering below deck as the pirates surged down the ladder towards them.

103

O'Rourke stirred. His head was banging. He felt sick. He tried to move his arms to feel the enormous bump on his head, but his hands were bound to the mainmast. He wrestled instinctively to free himself but an acute pain in his lacerated back forced him to refrain. His vision was blurred and, as it gradually cleared, he was met with the ghastly sight of Captain Moorcroft's tarred, naked, headless corpse, swaying from the yardarm, his feet bound with rope lashed to a spar. The deck was awash with blood. O'Rourke's head slumped to his chest. Then he felt the cold steel of a cutlass thrust under his chin. He opened his eye and saw a pair of blood-stained bandaged feet before him. The blade was raised forcing him to look up. He caught sight of brightly coloured yellow pantaloons and a grubby white, bloodied shirt and then he saw the scarred, dirt-streaked countenance of the Barbary pirate looming over him.

"This one is strong. He will fetch a good price. Attend to his wounds. We must look after our assets", Then he gestured to the swinging cadaver. "See your captain. He is a privateer. He is a pirate like me. Are you aware that captured pirates can be hung at sea? You are fortunate today. He is not."

The brig and the two pirate xebecs docked in Algiers after a few days. The Barbary pirates had taken advantage of the Royal navy's strategy of patrolling the coastlines of Spain and France and blockading French ports by probing for targets in the quieter shipping lanes. The surviving men, women and children were chained and led immediately to a marketplace where more slaves of white and black origin were assembled, of differing nationalities, waiting to be auctioned off to Arab buyers. The slaves were callously flogged by their new owners as soon as they were purchased, the white ones flayed with more gusto. Then the newly enslaved were then dragged off in all directions, screaming and pleading with the overseers who simply ignored them. Children were ripped away from their parent's grasp and sold individually to separate clients. O'Rourke stood in line, shocked and helpless, manacled in a coffle. He shuffled along next to Verzon who had been badly beaten about the face. His bald pate displayed a nasty gouge smeared with dried blood. The muscular mulatto, who had been offered employment by Captain Moorcroft, when a mate had died of dysentery in the Caribbean, had given a good account of himself during the fighting on board. There were several other mates chained in the coffle, but O'Rourke couldn't see McGinty. Verzon later confirmed that he had perished, throat ripped by a dagger, stripped naked and heaved overboard. The auction for the new arrivals began and the bidding intensified as it focused on Verzon. He was dragged away in his chains and flogged, beaten to the ground in front of his new master. O'Rourke was next. He stood there, naked, an iron slave collar chafing his neck, his hands and ankles manacled. Again, the bidding was vigorous with emirs, pashas and agents all admiring his tall and powerful physique. He suffered a blow to his kidneys by a carbine butt forcing him to his knees. One of the wounds previously inflicted by the mace opened up. He winced and gasped for air. Blood trickled down onto his bare buttocks. Two guards grabbed his neck brace and twisted him onto his back and zealously and intentionally pulled him roughly over the stony, broken ground to his master. He bit his lip and resisted crying out despite the excruciating pain. He was ordered to kneel up and forced to bow at the feet of the bey sat before him.

"The Pasha Yusuf of Karamanli will be pleased by my purchases and you infidels will repay him for keeping you alive by living in servitude, in perpetuity. Ha! Ha! Ha! Faisal, arrange the caravan! We leave at sundown."

The aide bowed and departed to arrange their journey to Tripolitania.

104

The enslaved, still in their coffle, were transported across the Maghreb to Tripoli, then onto the coastal city of Derna, capital of the Ottoman province of Cyrenaica. Some died from heat exhaustion and disease during the arduous journey, to the disgust of their masters. On arrival, O'Rourke and the male captives in his chain gang were immediately put to work constructing fortifications in the harbour, receiving only bread and water as recompense. The females and their children were allocated to the harems of the pashas, beys, and reis. Most of the women ended up as sex slaves. Verzon was the only other sailor from the *Mary Lou* who was chosen for Pasha Karamanli. The other survivors were dispersed to other areas of North Africa. O'Rourke and Verzon forged a strong bond. They got to know other *bagnards* in their penal gang as time went by. Nilsson, a blond-haired Swede. Penberthy, a Cornish fisherman from Penzance and Hutchinson, an American privateer. Hutchinson was hoping the American government would pay tribute and secure his release. He had been ransomed. He had survived for a year. His ship was taken by surprise in a lightning razzia by a Barbary xebec and two polaccas in the Atlantic. Penberthy had been enslaved for two years, plucked from the coast of Cornwall itself by the plundering North African raiders. His small hilltop cottage had been attacked in the dead of night by these terrifying itinerant corsairs. His wife and child were killed; chased over a cliff top as the pirates pursued them. He had been in bondage in Algiers first, then re-sold and brought to Derna. O'Rourke wondered how Penberthy still had the will to survive. Likewise, Nilsson, a Swedish midshipman whose merchant schooner was intercepted in the Mediterranean by the corsairs. He was singled out because of his blond hair more than any other *bagnard* and forced to endure the sexual predations of his masters, something which, to the captives' horror, they had all been subject to at one time or other. The men spoke constantly and longingly of escape whilst they ate their meagre rations of black bread before they were locked in their squalid *baños* for the night. O'Rourke dreamt of Kitty and the children. He did not know whether she had given birth to another baby boy or girl. He feared he may not ever see them again. He woke frequently during the night in feverish sweats disturbed by nightmares and fearing that both Kitty and the new born had not survived the birth. His chances of being released, like the lucky ones, through ransom, were slim to non-existent. He also feared that ophthalmia would ravage his one good eye and he would spend the remainder of his life in abject poverty as a beggar far from home. Death would almost certainly be preferable.

An unexpected opportunity to escape, however, arose when Derna came under attack from an American marine-led force of mercenaries sent via Egypt to attack Tripoli. The Barbary States had declared war on the United States in 1801 for failing to continue to pay tribute to the Berber Tripolitans for entering the waters of the Mediterranean to conduct business. In the early years of the war the United States had been allied with Sweden which had been in a conflict with the Barbary States since 1800. More American vessels were seized by the Barbary pirates and the crews ransomed, as in Hutchinson's case. The Americans had stepped up their efforts to minimise the threat by blockading the Berber ports and attacking Barbary vessels. The aggressive actions culminated in the raid on Derna in 1805.

O'Rourke was awakened at sunrise with a kick to his ribs by his cruel overseer Rafiq. The customary early morning routine. This brutal awakening though, on this particular day, was like being served a breakfast platter of bacon and eggs to the Irishman. Rafiq must have enjoyed his night of carnal pleasure, whoever that involved, male or female. A bad night would result in some poor unfortunate being bastinadoed until the skin of the victim's feet was raw and bloodied.

"Wake up slave!"

Rafiq went along the line of exhausted labourers meting out the same type of violent reveille. The captives stirred and dragged themselves to their feet except for the middle-aged Hutchinson. He remained comatose. The Berber overseer returned to him and booted him again in the ribcage harder, but he did not flinch. Rafiq snarled and snatched his caning rod from a subordinate. He kicked the prostrate slave again. He remained still. He turned him over. His pallid features explained all. The Tunis-born Muslim cursed and seethed with rage. Hutchinson was a prize. He had value, having been ransomed. Although no efforts had been made to pay the ransom, Rafiq knew he would be in trouble with his Bey. It was the overseer's job to ensure that valuable commodities like Hutchinson were kept alive, but he had taken a particular dislike to the American over recent months and treated him like any other loathsome, insignificant thrall in the chain gang, depriving him of food and sleep and subjecting the malnourished mariner to brutal beatings on a whim. Rafiq snorted grossly until his throat was full of mucus. He then spat the phlegm onto Hutchinson's sallow countenance and proceeded to urinate on the corpse.

"He was too white anyway. He's now green and yellow."

He laughed uproariously then suddenly stopped. An ice-cold steely glower bordering on the psychotic burnt into the hollow living-dead sockets of the frail and apprehensive onlookers.

"Laugh! Laugh you dogs!" he growled. He brought his iron rod down forcefully onto the emaciated flesh of one of the cowering captives. The others responded with tentative, contrived laughter as his new target wailed in pain.

"More! More!" he roared as he continued to strike broken bodies randomly. "Ha! Ha! Ha!"

Then suddenly he brought the feigned laughter to an abrupt halt. He picked on an individual, a quiet, unassuming Spaniard named Moreno and beat him with his fists, breaking his jaw, and not stopping until his face was a mass of crimson pulp. Eventually the last breath fled his weak, surrendering body. O'Rourke and the others burned with rage but felt powerless to intervene. Their shackles forbidding them. The terror gripping the shackled slaves spawned silence. A dreadful but ultimately cathartic silence, punctuated only by Rafiq's barking.

"Outside now!" The overseer laid into the rabble with the bastinado rod. The guards followed his example.

"There will be no food for you infidels today! It shall not be wasted! That's the bad news. The good news is that there is no work today for you either. Although it's not a holiday for you kafir. Today you will fight for your lives instead! The enemy is at the gates of Derna!"

He addressed his two flunkies. "Move these cadavers now!"

The coffle shuffled outside the ramshackle *baño*. Then the captives were escorted to the harbour fortress encouraged by the gouging lashes of the sentinels' whips. The local militia were already in situ poking muskets over the walls. At gunpoint, the men were herded into the fort, dragged over to cannons positioned around the ramparts and unshackled from their leg irons. Verzon peered out to sea. He could see a flotilla of ships approaching the harbour.

"Remove the manacles from their wrists!" Rafiq bellowed, his aides rushing forward to unfetter the slaves.

"Who's the enemy, gracious one?" Verzon dared to ask the overseer.

"American dogs, Greek mercenaries and treacherous Turks! Kill them or I will kill you!"

Suddenly a bombardment began from the American warships out in the bay and missiles rained down on the fortification. O'Rourke and the others had no alternative but to retaliate. Amidst the smoke and chaos and cries of the injured and dying, O'Rourke instinctively took command of the gun crew. He ordered Penberthy to seize the rammer and ram the load of gunpowder down the muzzle of the twenty-four-pounder gun. He then directed Nilsson to force in a wad of oakum which Penberthy rammed in also. Verzon, without waiting for the order, then heaved in the cannon ball and O'Rourke pierced the bag of gunpowder.

"Move the cannon forward to the parapet!" he ordered.

All four of them heaved the cannon forward. O'Rourke aimed it in the general direction of the flotilla of vessels but deliberately manoeuvred it so the missile would fall short.

"Move back!" he thundered amidst the din. He then lit the fuse. The gun discharged its ball with a roar and recoiled into the safety rope.

"Sponge!" he barked. Nilsson grabbed the sponger and cleaned out the barrel of the cannon and they repeated the process. In the meantime, the militia had begun to pour fire onto the American marines and mercenaries attacking the fortress as part of a land assault. The gun crew of slaves to the right of O'Rourke's party were blasted away by return fire, a ball smashing into the ramparts in front of them. Screams filled the air. Another missile sailed over their heads obliterating several militiamen manning the turrets on the far side. Verzon looked around for Rafiq. He was firing his weapon from the ramparts onto the attackers below who, having taken too many casualties, beat a hasty retreat. The bombardment continued in each direction. Reinforcements were brought into the fort and a militiaman was added to O'Rourke's party to ensure the range was accurate. They continued firing for the best part of an hour all whilst around them the casualties mounted but their luck held out. The militiaman was caught by flying debris from a near miss and was knocked unconscious during a renewed land-based assault which had gained momentum and then suddenly the fortifications were breached. All chaos broke loose. The militiamen fled for their lives back into the town. Rafiq cursed the pandemonium in his dispirited, fleeing fighters. Enraged, he singled out a white slave, a Maltese, Spiteri and shot him through the head with a pistol. He took aim again with a second pistol and downed another terrified black slave, known only as Zuri. Rafiq turned around to chastise his guards but was surprised to see they had already fled when his back was turned. His own minions had abandoned him. He was isolated. O'Rourke and the others seized their chance. They picked up discarded weapons and surrounded him. The brutal Rafiq cast away his pistols and withdrew his scimitar from the silk sash around his midriff. There was fear in his dark eyes which pleased the vengeful men confronting him but before he could react Nilsson drove a lance into his side.

"That's for Hutchinson!" he snarled.

Verzon then hacked at his neck with a cutlass. The brute screamed in pain to the delight of his tormentors.

"Who's laughing now?" Verzon asked. "That's for Zuri!"

O'Rourke drove a sabre into his guts, and he collapsed to the ground, squealing and shedding copious amounts of blood. Penberthy delivered the coup de grâce by lopping off his head with one swift blow of an axe, before saying.

"Louis Spiteri and Felipe Moreno, you also have been avenged! God rest your wretched souls."

105

The four fugitives fled the fort choosing not to follow the retreating rabble of defenders fleeing towards the town centre. Although the American-led forces seemed to have the upper hand, they thought it prudent to get away from the destruction in case the Arab troops rallied. They slipped away in the confusion and headed along the coast, donning Arabic garb after ambushing a cohort of Berbers escorting another coffle of human misery and degradation to the city. They slaughtered the escort and freed the black African slaves who chose to head inland rather than hug the coast. After hiding out at an abandoned caravanserai, the four escapees marched west until they came to a village. They rested until dawn then, still under cover of darkness, they overpowered some local fishermen who were preparing to set sail in a clearly misappropriated Maltese speronara. The four fugitives left them trussed up in some of the black slaves' fetters they had brought with them. They guided the boat out of the small bay but were soon bombarded by an American Navy cutter patrolling along the coast, the skipper failing to ask questions first, but they managed to outrun the craft. Fortunately, the speronara had provisions aboard. The men were careful to eat sparingly. They set a course northbound, hoping to head for Malta or Sicily but were blown off course eastwards during a squall. After several days, without further incident, they sighted an island. Anchoring in a cove, they swam ashore.

"We're free from bondage!" Verzon cried, splashing in the surf. They all lay on the beautiful beach laughing, much relieved to have escaped their oppressors.

Within a matter of minutes though, they were surrounded by a band of local peasants. The peasants took note of the lamentable condition of the new arrivals considering them to be no threat. One stepped forward, an older gentleman with a weathered, wrinkled complexion.

"Welcome to the Septinsular Republic. You are on the Greek island of Zakynthos," he said.

On arrival though at the main town the following day, after having enjoyed the hospitality of the locals who discovered them, the Greek authorities arrested them as French spies and incarcerated them but after a day of questioning they were released. Having no means of subsistence, the men were duly impressed into the Russian army whose forces controlled the seven islands of the Greek autonomous republic. They were sent to the island of Corfu to train and were subsequently despatched to a Jaeger Regiment. O'Rourke and the others did not complain. They were fed and watered and enjoyed the freedoms of army life and took the opportunity to build up their strength, taking advantage of the basic army medical facilities on offer to treat their various ailments.

In the autumn of 1805, the regiment was suddenly mobilised. With the Austro-Russian army having been defeated at Austerlitz, the Ionian Isles-based Russian forces landed in Naples with the intention of thwarting Napoleon's threatened invasion. Such was the alarming speed of conquest however, by Napoleon's troops in his latest European campaign, the Russian forces of the Septinsular Republic and their allies, the British, were forced to withdraw, fearing a decisive attack by the powerful French army. The four conscripted former slaves took the opportunity to abscond from the Russian lines to the British troops, who had arrived from Malta. They were subsequently evacuated and arrived in Sicily in January 1806, one step closer to home and feeling relatively safer in the bosom of the British army.

106

With Bonaparte's invasion plans coming to fruition though, the four companions found themselves unable to return to their homes. Instead, they were pressed into service to confront the French hordes. In July of 1806 they found themselves marching in echelon formation as part of the Royal Corsican Rangers battalion facing the French, Swiss and Polish forces of the French Army. The Battle of Maida, fought in the Calabria region of Italy, had begun. The Royal Corsican Rangers together with a Sicilian detachment, were positioned to skirmish with enemy *voltigeurs* but were pushed back. They were then reinforced by foot regiments and absorbed into the main body of troops. O'Rourke and his friends had only just formed up when the French infantry attacked in numbers. The British ranks heard the cry. "Make ready! Fire!" O'Rourke responded by raising his Baker rifle and firing into the mass of blue uniforms.

A return volley ripped into the British infantry shredding their numbers. Amidst the smoke and suffocating air, O'Rourke saw someone in his line lurch forward. The soldier hit the ground with a sickening crunch, like a felled tree. He recognized the bloodied blond hair of Nilsson. A musket ball had penetrated his frontal lobe. O'Rourke's racing heart ached for the unfortunate Swede. He gritted his teeth. Kneeling to reload with the enemy barely twenty yards apace, another deadly, deafening volley came from behind him obliterating the French ranks. A third volley from O'Rourke's line stopped them completely in their tracks. The acrid smoke drifted away to reveal an avalanche of bodies. Cries, screams and groans in French, Polish and Italian replaced the ringing in his ears. They could see the backs of the enemy. They were in flight.

"Charge! At 'em lads!" the order came.

The British broke ranks and went in pursuit of the enemy. O'Rourke ran, treading on the bodies of the fallen as he chased the French foot soldiers. He saw Verzon, outsprinting him, catch up with a limping French officer then bayonet him in the spine. O'Rourke caught up with a straggler who had fallen and was imploring him to spare his life. Without emotion, O'Rourke despatched him with his bayonet. Blood gurgled from the trooper's mouth. O'Rourke watched him in his death throes.

"That's for poor Nilsson, you bastard!" he replied in French.

Suddenly, a Polish cavalryman feigning death, sprang to his feet aiming his carbine at O'Rourke. Before he could pull the trigger though, a musket ball ripped through his skull. The Pole collapsed. O'Rourke looked in the direction where the shot came from. Verzon stood there holding the vanquished French officer's smoking pistol. O'Rourke nodded his thanks. Verzon, acknowledging his gesture, darted off in pursuit of more prey, happy in the knowledge he had repaid a debt to his former saviour. O'Rourke re-joined the hunt. He saw Penberthy joining in the killing spree, downing another fleeing officer with his musket, then gouging his bayonet into his chest. Rotelli, a Corsican, was then at his side, prising the sword from the grasp of the fallen major. Suddenly, a loud set of explosions occurred, the result of grapeshot, canister and mortar fire, the response of the French artificers and bombardiers. The blast of one projectile propelled the Irishman backwards. Dazed and deafened, O'Rourke struggled to his feet. He viewed the scene of carnage in front of him with scrambled senses and confusion. A crater now stood where Penberthy, Rotelli and the officer had been. Flesh, blood, and cartilage garnished his dark green tunic and blue trousers. He took one step forward but collapsed face down, in excruciating pain. He rolled over exhausted by his efforts and glanced down at his left foot. A shard of shrapnel from a howitzer shell was embedded in his boot. He tried to manoeuvre his left arm down to his foot, but his brain signals did not coordinate with his upper limb. He looked at his arm. It was flopping helplessly beside him at a disjointed angle. Suddenly pain skewered down his forearm. Another shard of shrapnel was protruding. He grunted, then passed out.

Fortunately for O'Rourke, the battle was short. Casualties were removed swiftly to the field stations. He awoke on a table in a marquee. He was groggy and nauseous. His vision was blurred. His damaged ear drums heard dulled voices.

"Orderly, damn it, man! He's awake. Strap him down. Put the block in his gob!"

"Yes, sir."

Then O'Rourke suddenly realized what was happening when the surgeon wrapped a tourniquet around his severely aching arm and reached for a curved blood-stained knife whilst an orderly forced brandy down his parched throat.

"No! Not that!" he screamed, choking and spluttering in equal measure.

He tried to wrestle free. The orderly forced his maw open and inserted the wooden block. He glanced down at the floor in his misguided desperation to find something with which to fight the orderly off. He was mortified. All he could see were sawn off limbs, arms and legs and severed feet strewn amidst a lake of blood. The surgeon brought the amputation knife down onto his forearm, then repeated the gory process, hacking at the tissue down to the bone. O'Rourke bit so hard on the block that he snapped a tooth, his agonising screams muffled. The surgeon took up his saw and its sharp, jagged blood-spattered teeth crunched into the bone beneath his elbow. O'Rourke's body arced in a spasm of pain and then he passed out again.

107

Twenty-four hours later, he awoke in a different tent, and was given a drink of rum by an orderly. He felt weak and drained, exhausted. For a while he dared not look at his aching arm. Then he plucked up the courage to glance at it. He cried out forlornly.

"God! No!"

Where his arm had been, there was only a blood-soaked bandaged stump.

Then he felt a shot of pain in his lower leg. He feared the worst. "My foot," he uttered to the orderly. "Is it..?"

"You still have it. We managed to save it. The shrapnel didn't penetrate as far. Your boot took the impact. We cauterized the wound."

O'Rourke let out a sigh of relief, then tears rolled down his cheeks. He sobbed plangently. A few hours later, the orderly returned with a surgeon. The surgeon examined his wounds, then, apparently satisfied, issued instructions to the orderly, then promptly left. The assistant carried out his orders and re dressed the wounds.

"Sorry, but we need the bed." The orderly pointed to a bath chair.

Another aide helped place the injured soldier in the bath chair and wheeled it outside. O'Rourke gulped fresh air into his lungs. He sat there, morosely, feeling despondent. Two stretcher-bearers came out of the marquee carrying a legless casualty. A cloth concealing the corpse's face slipped to the ground. O'Rourke was staring at a dead child. A drummer boy. The sobering sight of the deceased boy checked his emotions. Feeling guilt ridden, he sucked in some more fresh air, gulp after gulp and wiped the tears from his eyes. At least he was alive, although he was still at death's door whilst the wounds healed, due to the high rate of infection. He remained seated at a table in the shade of the tent watching prisoners file past, sharing a bottle of rum with a wounded bombardier. French, Poles, Italians and Swiss went by guarded by *Chasseurs Britanniques* and members of his own Royal Corsican regiment. He spotted the distinct, dark features of Verzon. He called out. His comrades halted the column and greeted him.

"Sergeant O'Rourke! Sergeant O'Rourke, we're glad to see you've survived. You will be going home now to your pretty wife back in England!" one Corsican, Ardelli said.

"Let's hope your important bits are still there for her sake," Verzon added as he placed his hand in front of his friend's stump. "Shake."

The soldiers laughed exhibiting the usual, perverse dark sense of military humour, forcing a tentative smile from the Irishman. Even some of the prisoners laughed.

"Take care," Verzon said. "I'll see you before you're evacuated, my friend. Penberthy?"

"He didn't make it. Nor Nilsson. I'm afraid."

"Life is cruel, my friend. Live each day as if it were your last."

The column set off again and disappeared out of view leaving O'Rourke reflecting on his deceased comrades. From despair to triumph and then back to despair. At least they were now forever free from their shackles.

108

For the next few days, O'Rourke remained at the casualty station near the beach. Despite his new-found resolve to live after witnessing the gruesome sight of the drummer boy and despite the camaraderie of his unit, O'Rourke felt himself sinking into a morass of despair and depression as he watched sailors and other orderlies stretcher a flow of corpses from the medical tents to be buried in pits under the parched, rocky terrain. He clung to his fragile life by a thread. Gradually, after a few more days of recuperation he felt slightly stronger which gave him the hope and strength to survive his latest ordeal. His wounds still caused him considerable pain but fortunately they did not become infected. After a period of reflection, he began to realise that he owed it to Penberthy and Nilsson to make it home. They had all concurred, whilst gazing up at the firmament festooned with a myriad of stars, on board the speronara, that someone had to stay alive to tell the tale of their misery and to make their sacrifice worthwhile.

At the end of the week, the field hospital received a distinguished visitor. Rear Admiral Sidney Smith who had supported the land forces with his squadron of Royal Navy ships and who had made several raids on the enemy's coastal forts came to inspect the makeshift hospital. He had left a contingent of his own sailors at the facility to assist the medical staff and was now tasked with organizing the evacuation of casualties back to Sicily. He toured the base with his entourage, pausing and speaking to some of the recuperating soldiers. O'Rourke was amongst them, sitting at a table with two other convalescing servicemen, slicing a melon.

"Be careful with that knife, sergeant," McCall, a Scot's dragoon said, holding the melon still with his one good arm.

"That's right, sergeant! He doesn't want to lose his other arm now, does he?" added the disabled bombardier, his left foot missing.

"I'm as steady as a rock," O'Rourke replied, hand shaking in mockery.

Sidney Smith's entourage paused in front of the convalescents. The Rear Admiral scanned the wounded men and then addressed them.

"Good day, gentlemen. I hope my men have brought you some comfort and tended to your needs."

"Yes sir," a corporal responded poised on a stool close by, head swathed in blood-soaked bandages. "But the extra tots of rum have given us the most comfort though, sir. We thank the Royal Navy for its generosity."

The Rear Admiral smiled, and the others laughed. The orderlies continued to scurry around busy. Another corpse was brought out from the marquee. Sidney Smith recognised the dead man as one of his own marines. He grimaced momentarily.

271

"It's time to get you men back to Sicily," he then said. "I've come to make the arrangements. Make sure you're still alive by the time we're ready!"

"If you double our rum ration sir, you can wager your life on it!"

The wounded men all laughed again except for O'Rourke who was distracted by an anxious looking orderly, a Swiss prisoner who was loitering behind Sir Sidney pretending to occupy himself with some supplies. Suddenly the prisoner lurched toward Smith clutching a dagger intended for the Admiral's back. Before he could strike, he let out a cry and gurgled as O'Rourke's own thrown blade pierced the would-be assassin's oesophagus. Wide-eyed, he dropped his weapon and sank to the ground clutching his throat trying desperately to stem the flow of blood. Smith spun around to see his attacker collapse to the ground.

"Good God! The scoundrel almost ran me through!" Smith cried, visibly shocked. An aide cautiously approached the stricken prisoner, with his drawn cutlass in hand. He turned him over. The death stare indicated that no further action was necessary except to call for the orderlies to remove his body.

Smith turned to his saviour. "My good man. Thank you. Your name, sir?"

"O'Rourke, sir. Sergeant Seamus O'Rourke of the Corsican Rangers, formerly of the Dillon's Regiment, sir."

"Sergeant O'Rourke, I am forever in your debt, sir. Surgeon Williams, please ensure that Mr O'Rourke is taken care of on board the *Pompée* when we evacuate. Double rations for him including the rum and make sure he has a comfortable berth."

"Yes, sir. I'll arrange it forthwith."

"In fact, double rations for all these wounded men. Good lord! I nearly did wager my life! The only other thing I would like to say Sergeant O'Rourke, is to practice your knife throwing. I expected it to be between his eyes."

The men laughed.

"That was with my bad hand, sir." He held up his stump. "I need to practice a bit more."

"Ah ha! Quite! Farewell Sergeant O'Rourke. Safe journey to you all and God be with you as he so obviously is with me."

The retinue moved on.

109

O'Rourke was transported to Malta from Sicily several days later after having staved off infection to his wounds. The British forces had retired to Sicily to defend the island after having made more raids on garrisons in the south of Italy ably assisted by Sidney Smith's flotilla. On the journey across the Mediterranean, O'Rourke pondered his future. His sailing days, he reckoned, were over. He wondered how the venerated Admiral Horatio Nelson had managed without his arm up until, that is, his tragic demise at the Battle of Trafalgar the previous year. His military career was all but over too. He feared for the future. As soon as he was able to, he had written to Kitty once he was acquitted of being a spy on Zakynthos. He informed her of his conscription and his move to Corfu, then Naples and finally he told her that he had joined the British Army again. He hadn't yet summoned up the courage to inform her of his injuries. Fortunately, his right arm was not the one amputated so he could still write. He composed his latest letter on board and was to despatch it from Malta. She had written once to him when he was in Zakynthos, telling him that she was overjoyed he was still alive. Previously, she had given up hope of him ever coming back. She had not known whether he was dead or alive. She had only heard that the *Mary Lou* was the victim of Barbary pirates, nothing more.

110

The frigate surged into Maltese waters and the distant bastions and cavaliers, spires and domes of the ancient citadel of Valletta could be seen shimmering in the mid-August heat. Constructed in the 1500s by the Knights of St John, the last time O'Rourke had set eyes on the fortress city, was when he was a passenger on board *L'Égyptienne*. At that time, he was not allowed to disembark due to a recrudescence of plague on board the ship which was quarantined in the bay whilst supplies were ferried to it. If he had been able to disembark, he would more than likely have stayed in Malta and re-joined his old Dillon's regiment which had since supplemented the garrison. But then, he would never have met Kitty. He could still possibly stay in Malta and arrange for his family to be transferred there. Or even Capri where the Royal Corsican Rangers were to be based. However, during the uncertain times of the Napoleonic era, Britain seemed safer, despite the threat of invasion. Ireland was out of the question, being a hotbed of unrest, where his allegiances would come under scrutiny.

This time his ship was allowed to dock. He was sent to the infirmary in Valletta for a health check. He waited, with others, to be seen. A nun came past issuing instructions to a young female nurse. He did a double take. He recognized the girl. It was Sanura. She walked off down a corridor before he could say anything. He then heard Gabriel Zammit's voice. The two of them came out of a room and they suddenly stopped, struck dumb by the sight of O'Rourke.

"My God! If it isn't Sergeant O'Rourke! See, Sanura!"

The two men embraced. Then Sanura approached and kissed him softly on the cheek.

"She's forgiven you. She loves Malta. See, I told you I would take good care of her. Your arm, alas, what happened? Why are you here?"

O'Rourke revealed all about his adventures whilst a guest of the Zammits. Gabriel had wed Sanura and they had two children. He stayed with them for a couple of days promising to stay in touch. The doctor had ordered him to convalesce for two weeks, so he went to see if any of his old companions from Dillon's were stationed there. O'Rourke hobbled through the narrow streets with the aid of a crutch, his foot still tender but gradually improving. He arrived at the garrison and found some old acquaintances. They were overjoyed to see their popular former sergeant, and they arranged for him to lodge at their billet. He reminisced regaling everyone with his adventures, his fortunes and misfortunes over several ales and dinner. Mulligan, one of the few remaining soldiers of Jacobite descent left in the regiment, joked about the two of them heading back to Ireland to fight the British.

"Come on Seamus, come back to the Motherland with me. We'll lead a new rebellion. Then, after we've kicked the English out of Hibernia, we'll restore the

Stuarts to their throne, open a tavern on the banks of the river Liffey and draw water from that fine watercourse and invent a brew, an elixir. What say ye?"

"Sean, the only fight I have left in me is to fight for my wife and family in Liverpool. That's it. I'm done with the military. I'm sick of fighting. Look where it's got me. I'm an invalid. It nearly sent me to my grave. I'll be on the first ship out of here to Portsmouth in two weeks' time. I have some business to attend to then I'll be on my way to Liverpool to see my Kitty and the children who I've not seen these past two years. In fact, I haven't seen the little lad at all. Charles Francis O'Rourke!"

"Let's toast him!" Mulligan roared. "*Et Jeanne D'Arc!*" he laughed. "Don't you fancy staying in Malta? In this beautiful Mediterranean climate? Re-enlist in the regiment. It's a comfortable, easy life at the moment looking after the French prisoners. We speak French and so we get the job of guarding them."

O'Rourke's ears pricked up at this. That was a job he could do. He recalled the French prison in Liverpool. That, he thought, could be his salvation.

"Mulligan, my incorrigible friend. It's a tempting offer which I have to unfortunately decline. You have though, given me food for thought. *Santé* Sergeant Mulligan!"

111

The barquentine deftly navigated the approaches to the harbour. The town of Portsmouth loomed up before it. The Bay of Biscay had been particularly stormy and treacherous, which assured O'Rourke and the other anxious passengers that Barbary Pirates would not be patrolling the seas in those treacherous conditions. The naval vessel was, in any case, well protected with its armoury. The passengers still suffered from *mal de mer* in the choppy seas and the decks were awash with vomit. The rest of the voyage passed peacefully and the weather in Portsmouth on arrival was cool but sunny. It was late September 1806. Had he delayed his sojourn in Malta for a month or so, then the ground at the cemetery in Gosport might be frozen and he wouldn't be able to extract his 'treasure'. He hadn't told Kitty about the tablet or where it was concealed. She would no doubt be apoplectic if he had told her. As it happened, it was a struggle to dig up the artefact. He'd waited until evening descended. Then, with a spade attached to his knapsack, two loaded pistols and a dagger hidden in his greatcoat, he had dug with one hand to unearth it. It was a real struggle and he felt vulnerable to attack by brigands. Several days later he stepped off the coach in Liverpool.

112

The October air of 1806 was typically cool when O'Rourke stepped off the coach. The usual tsunami of urchins surrounded it, each one jockeying for position, some coming to blows. The coach driver gave them all a rollocking and struck out with his crop. O'Rourke half-expected Francis to be amongst them but of course he was not. He waited for his goods to be offloaded before choosing one of the scruffy kids to carry his bag. He slung his knapsack over his shoulder and deliberately revealed his pistol to the urchin by opening his tunic as a deterrent in case the youngster had any ideas of scarpering with the baggage. He chose a gaunt, gangly youth called Arthur. Instead of heading straight home, he took a room in the Liverpool Arms. He tipped Arthur, who had never shut up on their short journey, asking one question after another, about his eye and his arm and inquiring about the contents of the sack. O'Rourke had to figure out where he was going to cache the Egyptian artefact. In the sack he also had some souvenirs from the Battle of Maida. Verzon had managed to secure them from the prisoners and the deceased foe and had shared them with him. It also contained the last of the Mameluke weapons; a dagger, pistol and sabre. He came to the conclusion that the sack would have to be hidden somewhere on the Great Heath but was forced to re-evaluate his strategy because the town had been expanding at a considerable rate and more dwellings were proposed for the Heath. He decided to opt again for burying his loot in a graveyard. Either that or risk depositing it at Mother Redcaps. That evening, having made his decision, he hired a cart and drove it up Dale Street, to St John's Church located near to the General Infirmary on Shaw's Brow. The conditions were perfect with a fog enveloping much of the town. Deceased French prisoners had been interred in the graveyard there. He tethered his horse and chose one of the rudimentary graves in which to conceal his horde. The final resting place of *Sergent-Chef* De Villiers, according to the wooden cross protruding from the earth. Again, he struggled with his one good arm to get the spade into the ground which was beginning to freeze over. Now and again, he could see the flicker of lights shed from lanterns inside the collection of buildings housing the Infirmary, the Seaman's Hospital and the adjacent Lunatic Asylum. He managed with some difficulty to dig down far enough to conceal the sack. He had just made good the soil, resting the spade against the wooden cross, when he heard the crunch of a twig behind him. He looked over his shoulder with alarm A garrotte was suddenly flung around his neck. It tightened and he started to choke. The shaven headed assailant snarled. Another footpad appeared in front of him, looming out of the fog, a strange looking individual in rags with thin wispy hair attached to his almost bald pate. The eyes were staring wildly, a lop-sided grin revealing an almost toothless mouth. The brigand brandished a knife. O'Rourke fought to stay on his feet. He was being dragged back by the other fiend. He clawed at the cord trying to relieve the pressure on his neck. He managed to squeeze his fingers inside the rope and jerked to his left, turning slightly, enough for him to make eye contact with the spade. He removed his grip momentarily on the cord which only served to tighten the garrotte and choke him more but in one movement he seized the spade and lashed out with it violently over his head. The metal edge of the spade met the forehead of the footpad behind him, causing a split across his temple. The man screamed and reeled back in agony relinquishing his hold on the rope. O'Rourke coughed and spluttered. He spun round at once to face the other wild-eyed, laughing villain in front of him just in time before he lunged with the dagger. O'Rourke evaded the thrust of the sharp instrument but lost his balance. Whilst falling, he managed to kick the blade from his opponent's grasp. He hit the ground, jarring his back, but swiftly pulled his pistol out of his belt and blasted the crazy standing over him. The other assailant bleeding from the injury sustained to his forehead, having recovered from his momentary pain and shock, snarled and moved menacingly towards O'Rourke brandishing the spade. The Irishman delved into his greatcoat inside pocket and withdrew the other pistol of the brace he always now carried. He cocked it in an instant and aimed it indiscriminately over his head and pulled the trigger. The gun flashed. His hat and hair was singed, and the din almost deafened him. The lead impacted on the footpad's shoulder, and he was thrown back to the ground. This gave O'Rourke time to drag himself unsteadily to his feet, unsheathe his dagger and dive onto the supine figure plunging the serrated blade into the bald cranium of his assailant. O'Rourke exhaled heavily and stared for a moment at the contorted face of the slain man he was lying on. He was shaking. He hauled himself up and proceeded to drag the bodies away from the disturbed grave with some effort. He laid them on the steps of the church and climbed exhaustedly back up into the cart and sped away.

The next morning, as he left the tavern, he saw Arthur. He gave him his bag to carry again. Arthur told him about the dead bodies being found at the church. Apparently, his assailants were deranged escaped inmates from the Lunatic Asylum. They trudged up past the Fall Well opposite the town's foreboding bedlam. O'Rourke glanced over. A shiver went down his spine. They continued on past the rope works, the windmills and the wasteland on which the limekilns had recently stood and strode out onto the Great Heath, with Arthur chatting incessantly.

113

O'Rourke stood on the threshold of the new mansion of Kitty's employer. Kitty had responded to a letter sent from Zakynthos, the first one her husband had managed to send since he was enslaved. It sent her into raptures when she received it. Once she knew he was alive, she had run around the cottage waving the missive and kissing and hugging the kids repeatedly. When she wrote back, she explained that they could not afford to stay in their home. She had taken on extra work as a seamstress to make ends meet but still struggled with the rent and the feeding and clothing of the kids. She had managed to gain access to O'Rourke's stash at Mother Redcaps but that had now been exhausted. She provided a new address for them and for her employer. She and the children had been forced to rent rooms in a court dwelling in Crosbie Street.

Once remunerated, Arthur departed. O'Rourke prayed that all was fine. He placed his knapsack on the ground and knocked. It was Kitty who came to the door. She stood and stared, momentarily in shock, then leapt on him smothering him with kisses. His one good arm wrapped around her back, and he squeezed her closer to him. She wondered where his other arm was, and she grabbed for it to wrap it around her. She fumbled around for it and felt the limp sleeve of his greatcoat. She pulled out of his grip when she realised it wasn't there. She grabbed at the sleeve.

"Dearest, oh no! Your arm! What's happened to your arm? Good God!" she said alarmed and in shock.

"I lost it," he said laconically. "Can you sew me another one on since I hear you're an able seamstress?"

She paused a moment, not knowing whether to laugh or cry, then burst out laughing, thumping his chest with her fists.

"Go to the court. Francis is there with the children. I'll see if I can get off early and make the time up another day."

She smothered him in kisses then assisted him with his knapsack pulling the strap over his left shoulder and closed the door slowly blowing a gentle kiss with her hand in the direction of her beloved.

He traipsed to Crosbie Street and ducked as he went through a low archway. He paused a moment, pressing his back to the tunnel wall, to allow a man tugging a hand-pulled water cart to squeeze by. Then he continued, emerging into a damp, narrow courtyard devoid of sunlight, named Zwill. The smell of sewage hit him full on. It seemed to be oozing out of every grate in the cobbled court. Two scavengers with the thankless task of cleaning out the communal privy were brushing and swilling away excrement with pails of water. Scruffy, snotty-nosed kids, faces covered in dirt were running around on the cobbles playing a game of tag. The players ranged from toddlers upwards to about ten-year olds. He stopped and watched them for a moment, not sure if his own son Patrick was amongst them. The unkempt kids stopped and fell silent and stared at the mysterious unknown character sporting an eye patch and minus one arm.

Suddenly, a shout echoed around the dour brick walls of the sun-deprived court. "Seamus! Your home!"

He turned and saw Francis, seated on the steps of a dwelling, holding a young child swaddled in a grubby shawl. Francis leapt to his feet with the bundle in his arms and ran to O'Rourke, hugging him. The toddler was smothered in his father's greatcoat, his dislodged bonnet covering the whole of his chubby red face.

"This is your second son, Seamus! Charles! Here, hold him!"

"No, it isn't Francis," O'Rourke said, as he took the 17-month-old little mite from his grasp. Francis re-positioned its bonnet. The toddler started to bawl. A quizzical expression crossed Francis's face.

"It's my third! There's you of course!"

Francis grinned and embraced him once more. He then realised alarmingly that his stepfather's arm was missing.

"Your arm, Seamus! My God, what happened?" he said in awe.

"I'll tell you all about my adventures inside. Where's Patrick?"

O'Rourke felt a tug on his armless sleeve. He turned to see a tousled-haired dirty-faced kid looking up at him.

"Mister, who are you?"

O'Rourke passed little Charles to Francis and knelt in front of the grimy faced child, tears welling in his father's eyes.

"Sonny, I'm your father. I should have guessed it was you with your red hair!"

He drew the child close into his chest and hugged him.

"Come on, I've got something for you three. Let's go into the house."

Francis led the way into the dark and dank three storey dwelling. Seamus crossed the threshold. He happened to peer down into the cellar and was shocked to see a gaunt figure with sunken eyes staring back at him from a broken windowpane. A shiver ran down his spine. For a moment he thought he was back amongst the slaves of the Maghreb.

"Lord God Jesus, who's that down there?"

"Mrs Bryant. Kitty lets the cellar to her. She has a baby girl. She's not too well. Neither is the baby. She pedals trinkets and sometimes looks after the babies if I'm not around. Kitty pays her or provides her with food."

The downstairs room, approximately twelve feet by fourteen, was cramped and sparsely furnished with an old rickety table and four chairs, a side cabinet with one wooden leg missing propped up by bricks, a blackened hearth with various rusting pots spread around it and a tatty looking rocking chair, its worn fabric ripped and torn. Upstairs was one bedroom with a battered wardrobe, a worm-riddled chest of rickety drawers, a stool and a bed, the only piece of furniture he recognised from the cottage. O'Rourke's heart sank. He felt guilty for having left his family almost destitute. However, the enthusiasm of the children raised his spirits.

280

Not long after, Kitty arrived. She swooped Charles up in her arms and the five of them hugged. The faces of the three boys were smothered in toffee apple red and they each held a wooden toy soldier, each with a different uniform on.

"My dearest Kitty, I'm sorry you've had to suffer living here in this awful, stinking, God forsaken place."

"It's not your fault, darling. You had to do what you had to do. I couldn't afford the rent at the cottage. I had to sell most of the furniture too."

"I promise I will make it up to you. I'm going to find work and as soon as we can afford it, we'll look for another cottage somewhere. I've had my fill of living in filthy, overcrowded hovels. I can assure you that."

"But, what work can you undertake, without your arm? Surely, that will restrict you."

"It didn't stop Admiral Nelson, did it?" Francis interjected. "His sword is in the Town Hall. The good burghers of Liverpool fashioned a new one for him, but he died a hero on the *Victory* before they could present it to him. Maybe you can have it instead Seamus!"

Kitty and Seamus laughed.

"No good to me son. My military days are over. Besides, there's many more army and navy war heroes who deserve it before me. I'll tell you about my plans shortly over a brew. And about my exploits! Anyway, I'm famished. We're going to have a celebration dinner tonight. Here, Francis, take this money. Go and buy a chicken and some vegetables. If there's anything left over, buy a pudding or cake. At least for one day, we can live like kings! Conceal the coinage well. Watch out for footpads and urchins."

The youngster's grin rippled from ear to ear, and he darted off with the coins afforded him, leaving his guardians in a loving embrace.

114

The icy wind gusted in from the Mersey causing O'Rourke to wrap the collar of his greatcoat closer around the nape of his neck. He stamped his frozen feet on the ground. He had been waiting for thirty minutes outside the Tower Gaol. Other men had gathered there. Some were beggars, others, like himself, were seeking employment.

The head gaoler, Thomas Morton finally arrived. He was a grey-bearded, snub-nosed corpulent man. He waddled over to the Tower gates, having made his way from the other side of the gaol from his shabby lodgings. He ushered the waiting men away by flapping his hand at them in a disparaging manner.

"Away with you, you loiterers! How many times do I have to tell you? There is no work for you here. Come on, shift! I've work to do. You vagabonds also, go on, hop it! Do you think I'm made of money? You'll end up *in here* if you don't stop pestering me! No alms today or any day! Especially for you!" he said, pointing at O'Rourke. "Ha!Ha!Ha!"

O'Rourke replied in French. "*Bonjour, monsieur, je n'ai pas besoin d'aumônes. Je n'ai besoin que d'un emploi.*"

The portly gaoler stopped in his tracks. He coughed up and spat out some mucus. "Zounds! Are you one of Felix Durand's French fugitives come to give yourself up after years on the run? Or are you one of Napoleon's spies? Or, has the damned invasion finally begun?" he said jocularly.

O'Rourke reverted to English. "None of those, I beg you sir. I am a pensioned soldier of the British Army, but I speak fluent French. I thought I might be of service to you. May I ask if you have in your employ someone who speaks the French language?"

"I have one person, a Huguenot, who speaks the language, but he can't work every hour God sends. Hmm, come and see me later my man, say at noon. We shall discuss this further, now good day to you, I have urgent affairs. We have had another escape. This time local debtors and felons!"

He barged forcibly through the crowd.

"Come on, out of my way. No alms! No jobs! How many times do I have to tell you?" he moaned pushing his way through the other remonstrating and imploring wretches.

O'Rourke distanced himself from the badgering pitiful rabble and afforded himself a smile and left to tell Kitty the positive news.

115

At noon prompt O'Rourke was outside the gaoler's dingy office. He was summoned in to be met by Morton and the Huguenot. The interview commenced and the Huguenot, introduced as Yves Drelincourt, was suitably impressed with the Irishman's command of the French language. Within thirty minutes, the meeting concluded, and O'Rourke left with a grin as wide as the Mersey. He was to report for duty the following morning at 0800 hours on the dot at the Tower Gaol.

Kitty and Seamus were delighted. The head gaoler had his doubts about the interviewee's physical condition but Drelincourt, believing his job would be easier with another fluent French speaker on the payroll, persuaded his superior that the benefits outweighed the disadvantages, and that the new recruit could also eavesdrop on the prisoners to discover their grievances, potential plots and intentions.

116

Six months into the post and O'Rourke had proved his worth by uncovering another plot by some of the French prisoners to escape. The ringleaders were punished with solitary confinement and reduced provisions, and one was moved to another gaol. None of the prisoners had been informed that he could speak and understand French, and they were astonished when it was revealed he knew exactly their intentions and what they had been saying about him and the other gaolers. They were a lot more circumspect from that point on about discussing things in his presence. In general, his appointment had led to improvements for both parties. The gaolers understood the needs of the prisoners more and relationships improved as a result. Drelincourt was mainly on duty at night so had little desire to address the needs of the prisoners. Indeed, he was always rather indignant when his slumbers were interrupted.

By June 1807, Kitty had given birth to her third child. A baby girl. The tiny bundle of joy was born premature but survived. They christened her Avril May O'Rourke. One day, a few months after the birth, O'Rourke was summoned to Morton's office. A young lad had passed a message on for him at the gates of the prison. He unfolded a piece of paper and read it. It was Kitty's handwriting imploring him to come home quickly. Avril May had taken a turn for the worse.

The physician breathlessly followed O'Rourke back to the court. He could not keep pace with the latter's strident gait. They disappeared through the dank and dirty covered passageway and emerged into the foul-smelling court. O'Rourke rapped on the door and an anguished Kitty opened it.

"The baby, Kitty, where is she?"

She pointed to the bedroom. Dr Phillips doffed his hat and went straight up the stairs. Francis was there watching over the baby who was wailing incessantly. The medic, who was employed by the Infirmary and the prison, ushered Francis out of the bedroom and then set about examining the bawling, implacable Avril May.

"Right, what have we here?"

"Ulcers and blisters on her feet and legs. Her glands look swollen. Has she been vomiting?"

"Yes," Kitty said. "And she's had trouble breathing. I was feeding her this morning and she kept stopping and gasping for air."

"Can you open her mouth for me please? Ah, she has a greyish-white coating at the back of her throat. I think she may, alas, have contracted Boulogne sore throat."

"Doctor Phillips, are, are you sure?" O'Rourke asked.

"Quite certain. And I'm very sorry to tell you Seamus and Kitty, sadly, there's nothing I can do. The Strangling Angel of Children has come for her. She's had the kiss of death. The malady has been passed on to her through kindness."

Kitty wailed and threw herself in anguish on to the bed. Tears ran down her gaunt face.

"Oh God, please don't take her away! Please don't take her away! Sweet cherub, no!"

"Keep giving her liquids Seamus. That will give her some comfort. I'm truly sorry. I can't do more," the surgeon added solemnly, before departing.

Seamus gently took his despairing wife off the bed and held her tightly. Francis entered, with tears in his eyes. O'Rourke shook his head sorrowfully. The boy ran out distraught.

Three days later, Avril May O'Rourke was laid to rest in her tiny coffin. Kitty, racked with guilt, blamed herself and fell into a deep depression. Her employer was kind enough to keep her position open and told her not to fret about it and that she could return when she felt she was able. O'Rourke bottled up his emotions and threw himself into his work. Gaolers and prisoners were united in sympathy. The popular Irishman had proved to be firm but fair in his dealing with the inmates. Kitty's depression lasted for several weeks until she realised that she had to be strong for her sons and she returned to work. Only through work could she help lift the family out of poverty. Seamus and Francis had helped enormously when she was in her plangent state and helped her get back on her feet. Her joie de vivre returned when she found out she was pregnant again and she took on her responsibilities once more with renewed vim and vigour. It was December 1807.

117

The prisoners burst out into the courtyards and into the September sunshine as enthusiastic and excited as school children at break time. Men and women, old and young, girls and boys intermingled and sought out their friends. Debtors, felons and the French sailors and soldiers, the prisoners of war, were mixing freely. O'Rourke and his fellow gaolers watched on, ready to intervene in violent disagreements which erupted from time to time. He particularly disliked the attempts of the criminal hierarchy to impose their tyrannical, brutal will on the weak and vulnerable, so he kept his eye on the troublemakers. The stench from the shit heap in one corner of the yard made him gag. The monthly disposal would occur in the next few days, thankfully. He wrapped his scarf tighter around his mouth and continued to observe the convicts. Some bantered, others exchanged spirits, wagered or played games. Women strolled around the grounds, arms linked, preening in front of the men. Children chased chickens around the yard whilst consenting couples engaged in sex in corners or up against the grimy walls in full view of the other inmates. His mind wandered to his new baby girl, Fleur-Rose O'Rourke. He prayed every day that she would survive. She seemed to have a stronger constitution than the tiny, premature, and ultimately tragic Avril May.

Kitty was ecstatic, but he feared for her mental health if God were to take this baby away as well. He also thought about Francis. The boy, as soon as he had reached the age of thirteen, had volunteered for His Majesty's Navy and vowed to follow in the footsteps of his hero Admiral Horatio Nelson. O'Rourke had tried to dissuade him, owing to his own maritime experiences but the youth was obsessed with the sea and his ardour had been enkindled by Nelson's victorious 1805 routing of the enemy at Trafalgar. At least it was one less mouth to feed. The last he had heard was that Francis was a ship's lad on the ship of the line *HMS Barfleur* serving under Rear-Admiral Tyler and the vessel was currently engaged in a blockade of Lisbon. Patrick and Charles, although a handful, were being looked after by Mrs Bryant. Her baby girl Daisy had sadly succumbed to Boulogne sore throat too, later to be known as diphtheria. There was consequently some kind of empathy between the two mothers. The antics of the two young tearaways allowed her to focus on something else and she doted on them as if they were her own. She shared in the benefits that Seamus's job had brought to the family with her hours of child-minding being rewarded fairly. She still had time for her trinket selling when her nurse-maiding duties were not required and she hoped to find herself a real man, the opposite to Daisy's father, a rogue of a sailor, who had abandoned her and the baby when it was born.

O'Rourke's thoughts were interrupted by a fellow gaoler.

"Seamus! Mr Moreton requires your presence forthwith."

O'Rourke proceeded to the office. He trudged through the ankle-deep mud in the passageway, passing a grunting couple locked in intercourse, and climbed the stairs to the chief keeper's room.

"Ah, Seamus, I have been informed we have more French prisoners of war coming to Liverpool in the coming weeks and months. I don't know where we'll put them all. We'll have to disperse them around the other gaols. I want you to liaise with the other prison officials at the Old Bridewell, St George's Dock and the Powder House on Brownlow Hill to see what capacity they have before they all start arriving. The first batch will be here next week."

"Right you are, Mr Morton."

"I also want you to liaise with the sea captains on arrival and arrange for the prisoners' initial transfer to the Tower. Once here, I will decide with the authorities where we can house them. It looks as if this will continue for some time. The Duke of Portland is getting twitchy with all the French prisoners being held along the south coast. They fear a mutiny, so they want to scatter them across the country."

"A wise move perhaps, sir. Fine, I'll take care of that. Any exact date?"

"No. I'll let you know in due course. Can you also go this afternoon to inspect the facilities at the House of Correction too? I'm too busy collecting jail fees today from our clientele or trying to. Here, take this missive. Give it to a runner. One of those kids that hangs around the gool will do it for a farthing."

Morton flipped him a coin and said, "Heads!"

O'Rourke caught it, opened his fist and looked. The copper coin had landed on the obverse side with the portrait of George III embossed on it.

"Correct, sir! Good call."

O'Rourke left and went outside the prison gates. Around the corner was the usual gang of bare-footed urchins larking around. He watched intrigued as they waited for a bag tied to a rope to be lowered from one of the prison's narrow windows. The debtors used this ruse to obtain money or food from sympathetic passers-by, but the impish lads had intercepted the bag. They giggled and bantered as they placed a stone in the bag. The hopeful recipient, up in the Tower, feeling a change in the weight of the load, hauled it up but its arrival back in the Tower produced a verbal volley of curses and insults. The street kids laughed heartily and danced around. Then the stone was launched out of the window and struck and floored one of the lads which sent the rest into more raptures. The stricken lad regained his feet gingerly and rubbed the tender bump on the back of his head. O'Rourke recognised him. It was Arthur. O'Rourke, laughing, beckoned to him. Arthur came over. He was even more wraith-like since O'Rourke had last seen him.

"Ouch!" Arthur complained. He rubbed the unkempt, curly blonde mass of hair on his head

"Serves you right for messing around. Listen, I need you to do a little job for me. Can you take this letter to the House Of Correction? Make sure it's delivered to Mrs Heavyside herself. It's from Mr Morton. Here."

He flicked him the farthing.

"No problems, sir. Rest assured it will be delivered promptly and I'd be happy to undertake any more errands that are required. I am at your service, sir."

Arthur dashed off, stubbing his toe in his eagerness to get away from the other lads who just sniggered anew. O'Rourke felt a pang of guilt. He had helped Francis avoid a life of misery on the streets and wanted to help Arthur, but things were still financially tight. Although Kitty's job had been kept open for her, she had not received any income during her period of stress and incapacity. They still hoped to move to a cottage away from the slum dwellings of the court and were trying to save what they could.

That afternoon O'Rourke set out to visit the House of Correction. He was trudging up Water Street when Arthur hailed him. The boy ran across to him.

"I delivered your message sir, to the lady, as requested."

"I'm grateful young man."

"Do you mind if I walk with you sir?"

"No, of course not, Arthur."

"Did you know there used to be a ducking stool in the House of Correction, sir."

"I believe so. Mr John Howard, the penal reformer urged them to do away with it several years ago, so I was told, but they still had it in later years. How do you know about the cuckstool?"

"I was born in the House of Correction, sir. My mother was an inmate there. She was a petty thief. An alcoholic. Always in trouble. In fact, I was witness to her being ducked there when I was little. I remember her screams. They'll stay with me forever. I was terrified I was going to be next. She was ducked once before at the Flashes, she told me. It nearly killed her. She was sent to the Infirmary on Shaw's Brow, I believe."

"What happened to her?"

"She died of typhus when I was seven, sir. At the Lunatic Asylum."

"And your father?"

"I didn't know him. All I know was that he was one of Pudsey Dawson's Liverpool Volunteers. Apparently, the men were being drilled at Moss-Lake Fields in preparation to fight the French invaders who had landed at Cardigan Bay in Wales with a force of two thousand. Rumours abounded they were headed for Liverpool to sack the town in revenge for the amount of destruction the Liverpool privateers and Liverpool-built navy frigates had wrought. They say that Liverpool's wealth has grown substantially as a result of privateering and ship building."

"Yes, it has, and of course, because of the abhorrent slave trade. All things maritime, eh?"

"And geography. Geography has dictated Liverpool's fortunes. And my misfortune, I suppose, because, anyway, the men got drunk, and my father was taken by a press-gang. I never saw him again. I still don't know if he's dead or alive. It sent my mam crazy. She reverted to theft to survive. Just like me, at times. By the way, sir, here's your purse back."

O'Rourke stopped and checked the pocket in his tunic.

"You cheeky bugger, Arthur!"

They both laughed.

288

"You're a very clever lad, Arthur. My wife Kitty works for a merchant who has connections. I'm going to see if he can pull some strings to get you into the Blue Coat. If you get in that school, you'll get the education your intelligence deserves."

"Gosh! Thank you, sir. I'd love to read and write. How's Francis sir?"

"The last time I heard he was blockading Lisbon with the British Navy."

"Wow! I've heard the British Army is on the Iberian Peninsula and was victorious against Napoleon's forces at Vimeiro. I suppose you'll be receiving more French prisoners in due course."

"That's why I'm checking out the House Of Correction now, to see if they have any capacity."

"Maybe you can move all the women to the House of Correction to create space at the Tower Gaol."

"That's a good idea Arthur, but it would cause uproar amongst the prisoners, to be sure, especially the debtors."

The two arrived at the main entrance in Mount Pleasant.

"I may have some more letters to send out in a few days so hang around the prison. Here, go and get yourself some lobscouse."

O'Rourke gave him another farthing, bid him farewell and then entered the institution alone.

118

Liverpool. Present day.

Jules switched off the TV. She was sick of endless debates about the stele and its authenticity and intended message. Paul was making dinner. Edmund had told him that, in the light of the team breaking up, his contract would be terminated in two weeks' time. He pondered his future as he stirred a pan of scouse. His circumstances had changed for the better, but he still feared being cast back onto the streets. Jules had been a wonderful lifeline for him, but he wondered whether their relationship was viable, once she felt safe and removed from any danger. Jules took a phone call. It was from Penny. She was flying out to Majorca with her family for two weeks. Paul served dinner. Jules blew on a hot chunk of beef before speaking.

"Do you know what? I think we need a holiday as well Paul. Some downtime in the sun will do us both good. I'm going to call Mum. We'll go to France. We can stay in one of the *gîtes* if it's not booked. You're still my bodyguard up until mid-September, so, wherever I go, you have to come too."

"Sounds fine to me, Jules."

She grabbed her mobile.

"Hold on. Finish your dinner first."

She concurred. Paul poured her a glass of red.

"Where exactly do they live again? Somewhere in the south of France, I think you mentioned."

The Charente region. More to the mid-west of the country. Near to Ruffec, about twenty miles from Poitiers. They live in an old mill house and rent out two *gîtes*. It's beautiful. They have large grounds with a lake in the middle, a stream that used to power a mill on one side of their land and a small river on the other. It's very peaceful. You'll love it. You can go only on one condition."

"What's that?"

"You fetch the croissants from the *boulangerie* in the village each morning."

"Sounds like a deal."

Jules finished her dinner and before a dessert of apple crumble and custard was served, she phoned her mum, Diana. They spoke at length and then she had a brief chat to her dad, Geoff.

"All sorted. It just so happens they've had a cancellation for next week and the other week was vacant anyway so, all we need to do is book some flights. Hold it, you have got a UK passport, haven't you?"

"I'm sorry, no," Paul said apologetically. "It expired."

"Oh, no! That's disastrous! We won't be able to go then," Jules groaned.

"But, I do have a French passport."

"What! You've got dual nationality? Oh, you big oaf!"

He cowered as she grabbed the cushion off the sofa and laid into him.

"My grandfather was French, remember. That's how I got it."

He was laughing as she belted him. The cushion then burst open showering them with cascading feathers.

"Ooh, look what you've done! Wait till I tell Edmund."

She jumped on him as he fell back on the sofa and continued to whack him with what was left of the cushion then she started kissing him. A further flurry of feathers floated down like a shower of confetti. One feather landed between their lips, and they laughed as they simultaneously tried to blow it away. They both slid lengthways on the sofa still embracing each other and kissing passionately.

119

The Ryanair flight from John Lennon Airport touched down in Bergerac. It was a beautiful late August morning. The sun was shining. It was going to be a warm day. They collected their hire car in the compound just across from the terminal and set off on the two hours plus journey to the *gîte*. It was situated a couple of kilometres from Ruffec in Aquitaine. They arrived in the town of Verteuil-sur-Charente and turned left across the bridge taking in the beautiful sight of the Château de Verteuil poised majestically on the banks of the river Charente. Five minutes later they were in the tiny village of Poursac negotiating the narrow road past picturesque old stone dwellings and farmhouses. Paul veered left up a track and they parked a bit further up on the right of a cluster of buildings to their left. There to greet them were Diana and Geoff and their dog Mylo, barking incessantly, tail wagging.

"Mum! Dad!" Jules said, embracing each one whilst Paul playfully fended off Mylo who was sniffing his crotch.

"Mylo! Get down!" Diana shouted.

"He's alright, Mrs Johnson, I'm fine with dogs."

"This is Paul, by the way. Paul, meet Mum and Dad."

Paul shook hands with Diana.

"*Enchanté,*" Paul said. Then he shook the firm hand of Jules's father. "Nice to meet you Mr Johnson."

"Call me Geoff. Come and see the place. How was the journey, Paul?"

"Pretty good. I love the *château* there in Verteuil."

"Yes, it's magnificent. Twelfth century."

"No way! Really?"

"Here's our place on the left. It was an old mill house."

"Wow! It's wonderful. On the right we have two *gîtes*, yours is that one, on the left. The other one is occupied by some guests. There's the lake and further over is the river and through here is the swimming pool."

"Gosh! It's beautiful. It's huge. Is this all your land?"

"Yes. To the river and to the trees on each side. Just make yourself at home."

"Thanks Geoff, I'll just grab our things out of the boot."

"I'll come and help you. The *gîte* is already open so you can take them right in."

Paul and Geoff unloaded the vehicle whilst Diana took Jules on a tour of her pots and hanging baskets. Then they all entered the holiday home. It was cosy inside with a spacious kitchen diner and satellite TV, comfy sofa and armchairs. Upstairs was a bathroom and two charmingly decorated bedrooms, one en suite looking out onto fields and woods beyond.

"Lunch is in fifteen minutes outside, under the mimosa tree," Diana said. "There's a freshly made cafetière of coffee on the side there. I hope you're hungry."

"Famished," Jules replied. "It's beautiful, isn't it?" she said turning to Paul. "We'll have lunch and spend the rest of the afternoon by the pool. I'm just going to take a quick shower."

They all sat under the shade of the mimosa and tucked into a meal of *charcuterie*, cheese, baguettes, chutneys and tossed salad followed by home-made gâteau and of, course, the obligatory wine. Paul felt immediately at ease with Diana and Geoff chatting to them as if he had known them for years. The tension in his neck and shoulders, caused by the drive, melted away as he surveyed the picturesque landscape leaving him totally relaxed. After a stroll around the grounds with the others during which they spotted a coypu swimming across the lake, red squirrels vaulting through the trees and a kingfisher skimming the river, Diana and Geoff left them to their own devices. They hunkered down by the pool in the late afternoon sunshine. It was still very warm. After a good couple of hours, they were interrupted by the children of the family next door returning from a day trip. They quite happily shared the pool, read their books, and watched the two young kids having a great time in the water. At 6pm they retired to their accommodation to prepare themselves for dinner. Diana served it on the patio of the mill house overlooking the stream that powered the old mill.

In the morning, after a superb relaxing night of sleep, Jules reminded Paul of his croissant duties. He seized a bike leaning against the wall of Geoff and Diana's house, leapt on it and raced off on the three kilometre round trip to the *boulangerie* in Verteuil. Forty-five minutes later he was back.

"Bloody hell!" he wheezed. "That incline is deceptive. I'm knackered!"

The others laughed, knowing full well what it was like.

"You were off like a shot before I could tell you to take Dad's electric bike. It's in his man cave."

"I'm afraid there were only two croissants left by the time I got there, so I got some *pains aux chocolats* and some *pains aux raisins*."

"Aye, you have to be up really early to get those croissants," Geoff laughed.

For the next few days, they were content to relax by the pool and in the grounds, venturing out only to Verteuil-sur-Charente to have lunch at a restaurant on the banks of the river in the shadow of the fairytalesque château or to take Mylo out up and along deserted tracks that led to dense woods and open fields and to the stream. The family on vacation next door were rarely seen. They had enjoyed the week previous staying local but had always planned to explore further afield so they were out most days only returning in the late afternoon. Jules, Paul and her parents did, however, also undertake an eight kilometre canoe trip down the Charente River, gliding past the fabulous château to the termination point just beyond. All this beauty and tranquillity was idyllic and therapeutic after the horrific murders of Simon, Lydia and Viren and the others, such a contrast to the life Paul had been living, which was something Jules had not revealed to her parents. Paul's mind, however, had started to re-focus on the clue he had unearthed from the Nelson Monument. Not the image of a bear which he had used to throw everyone off the

293

scent, giving them some breathing space, but that of a horse. He had tried to put the issue to the back of his mind but despite him enjoying the serenity and sun of rural France, the impulse to find the tablet was eating away at him. 'Curiosity kills the cat', he mused. 'A horse, linked to a lion.'

120

Midway through the following week, after a trip to the abandoned town of Oradour-sur-Glane, tragically frozen in time, the grim setting of a massacre by the Nazis, news broke over a French radio channel that a fourth letter purporting to be from the same mysterious English correspondent linked to the tablet had been found in an 19th century cabinet in an antique dealers in the south of France. Jules had been commenting on the lack of birds seen or heard within the confines of the village, just as she had experienced at Auschwitz, when Paul hushed her.

"What?" Jules shrieked. "Another letter? God! What are the chances of that?"

"I keep saying it's a hoax," Geoff said.

Diana scolded him. "Geoffrey! Don't say that! So, you don't believe your own daughter then?"

"Well, of course I do but-"

"People have died because of this. Do you think she'd be party to an elaborate hoax?"

"Shush a minute, you guys," Jules said. "Paul, see if you can get an English station."

He managed to locate one, but they only caught the last bit of the news bulletin when the news reporter said that those in possession of the correspondence were seeking authentication from experts before revealing its contents.

"They'll have to get in touch with the university then," Jules said. "They're holding the other letters. They'll have to carbon-date the paper again and confirm it's the very same handwriting. I'd be able to authenticate it, I reckon, right away."

"I thought you weren't getting involved again, dear," Diana sighed.

"I know, but it's a constant nag. It's as if I'm drawn to it. I don't think I'll be able to concentrate on anything else until this is solved."

121

Once back at Le Grand Moulin, Paul revealed to Jules that he felt the same. He couldn't get the tablet out of his head. They decided that Jules would call Edmund to offer help in any way, knowing that the French authorities would no doubt contact them requesting access to the other letters. Edmund agreed to pre-empt them by sending Jules to investigate. She would have a good idea whether or not the letter was authentic before sending anyone anywhere. The French authorities agreed to meet her, and her alone, to avoid any of the chaos that had been seen in Liverpool and Scotland. She was given a number to phone. She was passed through to a French minister and given a time and place to meet the following day, 2pm, in Montpellier, on condition that she told no one. A private flight had been arranged for her from Angoulême-Cognac airport. Paul dropped her off at the airport the following morning reluctant to let her travel by herself, however she assured him that she had every confidence in the French government to maintain her safety. On arrival at Montpellier airport, she was whisked away by the Minister of Culture himself, François Dupont, in an official vehicle. He had not told her the destination but, after a short while, having skirted the Étang de l'Or, she realised they were headed for the *commune* of Aigues-Mortes. Thirty minutes later they arrived. They parked in a car park just outside the walled town and Jules, accompanied only by the Culture Minister, walked through an arched entrance, part of the well-preserved medieval walls which surrounded the town. The Minister's bodyguard remained with the chauffeur.

"*La Cure Gourmande!* That's my favourite place in Aigues-Mortes!" she laughed as she went past the shop.

"So, you've been here before Dr Johnson?"

"Yes, many a time. We used to always holiday in the south of France when I was a child."

"Ah, yes, it's very beautiful."

Then she remembered her conversation with Edwin Calder, the antiques dealer. 'I wonder if it's his shop were going to. He did mention that he had an antiques business in Aigues-Mortes', she recalled as they walked up through the cobbled streets of the medieval town. They took a right, then a left and ended up in front of an antiques shop. She was right. The shop sign above read, '*Le Marchand D'Antiquités* Calder' and in an adjacent shop 'Calder *Brocante, D'Occasion, Bric-à-Brac.*' They stepped into the antique dealers to find that the two shops were actually one substantial adjoining emporium and there they found Edwin Calder in discussion with a customer on the shop floor. On seeing them, Edwin made his excuses handing his client politely over to another employee and greeted the two new arrivals.

"*Monsieur le Ministre et Mademoiselle* Johnson or Doctor, I should say. *Enchanté!*"

He held her hand and kissed it delicately again.

"Good grief! Dr Johnson I didn't know you were in France! All I was told by the Ministry of Culture was that an expert had been found to verify the authenticity of the letter I discovered, and it turns out to be you, my dear! *Quelle surprise!*"

"Ah, so you two know each other?"

"Yes, indeed *Monsieur* Dupont. We've met on a couple of occasions when I was in Liverpool, quite recently and we are both members of the Society of Antiquaries in London, although we have not met through that association to date but I'm sure we will in future."

"Yes, the last time I saw you was at Port Sunlight when you were with Ibrahim Shaqtar. Oh, my goodness. Simon! Do you remember him? God bless him! You did hear about him, didn't you?"

"Yes, I did! How dreadful! Shocking! I was really fond of him. He was a bright young man, and I was looking forward to meeting him again on my next visit to the Lady Lever."

"My apologies Dr Johnson. It was a French national who killed him."

"Thank you, Minister. You don't have to apologise on behalf of him. Well, Mr Calder, I'll just have to escort you on your next visit."

"That's very kind of you, Dr Johnson, I'll look forward to it. Now, would you both like to see the letter?"

Jules and the Minister were taken through to a back room, a spacious, comfortable, carpeted office, adorned with antique furniture. They were led to a beautiful early 19th century carved mahogany chiffonier.

"This is it. You won't believe this. As you've probably noticed in the main gallery, I'm obsessed with artefacts of the Napoleonic era."

"Yes, very impressive *Monsieur* Calder. An Englishman who loves Napoleon more than the French, it seems! Ha! Ha!"

"Quite *Monsieur le Ministre!* Now, I received a call from an antique dealer in Rome who said he had a cabinet that he thought belonged to Cardinal Fesch from when he lived in Rome. I was a bit dubious as I have had previous dealings with this gentleman who sold me something that proved not to be genuine. Anyhow, I went over to Rome, saw the piece, and fell in love with it all the same. It's beautiful don't you, think?"

"Wonderful. What craftsmanship."

"You're right Dr Johnson. Anyway, I managed to knock the price down because it's slightly chipped on the side and a leg has been replaced, then I brought it back here. The other leg wasn't too great so I thought that should be replaced also to match the new leg and then, lo and behold, as my carpenter was removing the old leg he found it to be hollow and hey presto! An old leather tube came out containing...this letter! Amazing!"

He produced the letter from his safe and handed it to Jules.

"Go on, read it Dr Johnson. Let me know if it's authentic."

297

Jules placed a pair of white latex gloves onto her hands provided by Edwin and sat reading the letter. She looked up at Dupont and Calder in astonishment, having half-read the cursively written missive.

"I think it's the real deal. Dated March 1815. The writing looks exactly the same at first glance. The tone of the language, the use of certain archaic words, the paper, it all looks kosher. It mentions an extra clue, another image."

"It also says," Calder intervened, unable to curb his enthusiasm, "that this extra clue, if resolved, will lead Fesch to a full print of the hieroglyphs on the tablet!"

"My God!" Jules cried excitedly. "A full copy of the message on the stele!"

"*Incroyable!*" Dupont added.

"It's almost as if the anonymous sender is making the 'game of clues' easier for Fesch to locate it. He's teasing him. He's teasing us all!" Calder laughed. "It's like a get out of jail card!"

Jules finished reading the letter. "Where is the clue, Edwin?" she enquired.

"Ah, it's tucked away in the safe. It's a priceless artefact. I'm sure there are legions of interested parties who'd pay a pretty sum to get their hands on it. What say you *Monsieur Le Ministre?*"

"Now, with all due respect *Monsieur* Calder, let's not get ahead of ourselves. It's worthless until we carbon date the letter and the image and authenticate both under laboratory conditions," he retorted.

"Besides, Edwin, you don't want to draw attention to yourself," Jules added. "Believe me, I know through experience. There are people out there ready to kill for this information. Lydia Longfellow was another of the team who was killed recently."

"Yes, I am fully aware of that. Poor girl! I saw it on the news. But, for me, it's worth the risk. I view this as my pension. I'm sure some mega rich individual or organisation would pay a fortune for it, as I say, even before it's validated, *Monsieur* Dupont."

"I don't doubt that *Monsieur* Calder."

"But that's why this meeting is attended by us three alone and whatever has been discussed today has to remain private until further notice. I'm sure the State will benefit from the interest generated by the find just as Liverpool has benefited, has it not? I trust you, Dr Johnson, and *Monsieur le Ministre,* will remain silent for the time being, until such time as I have a buyer in place."

"But what if the potential buyer is reluctant to divulge the nature of the image *Monsieur* Calder?"

"I will, of course, ensure that whoever purchases it will be duty bound to reveal the image within days. That will be stipulated in the contract."

"You're a savvy businessman, Edwin Calder," Jules responded with a smile.

"*Tout à fait!* Quite! Quite, my dear," the antiques dealer replied. "By all means, *Monsieur Le Ministre*, you take the letter, and have it carbon dated. I've made a copy of it. I'm sure by the end of the week, I'll have my offer in place. Maybe from the State itself?"

"Bah! Perhaps! We'll see!" the Minister laughed.

"If you could let it be known, through your preferred media outlet, *Monsieur*

Dupont, what I, the anonymous possessor, remember, of the image intends, that would be very helpful. Now, Dr Johnson, would you like to accompany me to lunch?"

"That would be lovely Edwin, but *Monsieur* Dupont is going to take me back to Montpellier airport."

"That's right. The aircraft will drop you off in Angoulême and then I'm flying straight back to Paris."

"Ah, ok. More's the pity! *Quel dommage! Eh bien, bon voyage, au revoir et à la prochaine Mademoiselle* Johnson."

Edwin seized the hand again of the beautiful academic. He held it for a moment longer, looking into her eyes.

"Such a shame, such a shame."

Jules smiled uneasily. Then he kissed her hand gently again and let go. The Minister shook hands with Calder, and then they departed.

122

Paul had returned to Le Grand Moulin after dropping Jules off at the airport. He took Mylo for a walk and then had lunch with Diana and Geoff. After lunch, Geoff showed Paul the old millstone, still in situ but now defunct. He also took him into his man-cave, his workshop and store attached to the main house, showing Paul an old shell from World War II. Geoff said there was no fuse in it but Paul, unconvinced, carefully handled the old piece of ordnance and was mightily relieved to find that Geoff was correct in his assumption. Paul's attention was drawn to something else on a dusty shelf. A toy model of a ship of sail.

"Hey, my grandfather, Étienne, the French one, had something similar to this. When I was a child, we used to visit my grandparents. They lived near Mourèze, Occitanie. They had a small farm down there. It's long gone now. I think it's a holiday home."

"Mourèze? Ah, I know it well Paul. We've holidayed in the south of France on many occasions. I love it down there. We actually stayed in Mourèze one year. The Cirque de Mourèze is spectacular. Have you been there?"

"Yes, I have. Many a time. I climbed all over those rocks when I was a kid pretending to be a Resistance fighter. That's what gave me a sense for adventure and an urge to join the British army. My grandfather was a *maquisard*."

"Was he? Gosh, tell me more."

"He said he used to hide out in the mountains. He wouldn't tell me much about the Occupation. It was all too painful, I suppose. Still raw, since the area was under Vichy rule. It was a community ravaged by division and mistrust."

"I imagine there were repercussions and bitterness that lasted for a long time."

"You're right. He survived of course. He was one of the lucky ones, hiding out in the Cévennes but many of his compatriots in the *Maquis* were betrayed and murdered by the Nazis, victims of another vicious reprisal."

"That's right, I remember visiting a memorial there."

"The Bir-Hakeim."

"That's it! Do you know, there's a little place near to Lac Salagou. Octon, it's called. We used to go there for lunch sometimes."

"I know it!"

"The square always reminded me of a war scene, when the Nazis would be sat at the restaurants and cafés outside and then suddenly the *Maquis* would surge into the square in trucks, guns blazing, and the proprietor would duck behind the bar. Thankfully, that's all in the past. We were looking at a property down there until we found this place. There are so many fantastic places to visit around there. Saint-Guilhem-le-Désert, Le Gorge d'Héric."

"Le Cirque de Navacelles."

"Oh, what a fabulous place that is!"

"May I?" Paul asked. Geoff assented. Paul took the ship of sail down off the rack.

A voice behind them said: "Jules used to love playing with that as a child."

Both men turned around. It was Diana.

"Diana, I'm just telling Paul of our love for Languedoc. His grandparents came from there, you know. We have links to France as well, you know Paul. My great, great, great-grandfather lived in Brittany. Although, he was born in Ireland. Members of the family at the time were Jacobites, I believe."

"Wow! Interesting."

"We don't have much information about him, but he finally settled in Liverpool, employed as an overseer. Apparently, that ship belonged to him. It's been passed down through the generations. It's in here because I want to repair it. It's normally in the house. It has a date scratched into it on the bow. It's a bit faded. 1809."

Paul blew and wiped some dust from the model. He stood and stared at it momentarily and then looked up at Diana and Geoff, in amazement.

"What's up Paul?" Diana asked.

"The name, on the ship."

"Ah yes, *L'Égyptienne*," Geoff said.

"No, I mean the name of the person who presumably made the ship. Pierre Cousseau. That's my great, great, great, great-grandfather! On my mother's side!"

"No way!" Diana replied. "That can't be!"

"It is! Pierre Cousseau."

"You just said your grandfather had a similar ship to this one," Geoff confirmed.

"That's right. And my great, great, great, great-grandfather's name was etched on the side of the bow exactly like this one. Pierre Cousseau, and the ship was a frigate named *L'Égyptienne*, the very same."

"That is bizarre. Plain weird. What are the chances of that then?" Diana said. "Wait till I tell Jules!"

"The only difference is that it says on it, *prisonnier de guerre,* Liverpool. Good God! He must have been a prisoner in Liverpool during the Napoleonic Wars. I never knew that! That's insane!"

Paul placed the ship carefully back on the shelf, stunned by the discovery.

"Speaking of Jules, she's just phoned to say she's on her way back. She couldn't get hold of you Paul, so she rang me."

"Oh, my mobile's in my haversack at the pool. I'd best go and pick her up."

123

The three of them left the man-cave and Paul retrieved his bag and set off for Angoulême. By late afternoon they were back. Jules could not believe the story about the ship. It was as if fate had brought them together.

"So, your great, great, great, great-grandfather Pierre made these ships and somehow my great, great, great, great-grandfather, Seamus, ended up with one. That is beyond weird. I wonder if they knew each other?"

"All I know is that he fought in the Napoleonic Wars. I have no other information about him but the revelation that he was in Liverpool as a prisoner of war has knocked me for six. My grandfather Étienne told me when I was young, and I became fascinated with Napoleon and military history in general."

As regards her own trip, Jules could only say that the letter looked authentic, and it was to be carbon-dated by the French authorities. She did not disclose Edwin Calder as the holder of the letter. She did, however, tell Paul and her mum and dad later over dinner about the letter's contents making reference to a second copy of the hieroglyphs. She couldn't contain her excitement any longer. She had to tell someone. Her interest in the project was well and truly rekindled.

"I'll have to make sure I don't tell you any secrets," Paul joked as they sat on the decking, enjoying drinks.

"So, what secrets have you got, Paul?" Diana asked innocently. Paul hesitated. Jules had not explained Paul's circumstances other than he was employed by the university as a result of his military background.

"He hasn't got any Mum. Look at that face, as honest as they come."

Jules pecked him softly on the cheek. Paul smiled uneasily.

"Paul, your ancestor's model ship. Is it still in the family?"

"I'm not sure Geoff. I don't know what happened to it. I just remember playing with it as a kid at grandad's place in Mourèze. It was never passed on to my father. My auntie in France apparently took care of the sale of the farm and farmhouse and the proceeds were divided up when my grandmother passed. Maybe she took it or perhaps sold it."

"Is your auntie still alive?"

"Mimi? Unfortunately, not. She died several years ago. My father sorted out her affairs. He never mentioned anything about a ship. She lived at Saint-Guilhem-le-Désert."

"I love that place!" Jules gushed. "It's so beautiful."

"I know, we were talking about it earlier. Dad always regretted not keeping hold of her house. It was run down, and he couldn't afford to maintain it. He had no option but to sell it."

"Was Pierre a sailor?" Jules asked.

"No. He was a soldier and a farmer. The only other information I have is that he fought at Waterloo. That's what my dad told me."

"Bloody hell!" Geoff said. "Interesting. Do you know what? I'm going to tell you something even more curious now. Do you remember, Diana, when we stayed at that *pension* in Saint-Guilhem that time, when Jules was only a toddler, and we were in the landlady's lounge? She'd kindly invited us in because our car had broken down and it was stuck in the car park, and we'd checked to see if she had any vacancies. She said no but she took pity on us and offered us the settees in the lounge to sleep on."

"I remember."

"Well, she had a toy model ship of sail as well."

"That's truly fascinating, Dad," Jules sarcastically and humorously opined.

"I haven't finished yet. Well, she let Jules play with the ship and of course, you broke it! The landlady was fine about it though. But when she took it back off you, as she was trying to piece the deck back in place, she noticed there was something inside it. It was an old leather tube, held fast to the interior of the model and in it, you won't remember this Jules, there was an old scroll, a print with hieroglyphs on! The landlady was so surprised, like I was. Fancy that!"

"What?" Jules cried in disbelief.

"Hieroglyphs And that's where I reckon your interest in all things Egyptian came from."

"You never told me that Geoff! Where was I?" Diana said.

"This was in the morning dear, when you'd gone to meet the mechanic because you were the one who could speak French. I remember you gushing about how good looking he was and how clever he was fixing the vehicle. I didn't really think it was that important to mention at the time. When Jules mentioned hieroglyphs before…What's up Jules?"

Jules had remained open mouthed, staring at Paul, then in turn at Diana, then her father. Suddenly, for Geoffrey, the penny dropped.

"Hieroglyphs, a print, of the tablet you've been searching for. Oh fuck!"

"Geoffrey! Enough with that language!" his wife chastised.

"Dad! You're a star!" Jules leapt up and kissed him on the forehead. "Can you remember what the guest house was called?"

"No, no way. It was about twenty-five years ago. We only stayed there one night."

"Can you remember what it was called Mum?"

"No, but when we went back several years ago, I remember it wasn't a B&B anymore. It was a private house."

"We so need to go there! Now!"

"We can't Jules," Paul protested. "We've had too much plonk."

"Tomorrow morning then!"

"I thought you weren't getting involved again."

"I know Paul, but this is huge! It could solve a lot of problems. Save a great deal of time. If it's a copy of the tablet, the world needs to know. I keep saying it, but maybe it's our destiny to find the stele. Besides, aren't you intrigued that this could

303

be the same ship that your ancestor made? Maybe he knew about the tablet. Can you believe that?"

"It's hard to contemplate. I can't get my head around it. Maybe you're right. Maybe it *is* destiny. Me, you, the model ship here with my forebear's name 'Pierre Cousseau' written on it. This other toy ship that was in Saint-Guilhem. Maybe it was my grandfather's. God knows where it could be now. It might not exist anymore. But it's a lead, I suppose. Ok, tomorrow. We'll go"

Jules kissed him. "Come on, we'd best have an early night. Mum and Dad, you'll have to come to."

"I'm afraid we can't. Your father's got a long overdue appointment with a specialist in Poitiers to check on a hip replacement. If he cancels now, goodness knows when he'll get a second opportunity. The best I can do is give you an idea where the *pension* was. I'll write something down for you and hand it to you in the morning. That'll give me time to think about it. Pack a bag as well. You'll have to stay overnight somewhere. It'll take you about six hours or so to get there."

124

Portsmouth, 1809

Pierre Cousseau languished in dark, fetid, cramped conditions. He sat crouched together with other prisoners of war in the depths of the prison hulk, *HMS Prothee*. He was exhausted. The detainees had been set to work at the dockyards in Portsmouth harbour and had been employed as labourers assisting in the building of nearby Fort Cumberland. They were all ravenous awaiting their evening meal of stale bread and what amounted to a slumgullion of offal and a tot of rum. He jockeyed for position, to maintain his precious bit of space, pushing his feet hard against a fellow prisoner. There was no angry reply. The soldier slumped over his legs, dead. He cried out to the guards for assistance. He prayed, like the others, that the deceased *voltigeur* had not died of anything contagious. Cousseau, after several years of martial inactivity that saw him concentrate on ovine breeding at his smallholding in the Languedoc and goat cheese production, was again conscripted into the ranks of *La Grande Armée* and sent to Spain as part of the French occupation force. Frustrated by Portugal's continuing trade links with Britain which damaged Napoleon's trade embargo strategy imposed on the British, known as the Continental System, the Emperor of France invaded Portugal through Spain in 1807 with a combined French and Spanish army thus provoking the Peninsular War. The duplicitous Bonaparte subsequently deposed the King of Spain and occupied that country also, turning the Spanish against him, hence the need for more reinforcements. Cousseau had arrived in Spain in 1808 but was captured at the Battle of Corunna which took place in January 1809. He experienced the same grim conditions on the Iberian Peninsula as in Egypt with stragglers from the columns being slaughtered by Portuguese and Spanish peasants. Sickness, hunger, and disease became the enduring narrative coupled with constant harassment by Spanish paramilitary units newly labelled as 'guerrilla' fighters. By this time, he had been rotting away in the hulk for over one month.

It was not long though before Cousseau and a contingent of men were withdrawn from the hulk, shackled, and escorted to a barquentine awaiting them in the harbour. They were not told why or where they were being taken. They sailed out of Portsmouth in a westerly direction and hugged the British coastline. They sailed around Land's End and into the Irish Sea. Unknown to the prisoners their destination was Liverpool.

The prison ship berthed in the dock of a wide river. The prisoners were relieved after navigating the roiling waters of the Irish Sea that had seen them swimming in vomit in their confined space for several days. They were brought up from the foul-smelling hold. They gulped in the refreshing cold March air, at the outset thankful, until it started to seep through their lightweight tunics and cotton shirts.

"Welcome to the town of Liverpool! Your new home! Now even further away from your families," mocked a sailor lowering the gang plank.

Crowds of jostling people gathered on the quayside gawping at the new arrivals, some jeering at the French prisoners and gesticulating. As they disembarked, their clanking chains added to the clatter of horses' hooves, the mewing of hungry gulls and the grunts of lumpers carrying sacks of grain slung over their arched backs on the busy dockside. Stones and bottles launched by youths hidden amongst the baying mob of gawking locals lingering on the quayside, rained down on the prisoners. The captives, huddled together, cowered and ducked as they shuffled though the gauntlet of verbal and physical abuse. One missile struck the master mariner, who was pole-axed, causing armed guards to respond by pushing aggressively through the intimidating crowd to try and apprehend the culprits who by this time had scarpered. The dock superintendent ordered the yeomen to clear the area. They forcefully shoved the curious spectators back. They drove their musket butts into the midriffs of some of the onlookers forcing the mob to disperse rapidly. The convicts were separated into groups on George's Dock and led off. Cousseau hoped that his cohort would not be force-marched to a long-distance destination in the chafing irons and the cold, biting wind that rattled through the sails of the moored ships. Although he had his military tunic and trousers on, he was shoeless. His boots had been stolen from him, ripped off his feet when he was first incarcerated in the prison hulk. His contingent was marched along the quayside past the forest of masts and then was ordered to halt. The guards liaised with an official. Cousseau and the other prisoners shivered. They surveyed the scene around them and listened to the raucous hue and cry, the shouting, the swearing, the bartering, the arguing, the banter and the laughter. The docks were a hive of activity. Cargo was being loaded on and off ships all along the waterfront. Further afield along the shoreline, in the distance, Cousseau could see boats being manufactured or repaired, no doubt to be put into service to reinforce Britain's supremacy of the high seas, he thought. An abundance of hand carts rattling and clattering noisily over the cobbles, skilfully manoeuvred by cussing carters, kept coming and going incessantly, dodging each other, laden with goods or otherwise. They competed for space with carriages and other horse drawn carts and wagons and packhorses that were being loaded and unloaded or in transit. Customs jerquers were lurking, boarding ships, checking manifests and searching for contraband. Barrels of rum and molasses rolled down the gangplanks and urchins and other opportunists were being constantly chased off or apprehended by irate guards and yeomen. The prisoners were ordered to march again but as luck would have it, they came to a halt after a short distance.

"Gentlemen, your accommodation awaits you. Let's hope you rot in hell there."

The taunting guard gestured theatrically to an imposing dwelling. Cousseau looked up at the building in front of him on the esplanade. The icy wind bit into his bones again. He shivered anew. From a tower looming above him, he could hear screaming and shouting. He, and his companions feared the worst. He wondered if he would survive another incarceration and speculated how long he would be held captive.

125

The conditions inside the prison were grim. The gaol was dank, cold, hostile and filthy, exactly as he had anticipated, but as the first few days passed, the new influx began to realise that the inmates were allowed more freedoms here than in the hulk. They could mix freely with the British felons at recreation time which brought its risks and inevitably caused some friction, but it was better for most than being locked-up for the better part of the day. Some of the debtor prisoners had their wives and children with them and liquor was even allowed. They were surprised that dances could be organised as well, in the hall, where visitors were allowed and where weekly markets were held. Gallic prisoners were permitted to sell the wares they had manufactured to the public.

The established French prisoners warned the new inmates not to mention any schemes or plots in front of a gaoler called O'Rourke, who, they were told, spoke fluent French. Cousseau was curious as to where this man O'Rourke had learnt his French and one day struck up a conversation with the gaoler during the midday recreation period.

"Excuse me, *Monsieur* O'Rourke. May I ask you how you came to speak fluent French?"

The gaoler looked around to ensure none of his colleagues were in listening distance. Then he spoke to the tall, lean prisoner in the confines of a dimly lit passageway.

"My family went to live in France when I was a child. We settled in Brittany. My grandfather was an Irish Jacobite as was his father who fought at the Battle of The Boyne in 1690. My great grandfather became a rapparee and rode with 'Galloping' Hogan, someone I doubt you've heard of."

"A rapparee. *Qu'est-ce que c'est?*"

"Much like your Chouans in Brittany. Some call them brigands, others guerrilla fighters. Anyway Padraig O'Rourke, my great grandfather, was one of the original Wild Geese that left for France with Hogan. However, he fell out with Hogan and elected to join other Jacobites serving in '*La Brigade Irlandaise*'. He served with the Dillon's."

"*Le régiment de* Dillon?"

"That's right. My grandfather, Michael O'Rourke was a young lad when he fought in Scotland during the Jacobite Uprising of 1715. He escaped back to France also, only to be killed at the Battle of Fontenoy in 1745 unfortunately, serving with the Dillon's during the War of the Austrian Succession."

"Oh! I'm sorry to hear this."

"My father, Sean O'Rourke fought alongside him and watched him die at the hands of the British led by the Duke of Cumberland. My father, then seeking some

308

form of retribution against Cumberland, fought at Culloden in 1746 during the Jacobite Rebellion."

"He obviously survived."

"Just. He was wounded but escaped to Ireland. He recuperated. He met my mother there. My father fled back to France and re-joined the Irish Brigade serving with the Dillon's again. He returned to Ireland with the family later on in his life once he'd retired from French service, but he could not settle."

"You see, his heart was in France."

"Perhaps so. When he was fifty, I was born in Ireland. My mother died giving birth to me. At the age of six my family returned to France. My father then married a Breton woman and as part of the family military tradition I became a foot soldier of the Dillon's."

"So, the Dillon's betrayed *La République* and this, I presume, is why you find yourself here in England instead of still being in the service of France?"

A noise emanated from further down the dark passageway. The gaoler glanced down it and saw someone approaching. He continued his conversation hurriedly.

"My allegiance was not to *La République*. Nor to the French people. It was to the King, King Louis XVI. Therefore, I did not betray anyone. On the contrary, *La République* betrayed Dillon's. I can't talk anymore now, someone is coming. They encourage us not to fraternise with the enemy prisoners."

Another gaoler appeared from the dim recess.

"Right, Seamus. Time for your break. See you in thirty."

O'Rourke set off down the passageway and unlocked then heaved open a sturdy wooden door. He closed it and locked it shut. After thirty minutes of respite, having demolished a plate of lobscouse and a half loaf of bread, O'Rourke was back on duty in the tiny guard room opposite the prison cell where the French prisoners languished. Cousseau stood by the bars, eager to continue their conversation but the gaoler ignored him. Later, in the afternoon recreation period, O'Rourke was locking the guardroom when he was approached by the French sergeant. The other prisoners had filed out into the light.

"*Monsieur* O'Rourke," Cousseau whispered, "can we continue our conversation? I am intrigued. You were saying that you were betrayed by the Directory."

O'Rourke looked up at the Frenchman whose gaunt features were illuminated by the lantern that the gaoler took from a hook on the wall.

"So, you did not agree with the revolutionary ideals of *La République? Liberté, Égalité, Fraternité?*"

"I switched my allegiance, like other Irishmen of Jacobite descent, because I am a Royalist and a Roman Catholic. I loathed the dechristianization of France."

O'Rourke's opinions tumbled out with a passion he'd kept bottled up for years.

"The Terror went too far. The Church was persecuted, marginalised. Lieutenant-General Arthur Dillon, the former commander-in-chief of the regiment was a victim of the Terror, guillotined in the name of *Liberté, Égalité et Fraternité* when he and generations of his family had rendered great service to France. That was betrayal! The Jacobins betrayed the Jacobites! That is why iron bars now separate us."

"I agree, the Terror did go too far but Napoleon reconciled the Catholic Church with the state with his Concordat of 1801 and so, as an Irishman, don't you hate the English, more than us French?"

"I hated the British hierarchy, for what they did to Ireland. The British imposed direct rule on the country and restricted Catholic's rights to buy land causing much poverty. Then they introduced the hated Penal Laws, which restricted our freedoms further, but the situation has admittedly improved over the last twenty years with Pitt's reforms."

"Is this right?"

"Likewise, I hated the Directory in France for its purges and its godless, revolutionary ideals which it tried to export to Ireland, but I do not hate the common people of England or France. I have friends amongst both. If the French invasion of Ireland had succeeded then maybe, not before long, the Irish would have turned against you, just as the local populace turned against you in Egypt, as I saw with my very own eyes. Yes, I had two of them before I set foot in that damned country. Allegiances change, as you can see."

"You, were in Egypt?" Cousseau said incredulously.

"Yes, the regiment fought at Alexandria and Aboukir."

"Aboukir Bay? That's where I was captured for the first time!"

"Then maybe we have faced each other in battle. Ha! Ha! Sergeant, you are most unfortunate to be a prisoner of the British once more."

"I count myself lucky. Egypt was a graveyard. Many of my friends died there," the Frenchman said solemnly. "Is that where you received your war wounds? On the battlefield in Egypt?"

"The eye is a souvenir from Egypt, but not as a result of combat. Ophthalmia."

"Indeed, I too saw many afflicted by this same malady. How about the arm?"

"The Battle of Maida, Italy. 1806. Shrapnel from your cursed artillery. Don't tell me you were there also!"

"No. But there are some amongst us who fought in that battle. I was at home, in Mourèze, Languedoc, attending to my farm, rearing livestock, in 1806 and caring for my wife and children. I was conscripted again for the campaign in Iberia. I pray I should see them again," he reflected morosely.

"Sooner rather than later, we all wish."

"When we were repatriated to France from Egypt, I arrived in ill health, in rags, penniless. I was disillusioned with life. I had joined up flushed with revolutionary zeal and fervour. I was a patriot, convinced of our destiny to emancipate the down-trodden of the world, led by *le petit caporal*. He though, had returned to Paris and left us to rot. He only believes in his own destiny."

"Then why are you still fighting his battles then?"

"I had no choice. We common people, peasants, call us what you will, have limited options. Then I was captured again at the Battle of Corunna in Spain. I must confess though, it's not the first time I have set foot in the British Isles."

"Oh, what affairs brought you here? Were you a mariner?"

"No. I took part in the invasion of Wales in 1797. It was a debacle!"

310

"Of course! Cardigan Bay! The Battle of Fishguard! Just like the aforementioned attempt to land troops in Ireland at Bantry Bay in support of the United Irishmen!"

"Yes, another disaster!"

"A street lad, Arthur, told me the Welsh invasion caused much consternation here in Liverpool. Although the local men, sailors and volunteers, were up for a fight I was told. Barricades were built. Many of the other townsfolk were in a frenzy. Some of them were panic-stricken and terrified and left in their droves in carts. Others wrenched travellers out of carriages and occupied the seats themselves in their desperation to leave. So, at least you had an impact somewhere!"

"I was with the small detachment of grenadiers, but the rest of the invasion force were nothing but drunks, deserters, convicts and even English prisoners, would you know? We were a diversionary force, nothing more. We were actually ordered to make for Bristol not Liverpool. Ireland was the main objective, to foment revolution."

"I remember, there was much mirth when we heard the French had mistaken Welsh women dressed in their traditional Welsh hats and red whittles draped around their shoulders for redcoats which discouraged you and contributed to your surrender! Ha! Ha! Ha! Was that so?"

"I reserve the right not to reply," Cousseau responded, smiling wryly.

"Ha! Alas, three times you have been a prisoner of the British, not twice! You are indeed fortunate, my friend, as you say. Your bones could be rotting on a battlefield somewhere. Right, enough of this. Recreation will be over soon, you'd best get some fresh air and exercise."

126

The noxious odours of a nearby brewery mixed with the choking fumes of the pottery furnaces made O'Rourke almost retch as he neared home. Kitty had a hacking cough, the boys also, no doubt caused by these works belching out their industrial vapours. Patrick, who was now almost six and Charles who was four were eager to play outside, now that the evenings were getting lighter, but Kitty was becoming paranoid about their health and well-being. O'Rourke, having received a small pay rise, and Kitty, who continued to work at the new mansion house, in addition to her seamstress work, were still not saving enough to rent a cottage. They were eating well and apart from the boys' and Kitty's coughs; they were generally in good health. He knew his wife was desperate to move to somewhere less polluted and each bone-jarring coughing fit she succumbed to made him feel guilty. There was also Fleur-Rose to consider. She had been wrapped in cotton wool so to speak and he had already had the physician out on two occasions to attend to her. They turned out to be minor ailments, and he thanked God, but it had still cost him money that he could ill afford. Consequently, O'Rourke thought hard about selling the artefact in his possession. He felt he needed more information about its value before he could part with it though. He intended to read more widely and keep abreast of the news. He asked Kitty if her employer would provide her with any unwanted newspapers or journals so he could peruse them for any information about 'Egyptology', as the new mania was called. Her employer was both a member of the Athenaeum Club and the Lyceum Newsroom and Club. Like everyone else, O'Rourke did keep himself informed of the progress of the war and the various battles taking place. He had kept in touch with his old comrades in Dillon's regiment still garrisoned in Malta and his friend, Frederick in the 8th (Kings) Regiment of Foot, who had fought in the Battle of Copenhagen in 1807 before being transferred to Canada. Patrice Verzon was back in the Ionian Islands still with the Royal Corsicans, having survived an invasion by French troops when stationed on the island of Capri.

"Hello, darling," Kitty greeted her husband. He kissed her on the cheek in return. "I have some good news Seamus. Arthur can start at the Blue Coat School. Mr Joseph has arranged it all. He's to attend Monday." She coughed.

"That's fabulous news! You must thank Mr Joseph for me. Could you also ask, if it's no great trouble, if he has any unwanted periodicals?"

"It's not like you to be an avid reader of the newspapers, dearest. Are your conversations with Arthur embarrassing you? He seems to know more than you do about current events happening and history."

"Sort of. Yes. He seems to know more than most. He's a very clever boy."

"Well, I'll do my best. I'll ask Mrs Wylie to discreetly enquire on my behalf. Mr Joseph can be extremely cantankerous at times. You don't know what mood he's in from one minute to the next. He does have a good heart though."

312

She coughed loudly again and drew in a sharp breath.

"It's also time for our boys to start learning to read properly. Do you think Mr Joseph has any spare books? We've only got the Bible to read."

"Well," she wheezed. "I might be pushing my luck, but I'll try."

"Thank you."

Suddenly Patrick, who was playing with his soldiers together with his brother in the corner by the fire, erupted into a coughing fit. Both parents looked on with some concern.

"I need to get you and the boys some cough syrup, don't I? Lord Almighty! We need to leave this dank death trap soon."

127

"Come here you thieving rapscallions! Give me them back!" the irate grocer bellowed.

The gang of destitute urchins dispersed rapidly in all directions. Arthur scampered up Hockenhall Alley to evade the chasing trader who soon gave up, pausing to catch his breath, his lungs bursting and stinging with the frosty air. The penniless boy laughed and nibbled on a carrot. He turned to glance back down the narrow thoroughfare. All was clear. He swung his head back around and suddenly bumped into someone emerging from the gloom, splitting his lip in the process. A thin-lipped, greasy-haired stranger grabbed him by the scruff of his neck.

"What have we here, then? A speedy little runt. Up to no good, I'll wager."

The man yanked the carrot from the lad's grasp and threw it down.

"But you're not quick enough, sunshine."

"Let me go!" Arthur wailed struggling to free himself from the grip of the stranger. Another creepy individual stepped out of the shadows and clouted the boy across the head.

"Stop squealing, you little brat!"

"Ouch!" Arthur complained.

"Shut it or I'll give you another cuff," the second man snarled. A tacky tattoo of a skull covered his sallow left cheek, a pathetic attempt to hide a large brown birth mark that disfigured his face.

"Methinks, you'll make a fine cabin boy for His Majesty's Navy," sneered the oily-haired press-ganger. He moved his ugly, scarred countenance closer to Arthur's face giving the boy a taste of his fetid breath.

"Get off will you, hound breath!"

Arthur suddenly kneed the stranger in his groin, taking him by surprise. The man gasped exhaling more of his vile breath, but Arthur escaped by darting away. He turned the corner with the tattooed thug in close pursuit but barged straight into someone else's midriff. 'Another press-ganger', he lamented. 'I'm for it now', he feared. He slowly raised his head up but was relieved to see the familiar features of O'Rourke.

"Woh! Steady on! Arthur?"

Before either of them could utter another word, the two pursuers hurtled around the corner and came to an abrupt stop when they saw O'Rourke. The Irishman instantly recognised one of the two as the villain who had attempted to impress him over the river at Mother Redcaps. The rat-faced fiend. He remembered his name. George, they called him. George Sewell.

"Hand the brat over! He's our property now," the tattooed hoodlum ordered.

"No, he isn't," O'Rourke responded determinedly.

314

"Are you sure about that?" Sewell sneered.

O'Rourke thought he would be instantly identified as the person who scarred the impress man but judging by his response, he failed to recognise him. Perhaps, thought O'Rourke, the blow on the head from Henry may have addled his brain or the mist that night may have prevented him from getting a good look at him. He observed the two ratings reaching for something inside their jackets. They both withdrew a hanger each and smirked. O'Rourke released his grip on Arthur as soon as he saw the knives.

"Go! Now!" he warned the lad.

It took little to persuade Arthur to flee. He turned and ran for his life. The smirks disappeared from the villains' faces when their adversary unfurled his greatcoat and withdrew a Mameluke scimitar. They circled him cautiously, probing with their daggers, the snarling tattooed opponent keeping to O'Rourke's blindside. O'Rourke slashed the cold air in front of him. Suddenly, he made the first serious move pre-empting the press-gangers by unexpectedly swivelling and smashing the sword down with a swoosh onto the collarbone of the tattooed thug severing his subclavian artery.

The mortally injured man cried out in anguish and dropped to his knees, blood gushing from the gaping incision in his flesh. Then he collapsed to the ground with his stunned companion, looking on in disbelief. The latter, feeling less brave without his partner, took off around the corner and disappeared into the murk. O'Rourke momentarily gave chase but gave up and returned to the corpse. He wiped his blade on the pressman's tunic, returned it to its sheath and departed through the ever-increasing darkness in the direction in which Arthur had fled.

The following morning when O'Rourke reached the Tower, Arthur was there, waiting for him. He crept out from a doorway to greet him, shivering with cold.

"Mr O, I'd like to thank you, sir, for coming to my assistance. I'm very grateful, sir. I heard a body was discovered on the wasteland, sir."

"I told you to stay out of trouble."

O'Rourke glared at him.

"I'm sorry, sir. I was famished, sir. It was just a carrot I stole."

O'Rourke's stance softened and he reached into his knapsack and pulled out a chunk of bread and handed it to the starving waif. Arthur thanked him and ate voraciously.

"Listen, I'm glad I've seen you. I've got some good news. My wife's employer has pulled some strings and got you a place at the Blue Coat school. Hopefully, you'll not experience hunger any longer."

"Oh, oh! That's fantastic news, sir! I'm flabbergasted!" he spluttered with a mouthful of bread.

O'Rourke could not help smiling.

"Keep your nose clean for the next few days. You start next Tuesday. I'll accompany you in the morning before work. Meet me at 7am at the bottom of Church Street on the Tuesday if I don't see you before then. Right, I have to go. Remember, no more thieving or making a nuisance of yourself and don't tell the other kids where you're going. Here's a farthing." O'Rourke flipped him a coin.

"Get some hot soup down you to warm you up, you look freezing."

"Thanks for everything, sir. I promise I won't let you down."

O'Rourke disappeared through the gates leaving Arthur in dreamland, the biting cold, momentarily forgotten.

128

O'Rourke, on arrival at work, was immediately despatched to the Pier Heads to liaise with the captain of another recently arrived prison ship. The motley collection of prisoners was herded down the gang plank by their guards. They sported different tattered uniforms, identifying them, not only as French sailors and soldiers but also Swiss, Italians and Germans who had fought on behalf of Napoleon. They shivered on the dockside. They were separated into groups. Some were to be imprisoned in gaols throughout other parts of Lancashire and Cheshire. After a few days transporting the prisoners around the two counties O'Rourke returned to his duties at the Tower. It was market day. The prisoners all looked forward to this day of all days. There was always a different ambience within the confines of the prison. They could, not only sell their wares and demonstrate their creativity and ingenuity, but also could meet members of the public who were allowed in to peruse and purchase the manufactured goods. O'Rourke noticed Cousseau behind one of the stalls. The gaoler approached it, something having caught his attention. There, amongst the various homemade toys and trinkets was an exquisite carved wooden ship, a frigate, replete with rigging and masts.

"Bejabers! That's amazing workmanship," O'Rourke commented. "May I?"

The French sergeant nodded his assent. The gaoler picked up the model and examined it closely.

"Such detail! What are the ropes made from?"

"Women's hair."

"Incredible."

O'Rourke noticed minute writing carved into the bow. "*L'Égyptienne!*" he read out aloud. "Hey, that's the ship on which I returned to England. *L'Égyptienne!*"

"You, were on that boat?" Cousseau inquired.

"Yes, I was on it returning from Egypt."

"That was the very vessel that conveyed me to Egypt. What a coincidence! Hold on, then you must have returned with the Rosetta Stone."

"That's right. With Colonel Turner accompanying it. The stone now resides in the British Museum I believe, in London. I was in the detail ordered to recover it from the possession of General Menou in Alexandria. I was an Interpreter."

"You were there? You saw it? The Rosetta Stone."

"To be sure. There was a right hullabaloo about it. The scholars, the *savants* and General Menou and his coterie were very unhappy when we confiscated it. We were spat on and cursed as we carried it away through the streets. It was not very pleasant at all, I can assure you, but these things happen alas, with the spoils of war! It's always an emotive issue."

"You will not believe this, *Monsieur* O'Rourke. I was in the work party that unearthed it. In Rosetta. At the fort! With Bouchard!"

"My God! You were there!"

"*Oui, monsieur.* Myself and my companions, we dug it up. Do you know how important a discovery it is?"

"Of course. I could tell from the passionate pleas and determined arguments of Menou and the *savants* how valuable it was. It's priceless, with its three languages."

"Bonaparte wants it back."

"That's not going to happen."

"Unless he invades!"

"He had his chance before Nelson obliterated the French and Spanish fleets at Trafalgar. I repeat, it's not going to happen."

"Then why are you strengthening the fortifications here in Liverpool? You must still fear him!" He paused a moment before continuing. "I had one, you know."

"One what?"

"An artefact. From Egypt."

"An artefact? What like? A scimitar? Or a vase?"

"*Non.* A stele. A tablet."

"A tablet?"

"*Oui.* Made from ivory."

O'Rourke felt his heart miss a beat. He paused trying to compose himself before replying. He hoped his expression would not betray his feeling of guilt.

"Ivory?"

"With hieroglyphs on it. About this size." The French man demonstrated the length and width of the item.

"Was there anything else on the tablet? Other languages, like on the Rosetta Stone?"

"No, just the glyphs."

"Where did you find it?"

"At Rosetta. The same day. Or, to be precise, the early hours of the following morning. We hid it, me, and some compatriots. We thought it might be of value given the furore over the Rosetta Stone."

"By Jove! Is it still in your possession?"

"Lamentably, no. My colleague, a *savant* named Antoine Demeraux tried to sneak it aboard the ship that was to repatriate us to France, but it was confiscated, by you!"

"By me?" O'Rourke responded defensively, a look of surprise on his face.

"*Oui, certainement!* The British!"

"Oh, the British!" the Irishman sighed. "I thought you meant me, personally."

Cousseau laughed tentatively, as did O'Rourke.

It dawned on O'Rourke that they were possibly discussing the same tablet that resided in its hiding place at St. Johns Church. He tried not to give anything more away in his expressions, but he could not resist asking one more question.

"Did your friend, the *savant*, know of the value of the antiquity?" he asked.

318

The Irishman, conscious that the hilt of his Mameluke sword might be protruding from his greatcoat surreptitiously adjusted his belt to conceal it further.

"No, but he hoped it would be valuable. We will never know unless it turns up in a museum or in someone's collection. The only thing I have left is a print of the hieroglyphs. My dear friend Demeraux made it for me. The British authorities allowed him to keep it as a consolation."

The French prisoner spat on the floor in disgust.

O'Rourke stayed silent for a moment. He nodded. His mind raced. This was the proof he required to confirm that the stele was one and the same. He recalled handing the print over to the bespectacled savant.

"Is your friend back in France?"

"*Non*. Unfortunately, he died. On the return voyage."

"I'm sorry to hear this."

"He was a sick man. Syphilis. Kidney failure. It was a shame. He was a very intelligent young man. He had a lot to offer. I blame Bonaparte, personally."

There was a moment of silence before they resumed their converstion.

"Do you have children, *Monsieur* O'Rourke?"

"Yes, two young boys and a beautiful baby girl."

"Here, take this toy ship. Give it to one of your children. It's special for you."

"*L'Égyptienne?* No, I can't accept it. Not for free. I am happy to pay for it though. How much?"

"A halfpenny."

"Deal."

"I will make two models more for your other two children if you like."

"For sure."

"Do you have fond memories of any other ships?"

"Not particularly fond memories, but vessels that have played a significant role in my life to date. The privateer, the *Mary Lou*. She was a brig."

"My, my, you were a privateer?"

"And a Barbary pirate vessel, a xebec, the *Crescent Moon*."

"Don't tell me you were a Barbary pirate as well!"

"No. I was their slave. I was captured on the *Mary Lou*."

"A slave! *Mon Dieu*, you've had some adventures *Monsieur* O'Rourke!"

"So have you, my friend, by the sounds of things. And your adventures are, unfortunately, ongoing."

"Tell me more, *monsieur*."

"Another time, perhaps. Here."

O'Rourke pressed a halfpenny into the prisoner's palm and took possession of the toy ship. He walked away feeling more than a pang of guilt for potentially dispossessing the Frenchman of something valuable, perhaps his future. They both knew the protocols and conventions of war as regards victors and the vanquished. The French sergeant would not have hesitated if their roles had been reversed.

129

It was a bright, crisp spring morning, in early April. O'Rourke lengthened his stride and a cheery Arthur, at his side, doubled his step to keep up with him. They were headed to the Blue Coat School and Arthur was nervously chattering away. They had met at the junction of Church Street and Paradise Street. O'Rourke and the boy paused, the former keen to purchase matches from a scrawny young match seller not much older than Arthur. His gaunt frame and hollow eyes betrayed his fate. The Irishman wished he could help more children and feared his own would end up destitute or become another inconsequential statistic of infant mortality. As they ventured up Church Street, they could see a commotion by the stocks outside the Anglican Church of St Peter. Arthur paused to take a look. O'Rourke walked on apace. A cowed man sat trapped in the stocks at the mercy of the street boys who were viciously pelting him with stones. Some of the urchins were Arthur's friends. O'Rourke stopped when he realised that the young lad was not at his side. He swivelled around.

"Arthur, what's up? Come on, boy. We're here now."

Arthur caught him up. "Look, the man in the stocks. It's him!"

O'Rourke glanced across. It was the greasy-haired rat-faced press-ganger, head slumped on his chest, half-dazed by the missiles that continued to pound him, blood streaming from his nose, lip, and a cut below his eye. He felt no sympathy towards him. Then one of the lads, Sam, saw Arthur.

"Hey, Arthur! Where are you going? Come on, we're having fun!"

Arthur gestured an apology then turned his back on Sam and the others. He felt a mixture of emotions. He was turning his back on his 'family', but he'd been given an opportunity for self-advancement which he had to take, otherwise he could be found dead on the streets of Liverpool like many of his brethren. Cries went up. Arthur didn't look back. He knew the gang was being chased away by the warden of St Peter's and the parish constable, as so often happened. A moment later Arthur and O'Rourke stood at the school gates, on the threshold of the charitable Blue Coat School established for orphans and destitute children and aided by donations since 1708. The two of them were greeted by the Principal who strode up, acknowledged them and then aspired to examine Arthur. O'Rourke had deliberately made no attempt to smarten up the unkempt, dirty, ragged, bare-footed child. He was a prime candidate for the school. A homeless, parentless, penniless youngster but with exceptional intelligence.

"Mr Dean, I presume," O'Rourke said. He removed his cocked hat. "This is the child that Mr Joseph informed you about. Arthur Pilgrim. Thank you kindly for agreeing to take care of him. I will act as his guardian. My address is in this letter. I will come and visit once he has settled in."

"Rest assured you will see a new person when you visit. We recommend the first visit takes place in eight weeks' time for new arrivals. Good day to you, sir."

Arthur, grinning from ear to ear, embraced O'Rourke, and then followed the Principal into the Blue Coat. O'Rourke looked up and saw a sea of infant and adolescent faces in the upstairs windows, all eager to catch a glimpse of the new arrival. O'Rourke smiled then turned away. He paused and pulled out a note from his waistcoat pocket.

'Don't forget to go to the Dispensary to fetch the cough syrup. The apothecary said it was ready to pick up. Love Kitty.'

130

As soon as the morning chores were over; the slopping out process, breakfast, the removal of the dead or sick, the removal of any blood-stained, urine and excrement-stained or pus-stained palliasses, O'Rourke wanted to converse with Cousseau. He chose him to fetch fresh straw for the cells accompanying him to the depot.

"Did you manage to see any of the pyramids or temples whilst in Egypt?"

"I saw the pyramids of Giza and other temples at Thebes, Luxor and Karnak. My dear friend Demeraux, the *savant* also explored the country and had the opportunity to study the ancient sites more."

"How about you?"

"I managed to see the Giza Pyramids, Alexandria and Cairo. We came across ruins on occasions and I had a brief visit to Rosetta too. Tell me, has this mania, Egyptology whet the appetite of the French people?"

"*Bien sûr*. Even Napoleon is passionate about it. The discovery of the Rosetta Stone caused a sensation, and of course, its subsequent theft by you British, caused uproar. The hieroglyphs, in particular, have stimulated everyone's interest. The *savants* are determined to unlock the codes and mysteries of antiquity. The Vatican, I believe, is also extremely interested in the hieroglyphs. It fears that this ancient language might divulge something that contradicts the events of the Bible."

"So, if you had kept your tablet, what did you intend to do with it?"

"Demeraux and I agreed to sell it to the highest bidder and split the proceeds between us and the family of Private Duval who also discovered it. Duval fell in battle, unfortunately."

"So, do you think the Catholic Church would have purchased it from you?"

"Yes I do sir. The Church or a wealthy aristocrat, a collector, or a merchant even."

"Probably the former or the latter since the Revolution rid France of most of the aristocracy. Ha! I would wager the Church more so, as you say, because the papal hierarchy fear it. They have most to lose, I suppose. How's those ships coming along by the way?"

"I've nearly finished the *Mary Lou*. I'll have both done by next week's market. Business is booming for all of us French. You see, we are capable of making anything. Bring us wood, ivory, bones, even this straw, and we can turn those things into toys or containers, dolls, trinkets, or anything."

"Good at turning your hand to most things, eh? Pity you're not so good at fighting."

"Ah! Ah! Ha! Ha! Ha! *Très drôle, Monsieur* O'Rourke. Oh, by the way I have made another replica of *L'Égyptienne*, this time, for myself, since we both have memories of that vessel. *Bonne journée*."

131

O'Rourke had left work enthused by his latest conversation with Cousseau. Walking home, he mulled over its content. The Church's fear of subversion and heresy would serve to increase the value of any hieroglyphic relic. 'Why didn't I think of that?' he mused. The Papacy would be in turmoil if anything contradicted and threatened the Catholic doctrine. He had been brought up as a catholic to never question the greatest story ever told yet these ponderances conflicted with his own faith. But just imagine if the ideograms did convey an alternate message to the scriptures. That would be quite incredible! Unthinkable. The damage it would cause. The power and wealth of the Church undermined. There would be mayhem. Perhaps resulting in a breakdown of law and order and a complete collapse of society. He had to think carefully about the decisions he was making and their consequences. On the other hand, the glyphs might confirm the veracity of the Bible bestowing the Church with even more power. Or maybe he was reading too much into it and his tablet merely conveyed another clerical decree of relative insignificance. This, the more likely scenario. Either way, the Church's interest could prove very fruitful

A few weeks later, on market day, O'Rourke walked around the stalls of the bustling market perusing the goods. The French prisoners were adept at creating things out of nothing. There were straw dolls, woven straw baskets, trinkets and trinket boxes, toys, detailed carriages made from wood, carved ships and animals. All sorts. The atmosphere was convivial. The French especially enjoyed the attendance of a procession of well-to-do local ladies, some of whom flirted with the better looking of the Gallic soldiers and sailors. O'Rourke, of course, knew all about the French penchant for the ladies. He found Cousseau's stall. The handsome features of the tall moustachioed grenadier were sufficient alone to attract the ladies. There he was regaling some of those interested ladies with anecdotes from his life. The gaoler waited until the trio of young ladies moved on. Their eyes sparkled and bosoms heaved with the thump of their hearts. They giggled about the dénouement of the tale they had just been privy to and left clutching their purchases, flattered by the compliments and attention showered on them by Cousseau and his admiring companions. The ladies glanced back coyly from time to time at the men with sweet smiles before forming a huddle from which lascivious cooing could be heard about the *je ne sais quoi* sex appeal of the French prisoners. The one-eyed gaoler stepped forward with a knowing grin on his face.

"Ah, *Monsieur* O'Rourke. I have something for you."

Cousseau presented him with the finished articles. The *Mary Lou* and the *Crescent Moon*. They were superb replicas, just as O'Rourke had described to the Frenchman. The detail was amazing and elaborate. The *Mary Lou* with its two square-rigged masts, a square mainsail and the gaff-rigged spanker behind replete with the topsail and topgallant sail and the foremast with its trysail. All attached to the rigging which was made of strands of women's hair. No doubt the prisoners had flattered the ladies by requesting locks of their hair to use on their models, he surmised. The xebec was an exact replica of the *Crescent Moon* with its square rig and two headsails and long overhanging bowsprit and mizzen mast, aft set with its lateen sails. A frisson coursed down O'Rourke's spine when he saw the miniature model, inducing lucid, traumatic memories of Captain Moorcroft dangling from the yardarm and the equally unfortunate Henry Roberts with his cleaved skull. Memories that often plagued his slumbers in the form of nightmares from which he awoke in cold sweats. He was beginning to regret this particular choice. As on *L'Égyptienne*, the skilful Frenchman had etched out his name, the year and hometown on the hull of the wooden ship, 'Pierre Cousseau *de* Mourèze, *prisonnier de guerre*, Liverpool, 1809'. Followed by the name of the vessel. The gaoler stood in silent contemplation for a moment.

"*Ça va, Monsieur* O'Rourke?" the French prisoner of war asked, witnessing the furrowed brow and look of anxiety displayed on the gaoler's face.

"Oh! Yes! Incredible!" O'Rourke enthused, snapping out of his trance. He pored over the models. "But I am not sure whether to be more impressed by your flattery of the fairer sex or your adroit creativity."

The French prisoners manning the stall chuckled.

"The children will love these. How much?"

"A halfpenny each to you, sir. I would be grateful if you would show these items to your friends in the hope that I may receive some favourable approval and more orders. Perhaps, a commission may be forthcoming if we can agree terms."

O'Rourke laughed at the proposition, but the toy ships were of such good workmanship that, in a maritime city, they might prove extremely popular, and this could be another method of supplementing his income.

"Alright then. I'll see if I can generate some interest for you. I'll show them off at the alehouses I mainly frequent, Ye Hole in Ye Wall and the Golden Lion."

"*Magnifique!* Then, I will eat and drink well, perchance. Can you let me know the names of Liverpool ships or vessels arriving at the port? Tell me what type they are, and I will re-create them. Oh, and some wood, would be helpful, of course. And perhaps you will even enjoy a bottle of French brandy for your efforts! Ha! Ha!"

"Now that sounds like a deal," O'Rourke confirmed. He produced a penny from his purse and left happy with his purchases. "*Adieu.*"

Giraud, another French prisoner, serving on the stall, commented when O'Rourke was out of earshot.

"You seem to have struck up a good rapport with Red Nelson, Pierre."

"It's always best, *mon ami*, to make the best of your circumstances. Who knows how long we are to languish in these infernal dungeons? Survive we must."

324

132

Kitty had managed to obtain some back copies of The Times from her employer. O'Rourke scanned through them for any articles related to the Rosetta Stone. There were the odd snippets of information. It was from an old, fading copy of The Times presented to him by Surgeon Phillips, however, that he found what he was seeking. Confirmation that relics containing hieroglyphic characters could have a considerable monetary value. The paper, dating back to 1804, had a name written on the front of it. Dr James Currie, Liverpool. Currie, O'Rourke was told by Phillips, was a Scottish physician who had treated many of the sick at the Borough Gaol and had railed against the unsanitary conditions in Liverpool. Phillips informed him that Dr Currie was an abolitionist too but had succumbed to illness in 1805. Surgeon Phillips had taken up the arduous challenge of treating the infirm at the prison and had followed in his mentor's footsteps by championing the abolition of slavery.

O'Rourke considered presenting the tablet to the Catholic Church but thought better of it when he realised that the ecclesiastical authorities might just confiscate it from him, leaving him without remuneration. Alternatively, there were plenty of wealthy merchants in Liverpool whom he could approach who had made their fortunes due to the Revolutionary and Napoleonic Wars with France. Others had benefitted from the abhorrent slave trade. He was still uncertain who he could trust. He thought about the possibility of approaching the British Museum, but the British Army might lay claim to the artefact and relieve him of his possession, again without financial recompense.

Events took a turn for the worse again where Seamus O'Rourke was concerned. In May 1809, O'Rourke had accompanied a contingent of French prisoners to the waterfront to dig out new foundations for the newly proposed Union Dock. After transferring them to the overseers organising the project, he was returning to the Tower when he noticed one of Arthur's destitute friends larking about by the Gaol. O'Rourke continued past but the boy called out to him.

"Beg your pardon, sir. What did you do with my friend Arthur? Where is he? In the Gaol?"

"No," O'Rourke laughed. "He's in the charity school. The Blue Coat."

"Oh, has he turned proper well-to-do now? In the school, eh? I reckon he's even got a pair of shoes," said the fair-haired, snotty-nosed waif.

"You never know, you could find yourself in there some day."

"Not likely. More like in 'ere. More's the pity," he lamented, indicating the Tower.

"What's your name, lad?"

"Sam, sir. Got a penny, sir?"

"No, but you might want to earn a farthing. I want you to go to the docks and find

325

out the names of the ships berthed there and what type of ships they are."

"I can't sir. I can't read."

"You've got a tongue inside that head of yours, haven't you? Just ask someone. The name and the type. Whether it's a frigate, sloop, brigantine. Got it? And make sure you memorize what they are. If you bring me five, that's a farthing. Ten a halfpenny."

"Right you are, sir!"

"And don't make a nuisance of yourself or you won't get paid."

"Understood, sir. I won't."

The young urchin rushed off eagerly towards the quayside and the gaoler returned to his duties.

The prison was receiving more inmates each week and the warders were struggling to keep up with the influx, hence the decision to put the prisoners of war to work, which they preferred, rather than languish all day in the 'trou à rats', despite the work being laborious. That afternoon O'Rourke and some wardens had to break up a fight in one of the courtyards between some French POWs and locals. Inmates were grappling with each other when the warders arrived. Blood had been spilt. O'Rourke waded into the melee with his baton. He caught sight of Cousseau who was involved in an altercation with another felon.

"Move apart!" he shouted at two other prisoners wrestling each other. There was no response. He was ignored, so he brought the baton crashing down on each of the napes of the grapplers. That did the trick. They separated, cowering in anticipation of more blows. He was about to repeat the procedure on two other brawlers when he realised one was Cousseau. He hesitated, and as the other fighter came into his range, he rapped the baton across his shoulders, forcing him to collapse. He pushed the Frenchman away from the stricken felon, grabbed the other convict by his scruff and yanked him to his feet, suddenly realising who he was. The Sewer Rat as O'Rourke had decided to nickname him. The greasy-haired exponent of impressment had recently been transferred to the Tower from another gaol where he had allegedly been a troublemaker. Sewell snarled.

"You! You're the bugger that killed my shipmate!"

"He deserved it, remember. You both drew hangers on me. I've a right to defend myself. What's more, you were targeting a bloody kid. Who knows what your evil intentions were? Now get out of here, arsworm, before you end up like that tattooed cur."

"Why didn't you hit that French bloody French poltroon, instead of me?"

O'Rourke raised the baton again menacingly which was enough to force the felon to seek refuge amongst his gang of cronies.

"What was all that about?" the gaoler asked the French prisoner.

"He snatched a trinket box made by one of my compatriots and smashed it!"

"Alright, enough! It's over now. I'll keep an eye on him. He's just a scoundrel. I'll find out what he's in for. Keep away from him."

"I can handle myself."

"If you kill him, you'll swing. If I killed him, probably no one would bat an eyelid."

326

Both sets of belligerents moved away from each other, and O'Rourke resumed his overseeing duties.

At the end of the shift, Sam was hovering by the prison gates.

"Sir, sir, I've got some names for you, sir. The *Mersey* and the *Avenger*."

"Hold on a minute, Sam. Walk with me. Now, slow down and tell me the first two again and what type they are."

"*HMS Mersey*, she's a naval frigate. The *Avenger*, she's a ship of the line in His Majesty's service too. They're both in for repairs and victuals before going to the West Indies. The frigate is in Canning Graving Dry Dock."

O'Rourke began to memorize them.

"*Mersey* - naval frigate. *Avenger*, ship of the line. Alright, anymore?"

"The *Americas* is a brigantine, she's a privateer based here in Liverpool. The *Sea Cloud* is a cutter for the excise. And the *Poseidon* is a whaler due to sail up north on the next tide to Iceland."

"Good work. Thanks Sam. For next time all I need to know is the name and type. I'm not interested in what their purpose is and where they're going."

"Got you, sir."

He tossed him the coin.

"Get me five more tomorrow and you can have another farthing and that'll be enough for now."

"Right you are, sir. Good day to you," Sam chirped. He skipped away, tossing the piece of copper into the air.

Cousseau was grateful for the information and over the next month, he and Giraud, who was a *matelot*, produced replica wooden boats. Giraud, who had fought at Trafalgar, on the French ship of the line *Achille* and had been taken prisoner, was able to describe the type of ships in detail. As an enthusiast, he would make sketches of any boat of the Age of Sail replete with its full rigging and spars. Business was brisk at the markets; however, a certain amount of resentment and friction had built up owing to the success of the French to generate income and provisions for themselves. The Sewer Rat was inevitably instrumental in this, and O'Rourke and his fellow warders had been kept busy breaking up violent confrontations. Sewell, he had discovered, had been convicted of rape soon after he had seen him in the stocks, his punishment for a brawl in a tavern where he had groped and punched a bar maid in a drunken stupor. The young girl being the victim of his sexual predations not long after his public corporal punishment and humiliation.

133

The letter, sealed within an envelope with the crest of the Blue Coat School on it, arrived at the Tower, addressed to Mr O'Rourke, which heralded eight weeks since Arthur's admission. It was another two weeks, however, before O'Rourke had a Sunday free, to visit the school. On the day of the visit O'Rourke stood alongside other guests, benefactors, and guardians in the school chapel. He acknowledged Surgeon Phillips who sat on the other side of the chapel with some gentlemen friends whom the Irishman did not know. Dr Phillips was the resident physician for the charity school also. The murmurs of the congregation subsided when a young girl took her place on the piano stool and started to play *Amazing Grace* on the piano. This was the cue for the service to commence and the other formerly indigent children entered the chapel in procession led by their school masters and the reverend. At first, O'Rourke did not spot Arthur amongst the children, and he became momentarily concerned but then he saw him. His wild, curly locks had been shorn. His flaxen hair was now clean and he had gained weight and seemed taller, appearing less sallow in his features. O'Rourke smiled. Arthur appeared sullen though, O'Rourke surmising that the young boy assumed his guardian had abandoned him, particularly when two weeks had lapsed since the arrival of the letter. The pupils of various ages, from what seemed nine or ten-year olds to young adolescents, were ushered into pews at the front of the chapel. Arthur's lugubrious eyes casually scanned the congregation. With a start he caught sight of the Irishman waving. His brooding mien transformed at once into a beaming smile. He waved back. Once the children and staff were settled, the child at the piano began the opening bars of a new hymn and the congregation stood up and burst into song. Arthur puffed out his chest and sang with gusto. They all sat down when the hymn had been sung and were urged to pray by the reverend. He then launched into his sermon. After more prayers, a Bible reading by one of the boys and two more uplifting songs, the service concluded. The children then filed into a hall where refreshments were being served; tea, coffee and an assortment of cakes and biscuits. Arthur ran up to O'Rourke and hugged him.

"I'll wager, you thought I wouldn't come."

"I did! It's been two weeks since the letter was delivered."

"I'm sorry I couldn't come any earlier Arthur. I was working last Sunday."

"I guessed as much."

"Look at you, you look amazing. Blue gown, worsted cap, stockings and even shoes! Goodness me! A right little well-to-do beggar as Sam, your friend said."

"All my friends are here now."

"That's true, Arthur, I'm happy for you but never forget where you came from. Humility is a virtue. Sam is still a friend and it's fine to have different sets of friends.

You never know, one day he might also get admitted here."

"Ah, Mr O'Rourke. I'm Mr Parsons, Arthur's schoolmaster," interjected a balding, bespectacled short man. "Nice to meet you. Arthur, can you go and help out with the refreshments whilst I have a private conversation with your guardian."

"Yes, sir. See you later, Seamus."

"Er, where are your manners, Pilgrim?" the school teacher demanded.

"Oh, pardon me, sir. Excuse me Messrs. O'Rourke and Parsons."

"That's better," Parsons gushed.

O'Rourke feared the worst. Was he going to be told that Arthur had not made the grade or was troublesome?

"Now, Mr O'Rourke, let me allay your fears," Mr Parsons said, detecting some anxiety in his guest's mannerisms. "Arthur is doing exceptionally well. He's turning out to be a model pupil. Extremely bright. His reading, writing and arithmetic skills are progressing well. We've been amazed by the speed in which he has learned to read and write, given that he has had no prior education. He has an aptitude for mathematics and is extremely knowledgeable about history and geography considering he has never left his hometown of Liverpool."

"He's spent many a day and night listening to seafarers' tales, I would imagine!" O'Rourke blithely quipped in reply.

"Anyway, I'd just like to say it is a pleasure teaching the boy. Your visit today has also been beneficial and comforting to him since his best friend unfortunately succumbed this past week to TB. Your presence has been a fillip to him."

"Oh, that's sad. I thought he seemed a bit subdued."

"It's one of those things, I'm afraid. Most of these boys and girls have led horrific lives thus far until they arrive here. A lot of them are still vulnerable to disease and illness owing to the vicissitudes of their poverty-stricken lives and unfortunately death visits the Blue Coat more often than we would like. Now, please excuse me, I must do the rounds, so to speak. Good day to you, sir and please visit again. Help yourself to refreshments."

O'Rourke did not have to be asked twice. He was ravenous and tucked into the spread like most of those present. He had just devoured his second cake when Surgeon Phillips approached him accompanied by three gentlemen.

"Mr O'Rourke, I'd like to introduce you to some colleagues of mine."

O'Rourke wiped a crumb from his chin, acknowledged the three gentlemen and rubbed his sticky hands on a napkin.

"May I present Mr William Roscoe, Mr William Rathbone the Fifth and Mr Richard Rathbone."

"Mr O'Rourke, it's a pleasure to meet your acquaintance, sir," Mr Roscoe said. "Forgive me for being a tad presumptuous, but pray tell me, what think ye of slavery?"

O'Rourke puffed his cheeks out and responded.

"Well, since I was a victim of slavery, I would say that it is, without a shadow of doubt, vile and abhorrent."

"How do you mean, a victim?"

"Well, I was abducted by Barbary pirates and enslaved in the Maghreb, chattel of the Pasha of Karamanli in Cyrenaica, Tripolitania. I was a wretched slave for one whole year. I managed to escape. Thank the Lord! Here, I have the scars."

O'Rourke moved his arm across his waist to pull back a cuff revealing the scars produced by the manacles, a permanent reminder of his bondage.

"There's more scars on my back if you want to see those as well. They've faded to some extent, but they are still very visible, unlike the mental scars that haunt me each day. They never fade."

"Good Lord! I'm sorry to hear that Mr O'Rourke," Mr Roscoe said. "Did your experiences prejudice your sentiments or were you always an advocate of abolition?"

"Sir, I'd seen slavery at its worst, in Egypt, prior to my miserable experience of it but I still accepted it as the norm despite my unease and misgivings. Prior to this I had little sympathy with people who were slaves because slavery had become so normalised. I suppose I closed my eyes and ears to it. It was someone else's problem. Slaves were just another source of labour. Bondage has always been with us through time immemorial."

"A modus vivendi throughout history," Mr Roscoe added.

"Yes, something that had become accepted, but after being enslaved myself I could now empathise with those unfortunates and from that moment on, I denounced servitude and all its intrinsic savagery. It is nothing but unjust barbarity."

"Do you feel that white slavery is on a par with black slavery?"

"In my estimation, sir," O'Rourke continued after pausing. "Regardless of colour, anyone who is enslaved suffers greatly but some slaves suffer more than others. Any vanquished foe could be potentially enslaved. That was one of the accepted rules of conquest. Just like, if the governors of a citadel under siege fail to accept terms of surrender and then are subsequently defeated, the victors have the right to slaughter all those in that city. Life, in our age, is brutal."

"Did you feel dehumanized yourself?" Richard Rathbone inquired.

"I certainly did Mr Rathbone. It was degrading, humiliating, to be treated like dog shit. Excuse my parlance gentlemen. Although my faith kept me strong. I did not give up hope of escaping or being rescued. St Patrick was enslaved when a boy, and he survived his ordeal. I was determined to survive mine."

"Of course, I understand. Black slaves from Africa, so-called savages, are considered chattel and a commodity rather than one of us, a human being. Abhorrent and incredible, is it not?" Roscoe solicited.

"It is, to be sure. The problem is however, in my humble opinion, that, as a man of limited means, my focus has always been on myself and my family. Where mine or my family's next meal comes from is my priority. Paying the rent to keep a leaky roof over our heads is another priority. How to pay a surgeon's fee is another worry." He indicated to Phillips who shuffled somewhat uncomfortably.

"These are my daily, my hourly concerns. Survival for my family and I is my only concern and for many here in Britain it is the same. Compassion for others therefore is in scarce supply. There is not much time nor capacity in my brain to consider

330

anyone else's plight except my own. Certainly not for savages from dark, far-off lands."

"So," William Roscoe said, intervening, "you are saying Mr O'Rourke that only when one is less concerned with economic worries; only when that financial burden is lifted can we make provision in our hearts and minds to find that compassion, to think about others, to champion another cause, to consider what is right or wrong in society."

"That's right, sir. As you can see around us, poverty is so endemic in our own society. We have enough to contemplate here. Never mind about the African continent and its peoples. Poverty engulfs us. Overwhelms us. Confines us, so that we can't see further than that wall of penury that surrounds us nor see over it."

"A plausible argument Seamus," said Dr Phillips nodding in agreement. "It's true, the majority of folk in these islands do not have the luxury or freedom to think liberally, so they remain indifferent, by and large, to other people's sufferings, having enough misery of their own to deal with."

"I buried my baby girl not long ago. The grief remains with me. It's difficult focusing on little else. When your heart and head are filled with grief, there is not much room left for sympathy for others. Do you understand gentlemen?"

"Yes, we understand you, Mr O'Rourke and we are deeply sorry for your loss," the young William Rathbone responded.

"Infant mortality sadly afflicts us all," Dr Phillips declared solemnly.

"I must say, as a nation we scramble up this barbaric staircase of humanity treading on and crushing the heads of black Africans and other unfortunates in our desperation to escape poverty ourselves. We seek to climb as high as we can away from destitution, and we, as a nation, are able to achieve this because we are more powerful than others, but we must use this power to change attitudes throughout the world. Only when our fortunes improve can we find time to consider others and question our sentiments and methods. And maybe in the future, those whose fortunes have improved can help pull others up from the trough of despair and deprivation that is manifested at the bottom of that staircase, having recognised the sacrifices of their forefathers."

Roscoe responded. "You speak eloquently, Mr O'Rourke. I am impressed. Can you find a way in your heart and mind to consider the issue of the abolition of slavery more? We need people like you for our campaign. Your experience would be invaluable."

"I'm not sure Mr Roscoe."

"Your heart and head may be full of the traumas and tragedies of our times, Seamus, but can you find a little bit of room in your soul to join us in the crusade for abolition?" Dr Phillips urged. "You once recounted your fascinating experiences and those of your black Haitian friend to me. What was his name?"

"Verzon. Patrice Verzon. He was a slave on Saint-Domingue, on the plantations. He told me of the horrors the black slaves faced. How the white plantation owners treated them. He was fortunate to win his freedom but had the misfortune of being enslaved again with me in Tripolitania. Twice his destiny was bondage. He is a free

331

man again now, well, I suppose, of sorts. He's in the British Army."

"Ah! Ha! Ha!" Richard Rathbone chortled. O'Rourke continued.

"From my own experience and his experiences of slavery, I do now always have reason to champion the cause of the abolition of servitude whenever I can."

"Clearly, your recollections would create much interest amongst our brethren, Mr O'Rourke. We understand that you cannot contribute financially but can you help us by distributing our pamphlets and perhaps you might entertain the idea of presenting a talk on your experiences at one of our meetings?"

"Mr Roscoe, you are very persistent and persuasive, sir. How can I refuse? To be sure, I'll give you my support. I'll come and share my experiences with you and your fellow abolitionists."

"That would be magnificent Mr O'Rourke. We have a meeting scheduled for a week on Sunday at Toxteth Unitarian Chapel. Mr Roscoe will be presenting a talk on the infamous *Zong* Massacre and the Middle Passage," Richard Rathbone added. "And there'll be plenty more cakes and biscuits, besides!"

The Irishman brushed imaginary crumbs from his face conscious and embarrassed that he had devoured his fair share.

Roscoe interjected. "Do you recall that confounded outrage Mr O'Rourke? When the slave ship *Zong* ran out of water mid-Atlantic, the crew outrageously threw one hundred and thirty natives over the side. Then, to compound this, according to the summation of a judge at the court case involving the ship owners and insurers, an African being tossed overboard, alive, was compared to a plank of wood being thrown overboard!"

"Yes, I remember. It was such a scandal. Heinous words, indeed."

"I am also doing a presentation on the life and times of the black freeman and abolitionist Mr Olaudah Equiano," Roscoe continued. "And we would be more than grateful if you could contribute with a session on your time as a slave and then perhaps, at the subsequent meeting, a discourse on Mr Verzon's servitude when Dr Phillips is to lecture us on the 1807 Slave Trade Act and extraordinary tales of manumission. Oh, and Edward Rushton, the local poet, is to read his poems. Do you know of him?"

"No."

"He's the founder of the Liverpool School for the Indigent Blind," Dr Phillips said. "He too lost his sight, but he has now regained it after an operation. He was a sailor on board a slave ship, scarred by the gruesome events he witnessed. Mr Rushton unfortunately contracted ophthalmia from the slaves. His experiences changed his attitude. He became an abolitionist. Maybe you and he have something in common Seamus."

O'Rourke smiled wryly.

"My contribution is a discourse on the Kitty's Amelia," William Rathbone said. "The ship that made the last legal slave voyage from Liverpool, in 1807. Proof that we are making progress, Mr O'Rourke, in our fight against slavery! But the global battle is far from over! Your experiences would benefit our cause greatly! Please I beg you. Do your utmost to attend."

134

So, O'Rourke committed himself to the abolitionist cause and officially joined the ranks of the anti-slavery lobby impressing those present at the clandestine meetings with his recollections and thoughts. Such meetings masqueraded as unitarian church gatherings or dinners.

In the meantime, at the Tower Gaol, O'Rourke had earned some commission on the sales of Cousseau's carved wooden craft and instructed Sam to provide him with five more ship names. Sam lurked on the docks, like many of the urchins who frequented the area, in the hope that they could pilfer food from a spillage or undertake a surreptitious theft of goods whenever a cargo was being loaded onto or off a vessel. This was not without its risks as theft could be punishable by death, and the guards were given the right to shoot perpetrators. Sam had already registered a Guineaman, a schooner, an East Indiaman, and a gun boat, having badgered cargo workers for the vessels' names when he spotted another ship sailing up the Mersey. A dock superintendent had already admonished him for being a pest, interrupting the work of the lumpers, carters and sailors. He had been chased away on two occasions. He waited until the boat, a corvette, captured from the French, had docked. As soon as the gang plank was down the disembarkation began immediately and the stevedores swung into action. The corvette had brought, amongst its cargo, cannons, and cannonballs, destined for the gun emplacements entrenched along the banks of the river. Sam managed to slip unnoticed past the chargehand and accosted the naval captain of the ship the minute he had disembarked. Sam naively rattled off several questions as quick as he could.

"Excuse me, sir. What's the name of this ship and what type is it and where have you come from? What's your cargo or purpose?"

"What? Zounds! Get away from here you filthy urchin," the irascible captain said, weary from an eventful sea-journey and he pushed the boy aside forcefully. "Guard! Chargehand! What's this disgusting little ragamuffin doing here accosting me? Get him out of here!"

The port supervisor intervened and grabbed Sam violently by the scruff of his neck. "I've already told you to beat it, you smelly little brat, poking your snotty-nose into other people's business."

"Wait!" the captain bawled. "Has he been enquiring about other ships as well?"

"He has indeed captain."

The captain yelled to a sailor who had followed him down the gangway.

"Bosun! Seize him!"

"Aye, aye Captain Dare."

Sam, realising he was in trouble, wriggled free of the superintendent's grip and tried

333

to barge his way past him, but the bosun lunged and grabbed him by his dirty, brown curly locks. Another overseer grabbed his arm squeezing it tightly until it began to bruise.

"Ouch! You're hurting me. Get off, you fat oaf!"

"Not so fast, you brat. Are you some sort of spy?" the bosun sneered.

"Exactly my thoughts, bosun. Who are you providing this information to, boy? Come on, tell me now!" the captain snarled.

"Sir, sir. I'm not a spy. Honest. Honest to God! A man asked me to get some names of ships at the docks and the type of ship they are."

"For what purpose?" Captain Dare enquired.

"I-I don't know. He just asked me to get some details for a farthing."

"Who is this man?" Captain Dare demanded.

"He's, he's Mr O'Rourke. He works at the Tower, sir." Sam indicated to the edifice along the docks.

"It's a prison, captain," the overseer confirmed. "There's criminals, debtors and French prisoners in there."

"French prisoners?"

The captain looked down at Sam accusingly, then back to the bosun, overseer and superintendent.

"Good sir, can you direct me to the port authorities whilst I carry out further investigation as to the motives of these potential traitors?"

"This way, captain. Shall I bring the brat?" the superintendent replied.

"Yes, keep tight hold of him. Bosun, you stay here with the overseer and supervise the offloading of the cargo whilst I sort this serious matter out."

Sam was led off, being ragged by his guard, followed by the naval captain.

O'Rourke was having his mid-day break when he was summoned to his superior's office. There he was met by Morton, the naval captain, the superintendent and two more officials of the port authority, who were also accompanied by two guards. Sam was also there, to his surprise.

"Ah, Mr O'Rourke, I'll get straight to the point. These good gentlemen have accused you of being a French spy. What say ye?"

"A spy?" he replied incredulously. "Mr Morton, that's preposterous!" he roared. "You jest!" he laughed.

His accusers remained silent. The gaoler observed their taciturn demeanour.

"On what grounds have you come to this conclusion?" O'Rourke snapped.

"The urchin," a sceptical Morton responded. "He's apparently been enquiring about ships and their cargoes at the dockside. He said you sent him to get information on the vessels."

"That's right, sir. I did. But it's a misunderstanding. I told him to get me some names and types of ships for the French prisoners. You see gentlemen, they make these fantastic very authentic, carved wooden boats that are named after the ships that come into Liverpool. It's all an innocent undertaking."

"He's been asking a lot more questions than that. About destinations and cargo, I can tell you," the superintendent said.

334

"Information that could be useful to the enemy, sir!" the angry captain continued.

"This is more serious than it appears! I believe you speak fluent French, sir, so, on that basis, *j'accuse, monsieur!* You are a spy intent on divulging information that can be used against his Majesty's government and its martial forces for the benefit of our great enemy Napoleon Bonaparte!"

"That's ridiculous, sir! I did not seek any more information other than that of the name of the vessel and type! In any case with whom am I to share this 'important' information? The French prisoners? What would they do with it anyhow? Samuel, speak up now boy. Tell them. Did I not tell you that all I was interested in were these details and nothing else?"

Sam snivelled and just nodded his bowed head.

"Look," O'Rourke added. "On the mantelpiece. There's one of the models. Even Mr Morton has one. Mr Morton, sir. You can vouch for me, can you not?"

Morton stayed silent, fearful of being implicated himself. O'Rourke glared at him.

Then suddenly, someone hammered on the office door. Another warden, Pearson, was summoned in.

"Excuse me, gentlemen, Mr Morton, sir. We have an emergency. Three of the French prisoners have escaped whilst building the Union Dock's foundations."

"What!" exploded Morton. "How?"

"They escaped in a boat after an altercation between some other prisoners proved to be a distraction and before we knew it, they were across the Mersey, sir and fled onto the Wirral. The vessel was a seized French fishing smack, *Le Morse*, sir. They seemed to know the location of it. They made a bee line right for it, sir."

"Damn you for not being vigilant! What are the escapees' names?"

"Schultz, Giraud and Cousseau, sir."

In the meantime, the overweening naval officer had sauntered across to the mantelpiece and had picked up the wooden toy. He read the engraving etched into the ship's bow with interest, contemplating its significance before speaking.

"*Le Morse*, Pierre Cousseau *de* Mourèze, *prisonnier de guerre*, Liverpool, 1809," he announced smugly, indicating to the side of the model.

Morton's cheeks went a bright shade of red and O'Rourke's spirits sank even further as he pondered the implications of this and the inconvenient timing of the escape.

"Seize him!" The two watchmen acted on the instructions of one of the aldermen and apprehended O'Rourke who deemed it unwise to react.

135

Kitty was furious when she heard her husband had been detained on espionage charges. She couldn't believe it. 'How dare they accuse him of being a French spy. After the sacrifices and hardships, he had borne for the glory of Britain!' He'd been temporarily incarcerated in Everton lock-up and guarded by soldiers from the nearby barracks, away from the French prisoners who were scattered amongst the local prisons. The three fugitives were still on the run. *Le Morse's* rudder was broken. That's why she had been laid up in dock, and so the smack drifted upriver and ran aground on rocks at Eastham. The whereabouts of the three occupants was unknown. Possibly, they had drowned. However, the magistrates decided to wait and see if the escapees could be found and returned to Liverpool to face trial with O'Rourke. Meanwhile, he languished in the tiny stone-built lock-up. O'Rourke had time to contemplate his fate. He knew that his Jacobite background might count against him and having served in the French military and lived in France, it was odds on he would be found guilty of high treason. His only hope was for people to vouch for him or for the fugitives to be captured and returned to clear him. For now, all he had to rely upon was the evidence of an urchin and a character reference from the feckless Morton, but he felt betrayed by his superior who had failed to support him in his hour of need. The consequences of being declared a traitor would be execution. He would be hanged, drawn, and quartered. He winced at the thought of evisceration, trying to visualize the agonising disembowelment, and then a frisson coursed through his nether regions as he contemplated emasculation. Of course, by the time he was beheaded, he would not give a tinker's cuss about the quartering. Dismemberment, by four chained horses. He wondered, in his case, whether it could be deemed 'quartering', given he was missing an arm. He allowed himself a smile at the absurdity of this notion. If the judge was, for some miraculous reason, lenient, given his service and sacrifice with the British Army, he might just spare his life by sentencing him to years of hard labour in a penal colony in Australia, perhaps, with his family even more impoverished than they were now. On reflection, he'd quite happily settle for this in the circumstances. Then again, he recalled the case of Edward Despard, a fellow Irishman and British officer, sentenced to be hung, drawn, and quartered in 1803 for an alleged conspiracy against the incumbent monarch, King George III. O'Rourke had read about Despard who'd also been sympathetic to the cause of black people, marrying a black woman and having a mixed-race child. He had re-distributed land to individuals in the Bay of Honduras in his role as superintendent regardless of creed, colour, sex or social standing. O'Rourke wondered whether his involvement with the abolitionists would turn out to be a case of bad timing. It could prejudice his impending trial.

From time to time, O'Rourke was moved to a lock-up in Wavertree. It was on such a day that he encountered Mr Joseph, Kitty's employer. The local hunt was mustering. The prisoner was being escorted up Wavertree High Street when several huntsmen emerged from the Coffee House Tavern in fine spirits. The gentlemen amongst them included the Earls Of Derby and Sefton and other dignitaries, landowners, and wealthy merchants raucously pontificating and joshing each other on the expected outcome of that day's hunt. Mr Joseph mounted a frisky horse that was being steadied by two attendants. The hounds were milling around excitedly, tails wagging furiously, with the whippers-in and terrier men struggling to contain their canines' enthusiasm, their leashes all a tangle. Mr Joseph's horse spun around as he tried to control it. The rider set eyes on the forlorn figure of the Irishman, clad in irons. The rich merchant controlled his steed and trotted over to O'Rourke who was flanked by four soldiers, one a corporal.

"Mr O'Rourke, I presume."

The group of guards flinched as the horse almost barrelled into them. It reared up at the side of the nervous troopers before the rider settled it down. The chained convict looked up surprised that his name was mentioned, but he could not identify the man who was eccentrically dressed in colourful riding attire, very much distinguishable from his counterparts.

"You may not know me, but I know you. I'm Kitty's employer."

"Mr Joseph? It's nice to meet your acquaintance, sir, albeit not in the most acceptable of circumstances. I've heard a lot about you."

"All good I hope!"

"Yes, sir. Thank you for your continued support of my wife. Obviously, in the current state of affairs, I would understand it if you decided you could not keep her in your employ."

"Nonsense, sir! She is an industrious worker and a fine seamstress, to boot. My wife finds her honest and trustworthy. She will always have a place of employment in my home for as long as I live. I am sorry you find yourself in such a predicament, Mr O'Rourke. From what I've heard from Kitty you are no more a Jacobin or Napoleonic spy than I! Rest assured you will have my allegiance when your case goes to trial."

"I'm very grateful for your support, sir."

The hunt master trumpeted the start of the day's chase. Mr Joseph tugged the reins of his steed and with a farewell, cantered away, lambasting the dog handlers to keep control of their hounds. He muscled his way into the pack, and then they were off into the countryside beyond the village.

The octagonal two-storey lock-up was opened and O'Rourke was shoved in. It contained a half-naked slumbering drunk from the night before. The corporal kicked him on the bare backside.

"Ouch!" he yelped. The detainee rubbed his bleary eyes.

"Get up you sot! And get your farting crackers on! Come on! Move!"

The now part-sober offender scrambled to put on his trousers and one of the other soldiers grabbed him and gave him a kick up the arse, for good measure, expelling him from the lock-up. O'Rourke sank down on the straw and retched. The stench of vomit combined with the nefarious whiff of a malodorous turd wafted around the claustrophobic circular bridewell, overpowering him.

"Hey!" he shouted to the soldiers. "Empty the shit bucket outside! And can I have some fresh straw?"

His request fell on deaf ears. He heard the key turn in the padlock and the laughs of the soldiers faded away. He sat in silent contemplation; his knees drawn up to his chest. Faced buried in his shirt to mask the foul odour enveloping him. At least he knew he had the backing of an influential member of the Liverpool business community and for the time being, Kitty would be able to remain where she was and feed the children, albeit on an even shorter shoestring. That, was undoubtedly, a relief.

136

A few days later, O'Rourke was informed that one of the French fugitives had been located. He hoped it was Cousseau. But when he was told the escapee had been shot dead since he failed to stop when requested to, he hoped it was not. He was subsequently informed twenty-four hours later that it was the Bavarian Schultz who was dead. He exhaled in relief when he heard this.

On the day of the trial, at Liverpool Town Hall, the assize court was packed to the rafters. O'Rourke had been secured in a coffle with other prisoners and ferried into a holding cell below the courtroom. Amongst those accused of other felonies was a serial debtor, a victorious duellist accused of murder, a suspected rapist, and others. One or two of the accused were unchained from the coffle every thirty minutes or so to go before the judge to receive their fate. O'Rourke was the last to be summoned. He was led from the dingy cell up the steps to the courtroom. A lively scenario greeted him with shouts and curses echoing around the assize. The indictable offence of treason was confirmed by the judge who was to sit alone in judgement on the case. The prosecution, led by Captain Dare himself outlined its case and recounted the story of Sam scouring the docks for information to feed to the 'traitor' O'Rourke who would subsequently pass this information onto the French prisoners, some of whom escaped with knowledge and location of a vessel provided by the accused. Witnesses produced included, of course, Captain Dare himself, his bosun, a chargehand, the overseer and the superintendent from the docks and even the young, arrogant amateur advocate had the temerity to call upon the despicable George Sewell, the Sewer Rat rapist who informed the judge of the time when O'Rourke beat him, an Englishman, with his baton, rather than Cousseau, the escaped French prisoner. A nervous Thomas Morton was also called on behalf of the prosecution and asked to describe the events of the escape. On hearing the evidence against O'Rourke, the judge called Thomas Morton again to provide evidence for the defence. This time he was asked to describe O'Rourke's role at the prison and why he had been given the post. The head gaolkeeper painted a favourable if somewhat skittish picture of O'Rourke and confirmed that there had been improvements at the gaol vis-à-vis the behaviour of the French prisoners which had made the gaol easier to govern. The employment of O'Rourke had been beneficial because of his command of the French language and as far as he was concerned no plotting or collusion with the French prisoners had taken place other than the usual daily banter. On the contrary, O'Rourke was employed to eavesdrop on the French to ensure that no plots to escape were being implemented and, in fact, he had actually foiled one conspiracy to escape, the culprits being dispersed to other prisons. O'Rourke, defending himself, pretty much reiterated what his superior had said. He elaborated though on his background and his Irish heritage and Franco-Irish upbringing that led to service in the French army. He explained why he had changed his allegiance from France to Britain emphasising his commitment to the King, Louis XVI rather than to the French people and highlighted the purges undertaken by the Directory of the Irish Brigade as another reason and finished his defence with the following words...

"Everyone can see the sacrifice I have made for Britain. How many of you standing in judgement can say the same thing?"

The spectators remained silent for a moment before Judge Harris spoke.

"We have heard the charges, the prosecution and the views of Mr Morton. I throw this case open to the public. Will anyone else vouch for the accused since treason is a serious offence punishable by execution."

"I will!" someone called in the row of seats in the gallery behind the prisoner. O'Rourke couldn't see who it was, but the voice was a familiar one.

"What say ye, Mr..."

"Mr Roscoe, Your Honour. William Roscoe"

"We have met before, sir?"

"Yes, Your Honour. I am a former lawyer and Member of Parliament. We have met in my capacity as a lawyer once or twice at the quarter sessions."

"Ah, yes. Now I remember. Well, Mr Roscoe, speak to me about the accused. Why do you vouch for him?"

"This man has every reason to hate the French. As explained, he is an ex-soldier who has fought against the French in Egypt and Italy, in his last two deployments. He bears the scars of those battles inflicted by Napoleon's soldiers. A daily reminder of the pain and suffering he has had to endure which has limited his opportunities for employment and curtailed his military career. He has fought for King George and for Britain. Besides, he is an abolitionist having suffered the fate of being a slave of the Barbary pirates. He only has good sentiments and is in no way like the character portrayed by the prosecution."

"I can vouch for him as well, Your Honour," came another gruff response.

Before the judge had the opportunity to ask the name of the gentlemen standing in the row of benches, the man spoke.

"I am a wealthy merchant and landowner in Liverpool, Your Honour. Mr O'Rourke's wife is in my employ, and she has told me everything about this gentleman and I find it incredulous that he stands before you accused of spying. It is indeed risible Your Honour. I have many business interests and contacts in Liverpool and not once has any intelligence arisen about this man in any negative capacity whatsoever. He is accused by people who know nothing of him. You should listen, Your Honour, to the people who do know him."

"Thank you, sir. Is there anyone else that wants to speak on his behalf?"

"I, Your Honour."

This time O'Rourke recognised the voice.

"My name is Frederick Kennedy. I was with Sergeant O'Rourke in Egypt and have charged into battle next to him. I swear by my life he is no spy or traitor. I have letters here for you, your Honour, for your perusal from the colonel of his former regiment, the Dillon's and from the Royal Corsican Rangers, his regiment in Italy all in support of this brave veteran."

"Kindly pass the letters to the constable, Mr Kennedy."

Frederick handed the letters to the court guard who passed them on to Judge Harris. There was a murmur in the auditorium. Frederick nodded in the direction of his friend who reciprocated. The magistrate placed his pince-nez on his nose and glanced at the correspondence.

"Would anyone else like to comment?"

"Yes, Your Honour."

Heads turned towards a dark-haired gentleman on the back row of the seating.

"And you sir, are?"

"Rear Admiral Sir Sidney Smith."

The court spectators gasped and became animated. Even the judge was taken aback when the man revealed himself to be the feted naval officer. He banged his gavel down several times before order was restored.

"Let the honourable gentleman speak!"

The racket subsided. Sidney Smith spoke.

"I know this man also, Your Honour. He saved my life in Italy. I owe him a debt of gratitude and can vouch that he is no traitor. I welcomed him on board my ship when he was injured and ferried him to Sicily. I repeat, he is no traitor. I just happened to be on a tour of the provinces when I heard about this trial. When I saw it was the one and the same Sergeant Seamus O'Rourke who was in this parlous state, I was determined to give something back to this fine man by supporting him in his hour of need. Captain Dare, you are sadly mistaken. I commend you for your diligence and desire to seek out every opportunity to defeat the enemy but, on this occasion, it is not prudent to pursue this course of action. Fool is he who questions the veracity of a knight of the realm and a rear admiral of his majesty's navy, and I think, sir, you are anything but a fool!"

"Right," the judge said. "Any more surprises, before I give judgement?"

A hooded figure leapt out of his seat in the gallery.

"One more, Your Honour."

"Good God man! Who the devil are you now?" Harris implored.

The whole court focused on the hooded individual. Then the intriguing figure removed his hood.

"I am, Pierre Cousseau! The French fugitive."

The court gasped again.

"Seize him!" cried the sergeant-at-mace.

Two constables moved to seize him.

"Let me speak, your Honour."

The watchmen grabbed the Frenchman roughly by his arms, but the judge ordered them to release him.

"Speak then, *Monsieur* Cousseau."

Sidney Smith peered long and hard at the Frenchman. Cousseau returned his stare. They both recognised each other. A faint smile pursed the lips of the famous naval officer. Judge Harris's deliberate cough brought Cousseau out of his momentary trance like state. He began his testimony.

"I have returned from my *misadventures* to speak out on behalf of this accused man, Mr O'Rourke. When I found out he was on trial for espionage I felt it my duty to return to tell you he had nothing whatsoever to do with the escape. Giraud, Schultz and I plotted alone to escape. He is an innocent man. The only assistance he has given us is to communicate our grievances to his superior and explain the procedures of the prison to us so we can understand things better. I asked him the favour of obtaining the names and types of vessels at the port, nothing else, so I could make and sell exact toy replicas of the ships to supplement our meagre fare. The prison encourages trade because, if we can supply our own needs, we are less of a burden on the state. No other information was required in relation to the ships. It was, I believe, the misguided attempts of a young, over-enthusiastic street waif who thought he could make more financial gain by providing more information as was necessary. Our actions were innocent, and our intentions misinterpreted. We only took the opportunity to escape on a whim much to our regret, because Giraud and Schultz are now both dead and so I alone have returned to face the consequences. That is all."

"Mr O'Rourke, did you gain from these model toys for the supply of information?" the judge inquired.

"Yes, Your Honour. A small amount. So did the boy. The French are very skilled craftsmen. They pocket more money than us gaolers from their endeavours."

There was a ripple of laughter in the gallery causing the tense atmosphere to break. Judge Harris called for a recess of twenty minutes whilst he gathered his thoughts and read the letters written by a colonel and a general. Those present filed out for some fresh air or refreshment whilst O'Rourke was escorted back to the holding cell. He sat there, trying to make sense of all that had occurred.

With the recess over and the court attendees settled down, O'Rourke reappeared followed by the court officials and the judge. Judge Harris paused for a moment, then began his summary of the case.

"Well, Mr O'Rourke. I agree with the learned gentlemen who mentioned that your accusers barely know you. Their accusations were based on the flimsiest of evidence. Your support has also convinced me that you are a genuine person, a patriot, although of course you are Irish! Your support comes from surprising but none the less worthy places. You have the scars of war, inflicted by the French. A part of you is buried somewhere on a distant battlefield in the colours of Great Britain. From the testimonies I have heard, especially from our esteemed visitor Rear Admiral Sir Sidney Smith, and the confession of *Monsieur* Cousseau, I have no reason to believe that you are guilty of espionage. However, I consider that, since you have taken to what amounts to a bribe, the only thing you should lose is your employment at the gaol and not your head, innards, or genitals! Case dismissed! You are a free man, Seamus O'Rourke!"

137

August, 1809

The courtroom erupted and a cacophony of noise echoed around the chamber. Some agreed with the sensational acquittal, others were against, including Sewell who scowled at the man who was rapidly becoming his nemesis before being led back to the Tower, his hopes of seeing O'Rourke hung, drawn and quartered, dashed. Sewell's feelings towards the Irishman only deepened when one of the spectators in the gallery, a member of the press-gang, that hunted the Irishman and Henry Roberts, recognised O'Rourke as the 'rogue' who scarred Sewell with his knife, informing him a few days after the trial, when on a visit to the Tower.

O'Rourke stood frozen to the spot in the dock. He then turned to the gallery and caught the eye of Cousseau who nodded at him. O'Rourke watched as the Frenchman was escorted away by the constables. The throng surged out of the court. Morton helped O'Rourke from the dock. He noticed that the Irishman had lost weight. He commiserated with him about losing his job. He wanted to retain him, but he could not go against the decision of the judge, besides, aldermen of the town council were present and had witnessed the outcome. The other members of the prosecution had dissolved into the crowd outside except for Captain Dare who consoled himself with the honour of formerly being introduced to Sir Sidney Smith, one of his heroes. In terms of daring-do and exploits, this dashing naval officer was on a par with Horatio Nelson in his eyes. It was a huge privilege to meet him. The rear admiral thanked the young captain for his devotion to duty, service and diligence and promised to put a good word in on his behalf with the Admiralty. O'Rourke emerged from the court. His first impulse was to look up towards the firmament and thank God. He felt a hand on his shoulder. It belonged to William Roscoe.

"See you at the next society meeting," said the abolitionist, a wide grin creasing his face.

O'Rourke was then approached by Sidney Smith who had freed himself from his admirers. The former sergeant saluted him.

"Thank you, sir, for your timely intervention and kind reference. I never expected we would meet again, not least here in Liverpool, in these circumstances."

"You're welcome, Sergeant O'Rourke. I'm repaying a debt which I thought I'd never be able to pay. I'm afraid I can't stay and talk. Good luck in your endeavours. I must go. I have a speech to make in Liverpool at the Lyceum and a ball to attend in Manchester later."

"Sir, we must leave forthwith," an aide urged.

"One moment." He addressed O'Rourke again.

"That French prisoner by the way. Cousseau? I know him! We confronted each other at the siege of Acre would you believe! I was on top of the breach looking down on him. I fired my pistol at him but missed. I was about to engage him with my sabre when the retreat was called. A most bloody affair! I'd love to tell you all about it one day. I've met him on one other occasion also. He was an emissary of the enemy arriving on my ship in Alexandria. It's a small world Sergeant O'Rourke and it's a bloody good job I didn't despatch him the first time I met him! My aim is not as true as yours! Farewell sergeant!"

They both grinned and saluted each other. The Rear Admiral was then spirited away by his entourage through the bustling scrum of admiring devotees.

The crowd surged after Smith, leaving only a few well-wishers scattered around. O'Rourke spotted a familiar, most welcome face. It belonged to Kitty. She stood with tears in her eyes. She had told her husband she did not want to attend the trial. She had already said her lachrymose goodbyes at the lock-up the day before, but at the eleventh hour she could not bear the tension anymore and decided to attend. She had confided in the lady of the house and in a flood of tears had told her about her dilemma. She informed her husband who immediately had summoned his carriage and horses and drove Kitty to the court himself, which was an experience in itself. She was battered and bruised. Flung from one side of the carriage to the other as Mr Joseph careered apace down the dusty, bumpy tracks and roads scattering townsfolk and uttering oaths without a care in the world. She had survived one ordeal. She had watched the courtroom drama unfold from the rear, a sickness manifesting itself in the pit of her stomach. She could not bear to hear the verdict, so she left prior to the judge's summing up and when she heard the tumult emanating from the Town Hall, she feared the worst until Mr Joseph ran out, one hand on his wobbling top hat, shrieking.

"He's a free man! He's a free man! Not guilty! He's done it! I'm off! To the hunt! Tallyho!"

He then lumbered into his carriage seat, took the reins from a watchman he'd employed to look after the carriage, tossed him a coin and set off at a frantic pace cursing and cussing with passers-by leaping to safety, not a moment too soon.

Husband embraced wife.

"Is Mr Joseph still here? I want to thank him."

"No, dear. I think he was in a hurry to leave."

"Darling. Thank God, you're a free man," she said, burying her head into his chest. "You'll be able to see the baby. I'm pregnant again," she whispered.

Her husband pulled himself slowly away from her comforting embrace. He did not know whether to laugh or cry. Another mouth to feed and now he was unemployed. Kitty was unawares he had lost his job. His legs felt like jelly, and he suddenly collapsed. He was caught in timely fashion by Frederick who had timed his arrival perfectly just before O'Rourke plunged to the ground.

138

France. Present Day.

Jules and Paul were up early the next morning. At breakfast, Diana handed a little sketched map of the main thoroughfare of Saint-Guilhem-le-Désert to Jules. At 8am both parties set off on their respective journeys. Paul drove to Limoges where they joined the A20, then took the N140 to Rodez, stopping there for lunch. They drove south on the A75, traversing the spectacular Viaduc de Millau, down to Clermont l'Hérault and eventually they arrived in Saint-Guilhem-le-Désert after a couple of delays, traffic accidents, later than they had hoped at 4.30pm. As soon as they parked up, they tried to follow Diana's map. Nothing much had changed in the beautiful medieval village nestled amongst the hills of the surrounding Hérault Gorge. They crossed La Place de la Liberté, ignoring the abundant inviting cafes and restaurants around the square, enjoyed by the many tourists. The two of them were desperate for a coffee but also keen to locate the *pension*. They walked down a steep narrow street festooned with floral displays outside every stone house and artisan's boutique. They paused adjacent to the magnificent ninth century Gellone Abbey and perused the map. They walked on, stopping a little further down the incline. They identified the property in question and knocked. A young teenage girl answered the door.

"Hello, is your mother in?" Jules asked politely.

"*Non, madame. Elle travaille.*"

"Can I leave you my phone number? I'm an English archaeologist and I just wanted some information about the house when it was a *pension*. We'll be staying local."

The girl took a piece of paper with the phone number on it and Paul and Jules turned away.

"Damn," Paul said. "Coffee? I'm gagging."

"Poor you, having to drive all this way. I'll make it up to you later," she teased him.

"I'll hold you to that. We'll ring around a few hotels to see if they've got any vacancies whilst we're having a drink. Let's go back to the square."

They sat in the shade of an ancient plane tree gracing the square, enjoying the late warm afternoon sun, listening to the noise of the square's small cascading fountain and the chirping birds. It was idyllic. Unfortunately, the only hotel they could find was in Clermont L'Hérault about 30 minutes away. They sat and waited in the square. 6pm came and went. Still no call. They decided to have dinner, so they sat and dined al fresco. Finally, at 8pm, they received a call. The woman was reluctant to see them not knowing who they were, as the night had drawn in, so she arranged for them to come and see her the next morning at 9am.

Upon arrival next day they met the woman at her house. She knew nothing about a toy ship. The house had changed hands a few times over the years, however, there was a glimmer of hope. She was still in touch with the previous occupant who now resided in the town of Pézenas about 40 minutes' drive down the A75. The address given brought them to a street in the historic, picturesque town that was crammed with boutiques and artisans' craft shops; sculptors, glassblowers, potters, and the like. A mecca for tourists. The premises were an antique dealer and *brocante* shop which lifted their spirits but again their hopes were soon dashed. The proprietor had purchased the property in Saint-Guilhem-le Désert with all its contents after the previous occupant had died suddenly, leaving no will. She had though found the toy ship in the attic and sold it to *Le Musée du Jouet*, the Toy Museum in Pézenas some years ago. Paul and Jules thanked her, their hopes raised again. After locating the toy museum, they purchased tickets and scanned the collection, to no avail.

"This is turning into a wild goose chase, Jules. Even if we eventually find it, the scroll might not be in it anyway. It's just a long shot."

Jules asked the manager if they still had the toy model, but he informed them that someone had purchased it several months ago. When Jules asked if he knew who it was, she was met by a Gallic shrug. The manager noticed Jules's disappointment. She was lucky that he had a soft spot for beautiful women.

"You look radiant *mademoiselle*, in that beautiful, green summer's dress. *J'adore les anglaises!*" The lothario pursed his lips.

Paul merely grinned whilst Jules blushed. The manager picked up the phone and rang the owner of the museum. They spoke. He then put the phone down.

"The proprietor has confirmed that it was an antique dealer who acquired it, an offer he could not refuse, several months ago."

"Do you have a contact number, a name?"

"Unfortunately not, but *Madame* Crilly, the proprietor said that the buyer had come from Aigues-Mortes to collect it."

Jules wondered if it might have been Edwin, although there were other antique dealers in Aigues-Mortes. An hour or so later they pulled into the car park outside the walls of the medieval town.

"Paul, listen. I'm going to go and visit the dealer myself if you don't mind."

"Oh, why's that?"

She hesitated.

"Hold on, this is where you went isn't it? For the letter!"

"You're right, but I promised the gentleman not to reveal his location to anyone. He was a bit sensitive about that. Please! Let me do this by myself."

"Ok, no problems. Give me a call if you need anything. Are you going to buy it if it's there?"

"Yep. I'll just say that you had one similar as a child and it's a birthday gift."

Jules left the car and disappeared through the stone arch. Paul decided to take a stroll. It was years since he'd been to Aigues-Mortes. He went through the arch and strolled up the cobbled street, window shopping, grabbing a *tartelette* on his way. Jules entered the emporium. Edwin was there alone. He was surprised to see her again.

"Dr Johnson! My goodness! What are you doing back here?"

"I've come to purchase something, for a birthday present. If you have one. Don't worry. I've kept schtum about the letter. No one knows I'm here," she fibbed.

"What is it you're looking for my dear?" Edwin asked, becoming more curious.

"A ship of sail. A model one. It's Paul's birthday next month. He told me he had one when he was a child. I thought it would be a nice surprise."

"Ah, well, you've come to the right place. I have a few of them. Different sizes. Different vessels. They're from the Napoleonic era, you know. French prisoners of war used to make them and sell them to survive in the prisons. There's some through here."

The antique dealer took Jules into another adjoined showroom of the emporium and showed her to a glass cabinet which he opened with a key.

"Here we are. We've got a sloop, a ship of the line, a barque and a frigate. This one, the frigate, has even got the name of the person on it that presumably made it."

The antiques dealer paused, pondering the inscribed details for a moment before reading them aloud.

"Pierre Cousseau, year, 1809. Oh, and it's called, *L'Égyptienne*."

Jules's eyes lit up on hearing the name 'Pierre Cousseau.'

"I'll take that one, most definitely. It adds something personal when there's a name attached to it, don't you think?"

"Most certainly. Very apt as well, being manufactured in Liverpool! It's 250 euros."

"Fine. No problem."

He took the wooden model out, locked the cabinet and carried the ship to the cash till. Jules took out her purse and paid Calder the sum immediately.

"Gosh! You're in a hurry, my dear. I like it when I don't have to haggle."

"I've a long journey back to Angoulême to drop the hire car back. We're flying back to the UK in a few days' time. My partner will love this. By the way, any news about the announcement of the image?"

"In the next day or two, I should know something. I've got some big offers on the table. My accountant is going to let me know which is the most lucrative. Where are you parked?"

"In the car park just outside the walls."

"Would you like me to carry it for you?"

"No, that's fine. I can manage it all right."

"Before you leave, I think a wee drinky poos would be appropriate to toast the deal. I always offer a glass of brandy to customers who've purchased high value items."

"That's very kind of you Edwin, but I..."

"I won't accept no for an answer, come, come, it'll only take a second, my dear.

My manager's up the other end he'll take care of the shop."

Calder, demonstrating all his gentlemanly traits held his hand out and gestured to Jules to lead the way to the office.

"Ok, very, very quickly. Edwin you're such a charmer!"

Calder called over to the manager and gestured. Arnaud nodded. Jules was shown to a brown leather settee in the plush office. Edwin took two glasses and a cut glass decanter of Courvoisier from a cabinet and poured two drinks. He passed one to Jules and then sat in his chair behind his desk, glass in hand.

"Are you ready? Down in one. *Santé!*" he yelled.

"*Santé!*" Jules reiterated. She tilted her head and let the brandy slip down her throat. She spluttered slightly due to its strength. As she lowered her head and glass, she stared at the man in front of her and shrieked, dropping the glass on the carpet. Calder was pointing a pistol at her.

"I wasn't toasting *your* health Dr Johnson, just mine."

"Edwin, wh-what are you doing?"

"Did you really think I'd let you destroy my chance of receiving a lucrative payday?"

"Wh-what are you talking about?" she stammered, shaking with fear.

"That toy ship. It's got something to do with the copy of the hieroglyphs, hasn't it?"

Calder paused and picked up his mobile and called someone, the barrel of the handgun still pointing at Jules.

"Get here. Quick!" he spat. He ended the call abruptly.

His attention turned back to Jules.

"There's something about that model that will lead you to the copy, therefore rendering the image in that safe meaningless, and worthless. Do you take me for a fool? All the attention would be on you again and you'd tell the world what everyone is desperate to know."

"D-don't you want to know what that tablet says?"

"Of course, I do, but the information on it might be dangerous for some people. Damaging. It could even be used as a weapon, in the wrong hands. Not to mention the huge financial value of it. Just imagine, every country in the world bidding to secure the rights to it. I expect to be a millionaire by the time the image is sold and a billionaire if I locate the copy or the actual tablet."

"So, you're just in it to line your own pockets."

"Not quite, Dr Johnson but it's certainly helpful."

Jules's phoned buzzed in her pocket.

"Don't answer it!" Calder raised the gun threateningly to her head.

Jules did not move an inch.

"Who's calling you?"

"I don't know."

"You didn't come with anyone else, did you?"

Jules was not sure if she should tell him. She hesitated enough for Calder to suspect that she had.

"You did, didn't you? You lying bitch! Who is it?"

He stood up and moved around the table and pressed the barrel to her head. Jules shook violently. Her phone rang again making her jump and her tormentor jumpy.

"Tell me, who is it?"

"My, my bodyguard," she uttered.

"Well, he isn't doing a good fucking job, is he?" Calder snarled; his gentlemanly demeanour transformed into something more perfidious. "Where is he?"

"I don't know. He...he was waiting for me at the car park. I-I suspect he's looking for me now."

Just then, the back door to the office opened. Calder wheeled around swiftly, pointing the gun towards it.

"Woh! It's only us boss. Take it easy. Wow! *Monsieur* Calder. Who's this babe?" one of the two cronies said, leering.

"The delectable Dr Johnson. Listen."

Suddenly, there was a rap on the office door.

"Take her to my mansion!" he ordered. "If she squeals, kill her on the spot."

With the gun still pointed at her head Calder yanked her from the settee and dragged her over to the two henchmen, both of whom pulled out their own weapons and forcibly removed her from the office, out through another door to the rear.

There was another knock on the door. Then a voice rang out.

"*Monsieur* Calder. It's Arnaud. I have a coachload of Japanese tourists out here. I need some help. Bertrand is not back from his break yet."

Calder sighed and cursed. He placed his gun back in the drawer and opened the door. The shop was awash with Japanese tourists.

"By the way, I've just sold that ship that was on the counter. For 200 euros!" Arnaud said, smiling, awaiting kudos.

"You what? You imbecile! I needed that! It's not for sale! Who the fuck's bought it? One of these idiots in the shop?"

"I sincerely apologise, *Monsieur* Calder. *Non*, it was to an English guy. He's gone. He asked if I'd seen his partner. The woman you were talking to before. I didn't see where she went."

"Get these Japs out the shop! Close it now! I'll call the police. When they arrive, tell them he stole it. I want it back!"

349

139

A distressed Arnaud began to herd the confused Japanese tourists out of the emporium making excuses as he went, and Calder returned to his office to call the police. Paul had earlier wandered up the street and located the shop just by chance, unintentionally, around the corner. He had walked casually past and saw Jules talking to the man he recognised as the antique dealer he saw at the Lady Lever at Port Sunlight. The man held a model ship in his hands. He did not want to intrude as Jules wished. When he sauntered past again, she was gone. That is when he phoned. He entered the shop. Some of the Japanese tourists were taking an interest in the ship, which was still on the counter, so he barged his way through the group, saw to his great surprise that his ancestor's name was on it and immediately offered 200 euros for the model. Arnaud snapped his hand off. He then assumed that Jules had returned to the car for her purse perhaps and had somehow missed her. He walked back down the street towards the arch only to pause at the bottom of the street when he saw *La Cure Gourmande*, the *confiserie* that Jules had spoken about being one of her favourite shops. He thought she might be in there, but she was not. He decided to venture in anyway, to purchase some sweets for her. As he perused the vast array of colourful goodies on offer, he noticed two agitated *gendarmes* talking and gesticulating outside. The woman they were talking to came into the *confiserie*. The police officers peered over to the shop also.

"What's happened?" the assistant at the till inquired.

"*Ils cherchent un anglais. Un voleur.*"

Paul immediately grabbed a random selection of items, raising his voice as he did, so the two women could hear his fluent French. He kept wittering on, engaging in tittle-tattle. One of the police officers popped her head in the door scrutinising Paul. When she heard the three people inside conversing in French, she left them alone. Paul paid for the items and strolled out of the *confiserie*, his haversack slung over his shoulder. The policewoman was checking out the other boutiques and stores. As she moved away, she almost bumped into Paul.

"*Je vous en prie,*" he said politely, as he let her pass first.

Paul went through the arch and across to the car. Two more *gendarmes* stood at the exit of the parking lot checking the identity of those leaving. He placed his haversack in the boot and as he went to get into his vehicle wondering where Jules was, Paul's eyes locked onto something familiar which his brain, at first, could not compute. He stared in partial bewilderment then in shock at a fragment of fabric caught fluttering in the door of a black Peugeot SUV. The same fabric of Jules' floral-patterned green, summer dress. He immediately got in the rental, gunned the engine, and steered the vehicle to the exit. He stopped and wound the window down, passing his French passport to the *gendarme* at the same time as offering them both a *bonbon* and conversing in French again. They declined the sweets, remaining po-faced but allowed him to leave without any suspicion. Paul tailed the SUV, obscured by two other vehicles in between them, consternation etched on his face, wondering why Jules was in the car and suspecting that she had been forced into it against her will. His mind was racing. 'Who's taken her and where the hell are they going?' The traffic was relatively slow until they reached the environs, then the target vehicle sped west towards Montpellier. Paul increased velocity accordingly and followed it at a distance. The SUV headed north on the Montpellier ring road and pulled into a service station. Two guys got out. One sprinted to the toilets, the other unhooked the gasoline hose. Paul deliberately stopped at a parking space where Jules might be able to see him. He hoped she had not been drugged or worse still, harmed in any way. He leapt out and grabbed a hoodie from the boot, donned it and proceeded to the toilets. The desperate man who had preceded him had opened the lavatory door and almost gagged.

"*Merde!*" he cursed. And there was. Lots of it. All around the *toilette à la turque*, the shit hole in the ground. He fumbled at his belt, pulled his trousers down and squatted over the hole, trying to avoid crapping into his pants. He heard someone else enter the toilets, he coughed as there was no lock on the door, then suddenly the door was booted open and before he could draw his concealed gun, he was knocked unconscious with his assailant's fist, one blow. He fell back, his arse squelching in the excrement already piled around the hole, his head banging against the shit-stained wall behind him. Paul wrenched the French thug's gun from his shoulder holster and left, exhaling deeply, keen to inhale fresh air.

"Christ! What's he been eating? *Andouillette?*" he muttered.

Paul strode resolutely towards the petrol station mini market. He entered just behind the other henchman who went over to the drinks fridge. Paul went down a separate aisle. There was no one else in the shop except for the cashier. He immediately reappeared behind the driver and grabbed the nape of his neck and violently shoved his head into the fridge door before he could react. The Frenchman collapsed to the floor.

"Heart attack!" Paul shouted. "Get the defib!"

As the cashier, alarmed, turned around to grab the defibrillator, Paul was gone. He held a coke bottle in his hand that he had grabbed from the fridge. He appeared at the side of the black Peugeot, startling Jules and a third crony who had a pistol dug into Jules's side in the back seat. She was conscious though agitated. Jules's eyes widened. She hoped her abductor had not noticed. The slimeball took his other groping hand off Jules's breast. Being left alone in the vehicle with the English woman was just the opportunity he had hoped for. Paul rapped on the darkened window and shouted in French.

"Hey, mate. Your girlfriend's got her dress trapped in the door. The door's not fully shut."

"What?" the guard answered, startled.

Paul sauntered around to the henchman's side of the vehicle. The guard wound his window down slightly.

"I said that door on the other side where your girlfriend is sitting is not closed properly."

As the thug turned to look, Paul squirted the coke that he had shaken up through the gap. It caught the henchman unawares. He put his hands up instinctively to protect himself, not realising what the liquid was at first. Jules sank her teeth into his hand hard forcing him to drop the gun on the front passenger seat.

"Ouch! You bitch!"

Before the thug could swipe out at her, Paul placed the barrel of his pistol through the gap of the lowered window.

"One fucking move and you're dead," he spat. "Open the door, slowly!"

The man pulled his door release and Paul yanked the door open and grabbed him by the scruff of his neck, pressing the gun to his head.

"Jules! Get out!"

Jules struggled to get out of her door. It was stuck, so Paul pistol-whipped the goon and ran around to her side and released her. They ran back to their rental and screeched out of the petrol station, just as the dazed, injured driver emerged from the mini market. He shoved the Asian cashier in the face as he was fussing over him and ran towards his SUV. He saw Paul's vehicle take a left. He checked his colleague. He was breathing and starting to stir. The driver hauled him to his feet and bundled him into the back seat. Then he scrambled over to the toilet block. He went in. It stank. He called out. Then he checked the cubicles and found his associate in the last one still unconscious. He baulked, then left leaving him lying in his mess. He ran back to the car and jumped in the driver's seat, glancing up at his mirror. His forehead was still bleeding. He dabbed it with a napkin from the glove compartment and set off in pursuit of his quarry. He took the same left turn and guessed rightly that they were heading for the A750 that led on to the A75. He called for assistance, and two other goons left Edwin Calder's mansion, situated north of Montpellier, and joined in the pursuit.

"Paul, thank God, you found me. I was beginning to think they'd killed you."

"Did those guys harm you Jules?"

"No, fortunately. They just roughed me up a bit, and that tosser was having a grope."

"Who are they, anyway?"

"Edwin Calder's henchmen. He's not the gentleman he portrays himself to be. He's a phony. A nasty piece of work. He was kidnapping me. They were taking me to his home. He's after the tablet for himself. The conniving, two-faced sod!"

Jules sank into her seat, exhausted by her abduction. She sat in silence, pondering the ramifications of her ordeal. Paul concentrated on negotiating his way through the traffic, remaining silent also. For the next hour, Paul had his foot hard on the accelerator reaching the Millau viaduct without incident. They pressed on over the iconic bridge, negotiating the toll without any significant delay. The SUV sped up the autoroute in pursuit whilst the summoned back up in a Renault Kadjar took the D911 to Rodez.

Towards Sévérac-le-Château, however, a roadworks sign came into view. A few

352

kilometres further ahead, the traffic came to a standstill. "Shit!" Paul cursed. He glanced in his rear mirror anxiously. The traffic in front was merging into one lane from two. He manoeuvred his Citroën C3, so it straddled the two lanes. One or two miffed drivers tried to squeeze past, but he forced them back giving them a one fingered salute for good measure. Further back, a lorry copied his straddling manoeuvre. He noticed a persistent black Peugeot attempting to get past it several times. It was his pursuers. The traffic crawled along agonisingly slowly. He repeatedly checked his mirrors and then spotted a guy jumping out of the SUV, running towards them. Paul saw an exit sign further ahead, number 43. He looked in the mirror again. The thug, the one who he pistol-whipped was getting closer. Paul snatched up his gun. Both he and Jules were frantically urging the traffic to move. Jules was beginning to panic.

"He's gaining ground Paul! He's nearly up to us! Move traffic, move, for God's sake!"

The thug was almost parallel with their vehicle. Paul turned his head. He saw the assailant with his hand in his inside jacket pocket reaching for a gun. He could see the nasty gash on his forehead that he had administered and could see his contorted face twisted in anger.

"He's got another gun," Jules cried.

Desperately, Paul swerved to the left almost catching the pursuer with a glancing blow, causing him to take evasive action to avoid his foot being crushed by the Citroën. The pursuer slammed his hand down on the rear window and managed to push himself away, but he stumbled. This gave Paul some vital breathing space. Suddenly their vehicle, tailgating the car in front, was at the merge point and the traffic filed into one lane and started to speed up. They both heaved a sigh of relief. The hoodlum, having picked himself up, stopped chasing and cursed. He waited for the SUV to catch up and leapt in. Jules and Paul momentarily relaxed but then as the traffic emerged from the roadworks and spread to the two lanes again, up ahead the traffic unexpectedly slowed down once more. There was a breakdown in the right-hand lane and a new filter was in place.

"Damn it! It's like the M6!"

He saw the SUV in the line of traffic behind him edging closer to the freedom of the two lanes. He positioned his vehicle to straddle two lanes again much to the annoyance of other drivers. The Peugeot surged forward, gaining on the Citroën, trying to bully its way through the jam. As the traffic slowed, the pistol-whipped henchman renewed his attempt to catch them up on foot. Paul could see the broken-down lorry that was causing the fresh delay slightly ahead, just before exit 43. Paul indicated right to move over to the other lane like most of the traffic before him, but other drivers were ignoring him. He cursed again. The motorway exit inched closer, but his path was still being deliberately blocked. He feared he would not get over in time. He looked over imploringly to another smug driver trying to gain his attention, a Dutchman, identified by his number plate, but the guy deliberately averted his eyes, looking straight forward. He glanced in the rear-view mirror again. The hood was approaching fast, close enough for Paul to see his bruised and swollen pate again, his hand in his inside jacket pocket once more. Paul suddenly beeped the horn hard causing the haughty Dutchman to glance across, returning the middle finger salute he had received off Paul several minutes earlier. He did a double take though, alarm spreading over his face, as he saw Paul brandishing the gun at him. He put his foot immediately on the brake almost causing a crash and Paul nipped in front of him taking a left onto the junction exit at the last gasp. The chasing henchman cursed again and ran back to his vehicle. The SUV braked abruptly forcing the driver of the car behind to slam on the brakes. The indignant, inconvenienced driver behind beeped his horn but wished he had not when the returning snarling thug hurled abuse at the occupants of the car and banged on their bonnet. He then jumped back into the SUV which indicated to change lanes. No one would give way again, so the driver just edged his vehicle in front of the adjacent vehicle, an MPV, clipping it in the process, forcing it to divert to the right and running it off the carriageway. The pursuers took the exit. They spotted the blue Citroën on an incline of the spiralling exit road and sped after it. The road off the autoroute was narrow, one lane either way. Paul, noticing that the SUV was still in pursuit, started to slalom his way through the traffic, taking risks, squeezing into impossible gaps in front of overtaken vehicles or only just avoiding oncoming vehicles with their lights flashing. This reckless but imperative act forced the SUV to delay its pursuit. Vital seconds were gained. Jules could barely watch. She was stricken with fear, shaking hands covering her face.

"Where are we headed Paul?" she screamed.

He did not reply immediately, his concentration firmly focused on another hair-raising stunt prompting a long blast on the horn from an oncoming truck.

"Paul! Where the hell are we going?" she barked as her heart missed a beat.

"The mountains! Trust me!"

140

Paul surged past a phalanx of cyclists clad in obligatory Lycra on a downward stretch and overtook a *'La Poste'* van on a bend, just missing a bus coming in the other direction. The SUV, now in hot pursuit, attempted the same manoeuvre but ploughed into a cyclist causing carnage amongst the six or seven or so riders, swerving to miss the oncoming bus. Paul wound his way down onto the D907, the spectacular gaping gorge of the fast-flowing River Tarn now coming into view, a torrent of water some 600 metres below them. Suddenly, the road narrowed, squeezed by the huge overhanging buttresses of rock on one side and a sharp drop down to the river on the other. Paul found it impossible to get past the tourist traffic in both directions. He cursed. Shortly after they arrived in the village of Les Vignes, with the SUV a little further back now accompanied by the other pursuing Renault. Paul, seeing the road ahead crammed with traffic and sightseers, suddenly veered off the road into a riverside car park.

"Quick! Get out Jules!"

Jules bailed out not knowing what to expect. Paul grabbed her by the hand and dragged her to the water's edge. Two excited tourists, paddles and life-vests in hand, were heading to a yellow canoe. They placed their accoutrements down for a second to take a selfie. Paul snatched up the paddles. Jules followed his lead grabbing the two life-vests. They threw them into the canoe and Paul dragged the vessel down the ramp and leapt in before the other couple realised what was happening. Jules scrambled in, her legs akimbo.

"Paddle!" he shouted to Jules who was still slopping around. The SUV surged into the car park followed by the Kadjar. Two of the thugs, one from each vehicle, jumped out and, on seeing their quarry escaping, dragged a canoe down to the river. They ran to the equipment store and grabbed a paddle each without paying, ignoring the shouts of the employee in the ticket booth, leapt into the canoe and set off, paddling furiously. The water at this point was a gentle flow, but Paul knew, having canoed here before, that there were sections on the watercourse that quickened with modest rapids. He paddled competently whilst Jules struggled, at first, to find her rhythm. She looked behind her.

"They're after us!"

"How many?"

"One canoe. Two blokes."

"Put your life vest on."

They both donned their yellow vests rapidly. Paul glanced back then increased his speed. He recognised one of the hoods as the driver he assaulted in the petrol station shop. Jules tried her best to keep pace with Paul, dipping her single-bladed paddle in the clear waters on the opposite side to Paul's. They kept ahead of the chasing canoe, Paul expertly negotiating the intermittent rapids. Jules's strength began to wane after twenty minutes. Her shoulders ached. She checked on their pursuers.

"I think they're closing Paul!"

"Keep going Jules!"

"I'm tiring Paul!"

Gradually the chasers reduced the distance between them, and a shot rang out whizzing past Jules's right ear.

"Shit! They're shooting at us!" she yelled. She responded by trying to quicken her paddle rate.

Another one whipped past her left side this time. She felt resigned to her fate, her stroke rate was now almost non-existent due to her exhaustion.

"Oh God!"

"Duck!" Paul screamed.

Jules ducked and Paul fired two shots from his gun. Both missed their target, but it was enough to disturb the rhythm of their pursuers. Jules placed her hands over her ears belatedly.

"Keep paddling!" he cried.

She was in tears as she picked up the paddle again and dipped it in the water.

Paul steered the canoe to the right side of the river to follow the course of the rapids and the craft swept down a narrow channel next to the bank. The overhanging canopy loomed above them. By this time the pursuing canoe was fast approaching when suddenly Paul yelled to Jules. "Shit! Lie back! Quick! Now!"

She saw him fall back and instinctively did the same closing her eyes in the process, expecting to be shredded by overhanging thorns and battered by twigs and branches. The foliage brushed her head, then suddenly behind her she heard a scream amidst the din of the foaming rapids.

She twisted herself around. Her heart leapt. Her terrified eyes fell upon a ghastly sight. The thug positioned in the front of the chasing canoe had been skewered through the neck by an iron rod which protruded out from amidst the foliage of the riverbank. The victim gurgled, his throat gushing blood mimicking the surge and sounds of the flowing waters that his torso was under. His partner had crashed into his suspended body as the canoe surged through the rapids. This had the effect of destabilizing the craft sending it careering into the riverbank. It overturned on impact pitching the other assailant into the Tarn. It remained there, pummelled by the force of the water, pinning the submerged, unconscious man against the bank. His skull had taken a blow from the heavy upturned canoe. The craft gradually released itself through the motions of the river and floated away, half submerged followed by the drifting corpse of the drowned man. As they hit a calmer, more serene section of the river both Paul and Jules, having witnessed the gruesome fate of their pursuers, collapsed back into their canoe, exhausted. The gentler current carried them away and a kilometre downriver the drifting canoe came to a rest on a shallow, shingle-covered area on the left bank. They stumbled out of the craft and collapsed onto the small, deserted sandy beach. They lay there for a good ten minutes, chests heaving, throats gulping for air, before speaking.

"My God! What just happened there?" Jules rasped.

"An iron bar used for holding back the foliage on the riverbank must have come loose," he choked. "A canoe before us must have hit the bank and dislodged it. I saw it just in time. It was hard to see in the shade of the overhanging branches of those trees. It almost skewered me. It's a good job you lay back otherwise you would have been a kebab too."

"It would have been a sheeeeesh kebab!" she snorted with nervous laughter. Paul relaxed enough to indulge in a smile.

"The French don't do health and safety, you see. I know from experience. I fell down a drain once in Vias Plage. The cover was loose. My brother called me 'the Grid Kid'."

Jules laughed hysterically as the image of Paul falling down a drain entered her head, releasing her pent-up tension.

"Look, I've still got the scar on my leg. I had a huge scrape on it."

"Where? There's nothing there!" Jules roared as she kneeled in the sand in front of Paul who had sat himself on a rock.

"Here! Look closer." He bent forward to show her. She lowered her head too to check out the scar. At that instant, a shot rang out from behind them, zipping over their bowed heads.

"Shit! Run Jules! To the canoe!"

Another shot rang out, just millimetres from Paul's ear as the two of them sprinted to the water's edge. He and Jules dived around the other side of the canoe just as another bullet hit the yellow kayak. He grabbed his pistol from its interior and fired two shots in quick succession at the copse of trees beyond the narrow stretch of sand and shingle. He snatched the paddles out of the boat, but another shot tore into one of the blades, shattering it and sending a small piece of jagged plastic into Paul's chin.

"Argh! Bastard!" he shouted angrily. He ripped the protruding sharp shard from his bleeding chin and tossed it away.

"Jules, we're going to have to swim for it. Take off your life vest."

She unclipped it and struggled out of it.

"On my count of three. One, two, three!"

Paul fired two more shots. Jules used this as the cue to run. She waded into the water and dived in. Paul followed her immediately, only just avoiding another bullet. They stayed submerged for as long as they could, the current allowing them to drift further down the river. They emerged to gasp some air and turned to see the assailant examining the canoe. Paul knew though that it was useless. A bullet hole had pierced it. They kept swimming and drifting with the current for about two or three kilometres, then Paul spotted one of the canoe company shuttle buses at one of the regular finish points on the right bank. They swam across to it and dragged themselves out of the water. An employee was securing a canoe to the side of the shuttle, so they sneaked on, being the first ones to board and hid at the back. About five other canoeists boarded after them and the employee took the wheel and set off for the departure point at Les Vignes. No one noticed them. An ambulance and police car drove past them, sirens on. On arrival at the car park the canoeists alighted. The driver got off and started to haul the canoes off to the riverside. The bedraggled duo sneaked off. As they deftly approached their car, Paul stopped abruptly. The groper was guarding it. He was eating an ice cream. Paul and Jules hid by a wall nearby. Paul took out the wet car keys from the pocket of his soaked shorts and pressed the unlock button. The thug spun around surprised, then began to circle the vehicle, looking around him. He was on his hands and knees looking under nearby cars when Paul leapt over the wall, stole up behind him, and hit him with his pistol.

"Careless, twice in one day," he said as he relieved the overpowered victim of his own weapon.

Paul bundled his unconscious adversary under a stationary minibus. Summoning Jules, they both jumped into the Citroën. Once out of Les Vignes they headed north on a narrow minor mountain pass away from the gorge. As they climbed away from the riverside town, they could see emergency vehicles down below in the valley, sirens wailing, trying to negotiate the line of built-up traffic piling into Les Vignes. They both heaved a sigh of relief.

141

Earlier, on the sprint up the A75, when they had momentarily relaxed, exuding a misplaced confidence that they had escaped the clutches of the gang and after Jules had recounted her experience at the hands of Calder, Paul told his side of the story. He told Jules he'd been window shopping in Aigues-Mortes, killing time and just happened upon the antique dealer's shop. He had seen Jules and Calder in conversation presumably about the toy ship and had recognised him from Port Sunlight and believed that Jules was in safe hands. When Paul told her he had the ship in his haversack in the boot, she couldn't believe him. She let out a spontaneous shriek of exultation spooking an already skittish Paul who, distracted, nearly hit the breaking vehicle in front of him. She planted a kiss on his cheek in thanks for him being her saviour, and in part to soothe his frayed nerves and heightened sense of acuity. Paul had not only saved her life, but he had recovered the model.

"My little meercat," she had cooed.

Now, as they continued to put some distance between themselves and their pursuers, Paul weighed up their options.

"I don't think it's wise to head back to your mum and dad's place. Does Calder know where they live?"

"No, but I told him the other day that I took a flight from Angoulême."

"He'll no doubt be staking out that airport from now on. I think we'd best head for Lyon and try to get a flight out of the country as soon as. Back to the UK. Sorry, but our wonderful relaxing south of France sojourn has come to an abrupt end."

"We can't go back looking like two drowned coypus. We'll have to stop somewhere. Besides, I'm exhausted, and I imagine you are as well."

"We'll find an Ibis somewhere near to a *hypermarché*, get some clothes and something to eat. I got you a present by the way."

"You got me a present? Oh, wow! What is it?"

"Your favourite sweets from the *confiserie* in Aigues-Mortes."

"From *La Cure Gourmande! Quelle surprise!* Ah, that's so thoughtful! I meant to get some after buying the ship."

"What? You paid for the ship as well?"

"Yep, for about 250 euros."

"Shit. That boat better be worth it."

"What do you mean?"

"Well, we don't even know if the scroll's in it."

"What? You mean you haven't checked!"

"I haven't had time to! I've been saving your ass for goodness' sake. You insisted on going by yourself."

"Pull over! Pull over somewhere. We need to check it out."

"No. We keep going until we get to Lyon. To a hotel."

Jules slumped in her seat with a face like a wet kipper and sulked, much to the amusement of Paul.

Three and a half hours later they were in Lyon. They did a supermarket sweep for clothes and victuals and headed to an Ibis on the same shopping concourse. The next available flight to Manchester was the following morning so they booked it. Once in their hotel room, Paul acquiesced. She was now able to see if the scroll was in the ship, but only after Paul insisted she made him a cup of coffee. She thumped him on the arm and forced him onto the bed pinning him down, then she relaxed her body and smothered him in kisses.

"Ouch! Watch my chin, it's still sore."

"Thanks for saving my life again. I'll make it up to you tonight, I promise. Oh, and thanks again for the *bonbons*."

She kissed him again seductively, arousing him and then slid off him, to his disappointment. She went over to the haversack and took the model out. It was undamaged. She stared at it.

"Pierre Cousseau. *L'Égyptienne* 1809. This is surreal. Your great, great, great, great-grandfather made this, and I played with this boat as a child. I can't believe we've managed to track it down. Have you got a knife or something sharp? We need to get the deck off it. I don't want to break it though."

"Again," Paul quipped as he reached for his haversack and pulled out a Swiss Army knife. "Here, let me."

He selected the blade tool and gently inserted it into the edge of the deck on the starboard side. He could see where it had been repaired. 'Was the scroll still there?', he wondered. 'Or did the woman take it out when Geoff and Diana had left? Or has someone else taken it?'

He carefully cut across the stern of the toy frigate then slid the knife around the edge on the port side. As he forced the last bit of wood with his implement the wood fell in. He held the boat up and Jules peered into the gap.

"It's there! It's there! The leather tube!" she exclaimed. She grabbed it with her long, slender fingers, and it detached itself from its two wooden holders.

"The moment of truth," Jules stated. She inhaled sharply. "Is it in there?"

She opened the top and there, inside, was a rolled-up scroll. She looked up and beamed at Paul then gently tapped the cylindrical case on the bedside table. The scroll slipped out. She unfurled the print on the bed, securing each corner of it with miscellaneous items, inconceivably thrilled to see lines and lines of hieroglyphic text. She began to read it assiduously.

142

"You fucking idiots! You let them get away. I've got two of our best men, Castaigne and Migaud, dead, as a result."

Edwin Calder launched the rare tome he was holding at the bruised head of Rambaud. The henchman parried it with his arm to prevent a third blow to his battered cranium. It landed at the feet of Peltier, the assailant who had fired the rounds from the copse without success. Vlissy, the WC victim, lowered his eyes.

"I gave you one job. One fucking job! To get that bitch to the *manoir* and you all screwed it up. I've got *les flics* crawling all over the place asking questions, not only here, but in the UK after Tufiq fucked up as well. Rambaud by name, but not by nature, eh! You big dickhead! And you, shithead! Take a fucking shower!"

Vlissy tentatively sniffed the air around him with his damaged nose.

"You stink!" Calder paused, still fuming. "So, have you got any idea whatsoever where they might have gone?"

"I'm afraid not *Monsieur* Calder," Peltier answered meekly

"Get out! All three of you. I need to do some thinking. Get out!"

Rambaud, Vlissy and Peltier swiftly fled the office, relieved to get out of the firing line.

Calder sat at his desk, his hands covering his anguished face. 'Who the fuck's this bodyguard? He must be ex-military,' he thought. 'Where would they have gone? The ship. Why would she come back to me and buy a toy ship? It's got to be something to do with the name of the artisan.' "Pierre Cousseau," he muttered. "As soon as I mentioned the name, she wanted it. Or is it something to do with the name inscribed on the vessel? *L'Égyptienne.*"

He went to his safe, entered the code and pulled out the rolled-up sheet of paper with the image on it. He sat back down and used his handgun and a crystal paperweight to hold the edges down and scrutinized the illustration. He then picked up his mobile, punched in his password and called a contact number.

"*Bonjour* Marie. I'd like you to do some research for me. Find out what you can, on one Pierre Cousseau. The only information I have is that he was possibly a Napoleonic soldier or sailor and was once perhaps a prisoner of war, probably from around these parts. Let me know as soon as possible if you unearth anything."

As soon as he put his phone down it rang again.

"*Bonjour* Bishop Ferrand...*Non*, I'm afraid she got away...I'm aware of the police interest. Two dead, I know. Rest assured, I won't let this happen again. We'll lie low for a while until I've figured out how much more she knows about the tablet. She's on to something...*Oui,* Bishop Ferrand. I promise not to kill the goose that may lay the golden egg..." The conversation ended. He placed the mobile down. "...yet," he sneered.

143

Jules sat at the desk in the hotel room concentrating, pen in hand, scribbling down her findings on a notepad, ignoring the pain in her arms caused by the intensity of the canoeing. Paul dozed on the bed. After thirty minutes, Jules clasped her hands to her face. She turned and looked at Paul. She stood up and just gazed into thin air for a good few minutes before heading to the en suite in a trance like state. She started to run a bath and poured lavender and patchouli *bain-mousse* into it. She then went to the bedside and gently tugged Paul's shoulder to wake him. He woke with a start. He rubbed his eyes and stared at the sheet of paper that Jules was proffering to him in silence. He sat up and took it from her grasp. She melted away to the bathroom without a word. Paul sat upright and began to read.

> 'This decree is a warning for future generations that your planet will witness the return of the Elohim. They will return in the year inscribed below, or earlier, if prompted by cataclysmic events caused by man alone or natural forces that threaten the very existence of your world.'

> 'This proclamation was written by the hand of Eloah himself and conveyed to your planet after the ice age by our heavenly vessel under the guardianship of the Elohim. It serves to forewarn you of the dire consequences of not treating your world with the respect it requires.'

> 'In the beginning, you became our Experiment, to see if we could transform sub-human species we found on your planet, into intelligent human entities who could sustain and preserve their world for generations. We inseminated some of these sub-human creatures with our seed and departed. We returned in later times to discover, to our surprise, that these creatures had not only survived but evolved into what you are today.'

Paul paused in thought, unconsciously fingering the wound on his chin. Then he continued.

> 'Eloah enriched the diversity of flora and fauna of the land and replenished the oceans and rivers abundantly, to help you evolve further. We taught you subsistence through agriculture, then we, the Elohim, departed but returned again to observe. Heartened by the success of our previous Experiment, we repeated the process of spreading our seed amongst you and the Nephilim were spawned. We returned again to find that the Experiment had gone awry as some of these monarchical warrior

giants had become too tyrannical, but the great flood devastated the land where the malevolent ones dwelt and rid the planet, for the most part, of their hegemony.'

'When the last of the Nephilim died out, we returned once more. The righteous amongst them were remembered as great heroes. We helped rebuild great cities in their honour. It was at this time we conveyed Eloah's wishes to the populace. We allowed the people to choose their own kings. We did not, this time, repeat the process of spreading our seed. We sent instead, our own, in human form, as prophets and monarchs, on occasions, to teach and guide the peoples of your world, to enlighten you and show you the path to righteousness, to remind you of your responsibilities in respect to Eloah's morals and to the planet on which you exist.'

Paul again paused in reflection for a moment and then continued.

'Those morals warned you about avarice. They warned against the indiscriminate raping of the pastures and forests. They warned against the excessive plundering and poisoning of the oceans and rivers. They warned against the wanton annihilation of the creatures that inhabit your world, and we warned you to beware of false prophets!'

'We warned that this sacred tablet must always be located within one of our hallowed structures that reach towards the stars. It must always be protected. We built these great structures, in diverse places, across your world for you, to remind you of our existence and to provide you with a constant reminder that one day we would return.'

Again, Paul paused for thought.

'If this very tablet and the message it conveys has not been respected, then woe betide! Those who have transgressed will be exiled to another planet. A barren planet. Pestilence and famine will follow. Only humans and those of the spirit world deemed evil will roam that world. Flesh of others will be your only sustenance. Their blood, the only liquid to slake your thirst. The flesh of children born unto you will be craved, as desirable as a lamb's. This will be the Darkness!'

Paul's eyes widened as he studied the stark, spine-chilling prophecy.

'We have taught you the language of the gods so we could communicate this proclamation to you. Do not forget our language. Pass it down, like the proclamation, from generation to generation and ensure, without fail, that you preserve this tablet and heed its message.'

363

'This sacred ivory tablet serves another purpose. Only by peering into it can we understand your personal journey, your personal history. Those who have been virtuous, lived peacefully and respected nature and their fellow man will be saved from the Darkness. Those who have been evil, corrupt and negligent will suffer the terrible aforementioned fate.'

Paul uttered the final sentence.

"The year we shall return to conclude our Experiment is -"

Paul stared at the date momentarily in awe, his hands clasped around his nose and mouth.

"2040"

He rubbed his perspiring forehead, removed his aching body from the bed and shambled over to the bathroom. He went in and knelt beside the bath and hugged a silent Jules, covering himself in *bain-mousse* bubbles. Then he stripped naked and slipped in behind Jules, hugging her and they lay there, motionless, and speechless, their minds elsewhere.

That evening they made passionate love to each other as if it was already the end of days, clinging to each other afterwards for reassurance.

144

Refreshed by a long and deep sleep, Paul and Jules headed to the airport early the next morning. On the flight they discussed the implications of the portentous proclamation.

"So, what now? Are we to be the harbingers of doom?" Paul asked.

"I don't know Paul. I'm still trying to get my head around it. It's…it's just incredible. Unbelievable. The implications of this are massive. What do we do? Tell the world of the horrors to come? Bury it? It's such a dilemma."

"We can't bury it. The way the world is heading, politically and morally in relation to the Earth's ecosystem, with plastic and other pollution poisoning the seas, rainforest destruction, wilful extinction of species, CO2 emissions and global warning, we don't stand a chance of impressing 'the gods', do we? How do they or we define what's acceptable?"

"We stop burning the rainforests down for a start. We try and reverse the effects of climate change immediately. Invest in conservation, new, cleaner technologies. We've got fifteen years or so to save the world. If it's not enough, we know in our hearts we tried. To have this knowledge and then do nothing with it is suicidal. On a personal level, I would think I'm righteous and respectful of other people and Nature. Or would they frown on me digging up sacred temples and mummies?"

"Again Jules, who knows? I think a good many of us do fit into those parameters, but we all have to work harder too. There's always room for improvement. Besides, the spectre of roaming a barren planet, murdering and cannibalising each other is one huge incentive to be kind to each other and the environment, don't you think?"

Jules smiled weakly.

"Paul, we'll have to call a press conference immediately on arrival. The sooner we disclose this information, the better. As we know all too well, people are prepared to kill for this information. I know Calder's motive was financial. He was hoping for a big pay day because he has in his possession the fourth letter and the animal image which he was circulating to the highest bidder and now there's me ready to usurp him. It couldn't happen to a nicer bloke though. The little shyster!"

"Others would love to suppress this information and still more will be bent on rubbishing it and disparaging you, citing you as the fraud. You'll become more of a target. Not only of vitriol, but of violent retribution. Are you prepared for that Jules?"

"What's new? Are you prepared for it, Paul?"

"It seems to be our destiny."

"I suppose there'll be many doubters when we reveal this."

"And the only way of proving it is-"

"By finding the stele," they said simultaneously.

365

"So, are you prepared to continue the search for it, Jules?"

"There's no option. We have to find it now. I've already been thinking of that image of the bear. Racking my brains. A bear linked to a lion. I'm drawing a complete blank."

"So will everyone else."

"Pardon?"

"I lied to you Jules, I'm afraid. To take the pressure off you. I'm sorry. It wasn't a bear I found."

"What are you talking about? It wasn't a *bear,* that *you* found?" She stared at him incredulously. "My God, it was *you* who called Radio Merseyside. You lied to me."

Paul fetched his haversack from the overhead cabinet. He sat back down and took out an old leather wallet. Jules looked at him, mouth agape. He opened it and took out a thrice-folded piece of faded, fragile paper to reveal an illustration.

"A horse!" Jules gasped. "You had it all along! I can't believe it! A horse, not a bear!"

"Again, I'm sorry I had to lie to you. I just thought we needed a bit of breathing space. We needed to recharge our batteries in France but fat lot that's gone and done us."

"It was nice while it lasted. You did the right thing. I'm not mad with you."

She pecked him on the cheek.

"Do we tell the world about this?" Paul said.

"Let me think about it. Oh, and get thinking about a horse and lion link."

"I have done Jules, but I haven't got very far."

366

145

The aircraft touched down in Manchester and they took a cab back to Liverpool. Jules had phoned her mother the previous day to tell her of their eventful trip and to warn her that she and dad might be in imminent danger. They chose to remain in France once their daughter had stressed that she had not divulged their whereabouts. After mulling over the situation Jules decided to see Edmund straight away. They arrived at the University and went immediately to the Chancellor's office. They recounted their dramatic experiences to him much to his consternation and revealed the lithographic print to him along with its transcript. Dr Parkes was, in his words, "gob-smacked". He immediately set up a conference at the waterfront Convention and Exhibition Centre for the following Monday. Being an environmentalist and a strong advocate of 'green' policies, he endorsed the view that the stele had to be found come what may. The fate of the world mattered more than an individual's life, even his own, he concluded. He resolved to re-deploy Team Quest as of then.

146

Marie Tulot had furnished Edwin Calder with the information he wanted. He stood in his office staring at the illustration he had taken out from his safe. A wild horned sheep, known in France as a *mouflon*, which inhabited the mountainous regions of the south of France, Europe and Asia. Marie had confirmed, after several hours of diligent research, that Pierre Cousseau had resided at *La Ferme des Mouflons*, in the *commune* of Mourèze, Occitanie. The secluded extant farm was now divided into three *gîtes*, now called *Les Gîtes de la Résistance*, 1, 2 and 3. The following day, his early Sunday morning arrival was well timed, just after the last guests had left. He and his retinue of henchmen surprised the cleaner and the owners. Rambaud pistol-whipped the proprietor and forced his wife and the female cleaner into the cellar of their cottage situated on the grounds of the old farm. Calder's men then set about tearing the three *gîtes* apart, digging up the tiled floors to each one, convinced that the original '*Ferme des Mouflons*', would reveal its secrets, namely, the print of the sacred text. It was late afternoon when he brought the proceedings to an abrupt halt when he watched a news broadcast on TV. Dr Jules Johnson was to hold a press conference the following Monday morning in Liverpool. The reason given was the discovery of something highly significant in the quest for the stele. Calder, flushed with rage, launched an empty bottle of Chateauneuf-du-Pape at the TV screen smashing the set into pieces and startling his bodyguard. Calder cursed bitterly.

"That bitch! She deceived me!" he bellowed. "The print must have been in the toy ship! Why didn't I think of that? The *mouflon* illustration is fucking worthless now!"

He downed the dregs of the wine he found at the cottage and slung his glass into the hearth shattering it.

"Get the others! We're leaving!" he growled.

He marched over to the cottage and down the steps to the cellar. He snatched the pistol off Rambaud and shot the three detainees without remorse. Rambaud, stunned, stared at the bloodied corpses, then scrambled up the stairs after his boss.

147

On hearing the news, Fatima left her holiday cottage and her parents on Anglesey. She returned to her apartment at Princes Park Mansions in Liverpool. Tom was already at home after spending a week in Italy and Randy too, having arrived from Singapore the day before, jetlagged but otherwise mentally refreshed. Penny was still in Spain with her family and had no intention of rushing back.

The re-formed members of Team Quest listened intently, shocked at the ordeal Jules and Paul had endured. Then Jules revealed the print of the stele. Fatima was transfixed, as Jules had been. Jules asked her to transcribe it to confirm her own findings. Within thirty minutes an incredulous, dumbstruck Fatima, was back with a translation. She passed it to Jules who read it and gave it her assent. It was almost verbatim, to Jules's own translation. She passed her own copy to Tom and the other to Randy. Both drew the same awe-struck response as Fatima's - complete shock followed by a moment of silent contemplation. Finally, Edmund spoke.

"This is utter madness. If only it were a hoax."

"When this gets out, everyone will assume it *is* a hoax. It sounds absurd," Randy blurted.

"Not really when you analyse it," Tom said. "A higher power, prophets, a Judgement Day, Hell, and a possible salvation for the righteous."

"I always believed that man alone was not responsible for the construction of the world's pyramids. There's my evidence," Fatima declared.

"And for ancient cities like Thebes, Cuzco, Ollayantambo - those huge blocks of stone, so perfectly aligned," Jules added.

"Well, it makes finding the tablet with its *sacred* text more important than ever. That's why I've brought you together. Are you all willing to take up the baton again?"

Each of the team nodded their assent to Edmund.

"Ok, good. Now, where did we leave off? The last clue. A bear. A bear linked to a lion."

"Er Edmund," Jules interjected. "Paul's got something to say about that, or rather show you."

She gestured flamboyantly to Paul. All eyes focused on him. He scratched the side of his unshaven face, fingered the still visible sore on his chin and shifted uneasily in his seat, then pulled out the wallet. He unfolded the fragile piece of paper and laid it on the table. Everyone's jaw dropped.

"A horse?" they all exclaimed.

"There'd better be a good explanation, Paul. I've spent hours thinking about a bloody bear in Liverpool!" Fatima said, raising her voice.

"As have we all," Tom added.

Paul apologized and explained his reasoning behind the subterfuge. On reflection, at the time, they realised they had all needed some breathing space. Everyone had been highly stressed with the killings. After his explanation, the forgiven Paul asked for everybody's thoughts on the lion-horse link. Randy offered his first.

"Well, when you think about horses and Liverpool, the Grand National, of course, springs to mind. When did that start?"

"Officially 1839," Paul tendered checking on his mobile. "But there seems to be some dispute as to when the first race was. Some race historians beg to differ. They reckon it might have been 1836. Nevertheless, William Lynn, the founder of the Grand National laid out the course and constructed the grandstand and Lord Sefton laid the foundation stone on the 7th of February 1829 at Aintree."

"We don't know if our mysterious writer was still playing his game of clues at this time, though," Jules said. "The most recent letter to come to light was dated March 1815. So, it's quite a long period. He, or she, might have passed away by that time."

Tom spoke next. "Any horses famous for unusual incidents or feats during that period? A horse might even be buried somewhere on the course, like Red Rum."

"That'll be popular. Digging up Aintree Racecourse," Fatima added. "Shall I call in the animal rights activists?"

"Lord Sefton, the 2nd Earl of Sefton, seemed to be an interesting character," Paul continued, reading from his phone. "He was known as Lord Dashalong apparently due to his love of driving a carriage and four horses through the streets of London at great speed. He was Master of the Quorn Hunt at one time too and on a sidenote, he established the Waterloo Cup at Altcar. The banned hare-coursing event. He was a bit of a gambler by all accounts. But I'm digressing."

"I'm definitely calling PETA. Paul, your good at the Lydia role providing us with all this information. God bless her."

"Thanks Fatima, but it's all here on the internet. Not to disparage Lydia, of course. She was the font of all knowledge. Anyway, there's a few things to consider as regards horses. The Grand National, carriage driving and fox hunting, even the carters that served the docks."

"Then there's coaching inns," Randy added. "And the names of other hostelries. The Horse and Jockey, for example. Or the Coach and Horses. Even the Hungry Horse chain."

Everyone laughed.

"But remember, it's got to be linked to a lion somehow," Jules reiterated.

"Of course, the influential Molyneaux family, the Earls of Sefton, had their ancestral seat in Liverpool at Croxteth Hall," Edmund said. "So, that's another avenue to explore, Croxteth Hall. Furthermore, you're forgetting Liverpool's other illustrious, wealthy, landowning family, the Stanley's, the Earls of Derby, the name deriving from the Hundred of West Derby here in Liverpool, not the city of Derby as many people think and whose ancestral home is Knowsley Hall, down the road. So, what's the horse link here?"

"The Derby," Paul said.

"That's right Paul. So, Liverpool can boast of two strong links to two of the greatest horse-racing events in the world."

Randy relayed the information this time from his phone.

"It says here the first Derby race was in 1780, so that fits in with our timeline and also that Leasowe Castle on the Wirral was built way back in the 16th century by one of the Earls of Derby and was most likely built to view horse racing on the Wallasey course, one of the oldest horse racing tracks in England. So, that's another area of equine interest. Viren would have loved all this, all things equestrian."

There was a moment of silence.

"And Simon," Tom said. "He loved the Chester races and the National."

"Well, listen. The news conference is set for 11am this Monday, so you've got the weekend to pursue the new lead. I'm going to be busy organising the event. Jules, you should think carefully about pressing charges against Edwin Calder."

"Edmund, I'm sure he's heard the news about the conference, so I don't expect him to be anywhere near here. He won't be happy, that's for certain."

"In any event, I'm going to place the print in a safety deposit box until Monday if that's alright with you. There's a company in the Liver Building who offer this service."

"Fine by me Edmund," Jules said.

"Ok, Randy can you check out Leasowe Castle on the Wirral? Tom and Fatima could visit Croxteth Hall, they do tours, and Jules you could take a trip to Knowsley Hall. Paul, you've got your job back. You go with Jules. Enjoy the Safari Park. Me? I'm going to check out the 12.30 at Newmarket."

They all laughed.

"Damn! We could do with another Lydia. Paul, you're not pretty enough," Randy joked.

"Know anyone up for a challenge?" Edmund asked.

"There's a guy who runs the Blue Badger Liverpool tours, Miles Rowson," Jules said. "He might be of use. He's a bit of an arrogant sod, but his knowledge of all things Liverpool is excellent. Maybe we can bring him on board."

"Ok, give him a call. If any of you come up with something interesting in the next 48 hours, we'll reconvene. And for the time being, it makes horse sense to keep this image to ourselves."

They all groaned.

Jules immediately rang the Blue Badger line. The receptionist informed her that Miles was already on a tour. He was over at the Cultural Quarter, the area of Liverpool dominated by a collection of historic buildings. St. Georges Hall, The World Museum, The Central Library, the Walker Art Gallery, and the County Sessions House. Paul and Jules decided to head down there.

148

As they traipsed over the cobbles in front of the grand façade of St Georges Hall, Jules spotted Miles holding a small placard up with a blue badger face on it, leading a band of nine or ten tourists towards the Walker Art Gallery, home of masterpieces by Rubens, Turner, Rembrandt, and Millais. Paul and Jules tagged on to the group, waving at the tour guide to gain his attention as he paused on the steps to address his cohort. Miles ignored them as he was in serious storytelling mode. Jules indicated to her watch and gestured to him that she wanted to talk to him later in the café. He understood her but carried on with his tour, leading his charges into the Gallery. Jules went to grab a coffee in the café whilst Paul wandered off to view the paintings in another of the Walker galleries. The sight of the Duke of Wellington imperiously perched on his column outside had prompted him to think about Wellington's horse Copenhagen and a possible Napoleonic link to the clue. He thought also of Bonaparte's famous grey stallion, Marengo. Bringing up information on his phone about the horse Copenhagen, he was interested to see that a thoroughbred mare named Lady Catherine was a daughter of 1793 Derby winner John Bull and this dam gave birth to Copenhagen. He strolled back to the café to find Jules ten minutes later. She was with Miles. The tour guide had given his sightseers some free time to explore the art gallery.

Paul greeted Miles. "Hello again."

Miles grunted a barely audible surly response.

"Paul, Miles has agreed to join our team," Jules said.

"Welcome aboard."

Miles remained indifferent to Paul's cordiality, barely registering him.

"So, you've finally come to your senses and condescended to ask, '*the Oracle of Liverpool*', for his help," he bragged.

"Something like that, I suppose," Jules retorted.

"Well listen, more or less straight up from here, past the Steble Fountain and up towards Islington." Miles pointed to his left. "Bear-baiting used to take place before any of the St George's Quarter was constructed. It was on the site of the Folly Fair. Also, the first zoological gardens in Liverpool were over by the Shiel Road, West Derby Road area. They opened in 1833 and would most definitely have had bears on show. Furthermore, over in Eastham Woods there's an actual bear pit…"

"Hold on, Miles. Let me stop you there," Jules intervened. "I'm afraid you've been led up the zoological garden path, as it were, like everyone else."

Miles slurped his latte, his brain computing the implications of Jules's statement. He stared at her, with a puzzled expression on his face. Jules glanced at Paul and gave him a dirty look, half in jest. Paul came clean.

"It's not a bear clue we're looking for. It's a horse."

"A horse! A horse? I've been racking my brains about a frigging bear in Liverpool! Ooh, I'd like to get my hands on that anonymous caller. The bozo who called into Radio City!"

Paul stifled his laughter and Jules smiled. Miles exhaled, put his anger to one side, and re-focused.

"A horse, then. Maybe something to do with the National?"

"We're on to that," Jules said. "And the Derby. We're just off to Knowsley Hall now."

"Of course, the Derby as well. The Stanley and Molyneaux families. There are also equestrian statues to consider."

"I was thinking Jules...," Paul said.

"Fox hunting!" Miles blurted out, rudely interrupting Paul who sighed indignantly.

"What were you about to say, Paul?" Jules asked swiftly, observing the peeved expression on her partner's face.

"I was thinking along the lines of Wellington and his mount Copenhagen. Or Napoleon and his horse Marengo. Wellington's Column outside prompted me to think along those lines."

"Don't forget, the horse must be linked with a lion," Jules mentioned.

Miles suddenly looked up, alerted.

"A lion? Of course! A lion-horse link!"

"Have you got something Miles?"

"Eureka!" he bellowed, startling the other visitors and café staff. "Have I, Jules. Have I!" He stood and held his blue badger sign aloft as if he were conducting another tour. "Follow me!"

Jules and Paul glanced at each other in surprise, then went after Miles who was striding off purposefully towards a gallery. They followed the 'Blue Badger' hurriedly through one or two exhibition rooms and then he stopped abruptly, with Jules concertinaing into the back of Miles, then Paul into Jules.

"Eh voilà!" Miles pointed at the painting hanging on the wall in front of them.

"A lion and a horse!" Paul gasped, taken aback.

"By George Stubbs, adjudged to be Liverpool's most famous artist, best known for painting animals. Horses in the main. No pun intended. Born in Ormond Street, off Old Hall Street in the 1700s, died early 1800s. The timeline probably fits. His birthplace doesn't exist now though. You've got the fabulous Albany Building on one side and that abomination replacing the beautiful neo-classical façade of the Cotton Exchange on the other. God, someone must have had their palms greased over that one. Just sheer corporate vandalism!"

"We need to check the back of the painting," Jules urged, desperate to take a peek at the frame.

"No way Jules, we might be accused of vandalism or worse still, theft."

"Well, I'm with Paul on this one. You can't just go manhandling the jewels of the city."

"Alright," Jules conceded. "You're right. Slap my wrists. This archaeologist should practice what she preaches. Penny! Of course! She's a trustee of NML. She can

373

probably authorize our access to it, under supervision, that is. I'll call her."

"Before you get your hopes up, I should advise you that...there are several George Stubbs paintings depicting lions and horses," Miles cautioned. "All different. Some are in the National Gallery in London and others are in overseas collections."

"Oh! Right. Well, let's start with this one on our doorstep. Excuse me."

Jules left the Gallery and phoned Penny. Ten minutes later she returned.

"Penny's flying back from Spain tomorrow morning. She's going to organize access to it sometime early next week. That break did her good, I think. She was happy to hear from me. Her tone has mellowed since we last saw her."

"Listen, I must go and round up my flock. St George's Hall next."

"Ok. I'll contact you when I have the details of the meeting. Thanks Miles. By the way, you're invited to the press conference on Monday. I'll sort out a pass for you."

Jules hugged him, Miles enjoying the close contact, then she and Paul left.

"Come on Paul, let's go and do our shopping and get back to the cottage. I've got some work to do for Monday's conference."

149

Edwin Calder sat brooding, clad only in shorts, in the extensive grounds that surrounded his sumptuous home, *Le Manoir de* Chamberte, situated north-west of Montpellier. He was ruing the loss of his lucrative deal. A deal that would have resulted in him splashing out on the expensive, grand *château* he always coveted. He had taken a dip in his swimming pool. The weather in early September was still burning hot. Beyond the steel meshed fence that surrounded the grounds he spotted a solitary *mouflon* emerging from the dense thicket to graze on the open meadow between the manor house and the woods. An unwelcome sight that made him dwell even more on his spurned opportunity. It was as if the *mouflon* was taunting him. He could feel the bile, the ire rising up from the pit of his stomach to consume him. Seething, he regretted the fact that his hunting rifle wasn't at hand. He watched it for a few moments before it was spooked, returning to the safety of the mass of trees. He drained his cup of coffee. His mobile rang.

"*Allô*," he answered irritably. His angry demeanour then changed. "*Ça va?* How's the weather in Zurich? It's glorious here."

"Warmish, my friend," Yves Malines responded. "Bishop Ferrand has asked if you're attending the news conference."

"In Liverpool on Monday? No, Yves. I am not. Since we let Dr Johnson slip through our fingers, my intention is to remain here in France. She has made accusations against me but fortunately she spoke to Inspector Duart of the Montpellier *Gendarmerie.* Being a fellow Graïlien, the complaints will go no further. He's also dealt with the aftermath of the fatalities on the river. He has assured me the spotlight will not focus on me or the sect."

"Good. That was my principal concern, Edwin."

"As it was for Ferrand. You can tell him the positive news. I was just mulling over our next move. I still have the letter and the animal image, but their value has diminished overnight. If Dr Johnson has the copy of the print and is to reveal it to the world's media on Monday, then we will have to just wait and see what message it contains."

"A wise move in the circumstances."

"The true value lies in the tablet itself. The artefact was already priceless but maybe Dr Johnson's discovery will catapult its value into the stratosphere, so, on reflection, that might be no bad thing, if we can get to it first."

"The Supreme Prelate is sending a delegation to Liverpool again with Ferrand at its head along with a team of Rainbow Angels this time," Yves said. "Our leader is convinced that the tablet is also the eternal supercomputer, and he is determined to be the one who delivers it to the Elohim on their return. His aspiration is to convert the multitudes to Graïlienism. One world religion, its billions of followers in total harmony with each other and he will stand at the head of it, bathing in the glorious light of our extra-terrestrial visitors."

"Yves, *mon ami*, it's all very well preaching peace and love to the world but to secure the tablet, force will inevitably be required. Every religion covets that tablet, and some, given the chance, will destroy it to preserve their modus vivendi. So, we must get to it first. Blood has been spilt and will be again in its pursuit."

"I realise this. My commitment to our mutual agreement has not wavered. We will succeed in selling the tablet to the highest bidder. We will first declare it won for the Grailien cause and then sit back and watch as the floodgates open."

"Indeed, the imploring, filthy rich will be tripping over themselves in their vulgar rush to convert to Grailienism in their desire to be saved. Amongst them, no doubt, those wealthy benefactors who will insist on contributing generously to our ransom fund in the hope of recovering the 'stolen' artefact, that is, after we have 'procured' it. I hope you still share my sentiments Guardian Cleric."

"Rest assured Edwin. I want the best of both worlds. Like you and Bishop Ferrand. I too aspire to reach the apotheosis of our ambitions. I long to join the ranks of the filthy rich. Sexual gratification and great wealth are two powerful, stimulating drugs."

"I concur. Perhaps our concept of Heaven is right here on Earth. We have the former and now seek the latter. Although recovering and preserving the tablet for the Elohim, I'm sure, will be seen as a righteous deed, no matter how it's done, still providing us with the opportunity to accompany them to 'Paradise', whenever that time comes."

"Edwin, you'll have to excuse me. I must go. My presence is required at an Inauguration. Boy, I love these baptism ceremonies and seminar camps. More naked grist to my sexual mill. Wish you were here?"

"Most certainly. Enjoy it, my friend. Ciao. Peace and love but mainly the latter."

"Ha! Ha! Sure, I won't let you down on that score. Take care."

150

"The date we shall return is…"

The mass of representatives of the world's media and the invited interested parties crammed into the riverside Liverpool Convention Centre, waited with bated breath, like the billions listening or watching live from around the globe. There had been gasps and screams as each section of the decree was announced by Jules. The Experiment, the Nephilim, the prophets and warnings of false prophets, the denouncing of greed and of the wilful destruction of the planet, the construction of the great ancient cities and pyramids, the portals, and the sacred texts. Further prolonged wailing and gnashing of teeth occurred as the hellish realities of 'The Darkness' were laid bare. The weeping transformed to sniffles momentarily as a little bit of hope for mankind shone through after the announcement that salvation, for some, was possible. She had already shared the events of how they came to track down the print in France prior to the revelation of the sacred script. Then, an emotional Jules stated, "…and this is why the people of this world have to come together as one, like never before."

She paused, amidst the now pervading silence, to survey the sea of dissimilar faces surrounding the dais. Bewildered souls who hung on to her every word. There were expressions of predominantly apprehension, but also of anger, sadness, dismay, and even happiness. Finally, she uttered the words everyone wanted to hear - the year of the return of the Elohim.

"2040."

The place erupted in chaos. Some delegates fell to their knees and instinctively prayed. Others fainted in the charged, frenzied atmosphere. Some laughed, still in denial, whilst others shouted "Hoax!" and "Shame on you!" Many remained stunned in silence. Jules, tears in her eyes, walked off the stage, straight into the comforting arms of Paul.

Edwin Calder alone, stared at his TV, deep in thought. Then his face relaxed and he smiled. He laughed uncontrollably, delighted that his name had not been revealed and even more so by the terrifying, ominous message of the sacred script.

"Our leader has been right all along!" he sang out ecstatically. He downed a shot of malt and licked his lips. "What price the artefact now?" he growled. "And Dr Johnson is still our best hope of finding it. We shall meet again, my dear, very soon. Very soon!"

The shocked delegates filed out of the Convention Centre, only for their confused and conflated emotions, to be tormented once more by the horrific spectacle of two Buddhist monks self-immolating on the concourse. People screamed and ran in different directions looking for assistance to help the burning monks. Others tried to get to them, to see if they could stop them somehow but it was all in vain. Those that had not averted their eyes watched on helplessly as the deadly flames devoured the silent men. Bizarrely, on the far side of the concourse, at another exit point from the arena, the departing crowds were met by Grailien men in alien costumes and topless female activists distributing leaflets on behalf of the sect.

Jules and Paul met with the others and Penny backstage. Penny hugged Jules tightly. It was the first time she had seen her since Simon's death. Edmund was going to be busy dealing with the Press for the rest of the day. The others arranged to meet Penny in the morning at the National Conservation Centre in Liverpool before slipping away from the frenzied posse of newshounds.

151

Liverpool, 1809

O'Rourke awoke with a start. He sat up in bed, bemused, uncertain of his surroundings.

"Mother! Father is awake!" Patrick screeched.

The younger child, Charles, dived onto the bed and hugged his father. His father exhaled, the impact winding him as a result of his frail body.

"Oomph! Steady son."

Kitty entered carrying her baby daughter. "Charles!" she screamed. "Get off your father!"

"It's alright, dear," he whispered.

Charles clung on despite his mother's rebuke.

"Oh, Seamus. We were concerned for you."

"What happened?"

"You collapsed after the trial. Don't you remember?"

"No, I recall the verdict and stepping out into the blinding light but not much else."

"You've been poorly for two weeks. The doctor diagnosed gaol fever. We thought you'd never pull through," she sobbed.

Patrick comforted his mother.

" Kitty, I've something to tell you about work. I-"

"We already know, father," Patrick interrupted. "You've lost your position."

"Mr Morton has been to see the authorities to champion your cause but I'm afraid, to no avail," Kitty said, wiping the tears from her eyes. "Don't worry yourself too much about it now. You need to rest and re-gain your strength. I'll fetch some broth. Kids, out! Leave your father to rest."

Patrick hugged his father. Kitty grabbed Charles by his scruff and tore him from his father's grasp unceremoniously. "Get off, Charles! Give him some air."

Kitty kissed her husband on the cheek, and he kissed the baby on its forehead, and then sank down into the pillow to rest.

Gradually Seamus regained his strength over the next few weeks. He was visited by Frederick who had since returned to duty with the King's regiment. Frederick had re-enlisted after being in the army since he was sixteen having completed twelve years of service. The visit had proved beneficial to Seamus. He had listened to his friends exploits and they re-lived old times in the military. It raised his spirits. Likewise, the gift of a bottle of brandy had revived him somewhat. His thoughts inevitably turned towards work after Frederick's departure. They could, perhaps, survive for the next month or so but no more. He thought about re-enlisting too if they would consider him. He also pondered a return to sea either as a privateer or in the navy. His linguistic ability could be a boon, although this skill had almost cost him his life. He was reluctant to pursue these potential opportunities, however, on the basis that they would again take him away from his family. He decided to pawn or sell his remaining artefacts. He had two Mameluke swords and a pistol to sell, items which he had recovered from the French soldier's grave in St John's one misty night. As for the tablet, he decided to bide his time.

Over the following few weeks Seamus was pro-active in attempting to find work. He frequented the docks and trudged over to the Herculaneum pottery works on the banks of the Mersey. He went to the sugar houses in John Street and Hay Market and visited the roperies of the 'ropewalks' area. He tried the chandlers, cooperages, victuallers, breweries, iron works, watchmakers and a plethora of other factories and businesses, all to no avail. He felt as if there was a stigma attached to him although he had been proved innocent of any wrongdoing. He also began to suspect that religious bigotry was a contributing factor for his constant rejection. Nevertheless, it was his disabilities that disadvantaged him the most. A merchant would always choose an able-bodied man or woman over an invalid. It was economically understandable.

Christmas came and went. They made the best of it but now the money was running out. The disheartened Irishman was becoming more and more withdrawn and depressed when Kitty made a proposition.

"Seamus, Mr Joseph is building some properties. I can-"

"It'll be the same response," he replied morosely. "I'm an invalid. I'll be slower and less dexterous than anyone else. Why would anyone care to employ me?"

"You can't give up Seamus! You mustn't think like that!"

Kitty snatched a bottle of whisky from his grasp.

"I see you're quick enough to pour that grog out so fast! Enough now! Get a grip of yourself! Stop wallowing in self-pity! Besides, once this has gone, how do expect to pay for more?"

He thought about snatching it back to drain the rest of the bottle's contents but stopped himself. Kitty's words struck a chord. What was more important? Something which amounted to water with a few ingredients in it or his family?

"Ever since I found Sam, dead in that doorway with his bony hands, chilblained feet and sallow face so blue with cold I've been in a downward spiral of melancholy. I-I mean, I could have saved him if I'd been working. His death is playing on my conscience."

"All the more reason why you should be thinking about your own family! That'll be us soon if you don't get your wits together! Would you like to see us all frozen to death as well, huddled in our rags in a doorway? That's our fate! Look, I know you tried to help Sam, you're a good man, but you can't help every destitute urchin you see. Life is so tough for a lot of people. Your family come first. Right, first thing tomorrow I am going to ask Mr Joseph if there are any positions available, so get yourself sober and presentable!" She stormed out.

152

Liverpool. Present day.

Penny met the team at 10am at the National Conservation Centre, the former Midlands Railway Goods warehouse in Victoria Street. They were ushered into a room where two technicians and one of the Walker Art Gallery's curators were assembled. The George Stubbs painting lay on a table.

"Now then, let's hope you're right Jules," Penny said.

"For everyone's sake," Randy added.

Penny nodded to the two technicians wearing white gloves who delicately began to detach the canvas from the ornate frame. In a matter of minutes, they had loosened three sides of the frame. As they were removing the bottom part with the assistance of the curator, something slipped into view below the frame.

"There!" cried Fatima who spotted it first.

"What the heck is that?" the astonished, hitherto doubtful curator asked.

The curator eased the last bit of the artwork from the frame and a slim, leather, rectangular-shaped wallet, approximately ten inches in length and two in width dropped to the table. Penny picked it up and with the consent of the others she opened it. In it was a thrice-folded piece of paper matching the shape of the wallet. She slid it out of its sheath and unfolded it carefully to expose the sought-after drawing.

"An eagle!" Fatima exclaimed. She looked around the relieved and somewhat euphoric team.

"Well done guys!" Penny gushed.

"Paul got the ball rolling by thinking about the paintings of Napoleon's horse Marengo and Wellington's Copenhagen and Miles led us straight to the George Stubbs painting," Jules said.

"And I'm going to tell you where the next clue will be found," said the conceited Blue Badger confidently. "You were heading there the other day Jules."

"Knowsley Hall!" Jules and Paul replied in unison.

"Exactly! The eagle and child is the heraldic crest of the Stanley family and synonymous with Knowsley," Miles said.

"And the horse link relates to the famous Derby race and the Earls of Derby as we previously reckoned," Tom added. "Penny, you know Lord Derby well. Do you think you can pull a few strings?"

"I reckon so. Being a friend of the Lord," she boasted playfully. "Give me a few minutes."

The team left to grab a coffee and Penny instructed the technicians and curator to reframe the masterpiece and return it to the Walker. Ten minutes later she found the team in the warehouse.

"All sorted. Lord Derby has given us immediate access to Knowsley Hall, providing we don't tell the media about our visit, but he won't be there. He's attending a Liverpool Chamber of Commerce function."

"Fantastic! Let's get going then!" Randy said.

They finished their drinks and arranged to split into two groups. Penny, Miles, Paul and Jules in one and Randy, Tom and Fatima in the other. Edmund was going to meet them there since he was also a friend of the 19th Earl of Derby, Penny having notified him.

153

They arrived at the Huyton Lodge Gates entrance to the magnificent, idyllic stately home, Knowsley Hall, which was only situated eight miles away from Liverpool city centre and gained access to the grounds. Despite the apocalyptic message Jules had conveyed to the world the day before, people seemed intent on carrying on with their daily lives, judging by the line of vehicles queuing to enter the Safari Park. The two cars drove up to the Hall, everyone admiring the 2,500 acres of verdant, lush grounds surrounding them. At the entrance to the imposing building, the manager of the Hall, James Green, greeted them as the team members climbed up the sweeping steps towards him. He took them into a private reception room, different to the one the tourists used, where they met Edmund. James addressed them beginning with an apology for the absence of Lord Derby. He then supplied the team with 'access all areas' lanyards, briefing them on health and safety issues and the do's and don'ts of the tour, what they can touch or more pertinently what they couldn't touch. James would be their guide.

"So, how can I help you folks? Where would you like to start first," James asked.

"We're interested in anything related to the eagle and child, or really just an eagle, I suppose," Miles replied.

"Anything that relates to the 18th or early to mid-19th century," Fatima detailed.

"We noticed the eagle and child statue on the façade of the Hall. Can we have access to that?" Randy inquired.

"There's no point, that's a 20th century addition. It's solid Portland stone, however there's plenty more to look at."

"Shall we start with the paintings?" Paul suggested, making reference to one epic watercolour of the stately home adorning the reception room. "It worked for us last time."

"Good idea, Paul," Jules said. "Have you works of art of eagles?"

"Several. Let's do them first. The ones that fit your timescale."

James led the team off into the Entrance Hall to view the paintings there, a mixture of portraits and landscapes. Then he led the team up the sweeping Grand Staircase to peruse those paintings hung alongside it and then he invited them into the State Rooms. None of the Stanley family were disturbed since they did not actually live in Knowsley Hall, opting to reside in other properties on the estate instead. The stately home's raison d'être now was principally functions, a spectacular venue for weddings in particular and tours. The group traipsed through the house. They passed a function room crammed with guests.

"Is that a wedding function?" Randy asked.

"No," James replied. "It's a party for retired ex-employees, those with long service and, believe me, there are some people in there, older than the Hall itself, I think. It's an annual thing. There's gardeners, nannies, librarians, curators, chefs, people who were in service, maids and butlers and the like."

They arrived at a magnificent work of art depicting the eagle and child, everyone appreciative of the vivid, dramatic painting.

"If we can, we need to look at the frame," Penny said. "We need to detach the painting from it."

"I'm afraid I can't help you with that. Lord Derby would have to give me permission. Otherwise, I reckon I would not be attending any long service functions if I gave you access to it without his consent."

Edmund intervened. "Let me speak to him." He took his mobile out and went off to have a private word. Five minutes later, he was back.

"James, he's given the green light to us providing we draft in Penny's team of technicians from the NML. He wants you to call him immediately to confirm it."

James went off to call Lord Derby and Penny used her phone to mobilise the NML technicians. The manager returned shortly.

"Lord Derby wants one of our curators to supervise the operation."

"It'll take a while for the NML team to arrive, so why don't we look at something else?" Penny suggested.

"Sure, the coat of arms displays the eagle and child crest and furniture as well. Come along. Lord Derby has given you carte blanche. You can go anywhere in the house, but if you want to examine anything, he wants one of the experts to accompany you and they'll do it for you."

The team spent the next hour in the company of historical experts and other curators examining the fabulous array of furniture on show. None of the experts had come across any secret compartments other than those they knew about, and they had recently examined all the furniture in the light of the revelation of the anonymous letters. The technicians arrived soon after and began the process of checking each frame of interest. An hour later they had still drawn a blank. The whole team was invited into the retirees' function room and offered refreshments on account of Jules being recognised off the TV. The team gladly partook of the buffet on offer and were only too happy to mingle and chat with the pensioners. Jules realised it was a good opportunity to pick their brains, given their wealth of knowledge and recollections of Knowsley Hall.

154

Jules sat down at a table and introduced herself to the three ladies there. One in her seventies. One who divulged she was eighty-two and one who proudly volunteered that she was ninety and, overall, all three were compos mentis. Joan, Mabel and Irene, respectively. Joan had been a stable hand and keeper at the Safari Park; Mabel had joined as a secretary and Irene had been a librarian and curator. All had been volunteers at the Hall after their retirement. They were extremely interested to hear how the hunt for the stele had led the team to Knowsley Hall. Jules explained the lion-horse link and the discovery of the eagle clue and asked them to think for a minute of anything that might be of interest to her in respect to an eagle. The ladies were pensive for a moment but couldn't recall anything and so they continued to reminisce about the good old days and Jules enjoyed listening to them, but she was eager to mingle with the other former staff members. She stood up and was in the process of politely excusing herself when Irene stopped her.

"I've just remembered something my dear. About a horse."

'Ah, God bless her cotton socks,' Jules thought. 'She must have got confused. She's thinking about a horse, not an eagle. I'll just let her finish her story then I'll move on. I hope it's not too long'.

"Well, I remember back in the sixties, when I was a newly employed librarian and dogsbody. Excuse me."

She paused to cough. It was a raucous cough. She apologized then resumed.

"There was a family gathering, a celebration of some kind, maybe a birthday. I was tasked with looking after Edward, the present Earl and his friend Peter whilst the adults enjoyed each other's company. Edward and Peter were only about four or five at the time. We were in the library reading. I was momentarily distracted by the phone. I answered it, turned round and Edward and Peter had gone."

She coughed again.

"Are you alright, Irene?" Jules asked concerned.

"Yes thank you, dear. Anyway, where was I? Oh yes, I chased after them. They both thought it was a great joke. I managed to catch up with Edward, but Peter managed to open a door to the parlour where his mother and father were with other guests and ran straight into Edward's Uncle John."

"The 18th Earl of Derby," Mabel confirmed.

"He also collided with a side table on which was a bronze statuette of a horse and he subsequently fell on the floor. Uncle John was not amused. Nor were Edward's parents and I got some severe looks."

"We've all been privy to those at some time or other," Joan chuckled.

"Haven't we just," Mabel chortled.

Irene continued. "Well, the boy just lay on the floor, with a startled look on his face, his legs akimbo. Now, the statuette had crashed to the floor also and the wooden plinth broke off."

Jules's interest in the story began to wane, despite her best intentions to remain interested. The pensioner had a slurp of tea and then droned on.

"I remember Uncle John saying that it was an heirloom. It had belonged to the 12th or 13th Earl, a gift or prize from a wager, from a friend, a gentleman who was one of the horse racing and hunt fraternity. Are you still with me dear?"

"Oh, oh yes, Irene. Please, carry on."

"Well, someone picked up the plinth and read the engraving on it. 1795 Derby Winner - Spread Eagle."

"Spread Eagle!" Jules repeated.

"What's up dear? Did you forget to pick your winnings up?" Mabel joked.

The three ladies tittered. Then Irene spoke again.

"Yes, Spread Eagle. Then this tipsy guest, a gentleman, looked and gestured towards Peter who was still lying there, legs apart on the carpet and quipped, 'Spread Eagle'. Everyone just laughed as Peter was spread-eagled, on the floor. Then the slightly inebriated chap noticed something inside the fractured plinth. He picked it up to peruse it. He pulled out a slim, rectangular leather wallet which when opened contained a piece of paper and on it was a drawing."

"A drawing! Of what?" Jules said with a heightened sense of urgency.

"Of a..., oh erm...a drawing of a..."

"Come on Irene," Jules excitedly squeaked in encouragement.

"Oh! Drat! I've forgotten, dear. Was it a rabbit, or dog? Definitely an animal. Ooh, silly me I can't remember which. Funny how the brain works."

"Irene, you're a star!" Jules cried. Jules planted a kiss on her cheek and gave her a hug. "Can you remember please what was on the paper?"

Irene thought for a moment. "No, it's completely gone. That's ridiculous isn't it? I can remember all the other details of that incident as plain as day."

"What happened to the bronze horse?"

"The horse was given to Edward as a toy to play with, if I remember rightly but I'm not sure what happened to it after that."

"Oh, that's a shame. Maybe they got it repaired and it could still be in the Hall somewhere."

"Perhaps. There is though, a slim possibility that we might be able to find out what was drawn on that paper."

"How do you mean?"

"Well, the illustration was also given to Edward, and I recall we used it for a bookmark. It could well be amongst those 5,000 books displayed in the library or stored in the vaults."

"Really? Do you mean it could still be there? Amongst all those books? Irene, thank you so much for your help! I'll see if we can check through them now. I'll go and tell the others. Thank you so much, ladies. It was a pleasure meeting you."

She hugged the three pensioners.

155

Jules quickly left the function and searched for the others who had gone into the landscaped gardens for a stroll and some fresh air. She located everyone and urged them to accompany her to the impressive library where two curators were on standby clad in white gloves. Before finding the rest of the team she had spoken to James who had advised her that only the two expert employees could handle the books after he had liaised with the Earl. She recounted Irene's story to the amazement of the others. Everyone's attention turned to the books. They peered through the glass panes of the bookcases trying to spot anything like a bookmark protruding from a tome. The curators began their search methodically choosing one bookcase at a time. They took each book carefully and leafed through it. Jules realised it was going to be a painfully slow process. She saw that each book was marked with the eagle and child motif. Suddenly they were interrupted by Irene and her two friends, Mabel and Joan who were either side of Irene's Zimmer frame, Mabel with her walking stick, both commendably helping their older friend.

"Can we help?" Joan inquired.

"Oh, ladies. Thanks for the offer but I think it will take a while to check all the books. You're better off staying put at your party," Jules replied.

"I don't suppose Edward remembered what happened to the illustration. He was probably too young," Mabel said.

"Has anyone contacted him? I guess it's worth a try," Joan declared.

"I did ladies. I texted him," James said. "He's busy right now. He responded saying he vaguely remembers the incident, but he does recall the bronze horse but not the drawing. Now, can you excuse us ladies?"

"We might be able to save you a lot of time," Irene insisted. "Two books, the child I recall, enjoyed. One contained the poem of the *Owl and the Pussycat*."

Mabel began to warble theatrically.

"O lovely Pussy, O Pussy, my love,

What a beautiful Pussy you are

You are, you are!

What a beautiful Pussy you are!"

Everyone stood slightly bemused or amused at Mabel's outburst.

"Edward Lear, the poet. Of course, he was an employee at the Hall here for several years and I remember telling the young child that he helped look after the animals in the menagerie and the birds in the aviary. This he very much liked to hear," Irene added.

"Did you tell him about that other famous bard William Shakespeare and his links to Knowsley?" Joan asked.

"Yes dear but he preferred hearing about Edward Lear. He liked looking at owls and other birds. The second book was an Audubon book. Not the famous tome in the Liverpool Central Library that's worth millions, the one which I, incidentally, used to look after. No, a smaller, different book. A publication from the Audubon Society. I left shortly after the spread-eagle episode after ten years' service here to take up a position at Speke Hall as a librarian and curator and then I went to work at the Central Library, you see. My great niece Lydia worked in the Record Office, until recently. God bless her."

"Oh my God! So, you're Lydia's great aunt! Lydia was our dear friend, God love her. Now I know who she got her intellect from!" Penny roared.

"Yes, that's probably true. I couldn't attend the funeral. I was ill. Poor girl. But I know she was a hero. She was trying to save the world when she was so viciously taken away from us."

"Audubon was born in Haiti, you know, when it was called Saint-Domingue," Mabel swiftly said so as not to dwell on the demise of her friend's great niece.

"Haiti?" Penny inquired. "I never knew that. One of my forebears came from Haiti. He was a former slave you know. Ended up in Liverpool."

"Ladies! We're digressing!" Miles interrupted sharply. "Madam, are you suggesting that we should check the library for anything related to Edward Lear or John James Audubon first?"

"Precisely, young man!" retorted an indignant, tetchy Irene, not warming to Miles's abrupt tone. "That's my advice. That's if you all don't want to spend days on end looking for the fucking drawing!"

Everyone was rooted to the spot. They glanced at each other in silence, some holding in their laughter, others in shock, taken aback by the nonagenarian's expletive.

"Excuse my language. I think you'd better get on with it."

"She's right!" Jules said breaking the silence. "Thanks again, Irene! Come on, everyone, have a look for Edward Lear and John James Audubon books."

The members of the team started to scour the bookcases but Margaret, one of the curators went straight over to one of the cabinets, opened it and selected a book off the shelf. She passed it to Eric, the other curator and then took another book off the same shelf. Both were books about Audubon by other authors. They delicately turned over each page without finding any bookmark.

"I'm afraid our chances of finding it are a million to one after all these years," she sighed lamentably. "Some of the collection has been sold."

"Oh! That doesn't sound too encouraging," Fatima said.

Eric headed straight for another bookcase followed by Tom. Before the curator had managed to select the correct key to unlock the cabinet Tom bellowed.

"*A Book of Nonsense*! By Edward Lear!" He beckoned to the others. "Over here! There's several. *Nonsense Limericks*, *The Jumblies*, etcetera!"

Everyone congregated around Eric and Tom who was jabbing his finger at some books by the poet and author on the last shelf of a cabinet. Eric looked flustered as he was jostled in his attempt to open the door of the glass-panelled bookcase. The others drew back as they registered his peeved expression and allowed him some space to pull the door open. He withdrew three copies of the Nonsense books, different editions, the oldest being from 1861.

"There was an Old Man with a beard, who said,
It is just as I feared!" Joan chirped.
Tom completed the limerick.
"Two Owls and a Hen, four Larks and a Wren,
Have all built their nests in my beard."
He tugged at his own whiskers and chuckled.

Again, Eric and Margaret carefully examined the books and cautiously went through the pages. There were about ten tomes in all, of the writer's works. The work was laborious and slow. Then Margaret pulled out the penultimate book, a rather tatty, battered hardback version of the *Book of Nonsense*, published by Routledge, Warne and Routledge dating from 1863. As she delicately removed it from the cabinet, something could just be seen protruding from the bottom of the book. She looked at Eric purposefully. "We have something! I think!" she called, alerting the others who were idly chatting in groups, slightly weary of the tedious, over-cautious approach. Margaret meticulously leafed through the pages until she came to the one of interest and there, she found a folded piece of paper inserted on the page of the verse of the *Owl and the Pussycat.* Everyone crowded around, invigorated by the find. Eric in dramatic limp-wristed fashion slowly extended his gloved hand towards the book and extracted the paper from the page, holding it gently by the edge. He took it over to a table, followed by the others, all exuding a rekindled but impatient curiosity, and painstakingly unfolded it revealing an illustration.

"A bird!" most said in unison.

"It looks like a bird-of-paradise," Edmund said.

"Is that what you're looking for?" Eric asked, scanning the puzzled faces of those around him.

"Oh, of course! It was a bird-of-paradise! I remember now!" Irene squawked. "Why didn't I make the same association with the Spread-Eagle Derby winner? Two birds. That is so bizarre. It just shows you how the mind works, as I said."

"That's definitely it then," Paul said. "A bird-of-paradise. But what's the link?"

"Yes, an eagle and a bird-of-paradise," Jules reiterated. "Think everyone. Maybe there's another clue to be found here at Knowsley Hall or some other link to the Stanley family."

"Perhaps," Margaret concurred. "Maybe it's linked to Edward Lear and the aviary."

"When was he employed here?" Tom inquired.

"1832," Eric replied. "Stayed for four or five years. He was a fine illustrator of birds. He wasn't just known for his nonsense verse."

"Hmm. Interesting, very interesting," Edmund muttered.

"Does anyone know what type of bird-of-paradise it is?" Fatima asked.

"Good shout Fatima," Randy said. "The clue might be in the name."

"Got it!" Penny screeched, startling everyone in the room. Everyone glared at her.

"Guys! Fall in and follow me!" she barked, abruptly, like a parade ground sergeant major. She strode resolutely to the exit of the library.

"I know where the next clue is! Trust me!"

The others looked at each other hesitantly, all slack jawed.

"Come on! Move!" she ordered. "At the double! Get your lead-laden backsides moving!"

"Oh! I know exactly what she means," Miles exclaimed. "The penny's just dropped! No pun intended! Come on!"

"But aren't you going to tell us?" Irene protested. But Penny and Miles had already left the library hastily. Jules and Edmund apologized for their colleagues' sudden departure and quickly thanked James and the curators for their assistance. Jules embraced the ladies again who were bristling in faux high dudgeon, thanking them too for their assistance and then Paul, Edmund and Jules quickened their step to catch up with the others.

"Edmund, can you call the Earl and thank him for his invaluable assistance?" Jules requested.

"Will do."

"Penny! Hold on. Where are we off to?" Paul shouted pulling the car keys from his pocket.

"The Pier Head! Museum of Liverpool Life!" she shrieked as she made her way down the flight of steps outside the Hall.

They all dispersed to their cars.

"We're on a roll!" Randy cried. "How many clues have we found now?"

"Penny's obviously confident about this one, so it will be four," Jules replied.

"Hurrah! Three to go then!" Edmund whooped like a nipper as he veered off in another direction.

156

Penny parked her car adjacent to the Port of Liverpool building at the Pier Head, one of the so called Three Graces that lined the Liverpool waterfront. The others found parking spaces nearby. She waited on the plaza impatiently outside the Museum of Liverpool for everyone to assemble. Ten minutes later everyone was there. She marched them into the atrium of the museum overlooking the Mersey ignoring the greetings of staff familiar to her and turned left and stopped and whispered, "*Eh voilà!*"

She was referring to a large, wooden gilded carving of a bald eagle, displayed on the wall of the foyer. Miles butted in.

"This gilded bald eagle was originally perched above the former American consulate in *Paradise* Street," he said before Penny could expand. "The consulate building dated back to 1790 and was the first ever consulate of the United States on British soil. So, it fits the timeline. The Yanks off the cruises love this when I bring them here on my American Civil War tours."

"Of course, the bird-of-paradise clue links to Paradise Street and the American eagle," Tom said.

"And this is definitely the original one. Right?" Fatima cautioned. "Because there's one also still in situ above the original building in Paradise Street which is now a boutique and apartments."

"Yes," Penny answered swiftly, beating Miles to the draw. "This is the original one. We restored it. The other's just a replica but this one now belongs to Grosvenor, the Liverpool One owners. Marcus!" She beckoned a member of staff across. "I need this taking to the Conservation Centre immediately."

"Are you sure Ms Carter? Have you requested authorization from Grosvenor?"

"No, time is of the essence, Marcus. I'll sort that out in due course."

"But…"

"No 'buts' Mr Cheeseman. Let's get it done, thank you!"

"Yes, Ms Carter."

"Right, grab a coffee, you guys and meet me at Victoria Street in thirty minutes."

The team retired to the café. As arranged, they all met later at the Conservation Centre. Penny had supervised the removal of the artefact which had taken four members of staff to carry the heavy gilded bald eagle to a van. On standby at the Conservation Centre was her team of technicians who had returned from Knowsley Hall earlier and a few other on-site technicians. She instructed them to make an incision into the back of the wooden sculpture. They hesitated.

"Do it," she said sternly. "I'll take the rap for it. Be incredibly careful and precise though. Make it big enough to get your hand in."

The technicians cut a small square of wood out from the back of the gilded eagle and removed it. They were surprised to see that the top half of the eagle was hollow inside. Penny then inserted her hand in the gap and felt around.

"It's hollow where the eagle's neck is! I can't insert my hand any further though. Fatima, you've got thin arms and small hands. Do you know, I should be called Fatima. Not you. Can you squeeze your hand in?"

The slender Fatima placed her hand in the aperture and felt around with her fingers. She pushed as far as she could manage then her expression changed.

"I felt something! There's something definitely there, in the neck. It felt like leather." The team members exchanged glances of anticipation. "I can't quite grasp it though. Jules, you have a try."

Jules thrust her hand into the gap.

"You're right Fatima! There is something leathery there. My fingers are touching it. Let me see if I can get some more purchase."

She withdrew her hand from the void and repositioned herself then repeated the process. She grimaced as she tried to shove her hand further in, wood chafing on her wrists, her long, slender fingers searching around for the elusive item.

"Ugh!" she strained. "I think I've got it!" Her grasp was weak though and she let go of it. "Damn!" She trawled around for it again and clasped onto it more firmly this time and yanked at it.

"Yes! Got it!" She withdrew her hand slowly. She pulled out a cylindrical tube identical to one previously found and handed it to Penny whilst she nursed her wrist. Penny shouted in triumph.

"Hurray! Good job, Jules!" She then opened the case cautiously and pulled out another fragile piece of paper. The next clue. She turned away from the others, shielding the illustration from them, in a mock pretentious manner. They all waited in anticipation, amused by her antics. She then unfolded the sheet of paper and turned theatrically and thrust it into their view.

"It's a bird! Not another one!" Penny quipped, mimicking a Bristolian accent.

Paul commented. "It looks like another eagle."

"No, it's not, you divvy! It's a *liverbird*. Based on the cormorant," Miles witheringly sneered. "And it's holding a sprig of laver seaweed or broom in its beak."

Paul glowered at the arrogant Miles, furious at the unwarranted snide remark."

"Oh, I thought it was a heron!" Jules laughed, diluting Miles's verbal attack on Paul.

"And me an imperial shag," Penny followed up. "Not the Prince Harry type."

"Oh, Penny. Typical of you, lowering the tone. Ha! Ha!" Fatima giggled.

"Ok, well I see everyone's point," Miles stated, in a more conciliatory tone. "It doesn't quite look like Bella or Bertie on the Liver Building, I must admit. Oh! Great! This is going to be a good one. There are dozens of liver birds dotted around the city."

Penny addressed the technicians and told them to make good the American bald eagle, then she spoke to the team.

"Well, we've had a very productive day. Do we carry on folks? What's the consensus? What do you reckon Edmund?"

"I think we've done enough for today, don't you think?" Edmund said. "My head's in a spin."

"I agree," Jules concurred. "We'll have to think this one through. How about meeting for breakfast tomorrow at ten? I recommend the full English at the Milo Lounge, Lark Lane."

"Sorry, no can do," Penny responded. "I'm busy with other things tomorrow."

"Me also," Edmund added. "But that doesn't stop the rest of you from meeting."

"Ok then, the rest of us will meet at ten for brekky."

Penny passed the illustration and leather tube to Jules.

"Just one thing," Randy said. "Are we going to tell the world about our recent successes?"

"I think we should keep it to ourselves. We're doing just fine at the moment. Who agrees?" Tom asked. "Jules?"

"Let's ask the security manager. Paul?"

"Keep it to ourselves for now."

The team, to a person, accepted his judgement. They briefly discussed the safety of the group but declined an offer from Edmund to beef up security. The consensus was that they could not trust anyone else after recent events. They bade farewell to each other and left.

157

"So, you see, King John granted Liverpool town status in 1207 and his seal for Liverpool was an eagle originally, but gradually it changed to, some say a 'lever' or 'laver' bird probably around the beginning of the 17th century," Miles explained whilst devouring his breakfast.

"More toast?" Jules suggested.

"No thanks." The tour guide slurped some tea, then continued. "The presence of cormorants in and around the pool that drained into the Mersey, the site on which 13th century Liverpool was built around, perhaps played a part in the seal being changed. The 'laver' referring to laver seaweed that must have been in abundance in the estuary."

"So somewhere along the line it subtly changed to 'liver' bird," Jules said.

"Precisely. And 'Leverpul' or 'Leverpoole'". He spelt out the words. "Became Liverpool. However, the origin of the liver bird is still in dispute today. The British Museum in London holds a seal from the 13th century which looks nothing like an eagle nor a cormorant. More like a dove. Sounds like something you'd make Paul. Anyway, what's the plan of action for today?"

Paul ignored the jibe. Jules jumped in.

"Well, as you are aware, liver birds are displayed all around the city, but most do not fit the timeline of the 17th or early 18th century. But, as we've seen, the penultimate clue could be linked to a book or painting or whatever. Even a building."

Paul, undeterred by Miles's strategy to belittle him at every opportunity, chipped in. "Maybe one that's been demolished courtesy of the Luftwaffe."

"That's a point," Fatima said.

"Or courtesy of our own unimaginative councils over the years," Miles added caustically.

"Well, we can only concern ourselves with what's still extant," Randy declared.

Jules spoke again. "What I propose is that we split up again to cover the whole Merseyside area. Tom, Fatima, and Randy, you scour the suburbs and Miles, Paul and I will concentrate on the city centre and the Wirral."

"Ok. Sounds good," Tom agreed.

"Go to those places that were in existence at the time. It might mean revisiting Knowsley Hall and then there's Croxteth Hall and of course Speke Hall. I'm not aware of any link with a liver bird there off the top of my head, but who knows?"

"Bear in mind that the liver bird we seek may not look like the liver bird we are all familiar with, hey Paul?" Miles said, unable to resist another dig.

Paul undaunted, spoke again. "Don't forget the bird-of-paradise link either."

"Another good point Paul," Tom agreed. "We'll have to check out their names. Maybe there's a clue there. The illustration didn't identify what type of bird it was."

395

"I can do that on my iPad. I've got it with me," Fatima volunteered. Jules passed her the illustration.

"Well Paul will probably-"

"All clear? Any questions?" Jules hastily asked cutting off Miles. "No? Ok, keep in touch. If we draw a blank today, then I will consider revealing this clue to the media."

The others upped and left, leaving the condescending Miles peevishly slouched on the table feeling robbed of another opportunity to humiliate Paul.

158

Randy's sub team decided to visit Speke Hall first, then the village of West Derby and ultimately Croxteth Hall. Jules led her team to the city centre. They decided to start at the waterfront and work their way through the city centre noting any reliefs displaying the mythical bird. Randy, Tom and Fatima arrived at the 16th century Tudor house, Speke Hall and were given a private tour of the National Trust manor house and grounds. Nothing significant came to their attention, so after an enjoyable but fruitless two hours they headed to the suburb of West Derby, a Domesday Book village that was once of great importance in Lancashire prior to Liverpool's expansion. After lunching at the Hare and Hounds pub they checked out the historic Elizabethan Courthouse and Yeoman's House, and other points of interest in the village, then strolled through the grounds of Croxteth Park to Croxteth Hall. Fatima was placed in charge of notetaking and anything of interest was input into her iPad. By the time they returned to the car it was 5.30pm. They decided to have a pint in the Hunting Lodge pub since it was a pleasant evening. After their fact finding mission, their limbs were aching, and so they took the opportunity to decide on their plan of action for the following day. They agreed on targeting South Liverpool, quaint Woolton Village the starting point and then Gateacre Village, Allerton, Aigburth, Mossley Hill and Childwall, taking in the abandoned derelict Grade I listed Woolton Hall which bewildered and angered them with its lack of upkeep and Sudley Art Gallery.

By the time they left the pub just after 7pm the late September sun was setting. Randy was first back to his car.

"Shit!" he yelled. "Someone's smashed the window."

"Oh no! I left the iPad on the back seat. I hid it under that blanket. It's gone!" Fatima cried as she searched in vain for it on the back seat.

"Thieving sods!" Tom snarled.

"I've got everything backed up on my pen drive so work wise I'm ok. I can claim the iPad back on my insurance, but I'm sorry about your window Randy."

"It's ok, the car insurance will cover it. It's just the inconvenience of it. We'll have to stop off at a police station and report it. Not a great end to a pleasant day."

They cleared the shattered glass from the interior of the car as best they could, and Tom patched up the gap with some plastic bags and tape bought from a convenience store, before heading home. Tom volunteered to ride in the back.

They were to drop Fatima off near Princes Park first. Randy took the wheel and drove up Mill Lane and headed towards Tuebrook as there were roadworks along Queens Drive. As he came up alongside Newsham Park he took a left on Orphan Drive, parked up and went to report the offence at the police station located nearby. Ten minutes later he was back in the car. Instead of getting back onto the main thoroughfare though Randy drove along Newsham Drive, then onto Belmont Drive running parallel to Rocky Lane. A bit further up Randy halted the car and pointed to the Belmont pub across the traffic junction.

"There's a liver bird, on the façade of the pub. I remembered there was one there when one of the police officers mentioned that there'd been a fracas in the pub. Stay here. I won't be a second. I'm just going to take a closer look and pop into the pub to see if there's anything significant. Five minutes tops."

"I'll come with you," Fatima said.

They crossed the lights leaving Tom in the car. Five minutes later, as suggested, they were back. Fatima climbed into the passenger seat. As Randy shut her door, he noticed a silver Audi a little further down the road, parked up, with its side lights on. He had seen the same vehicle parked up in West Derby village by the Village Cross monument. The two men inside had followed them into the Hare and Hounds and left shortly after Randy, Tom and Fatima had finished their lunch. The next time he noticed them was at Croxteth Hall, the two having arrived before them. Randy figured that the men must have been eavesdropping on their conversation and knew they were to visit the stately home next on their itinerary. He decided to approach the silver Audi but as he drew nearer, he started to regret his decision as the passenger door opened and a burly, shaven-headed black guy emerged. Randy froze, the moment he saw the menacing expression on the stranger's face and backtracked. He ran back to his Toyota Land Cruiser, got in and turned the ignition key.

"We're being followed by two guys! Call the police!"

Tom, agitated, extracted his mobile from his pocket. He looked back towards the vehicle in question. His hands were shaking, and he fumbled it. It fell down between the seat and the gear stick.

"Oh shit! I've dropped it!"

Tom tried to recover it, but his stubby fingers could not reach it. The more he tried, it slipped further out of range. Fatima glanced back as Randy gunned the engine and put his foot down disappearing around the corner. The Audi surged after them, Peltier having returned to the vehicle.

"Fatima, use yours!" Randy cried.

Fatima took her phone out of her pocket. "Oh no! The battery's dead!"

Randy felt for his phone in his jeans pocket.

"Damn! Mine's in my jacket in the boot!"

Not being familiar with the lay out of the park Randy weaved through a couple of roads not sure of where he was heading. As he turned a corner, he accelerated up the road with the pursuing vehicle behind. Suddenly Fatima screamed.

"Bollards! We're trapped!"

"Bollocks! Hold tight!" Randy screamed.

Randy swerved to his left. The front left wheel of the vehicle clipped the pavement with a thump, jarring the occupants and he careered onto the green grass of the park just opposite The Judge's House, missing a tree by inches. The manoeuvre bought him some time, however as the chasing vehicle also skidded to a halt in front of the thick concrete bollards. Randy steered the car between two more trees, leaving churned up grass in his wake but realised he couldn't get back on the road due to a low steel barrier running along the edge of the grass.

"Shit! We'll have to go across the park!"

He veered left and headed for a clump of shrubs and saplings.

"Hold tight!" he yelled.

"Randy, for God's sake!"

"Trust me, Fatima!"

The saplings and bushes whipped noisily against the front and side of the vehicle scratching the bodywork and tearing Tom's makeshift side window off. The car raced across the deserted verdant acres of the park pursued by the Audi which had taken the same route. Randy spotted a gap between two of the barriers wide enough for his vehicle to get through, so he shot through the gap and landed the car again onto the pavement, then flung it onto the road with another few uncomfortable bumps. He found himself speeding along the edge of the park. In his mirror he saw his pursuers take the same course of action. His intention was to get back to the police station on the far side, but the Audi seemed to effortlessly power up behind him. As he streaked down Gardner's Drive, he saw a couple of teenage cyclists, their flashing rear lights blinking in the dimly lit near distance. He braked suddenly and considered overtaking them but was thwarted by an oncoming vehicle, so he swerved across the road at the bend with the Audi right behind him and he took a sharp left up Lister Drive. He rounded the bend and sped down towards Green Lane, the Audi again in pursuit but a little further away. He screeched to a halt at the junction. Not sure which way to go after becoming ever more disorientated, he dived out in front of a bus just avoiding a collision and did an immediate U-turn cutting up a van coming in the opposite direction.

Rambaud cursed as the bus blocked his view then suddenly, he was surprised when he saw the Toyota shooting back up Lister Drive, the same way as the tailed car had come. He reversed his vehicle hastily, flinging it into a three-point turn and screeched after his quarry.

"You just missed the damned bus!" Fatima squealed, quaking with fear, more so through Randy's reckless driving than with her pursuers. "Where are you going now?" she shrieked.

"Back to that police station!"

Randy accelerated when he observed the chasing vehicle coming after them again. At the crest of the small hill, he realised that he was going into the sharp bend too quickly. He hit the brakes. It was too late. Randy lost control of the Land Cruiser. All three screamed as the car's momentum could not be controlled. It spun and smashed side on into the barrier on the other side of the road, the vehicle's airbags inflating on impact, then it rebounded into the middle of the road and wheeled down the incline, hitting a low concrete wall before coming to rest in an overgrown thicket of bushes. Randy was slumped back in his seat. Blood trickled from a gash on his temple sustained when the vehicle careered into the wall at the crest of the hill, his cheek pockmarked by broken shards of glass from the obliterated window. Tom was screaming in agony. His left leg was lacerated, and blood oozed from his ripped trousers. Fatima's face was red and swollen, her cheekbone sore from the force of impact with the interior door panel. She was dazed and in pain.

"Randy!" she gasped. "Randy!" There was no response. Her friend lay motionless. She came to her senses quickly.

"Tom, we have to get out of here!"

Fatima, frightened and shaking, glanced back but couldn't see the Audi. She looked around the vehicle but couldn't see anyone. She opened the door, staggered out and yanked open the rear passenger door with some difficulty owing to its battered condition, then helped Tom out.

"Come on, Tom. We've got to get out of here! Stand there for a second."

"What about Randy?" Tom said gritting his teeth, grimacing with pain, clinging to the open door.

"I think he's done for," she said, opening the boot.

Fatima grabbed Randy's jacket and searched for his phone. As she did so, Rambaud, his long black curly hair streaked with blood, appeared at the top of the hill followed by Peltier, whose left arm lay limp at his side. Both were struggling to walk. The pursuers had made the same mistake in taking the notorious corner too fast and had smashed into the wall themselves, the car rebounding back in the direction they had come, hiding it from view.

As Fatima grabbed the phone, a bullet whizzed past her ear.

"My God! Tom, they're shooting at us!"

She seized Tom by the scruff of the neck and dragged him. The pain seared through his leg, and he crumpled.

"Argh!" he cried.

"Can you run, Tom?"

Another bullet fizzed past Tom's shoulder. "Shit! We've got no choice!"

They started moving around the front of the wrecked vehicle and stumbled their way across the road and ran. Rambaud and Peltier limped over to the castellated wall and took aim at their quarry below. Two bullets buried themselves in a row of plane trees that sheltered Tom and Fatima's escape. Their assailants cursed and took off in pursuit, half-limping down the steep road, not aware, in the gloom, that there was a path to the right of them which, if taken, would have led to the henchmen intercepting their quarry. This gave Tom and Fatima the chance to increase their distance from them. They ran alongside a low wall to their right.

"The police station! It's not far from here! Down the road."

Tom looked back in fear. "I don't think I can make that!" he said breathlessly as he limped along. The two thugs had turned the corner and come into view. Another bullet zipped by. Fatima clutched the struggling Tom's arm.

"Follow me!" she urged, leading him up an alley to the right. A wall topped by railings stretched the length of the path. She found a foothold in the crumbling brick of the wall and hauled herself up athletically and over the railings and dropped down into some dense bushes.

"Ouch! There's razor wire here and brambles." She looked down at the lacerations on the palms of her hands and fingers. "Shit! I'm bleeding! Be careful."

Tom planted his right foot into the same foothold and hauled himself up. His face creased with pain. Then he placed his hands in between the vertical iron railings and, assisted by Fatima, as ably as she could, lifted his injured leg slowly over the top. He wailed in agony, then wobbled precariously as he sought to avoid the spikes piercing his nether regions. Fatima unceremoniously grabbed him and bundled him over. He landed awkwardly amidst the razor wire and brambles. "Ow! Bugger! I'm cut as well."

"Sorry Tom! Come on, stay low," Fatima cautioned as they moved through the tangled undergrowth of weeds, shrubs and trees. "Watch out. It's full of nasty thorns."

"Where are we?" Tom whispered, glancing up at an imposing Gothic looking tower.

"It's the grounds of the old Seaman's Orphanage. It's derelict. I've done a ghost hunt here before. It's real spooky but it might be our only chance of hiding out. This way."

"Ouch!" Tom complained anew as a vine of vicious thorns was catapulted into his temple as Fatima forced her way through the dense foliage.

"Oh Tom, sorry! Ooh!" She paused as she herself was snagged on a bramble bush, the sharp points ripping at the flesh on her arms. She managed to extricate herself, delicately picking off the vines entwined in her cardigan. Her fingers bled. She grimaced. She snapped back the invasive shoots of the plant as best she could so Tom could follow but he too became entwined. The sleeve of his shirt ripped as he tried to yank it free. He winced and filled the air with expletives. They gradually made their way through the undergrowth, their scratched arms, hands and faces bleeding, thorns protruding from their torn skin.

Their pursuers paused at the entrance to the alley unsure whether they had taken that route to the end. Tom inadvertently stumbled over and kicked an empty beer can that had been discarded in the overgrown grounds along with heaps of other refuse. Alerted, the two henchmen leapt on to the wall and hauled themselves up. Rambaud assisted the injured Peltier by unceremoniously bundling him over the pointed railings but they both met the same fate as their quarry in their haste to negotiate the impediment. They jumped down into the mesh of sharp metal and brambles. The razor wire sliced down Rambaud's face.

"Argh! *Putain!*" he cursed loudly. He dabbed his bloodied cheek.

Peltier too had come a cropper. He had been momentarily relieved to overcome the obstacle with his injured arm but as he jumped down his hand was gouged by one of the vicious steel blades of the wire. "*Merde! Putain!*"

They both stopped temporarily to check the extent of their injuries. Peltier wrapped his hand in a cravat and Rambaud dabbed his cheek with the sleeve of his hoodie. They set off again in pursuit but were soon delayed again, hampered too by the mass of nasty thorns and brambles that snagged on their clothes. In the meantime, Fatima had led Tom to an iron gate just past the locked main door of the building. There was a small gap in the gates where a rod had been bent. They

401

squeezed through on all fours and found themselves emerging into the courtyard behind the eerie, neglected Victorian building. Tom tripped over some more debris in the dark, wailing in distress again. Fatima picked him up and pulled him over to a doorway. She ripped away some wooden panels covering the gaps at the base of a time-weathered door. Tom followed her example. They made a hole big enough to squeeze through. Tom was suffering in anguish as his damaged leg scraped along the ground. The two Frenchmen followed a blood trail to the gate with their phone torches. It was too narrow for them to crawl through so Rambaud attempted to bend the skewered bar further to one side with brute force. He succeeded but only slightly. Peltier took his turn, kicking at it. One more effort from the muscle-bound Rambaud managed to bend it enough for both of them to squeeze through. They arrived in the rubble strewn yard. The assailants shone their phone torches around the eerie space, creeping cautiously around it, searching every nook and cranny in the courtyard of the foreboding Gothic style edifice, testing each weathered door until they found one that had been breached. Rambaud tried to scramble through the gap but was again thwarted by his bulk, so he ripped away the remaining part of the wooden panels and entered forcefully with Peltier in the rear. They walked along a short corridor, pausing to check a derelict office or reception room on the way and entered a large, cavernous Hall partially illuminated by their phone lights that weakly penetrated the pitch-black interior. They crept through to another corridor after being alerted by a clattering noise ahead. Tom had walked straight into a rusted mobile commode which lay eerily abandoned along with bedframes and other equipment on the former hospital wards. The orphanage built in 1873 had also been used as an asylum before being converted to a hospital. Fatima went to pick him up. She shined Randy's phone light down onto the floor and noticed the bloody footprints Tom had left in his wake.

"It's no good Fatima. That blood trail is going to lead them straight to us. Save yourself. Go and find somewhere to hide and phone the police. You can move faster. I'm going to try and delay them."

"No Tom. Come on, we can both make it!"

"No, we can't. I've lost a lot of blood."

"Tom don't leave me here all alone."

"Fatima, I'm exhausted. I can't go on. Besides, you're not alone. You're right. This is the most haunted looking place I've been to in my life."

"Tom, I beg you!"

"Go now, Fatima, please!"

Fatima, tearful, hugged her companion and disappeared into the gloom. She crept through to another ward and found a staircase blocked off by a barrier. She surmounted the obstacle and climbed the stairs as quietly as she could. Tom groped around in the dark and found a discarded iron rod from a broken metal framed bedstead. He dragged himself into one of the creaking mobile commodes and pushed it back the length of the ward and waited behind an old, torn, dirty dressing screen, weapon in hand. It was not long before he heard someone entering the long, narrow spooky ward. He peered around the screen and saw two dim lights dancing in the distance. They appeared to be getting closer with every second. It was time to make his move. Suddenly, he manoeuvred the wheelchair-cum-toilet aid out of its hiding place and with his good leg, pawed at the floor with his trainer. The wheels of the rickety mobile commode started to creak, making a strange, unidentifiable clicking sound. He built up some momentum, more and more, pawing with his foot until it sped along towards the flickering lights at the other end of the ward. The wheels were spinning as fast as they could go now, creaking and clicking and grating on the floor, down the long ward, gaining speed with every drag of Tom's right foot.

"*Putain!* What the hell is that?" Peltier asked, perturbed by the eerie sound. He felt the urge to flee in fear as the strange noise became more audible. He peered into the darkness. Suddenly, out of that blackness, Tom's ghostly apparition materialized, his pallid face contorted with rage. He wailed like a sword-wielding snorting banshee. Peltier, who was rooted to the spot, screamed, as Tom thrust the iron rod he was brandishing like a jousting lance, forwards. The metal spear rammed into Peltier's open mouth smashing his teeth and gouging the back of his throat. Rambaud looked on in terror before reacting, pumping three bullets into Tom's chest and face. Tom and his chariot tipped over with a loud crash. Peltier staggered around momentarily, clasping the improvised spear which protruded from his contorted mouth, then collapsed to the floor. Rambaud, shaking in fear and rage, gritted his teeth and cursed. He callously abandoned Peltier to his fate, aware that he would not survive and continued his search for the woman. He came to the staircase and leapt over the barrier. The stone steps were littered with detritus from the derelict asylum. Fatima sat, trembling, hidden in a cupboard in one of the deserted rooms situated along the corridor. She had phoned 999 and waited in hope for salvation. She prayed to Allah, trying to stifle her sobs. She had heard the gunshots. Then she heard the crunch of broken glass under foot by the doorway and froze in fear. Rambaud stood there listening intently. He was about to enter the derelict room when suddenly he heard another spine-chilling noise similar to the mobile commode emanating from the darkness around him. He spun round and shone the phone light into the room opposite. He stole tentatively in, his senses alerted, his gun in hand. He raised the phone light and there, coming towards him slowly out of the tenebrosity, was another mobile commode, creaking and clicking, but this time, moving by itself. His eyes widened in terror, and he screamed, firing shots indiscriminately into the dark. Fatima instinctively cowered fearing the worst, then she heard screams again, nearby, followed by shouting and cursing in French. There was the sound of heavy footsteps stomping along the corridor, then fading. She then heard another sound, this time the welcoming shrill of wailing police sirens. Closing her eyes, she wept. Deep, remorseful sobs. She soon heard noises coming from the ground floor of the building and shouts of her name. She opened her eyes suddenly and sighed heavily with relief. She glanced to her right and her heart leapt as she saw the apparition of a thin, wan-faced little boy dressed in a Victorian school uniform, sitting next to her, knees drawn up to his chin, smiling at her but she did not freak out. She was too exhausted to react and in an extraordinary way, she was comforted by his presence. The spectre disappeared just as the cupboard suddenly opened, startling her. The snout of an Alsatian, sniffing ten to the dozen, came into view, followed by the relieved face of its handler. The dog licked her face. She half-sobbed and half-laughed. Fatima was led out past the bodies of two people. She recognized Tom's trainers protruding from the blanket that covered his lifeless body. Her heart sank. She glanced down at the other corpse.

'Good on you, Tom. You died like a true man. Thank you, my courageous friend. You're my hero,' she reflected, before being led to an ambulance.

"My friend, in the car crash…," she muttered to the paramedic.

"Don't worry. He was only concussed. A couple of broken ribs I reckon by the looks of it too, but he'll pull through."

She placed her lacerated, bloodied hand over her face and rubbed her forehead, her fingers leaving a smear of red on her brow.

"Thank God!" she gasped as she was laid on the ambulance stretcher.

159

The news of Tom's death hit the others like a bombshell and the spotlight once again was focused on Team Quest. Fatima and Randy both confessed that they had had enough after their ordeal and quit the group. They both needed a period of convalescence. Jules, Paul, and Miles stoically agreed to soldier on despite the stark reality that their lives were in danger. Jules had no doubt that Calder was involved after Fatima told her that she heard one of their attackers uttering French expletives. Jules contacted Merseyside police who carried out further investigations. They had already announced that they were on the hunt for a killer, possibly of French nationality, and had alerted all ports with a description of the suspect. She expected another visit from Armitage and Noades.

This latest setback sent Edwin Calder into meltdown. He cussed and raged when he heard the bad news. He knew that it was Peltier who was dead after hearing the brief description of the deceased reported by the media. A black, shaven-headed, possibly French male was the only reference to him.

"That idiot Rambaud has fucked up again! I asked him to just shadow them. Not fucking try to kill them," he seethed as he paced around the bureau in his home, phone glued to his ear. "Sooner or later the trail will lead right to my doorstep and Duart will not be able to protect me. It's time to go to ground."

Calder threw his mobile onto the settee. He paced up and down for another minute, grabbed an empty wine bottle from a table and launched it down the steps of the terrace that led to the garden and swimming pool. It smashed into pieces. Then he retrieved the phone and called his chauffeur, ordering him to have his Daimler ready to leave within thirty minutes. He took another henchman with him, Troussard and left 'Le Manoir' without informing his mistress, Martine. She was blissfully unaware of his ruthless nature and was content just to spend his money and lie in his bed. He was heading for Île de Ré, just off the coast of La Rochelle where he had a modest yacht moored on which he could rest up. No one other than himself and the skipper knew about the vessel which would serve as his bolt hole for the foreseeable future. He determined that only he, Edwin Calder, could be trusted to get his hands on the tablet.

160

After a discussion between Edmund and the remaining members of the team, it was decided that the liver bird clue would be revealed to the world. Edmund contacted the local media outlets immediately to disclose the details of the team's recent bitter-sweet success. There was a furore and a scathing backlash over the revelation that everyone had been misled with the false bear clue. The overriding consensus was that the team had acted irresponsibly and inconsiderately but Edmund defiantly defended the team's deception in a hostile interview with the BBC, pointing to the recent death of Tom as to why they chose that route. However, the scandal was short lived as the exposé of the fifth and newest clue, and the story that led them to discovering the other clues, served to reinvigorate everyone's interest in the hunt for the tablet. It acted as a beacon of hope for all. Only two more clues remained until possible 'redemption.'

By the end of the week, Miles had methodically logged all the liver birds that the two teams had found, but others were still to be found across and beyond the region. It was a case of investigating each one. Most could be discounted because of the timeline. Miles feared that this clue might have been buried in the rubble of the Blitz, as Paul had suggested, or according to his own theory, bulldozed away on the authority of uncaring, zealous politicians afflicted by ideological puritanism or by indifferent developers employed by corrupt officials casually sweeping away Liverpool's history. Greed was the message conveyed on the ivory stele's proclamation and greed might just be man's downfall, he steadfastly believed. From his apartment in the Baltic Triangle, Miles set out. He walked towards the former Victorian Cain's brewery, now a kaleidoscope of bars, pubs and a vintage emporium and paused to watch tourists taking photos against the backdrop of Paul Curtis's angel wings mural. This caused him to wonder how the Elohim would look. With the tablet's inscribed prophecy now conveyed to the world it had perhaps proved that the scriptures had been wholly accurate in depicting certain events and characters. He thought too about the Apocryphal Books of Enoch and the saga of the Watchers, the Anunnaki as they were also known and their giant and, in some cases, destructive hybrid offspring the Nephilim. Then he mused about the story of Noah and the Great Flood, caused, he always believed by the melting glaciers of the Ice Age that heralded the prevailing interglacial period. Everything seemed true. He headed for the Anglican Cathedral. A service of remembrance had been scheduled for Simon and Lydia and the other recently murdered victims of the quest for the tablet. Tom had been hastily added to the heart-rending list and his distraught family had found themselves reluctant invitees. As he trudged up Upper Parliament Street, Miles looked across the road to the blue plaque on the front of an elegant town house bearing the name of George Stephenson who resided there during his time

406

constructing the world's first locomotive-hauled inter-city railway, the famous Liverpool to Manchester Railway. He disappeared into the sunken cemetery ensconced in the shadow of the imposing Anglican Cathedral. He had trod this route many a time in his role as a Blue Badger. He walked past the next point of interest on his Railways Tour, the mausoleum of William Huskisson. The statesman and member of parliament held the dubious honour of being the first ever rail passenger fatality, struck by Stephenson's *Rocket* as he sought a reconciliation with the Prime Minister of the time, the Duke of Wellington, who was on the adjacent track, in a carriage pulled by another locomotive, the *Northumbrian*.

Miles met the others at the cathedral entrance. After the service, Paul, Jules and Miles mingled with Tom's friends and family, offering their condolences. They also met the relatives of the other victims, being reacquainted with the nonagenarian Irene. Then they left, leaving Edmund and Penny to liaise with Tom's distressed family and his estranged wife. They solemnly strolled down the path leading to the cemetery. Jules wiped a tear from her eye. Paul placed an arm around her. They had all been to visit the scene of his death the day before.

"Did you notice the liver bird on the Seaman's Orphanage yesterday?" Miles said, breaking the silence.

"I did," Jules said sniffling. "Paul pointed it out. It's not in the timeline though, is it?"

"No, The Orphanage was built in 1874. Too late I think."

"Tom's death stopped us in our tracks," Jules snuffled. "But there are still numerous liver birds out there to discover and catalogue."

"Miles, shouldn't we just target those buildings that were built prior to, let's say, 1850 and forget the rest?" Paul suggested.

"Take your pick then Paul," Miles replied cattily. "Where do you want me to start? We've got dozens of places like the Lyceum, the Wellington Rooms or the Union Newsroom building in Duke St, Liverpool's first public library. The Georgian Quarter, Blue Coat Chambers, the Town Hall, Rodney Street and further afield the Judges' House at Newsham Park, the Ancient Chapel of Toxteth, Toxteth Reservoir, Woolton Hall. Even Ken Dodd's friggin' cottage in Knotty Ash, perhaps, to name but a few! Some display liver birds on their façades or reliefs, many don't, but, as per the Knowsley Hall clue it could be anywhere inside one of these places, knowing our friend, the mysterious writer."

"Or not knowing him, rather," Jules quipped. "Let's hope it's not under the liver bird on the Minton flooring at the Town Hall!"

"God no! Besides, as I've said before, we've lost so many historic buildings over the years. I'm sure one or two of them displayed the liver bird motif. Perhaps the stunning neo-classical domed Customs House or the Cotton Exchange. The clue could be lost forever."

"I was chatting to a friend of Tom's before the service, a musician, who told me that there's a stained-glass window in the Bombed-Out Church that depicts a liver bird, and he told me there's a crypt lying under the church. Maybe that's a possibility."

"Good choice, Paul!" Miles spat in a patronizing manner. "Thanks for that little gem, which I already know about. It was built in the early 1800s."

Paul squirmed and felt a flush of anger, but Jules warned him off behind Miles's back.

They took the path that led to the chalybeate waters of the Liverpool spring, which was said to have curative properties, now just a trickle oozing from the former sandstone quarry rock.

"This place also fits the timeline, I would think," Miles said. "Built in 1829, if I remember rightly. Once the non-conformist Liverpool Necropolis had been built on Low Hill about 1825 there was a desire to construct a Church of England burial ground somewhere and this, a former quarry site, was chosen, after the sandstone rock had been exhausted."

"I read somewhere that there's about 57,000 bodies in this cemetery alone. It's hard to believe."

"That's right Jules. The poor were buried in deep pits. Coffins piled one on top of the other. Goodness knows how many of the deceased we're standing on right now."

"The catacombs built into the rock are interesting too."

"About one hundred odd. You wouldn't think so, looking at the rock. See Jules, you don't need to go to Egypt to excavate. You can do it here."

"I agree, but I don't think we'd find any Egyptian mummies here."

"Where is that Necropolis you mentioned?" Paul asked. "I've not seen a cemetery up there."

"It's actually on West Derby Road opposite the Quilliam Centre, Brougham Terrace," Jules confirmed.

"What? That piece of non-descript parkland?"

"That's it. It's called Grant Gardens now. There's another 80,000 bodies under there," Miles added.

"80,000? God, I never knew that. You see a few kids playing on there from time to time but as a park it always seemed sparse. No play area, nothing. That's probably why."

"No shit, Paul!"

Paul clenched his fist and curled his lip. Jules shot Paul a furtive look of disapproval. The trio continued their stroll around the graveyard now deemed public gardens, arriving at the Huskisson memorial. Paul was half-listening to the pompous tour guide who was, in the main, wittering on to himself, divulging the sequence of events that led to Huskisson's demise, whilst Jules sauntered over to the grave of Kitty Wilkinson to pay her respects to the 'Saint of The Slums'. Kitty, an Irish born working class woman, founded the first public washhouse in Britain at her home, where people were allowed to wash their clothes during the 1832 cholera epidemic, saving many lives.

"There was a riot when the *Rocket* finally arrived in Manchester," Miles declared. "The waiting crowds had become restless and were tanked up on ale and the Prime Minister, the Duke of Wellington, was pelted with vegetables."

"Nothing new there then in terms of respect for politicians," Paul quipped.

Jules wandered over to the row of gravestones lining the flower borders. The two guys remained at the sandstone-built Huskisson Monument. She paused at the moss-covered gravestone inscribed Liverpool Female Orphanage Asylum. Her eyes scanned the poignant names of the deceased orphans and the pitifully young ages they passed away at - six, seven, nine, twelve years of age. Her heart melted. There were columns of them. 'What lives these children must have led', she wondered. 'And what was the cause of their death? Typhoid, plague, smallpox, cholera? Or perhaps something more sinister? Life was tough. Very tough, unimaginably tough, because most people struggled to survive themselves and when your belly is groaning through hunger, or you are struggling to pay the rent of your hovel, or feed and clothe your kids, little thought and consideration can be given to others. It took a special person to be considerate of others during those times.'

She glanced back at the gravestone of Kitty Wilkinson. Someone who bore the scars of tragedy from an early age but still managed, in later life, to help others. Her father and sister drowned on the ferry crossing from the Emerald Isle. Jules read some of the dates of the orphans' deaths - 1847, 1850, 1865. She wondered where the orphanage had been. Likewise, the Liverpool Orphan Boys' Asylum, the name of which was inscribed on the adjacent fading gravestone.

"Miles, excuse me. Where were the orphan asylums?"

Miles walked over with Paul. "Myrtle Street. No longer there though."

She looked at the next gravestone inscribed with more children's names.

"That's still there, as you know. The Liverpool Blue Coat Hospital. Well, former hospital, boarding school, charity school, call it what you will. Arts centre now, of course. The Blue Coat Chambers."

Jules remained momentarily silent, staring at the names, the woefully young ages and year of passing again.

"It's ironic isn't it?" Miles mused. "That a rich slave trader could be so philanthropic, founding a school for street kids and orphans and yet being so indifferent to the suffering of others, treating black people like chattel, like a commodity rather than not seeing them as another human being."

"Who's that?" Paul inquired.

"Bryan Blundell, the sea captain of the *Tarleton* slave ship, co-founder of the Blue Coat."

"It's unreal, but not so unusual," Paul replied. "The Nazis treated the Jews and others as sub-human slaves in the death camps and then amazingly after a day of vicious murder and brutality Nazis would return to the bosom of their families and become loving, caring individuals, playing with their young children, some of whom were the same age as some of the poor kids they'd just sent to the gas chambers!"

"As if nothing had happened!" Jules commented. "The more you dig into the layers of history the more you realise that mind-sets were not the same. The layers of history are like different strata of rock. The consistency of each stratum being different to another. Like people in the time of the pharaohs happily accepting their fate, being entombed with their king. Like human sacrifices in Mesoamerica. It's not right is it? But it was accepted then. They believed that they were doing the right thing, however ludicrous and terrifying it sounds. You're born into an era, and you grow up in those times and experience the mores, the values of that age."

"In years to come people will question how on earth we all drove around in vehicles belching out exhaust fumes that harmed us in countless ways and were detrimental to the planet," Miles said. "Or flew on aircraft poisoning the skies, emitting toxic pollutants. We're all guilty of using these forms of transport because we were born in the era of the internal combustion engine. I agree, we have to contextualise history. We have to learn the lessons and not repeat the mistakes of yesteryear."

"I suppose it's always been a case of, until something better comes along," Paul added. "But you're forgetting Miles, we may not be here in 'years to come'."

Jules remained rooted to the spot in contemplation once more when suddenly she felt an unusual warm radiance wash over her, as if she had been embraced by something ethereal. Then she touched her cheek as if something delicate had brushed it. The strange sensation did not faze her though. Her eyes focused on a gravestone. They settled upon a particular name inscribed on the Blue Coat gravestone, one she felt an immediate affinity for, 'Mary O'Rourke, aged twelve. Died 1860.'

"O'Rourke," she muttered.

"What did you say Jules?" Paul said.

"O'Rourke. Mary O'Rourke, aged twelve. Died 1860. God bless her. The name O'Rourke exists in my family. Maybe she's related to me. You never know. Do you know what? I must do my family tree sometime. I barely know my ancestors. I feel ashamed that, being an archaeologist and historian, I've not traced my family's origins back. I only know snippets of information from my parents or grandparents. Miles, just a thought, does the Blue Coat have any liver birds on it? I can't remember. I go to the Athenaeum regularly, opposite it, but can't quite recall if it has."

"Actually, it has. One on the gates and one or two on the front of the building itself. I don't normally go that far up into town for a tour unless it's a Beatles tour. Too many shops. The tourists get too distracted. I'd actually forgotten about that one. Well, I hadn't, I just haven't got round to logging it. You know how meticulous I am."

"Well Miles, something tells me we should go and check it out right now."

"Fine by us," Paul said glancing at Miles.

161

Montpellier, France. Present Day.

Calder's housekeeper Muriel looked bemused. She tried to explain to the police detectives who had surrounded *Le Manoir* with a force of armed officers that the owner had departed without informing anyone of his whereabouts. Not even his mistress who had taken herself off to bed with a bottle of champagne to console herself and currently lay comatose on the four poster. The attendant officers had combed the grounds and outhouses and the interior of the manor house but there was no clue as to where he had gone. Muriel suggested he could be on one of his many business trips. He took them at the drop of a hat whenever an item of interest came up on the antiques market. No records of any phone conversations or financial transactions had been made in the last twenty-four hours. Unbeknownst to them, the antique dealer's yacht had slipped anchor and was headed across *'La Manche'* with Troussard and another henchman, Dreyfuss, who skippered the boat.

162

Jules, Paul and Miles arrived at the gates of the Blue Coat Chambers and stood there inspecting the small liver bird that adorned them. They immediately discounted it of being of any significance. The liver bird that attracted their attention more was perched above the entrance, below the clock. The edifice, completed in 1725, had been bomb-damaged during the Blitz. They walked to the entrance of the building and peered up at the sculpture. The liver bird was sculpted as a relief on an elliptical-shaped piece of white granite. Above the liver bird, which was placed centrally in the stone oval, was a cherub, face cushioned by angel's wings.

"We need to see if this is the original sculpture. It looks relatively new," Paul said.

"Of course, it is. They renovated the Chambers in 2008 and built an extension. Isn't it obvious?" Miles sneered contumeliously.

Paul bristled.

"I suppose anything out of the ordinary would have come to light during that renovation then," Jules added swiftly.

"Even so, it would be nice to get a close up. There seems to be a gap between the sculpture and the brickwork," Paul said.

"You're right. Maybe we can see better from the window above it," Jules said.

"Or failing that, a ladder might suffice," Paul replied.

They entered the Arts Centre and asked for the manager. He greeted them and listened intently to their request. He took them up to the window above the liver bird. Paul hung out of the arched sash window but did not notice anything peculiar. The sculpture was a solid piece of granite. There was nothing in the gap behind it. Disappointed, he drew his head back in but then noticed the liver bird above another door in the quadrangle.

"We should also have a closer look at that one, over there."

He pointed down into the cobbled courtyard.

"Ah, yes, the gold one. Above the shop. There's another opposite," the manager said.

They went downstairs and out into the courtyard and went across to the steps that led up to the entrance of the bookshop and scrutinised the liver bird above the blue door.

"Do you think we can take a closer look at that one?" Miles asked. "Do you have a ladder we can borrow?"

"Er, sure. Just one moment."

The manager returned with a member of staff carrying a ladder. Miles, half pushing Paul out of the way, to the amusement of Jules, scrambled up it and examined the gold-leaf embossed figurine that was perched on a narrow pedestal. Again, there was nothing of interest except the fact that this liver bird was probably the original and so one of the oldest liver birds in Liverpool. He took the ladder over to the shop door opposite and examined that sculpture. He came down the ladder satisfied that there was nothing to get excited about.

"What happened to the original liver bird sculpture above the main door?" Paul asked.

"I would think it got destroyed during the Blitz," the manager answered. "You might want to check out the Liverpool Record Office. They hold an archive on the Chambers. Maybe there's some pictures or documents you can lay your hands on. I don't think there's anything else related to liver birds here, but you're welcome to have a tour of the building and garden."

"Ok, thanks. What do you reckon Jules?"

"It sounds as if the building has had several refurbishments over the years. It's worth checking out, particularly the refurb after WWII."

"I don't mind doing it," Miles volunteered.

"Fine. Maybe Paul and I can go and check out the Ancient Chapel of Toxteth and the Toxteth Reservoir whist you're doing that. That'll cross off another two of the timeline sites on our list."

"By the way, did Fatima get back to you about the birds-of-paradise, Jules?" Paul asked.

"No, she didn't. With everything that went on, I'm not surprised. We'll have to check it ourselves."

"Ok, I'll look into it. I'll ask her to send me a copy of the illustration."

"Thanks Paul."

The trio split up. Miles headed over to the Central Library and Paul drove Jules to Toxteth after recovering the car from outside Gambier Terrace.

"Do you know?" she said. "I was convinced that the Blue Coat would unlock some secrets for us. Never mind. I just had this feeling."

"It still might. We'll just have to wait and see. I've just had another hunch. The Liver Hotel in Waterloo. I think our mysterious friend likes his Napoleonic era links, the town of course being established in memory of the Battle of Waterloo."

"I think you just want to go on a Napoleonic pub crawl, don't you? Why not try the Lord Nelson in Knotty Ash and the Welly in Picton, to boot. No pun intended! There's two off the top of my head."

"Ah, clever, the Wellington. How do you know all these Liverpool pubs anyway?"

"Ex-student of course in Liverpool."

"That figures. Well, since you mentioned it, we might as well have a quick visit to each one and catch a bite to eat somewhere."

Jules and Paul, after spending time at the Toxteth Reservoir and the Ancient Chapel of Toxteth, were dining in a bistro when Miles phoned.

"Hi. Bingo! I've got something. Where are you guys?"

"Up in Waterloo," Jules replied. "You've got something?"

"Waterloo? What the hell are you doing there?"

"Paul had some idea about the Liver Hotel in Waterloo. You know, his Napoleonic theory. It's a military thing." She smiled at him.

413

"Well, you can forget that ridiculous notion. You'd best get your backsides back here pronto. I've cracked it."

"What have you found? Go on, tell us!"

"No way! You'll have to wait. Are you guys eating?"

"Afraid so."

"Great. There's me having nothing to eat all afternoon and you two stuffing your faces. What's on the menu? Steak, Scouse? Fish? Ooh! That's what I fancy, fish and chips. See you soon."

Miles rang off and Jules and Paul finished off their meal, paid and returned to the city centre. Paul's mobile pinged on the way. Jules picked it up and checked it. It was a text from Fatima with the photo of the bird-of-paradise illustration attached.

"She says it's likely to be a blue bird-of-paradise, although it doesn't quite resemble an actual blue bird-of-paradise. She says it's more like a combination of several different birds-of-paradise because of the different colours displayed on the plumage. Furthermore, she states that the blue bird-of-paradise was discovered in 1884 in Papua New Guinea, however she qualifies that by saying that specimens of different types of birds-of-paradise arrived in Europe as early as the 1500s."

"Well, Spanish explorers were in that vicinity in the early 1600s, hence the Torres Straits between New Guinea and Australia."

"That's right, so were the Dutch who actually discovered Australia first so I'm sure some trading went on and tales were told of exotic-coloured birds, of myth and legend."

"Much like our own mythical birds, Bella and Bertie."

"Anyway, Fatima ends by saying that she's also come to this conclusion on account of the dominant colour of the bird being blue. It looks like it's wearing - a blue coat."

The two exchanged glances and smiled.

"It's all a bit speculative though, perhaps a tad unconvincing but it will have to do."

"I agree Paul. Let's go for it."

"It may not matter anyhow. Smart-arse reckons he's cracked it."

They found Miles at the café in Central Library. He rose from his seat on their approach.

"Come on. We're going to the Record Office."

They followed him to the archive room. His jacket was placed over the back of a chair reserving his microfiche reader. He logged in and searched for the *Liverpool Echo*, 3rd May 1941. He scrolled down a few pages and came to a small article with the headline, 'Leather Cylinder Found In Rubble Of Blue Coat'.

"What the -," Paul uttered.

Miles grinned smugly then read the piece. "Volunteers and ARP Wardens were surprised to find a leather tube containing nothing but an illustration amidst the rubble of the Blue Coat Chambers yesterday. A spokesman said that they first thought it was some sort of time capsule hidden by a child or class somewhere on the premises at the former charity school. No date was given as to the age of the

414

mysterious object. The occupiers of the building reckoned that the cylinder must have been hidden either in the clock that was destroyed above the liver bird that stood defiantly over the main door of the building facing School Lane or behind a brick in the wall around the vicinity of the liver bird sculpture. The foreman's young son, much to his delight, was given the tube containing the drawing of, a fish!"

"Miles! I can't believe it! You're a brick!" Jules exclaimed.

"A what?"

"A brick. It's a bit dated. It means a helpful and reliable person."

"Oh, I thought you said something else!"

Paul smiled wryly.

"That's it!" Jules said. "Gosh! How lucky is that? Found during the Blitz! I knew I was right about the Blue Coat!"

"Brick. Genius. Superstar. Keep the plaudits coming. What would you call me Paul?"

"Er...special?"

Miles peered over his specs at Paul.

"I wouldn't have expected anything else from someone with your intelligence quotient."

Paul just laughed.

"Guys! Please! Let's just concentrate on this now. So, we've established the link! A fish and a liver bird or sea cormorant but what type of fish is it? There's no description. No photo. Damn! Maybe we can trace the kid, if he's still around."

"What do you think, Paul? Any more of your hare-brained Napoleonic ideas?" the goading Miles said sarcastically. "I even dropped a hint at the restaurant and neither of you numbskulls took the bait."

"Very funny," Paul said. "You can add comedian to your endless list of talents and-"

"Right guys, that's enough," Jules said swiftly sensing the heightened animosity. "Time for a brain-storming lesson. Let's grab some refreshments."

163

They went over to the Wetherspoons pub opposite St George's Hall housed in the former opulent Victorian, Gothic-styled North Western Hotel which was built in 1871 and designed by one of Liverpool's greatest architects Sir Alfred Waterhouse. Miles predictably ordered fish and chips for himself and a beer, plus two coffees for the others. The dilemma of the new clue weighed heavily on their minds.

"Should we reveal it, or shouldn't we?" Jules asked.

For thirty minutes they debated what to do. They felt that their lives were still in danger, but they felt burdened by a responsibility to continue. Donations had poured into the University of Liverpool to fund the ongoing quest for the stele from a plethora of individuals and organisations. People realised that the team had shown itself more than capable of unearthing the artefact first. Jules called Edmund to inform him of their latest remarkable but appallingly costly success, given Tom's death. Edmund relayed the news to the recuperating Randy and Fatima and Tom's next of kin and took the decision, after further discussion with the team, to announce the discovery. Once again, the world went into meltdown. Everyone wanted to know what type of fish was effectively on the menu. In the ensuing days, attempts were made to trace the child who inherited the illustration. The media hunt was successful. The young child was, obviously, not young anymore. He was in his late seventies, a resident in a local nursing home in Anfield, afflicted by Alzheimer's. His memory, all but erased. The team's first fish-focused meeting at the Wetherspoons had been interrupted by a rather pushy and annoying local journalist who recognised Jules and tried to gate crash. They had to abort the session. They met up the following morning at Spital on the Wirral for Tom's very poignant funeral. Out of courtesy they did not discuss the vital new clue. They reconvened at Jules' university office the next day.

"We need to focus on Liverpool's 18th century and early 19th century maritime history," Jules stated. "Any ideas?"

"Are we talking about freshwater or saltwater fish?" Paul asked.

"Good question, but I would think it would be saltwater," Jules replied.

"Well, not necessarily," Miles said. "Otterspool was renowned as an important salmon fishery. Also, the River Jordan still flows into the Mersey at Otterspool Promenade although most of it is now culverted. In the 17th century though Otterspool was just a creek and the River Jordan had two tributaries or brooks, one of which was later dammed to form a lake in Greenbank Park and both brooks were then re-directed into Sefton Park Lake."

"Greenbank Park was part of the Rathbone family estate."

"You're right Jules," Miles said. "The renowned Rathbone family sold part of the estate to Liverpool Corporation but Greenbank House, which is within the University of Liverpool's Greenbank Halls of Residence complex, as you know, was built in the late 18th century. That fits our timeline but I'm not aware of any connection between the Rathbone family and fish."

"We'll just have to reconnoitre the park. There might be something of interest there," Paul added.

"I haven't finished yet! May I continue Paul? Of course, the Rathbone family connection is with the abolition of slavery, but not fish, although William Rathbone III was a Liverpool ship owner and merchant involved in sea trade with the Americas. Maybe we should emulate another of the wider Rathbone family, Basil Rathbone, the famous actor who used to play Sherlock Holmes, and go and investigate Greenbank House and Park."

"And Otterspool, I suppose, with its salmon links," Paul suggested.

"No shit Sherlock!" Miles retorted acerbically. "Well, you wouldn't know this, Paul, but there were many small fishing villages on the Mersey like Hinderton which was over on the Tranmere side and Seacombe Bay also on the Wirral side and others on the River Dee like Parkgate, Hoose, which is now absorbed into Hoylake and also Dawpool, so there's more than one place to check out if we're talking fishing villages or fisheries from that time."

Miles stood up and walked over to the window and stretched.

"So, where do you want to start, Sherlock Holmes or should I say, Sherlock Homeless?"

Paul made a sudden aggressive movement towards Miles, leaping out of his chair only for Jules to bar his way. He seethed with ire, wanting to punch the pompous gits' lights out, but he refrained because of Jules's presence. Miles had become increasingly hostile to Paul over the last few days particularly since he had found out that Paul was a former down-and-out. Jules had told him not to react to Miles' puerile jibes and deep down Paul knew she was right. He was aware Miles was just jealous of his relationship with the eye-catching Jules. Miles, in his deluded scheming mind and highfalutin, egocentric opinion of himself, hoped that Paul would be kicked off the team if his aggression boiled over, leaving him as Jules's only shining knight in armour. She was worth a bloody nose.

"Maybe it's allegorical. The fish," Jules mentioned swiftly to ease the tension again. "Maybe it symbolises something else."

"What like?" said a curious Miles.

"Neptune or the merman Triton."

"As in the Liverpool coat of arms?"

"Precisely Miles."

"Hmm, it's something worth checking. So, the Town Hall in that case or anything with the Liverpool coat of arms displayed on it. Damn. I wish you hadn't come up with that one. It'll be like the liver bird quest all over again."

"Well, listen," Jules said, "Paul and I will pay a visit to Greenbank House whilst you Miles, can visit the Town Hall and do some research on the coat of arms and any of the old fishing villages. Then, if there's anything of interest we'll follow that up. Ok?"

417

"Anything more you want to contribute, Paul? Any more of your inane comments or crap Napoleonic theories you want to share with us, or would it be just another case of a red herring?"

Miles grinned. His constant goading forced the grimacing Paul to storm out of the room to prevent himself from wiping the smile off the tour guide's smug countenance. Jules stood for a moment glowering at the immature Miles, before rushing out after the person she had fallen for.

164

A few hours later, Paul and Jules returned to the city centre having explored Greenbank House. Access was no problem because of her university links. They also went to nearby Greenbank Park and strolled around the lake but both destinations hadn't come up with anything of merit. They had also ventured into Otterspool Park and walked along Otterspool Promenade trying to imagine it when the area was just a creek and a fishery. They lunched at the Royal Albert Dock and then strolled along the waterfront past the Three Graces. A huge, spectacular cruise ship was moored nearby at the cruise terminal.

"Ever been on a cruise Jules?"

"No. Why? Are you offering to take me?" Jules wrapped her arms around her lover's firm left bicep.

"Yes."

"Wow! When?"

"Right now."

"What?"

Paul led her to the ticket terminal for the Mersey Ferry cruise.

"Oh! You joker!" She grabbed his cheek gently and squeezed it. Paul laughed. The tension of a few hours earlier had dissipated. He always felt relaxed around Jules when they were alone. He purchased two tickets for the ferry that was just berthing at the landing stage.

"I've been wanting to go on the ferries for ages but never had the money," Paul said. "I've dreamed of going on a real cruise ship too. Many a time I've watched, envious, as the tourists were flocking back to the ship to gorge themselves on a sumptuous buffet."

"Then maybe we should go, once this is over. I'm sure everyone wants to fulfil at least some of the goals on their bucket lists given what the future holds."

"Just being with you is on mine."

"Ah, that's so sweet!"

They embraced and kissed. The disembarking passengers alighted from the ferry to the strains of Gerry Marsden's 'Ferry Across The Mersey' and climbed the ramp of the floating landing stage, setting foot back on terra firma. Once clear, the new passengers were allowed on. Paul and Jules sat on the top deck and waited for the multi-coloured 'Dazzle Ferry', *Snowdrop*, to depart. It was not long before the boat's ropes were cast off their moorings and tossed back onto the deck, the vessel setting off on a 50-minute River Explorer sightseeing cruise heading first past the Tranmere shoreline and the historic Cammell Laird shipyard. Paul began his own exclusive commentary for Jules, usurping the recorded information for tourists over the tannoy, mimicking Miles's voice and mannerisms.

419

"Over to your right we have the famous Cammell Laird shipyard renowned for its expertise in building ships like the *Mauretania*, the Confederate American Civil War ship *CSS Alabama*, the first British ship to be built and designed as an aircraft carrier, *HMS Ark Royal* and the *Ma Robert*, David Livingstone's Zambesi River vessel."

Jules shrieked with laughter as the ferry ploughed through the churning waters of the Mersey, the wind throwing up her beautiful auburn hair. Paul thought she looked more vivacious than ever.

"And don't forget *Boaty McBoatface!*"

"Ah, yes. And the *RRS Sir David Attenborough*."

"How do you know about all these ships?"

"Books, my dear, books."

He reverted to his normal voice. "Public libraries are a godsend to homeless people. Warm as well as educational."

He pointed to the shipyards.

"I've always thought Laird's should have its own purpose-built museum in Birkenhead at Woodside given its illustrious history, around the corner from that ostentatious hidden gem, Hamilton Square."

Then he resumed his commentary mocking Miles again to the delight of Jules.

"Yes, Georgian masterpiece Hamilton Square, Grade I listed, you can just see the clock tower atop Birkenhead Town Hall. And as we pass the Tranmere Oil Terminal, you will notice the line of impressive waterfront villas adjacent to it that form part of the Conservation Area, Rock Park Estate, a notable former resident being American novelist and U.S. consul Nathaniel Hawthorne."

She laughed hard.

"See, you would make a fantastic tour guide! Don't let Miles put you down ever again. He's just a jerk. You should set up a rival company. That would piss him right off."

"Actually, since you mentioned previously that I could be a tour guide I have been giving it some thought and genning up on the local history. The search, of course, has broadened my local knowledge considerably."

"Carry on but let me hear your own tour guide voice now. Have a practice."

"Along this stretch of the shoreline at New Ferry, Brunel's *Great Eastern* was scrapped across from its homeport of Liverpool, its topmast can still be seen today at Liverpool FC's hallowed ground Anfield, courtesy of Everton FC, the Blues having originally played there."

"Wow! Impressive. You've got something for everyone. Football, the American Civil War, maritime history and ship building."

"And before we turn the Dazzle ship around and head towards the open sea, we can see the quayside of Eastham Ferry. This site has been used to cross the river since the Middle Ages but is no longer in use."

"Go on. Any more?"

"However, the Eastham Ferry Hotel, as you can see, is still very much in use. It backs onto Eastham Woods the former site of the mid-19th century Pleasure Gardens and Zoo where you can still view the bear pit where smart-ass Miles went to, thinking he'd cracked the clue by himself, the arrogant bastard, when I told the world we were looking for a bear connection."

Jules shrieked with laughter again.

"The road takes you up to Eastham village which is one of the oldest villages on the Wirral. Just beyond the quayside we can see the entrance to the Manchester Ship Canal built in the late 1800s to connect 'Cottonopolis', i.e., Manchester, with the Irish Sea."

"Bravo!" Jules clapped. "Now, it's bloody freezing. Can we go below to get a hot drink?"

"No probs. Come on."

165

The pair went into the saloon on the lower deck and purchased hot drinks. They sat and pointed out Otterspool Prom where they had been earlier and the locations of the mid-19th century Conservation Areas of Cressington Park, Grassendale Park and Fulwood Park replete with their Italianate Victorian villas. The ferry swept past the Royal Albert Dock and the Three Graces; the Port of Liverpool building, the Cunard building and the Liver building then headed down river, passing the 'docker's clock', the Jesse Hartley designed Victoria Tower and further down the Mersey, the Stanley Dock Tobacco Warehouse, the world's largest brick warehouse, newly converted into apartments. Jules and Paul returned to the top deck to escape a bawling baby and braved the breezy conditions as the boat headed towards the mouth of the river. They looked over again to the Wirral side of the Mersey, having passed the ferry terminals of Woodside and Seacombe, and saw people in Vale Park and on Egremont Promenade enjoying the views, walking and cycling and others on the beach, amongst them children playing excitedly on a driftwood pirate ship. Paul also made Jules aware of the castellated remains of the Magazine depot where ships entering the Port of Liverpool in the 19th century were impelled to deposit their gunpowder before berthing at the docks. Then suddenly Paul stood up from the bench they were sitting on and pointed excitedly.

"There's our fish!" he cried. "Of course!"

"Where? What are you pointing at?" Jules joined him leaning on the edge of the rail. She scanned the foaming waters. "Not the ubiquitous Mersey brown trout."

"No! They're long gone! The river's been cleaned up considerably. There's all sorts in there; flounder, eels, smooth-hound, salmon, cod, plaice, dab, sole, whiting."

"How do you know all this?"

"I've watched the anglers on the promenade many a time catch all of these. And heard them talking to other people. When you're homeless you have to fill your day somehow."

"So, what fish are you talking about? I can't see anything."

He pointed in the distance and waited for Jules to figure it out.

"Where?"

"There!"

"Ah! Do you mean Fort *Perch* Rock?"

"Yes! The old Napoleonic fort built, let's see…" He took his mobile out.

"Built between 1826 and 1829. It fits the timeline."

"But Napoleon was dead by 1821. How come it's classed as Napoleonic?"

"Well, it says here that it was proposed in 1803 by merchants in Liverpool to protect the mouth of the river from the threat of invasion by the French, so maybe that's why it's considered Napoleonic. But that's not the point. It's the name that's of interest, of course.

"Hold on," Jules said, reading text on her own phone. "The *perch* refers to a warning beacon or light that was on the Black Rocks or Rock Perch site before the fort was built. The current lighthouse replaced the light that was mounted on a perch or some kind of tripod as such. It's got nothing to do with a fish."

"It doesn't matter. It's metaphorical. It's a better bet than what we've come up with so far and if there is something unearthed here I'd like to shove that perch or pole, whatever it was, right up that arrogant sod's -"

"Paul! No need for that!"

"I'm sorry but he's getting on my last nerve."

"I understand your feelings about him but just try and ignore him. He's an overbearing narcissist. But love him or loathe him, we're stuck with him for the time being. We'll go and check it out ourselves and run it by Miles later."

"We can take the underground over to New Brighton once we're back on terra firma."

He lapsed into tour guide mode again.

"And there's the former site of the New Brighton Tower, a steel tower dwarfing Blackpool's own tower, sadly demolished soon after the Great War."

He suddenly stopped, as he remembered Simon's demise. He smiled ruefully. Jules glanced at him and understood. She peered into the distance towards Liverpool Bay, the spray of the waves stippling her face. She blinked as the droplets penetrated her eyes. She wiped the moisture away as if it were tears.

The Snowdrop sailed past the quadrangle-shaped, sandstone-built coastal defence battery and the white-washed Perch Rock Lighthouse and headed towards the open sea. It arrived parallel to the Crosby littoral and tourists, congregating on the starboard side of the vessel, spotted the Anthony Gormley '*Another Place*' cast iron sculptures of men eerily emerging out of the water as the waters receded. They appeared like lost souls delivered up from the submerged wreck of the *Titanic* watched over by the ghost of the ship's captain, Edward Smith, from the window of his nearby former home in Waterloo. Soon after, the Mersey ferry turned and headed back into the narrow of the river.

166

Jules and Paul disembarked a while later and headed for James Street underground train station, passing the former White Star offices from where the tragic news of the *Titanic's* fate was made public from the balcony above to the anxious and distraught crowd of relatives of the lost below. Ninety of the crew were from the environs of Liverpool or had close links to the city. Jules and Paul bought two return tickets for the underground Merseyrail service and arrived in New Brighton, twenty odd minutes later. They walked down the steep road to the beach and waterfront and strolled along a short stretch of promenade named in honour of Victoria Cross recipient Lt. Commander Ian Fraser who commanded a midget submarine which had attacked an anchored Japanese cruiser in WWII. Paul paused to read the dedication and pay his respects, then followed Jules who had strolled on towards the fort. They both went along the causeway to the arched entrance of the sandstone-built sentinel. The imposing structure was closed but they combed every part of the solid twenty four foot high walls that faced landwards and the thirty two feet high walls facing the river, searching for anything out of the ordinary. They circled the structure stopping to analyse the lighthouse as well but did not find anything pertaining to another animal except when a seagull dumped its load on Paul's back much to the amusement of Jules. Paul cleaned up his jacket in the toilets of the nearby Floral Pavilion Theatre whilst Jules phoned Miles to inform him of their potential discovery and contrary to Paul's sentiments, Miles surprisingly offered his congratulations and reckoned Fort Perch Rock was a strong possibility. She then phoned Wirral council to try and contact the owners. An official told them the fort had just been sold but they had no contact details for the new owners who were overseas buyers, and they were not at liberty to disclose such information. Despite arguing her case, the jobsworth was unwilling to help further, so Paul decided to tackle the problem head on. He ordered two grappling irons off the internet and arranged with Miles to meet them at the New Brighton pub, the James Atherton, the following evening. When Miles discovered the plan, he was mortified. He was to accompany Paul scaling the heights of the fortress to gain access to the interior for a recce.

"You mean we're going to use grappling hooks to climb over the wall of the fort? No way! Besides, I don't like heights!"

"There's no one else I can rely on Miles. I need someone to go with me. You wouldn't expect me to ask Jules, would you?"

"I'll do it if you want me to," Jules said draining a glass of white wine and spritzer."

"No, I need you to keep a watch out Jules. I want you to stay in the car whilst Miles and I have a mooch around. The fort's been closed for some time. We're not going to break into any of the rooms or cause any damage."

"I came here as a child and remember there was a little war museum inside. There

424

were aircraft parts dug up from crash sites, bits of fuselage from R.A.F. WWII fighters, American bombers and the Luftwaffe and an exhibition about the RAF and Speke Airport."

"That's right Jules. It was an aviation archaeology museum," Miles continued. "There were also exhibitions about the *Thetis* submarine that sank at the mouth of the Mersey and *Lusitania* and *Titanic* displays and a museum of ship radios if I remember rightly."

"There was an exhibition about the Beatles and Elvis too. I went when I was a kid also," Paul added.

"What time are we doing this then Paul?"

"About midnight."

"It's only 8.30pm now. We can't stay in here all night. We'll all be blotto."

"Don't worry Miles. I've booked a session at the Bowling Alley for 9pm. That'll keep us occupied for most of the evening."

"Ok, fine. Can we go now so I can grab a pizza? I don't do climbing on an empty stomach. By the way. I'm a hot shot when it comes to bowling. I'm going to kick your ass good and proper."

"We'll see."

167

After spending the rest of the evening in the bowling alley, the trio retired to Jules's car which was parked just outside. They sat and waited until the venue closed and the employees had left. It was a quarter past midnight. The place was almost deserted. Paul got out of the car and delving into the boot, pulled out a rucksack. He told Miles to follow him across to Fort Perch Rock. Miles was dressed in black as Paul had asked him to. Paul likewise was head to toe in black, carrying his backpack, slung over his shoulder. They went on to the beach and around the side of the imposing fortification. The tide was out. The lighthouse, solid as the rock it was built on, loomed large in the light of a full moon. Paul halted once he was under two former gun emplacements. He looked around to ensure all was clear, then he knelt down and opened his bag and took out a grappling hook. He unfurled the rope from it. He stood up and told Miles to stand back. He swung the steel hook to and fro and then cast it over the gun turret. It held fast first time to the iron-framed structure. With the other hook slung on his back, he tugged on the rope to ensure that it was secure and then scrambled up the sandstone block wall using the rope. On reaching the emplacement which jutted out of the fort in an arc, he removed the other iron hook from his back and threw it over the top of the sandstone block wall. Once it felt secure, he called for Miles to join him. Miles tugged on the first rope and started to climb the structure. His foot slipped on the green moss at the base sending him dangling much to Paul's amusement. Gradually he managed to heave himself up and Paul grabbed his arm and dragged him unceremoniously over the balcony-like gun turret. By the time Miles had picked himself off the debris-littered floor, Paul was already pulling himself over the top of the wall above. He sat and waited for Miles to climb up to him. He hauled him on to the wall and then they both climbed down together into the courtyard.

Jules sat in her Range Rover and waited. All was quiet. An embracing couple had passed by on the other side of the road behind her and a few cars had left their parking spaces a bit further up the road but other than that it was practically deserted. Her phone rang. It was Paul notifying her that they were inside the structure. He rang off. Paul took two flashlights off his military style belt and handed one to Miles and the two of them began to search the uneven concrete and part-cobbled courtyard. Jules switched on the radio and sat and waited. She closed her eyes and hummed the tune she was listening to. Suddenly there was a rap on the front passenger window. Startled, she looked to her left but saw no one. Then, her window was smashed by someone wielding a hammer. She screamed in terror. A burly, menacing guy released the lock mechanism, yanked open the door and held a handkerchief over her mouth. She struggled, trying to start the ignition, but a second assailant had opened the passenger door and forcefully pinned her down.

She fainted due to the effects of the chloroform-soaked handkerchief. The muscular Rambaud dragged her out of the car and he and Troussard carried her along to another vehicle along the deserted stretch. They bundled her in, making sure they got a good grope of her assets.

"*Ça suffit!*" Calder, at the wheel, barked. "*Ne la touchez pas! Allons-y!*"

Dreyfuss, the skipper of Calder's yacht, got out of the passenger seat and sat in the back with the unconscious Jules. Troussard checked his gun and Rambaud, who had been found holed up in a Welsh hotel in Llandudno after having the wits scared out of him, took a rope and grappling iron from the boot. Rambaud secured his pistol in his shoulder holster and both he and Troussard set off towards the battery. The hired vehicle reversed and sped off along the waterfront away from Fort Perch Rock.

168

Paul and Miles continued to scour the grounds of the fort. The place felt eerie. Paul flashed his torch along the flaking white-washed walls of the buildings that used to house a garrison of approximately one hundred soldiers. Miles was nervously wittering on about Fort Perch Rock's history.

"Britain's first shot in anger in WWI was fired by the battery, a warning shot across the bows of a Norwegian vessel. The shell apparently ended up on the other side of the Mersey, in some understandably irate person's garden."

Paul, barely registering Miles's anecdote, climbed up to the ramparts and walked along scanning each red sandstone block and the surface below his feet whilst Miles shone his torch into every nook and cranny of the courtyard. He examined an old cannon mounted on a four wheeled wooden carriage. The task of finding something tangible remained immense. Miles figured they would have to get access to the units that housed the various exhibitions unless Paul intended to break into them, despite what he had previously said. Then suddenly Paul called to him from the upper level. Miles made his way up two small flights of steps and found Paul near the ramparts. He was crouching down scrutinizing a sloping walkway or ramp of granite setts.

"Miles! Look!"

Paul's flashlight shone on one particular stone sett. Miles stooped down and peered at it. Then he gasped. There, scratched into one of the brown coloured stones, barely visible, after almost two hundred years of weathering and the scuffing of boots, was the tiniest of fish.

"Bloody hell! How did you find that? It's a tiddler!"

"I was looking for anything that dates back to the original time. Obviously, the sandstone walls and granite setts fit that parameter. Most of the former parade ground has been concreted over so I guess I'm just lucky it wasn't anywhere else.

"I take back everything I said mate, about the Napoleonic theory."

"Well, not everything's been related to that. You were right to query it. It might be just something of nothing. Maybe a soldier's carving perhaps. Let's see though."

Paul reached into his haversack and pulled out a club hammer and chisel. He started to chip away the mortar around the engraved stone in the beam of Miles's flashlight. It was not long before he had loosened the granite sett. He tugged at it and manoeuvred it out. Miles focused his torch on the surprisingly deep hollow of the hole then suddenly the beam illuminated an object.

"There's something there! I don't believe it!" Miles cried.

Paul inserted his hand into the hole and pulled out another cylindrical shaped leather tube. They both looked at each other.

"Paul, don't open it yet. Let me video it. It'll be cool."

Paul merely shrugged. Miles put his hand in his windcheater pocket. "Shit! My phone! I've left it in the loo. I found it open, so I went in. I needed a crap. Nerves. I put it down on the sink when I was washing my hands when I was disturbed by a noise outside. I rushed out thinking that it might be you looking for me, but it was a friggin' cat, would you believe? I chased after it reckoning it must have access to one of the museum rooms, but it disappeared. Then you called me, and I completely forgot about it. I'll nip down and get it."

"I'll come with you. We're done here. We've got what we came for."

Paul collected his tools and placed them in the haversack. Then they made their way round to the steps and came down into the courtyard.

"I'll wait here while you get your phone." Paul placed his bag down, zipped it open and placed the cylinder securely at the bottom of the haversack, forgetting that Miles wanted to video the moment of the reveal. Paul's thoughts were with Jules. He just wanted to get back to her and open it in her presence. He removed the hammer momentarily placing it on the ground and inserted his hand in the bag again to recover the tube after remembering Miles's request. Miles was a few steps away from the toilets.

"Hey! There's the cat. There's actually two."

Suddenly, Paul and Miles both heard a faint noise behind them then unexpectedly the glass pane of one of the former barrack room windows shattered.

"Fuck!" Miles screamed. "What's that?" He ran back towards Paul.

Paul grabbed Miles and dragged him headfirst down some steps leading to another exhibition room. Then he scanned the immediate vicinity keeping his head low. Another bullet fizzed past and hit the wall behind him whilst another hit a metal lamppost nearby, ricocheting off it. He grabbed his rucksack and pulled it down the steps, as yet another slug smashed through another window pane showering them with shards of glass. From the trajectory of the shots, he realised that there was more than one assailant. From his haversack he pulled out a Glock 17. Paul identified that one of the shooters was positioned on top of one of the white towers that dominated each side of the fort.

"Where did you get that from?" Miles squealed, cowering at the foot of the stone steps.

"An old mate, ex-army. Enough's enough. Time to fight back."

Paul pointed the hand gun at the white tower to his left and squeezed the trigger several times. The 9mm slugs spat out. The discharge was met with no immediate response from the vicinity of the tower, but another bullet fizzed past from a different direction almost creasing the hair on his head, but this shot served to expose the position of the second shooter. Paul fired again across the courtyard to his right towards the other white tower and then pointed the pistol towards his other gun-toting opponent letting loose once more. Up on the tower to the left, Troussard cursed his luck. One of the bullets from his quarry had found its target more in hope than skill, he imagined, impacting on his shoulder. The pain pulsed through flesh and bone. He grimaced. He hadn't expected his opponent to be armed. He had become careless. Another volley of bullets spat from Rambaud's gun giving Troussard the information he sought. Rambaud was still operative. Troussard

429

fired his own Beretta M9 pistol this time with less accuracy due to the pain he was in, the bullets peppering the brickwork above the stairwell harmlessly. Paul responded in kind.

"How the hell are we going to get out of this one?" Miles screamed in desperation.

"Shush! Keep quiet! Let me concentrate."

"How many of them are there?"

"At least two."

He was in the process of reloading the Glock when suddenly out of the gloom, a huge mass appeared. It was Rambaud sensing his opportunity, baring down on him. Paul tried to insert the magazine into the pistol but distracted, fumbled it. It clattered down the steps. Realising it would be too late to retrieve and insert, since the gunman would be on him, he instead tossed the weapon to Miles and launched himself out from the steps, diving to the ground to seize the club hammer. He reached it with his left hand, rolled over and swung the heavy object at Rambaud whose momentum carried his bulk forward like a juggernaut. It connected with his patella. This unexpected move came as a surprise to the hulking Frenchman. Bone and cartilage crunched in his knee cap and Rambaud screamed in agony. He was felled like a giant redwood, loosening off some rounds from his automatic weapon before landing with a thud on the ground. His anguished face appeared over the top step of the stairwell. His eyes widened in astonishment as he was met by the sight of the quivering Miles holding the handgun. Miles fired instantly and indiscriminately at the menacing countenance. The recoil sent him back down the steps. He then looked up and shuddered. The bullets had made a vile mess of Rambaud's face. Paul shouted to Miles to let him know he was returning immediately. Bullets sprayed around him as he dived over the lifeless bulk of Rambaud, snatching up the dead man's weapon as he did. He clattered head first down the steps where the hysterical Miles was sobbing at the bottom. Paul ignored his whimpering and swiftly got to his feet snatching the Glock off him. He checked the cartridge. There were still some bullets in it. He crept back up the stairs and returned fire at the tower. Once spent he tossed it down to Miles.

"Miles! Miles!" he hissed. "Load the gun again. Now!"

Troussard responded with more venom. The bullets were smashing up everything around them.

Paul responded once more with the dead man's automatic weapon, ever alert, fearing another assault.

Miles belatedly came to his senses and dived into the bag, searching for another cartridge. He found one. The last one. He scrambled up the steps. Miles, hands shaking, placed the magazine into the chamber and put the gun on the steps nervously. He stared at the gruesome sight of Rambaud's blood-filled mouth, ripped gums, twisted lips and smashed teeth. He felt like puking.

"Listen Miles, listen!"

Another volley slammed into the wall and through the shattered windowpane of the exhibition room ripping up the abandoned museum displays.

"Shit!" Miles screamed.

"I want you to make a run for it. Take the cylinder. I'll give you covering fire. Get out the same way as we came. Here!"

Paul passed him the leather tube and the pistol. A reluctant Miles felt a pang of discomfort holding the lethal weapon again.

"Be careful, there might be more of them waiting outside. Check if the ropes are still intact. If they're not, just wait for me on the ramparts. Make sure you take cover."

"What are you going to do?"

"Go on the assault. Right, ready. After three. One, two, three. Go!"

Paul opened up as Miles surged from the steps. A flurry of bullets smacked around Troussard's position. The Frenchman squeezed the trigger of his weapon in response. Paul's military training kicked in and he moved deftly from position to position taking cover, when required, towards the whitewashed tower. He'd just managed to reach the foot of the tower when suddenly he heard shots being fired from the direction of the ramparts where the grappling irons were positioned. Miles was shooting at something or someone. Paul cursed. He climbed on to the ramparts and shuffled along, keeping one eye on the tower. When he was confident no one was there, he sneaked along with more urgency, then he stopped in his tracks. He could hear Miles screaming and swearing and could see the silhouette of a gunman in the moonlight on the ramparts looking over the side of the fort, laughing raucously and saying in a mocking tone.

"Marionnette! Marionnette!"

Miles was dangling on the rope, struggling to hold it with one hand whilst his other hand held the Glock. He had made it down to the turret and then proceeded to climb down the sandstone wall with the aid of the second rope when Troussard caught up with him, the sword of Damocles literally hanging over his head.

Miles fired the pistol wildly three more times in the direction of Troussard. Then he pressed the trigger again. Nothing happened. The magazine was spent. He cursed and dropped the pistol onto the rocks below and gripped the rope with two hands. The tide was lapping at the rocks now. Miles glanced down. If he let go of the rope he would crash onto those rocks and do himself considerable harm. If he stayed dangling on the rope Troussard would finish him off. The assailant's gun was already pointed at his head. It was a classic case of Hobson's choice. He was literally stuck between a Rock and a hard place. Then suddenly he remembered he had the leather tube. It was tucked inside his belt. He took it out and waved it.

"Is this what you want you ugly bastard? Can you swim? You're going to have to!"

Troussard did not relish recovering the cylinder from the sea. He could not swim. Besides, Calder would be furious if he had it almost in his grasp and relinquished it. Suddenly he fired off some shots into the darkness. Paul, who was sneaking up on him, immediately felt pain. He dived for cover and checked his arm. He winced. It was bleeding but he was relieved to see the bullet had only nicked him. It was not too serious. Paul tried to return fire with Rambaud's automatic pistol, but the trigger just clicked. He too had run out of ammunition. Then he saw Troussard leap over

431

the side onto the balcony. The henchman was pointing his pistol at Miles's head. "Throw it on to the balcony! Quick! And I will spare your life."

Miles naively thought that was an acceptable trade and threw the cylinder. It landed exactly where it was required. Troussard picked it up off the emplacement floor and smirked. Then, calmly and callously, he shot Miles through the head. The tour guide's body crashed onto the black rocks below, his blood and brains mingling with the encroaching tidal water crashing up against the solid foundations of the fort. Suddenly, it was Troussard's turn to feel pain as he felt the full force of Paul's boots connect with his back and neck. Paul had leapt from above, crashing down on him. This propelled Troussard towards the edge of the gun turret. His momentum took the upper part of his body over the balcony rail, and he had no option but to let go of the leather tube and his firearm as he desperately reached out for something to prevent him from toppling over the side. He managed to grab the railing, but his weight caused the rail to bend and almost break. For an instant he wobbled just able to push himself back before part of the rail on the balcony snapped completely. He managed to re-gain his balance and turned to face his opponent who had gingerly and slowly picked himself up from the floor after landing awkwardly. For a moment, they sized each other up, then Troussard charged forward and barged into Paul forcing him back through the narrow aperture of the gun turret. Paul landed heavily on some debris, winded and with Troussard on top of him. The two grappled with each other. Sweat from Troussard's ebony brow was dripping onto Paul's contorted features. Paul managed to free his uninjured arm sufficiently to punch Troussard in his wounded shoulder. The Frenchman grunted in pain and Paul took the opportunity to manoeuvre himself to one side, enough to wriggle free from his assailant's grasp and turn the tables. Troussard, now supine, responded by levering Paul away with his foot and then sent him sprawling backwards with a powerful kick. Paul was propelled back towards the balcony. His back arched over an intact part of the railing. He grabbed the railing to steady himself. His heart pounded. He looked down to the rocks and the foam of the churning waters, half-expecting the section of railing to break, but it remained intact, and he was able to straighten himself up. He turned to face Troussard again. The Frenchman had pulled a knife from a sheath attached to his lower leg and was stood there waving it menacingly. The evil smirk had returned. Paul looked around and spotted the grappling iron. He seized it swiftly and began to swing it like a mace keeping the killer at bay. They both circled within the confined space like two gladiators in a miniature amphitheatre. Troussard thrust the knife at his foe. Paul parried with the grappling iron. The Frenchman dexterously passed his knife from one hand to the other and picked up a jagged piece of metal debris. Then he flung the debris at his opponent to create a distraction, rapidly transferring the sharp blade back to his good hand. Paul had instinctively lifted the grappling hook up to protect his face as his opponent had intended, allowing Troussard the briefest of opportunities to drive the knife into his enemy's unprotected body. He launched himself forward, but Paul brought the iron swiftly down onto Troussard's skull. One of the hooks penetrated the back of the Frenchman's head. Simultaneously, Paul felt the blow of the knife in his gut, but his stab vest under his t-shirt had protected him for the most part. He was winded again but still kept control of the grappling iron. Troussard screamed in agony and writhed around like a hooked perch on a line. Paul secured the end of the rope to the railing and then with all his might flung Troussard off the balcony and onto the rocks below. The rope, taut, held fast, just, with the railing weakening at every second, allowing Paul to abseil down it before it gave way. Paul fell back into the foaming waters surging over the rock which cushioned his fall. He bruised his coccyx but stifled his cry of pain. The hook had buried itself deeper into Troussard's cranium as he lay lifeless, buffeted by the waves.

Paul immediately waded over to Miles's floating body. He dragged it back onto the beach, seeing from his injuries that he was already dead. Then he frantically went in search of the leather tube, wading waist high through the surf, pounded by the waves, peering into the darkness. He found it around the other side of the fortress being pummeled against the walls, bobbing around in the water. He seized it and staggered to safety up the beach. He could hear sirens wailing along the promenade. He opened the leather cylinder to find a soggy sheet of paper inside. He clawed at it. Alarmingly, it began to disintegrate in his hands. He managed to get some purchase on the sodden paper but as he attempted to extract it, the illustration ripped again. The saturated limp bit of paper he held in his hand was enough though for him to identify the animal. He let out a huge sigh of relief and flopped down on the beach and lay there exhausted until, shortly after, members of the armed police surrounded him, weapons pointing at his head. They arrested him and hauled him away. He looked back to where he had been lying and the waves had already devoured the shreds of paper, leaving just the tube to be tossed around in the surf. He looked across to the parking bays hoping to see Jules but became anxious when there was no sign of her or her vehicle. He remembered his phone was still in his backpack in the fort. He tried to remonstrate with the officers, but they bundled him into a van at gunpoint. Although once it became apparent who he was and what he was doing, he was treated more respectfully as a victim rather than a perpetrator. He pleaded with them to recover his phone, warning them that another body was in Fort Perch Rock itself in addition to the other two they had retrieved from the sea. His mobile was eventually recovered, and his worst fears were confirmed. Jules had been kidnapped. A solitary text message bore witness to this.

"Paul, I've been kidnapped. Do not attempt to call. They will call you. If you have the final clue do not reveal it to anyone otherwise my life will be in danger. Do not involve the police."

He hammered his fist on the interior of the van in anger as the police took him off for more questioning. He was taken to the Birkenhead custody suite to dry off and have the superficial wound on his arm attended to. He thought about Miles. He disliked the prat intensely, but he would never have wished it would end so disastrously for him. Then he dozed off with exhaustion.

169

Paul awoke to find detectives Noades and Armitage waiting to interview him. He showed them the text and answered most of their questions, imploring them to help him find Jules despite the ultimatum. They advised him to wait until contact was made. However, he steadfastly refused to confirm whether he had found the final clue or not but reports of an empty leather pouch being found and a loosened cobble stone with a fish engraved on it was reason to believe that he had done so. Despite the dead bodies and in spite of the fact that he had an unlicensed weapon and had been trespassing, Paul was released, the police commander cognizant of the bigger picture. Only one prerequisite was made, that he worked with the police to secure the safety of Jules Johnson. Although he agreed in principle to this and desperately wanted this, he knew he would have to act alone when the time came. Later that morning, at Police HQ, Paul's mobile buzzed. He was prevented from snatching it off the table by Armitage until a police officer tasked with tracing the call was ready. Then he got the green light. He picked up the mobile and answered.

"Jules?"

There was a pause.

"No, my friend."

"Calder? Is that you? Where is she?"

"She's right here, Paul."

"You'd better not have..."

"She's fine Paul. Stop bleating man!"

"Prove she's still ok."

"If you must insist," Calder sighed. He nodded to his henchman who slapped Jules across her face hard.

"Ouch! You big ugly brute!"

"Hey! What are you doing to her?" Paul screamed.

Dreyfuss stuffed a gag back in her mouth. Her cheek blazed red.

"Nothing now. Maybe later. Perhaps I will do to her what you did to my men. Bad news travels fast. Now, listen. If you *do* want her back in one piece you do as I say. First of all, I want you to tell me what the clue is. Not now! In private, when every copper in the world isn't listening in. Then, you can instruct me where this clue might lead to. I feel that we are so close to finding the tablet and then we can notify the world whether it is genuine or not or just a charade. I hope for my sake and your sake it is not a charade. We both have something to lose."

"So, if I tell you what the clue is, you'll let Jules go?"

"Not quite. I want you to lead me straight to the artefact. Then, I shall release her. You telling me what the clue is only serves to keep her alive for the foreseeable future."

"If I tell you the clue, you might be able to work it out for yourself. I'd rather take

434

you to the place where I think we will find it. Besides, I have no evidence of the drawing. It's lying in bits at the bottom of the Mersey."

"Ok, Mr De Vere. This is what we'll do. At your love-nest, you'll find another mobile. There's a number on it. Call me as soon as you get it. Do not involve the police again. I will tell you where to meet. By the time this conversation is finished your beloved will be on her way to the next safehouse so it's no use tracing the call. Do you think I am *'un imbécile'? À la prochaine, mon ami*."

The call was traced to a warehouse in Bootle, north of Liverpool, just before the line went dead. Armitage responded swiftly, sending an armed response team to investigate. Paul was already out the door.

"Paul! Paul!" Noades shouted running after him. "Can't you just give us the clue?"

"No chance. I'm sorry. I have to do this on my own!"

"Well, just give me a call when you find out the rendezvous."

"No can do."

170

Outside the police compound Paul hailed a cab to the cottage. He was about to enter when he heard a noise inside. He peered through the window furtively and glimpsed the back of someone entering the bedroom. Putting the key in the lock, he quietly opened the door. He stealthily crept to the bedroom and grabbed the intruder entering the lounge. He was about to punch him when he realised it was Brian the warden, back from his leave, having recognised him from a photograph on the cabinet.

"Don't hit me! Take what you want!" he cried.

Paul released him.

"It's ok. I'm not going to hurt you. Mistaken identity."

"Who are you?"

"Your guest. Now have you seen a mobile?"

"Oh, your Jules's friend. Not quite what I imagined. I picked one up and put it in the bedroom on the side table. I thought it might be Jules's."

Paul dashed in, picked it up and rang the number.

"You should have moved out by now!" Brian said indignantly, picking up a discarded pair of knickers. He looked at Paul enquiringly from the threshold.

"Not mine," he replied.

The call was answered. Paul held up his hand to Brian.

"Ah, *Monsieur* De Vere, you are concerned about the delectable Ms Johnson, aren't you? Will it be a fleeting love affair or a long term one? Your choice."

"Just tell me where to meet."

"Exchange Flags. That's where business traditionally took place, I believe, in Liverpool. Let's say we're trading lives just like the slave ship owners did."

"What time?"

"One hour. Two pm. Remember, on your own, or the chattel will be jettisoned overboard, as it were."

Calder ended the call.

"Do you want a coffee?" Brian asked. "You look as if you could do with one."

"Cheers."

"Where's Dr Johnson by the way?"

"That's what I'm trying to find out."

"You're her bodyguard, aren't you?"

Paul had stripped to his underwear and grabbed a towel.

"Excuse me. I need a shower."

"Be my guest."

Ten minutes later he was in the bedroom putting on fresh clothes.

"Or maybe you're more than just a bodyguard," Brian observed.

Paul's own mobile rang. It was Penny. She had heard about Miles's death. It was on the news.

"Hi, Paul. Are you ok? I've just heard the dreadful news about Miles. Where's Jules?"

"Listen, Penny, you must keep this quiet. Do not tell anyone. Her life depends on it. She's been kidnapped."

"Oh my God! By whom?"

"Calder and his cronies."

"Where, when did this happen?"

"Last night. When I was at Fort Perch Rock. She was waiting in the car. She's somewhere in Liverpool. I have to meet Calder. He's after the last clue. Well, he wants me to take him to where the tablet is."

"You know where it is? So did you find another clue last night?"

"Yes, but I can't tell you what it is for Jules's sake. We found a stone sett with a fish engraving on it in Fort Perch Rock. We took the stone out and another leather tube was underneath. All I'll say is that the tablet is buried underground. In the event that Jules and I don't make it, at least you might be able to find it. I don't intend to let Calder get his grubby hands on it. I must go. If Jules does make it and I don't, tell her I love her so much."

Penny remained silent, surprised by Paul's heartfelt declaration of love for her friend.

Paul finished the call, drained his coffee mug, and thanked the warden.

"All I'll say Brian is that we'll be out of here by the weekend. One way or another. Nice to meet you. Take care."

171

Paul called for a taxi. It picked him up five minutes later and dropped him off twenty minutes later in Pall Mall next to the former Exchange Station. Crossing the road, he surveilled everyone and everything around him, senses heightened to the maximum as if he were back on patrol in the Badlands of Afghanistan or Iraq. He walked along Tithebarn Street and went through the passageway leading to Exchange Flags and glanced left and right, taking in the war memorials and the people viewing them. Then he spotted a lone familiar figure circling the Nelson Monument. Paul glanced swiftly around the concourse to see if a weapon was trained on him. He didn't see anything that caught his eye. He approached Calder cautiously and stood facing him. The antiques dealer recognised him.

"Such a magnificent statue so fitting for a great hero, don't you think? I wonder if they'll raise one to you or your unfortunate dead companions when you find the tablet. I always think people should be dead before they are cast in bronze though. You know, I think it gives everyone a little bit of time to dig some dirt on *the hero* before a statue is erected of them. Yours would be a marvellous story. Addled tramp or beggar elevated to a man of stature and reverence. A classic case of zero to hero."

"I've never begged in my life. Besides, you know nothing about me."

"You'd be surprised, Mr De Vere. Indeed, they may find room for you right here. Two monuments to two dead British heroes, side by side."

"So, of course, you intend to kill me once I've led you to the stele and I dare say Jules will suffer the same fate. Why shouldn't I just kill you now with my bare hands?"

"Because of this gun I have in my pocket."

"I just thought you were pleased to see me."

"Oh, I am. But there's also a gun pointed straight at your lover right now. One signal from me and she's dead."

Paul scanned the square but he couldn't make out where Jules was.

"Enough of this chitchat. Let's get down to business. First, the illustration. What was it?"

"What guarantees do I have about Jules?"

"As I previously stated. It guarantees her a few more hours of life. Not days. I hope it doesn't come to that. I'm getting tired of all this running around. I'd much rather be on my billionaire's yacht. At the moment, I've just got a millionaire's yacht. Well, not even that. It's *d'occasion*. Second or maybe third hand but once I recover the tablet and sell it to the highest bidder, I'll be able to purchase my billionaire's yacht."

"So, that's your motive. Financial gain. Pure greed. How can you contemplate that when the message on the stele is stark?"

438

"What guarantees are there that such cataclysmic events would ever take place? The gods could be dead. Thousands and thousands of years have passed since this decree. Nevertheless, I am a religious person, believe it or not. My faith is Grailienism. I am a Grailien."

"A what?"

"A Grailien believes in the existence of extra-terrestrial beings, unsurprisingly. It is a UFO religion. However, I'm only really there for the sensual pleasures of the flesh. And that's my holy grail. Exclusively available for members only. It distinguishes us from other faiths."

"Is that so? It sounds like a church of perverts to me."

"Each to his own, Mr De Vere. Each to his own. The delightful Ms Johnson would be perfect as one of our Shining Light Angels but that would place her off limits to the likes of me, a mere foot soldier. Do you think there's any chance of me persuading her to become just a common or garden disciple so we can both partake in the frequent orgies that the order likes to encourage?"

Paul bristled at the provocation but remained calm.

"Anyway, we're digressing. Back to the issue in question. There's many others out there who want to get their hands on the tablet for varying reasons - theologians, clerics, politicians, heads of state and all manner of believers. Some want to destroy it in order to preserve their way of life. Others want to protect it, but I couldn't care less who I sell it to as long as they're the highest bidder."

"You might be a friggin', what Grailienist? But I'm a realist. You'll get nothing out of this, except notoriety."

"Grailien, my dear boy, Grailien, but now, less of your insolence, we're wasting precious time." Calder raised the pistol in his jacket pocket.

"The drawing. The image. What was the animal? You have ten seconds to tell me before I raise my arm to give the signal to a very edgy *Monsieur* Dreyfuss. Ten, nine, eight, seven, six, five, four, three, two..."

"Ok, stop! It was - it was, a mole."

"A mole? Are you sure? You're not bullshitting me?" He raised the concealed pistol anew.

"No. That's the truth."

"Then where does the connection to the previous clue occur? A mole and a fish? It can't be, you lying bastard! She dies!" He half raised his arm.

"No! Think about it. If you're a nautical man. Remember a mole is also a breakwater, a causeway made of rocks, boulders!"

"Ah! Yes, of course, it is! Maybe I don't know you. At least, I've underestimated your intelligence. Now, to go further up in my estimation, where are we going to find the stele? Underground somewhere, I presume."

"You'll have to follow me. It's a bit of a distance."

"Lead the way."

Calder took his mobile out and called someone. "Take Dr Johnson back to the car and await my instructions."

439

172

Paul set off with Calder behind him. The antique dealer's left hand stayed permanently in his coat pocket firmly fixed on the handgun he carried. They walked along Dale St and up past St John's Gardens and proceeded up London Road. Halfway up, Calder paused, wheezing. He took out a handkerchief and mopped his moist brow.

"I told you it was a slog."

"Carry on. I'm alright."

They passed Pembroke Place and crossed a junction further along the road and continued uphill. Paul then turned right and stopped outside the former Bear's Paw pub. We're here," he said.

Calder, breathing heavily, sat on a low wall. His hand was still grasping the pistol inside his pocket.

"There's nothing here," Calder gasped. "You better not be taking the piss."

Suddenly, a figure wearing a hard hat and yellow hi-vis vest seemed to emerge from nowhere behind Calder chatting to someone else. The sweating, skittish middle-aged man rose to his feet sharpish and turned anxiously to see who it was.

"Ah, you've made it," the man in the hi-vis jacket said. "You're our last tour today. I'm Tony. Welcome to the Williamson Tunnels!"

173

Liverpool, 1810

At work the following day, Kitty tentatively approached Mr Joseph's wife Eliza, as the conduit for contacting her husband about the possibility of some work for Seamus. Eliza was sitting, playing her harp gracefully in the parlour. Her slender fingers caressed the chords, her kind face a mixture of concentration and contentment. Kitty waited respectfully outside the door until Eliza finished playing. She was hesitant but knocked. She was invited in.

"Excuse me, ma'am."

Before Kitty could continue Eliza spoke.

"Oh, Kitty. I was just playing that requiem in memory of those poor folk who were crushed by the spire at Our Lady of St. Nicholas's Church. A most dreadful affair! Don't you agree?"

"Yes ma'am. Ma'am -"

"Especially for those poor girls! Fate has dealt them an awful hand. Born into destitution or orphaned and rescued by the Moorfields Charity School only for their lives to be cruelly taken away. I suppose it is the will of God if something so unusual happens, like the church spire falling on the congregation on a Sunday. Any other day and lives would no doubt have been spared."

"Quite, ma'am. Dreadful."

"I do worry about Mr Joseph's building work. One day I'm sure the roof of some house or an arch will collapse on top of him. He tells me though he has great faith in his workforce." Eliza shook her head. "Now, forgive me for prattling on. What would you like to say?"

"I was wondering ma'am if Mr Joseph required any more labour for his housing project. You see, Mr O'Rourke has not been able to gain wilful employment as of yet, since the trial."

"Oh, that's a shame! You should have mentioned it earlier."

"Well, ma'am, my Seamus is a proud man and I think he thought he could find something himself."

"You should have asked Mr Joseph before he went off to London."

"I never like approaching him, ma'am. He's always busy. And he's already done a lot for us."

"I know he's a cantankerous curmudgeon at times but you're one of his favourites, Kitty."

"Well, he's back. But he's in the ground."

"I beg your pardon, ma'am!"

"Oh! I don't mean, departed. Ha! Ha! I should re-phrase that, he's *under* the ground. You know, digging those infernal tunnels for what reason no one knows! Like a mole! That's what I call him! When he resurfaces, I'll ask him on your behalf."

"Thank you once more, ma'am."

Later that day, Joseph Williamson emerged from a hole in his wine cellar, plastered in dirt. He dusted down his shabby garb and whacked his shredded top hat against the wall, shedding more dust around the place. He re-positioned his hat on his head. Tufts of his hair protruded through holes in the worn material. Three more grubby looking men emerged from the hole after him and bid farewell to their employer. They trudged up the staircase in a cloud of dust. The wealthy tobacco merchant continued to pat himself down, then went to the parlour, encountering a maid on the way.

"Have my bath ready in ten minutes."

"Yes sir," countered the maid.

Joseph found his wife Eliza, sitting in the drawing room, sketching.

"Ah Eliza, I'm just going to take my bath and change for dinner."

"Oh, Joseph, one minute, I need a quick word. Kitty, she asked if you have any work available for her husband Seamus. He can't find any employment."

"Well, I prefer able-bodied men of course who can swing a pick or use a saw. Hmm, tell you what, have Kitty tell him to come along and see me on Friday. I have some affairs to attend to in Warrington over the next few days but then I'll be free."

"Oh dear, Joseph, you're getting dirt on the carpet again. Please go and change. But thank you for considering him."

Joseph Williamson trudged out leaving a trail of muddy footprints behind. Eliza, tutting, rang the servant's bell for assistance.

Friday came and Seamus, having smartened himself up, accompanied Kitty to Edge Hill. On arrival he was directed along the street to a building site where he would find Mr Joseph, as everyone familiar to him called him. Kitty wished her husband good luck and reassured him with a peck on the cheek. Seamus arrived on site and watched the activity for a moment. Labourers, carpenters, and bricklayers all toiling in a sea of mud.

"Can I help you my man?" a foreman enquired.

"Er-Mr Joseph. Mr Joseph Williamson. I'm after him."

"Mr Joseph? Down there. With that woman."

O'Rourke walked further along the road. He stopped and waited, keeping his distance respectfully, but could not help but overhear. The tall, well-built merchant was remonstrating loudly with a diminutive lady. Once the argument had abated, the woman having strode purposefully away with a face like a smacked kipper, O'Rourke approached the tall merchant.

"Ah, Mr O'Rourke, just sorting a rental out with that damned lady. I admire her though. She gave as good as she got! Now, you're seeking work, eh? Let's see, one eye, one arm. Such a disadvantage when I have plenty of unemployed labourers seeking posts!"

442

O'Rourke's heart sank. He felt he could no longer face Kitty if he were to be rejected again such was his fragile state of mind.

"Well, you need two hands to knock a nail in," Williamson continued. "One to swing the hammer and one to hold the nail in place. You need two hands to saw a piece of wood. One to hold the saw and the other to hold the wood."

O'Rourke was about to apologize for wasting the gentleman's time, turn on his heels and walk silently away to the beckoning Mersey. A pale imitation of the man he once was.

"Bricklaying? Well, I suppose you could do that, albeit slowly."

The crushed, disabled Irishman raised his eyebrows.

"Although, again, you need two hands to set it properly."

With his hopes dashed once more, O'Rourke's chin dropped to his chest as he prepared to utter his abject apology.

"Hmm Mr O'Rourke, what can we possibly do with you?"

O'Rourke raised his head.

"Let me ask you something. Are you claustrophobic? Can you work in dark, cramped, airless conditions?"

"You mean, like in a mine or something, sir?"

"Something similar, exactly."

"Well, I've just spent time languishing in dark, cramped conditions in various lock-ups sir, as you know and of course, when I was a slave."

"Ah, yes, Kitty told me you were in bondage. Fascinating. You'll have to tell me more sometime. No doubt you are not averse to hard labour then having been enslaved."

"I was also in the British Army, sir. I was a sergeant."

"Yes, I was aware of that. You were in Egypt, were you not?"

"That's correct, sir. And more recently Italy."

"Two places steeped in antiquity, history and architecture. Tell me, did you get to see any of the pyramids and temples whilst in Egypt?"

"I did indeed, sir. I saw the Great Pyramids of Giza and some ancient sites in Alexandria and other ruins."

"How interesting! You'll have to tell me all about the workmanship you saw. So, you were a sergeant. You know how to control and supervise men then. Well, Mr O'Rourke, I am doing some underground excavations under my home and around Edge Hill."

"Excavations? What are you looking for, sir?"

"Ah, that's for me to know! And me alone!"

"I need an overseer, someone with authority, to keep the work ticking over whilst I'm away on business. My previous overseer passed away recently, consumption. God bless old Riley! So, I'm thinking, perhaps you fit the bill with your gaoler and sergeant's supervision skills. How does that sound?"

"It-it sounds fine and dandy indeed, sir! I'm up to the job, to be sure. I won't let you down, sir. All I need is a big gob and a foot to boot someone up the arse with now again."

443

"Ha! Ha! Well, I might still need you to do some digging as well. I'm sure you're capable of swinging a pick with one arm or digging away sandstone or rubble with a trowel or shovel. Right, the position's yours Mr O'Rourke. I'll sort out the fine details tomorrow and you can start on the Wednesday."

"That's fantastic news, sir. I won't let you down."

"See you 7am prompt. Come to the house. I must go. Good day to you."

Joseph Williamson strode off towards the building site, haranguing the foremen who had also come looking for him on a pressing matter. O'Rourke crossed himself and looked to the sky, muttering thanks to the Almighty.

174

It did not take long for the recaptured Pierre Cousseau to settle into his new surroundings. After three weeks of solitary confinement and a flogging as punishment for his abscondment, he was transferred to the Powder Room on Brownlow Hill. The French prisoners held there were keen to hear about his adventure. He told them, as he had told Morton and the authorities how he had evaded capture and lived off the land. He had regretted his decision to escape given that Giraud and Schultz the Bavarian were dead. He could never understand how sailors went to sea without being able to swim. Giraud had drowned when *Le Morse* smashed onto rocks and catapulted them into the Mersey. Cousseau managed to scramble ashore having learnt to swim in the bountiful rivers of the Languedoc. Schultz also proved to be a strong swimmer. The two survivors had initially set out on land together, hiding during the day in barns and haystacks, travelling by night across the Cheshire peninsular, living off the land, and stealing what food they could to survive. Initially, disorientated by their calamitous capsizing they had ventured the wrong way, heading for South Cheshire. They stumbled across some of the villages of the Hundred of Wirral, Hooton and Willaston until they realised that they should have been heading north to Hoose. O'Rourke had inadvertently told Cousseau, when discussing Jacobite history, about William of Orange, setting sail nearby this sleepy fishing village, with his 10,000 strong army to conquer Ireland from a departure point now known as the King's Gap, to participate in the Battle of the Boyne in 1690. It was Cousseau's intention to get to Hoose and follow the same route to Ireland where he hoped to find some sympathetic Irishmen who might help them return to France. They found themselves at Puddington before heading north and followed the coast of the River Dee through Gayton and Heswall. They were discovered in the hamlet of Thurstaston, in the grounds of Thurstaston Hall where they had sought refuge in a barn, after disturbing pheasants. They had heard of an anchorage at Dawpool, close by, which was another possible escape route. This information was provided by a French major on parole who had furtively sheltered them for one night only in the cottage he had been billeted in, at Gayton. The two fugitives split up and ran in different directions pursued by gamekeepers, farm hands and the local constabulary. Shultz ran through the adjacent churchyard to escape but was shot dead by a blunderbuss wielding yeoman after failing to halt. Cousseau evaded capture but was forced south again. He ended up in the village of Thornton Hough, befriending an unsuspecting old man who took pity on him and employed him as a labourer around his isolated cottage. He said he was Swiss. On hearing of O'Rourke's trial Cousseau decided to return to Liverpool, out of guilt.

Now that he was incarcerated again it was not long before he started to produce his wooden toys again at his new gaol.

175

O'Rourke stood outside Joseph Williamson's mansion house in Mason Street. It was ten minutes to seven. Sleet cascaded down into his chilled face, illuminated by the lantern he held. Ten minutes later an exuberant Joseph Williamson burst out of the front door to meet him. He wore his tattered top hat with his unkempt hair still sticking out of the holes. He was dressed in a patched up brown jacket that had seen better days, corduroy breeches and a pair of battered boots. He also carried a lantern.

"Ah! Mr O'Rourke, very punctual. Come, I'll show you to your place of work. Not the day to be working outside. Bugger! It's frightfully cold!"

Williamson led him to the rear of his property. They passed beneath a brick-built arch, then descended into a tunnel.

"This is where you will be working. The men are due to arrive at 7.30. Don't take any flimflam from them. They can be surly and confrontational at times. I'll make sure they know you're in charge before they come underground."

O'Rourke raised his lantern. He gasped when he saw several different subterranean passageways disappearing into the dark. They moved further down a passageway, Williamson pausing to light a few lamps along the way and then he led his new overseer into a dark chamber. Williamson lit more lanterns which flickered into life, shedding light onto a huge vault adorned with brick arches.

"Better than the pyramids, eh?" the wealthy tobacco merchant joked.

"My God! I did not expect this, sir!" Seamus said. "Have the other passageways got chambers at the end of them as well?"

"Some have. Some haven't. I've yet to decide what I'll do with them."

"What do I have them do then, Mr Joseph, the labourers?"

"Dig and hack, Mr O'Rourke. Dig and hack. Through the stone. Cut and shape sandstone into rough blocks. Remove the quarried sandstone and any rubble accrued from the tunnels. Liaise with merchants and builders who require said stone."

"Yes sir."

"Ensure there is a ready supply of stone bricks for my arches. Continue with the bricklaying. You can knock all the brick arches down if you like and have them start again if they're idle. You can swap the labourers over from time to time, so they all learn the different skills required. We'll turn them all into craftsmen."

"What's the ultimate purpose, sir? Why are we digging and where to?"

"As I said previously Mr O'Rourke. That's my secret. Just keep them tunnelling. It provides them with a wage. By the way, come and see me at 5 o'clock prompt, when we down tools and I'll sort out your wage."

"Thank you, sir."

"If you need me I will either be supervising the house building or in my wine cellar where I have another excavating operation in progress. No wonder Betty calls me a mole, eh!"

Williamson departed and O'Rourke took the opportunity to light up his clay pipe. He sat on an upturned bucket and surveyed the scene. The flames of the many lanterns flickered casting light on the man-made structures. He marvelled at the workmanship of the random brick arches. He pondered the motives of his new employer. 'Was he searching for something? Was he crazed? Or was he just being benevolent by providing work to unemployed men?'

The men filed in at 7.40am having been briefed by their benefactor about the new overseer. Some of the men he knew; ex-cons or debtors whom he had supervised in the Tower, others ex-army or sailors. Most of them knew who he was. They knew of his reputation as a firm, but fair overseer and the sobriquet 'Red Nelson' was used amongst the workers, a nickname the French prisoners had bestowed on him. He was shown around the other vaults by another foreman, William Meadows who walked with a limp. O'Rourke expressed amazement at the vaulted brick passages and large galleries hewn out of the solid sandstone. After arriving in one chamber Meadows grabbed his arm. O'Rourke had been slightly impatient with the slow pace of the former military artificer who, he discovered, had suffered his wounds at the Battle of Vinegar Hill in Ireland during the Irish Rebellion of 1798 and had moved past him eager to see the extent of each vault. O'Rourke turned to Meadows and glared at him thinking the cripple was exerting his authority in the hierarchy or had anti-Irish sentiments due to his war wounds. Meadows stared back, remaining silent. He simply raised his eyebrows and moved his head in a downward motion. O'Rourke raised his lantern and looked down to where Meadows was indicating. O'Rourke recoiled in fear, thankful that his new colleague had checked his progress and kept firmly hold of him. A yawning chasm dropped away beneath his feet. At the bottom was a pool of stagnant water emitting a repugnant stench. O'Rourke nodded his thanks to Meadows. In return, a brief smile fractured the stern face of the veteran whom O'Rourke, judiciously, invited to lead the rest of the way along a ledge around the edge of the gulf. The two overseers negotiated another narrow-vaulted passage and skirted around another drop. Down in the darkness there was another deep pit, but it was devoid of water. A third tunnel, accessed only by crawling through on one's hands and knees, which the Irishman initially struggled with, emerged into a gallery in which they were able to stand up. On the far side there was another deep gulley with a fetid pool of water below. They returned to the chamber the labourers were toiling in, O'Rourke's tour of the arcane, subterranean labyrinth complete.

The work at times was dangerous and several breaks were required throughout the course of the day due to the choking dust. The men were allowed up into the fresh air to smoke their pipes and imbibe the supplied water provided by the water carters who would visit at certain times of the day. From time to time the labourers were provided with liquor, ale or porter, courtesy of their benefactor who they

447

found quite odd and cantankerous but at times kind and convivial. They were indebted to him for providing them with a wage with which to feed their families despite the fearsome capricious rants that he was capable of unleashing without rhyme or reason.

After a few months Seamus felt comfortable in his new role. The men had accepted him, and the work progressed to the satisfaction of their employer. From time to time Mr Williamson would engage him in conversations about Egypt and its plethora of temples and pyramids and the possibilities of subterranean passages beneath them and the many secrets they may hold. Although the overseer had limited knowledge himself of Egypt's rich historical tapestry, he had become interested in the subject since acquiring the tablet. He had also discussed Egypt with Cousseau whose military expeditions in the country and those of the savant Demeraux, had increased his knowledge of ancient sites.

It was May 1810, when the baby was finally born, a boy. But there was something immediately apparent and concerning, about the state of his health. Kitty suffered a painful birth but fortunately came through it. The child, named Michael Stuart O'Rourke, had an abnormally large head and 'sun setting eyes', as the physician called them since the baby seemed unable to raise his eyes. Dr Phillips diagnosed it as hydrocephalus, 'water on the brain'. Kitty and Seamus were heartbroken, however, they had seen children survive with the same symptoms. Soon after the birth, Kitty's mother moved into the court dwelling, having been ejected from her croft in Scotland when Kitty's father had passed away. Her mother, who was in her fifties and not in great health herself, came to reside permanently with them, which increased the pressure on both Kitty and Seamus to provide for everyone. Kitty returned to work as soon as her strength allowed. At least her mother could help with the housework and look after the kids, a duty she shared with neighbour Mrs Bryant, whom they still paid a small amount to for childcare.

176

During a business trip to London Williamson took the opportunity to see the Rosetta stone for himself. He returned to Edge Hill wildly enthused about all things Egyptian. O'Rourke had decided that he could confide and trust in his employer after their many chats about ancient Egypt and determined to inform him of his secret. The overseer felt he could no longer keep hold of the tablet. He was desperate to secure his burgeoning family's future and so he sought out Mr Williamson on his arrival back in Liverpool. O'Rourke was invited into his home and was guided to the library by a servant. He entered the room admiring the paintings and engravings adorning the walls, some of which were painted by the hand of his wife Eliza. There were also portraits of Nelson and Samuel Johnson and other distinguished notables together with several landscapes of verdant pastures with a horse or two in the forefront. The bookcases were festooned with volumes of literature, amongst which were biographies and science books. Mr Williamson greeted his employee heartily and placed a Bible he was reading, on a bureau. Then he offered a choice of beverage to his charge hand, on tap ale, sherry or port.

"The Bible tells me what a rascal I am, Seamus!" he said indicating to the Good Book.

Williamson poured porter direct from a cask into a tankard and thrust the flagon into O'Rourke's hand.

"Thank you, sir."

"Betty is a talented artist, would not you agree, Seamus?"

"She is, indeed, sir. Very talented."

Williamson himself had already partaken of several jugs of the ale and finding himself in a good humour, regaled O'Rourke with an amusing story about the day the tobacco merchant married his wife Betty, as he called her. Immediately after the ceremony at St Thomas's Church in Park Lane, which he attended dressed in hunting pink, he rode off on his horse to join up with his fellow huntsmen for the Liverpool Hunt that was taking place on the same day, telling his newly-wed to have his dinner ready when he got home. In that fleeting moment Seamus visualized Kitty smashing a tankard of porter over his head if he had said something similar on their wedding day. Of course, Seamus had left his wife on the quayside, on their wedding day, abandoned and alone, but the circumstances were different. He thought of how Mrs Williamson coped with the eccentricities and mood swings of her husband. Although Kitty had told him that Eliza could also give as good as she got.

"Now then Seamus, what did you come to see me about?"

"I believe you got to see the Rosetta Stone in London, sir."

"Yes, indeed, Seamus! It was magnificent! I met a very learned scholar there at the same time. One Mr Thomas Young and we spent more than an hour in

449

conversation about Egypt. Mr Young was especially interested in the hieroglyphs. Ah! I wish I could see those pyramids! I wish I could transport myself to ancient Egypt, to the realms of antiquity: to Giza, to Karnak, Philae and Saqqara."

"Well, sir, it's still a very dangerous place, as you are aware, in the Mediterranean and in Egypt, but perhaps I can bring a little bit of ancient Egypt and antiquity to you."

"You, Seamus? In what way my good man!"

"I have an artefact in my possession that I acquired from Egypt."

"Oh, Seamus, I'm not interested in swords or pistols, dear God!"

"Quite, sir. But this is different. It's a tablet, sir. A stele with hieroglyphs on it."

"What? Hieroglyphs! On a tablet of stone?"

"Yes, Mr Joseph but it's an ivory tablet, not stone."

"Good Lord!"

"I have it hidden. I am looking to sell it, sir and wondered if you would be interested in such a thing, given your interest in the subject."

"Does anyone else know about it?"

"No, sir. You're the first person I could trust to share it with. I've not even told Kitty about it. Not that she's untrustworthy. It's just that I've been waiting to discover the value of the item."

"Does it have other scripts on it, like the Rosetta Stone?"

"No, sir. Just the glyphs."

"Hmm. Of course, the Rosetta Stone's value lies in the fact that the other two languages, cursive Egyptian and Ancient Greek will eventually be the key to deciphering the hieroglyphs."

"That's correct, sir."

"So, I would deduce that it is of lesser value than the Rosetta Stone and as yet, we do not know what it says. It could just be a religious decree like the message on the Rosetta Stone. Or, it could reveal something else of real interest. Who knows?"

The tobacco merchant picked up a crystal glass decanter and poured some port into a glass and sipped it. He paced up and down before speaking again.

"Hmm. Intriguing, Seamus, very intriguing. Listen, what I propose is that I will purchase it from you for, let's say, ten guineas initially. I will take possession of it and conceal it. Let's just say I have the perfect hiding place for it!"

"Undoubtedly, Mr Joseph."

"Then, I will take steps to find out if this item has an increased value. I shall make some discreet enquiries. If we find out that it is more valuable than at first thought, I will guarantee that I will re-visit our agreement and come to an improved financial settlement. How does that sound?"

"That's sounds very fine to me, sir. It's a deal."

O'Rourke held out his stump since he was holding his tankard in his other hand. Mr Williamson laughed then shook it.

"Gadzooks! It's about time we fixed you up with a hook! I'll throw one in as part of the deal! You got me hooked on Egyptology, so I'll get you hooked!"

"Gads-hooks, sir!"

"Exactly!"

They both laughed and brought their drinks together in celebration. O'Rourke was pleased with the initial arrangement, and he trusted his employer. Mr Williamson was already a wealthy man due to his tobacco business and landowning interests and had no reason to swindle him. On the contrary, he was a philanthropist. It was a win-win situation. The overseer was desperate for more money, and he had an insurance policy to boot.

"When can you bring it, here, Seamus?"

"Tomorrow night, sir. About ten or eleven. I'll wait until it gets dark before I recover it."

"Fine. I'll have your monies ready. Thank you."

"No, I thank you, sir."

"Just make sure no one else hears about our arrangement."

O'Rourke made his excuses and left otherwise he would have been there half the night, with his gregarious boss in a jovial, exuberant mood.

The next evening, just before 10.30pm, there was a rap on the door of the Williamson household. The butler answered. A rain-soaked O'Rourke stood on the doorstep. The butler was just about to remonstrate with him about his tardy arrival when the head of the household intervened.

"Ah, Mr O'Rourke!" Williamson boomed. "Let him in, Sykes, there's a good chap. I'll see to him now."

"Yes, sir."

As soon as Sykes was out of earshot, Williamson ushered O'Rourke into the dining room. As he entered, an eight-day ornate clock chimed on the half-hour.

"I'm making a mess, sir, on your floor."

"Don't worry about that Seamus, I'll have someone clean it up," he said. He removed candelabras and a vase holding cut flowers from the mahogany dining table.

O'Rourke placed the dripping dirty wet sack on the table and Williamson stuck his hand in and carefully manoeuvred the tablet out. He unwrapped the protective cloths around it and brushed away some dust and soil that had penetrated through holes in the sack and stared at the stele.

"My goodness! What a beautiful piece. Just as you described! I wish we could read it! Rest assured, I'll take care of it. Here we are, Seamus, ten guineas, as agreed. This is cause for celebration! Here!"

Williamson thrust a tankard of porter into his hand. "Drink to us, my man! And the pharaohs of Egypt!"

O'Rourke gladly accepted the alcohol. They touched tankards again and drank.

"I have to go sir, after this one. Kitty's expecting me home. I said I was only nipping out for half an hour or so on an errand for you."

"That's right! Leave a man to drink all on his own! Well, I suppose I've some thinking to do about the tablet. We need to find out its value. Before you leave, any ideas? Maybe I should just take it to an antiques valuer."

"At this stage, it might not be prudent because if the Army become aware of it

451

and take an interest in it, they might confiscate it and claim it as their rightful property as per the articles of the Capitulation of Alexandria."

"Hmm, quite so. Quite so."

"I was informed however by Cousseau, you know the French grenadier, the prisoner of war, that the Vatican had taken a keen interest in the Rosetta Stone. Apparently, the Catholic Church is concerned, God forbid, that something, somewhere, written in hieroglyphs will contradict the events of the Good Book."

"What? You mean to say that I have been wasting my time reading the Bible all these years! Confound it, man! What does this Cousseau know about anything anyway?"

"Sir, a lot more than you think. He was there when the French unearthed the Rosetta Stone. He was in the working party that dug it up. And he and some companions found the ivory stele the day after and hid it."

"So, how did you acquire it?"

"I relieved his friend, a savant by the name of Antoine Demeraux, of the artefact when he tried to sneak it on board a ship returning him to France, in contravention of the orders of my superiors. And poor Cousseau, he doesn't even know I've got it, here, in Liverpool!"

"Heavens! What a coincidence you've both ended up in the same place! So, it too was discovered under the shadow of the eagle, then. The French imperial eagle. An eagle that has cast its broad, insidious shadow over too many lands for too long. A shadow that threatens my affairs and every British person's livelihood with this damned Continental System! They are laying claim to everyone, everywhere and everything!"

"To be sure, sir. No doubt the artefact as well, sir! Although Cousseau already has a copy, a print of the hieroglyphs of the stele back home in France somewhere."

"Ah, he has a copy! That's interesting. That's what we'll do, Seamus. We'll make a copy of the script, and I can perhaps send a line or two to the Vatican or to a member of the French catholic clergy and see what reaction we engender."

"That's a wise proposition, sir."

"If we get some sort of response or interest, we'll know how serious the threat of these hieroglyphs are to the Catholic Church and perhaps they'll be prepared to pay to acquire the tablet! That's it, man! Right, I'll let you go, Seamus! I've got some thinking to do!"

O'Rourke downed his porter and bade good night to his employer leaving the 'King of Edge Hill', as some called him, to mull over the possibilities.

177

Over the next few months Joseph Williamson was principally preoccupied with his commercial interests. Not only was he involved in his tobacco business where most of his wealth originated from, but he was busy constructing the most varied kind of houses on land that he owned. He was determined to master the art of lithography and so acquired the equipment necessary for the printing process installing it in a workshop for the express purpose of making a print of the glyphs. He still found time to pursue his activities underground like a troglodyte. Somewhere, within that sprawling labyrinth, he had hidden the stele.

One cold, January morning, he called O'Rourke to Mason Street to show him the print of the stele.

"It took me a few goes to master the technique. Here, take a look."

He presented O'Rourke with a printed paper copy of the hieroglyphs. The Irishman was astonished by the quality of it, and he knew that when Joseph Williamson did something you could guarantee he would do it to the utmost of his ability whatever the undertaking.

"I've made a couple of copies. This one, I'm going to cut into portions. I have identified someone who might take an interest in the tablet and to this end, I have drafted a letter to be sent to them accompanied by the first few lines of the script. We'll see if they elicit a response."

"Who is it, sir? Someone at the Vatican? In the Curia."

"No, Seamus. Someone who resides in France."

"In France? Who?"

"His Eminence, Archbishop of Lyon, his highness, Prince of France, Cardinal Joseph Fesch. Call him what you will. He's Bonaparte's half-uncle."

"Interesting, sir."

"Yes. Very. He's an ecclesiastical diplomat to Pius VII. He has the ear of both Napoleon and the Pope. An erudite man. A man of sophistication and good taste. A former successful merchant and a renowned collector of art and antiquities."

"But, sir, how are you going to get a letter to him? With the embargo and all? The mail is restricted as well."

"There's ways and means, Seamus. Ways and means! Napoleon's Continental System has great flaws in it and men of international commerce, like me, know exactly how and where to exploit them. Rest assured he'll receive the letter. I am going to send it anonymously. I will seal the envelope only with the word 'Liverpool'."

"Well, sir, how will he communicate with you?"

"Ah, good point, Seamus. I hadn't thought of that! I know, I'll write 'Ye Hole in Ye

Wall' on the letter so they can address any correspondence there, then I'll arrange to have it picked up discreetly from the landlord. You know him, don't you?"

"Yes sir. Ralph. He receives letters on behalf of many a lodger or guest. He's an honest man. He can be trusted."

"I should think. It's the start of a game, Seamus. An intriguing game. Let's see if the Fesch bites, as it were. Ha! Ha! Ha!"

178

Cardinal Joseph Fesch stood at his window overlooking the banks of the River Saône from the Palais Saint Jean, the archbishop's see in Lyon, deep in thought. Something curious had transpired. Something that had gained his attention. Two months prior he had received an anonymous missive from someone based in the town of Liverpool, Lancashire, England. This was the only information that he could possibly glean from the correspondence by dint of the wax seal on the envelope and by an obscure return address on the letter itself - 'Ye Hole in Ye Wall, Hackins Hey, Liverpool'. An unknown envoy had delivered a sealed leather cylindrical document holder to the Palais and then, melted back into the crowds of the bustling streets of the city without divulging the origin of the item.

Inside the leather tube was the letter and a partial rubbing of pictograms taken, the writer claimed, from the carvings of an ancient Egyptian ivory stele. The correspondence dated 29th January 1811 was written in English and explained that the stele had come into the possession of the letter writer by means of a British soldier who had fought at the Battle of Alexandria in 1801. It also stated that the hieroglyphs conveyed a different, unknown message to those inscribed on the Rosetta Stone. The anonymous letter writer then went on to say:

> 'The artefact may be of interest and value to the papacy, if it communicated a profoundly disturbing and potentially catastrophic contradictory message to the Scriptures that would threaten the very foundations of our Christian faith and life as we know it' continuing that...
>
> 'Your Eminence, Cardinal Fesch, being an intermediary between your exalted nephew Emperor Napoleon Bonaparte and the Vatican, was deemed the right person to approach, given your intellectual acuity, ambassadorial adroitness and penchant for collecting fine works of art and other sought after collectables.'

Fesch, like many around the world, had taken an extreme interest in the discoveries of Ancient Egypt made popular by Napoleon's troops and savants during the Egyptian campaign of 1798-1801. The Cardinal, due to his family links, had taken advantage of his nepotic and eminent position to amass a collection of valuable works of art from all corners of Napoleon's Empire. A knock on the door to the chamber interrupted his thoughts. He responded by calling out and in came a young '*diacre*', a deacon called Jean Lefèvre.

"Ah, *Diacre* Lefèvre, welcome back."

"*Merci Votre Eminence* Fesch," the deacon replied. The young, thin, hook-nosed, black-haired prelate kissed the gold ring on his superior's finger.

"Tell me, have you discovered anything else about our anonymous friend?"

"My spy in Liverpool reported that Ye Hole in Ye Wall is in fact a tavern in the town of Liverpool, at the said address in Hackins Hey, a narrow thoroughfare, I believe. The tavern is frequented by many. It is a popular hostelry frequented by foreign sailors of every nationality and local residents, of all class."

"So, the sender could either be the landlord, the proprietor of the tavern or just a patron. More likely the latter. We must discover who this person is."

"Your Eminence, have you informed His Holiness or our great Emperor about the missive?"

"Not as yet. I will wait until we have more information about the correspondent and the stele. Then if there is any intrinsic value in this tablet, I will notify both parties. I suggest that your spy poses a few discreet questions to those employed in the tavern or befriends those that indulge themselves there."

"I will Your Eminence."

"Send your spy a purse of silver so he can lavish ale or good French brandy on those he might think may have information about the anonym."

"*Bien sûr*, Your Eminence, I will pursue this straight away. *Au revoir.*"

Deacon Lefèvre took his leave. He paused outside the chamber, pleased in the knowledge that he and Fesch were the only one's privy to the letter. It could be a hoax he thought, or it could be something much more significant. In any event he was determined to eradicate any potential threat to his personal ambitions. Bent on a strategy that with the right approach might propel him to the highest echelons of the Curia where his insidious aspirations lay, he was determined nothing, or no one was going to stop him from achieving those goals.

Cardinal Fesch cached the cylinder and its contents in a secret compartment only he was privy to. He had not, up to that point, been able to properly lend his attention to the worrying conundrum owing to his nephew's marriage to the young Austrian Marie Louise, the Duchess of Parma. He, as Cardinal, had conducted the wedding ceremony. Since that glittering event had now taken place, he now had time to reflect on the artefact. If it did exist, then he thought it would be a nice addition to his growing collection of art and antiquities. Alternatively, he could forward it to the sanctuary of the Vatican vaults where the item would be hidden away until such time that the hieroglyphs could be transcribed. Either way his curiosity had been piqued. If Lefèvre couldn't obtain any more information via his agent, he intended to reply directly to the missive.

179

O'Rourke, smothered in red dust from the quarried sandstone, was overseeing the depositing of the debris outside the entrance to the tunnels when Joseph Williamson approached. The overseer had given up on receiving a response from abroad. It had been months since the correspondence had been sent. A tumbril rumbled away transporting its load of surplus quarried sandstone spoil, gratis to anyone who could put it to good use for building schemes elsewhere. O'Rourke unobtrusively spoke to his boss.

"Good morning, sir. I don't suppose you've heard anything about the letter?"

"Not yet, Mr O'Rourke, we'll give it another month or so. These things take time. Especially when the missive has to travel through one or more war zones."

"I'm doubtful whether it's made it to its intended recipient."

"Well, you have to trust me. I've sent mail by courier before to the continent and it's always arrived eventually at its destination. I would imagine the addressee is weighing up his options and could even be making covert inquiries about us right now. Patience, Mr O'Rourke, patience. Keep the faith."

180

September, 1811

Angus MacShane downed his ale and slammed his tankard onto the uneven wooden table causing it to wobble. The contents of other drinks on the table spilt out.

"Woh! Easy, Angus! This nectar is precious to us seafarers!" a beer toting mariner cautioned.

"Pray don't waste it, my ugly looking Scots companion!" ribbed another.

"Sorry, gents! It hasn't cost you a penny though since I bought it for you! Now, excuse me, I'm off to the Mariner's Arms to meet with someone."

"Ah! No doubt someone of the female variety! What's up with the whores in this establishment Angus? Not ugly enough to match your lugly physiogn-, your ugly phylsiogno-, your ugly mug!"

"Physiognomy is the word you're trying to pronounce, you tosspot! Ha! Ha! I bid you farewell you lushy-eyed fuddlers!"

As soon as he departed the premises of the Ye Hole In Ye Wall, upon striding to the nearby popular sailors' inn, the Mariner's Arms, the rugged, square-jawed Scottish privateer's, sociable, 'one of the lads' demeanour was instantaneously transformed to one displaying contempt for his fellow bibulous companions. On entering the next public house on his rounds, he purchased another flagon of ale and was handed a package from behind the bar by the taverner. He passed the landlord some coinage for the stout porter ale which amounted to more than its cost as per their private agreement. The publican swiftly pocketed the excess sum of money. The brown-bearded Jacobite-sympathising Highlander placed the package in his tunic and sat alone in a dim corner of the alehouse. He discreetly unfastened the jute sack which was wrapped around the parcel and took out a small tin container. He promptly prised it open and pulled out a spyglass. He held it to his eye purposefully and scanned the room to demonstrate its functionality to anyone watching. Then he then placed it on his lap and furtively unscrewed the top. A purse of coins slid out. He extracted a letter from it as well. He pieced the spyglass together again and laid it on the table. Lighting his clay pipe, he proceeded to read the letter under the light of the lantern on the table. It was from Lefèvre. He had arranged, with the blessing of the Vatican, to visit the French prisoners of war in Liverpool, in his capacity as an emissary of the Catholic Church. The humanitarian visit had been sanctioned by the British Transport Board which had taken over the role of the Board of Sick and Hurt Commissioners in caring for the interests of captives. He would be arriving on or about the 25th of September 1811 and would liaise with the prison agent for access to the French prisoners. On his arrival they were to meet clandestinely in the grounds of Speke Hall where he had been invited to stay. The

458

despatch also made mention of a mysterious letter being received relating to an artefact, an ivory tablet with hieroglyphs on it, the origin being Liverpool. It asked MacShane to eavesdrop on random conversations in the taverns and coffee houses to garner information about it.

Deacon Jean Lefèvre arrived in Liverpool off a carriage on the evening of 24th September. On the 25th, he met the local Transport Board Agent and toured the prisons, The Tower, and the New Borough Gaol in Great Howard Street. The street name, on enquiring, was a dedication to the deceased penal reformer John Howard who had given advice to the architect of the newly commissioned gaol and house of correction on how to build the installation. Pierre Cousseau had been recently transferred there. Lefèvre conversed with the captives, taking note of their grievances, and collecting letters to deliver to loved ones back in France. In reality, he could not care less about his incarcerated compatriots. His sanctimonious attitude was that it was the imbeciles' own stupid fault for being captured. He himself had only joined the clergy to escape conscription having no desire to fight. He asked where the men had been captured. Some recounted their stories. The dissembling clergyman feigned sympathy for their plight. Then he asked if anyone had been to Egypt. Cousseau and one or two other prisoners put their hands up. Whilst the Agent was busy verifying potential prisoner releases, namely invalids, which Lefèvre insisted upon, to enhance his own well-being and standing, the unctuous deacon asked if anyone had heard of a tablet coming to light in Liverpool.

"A tablet?" Cousseau enquired curiously. "What type of tablet?"

"An ivory one. With hieroglyphs written on it."

"A stele. An ivory stele. But this is impossible. I found an ivory stele in Egypt. A friend of mine was to return it to France, but it was confiscated before our repatriation. Before the sea voyage, by the British. Maybe this is the same one we are talking about. How do you know about this, *monseignor*?"

"A compatriot in the Catholic hierarchy received an anonymous letter advising that a stele was in Liverpool and would we, the Catholic Church, be interested in purchasing it. I was thinking this was a hoax but perhaps, from what you have just told me, this could be the very same ivory tablet. Do you know anyone here in Liverpool that might have taken possession of it?"

Cousseau hesitated, before replying. *"Non, monseignor. Aucune ideé."* His immediate thoughts though gravitated towards Red Nelson. He remained pensive. *'Non, c'est impossible,'* he thought. The Agent returned to Lefèvre shortly after to escort him to a meeting with the prison officials.

That evening, after being wined and dined at Speke Hall by Father Price, a local Catholic priest who had been authorized by the current owners to allow the Vatican's emissary to lodge at the Tudor manor house whilst it was being renovated, Lefèvre made a polite request to be left alone whilst he took some air outside. He took a lantern and strolled outside the Hall into the gardens. He had been given a tour of the medieval house earlier and learned about its history. He inspected the priest holes, admiring the Catholic Norris family for their fortitude in standing up to years of Protestant persecution. He loitered in the gardens for a few moments. A

459

dark shape stepped out of the shadows. It was MacShane. He joined the deacon at the entrance to a short maze in the landscaped gardens.

"Greetings, deacon. I hope you have partaken of our British hospitality," MacShane whispered.

"The food is foul here in England, but the scotch is good," the Frenchman retorted.

"That's because it's Scottish. The clue is in the name."

"Enough of this tittle-tattle. We haven't got much time. Here, take this other purse of money to loosen tongues with. Have you any information to assist the war effort?"

"There's unrest in certain parts of the country. Food prices have increased. There's been rioting. People say the prisoners of war are better off than them. Because of the growing numbers of captives, folk claim they're being deprived of their essentials. There's tension also in the textile mills and other industries. Luddites are rebelling."

"Perhaps this is Bonaparte's ingenious master plan. To have his troops captured so they are a burden on the state. I take back what I really feel about the prisoners of war."

"Well," the Scot laughed, "if it is a strategy, it's working. The country is ripe for revolution. If only Bonaparte could witness these events, he would load his *Montgolfiers* and barges up with his Army of England forthwith and unleash them across the Channel. I also have some naval ship and land troop movements for you also. I've written them down."

He passed him a note which he placed in his cassock pocket.

"Thank you, MacShane. You are a loyal Jacobite. Now, as regards our other affairs, I had an interesting conversation with a prisoner this afternoon. A grenadier, by the name of Pierre Cousseau. He told me he had unearthed an ivory tablet when he was in Egypt, but it was confiscated by British troops at the point of embarkation on the return journey to France. I'm now convinced the story is true then. It could be the same one. Therefore, I am at liberty to divulge that the Catholic Church and the French authorities would be intrigued by this tablet. Make some more discreet enquiries on this matter, would you?"

"Rest assured, I will Deacon."

"I must go. Take care. I leave tomorrow for Hull, then Portsmouth the following day. Keep in touch. Your rewards will be substantial if your questions unearth more answers about the artefact. *Adieu, mon compagnon*."

Lefèvre took his leave and his spy melted back into the darkness.

181

O'Rourke was sat in the Liverpool Arms enjoying an ale with some friends when someone he recognised entered. Hansen, a Dane, a prisoner of war, from the ongoing Gunboat Wars. He hobbled over to the bar. He was from the Tower.

"Hansen! You're a free man, I see. Come and have an ale!"

"Ah, Red Nelson! Right you are, sir! I am a free man. You don't have to escort me back to gaol. I'm not an escapee. Nice to meet your acquaintance again, sir. I will take you up on that porter. Very kind of you, sir!"

The barman pulled a glass of porter on O'Rourke's authorization and delivered it to the table.

"Who sanctioned your release?" the former gaoler asked.

"An emissary of the Vatican. A deacon. He arranged it with the agent to release some of the invalids."

Hansen pointed to his left leg and lifted his pantaloons slightly to reveal a wooden peg leg.

"That's the work of your damned navy! A relic of the Gunboat Wars!"

"The Gunboat Wars are ongoing, so why the devil are they releasing Danish prisoners of war?" queried Foster, a carpenter also employed by Williamson. "You'll just join up and serve again!"

"No. Definitely not! I pledged I will not serve again. I'm on parole. I'm just waiting for my passage home via Sweden. Your government is too niggardly to repatriate me, so I have to make my own arrangements."

"That's because there's been tens of thousands of prisoners over the years," added Parry, a gaoler. "Each detainee has to be cared for and paid for. It costs a fortune to incarcerate you prisoners. If our navy wasn't so victorious in battle, then maybe we could afford to send you home ourselves. But that's why you have to find your own way back to Denmark."

"That deacon though seemed more interested in treasure than our welfare," Hansen lamented.

"What do you mean by treasure?" O'Rourke said, intrigued.

"He asked if anyone knew about a relic. A tablet made from ivory with Egyptian script on it. Hieroglyphs, that's what they're called."

O'Rourke nearly choked on his porter.

"Your old *camarade*, Cousseau -"

"Hansen, he's not my '*camarade*'," O'Rourke objected sternly.

"Well, saviour then or whatever he is. He told the deacon he'd found a tablet in Egypt, but it was confiscated by pilfering British troops. The deacon reckoned this might be the same one and the Vatican wants to get its hands on it."

Hansen gulped his ale down swiftly.

"Ahh, I like your British ale. Maybe I should remain in England. However, I have a wife and children to return to. Right, I'm off to the Pier Heads. If anyone knows of a ship leaving for Sweden, let me know. I don't want to be a burden anymore on you British!"

"Beware of the impressment! They're floating around," Parry warned.

"There's employ for you as a privateer, my friend, if you fancy it."

The table of men looked over towards a lone man sat in the dark recess of the corner of the saloon. The man with the broad Glaswegian accent, continued.

"Tomorrow morning, we sail. Not to Sweden though. The Azores. Better than being impressed."

"An English privateer? No, my friend, with respect, if I get captured by the French, I'll end up a prisoner of them! Thanks for the offer my friend! Farewell all!"

Hansen departed. Tock, tock, tock, his wooden peg striking the stone floor. MacShane puffed on his pipe. Having studied the expression on O'Rourke's face when Hansen mentioned the tablet, he was convinced that this man Red Nelson, knew more about it. The group of friends supped their ale to the last drop. Foster burped loudly, Parry farted and then they got up to depart. The smoke dispersed from MacShane's pipe enough for him to acknowledge the leavers with a cursory nod. As soon as they had left, he scribbled a note on a piece of paper with a Conté pencil, a gift from the deacon. He placed it in an envelope and sealed it and addressed it to Lefèvre. The note was in code. He intended to send it with the French prisoners' mail which was censored but the secret coded language, which was disguised within normal French cursive script, would not raise suspicions amongst the agents of the Transport Board. He rued the timing of his potentially incriminating discovery since he was due to leave on the morning's tide on the privateer *Harp Seal*. He notified Lefèvre in the memo of his intentions to pursue the lead on his return.

462

182

O'Rourke trudged home, elated and in good spirits but simultaneously anxious that the Vatican had shown an interest in the relic. This was the confirmation he was waiting so long for. His employer had told him there were ways and means to communicate and this was the evidence needed. Unfortunately, the timing was wrong for O'Rourke too since Mr Joseph had travelled to London to conduct some urgent business and would be away for at least two weeks. The overseer kept the men at the 'coal face', as it were, in his absence. He knew that his boss knew every single part of his subterranean labyrinth and any apparent slacking would be noted immediately and duly addressed. The foremen on the building sites also intended to keep their charges' noses to the grindstone. On the day he expected Mr Joseph to return he was notified that he had been struck down by a virulent cold and advised by his physician to take advantage of the benefits of the sea air on the south coast. Betty was summoned to the capital and then they departed for Lyme Regis. She went with a retinue of personal attendants. Kitty was not amongst them due to her family commitments. She would have liked a change of scene, however.

It was five weeks later, when the itinerant party returned to Liverpool. Williamson was up bright and early to inspect the work completed in his absence. He was invigorated by his sojourn in Dorset and keen to crack on.

"Good to see you back, sir," O'Rourke said eagerly. "I have news for you, sir. We've had a visitor."

"A visitor? Not that confounded woman again from 'Ye Ugly Face Club'!"

"Ha! Ha! No, sir. A visit from the clergy."

"Aha! Are you telling me Seamus that the Fesch has taken the bait?"

"To be sure, sir. A French deacon came to see the prisoners apparently in his role as an emissary of the Vatican. However, he asked pertinent questions about the ivory tablet, sir. Cousseau allegedly confirmed the existence of such a tablet and the deacon departed convinced that it was one and the same!"

"Very interesting developments indeed. Well, we'll see what happens next Mr O'Rourke. I'm certain they'll follow up their fact-finding expedition with a missive. Now, take me to see what the lads have been up to."

The overseer led his boss into the tunnels.

183

It was mid-November 1811 when a letter arrived at Ye Hole in Ye Wall. Frederick's uncle, Ralph had been asked to watch out for a letter addressed to 'Anon'. O'Rourke had slipped him some money, a gift from Mr Williamson, on the understanding that he would only inform O'Rourke discreetly of its arrival. O'Rourke was duly notified on its arrival and he in turn told Mr Joseph, who despatched his butler Sykes and coachman Dickins as arranged, later that evening, to recover it after the patrons had all stumbled out of the premises. They took a circuitous route back to Edge Hill in the pony and trap just in case they were followed. Mr Williamson took receipt of the letter and opened it in private. It read:

> 'To Anon,
>
> Sir,
>
> In the first instance we believed your correspondence to be a hoax established to extort funds from the Catholic Church. However, we have made some enquiries since and believe that your intentions are honest and genuine and that you do, indeed, have in your possession something that may be of interest to the Vatican. Unfortunately, we have no intention to remunerate you for something that belongs to the French people. We believe that you obtained it through misappropriation in Egypt during the evacuation of French troops. We demand that you relinquish the artefact into our possession henceforth. Deacon Lefèvre will be the intermediary on behalf of the French government. He has arranged a further humanitarian visit to attend to the needs of the French prisoners of war in the new year. We await your reply detailing how, when and where you should meet with the deacon on his arrival to execute the transfer.
>
> Yours faithfully,
>
> Your Eminence Cardinal Fesch.'

Williamson guffawed loudly when he read the letter.
"The sheer hubris of these French scoundrels! Ha! Ha! Ha! I shall respond immediately!"
The 'King of Edge Hill' sat at his bureau and swept to one side documents relating to his tobacco, property and shipping interests. He took a piece of paper, located his

464

quill, and dipping it into the ink pot, began to write, the dim light of the lamp flickering beside him, joining the dancing shadows of the flames that leapt out from the crackling red glowing logs of the fire roaring in the hearth.

184

Cardinal Fesch opened the missive from the same mysterious sender. It was January 1812. He read the letter out loud to Lefèvre who had been summoned to the cardinal's library in the Palais Saint Jean.

"Your esteemed Eminence,

Thank you for your previous correspondence. It arrived on the 17th of November last. Allow me to get straight to the point. I most strongly have to disagree when you say the relic in my possession belongs to France. If anything, it should be bequeathed to the Egyptians. Or perhaps the Ancient Greeks or Copts or whoever. Certainly not the French. Let me kindly remind you that you lost all rights to your accrued state acquisitions as per the terms of your tame capitulation. Needless to say, we will not be relinquishing the artefact to you in the foreseeable future. Unless, you are prepared to pay for it. It is patently obvious that it is either of serious interest to you personally or a grave threat to the Catholic Church, so perhaps a financial settlement can be arranged expeditiously. Or, perhaps I should forgo the middle man and go straight to the supreme pontiff or the Emperor himself.

I await your reply with interest!

Yours faithfully,

Anon."

"This man is mocking us, Your Eminence," the scowling deacon remarked. "I believe, Cardinal Fesch, it's time for us to take positive action. If we pay a sum to recover the stele then this extortionist might apprise other reprobates of his success and leave us vulnerable to other threats. We would be swamped like the Egyptian army at the Red Sea."
After a period of silence, the ruminating Cardinal spoke.
"For now, Deacon Lefèvre, we have sutured the wound. We have stemmed the flow, the haemorrhaging, of artefacts from Egypt but the floodgates might open once more if the Emperor makes his peace with his enemies again. We need to protect the Church from any possible contradictory evidence of the Holy Bible."
"I concur Your Eminence."
"This artefact does also interest me from a personal point of view. It would indeed

be an asset to add to my burgeoning collection of art and antiquities. Whether it comes into my possession or into the safe hands of the Vatican is immaterial, the fact is, you are right, Deacon Lefèvre, we need to secure it now. What measures can you take?"

"When my spy, God forbid, returns from his voyage safely I will arrange my next visit to the prisoners. I will spend a few more days in Liverpool to try and establish the identity of our mystery man. If we are successful in identifying him, I will have MacShane follow him, to try and ascertain the location of the relic. MacShane has indeed informed me he might have a lead."

"Whilst you organise your visit I will respond with a more robust response. Our mystery man must, in no uncertain terms, know how determined we are to obtain that artefact. Besides, another letter might flush him out. He might reveal his identity this time when claiming the missive."

"A wise move, Your Eminence."

"Social order as we know it and the Catholic Church's place in that hierarchy is at stake. It will be destroyed and forever transformed, if God forbid, that stele or any other undermines the authority and beliefs of Catholicism."

"I concur with every sentiment you express, Your Eminence. It is truly, potentially destabilising, and would be fundamentally disastrous to our faith and to our sacred way of life which has underpinned society for centuries. I fear for our future. I will make the arrangements forthwith."

Lefèvre took his leave, then he paused outside, muttering to himself.

"Yes, indeed Cardinal, I couldn't agree more. *My* future in Rome is at stake. Rest assured, I will find our anonym and eliminate him." He strode along the hallway and paused at a mirror. He ran his hand down each side of his face, liked what he saw and sneered. "Those who seek to harm the Church must suffer the consequences. The only payment forthcoming to our mystery friend, will be made in blood, in reparations to the Catholic Church."

185

MacShane returned to Liverpool after delivering his share of the treasure, plundered from a French ketch and Dutch West Indiaman, into the care of Mother Redcaps. The hostelry continued to provide a service to their customers despite the passing away of Poll Jones in 1810. The Scotsman had taken to the rowing boats to avoid the threat of impressment along with other hands before the ship had eased into port with a skeletal crew. The crafts landed near the Red Noses rocks on the Wirral shoreline and the men had split into groups and dispersed to make their way to their refuge. MacShane's new mission was to carry out surveillance on Red Nelson whom he was convinced was involved in the conspiracy. The spy, who expressed Jacobite sympathies like O'Rourke, still remained faithful to the cause, his anti-English sentiments fuelled by the fate of the grandfather he never met, executed by the British after Culloden.

It was late afternoon. He went straight to Ye Hole In Ye Wall, resisting the urge to visit his favourite Paradise Street brothel, but O'Rourke was not in there. He knew that he frequented other town centre taverns – the Cross Keys, the Talbot, the Golden Lion, the Liverpool Arms and the Mariners Arms. The privateer checked each one, but he could not be found. He checked a number of coffee houses also, to no avail. O'Rourke, in fact, had been attending the funeral of his little son, Michael. The perpetually smiling toddler whom everyone loved had succumbed to a violent, epileptic seizure. Seamus and Kitty were cast into a void of despair. MacShane returned to 'Ye Hole' and retired to his customary corner in the dark recess of the saloon with pipe and ale. He was the last one to be shown the door. Lefèvre had notified him that another letter had been despatched to the anonymous contact. He was not sure whether this letter had already been delivered to its intended recipient. He had received his own communiqué at his lodgings at the Mariner's Arms on his return. The proprietor told him it had arrived that morning so he figured that Cardinal Fesch's letter would arrive at the same time, approximately. His instinct told him to surveil the inn. He loitered outside the premises for a moment and then hid in a doorway, in the dark. He was rewarded when, twenty minutes after its closure, two men turned up in a horse-drawn cart and straddled the entrance to the narrow Hackins Hey. A bald, stout character leapt from his seat and banged on the tavern door, playing out what sounded like a rehearsed rhythmic coded rap on the wood. The landlord unlocked the door and thrust a letter into the recipient's hand. The two exchanged succinct farewells. The man returned to the cart and it rattled off up Dale Street. MacShane dashed out of the shadows and followed it. They were headed in the direction of Shaw's Brow. A beggar, pleading for alms, tried to intercept MacShane but the cussing Scotsman, ruthlessly bundled him aside. The wretch's head hit the cobbles with some force. He lay there lifeless.

468

MacShane stumbled, managed to regain his balance almost immediately and continued his pursuit of the cart. At the junction with Byrom Street, he saw it turn onto Shaw's Brow and head towards the Seamen's Hospital and Infirmary. He took a gamble and took a detour along Hay Market past St John's Church into St. Johns Lane hiding at the junction with Lime Kiln Lane where he intended to intercept them if perchance they took that route.

The cart rumbled down the lane. His hunch was right. It passed the intersection. MacShane, loitering with his dirk drawn, leapt onto the back of the rattling transport. He seized the stunned passenger by the neck and held the knife to his throat. Sykes shrieked.

"Drive on carter, or your companion dies!" MacShane spat venomously. "Who's your master? You bald little bugger."

Sykes trembled in fear.

"Don't tell him!" the carter screamed. The dithering butler feared for his life.

"Oh Lord, forgive me. It's…"

Just then the horse was spooked by a rabid stray dog that ran at it, snarling. The horse reared up in fright. Dickins, the carter, distracted by the Scotsman, had failed to give his full attention to the road ahead and couldn't control the beast. The horse panicked and the cart tipped. MacShane and Sykes were flung backwards. The sudden jerking movement caused the Scotsman's lethal blade, still pressed firmly to Syke's gullet, to inadvertently slit the butler's throat. Sykes gurgled and he thrashed around. The demented horse reared up again and the two of them crashed off the back of the cart. The carter shouted in vain.

"Sykes! God, no!"

The dog turned its attention to the sprawled bloodied body. Dickins, despite his shock, managed to steady the horse. He cracked the whip and steered the beast at a frenetic pace down the thoroughfare, too afraid to glance back. MacShane rose to his feet dazed by the impact his head had made with the ground. The rabid, salivating beast growled menacingly at him. He froze. Then slowly he backed off and recovered his dagger. The dog considered that enough territory had been ceded for it to claim possession of the corpse. It licked the blood from the butler's neck and found it was to its liking. The half-starved drooling dog then sank its teeth into the gaping wound, forcing out another spurt of blood. The canine's face was immersed in red as it tore at the flesh dementedly. MacShane looked up momentarily to see the cart hurtling down the lane, careering from side to side only to disappear left around the corner into Ranelagh Street. He cursed. His eyes shot back to the dog but its focus was well and truly on its prey, affording him the opportunity to hobble away towards the church, fingering the bruise amidst his curly shoulder-length hair.

Coachman Dickins had managed to keep the letter tucked under his thigh. In shock, he went straight to the mansion at Edge Hill to report the crime to his employer. Williamson was outraged when he learned what had happened. He grabbed his sword and pistol, alerted another live-in servant and the three of them returned to the scene of the crime. Several townsfolk were already present. Doctors from the infirmary attended too. The rabid dog lay dead in the lane despatched by

469

a ball to the brain. Sykes's face had already been disfigured, ripped to shreds in the violent frenzy. Williamson turned away barely able to look. The guilt began to torture him. Repton, the young servant vomited. Two tragedies in a week, thought Williamson. Maybe this stele was cursed.

186

April, 1812

MacShane laid low for several weeks after retrieving some of his money from Mother Redcaps. He returned to Scotland to visit family. He mulled over his suspicion that Red Nelson was implicated in the ruse. He had expected O'Rourke to pick up the letter himself, but he was thrown when two others had collected it. Fortunately, the carter had barely got a glimpse of the assassin. His back had been turned to him and the Scot had worn a cloak and hood. Williamson had ordered the carter to remain quiet about the affair in case the assassin returned for him if his identity was revealed. Dickins, fearing for his life was more than happy with this arrangement and the pecuniary incentive offered by his employer. The merchant privately and surreptitiously arranged for Syke's funeral to take place in the bachelor's hometown of Warrington stating that he had died of natural causes. The Liverpool Mercury newspaper merely reported that an unidentified man had been assailed by footpads and left to die when the rabid dog attacked him. His face had been chewed away to an extent that concealed his identity. When MacShane returned to Liverpool he was none the wiser about who he had killed.

Williamson felt compelled to respond to the correspondence in his possession. The letter received from Lyon had been more hostile in tone and made a biblical reference to the wrath of God 'bursting upon the head of the wicked'. He bristled with anger at the thought of being threatened and having one of his most trusted employees slain. He responded in a typical pugnacious manner. He made reference to the death of Sykes without revealing his name and claimed that if the Catholic Church was prepared to kill to obtain the artefact, then this proved that the relic was of considerable value to the Vatican. As a riposte, he himself quoted from the Good Book:

> 'For the wrath of God is revealed from Heaven against all ungodliness and unrighteousness of men, who by their unrighteousness suppress the truth.'
>
> Romans 1 v 18

187

13th May, 1812

Kitty stood at the threshold of the parlour listening to the dreamy and relaxing sounds of the harp again. 'Eliza plays with much grace and finesse,' she thought. The last melodic chord drifted away. She knocked on the door which was partly ajar. Eliza had already sat herself at the grand piano and was about to play another tune.

"Oh, do come in Kitty. How are you today?"

"I'm fine ma'am. Seamus is alright, too."

"I'm glad to see you back at work. It was heart breaking news about little Michael. Poor soul!"

"Yes, ma'am it was, although Seamus and I half-expected it. We were warned by Dr Phillips that he could have a seizure at any time. We knew his life could be short. He was a lovely, happy child who gave us some beautiful memories. We had braced ourselves for the inevitable. Thank you for your kind words. Here's the newspaper you requested ma'am, the *Liverpool Mercury*."

Eliza took the paper and jabbed her index finger at the front page.

"That...that has shocked me to my core. Our very own Prime Minister! Assassinated! In this country of all countries! These things don't happen here. It's an absolute scandal! John Bellingham of all people! Mr Joseph always thought him a bit odd. He resided in Duke Street, you know. I mean, he had some grievances, valid or not, but to actually shoot Spencer Percival, my God! He's brought shame on the people of Liverpool, he has!"

"I've heard he's already been committed to trial already."

"He'll swing for this Kitty. No doubt about it! Oh, it says here Mr Bellingham was actually born in St. Neots, Cambridgeshire. Well, he's certainly caused more friction between Liverpool merchants and the government. They'll think it's a conspiracy!"

188

Lefèvre was incensed when MacShane reported that he had killed someone but not gained any more intelligence from the incident, confirming the anonymous writer's narrative that blood had been spilt. Cardinal Fesch ordered the deacon back to Liverpool to continue in his role as a humanitarian, concerned with the welfare of prisoners, a front for his covert activities. His ship sailed to Malta first to report on the condition of prisoners there and then, during the voyage to England, *La Grande Armée* had launched their offensive across the Nemen River, unknown to the occupants of the brigantine. On landing in Portsmouth Lefèvre encountered a convivial ambience, engendered by the news that Napoleon had invaded Russia which removed any imminent threat of the invasion of Great Britain.

After touring some of the squalid prison hulks on the south coast of England, Lefèvre arrived in Liverpool at the end of June, a week later. The port was a hive of activity. A squadron of Royal Navy vessels were being victualled before setting sail to the U.S., the War of 1812 having already begun the same month. He toured the New Borough Gaol in Great Howard Street and liaised with the agents. Cousseau and the rest of his fellow prisoners were craving information about Napoleon's massive push into Russia, but they were disappointed when Lefèvre informed them he knew little himself. His attempts to meet up with MacShane were stymied when, at short notice, the Glaswegian was requisitioned for a voyage on his privateer to the Americas to capitalize on the abundant prizes made available by the declaration of war by the U.S. on Britain. They were due to meet up that evening at Speke Hall again. Lefèvre decided to conduct his own furtive investigations. He again asked the French prisoners about the stele. Cousseau did not volunteer any more information this time. Frustrated with his lack of progress, Lefèvre left Liverpool to visit Hull and other towns in the north where prisoners were held. He took it upon himself to carry out some espionage for his country because he was certain once Napoleon had conquered Russia, he would turn his attention back to Britain. This intelligence, he calculated, would raise his profile with the Emperor and stand him in good stead for future promotions or appointments. From his devious perspective, the conniving deacon had convinced himself that Napoleon was in need of an ecclesiastical ally, the Emperor having imprisoned two popes already, Pius VI and the current pontiff Pius VII, resulting in the straining of relations with his uncle, Cardinal Fesch who had vehemently opposed the scandalous manipulation of the papacy. Lefèvre also saw himself as a go-between. The man who could bring the two estranged parties together. He went as far as Glasgow on his travels and returned to Liverpool on 6th[th] August. However, MacShane was still at sea. He had seen action boarding a U.S. West Indiaman merchant. The affray had cost him the fingers on his left hand. A swipe of a cutlass severing four digits a moment after he had fired his pistol into the

473

melee. A fresh scar ran underneath his chin also. The *Harp Seal* limped back home towards Liverpool victorious, laden with abundant booty but in a parlous state and needing substantial repairs, arriving four days later. Notes had been left at the Mariner's Arms where the Scotsman lodged. The most recent one instructed MacShane to meet on 11th August at the maze at dusk if he was returned to Liverpool.

Lefèvre made his excuses again to Father Price who had again arranged with the Watt family for the Vatican envoy to stay at Speke Hall and made his way to the maze entrance. The evening sunshine had dissipated, and his path was lit by a full moon. He approached not knowing whether MacShane would be there. A figure suddenly loomed large out of the gloom making him start. It was the Scotsman.

"Good grief! MacShane! I thought you were never going to return. Your *visage*, is that a souvenir of your voyage?"

"Aye, it is, monsignor. And this! Confound it!"

He held up his mangled hand. Only the thumb had survived.

"Mon Dieu!"

"Och! It's useless. I can't fire my pistol with it or hold my dratted broadsword anymore with it!"

"Listen, about our affairs, any more news of our friends?"

"I saw the Irishman O'Rourke, the former gaoler in the Liverpool Arms earlier this evening. I still believe he's involved. I eavesdropped on him and some companions. They're going to watch the aeronaut, James Sadler, tomorrow. They're going up to a village called Everton to watch the balloon spectacle. I know where they're going to meet. You need to come with me. There'll be thousands of people there. We need more eyes though."

"Do you know anyone else who could help? Someone you can trust."

"Aye, a lad newly released from gaol. I got talking to him this afternoon in the Mariner's. I bought him a few ales. He needs money."

"Fine, recruit him. Where are we going to meet?"

"Prince Rupert's Tower. It's in Everton. If you don't know where it is, just ask. It's a well-known local landmark. Meet me there at noon. Sadler's hot air balloon takes hours to inflate. Weather permitting it will make an ascent. It's taking off from the Pilgrim Pleasure Grounds on the St. Domingo estate. O'Rourke is meeting his friends outside Molly Bushell's confectionary shop at 12.30pm. We'll tail them from there."

189

The heights of Everton were thronged with tens of thousands of people. It seemed that the whole of Liverpool was present to witness the courageous James Sadler's bold and daring attempt to fly above the town. The fine ladies and gentlemen from the district and beyond were all bedecked in the latest fashions, preening, and posing whilst toiling servants trailed in their wake heaving picnic baskets, chairs and tables. Hundreds more had paid to get close to the balloon that Lefèvre called a *Mongolfier* after the famous eponymous French brothers, the pioneers of hot air ballooning. A carnival atmosphere prevailed. The August sun was shining. The sutlers were out in force selling their wares; food, drinks, souvenirs, parasols, and all manner of things. Troupes of actors, dancers and musicians entertained the masses, jockeying for space and attention alongside jugglers, conjurors and shoulder-borne performing monkeys. Molly Bushell's toffee shop was doing a roaring trade with her speciality Everton mints, the guarded recipe having been passed to her by local physician Dr James Gerrard. The nearby famous Prince Rupert's cottage proved to be as popular as ever with the tourists as well, the site of the village providing panoramic views of the town, river and Welsh mountains in the distance. At noon precisely, Lefèvre appeared trudging up the hill. He approached the lock-up, or Prince Rupert's Tower as it was known, spotting MacShane and his accomplice. His wiry associate's features were evocative of a rat, he thought. MacShane introduced him.

"Monsignor Lefèvre, this is George Sewell, he is assisting us today. He knows who we're looking for. Red Nelson and he have had some unfortunate prior altercations and as far as George is concerned he has unfinished matters with this man."

"Good day, *Monsieur* Sewell. I'm happy to meet your acquaintance but let's get one thing straight right away, we are here to monitor our quarry's movements, not assail him. Is that understood?"

"Yes, sir."

MacShane had told Sewell very little about the mission. Sewell was only informed that Lefèvre was a Catholic emissary sent by the Vatican. Lefèvre bought some Everton toffees and shared them with his hired hands. They loitered, scanning the crowds for any sign of their target. Sewell was the first to sight O'Rourke with his group of friends and family scrambling up the hill, amongst them the boys, Kitty and little Fleur-Rose. They all paused breathless at Molly Bushell's and joined the queue for the treats. Genteel ladies and upstanding gentlemen waited in their carriages whilst their attendants queued for the delicious, prized sweets.

A Welsh gaoler, Emlyn Parry arrived not soon after with his family and then the party of day-trippers all set out merrily to the heights. They were followed at a distance by Lefèvre, MacShane and Sewell. The minute Sewell set eyes on O'Rourke, he swore and cussed and MacShane had to chastise him and remind him of his obligations. Because the group were twenty plus in number with numerous children to supervise, it proved easy to keep them in sight despite the enormous crowds. The happy excited group found a site set back from the ridge and picnicked on apples, cakes, bread and ham and pickles. A military band struck up to entertain the masses nearby and by 2pm the balloon was ready to be released vertically towards the drifting clouds of the glorious, cerulean firmament. Just before three in the afternoon James Sadler made his ascent. The spectacle of the magnificent, unique and awe-inspiring fire eating balloon thrilled the multitudes as it ascended. The spectators gasped as the curious flying object drifted away gracefully, eastwards towards the village of West Derby to great approbation and applause. Legions tried to follow it. Gangs of kids raced after it and people on horseback galloped away to track it. Carriages followed. O'Rourke recognised Mr Williamson's carriage as one of those. He was at the reins, cursing rudely, trying to make haste through the hordes. O'Rourke laughed as he passed by.

"Mr Joseph, sir! Refrain from your endeavours! You're not going to win that race!"

"Ah Seamus, Kitty did you see it? What a stupendous spectacle! Maybe I should become an aeronaut. Bah! You're right! Too many damned people here! I've got no chance of catching it! At least I got as close as I could to examine it. It cost me though! In any event I shall catch up with the daring James Sadler this evening. Eliza and I have been invited to the Mayor's banquet in his honour. Gosh, my man! Are all these youngsters with you?"

"Yes, sir. They belong to my friends' families."

O'Rourke's companions all acknowledged the gentlemen, some of whom were the philanthropist's own employees.

Eliza poked her head out of the carriage window.

"Aww, Joseph get the children something to eat. Treat them all to a stick of sugary rhubarb or something."

"Righty-Ho, my dear. Here, Seamus. Take this." Williamson deftly passed him some coins.

"That's very generous of you, sir. Thank you. What do you say to Mr and Mrs Williamson, kids?"

The snotty-nosed minors, astonished by the wealthy couple's generosity, thanked them and jumped wildly around.

"Ha! Ha! See you tomorrow Seamus, bright and early!"

Williamson climbed back into the driver's seat and snatched the reins from his jarvey. Lefèvre, surveilling, obscured in the swathe of humanity drifting along the ridge, nudged MacShane.

"He's our man, atop the carriage," he sneered. "Come on, follow him."

"But what about Red Nelson?" Sewell complained.

"Forget him!" the deacon snapped. "I think *Monsieur* Williamson will lead us right to our sought after prize."

"What prize?"

"It's not for you to know. MacShane tell him to be quiet, for God's sake."

MacShane grimaced at the ex-convict, gripped Sewell's arm forcefully and held his solitary thumb to his lip.

190

The three of them pushed and shoved their way rudely through the crowd to keep pace with the carriage. Williamson was making slow progress through the throng. The cussing merchant guided the fiacre down a stony path. It started to pick up momentum. People dived out of the way. MacShane saw a man climbing into another cart. He dragged him out unceremoniously, leapt up into the driver's seat and cracked the whip. The horse set off startled. He brought it under control, picked up Lefèvre and Sewell further down the track and set off in pursuit of their new target, the shocked owner's remonstrations drowned out by the band and cacophony of the multitude. They followed the fiacre the few miles to Edge Hill, struggling to keep up with it and just managing to keep it in their sights. They saw the gentleman and his lady alight at a mansion. The coachman took the reins and departed whilst Williamson escorted his wife in. Lefèvre waited with the others wondering what to do next. A few minutes later his mind was made up for him. Williamson stepped out of the house. He wore his battered hat with his unkempt hair sticking out of it, a grubby, unbuttoned shirt and tatty, filthy boots. They looked at each other bemused by his appearance and wondered where he was going dressed so slovenly. They followed him at a distance to what looked like a quarry. There were heaps of rubble and large red sandstone rocks strewn around. Then Williamson disappeared out of view. They inched closer. They realised there was an entrance to a tunnel. The trio looked at each other mystified. MacShane took out his tinderbox and passed it to Sewell who lit the candle in the container. Then he lit a lamp that they found near to the entrance and the three of them furtively followed Williamson into the subterranean passage. They were stricken by a sense of unease and apprehension. They progressed deeper into the tunnel. Their eyes focused on strange brick and sandstone arches and other hewn out passageways. In one of the tunnels, they identified a light source and followed it. The trio stopped abruptly when they heard the crunch of a pickaxe being struck against rock. They proceeded with caution only moving in synchronization with the strike of the tool for fear of being discovered. They heard no other voices. Heard no other evidence of metal striking rock for Williamson had given everyone the day off to attend the ballooning event. They extinguished the lamp. They squeezed through a narrow groove between two walls of sandstone rock and entered a large vault. They spotted Williamson on the far side of the chamber, so they hid behind a mound of spoil and watched as the wealthy merchant and landowner, pickaxe in hand and back turned to them, pounded the vast stone strata of rock. The loosened chunks of sandstone flew in all directions shrouding Williamson's shabby attire in red dust. MacShane furtively crept nearer and nearer, on every strike of the pick. He reached for a rock. Shortly after Williamson had struck the rockface one more time, he received a vicious blow to the head. He blacked out. When he came to, he found his hands tied behind his back. He had been dragged to another cavernous vault and lay perilously close to a fifty foot drop. His head ached and he longed to rub the back of it. His unkempt hair was matted in blood. Still groggy, he looked up at the three imposing figures astride him.

"Ah, *Monsieur* Williamson, you are awake. I feared my overzealous colleague here had done for you. It would have been a disaster."

MacShane stood over him in a threatening manner.

"Who, who are you? What in damnation do you think you are doing? This is private land!"

"You do not seem to be the same self-assured person now that we have revealed your identity."

"What do you mean? Damn you!"

"Does the name Cardinal Fesch appear familiar to you?"

Williamson hesitated. He stirred at the French cleric.

"What! You are Fesch?"

"*Non, monsieur*. I am just his humble servant, his emissary."

"You are a man of the cloth, and you have the temerity to authorize and assail a gentleman! Zounds! I will take you in a duel for this!"

"You, sir, are in no position to request anything." He turned to his lackeys. "Did you hear that my companions, Mr Williamson wants a duel?"

The three intruders laughed raucously.

"*Monsieur* Williamson," Lefèvre continued, "where is the Egyptian stele?"

"The what?"

"Now, come, come *Monsieur* Williamson. Don't play games. Although I enjoy playing games this is not the time. My spy, MacShane here, reckons Red Nelson is aware of it and you, being his employer, would undoubtedly be a strong candidate to be implicated in this heinous plot to extort funds from the Catholic Church. You know very well what I'm talking about, don't you?"

"Certainly not, you charlatan!"

Lefèvre, losing his patience, indicated to Sewell to intervene.

"*Monsieur* Sewell, earn your purse."

Sewell obliged by suddenly kicking Williamson in his groin.

"Aaargh! You little lick-spittle sewer rat!" he gasped. The merchant writhed in agony. "An apt soubriquet for your rodent-like features and offensive effluvium!"

Sewell, offended, delivered a vicious kick to his victim's abdomen this time.

"Aaargh!"

"You're calling me a sewer rat when you're the one crawling around underground, you mumbling cove!"

Sewell knelt on one knee and delivered a swift fist to the prostrate gentleman's jaw. Williamson winced in agony. Lefèvre intervened.

"*Monsieur* Williamson, we are wasting valuable time. If your pain is increasing due to a punch or kick or two, then how will you react when I torture you to obtain the information I seek?

"Damn you, man!"

"The Catholic Church, thanks to the Inquisition, knows how to extract confessions from reprobates like you. Indeed, and since I am an expert on the subject of the history of the Inquisition and the imaginative techniques and interesting methods employed to elicit information from heretics and other offenders and the like, I am sure a swift resolution will avail."

"Confound it! Leave me be!"

"Unfortunately, we don't have time for lingchi although MacShane's razor-like dirk is more than capable of a thousand deep cuts. I find scaphism quite appealing though, considering the amount of vermin that will be in and around these tunnels, however, we do lack milk and honey and, of course, time again. On the other hand, this rope and pulley, is perfect for, strappado."

Williamson stared in horror at the wooden construction that hung over the drop to the bedrock below. It had been erected to bring up spoil and rocks from the lower vault to then be removed from the labyrinth. A battered tin bucket sat at the end of the rope that worked as a pulley. The phrase 'hoisted with his own petard' flashed through Williamson's mind.

Suddenly MacShane yanked him to his feet and bundled him over to the pulley. The Scotsman drew his dirk. Williamson's face expressed renewed fear, but the knife holder merely sliced through the cord holding the metal bucket and then his captive's bonds. The merchant went to finger the bump on his cranium, but the pistol toting Sewell yanked his arm down with such force that it came down unexpectedly on MacShane's wrist, dislodging the blade from his grasp. The dagger sailed over the precipice and clattered onto the bedrock below. MacShane glared at the hapless Sewell, beginning to regret his choice of partner. The rat-faced thug bowed his head avoiding eye contact. Williamson, momentarily, sensing an air of animosity between the two henchmen, thought about exploiting the discord between them by launching a surprise attack on one of them but he suddenly stiffened when he felt the sharp point of another blade in the small of his back.

"Do not even think about it *Monsieur* Anonym," the knife-wielding deacon warned, having read his intentions.

Sewell then turned his ire on his captive. He manhandled him, swiping him with one flourish of his back hand across his cheekbone. Williamson grimaced. Sewell forced the captive's arms behind his back, then bound him securely by his wrists to the rope which was moments earlier attached to the bucket. He tightened the cord with a sharp pull making his captive wince. Sewell manoeuvred him, with MacShane's help to the edge of the chasm. On the orders of Lefèvre, the two henchmen pulled the levers of the pulley towards them. The rope tensed and the pain seared through their victim's arms. He cried out.

"Now, now, *Monsieur* Williamson. That was only the first little wrench of the cord and, of course, it hurt. The pain is unbearable already. When we dangle you over the edge of the precipice, your shoulders will dislocate. And when we attach rocks to your feet and legs well then, your arms will be ripped from their sockets and no one will hear your screams of agony, just us three. Pray tell me where you have hidden

480

the tablet in this labyrinth of yours because, without doubt, this is the most commendable of places to cache something of value."

"Go to blazes, you hypocritical bugger!" Williamson cried.

"Blazes is somewhere below your subterranean labyrinth, *mon ami*. Maybe you knew all along where you would end up and were excavating a route to it already. A bit more please, gentlemen."

MacShane tugged on the pulley anew. Williamson's back arched. The sinews in his limbs were stretched to breaking point as his feet scrambled to gain purchase on the stone ledge overlooking the precipice. Then he found himself bent double. He screamed. Suddenly, a sword-wielding figure burst out of the shadows. It was O'Rourke. The Sewer Rat, oblivious to the danger about to engulf him, was chuckling like a demented child anticipating the forthcoming savagery to be meted out to his helpless victim. The Irishman slashed at Sewell's hand with the scimitar, swiftly and without mercy. Severed digits dropped to the ground. The sadistic laughter was instantly replaced by screams. He half turned to see who had disabled him, but a boot was immediately thrust into his gut, and he flew backwards over the edge catching Williamson's feet with his own skewed leg as he went, sending the strung up merchant dangling over the ledge. Williamson's shoulder ligaments strained. He cried out in agony. A shocked Lefèvre turned to run when he set eyes on the fierce-looking Irishman brandishing the razor-like weapon. O'Rourke flung the scimitar at him. Its tip piercing the back of his thigh. He screamed in pain but continued to limp away as fast as he could. The embedded sword clattered over the stones and then dislodged itself. In an instant, O'Rourke had used the hook attached to the stump of his left forearm to drag back the rope and haul his employer back onto terra firma. In the seconds it took all this to happen, MacShane instinctively had plunged his hand into his tunic to retrieve his pistol when he realised that he couldn't grab it with his gnarled hand. He fumbled for the weapon with his other hand presenting O'Rourke with a split-second opportunity to beat him to the draw. Twisting his body around he fired his pistol. The noise of the gun shot echoed through the chamber. The vault lit up momentarily, illuminated by the sudden flash. MacShane staggered backwards and leant against the sandstone wall of rock, a bullet lodged in his chest. O'Rourke scampering, recovered his sword, cut down Williamson and then finished off the spy with a thrust of his blade through the heart. The blood gurgled from MacShane's mouth before he expired, crashing to the floor.

"Mr Joseph, sir, my God, are you alright?"

"Argh!" Williamson cried. "My shoulders, the ligaments, they're burning with pain. Good God! I can still move my arms though, they're not broken. Go after that villain, the cleric, will you? Don't let him escape!"

191

O'Rourke turned and went in pursuit of Lefèvre. He took a lantern and delved into the dark recesses of the labyrinth. He was confident that Lefèvre was still in the maze of tunnels and vaults. There was a blood trail. He followed it. It went down a narrow passageway into a large chamber and led to a heap of rubble and rocks. He crept closer to the mound of spoil. He had the sword in his hand and the lantern dangled on his hook. He was about to scramble up the scree to seek out his prey on the other side, when suddenly, a crunch of stone behind him betrayed the position of his adversary. He had been tricked. Somehow Lefèvre had stemmed the flow of blood and hid elsewhere to deceive his opponent. Lefèvre swung a pickaxe ferociously at O'Rourke's head, but the Irishman anticipated it sufficiently to turn his body and avoid it connecting. The axe head buried itself in his shoulder instead. O'Rourke grunted in pain, his back arching in response to the contact. He staggered backwards but managed to fling the lantern from his hook in the direction of Lefèvre, before collapsing to his knees. The missile connected with Lefèvre, a glancing blow on his temple, enough to cause him to lose his footing temporarily amidst the stone and spoil strewn around the bed rock. O'Rourke clawed desperately with his hook at the axe blade embedded in his shoulder, eager to seize it before the deacon could recover and extricate it. But Lefèvre, having regained his balance, acted first yanking the weapon from the Irishman's flesh. O'Rourke cried out anew. The deacon raised the axe, poised to strike his enemy again. O'Rourke, one knee on the floor, launched himself at his opponent, his curved blade piercing the left armpit of the French cleric. Lefèvre gasped. His eyes betrayed a look of terror and disbelief. He remained momentarily frozen like a statue, the pickaxe poised above his head. O'Rourke withdrew the blade and then plunged it back into the deacon's gut without hesitation. The pickaxe crashed to the ground. Lefèvre staggered around clutching the hilt of the weapon with one hand whilst trying in vain to stem the flow of blood from his midriff with his other. Then his body stiffened, and he collapsed face down onto the heap of detritus.

Blood seeped from O'Rourke's wound. Fortunately, the pickaxe edge had been blunted. Its end had been broken off limiting the damage. The pain was still manifest though. He went over to the corpse, turned it over and recovered his blade which was sunk to the hilt in the deacon's stomach. He wiped the blade on Lefèvre's cassock and momentarily asked for God's forgiveness, then he turned into the dark and stumbled through the passageway where he could see a dim light. Williamson was sat upright against the rope-secured pulley, clutching his shoulders.

"Thank God. You're safe. Are you hurt?"

O'Rourke turned to reveal his wound. "He caught me with a pickaxe, but he came off worse. I think we both need some attention."

"Come on, we need to get out of here. I'll give everyone another day off with pay whilst we consider how to dispose of the bodies. Fortunate scoundrels!"

"Excuse me, sir, for my inappropriate methods."

O'Rourke managed to help drag his employer to his feet by the scruff of his neck using his hook and injured arm despite the excruciating pain in his shoulder.

"Your investment in my hook has paid dividends," he gasped between grunts.

"Aye. Foresight is just one of my many mercantile abilities."

"Sir, by rights we should inform the authorities and say that we were assailed by these henchmen."

"No, they would question the presence of the cleric," Williamson cautioned. "Although that Scot, MacShane was a spy. We could concoct a story about him, but it would have to be very elaborate. For now, we'll say you fell and hurt your shoulder on the axe and went over a ledge and I hauled you back, hence my strained ligaments or something of that ilk. Here, take the lantern. Let's go."

192

August, 1812

"Now Mr Williamson, you need to rest up for the next few weeks. Your ligaments are severely strained. No labouring for you for at least a month if not longer. You've had a most frightful experience."

"But, I-"

"Sir! I must insist! It's serious. Your shoulders may suffer permanent damage and constant pain if you don't adhere to my advice. The most I am allowing you to do is pick up a quill, newspaper or a glass of port, a book at most. No heavy objects. No hunting, no riding and certainly no digging! You have servants to cater for all your needs. You have men to continue your excavations. And overseers whose job is to naturally oversee. With respect they don't need you to be looking over their healthy shoulders. Is that understood, sir?"

"Yes, if you say so Dr Phillips! Tarnation!"

"As for Mr. O'Rourke, he was fortunate the pickaxe didn't penetrate further into his flesh or bone. I've sent him to the Infirmary at Shaw's Brow to see a colleague of mine. He should be fine within a day or two provided no infection sets in."

"Oh, that's good news."

"I'm sorry you had to miss the banquet for Mr Sadler. Eliza had a grand time though. I'm sure she's told you all about it."

"Humph! The woman's never stopped blabbing about it since! 'James did this and James said that,'" the grumpy patient retorted.

As soon as Dr Phillips had left in his fiacre, Williamson ordered a footman to organise his own carriage, despite the protestations from Eliza. He was helped into the transport by several struggling, harangued valets and driven off to the Infirmary post haste. Once there he was again given assistance alighting from the carriage by the two fussing footmen who had accompanied him there, both enduring another volley of verbal abuse from the waspish grouch. He sent one of the attendants to seek out O'Rourke whilst he went alone to the morgue. He entered much to the surprise and consternation of the mortician who tried to usher him out.

"Sir, alas, my employee is in here. I have come to identify the poor wretch!"

"Oh, well, sir. You should have made an appointment."

"My apologies, my good man."

"What's his name?" the mortician said, softening his stance.

"Seamus O'Rourke."

The hospital employee, not recognising the name, began to check the cadavers lying in each coffin. Whilst he was otherwise occupied, Williamson surreptitiously helped himself two glass bottles of embalming fluid and placed them swiftly into the inside pockets of his coat, grimacing with pain as he did so.

Suddenly, someone burst into the basement room. It was O'Rourke. The mortician looked up. Williamson feigned shock.

"My God! Is that an apparition I see before my very eyes? Can you see him, sir? God rest his soul!"

"Mr Joseph sir, what's happening?" O'Rourke inquired, unawares.

"He speaks! He speaks! Oh, good Lord! I feel faint!"

The confused mortician ran to assist him, placing his hands on his sore shoulders.

"Ouch!"

"Sorry sir, here, take a seat."

He guided him to a bench with O'Rourke looking on, bewildered.

"I'm alive, sir. Who told you I was deceased?"

"Oh! So, you're not a spirit, then? Oh, thank the Lord! Someone told me you had expired at the Infirmary. Come then, that's cause for celebration!"

He turned and addressed the non-plussed embalmer.

"Thank you for your assistance, kind sir! He's lives! He lives! See? There is a God! Maybe these corpses will also be resurrected sometime soon. Go easy with the arsenic or whatever you give them."

The embalmer seemed to be exhibiting traits of a newly acquired nervousness. The two of them took this as their cue to leave, leaving the concerned worker in a state of flux, warily eyeing up the lifeless bodies around him.

"What was all that about, sir?"

Williamson paused along the corridor to reveal the bottles to O'Rourke.

"We have some preserving to do. Come, I've got a plan."

485

193

Despite the reticence of his attendants, Williamson insisted that he and O'Rourke were to be dropped off at the tunnels. His aides were warned not to tell his wife their whereabouts. They procured some canvas that was used for dragging debris out of the tunnels and proceeded to the chamber where MacShane lay. The rats had already made their mark chewing the soft tissue of his ear lobes and nose and soaking him in urine. Searching his body, they found hidden in a sewn up inside pocket in his tunic, a crude map of the port of Liverpool with its gun emplacements and barracks, incriminating evidence of his spying activities. O'Rourke dragged the stiff, musty cadaver onto the canvas with some difficulty, aggravating his shoulder wound. Williamson took MacShane's dirk and made an incision in his jugular. Blood spurted out. He lifted the bottle to the aperture in his neck, cringing as he did so and attempted to pour the embalming fluid in. Then he incised his femoral vein and emptied more of the liquid into his body. They forced his mouth open and poured some down his throat, then rolled him up in the canvas.

"I've learnt how to print and now, damnation, I'm learning how to embalm corpses! That should stop him from reeking for the time being, I hope."

They repeated the process with Lefèvre's corpse. They stripped him of his personal effects; a gold ring, a silver cross, a gold pocket watch, and a list of navy vessels operating out of Liverpool and Hull which also confirmed the deacon's spying activities.

"What shall we do with these articles?"

"I'm no thief, Seamus. We either send them back to the see in Lyon or to the Vatican or sell them and use the funds for the charitable schools."

"Right you are, Mr Williamson. I'd say the latter. Now, where are we going to put the cadavers, sir?"

"In one of the chambers. I'm afraid you'll have to do the lugging. We'll use a hand cart to transport them where we can. I hope your shoulder's up to it."

"It's not too bad, sir."

"I'll say we've had an infestation of rats and I've killed some, hence the smell. It'll be off limits until I say. That will give us time to figure out what to do with the bodies in the long term. We'll use debris to cover them. I told you that you might have to do some digging sometimes. Now's the time, but first we have to bring the Sewer Rat's corpse up from down in the vault."

"We can use the winch."

"Good idea."

O'Rourke descended down the rickety wooden staircase Williamson's carpenters had made. With a lamp in his hand, he went over to the spot below the ledge to locate the corpse. He swung the lantern around. His heart missed a beat. He became defensive and cautious. The body was not there. Just a couple of his rodent-gnawed severed fingers and a broken hand trolley with buckled wheels and sheets of blood-spattered canvas in it. The Sewer Rat had survived the fall. O'Rourke made his way back to the staircase and lowered the lantern, only then laying eyes on the specks of blood on each step.

"Mr Joseph, sir," he shouted upwards. "We have a problem. There's no corpse! The Sewer Rat has miraculously survived the fall somehow and must have escaped."

"Damn it!"

"I'll have a search around, but I reckon he's long gone now. Then I'll clean the blood stains away around the chambers and get on with the removal of the other two bodies."

194

20th August, 1812

A week or so later, O'Rourke was summoned to the mansion.

"You've done what, sir?"

"Told them to start building once the new tunnel is dug. The stonemasons have my design and plans. They're perusing them now."

"It's, it's ambitious to say the least, sir."

"You know me by now, Seamus. I don't do things by halves!"

"And what about the bodies, sir?"

"I've had the bricklayers brick up that particular tunnel. Stop the rats from getting out."

"And the stele?"

"Still securely hidden but it will be moved to the new site on completion."

"Do you think Cardinal Fesch knows our identity?"

"I'm not sure. I have a hunch that their belligerence was a spontaneous act. If that's the case, then we still remain anonymous to Fesch. They must have followed you at Sadler's balloon spectacle, saw me interacting with you and chanced their luck. We don't know how much Sewer Rat knows."

"Probably very little. I'd be surprised if they had divulged to him the real reason why they targeted you. The rogue can't be trusted. It would be your word against his. I doubt he knows it was me who kicked him off the ledge."

"Nevertheless, we still have to be on our guard. Stay alert. The next few months will be critical in determining if we are still in danger. If more visitors arrive, then we'll know for sure. Oh, now, I still haven't thanked you Seamus for saving my life. I am eternally grateful."

"I was only doing my duty, sir."

"Notwithstanding, as a reward I am offering you one of my cottages, rent free, on my land at Edge Hill. Liver Bird Cottage with a renumeration increase of ten shillings to your weekly purse. How does that sound?"

"That's, that's very generous of you, Mr Joseph but as I said I was only doing my-"

"Above and beyond, Seamus. Above and beyond. Now, go and break the good news to Kitty. I won't take no for an answer. I have correspondence to write to his Eminence, Cardinal Fesch. Since that dastardly Deacon Lefèvre was so keen on playing games, I too will play a game."

"A game, sir?"

"Yes, a wily game Seamus. One which might take time to reach its conclusion though. I have been considering the rules of this game over the last few days. Besides, I need some amusement. I fear I will be incapacitated for several weeks or perhaps months. I yearn to dig but my ligaments ache so. It seems I will be making more frequent appearances at the Athenaeum and Lyceum. And of course, taking Betty to the Theatre Royal. Hey-Ho!"

"That doesn't sound too taxing, sir."

"You'd be surprised Seamus where Mrs Williamson's concerned! You'd be surprised! But don't tell her that, will you?"

"Of course not, sir.

"And as for poor Bobby, he won't be able to attend church with me."

"Bobby, sir? Who's Bobby?"

"My trusty steed, of course!"

"Oh! That Bobby."

"Yes, normally he accompanies me to St Thomas's on Park Lane. He sits behind the pew and places his front hooves over my shoulders in repose. He carries me, you see, all the time, so I like to repay him."

"Quite, sir. I understand," the bewildered Irishman lied. "Right then, I'll be off to see Kitty and later I'll be back at work. I'll arrange our transfer to the cottage in due course, sir, once I've settled my affairs with my current landlord. Thank you once again."

"The pleasure's all mine."

195

Williamson sat down at his bureau in the library. In front of him was a blank sheet of paper. He took his quill and dipped it into the ink well. His shoulder ached. He paused, to reflect for a moment, then started to write cursively, a sly smirk creasing his countenance.

'22nd August 1812

Sir, Your Eminence, Cardinal Fesch of Lyon, Prince of France, ambassador, senator, diplomat, Grand Almoner, Count, Sovereign Prince, Knight of the Order of the Golden Fleece, (your titles and positions are legion).

I was extremely surprised to say the least when I was assailed by a member of the Catholic clergy and some other villains acting on his behalf. I survived this attack - just. However, the deacon unfortunately, did not. I have bequeathed his personal effects to a charitable cause and thus being men of the cloth, you and he would most certainly consent with this option, would you not? I discovered to my cost (and to his) that Deacon Lefèvre was not acting in good faith in his role as an emissary of the Vatican addressing the concerns of the French prisoners of war. On the contrary, he was involved in espionage for Bonaparte and was also here to effectuate a scandalous and murderous mission to silence me and recover the artefact. What would it do to your standing in the Holy See of Rome, Joseph Fesch, if they knew you had spies working for Bonaparte, given the fact that you have been acting as a conduit between the Vatican and your nephew? Since matters have taken this grave turn for the worse and the Catholic Church is prepared to kill to achieve its aims of procuring the tablet, the stakes have been raised. I suggest we come to a swift agreeable financial arrangement to settle this affair. If not, your only opportunity to acquire it, short of an invasion of these lands, is to play a game. Games are preferable to violence, don't you think? Treat my agreeable offer as an act of benevolence to the Catholic Church on my part. (At least one of us is demonstrating a degree of respect.) Deacon Lefèvre was fond of games. Let's play mine in memory of him. How did I know he was fond of playing games? In his desire to torture me in the best traditions of the Inquisition he so obviously approved of, he referred to those punishments as 'games'. So, now, to the simple rules of my 'game of clues'.

If you want to find the stele, you must find certain clues. There are seven in total to locate. Each clue found will reveal the whereabouts of another one. Moreover, each clue links back to the previous one. The final clue will lead you to me and the artefact. Each clue is an illustration of a creature. To commence the game, I have enclosed two illustrations of animals. Solve this initial particular conundrum by identifying the link between them and you will be up and running. *Bon courage*, Your Eminence! You will need it!

I have the honour to be, My Lord Cardinal, Your Eminence's devoted and obedient servant.

Anon.

Enc. The illustrations which will lead to the first of seven more clues and a print of the next three lines of the coveted tablet.

PS Any correspondence can be forwarded to Ye Hole In Ye Wall, Hackins Hey, Liverpool as per previous correspondence.'

Williamson, chuckling to himself, started to draw his first clue on a separate piece of paper.

"Bah!" he moaned, moments later. He screwed up the paper, took a fresh sheet and commenced drawing again. Once he had finished the first illustration, he put it aside and started to draw the second creature on another sheet. Thirty minutes later, with scrunched up paper surrounding the bureau, he bawled for the butler.

"Myers!"

Myers arrived. "Yes, sir!"

"Can you find Mrs Williamson and ask her to come here immediately. I have a very important task for her. I need her expertise. Check the garden first."

"Yes, Mr Joseph."

One hour later, the gentleman of the house was screeching again.

"Myers! Get my carriage, forthwith!" he ordered.

Sykes's replacement entered the library again.

"Yes, Mr Joseph. Straight away. Affairs, sir?"

"No, Myers, pleasure. Just pleasure. Well, it's reconnaissance, truth be told. I'm setting a trail for a new hunt and I'm the damned fox! I need to find a foxhole."

"A game is it, sir?"

"Yes, Myers. A deadly game. It's always a deadly game when a fox is involved."

He thrust him a compact, sealed leather cylindrical tube with the letter, print and Eliza's illustrations enclosed.

"Ensure that this is sent, will you Myers. It goes via Spain."

"Right you are, sir."

"*Blocus continental,*" the merchant said in his best French. "And all that nonsense. The address is on the tag attached to it, by the way. Make sure it's secure before it's sent."

"Most certainly, sir. I'll away to see to your carriage, then "

"Yes, yes, do so. Make haste."

196

Cardinal Fesch, muttering oaths and cursing the anonymous sender, flung the letter across the chamber. It fluttered down onto the tiled, patterned floor. Then he swept the illustrations and print from his bureau onto the tiles. When Lefèvre had not returned to Lyon he'd raised the alarm with the appropriate authorities and the Curia in Rome. He thought at first that Lefèvre had returned to Malta and succumbed to the outbreak of plague which had devastated the island, killing thousands. Representations had been made to the British government and accusations of malpractice ensued. Members of Lord Liverpool's government protested their innocence furiously and conducted an enquiry into the mysterious disappearance of the deacon. *The Liverpool Mercury* newspaper speculated that he had been abducted, having tracked down witnesses who claimed that the cleric was last seen with two dubious looking men in a tumbril at the James Sadler balloon ascent, characters he would not, one would assume, normally associate with. A description of the two men had been published and circulated. Since no ransom had been made it had been reckoned that the potential kidnap had gone wrong, and the deacon had died somehow. But now the Cardinal knew the truth. He was loathe to reveal the letter's contents to anyone, so he was prepared to let sleeping dogs lie.

His other area of concern was with the fate of his nephew. Matters had taken a turn for the worse for Napoleon's Grande Armée in Russia. The army was starving in the winter quarters of a deserted Moscow. The Battle of Borodino in September had been nothing but a pyrrhic victory for the French Emperor. Fesch feared for the success of the invasion and its repercussions if Bonaparte was forced to retreat. What would that mean personally for him? Despite his best intentions, his mind began to focus again on the contents of the leather tube. The illustrations of the animals intrigued him. He picked them off the floor and analysed them. He recovered the print of the hieroglyphs, stared at it momentarily in a trance and yearned to know what secrets they held. What message they conveyed. What repercussions they would have for the Catholic faith, if any. It was this that gnawed at his soul. He decided to resist responding to the anonymous letter, on the understanding that the anonym's challenge of a game of clues was futile, and not least impossible. He then retrieved the letter and placed it and its accompanying contents back into the leather tube. He went across to his ornately carved and upholstered grand canapé and banged twice with his fist on the elaborately carved right arm of the sofa just in front of the griffin's claws. The arm immediately clicked detaching itself slightly from the leg. He placed his middle finger into the small aperture that had appeared and brought it forward, releasing a lever. He then lifted the arm and placed the tube in a hidden compartment concealed within the leg of the item of furniture.

197

It was another letter received, dated April 1813, that prompted the Cardinal to review his stance and act. The note was from a person named only as George who claimed to know where the tablet was and what happened to Lefèvre and would reveal all for a sum. The Sewer Rat had managed to escape from the tunnels after lying unconscious for some time. The handcart and tarpaulin had cushioned his fall. He had awoken to find his mangled fingerless hands bleeding profusely. Only his little fingers and the stumps of his thumbs and fingers survived. He had crawled up the steps and discovered MacShane's body which he had searched. He found a purse of money in one pocket and a bottle of whisky in another. He poured some of the whisky on to his disabled hands, wincing in the process and drank the remainder. He used the Scotsman's dirk, still in its sheath, to cut away some of his shirt sleeves and wrapped them around his gnarled hands. The cutting process was painful and laborious. Then he went straight to the infirmary to seek out a physician to tend to his 'industrial injury'. There his wounds were cauterized and bandaged, and he left in the early hours. He took a coach to Preston where he had a relative and stayed for several months, lying low. He had not known much about the deacon, and it was only when they were about to torture their victim, he found out that Lefèvre was after some sort of relic which he assumed was in the tunnels. He had subsequently heard of the furore over the cleric's disappearance and saw an opportunity to blackmail Cardinal Fesch who had first raised concerns about the deacon's no-show. The Sewer Rat had, in the meantime, become a 'bilge rat', employed on the same privateer, *The Harp Seal*, as MacShane, and had set sail to the Caribbean. Sewell had been dismissed from the navy after his conviction for rape. He changed his appearance. Gone was the greasy, lank, dark hair. His pate was now bald. His thin lips were camouflaged by a drooping moustache and beard. The crew had joked that when MacShane was on board they needed another hand. Now they said they needed two more hands when Sewell showed up as his replacement.

Fesch decided to write to 'George', not knowing but suspecting it may be one and the same person who had the stele although the handwriting was different, and the spelling was full of errors. He wrote saying he would not pay anything until the tablet was in the possession of the claimant and until 'George' had identified the first few lines of script on the antiqulty. The return address was 'Mother Redcaps, Wirrall, Cheshire, England'. The Cardinal then finally wrote back to 'Anon' stating that a new agent had been appointed to track down the article and that he was close to locating and solving the first clue all in the hope of calling the stranger's bluff and to heighten his sense of anxiety.

198

It was a delightful, warm mid-June summer's evening when O'Rourke received notice of a new letter. He had shared a few porters of ale with his companions in some of the town's many taverns, the workers having earned them by spending most of the day deep underground in the choking, dust filled conditions, toiling away, hacking at sandstone, clearing rock and debris, building brick arches and excavating tunnels and vaults. When each letter arrived at Ye Hole, as they called it, O'Rourke was notified discreetly by Ralph, the landlord. He didn't immediately lay claim to it. He endeavoured to adopt the same precautions as before. After finishing their much needed drinks, the group of colleagues all left. They went their separate ways to their homes. O'Rourke, however, went to the Piers Head where he had seen some urchins pestering traders on the George's dock. He loitered for a moment watching them fooling around, then he called one over, a boy who introduced himself as Marcus and entered into conversation with him. The lad shot off with two other waifs. They entered the premises of Ye Hole, the two other street kids causing a distraction by begging at the crammed tables of revellers. Marcus went straight to the bar, identified Ralph from the description O'Rourke had given him and asked him for the letter, name-dropping O'Rourke in the process. The other lads were now making a nuisance of themselves, so all heads were turned towards them. The landlord furtively slipped the envelope to Marcus who concealed it in his tattered shirt and then chugged an ale on the bar belonging to a patron.

"Hey! That's mine, you thieving little brat!" a berating bespectacled clerk shouted.

The three boys took flight. They returned to George's Dock and delivered the missive to the one-eyed, one-armed man who rewarded them handsomely for their efforts. O'Rourke slipped the letter into his shirt and set off home in a wagon.

The family had spent a wonderful Christmas at the cottage and Kitty had recently given birth to a baby girl, Mary Catherine. Kitty was convinced their fortunate change of circumstances, away from the poisonous air of the tanneries and sugar refineries and noxious odours of the breweries and open sewers, had resulted in the good health of her new baby girl. The outcome would not have been the same she thought if they had stayed in the impoverished confines of the court. They had also received notification from Francis that he was no longer the ship's lad, he was a bluejacket, and the crew were due some respite from their blockading duties sometime soon. O'Rourke, arriving home, slipped the letter into a bureau and locked it. Mr Joseph was currently away, repeating the process of conducting business in London and then holidaying in Devon, taking the sea air at Salcombe, this time with Eliza and they were not expected back for a number of weeks. The following evening O'Rourke was invited to talk at a dinner party at Greenbank House, home of the renowned abolitionist Rathbone family, about his experience of slavery and that of his friend Patrice Verzon. He had politely declined the offer of joining the notable guests for dinner, including Dr Philipps, who later presented a talk on the life and works of Dr Currie. William Roscoe, also a guest, regaled those present with his experiences of being an abolitionist in Liverpool, recounting the time he was stoned by Liverpool merchants and seamen opposed to the restrictions imposed on the slave trade. He also expatiated on the life and work of influential abolitionist William Wilberforce.

199

The Gallic prisoners were reeling when they heard the latest news. A British, Portuguese and Spanish alliance under the command of Dublin-born Lieutenant General Arthur Wellesley, later to become the 1st Duke of Wellington, had defeated a French army under Napoleon's elder brother Joseph, at the battle of Vitoria in Spain. Several months earlier they had been informed of the debacle of the retreat from Moscow in December 1812. Almost all knew of comrades who had not survived the campaign. More than half a million men had set out to invade Russia with only fewer than 65,000 returning, frost-bitten and starving. The French prisoners knew this humiliating retreat was pivotal. Although they lamented the loss of life, they knew their hopes for freedom and repatriation had come a step closer. The enemy was now knocking at the door.

"I tell you, we will be back on French soil soon," Cousseau declared. "Perhaps before Christmas. *Le petit-caporal* has bitten off more than he can chew this time. This latest defeat at Vitoria leaves the motherland open to invasion by Wellington from Spain. Too many fronts have opened up. I doubt the truce will hold with the Prussians either."

"Those duplicitous Prussians!" Moreau, a Swiss captive raged.

"Who can blame them, Moreau? They've been forced to fight for Napoleon, like others. They too have seen the writing on the wall. The Swedes as well. They've allied themselves to Britain and Russia. All it needs is for Austria to take up arms again against us and that would be too formidable a coalition to defeat this time."

"Napoleon's fortunes are on the wane," the *Marseillan*, Glory added. "Moscow was the turning point."

"Precisely, *mon ami,*" Cousseau stated.

"*L'Empereur*, he'll never surrender!" Moreau declared defiantly.

"Well, his good fortune is deserting him. Moreau, the Empire. It's finished."

"Glory, I beg to differ! I still believe in the cause!"

"Your sentiments are bold, citizen. But they are foolish."

Moreau stood up to confront Glory.

"*Arrêtez! Ça suffit!*" Cousseau warned. "And that's an order!"

The two would-be belligerents backed off and settled down in the cell.

"Hey boys, it's time for recreation. Here comes gaoler Parry."

They filed into the sunshine. Glory and Cousseau continued their discussions.

"Cousseau, will you try and leave immediately when the wars end?"

"I have some affairs to attend to here in Liverpool and then I shall return home to my wife, Odette and children who sadly will not recognise me. How about you?"

"Yes, I will return to Marseille. I have a wife but no children. I suppose I am fortunate unless my wife has left me for another!"

200

August, 1813

The sloop glided up the Mersey, passing George's Dock, jammed with jostling ships unloading and taking on cargo. The Goree Causeway was rammed with traffic, tumbrils and wains and other horse drawn carts and wagons of every description coming and going. Fishermen disgorged their catches onto the dock attracting an airborne invasion of mewing seagulls swooping and diving in an excited frenzy. The boat slipped into Salthouse Dock and was made fast by dockworkers and sentinels. The privateers assisted in unloading the cargo whilst the captain and the waiting owners struck up deals with dock officials and curious merchants interested in the booty being off-loaded. Once the work was complete two hours later, the seamen dispersed in all directions carrying their prize money and possessions. Sewell walked down Bridge Street and crossed over the channel feeding into the Old Dock. The Custom House, at the far end of the dock was hidden by a phalanx of spars from a plethora of moored vessels. He proceeded along to the Goree to find a captain of a fishing smack he could negotiate with to obtain a passage across the Mersey. He wanted to deposit his booty at Mother Redcaps and see if there was any post for him. It was not long before the smack departed for the short crossing to the Wirral shore. The irony of the situation was not lost on him. He had previously attempted to impress privateers for the Royal Navy, the scar on his face a constant reminder. He still had not found out who had maimed him but the same man who had disfigured his face, was a prime suspect. The boat came alongside the berth. He spat venomously into the wind-roiled, turbid waters of the Mersey as the image of O'Rourke festered in his mind.

With his booty safely secured, he proceeded to his lodgings, a letter that was awaiting him tucked into his belt. Once inside his spartan accommodation he awkwardly sliced open the envelope with MacShane's dirk and read the text eagerly. He was disappointed. The Cardinal would only negotiate once the tablet was 'in George's possession' and once he had confirmed the type of text written on it. The missive stated that the Cardinal would not tolerate any form of extortion. Sewell, with his blackened teeth, uncorked the bottle of scotch he had purchased at Mother Redcaps and held it to his lips in his gnarled hands. He took a few swigs and placed it on a side table and lay down on his bed. He lay thinking for a while and then drifted off to sleep after a few more gulps.

201

"I hope you enjoyed your vacation on the south coast, ma'am."

"Thank you, Kitty. I did. Most agreeable. The fresh sea air did Mr Joseph and I so much good. He was swimming most days, which has really benefited him. His shoulders no longer hurt after his accident, and he's got his strength back in his arms. I suppose I won't see him now he'll be off down his damned rabbit holes, I dare say."

"Is that a new book you're reading, ma'am?"

"Yes, *Pride and Prejudice* it's called, by Jane Austen. It's really good. I've nearly finished it."

"Here's your newspaper, ma'am."

"Ah, thank you Kitty. I see Austria has declared war on France. First Prussia and now Austria have turned against Napoleon. And Field Marshall Wellesley, God bless him, is striving to cross the Pyrenees. The end is nigh, me thinks, for Bonaparte. And Wellesley is destined for great things. They'll be erecting monuments to the Irishman all over England if his success continues. Mark my words!"

"Can you fetch me another pot of tea, Kitty?"

"Yes, ma'am."

Kitty headed towards the kitchen just catching the tail end of the head of the household disappear out of the door, attired in his shabby garb, torn top hat and worn boots. She smiled and shook her head in amusement.

First, Williamson went to inspect his houses, to check on their progress. He was greeted heartily by the carpenters, bricklayers, and labourers he employed, who constructed the dwellings according to their master's eccentric designs without question. Then he met O'Rourke at the tunnel entrance for a tour of the newly excavated passage and chamber. He restricted access to this passageway and chamber to only a handful of trusted, skilled stonemasons and carpenters who were sworn to secrecy about their work. Since he had been invigorated by his pleasant sojourn in Devon, the wealthy merchant was raring to go and threw himself into his excavations with renewed vigour whilst handling his affairs in the tobacco business with his usual self-assurance and commercial acumen.

202

The Sewer Rat sat in the saloon of Mother Redcaps listening to the banter of the other privateers, smugglers and merchant seamen. They talked animatedly about the intensifying battles in Europe and the news that Napoleon had defeated an army of the Sixth Coalition at Dresden only to suffer a reverse a few days later at the Battle of Kulm in Bohemia. Sewell had been placed on alert again by the captain of his privateer. They were to make one more sortie before the onset of winter. Sewell had made one recce of the environs of the tunnels. It was swarming with workers, so he observed from afar. Most of the men had left at six pm. He had witnessed Red Nelson bantering with a few other overseers as he locked the large wooden gates at the entrance to the underground passages. He was even more convinced, after seeing O'Rourke pocket the keys that it was the Irishman who had attacked him that afternoon, leaving him for dead. It was dark in the tunnels and the attack was lightning fast, and he had not seen a thing before he was launched off the edge of the precipice. He wanted to kill him there and then, but he knew he had to bide his time. He had to get into the tunnels and survey the labyrinth and find out where the tablet was being hidden. He had kept a low profile and remained on the Wirral side of the river, venturing over only now and again to Liverpool. He decided to respond to Cardinal Fesch, to inform him that he was making progress, but he had to leave Liverpool for a few months. At least by responding the Cardinal would know that he was committed to helping him find the artefact. He slugged back his shot of whisky and went to find a prostitute to abuse for the evening.

203

Joseph Williamson had taken a keen interest in the progress of the monument dedicated to Horatio Nelson that was to be erected at the Exchange. After all, he had contributed considerably to the subscription fund which would be used to create Liverpool's first public statue. On occasions he had been invited, with a few select guests, to attend a progress meeting and to get a sneak preview of the sculpted works. The monument was unveiled to a cheering crowd on 21ST October 1813, the apogee of an idea that had been nurtured since the tragic death of Britain's greatest naval hero, Nelson in 1805, and a few days after the momentous Battle of Leipzig that saw Napoleon's armies arrayed mainly against the Prussians, Austrians, Russians and Swedes. The news gradually filtered through in the next few days that the Sixth Coalition had been victorious, and the French were on the retreat once again. They had been repulsed from the German states, the German troops having deserted from Napoleon's army and switched sides.

204

George Sewell was frustrated in his attempts to return to England. In action against an American privateer off the coast of Boston, his schooner, *The Harp Seal* was badly damaged, likewise the American sloop. Both limped away from the confrontation with considerable fire and cannonade damage incurring heavy casualties on both sides and with no financial gain for either side. Sewell was fortunate enough to avoid injury. The crippled *Harp Seal* managed to limp to Liverpool. However, it was not the Liverpool that the remnants of the crew wished for. It was Liverpool, Nova Scotia. The battle-scarred vessel was laid up over the harsh winter whilst repairs were made. It was late March when she set sail. *The Harp Seal* ventured south first, not wanting to complete the long journey home without a prize. She patrolled the American coastline searching for American merchantmen which may have slipped through the Royal Navy blockade and ended up as far south as the Leeward Islands where she found and attacked a French privateer that had, in turn, raided a brig leaving the Swedish possession of Guadeloupe bound for Europe, garnering coffee, cocoa, sugar, rum, and molasses as a reward. The shattered French vessel was towed but sank on the voyage home. Meanwhile, in Europe, the armies of the Sixth Coalition were now fighting Napoleon's forces in France. The British invasion of south-west France under Wellington, in November 1813, assisted by the Portuguese and Spanish armies, had suffered a series of setbacks, defeats. In north-eastern France in the new year, the Coalition forces' strength, unity and superior numbers finally prevailed culminating in the Battle of Paris at the end of March 1814 and the surrender of Bonaparte's forces. On April 11th 1814, Napoleon's fate was sealed - exile to the Isle of Elba, much to the relief of his many adversaries and a war-weary Europe.

205

The French prisoners filed out of the New Borough Gaol and paraded down Great Howard Street. They were exuberant, in good spirits, defiantly singing *La Marseillaise* and other French ditties. They were going home, and it was time to celebrate. Townsfolk along the route cheered and clapped them in this longed-for moment of peace and new-found spirit of reconciliation. There was a carnival atmosphere.

"*Mon Dieu!* Cousseau. The English. They are cheering us. Celebrating, like us," Glory said, moments before a missile dislodged his hat. "*Putain!* What was that?"

"Ha! Ha! It was a stone!" Cousseau replied. "Some of the English aren't cheering us. It's those damned urchins. Mind you, they treat everyone with disrespect. Just keep an eye on them. Aha! They're being chased away by a constable."

Cousseau detached himself from the line of *détenus* surreptitiously.

"Cousseau! *Où vas-tu?*" Glory implored.

"Remember, I have some affairs to attend to. It will take hours for us all to be processed and accommodated on the ships. Here, take my knapsack. I will be back before the last ship sails today. Take care, *mon ami*. Enjoy your freedom. I'll see you on the other side of *La Manche*, if not before."

206

Cousseau was bent on finding O'Rourke. He was intent on challenging him about the stele but not in a provocative way. His liberty, after so many wasted years in gaol, was too precious to lose. He was not one hundred percent certain that O'Rourke had anything to do with the tablet anyway, but he wanted to put his mind at ease. He slipped away from the crowds and headed for Edge Hill. He had been told by another gaoler where O'Rourke's place of work was. Once there, he watched from a good distance away. The carters came and went filling their tumbrils and wagons with blocks of sandstone and spoil from the tunnels. Some of the detritus was destined for the port of Liverpool dock system, which required the building materials due to its exponential expansion. Cousseau was accustomed to seeing these carters transporting their loads having spent time labouring on the waterfront digging the foundations for the new docks. Canals, roads, and fortifications had also benefited from the unwanted stone and rubble. He often made a fuss over the horses and other beasts of burden, as did many of his fellow prisoners. At 12 noon, the labourers spilled out of the tunnels, blinking in the bright, spring sunshine. Some headed off to nearby homes for their sustenance. Others stretched their aching limbs and backs and headed off into the surrounding countryside to locate a picturesque spot to eat their lunch. Cousseau did not see O'Rourke come out. Perhaps, he thought, he was not there. In any event he decided to enter the tunnels. He was just about to get up from his concealed position from behind a wrecked tumbril when he saw another man carefully picking his way through the rubble crossing the wasteland heading towards the tunnel. He assumed it was a labourer who had returned to collect something from his workplace. He waited for the individual to re-emerge, but he didn't.

Cousseau decided that he could not wait any longer. He ran across the wasteland that scarred the immediate surrounding area avoiding a stationary horse and wain, the driver of which was occupied, extracting suitable lumps of sandstone from the mound of spoil. The Frenchman passed unnoticed and cautiously crept down some steps carved from the sandstone. He heard voices further along a passageway that was dimly lit with oil lamps. One of the voices belonged to O'Rourke, his Irish dialect distinct. He was reprimanding the individual who was with him who was protesting his innocence about some incident. After a few minutes, the conversation ended with a stern rebuke which the chastised worker accepted. He then departed. Cousseau crouched in a recess, hidden from view and watched the admonished individual scramble up the uneven hewn steps. O'Rourke turned and disappeared down another poorly lit passageway. Cousseau waited a moment and then was about to follow him when he saw someone else step out of the shadows and follow the overseer. He hesitated. He had assumed that the person he had spied entering

503

the tunnels was the upbraided worker. Cousseau followed both of them from a distance. The intruder seemed to be stalking O'Rourke. The Irishman stopped fleetingly and turned, holding his lantern up to peer back into the gloom. Both the intruder and Cousseau hid themselves instantly The rest of the labyrinth was silent. All work had stopped for the lunch break. The other intruder continued on after O'Rourke who pressed on into more vaults, passageways, and chambers. Cousseau was amazed by the subterranean labyrinth and wondered what on earth was happening within there. He continued to maintain a distance between himself and the other two but in doing so he lagged behind the stranger, becoming more circumspect at every turn in the tunnels which would suddenly and unexpectedly reveal another vault, pit, abyss or chamber. Suddenly he heard some sort of commotion up ahead, then someone crying out. He heard the slamming of a heavy door somewhere. He proceeded cautiously and located the door, a large, heavy, wooden, oak door with a key still in the keyhole. There was a smear of blood on it. He twisted the bronze, circular handle and the door creaked open. He left it ajar ensuring that he was as quiet as possible. He emerged into a small chamber that had two exits into new passages on the far side. He cursed as he was unsure which tunnel the other two had taken. He chose one. The wrong one. The narrow passageway seemed to be on an incline. He could see a shaft of light ahead. He could hear raised voices. He quickened his step and then stopped suddenly. The excavated tunnel had come to an abrupt halt overlooking another huge chamber with a forty foot drop. He dropped on to his stomach and crawled to the edge making sure he was not seen. He was aghast when he saw what was happening in the chamber. There below him was O'Rourke pinned to the rough sandstone wall by a foil at his throat held by the aggressive intruder and filling the middle of the cavernous chamber was a structure in the process of being constructed, which he could only describe as being extremely odd and incongruous to its surroundings.

207

"I knew you'd be back sometime, you sewer rat!" O'Rourke snarled, blood seeping from a wound on his head.

"Been playing on your mind, have I O'Rourke? No need to fret anymore. Alas, this is the last time you'll see me."

Cousseau half-recognised the voice. It sounded familiar. Then suddenly he realised who it was. The convicted rapist from the Tower, with whom he had fought, bereft of his greasy, lank hair.

"*Putain!* Sewell!" he whispered under his breath.

"Where's the tablet, you Irish cur?"

Cousseau, up on the ledge, gasped in astonishment at the very mention of the artefact.

"Tablet? I don't know what you mean."

Sewell pushed the sword that he now favoured, because of its light weight, further into his victim's pharynx, drawing blood. O'Rourke grunted.

"You know exactly what I mean. I was there when Lefèvre, the deacon, was in the tunnels. He was prepared to kill for it. And now I am!"

Again, the concealed Frenchman recoiled in amazement.

"You did this to me, didn't you, you vile wretch?"

He raised one disfigured hand. The other mutilated hand was wrapped firmly in a neckerchief or some sort of cloth which helped him secure the lightweight sword more firmly in his grip.

"Tell me! Where is it? It's got to be in this labyrinth somewhere. If you don't tell me I will slaughter you and your family! Yes, I know all about your beloved whore of a woman Kitty and your leprous offspring!"

The Irishman bristled with anger. "Leave my family out of this, you dog! They don't know a thing!"

"Stop lying you pitiful leasing-monger!"

Sewell, without warning, jabbed the sharp foil into O'Rourke's forearm. The Irishman winced with pain, but it angered him enough to launch himself at his attacker just as the sword was withdrawn from the piercing hole. O'Rourke, unarmed, having been disarmed by Sewell when he first sprang out of the darkness at the oak door, and still dazed by the blow to his head caused by a sandstone rock wielded by the furtive intruder, managed to administer a succession of swift punches to his enemy's face in spite of the wound to his arm that seeped blood. The Sewer Rat reeled away, stumbling in the face of the onslaught. O'Rourke continued to advance, despite the danger, enraged by Sewell's threat to his family and the unforgivable slur on Kitty. Sewell gained his footing again and jabbed the sharp point of the sword towards O'Rourke several times. O'Rourke backed off. He held his prosthetic leather bound, wooden arm up to protect himself parrying stabbing thrusts from his adversary and then he attacked again swiping out at his assailant with his sharp hook. Sewell just managed to avoid it and then countered by plunging his foil into the skin of his adversary's shoulder. The overseer grimaced. Sewell struggled momentarily to extract the sharp tip from his opponent's flesh. He succeeded but O'Rourke flew at his aggressor again, this time seizing the cloth around his adversary's gnarled hand ripping it and the foil from his grasp and butting him in the face in the process. Sewell's nose exploded and he cried out as he was propelled back. The sword clattered to the floor. The Sewer Rat managed to regain his balance and immediately reached behind the back of his tunic to produce a small Queen Anne pistol. He held the concealed weapon in his crooked hands and pointed it at O'Rourke who was about to reach for the foil. He fired but just as he discharged the pistol, a huge weight slammed into his nape and there was a jarring crack of bone. The heavy load was Cousseau. He had leapt from the ledge above. The impact had propelled Sewell forward and now he lay lifeless, his neck broken, his head lying at a twisted angle to his body. Cousseau had crashed to the ground, banging his head on the bedrock and lay motionless, too. O'Rourke lay sprawled against the partially built structure, mortally wounded, the ball nestled in his chest. Shortly after, the oak door was pushed open, and the barrel of a blunderbuss protruded through the aperture. It was held firmly by Joseph Williamson. He entered the chamber cautiously and found the three men collapsed on the floor. He was followed by two other men armed with pistols. Williamson raced over to O'Rourke. He looked on in horror. A mass of blood covered most of his torso. He checked his pulse. It was faint. He shook O'Rourke's shoulder.

"Seamus! Seamus!"

He opened his eyes, barely.

"Mr Joseph, sir. The Sewer Rat...he returned. He's done for me."

He then convulsed, coughing up more blood.

"He said he'd kill Kitty and my young ones."

"Don't worry, Seamus, he won't. He's dead."

"This one's still alive, sir!" shouted one of the other men.

"The brigand! I'll blast him to hell!" Williamson snarled.

"No! Sir, it's Cousseau," O'Rourke wheezed, blood oozing from his mouth. "The French prisoner. He tried to save me. He leapt from the shaft above. He killed Sewell."

"Good God! He jumped from up there! To save you? Alright, Seamus. I'll look after him. We need to get you to a surgeon."

O'Rourke spewed up more blood and bile.

"Too late, sir," he sighed. "Look after my family, if you will, sir. Tell Kitty, I love her."

And then he drifted away, exhaling his last breath.

208

Williamson stood solemn for a moment, burning with rage, tears in his eyes. Then he instructed the men to carry each body outside the chamber. The two assistants were stonemasons who were already privy to the secret chamber and involved in building the sensitive construction. He locked the door and told the men to fetch a stretcher and to find Rafferty, another overseer to intercept the workmen returning from their break and inform them that they had been granted the day off with pay. Williamson, in the meantime, dumped Sewell's corpse onto a wheelbarrow and pushed it away down another tunnel in the bowels of the labyrinth. He emerged into a vault, placed the wheelbarrow down and took a sledgehammer from it and stared at the brick wall in front of him.

"This is where you belong, Sewer Rat. You can join your vile friends."

The philanthropist used all of his six foot powerful frame to smash the heavy sledgehammer against the brickwork. He pounded and pounded, taking his frustrations out on the brick wall until it was breached. Then he clawed at the bricks until he had pulled away enough of them to crawl through. He tipped the cadaver unceremoniously out of the wheelbarrow and dragged it towards the aperture. He crawled over the rubble and heaved the body through the gap. He returned to the wheelbarrow for a shovel and then began to dig furiously into a huge mound of spoil within the chamber, beads of sweat dripping from his furrowed brow. He dug without pause in a frenzy and then abruptly stopped. He had unearthed MacShane's putrefying head. It spooked him momentarily. He heaped spoil over it and dug adjacent to it hoping he would not disinter Lefèvre. He managed not to and succeeded in excavating an area large enough to conceal the fresh corpse. He dumped the Sewer Rat into it and started to shovel the detritus on top of him. As he did so, his attention was drawn to something protruding from the inside pocket of Sewell's tunic. It was an envelope. He retrieved it. He opened it up and pulled out a letter and glanced at it in the light of a lantern. It was a letter from Fesch. He placed it in his pocket and piled the waste vigorously onto the body until it was completely covered.

Afterwards he paused to read the letter. From the substance of the text, he realised that Fesch still had no idea about his identity nor of the whereabouts of the stele. Sewell, he deduced rightly, was intent on extracting tribute from the cardinal. He returned to the secret chamber to find the two stonemasons waiting for him. They had placed O'Rourke onto the canvas stretcher and covered him with a sheet. Sitting upright against the sandstone wall was Cousseau, his aching head in one hand and his other hand fingering the enormous, contused bump on his cranium. When Williamson appeared, the injured Frenchman spoke to him in French.

"*Qui êtes-vous, monsieur? Où sommes-nous? Je ne connais pas mon nom. Qui*

507

suis-je?" he asked in a state of confusion looking forlornly at those present.

Williamson instantly realized he had lost his memory. He was sympathetic towards the French soldier and grateful for his courageous attempt to save O'Rourke.

Williamson tried to explain. "Your name is Cousseau. You are a French prisoner of war. You have lost your memory. You had a frightful blow to the head."

"You're being repatriated today. To France," added Hughes, one of the stonemasons.

"Check his pockets. See if he has any identification papers," said the other.

Williamson gestured to Cousseau to check his pockets. He pulled out a letter. It was from the Transport Board confirming his release and repatriation on parole and had his name, rank and home address on - *Sergent* Pierre Cousseau, *La Ferme des Mouflons*, Mourèze, Languedoc, France.

"You see, Pierre, Pierre Cousseau. It's you," said the merchant indicating first to the letter and then to the concussed man.

Williamson memorized the address. He was uncertain when the Frenchman would regain his memory, but he saw an opportunity. He was in no doubt why Cousseau had come looking for O'Rourke. To see if he genuinely had the tablet here in Liverpool. As to his motives, he was not quite sure. Attempting to save O'Rourke for a second time and endangering his own life in the process, meant either that they had struck up a bond, a friendship perhaps, which would have led to frank but amicable exchanges about the ivory stele or he was only attempting to keep the overseer alive in order to extricate the truth from him about its whereabouts and recover it for himself. He decided that they would get Cousseau aboard a ship as soon as possible.

"Mr Hughes, take Sergeant Cousseau to the port at once. We don't want him to be stranded in England. Explain to a surgeon that he has had a nasty concussion to the head. A victim of an attempted robbery by rapscallions. We found him and rescued him. Make sure they treat his wound accordingly and make sure he gets priority boarding." He reached into his coat pocket. "Here, take this purse. That should speed up the process."

Hughes pocketed the coins and helped Cousseau to his feet.

"Use some of it to reward yourselves, Rafferty and young McGuire for his vigilance," he whispered out of earshot of Cousseau. "He informed me of the intruders. Tell him his reprimand for ill-discipline has been rescinded."

He turned his attention back to the Frenchman.

"And as for you, *adieu, Monsieur* Cousseau. *La belle France* awaits you."

The Welsh craftsman Hughes led the injured Frenchman away through the tunnels.

"Come on, Mr Patterson," Williamson urged, "grab the other end of the stretcher. Sadly, I have to break the news of Seamus's passing to his family. Sweet Jesus!"

508

209

The frigate reached the open waters of the Irish Sea, the Lancashire littoral diminishing on the starboard side. Many of the freed French soldiers stood on deck in silent contemplation watching it disappear over the horizon. An hour had passed since Cousseau was helped on board. He was given an opium-based sedative to help him sleep. At his side was Glory who had waited for him on the quayside with his personal belongings. The sergeant woke up the following morning feeling groggy when the vessel was somewhere off the coast of Cornwall. As Glory's features came into focus, he recognised them vaguely.

"Pierre. *C'est moi*. Jean. Jean Glory. Do you know me?"

"Jean?" Cousseau replied. "Jean Glory? Yes, you are vaguely familiar."

"I am your friend. Remember? We've shared a prison cell for goodness knows how many years. Here, drink this."

Cousseau drank from a canteen held to his lips. He spluttered. It was brandy. He expected water. He took another slug. His head still throbbed. He fingered the back of his skull.

"You were concussed. Attacked by those wretched street urchins."

Then, suddenly, he shot up with a start from his palliasse.

"No, I wasn't."

"Yes you were. There's a contusion as big as my fist on your head."

"No, I mean, I was concussed but it wasn't because of an attack by waifs. I was in the tunnels."

"The tunnels? What tunnels? Are you sure you are alright Pierre? You are talking *'non-sens'*. The bang on your head was truly severe."

"No. I was in these tunnels. They exist. I went there to find someone. Red Nelson, the gaoler. I think he had something of mine. I remember everything now. He was shot. I jumped from a ledge above and landed on the assailant. Sewell! Sewell! That was his name! That's the last thing I remember before I blacked out. I recall too speaking with a grubby looking overseer in a battered top hat. I have to get back to Liverpool!"

"*Désolé, mon ami*. We are destined for La Rochelle. We're in the middle of the ocean. We're going home! What happened to Red Nelson?"

"I'm not sure. I can't even remember how I boarded the ship. It's all a blur."

Cousseau felt overcome by exhaustion.

"Come, you need to rest. Doctor's orders. Try and sleep. Perhaps you'll remember more when you wake up."

Glory helped him to lie down again. Cousseau closed his eyes. The swell of the sea rocked the vessel, making him feel nauseous. The next time he opened them he was back in France.

210

Seamus O'Rourke's coffin, resting on a cart pulled by two of Williamson's finest horses, was transported to St Peter's Church in Seel Street, the mournful toll of the bells and the clatter of the horses' hooves, the only audible sounds as the solemn cortege arrived. The funeral was well attended by O'Rourke's friends and work colleagues from the tunnels and the gaols. His fellow abolitionists William Roscoe, William Rathbone V and Dr Phillips were also present. The congregation filled every available space with some having to pay their respects from outside. Arthur read a lesson from the Bible, William Roscoe delivered the eulogy, and a chorister performed an emotional requiem. Kitty and the children were inconsolable. He was laid to rest in the church burial grounds. It was a morose, sombre affair until the wake commenced. Williamson had booked the Theatre Royal to celebrate the life of the Irishman. He arranged and paid for everything. Kitty had been told that she and the family could stay at Liver Bird Cottage indefinitely rent free and if he ever had to sell the land, which was a possibility, given the borough's burgeoning demographics, he would arrange for the family to be housed in one of his other properties. This was indeed a relief for Kitty. As was the monthly stipend she was to receive from her employer as part of the promise to her husband that he would take good care of her and the children in the event of his death.

Over the next few weeks Williamson, during a bout of depression, questioned the worth of the stele. He came to the conclusion that he was not interested in its economic value anymore. It had led to the deaths of two of his employees and almost resulted in the taking of his own life. The only consolation was that it had ironically brought O'Rourke's family some sort of prosperity despite the loss of its major bread winner. However, his melancholy and sullen disposition were short-lived. The tablet seemed to have some sort of perverse, talismanic hold on him. Despite the tragic consequences accrued since its possession he felt compelled to continue playing his potentially lethal game. His desire to flirt with danger, to gamble with his future, grew stronger day by day. He was a hunter and now he had become the hunted but felt like a wily fox who had outsmarted his tormenting opponents. His survival instincts were aroused, and he still savoured the opportunity to live life to the full. He began to exude a confidence, emboldened by the letter, that Fesch still knew nothing about him or the existence of the tunnels, despite Sewell's involvement. However, he loathed to touch the artefact again. He was ever more convinced that the script conveyed an ominous portend. It had, to all intents and purposes, become synonymous with tragedy so he determined that the stele would remain hidden until such time Egyptian hieroglyphic pictograms could be fully deciphered or until someone intelligent enough could follow the trail he was to set down. Only then might the potentially portentous message be revealed to the world. He privately hoped this would only be achievable in generations to come but nevertheless he relished a battle of wits with his contemporaries. To the victor, the spoils. For the time being, he immersed himself in his mercantile affairs; his tobacco merchant's business and house construction and returned to his subterranean enterprise, validating his soubriquet - 'The Mole of Edge Hill'.

211

Cardinal Fesch had heard nothing from his contact 'George'. He had received correspondence from Sewell in July stating that he had arrived back in Liverpool in April and was confident of laying his hands on the artefact but had received no word since. The trail had gone dead. With his nephew Napoleon's exile and France's defeat he had more pressing personal matters to attend to, starting with his reconciliation with Pope Pius VII. The letter had been forwarded to the Palazzo Falconieri in Rome where he had taken up residence. His world was turned upside down again in March of the following year when his nephew threw Europe back into the maelstrom of geo-politics by escaping from his exile in Elba. Fesch was subsequently recalled to Lyon to resume his pastoral duties. Whilst he was back at the see in Lyon, a letter arrived from England. It was not the one he hoped for. It was from his anonymous correspondent. The letter detailed that again blood had been shed in pursuit of the artefact. This time it had been, lamentably, someone close to the letter writer. It also confirmed that someone named 'George', who he assumed was the person he had corresponded with, was also dead.

The last tenuous link to the artefact had gone or so it seemed. However, curiously, accompanying the missive, was another drawing of an animal. This time, a *mouflon*, a wild sheep, which was native to his homeland of Corsica and to mainland France. It said that this clue would lead to someone who could possibly reveal the lines of all the hieroglyphs but not the whereabouts of the stele. Someone closer to home. The letter stated that this person was innocent and not privy to the twists and turns of 'our little game' and it urged the Cardinal to ensure that the individual was not threatened or harmed if the Cardinal solved this particular conundrum. Fesch had no intention of seeing anyone else die because of this artefact anyway. He had been shocked by Lefèvre's ruthlessness and spying activities and would never have sanctioned murder as a means to an end. Coercion perhaps, but not assassination. Although it did give him food for thought. It was as if the anonym was admitting that the riddle would never be solved and that he was making his 'game of clues' easier by dangling a tantalising carrot before his eyes. Either that or he was scared that the recipient of the letter might know more about the tablet than was actually perceived and wanted to deflect attention away from himself and onto someone else who was privy to the full text on the artefact. Someone in the south of France perhaps where the *mouflon* prevailed, Fesch assumed. For the time being, he was preoccupied with the events happening so rapidly in France. The Napoleonic Wars had recommenced, and all his thoughts were focused on his resurgent nephew and his newfound ambitions. He placed the letter in another hidden compartment concealed within a chiffonier that stood in his library.

212

Pierre Cousseau had returned to his wife and children during the month of June 1814. The children did not recognize him. Nor he, them. They had grown. He had aged. His wife, Odette, had recognized him only when he had drawn closer. He had appeared over the ridge and made his way down the track to the small holding. She fainted in his arms. They all looked malnourished. Him because of his years of incarceration and his family because of the prevailing harsh conditions in France where food had been requisitioned to feed Napoleon's armies. Nevertheless, they had all survived. Pierre returned to his husbandry, eking out a living.

One day, some months after, he received a notification from a bank in Montpellier. An account had been set up in his name and funds were available for him to withdraw. He could not believe what he was reading. He raced into the ramshackle farmhouse to show Odette. He had no idea who his benefactor was, only that the bank transfer had come from England. When he arrived at the bank two days later, he was passed another letter. Intrigued, he opened it hurriedly. The correspondence stated that this stipend was for his courage and bravery shown when trying to save the life of Seamus O'Rourke. The only condition to him signing the agreement, to give him access to the funds, was a request for him never to set foot in England again. He realised his quest for the stele would have to be surrendered but these funds more than compensated for it. They exceeded his wildest dreams, and he was not in a position to look a gift horse in the mouth. Curiously there was a picture of a *mouflon* with the note. The mysterious benefactor asked him to keep the picture of the wild sheep safe with the print of the hieroglyphs he had in his possession. The letter he could destroy. He stood for a moment perplexed and pensive. Who had he told that the hieroglyphic print existed? He then snatched the quill enthusiastically from the bank clerk's grasp and signed the document without hesitation. Whoever had possession of the stele therefore, he surmised, was already wealthy or had perhaps sold it on at a profit.

On his jubilant return to the farm, he placed the illustration and hieroglyphic print into the base of a wooden craft he had manufactured in the Tower Gaol, a souvenir of his time there. He paused to reflect on the item that reminded him of Red Nelson. He had made the same, identical vessel for himself, the frigate l'*Égyptienne* since they both had memories of it.

213

The Battle of Waterloo on the 18th of June 1815 proved to be Napoleon's final attempt to resurrect his empire. The armies of Wellington and the Prussian Blücher, however, won the day. Cousseau, despite his upturn in fortunes and despite the imploring of Odette, could not ignore the cajoling of some of his old comrades in the guards and could not resist the patriotic call to arms.

214

It was late July 1815 before Pierre Cousseau returned to his family. Fortunately, he had again survived the carnage, just, as part of the Old Guard, thrown into the fray at the last moment to salvage the day. The Middle Guard had been annihilated by fierce withering fire from the British and Prussians, but the Old Guard held firm fighting a rear guard action to secure the safety of the remnants of the French army. He was involved in a skirmish with a British unit which resulted in the death of Glory, his old companion in arms from the Peninsula Wars, cut down by a sharpshooter. He returned fire at the marksman who had killed his friend, his black features distinctive under his Belgic shako. He missed by inches, seeing the British marksman flinch. Having reloaded his Brown Bess, the British soldier took aim again. Cousseau instinctively ducked and seconds later his bearskin was ripped off his head by the lead shot. His company was ordered to retreat. The situation had become more acute and chaotic with French foot soldiers and cavalry fleeing in every direction, but the grenadiers remained steadfast and orderly until the realisation that all was lost. Once the enemy had stopped pursuing them they joined the massed but ragged ranks of the defeated on their solemn march back to French territory.

215

Patrice Verzon watched from a ridge, exhausted, next to his fellow sharpshooters, in the immediate aftermath of the battle as human vultures swooped down on his fallen comrades and the dead of the enemy, scouring the battlefield for souvenirs and possessions. The opportunists stripped the bodies of anything valuable, even prising teeth from the twisted mouths of young, deceased combatants. The much sought-after dentition to be sold on, to be marketed as 'Waterloo teeth'. The former slave had survived another battle. He had found himself back on the island of Zakynthos in the Ionian Islands with his regiment expulsing the French garrison and then he had been part of the Royal Corsican forces that captured Fort Cattaro in 1814, modern day Kotor on the Adriatic. He decided to desert from there, taking advantage of the ending of the War of the Sixth Coalition with Napoleon's abdication and exile on Elba, by joining the swell of displaced refugees, ex-combatants and newly released prisoners migrating across Europe. He made his way across the continent to Brussels taking labouring jobs where he could, but he struggled to find meaningful work and when Napoleon's resurgence prompted the Hundred Days War he volunteered his services again, re-enlisting with the Rifle Corps, the 95th Regiment of Foot on its arrival in the country from England. At least the half-starved drifter was guaranteed to be fed each day. It was a stark choice. Defeat at Waterloo for the French meant that the vanquished Napoleon was sent into exile again, this time for good, to the island of St Helena in the South Atlantic. As for Cardinal Joseph Fesch, he was allowed to retire to Rome, where he lived peacefully until his death in 1839.

Back in Liverpool, Joseph Williamson's subterranean and terrestrial works continued. A steady flow of unemployed and disabled soldiers returning from Waterloo or beyond turned up at the gates to the tunnels. The philanthropic gentleman took on as many as he could. Frederick Kennedy was one, identified by Williamson as Seamus O'Rourke's companion. He was immediately employed as a carpenter. One cold, rainy December morning a solitary figure stood at the gates, huddled in his great coat to protect him from the elements. Joseph Williamson appeared in a jaunting car shortly after. As Williamson instructed the jarvey to park up his carriage he noticed the shivering black man attempting forlornly to shield himself from the elements. He looked as if he was waiting for someone. Williamson approached him and inquired of his presence at the gates.

"Hello, sir! You seem to be awaiting someone. May I inquire whom it is?"

"Oh, good morning, sir. Indeed. I am waiting for a friend. Name of Seamus O'Rourke. He told me he might be able to fix me up with some employment if I was ever in Liverpool. I have just returned from the United Kingdom of the Netherlands. I fought at Waterloo."

"You and your brethren in arms did a fine job, let me say, my man. Let's hope Bonaparte does not escape from the South Atlantic or you'll be obliged to take the King's shilling again! A friend of Seamus O'Rourke's, say you? Well, you'll have a long wait. I'm afraid he passed away last year, sadly."

"He's deceased? Oh, my good lord! How?"

"He was assailed by a scoundrel seeking vengeance. He was shot, I'm afraid. I held Seamus in high regard. He was an overseer here in the tunnels."

"He was a good friend to me. I will seek out his family to see if I can help them in any way," Verzon stated solemnly. He stayed silent for a moment.

"His family are fine. I'm taking care of them. They want for nothing. I'm Joseph Williamson by the way."

Verzon bowed theatrically. "Ah, so you sir are the 'King of Edge Hill'. Seamus mentioned you in a letter and spoke fondly of you. He told me of his employ excavating tunnels." He bowed again.

"No need to do that my good sir. Pray tell me, did Seamus owe you anything?"

"I saved his life once, but he also saved mine, so I think all is even."

"Well, a friend of Seamus's is a friend of mine, Mr..?"

"Verzon. Patrice Verzon at your service, sir."

"Well, Mr Verzon, I may then have a position for you."

"What? That's wonderful news, sir!"

"You're big and muscular, I see. Have you had any experience of overseeing men?"

"I was a sergeant with the Royal Corsican Regiment."

"My, how exotic. The Royal Corsicans, eh? Splendid! Just the calibre of man I need to oversee in my tunnels. I have not really had anyone as good as Seamus since. I was waiting for someone with a similar physique and affable disposition to come along and you seem to be suitable, Patrice. Your first concern was to take care of his family, although I suspect you're finances are diminished. I like those qualities in a man. Come, we'll get out of this damned rain. There's a hut and brazier just outside the tunnels. You dry off in there and have some hot tea and a biscuit whilst I make some arrangements for you to tour the site and meet the labourers, craftsmen and other foremen. They'll set you right and you can start officially tomorrow. I'll pay you for today as well. I'll sort your terms out later."

"Mr Williamson, sir. Thank you so much for your kindness. You truly act like a benevolent king. God love you!"

"Oh! For goodness sake! All this approbation is too much for me. I think I'll just persist with the soubriquet the 'Mole of Edge Hill' instead! Betty, my wife, calls me so. I'm certainly no king by her reckoning."

517

216

Joseph Williamson never did hear from Joseph Fesch again. His 'game of clues' had offered up seven illustrations to discover in total, excluding the *mouflon* illustration. He continued to philanthropically employ returning Napoleonic British soldiers, especially those who had been maimed or stricken with illness due to their wartime experiences. His subterranean labyrinth continued to expand exponentially, year on year. In later years Patrice Verzon, who married and settled in the area, loved to tell his children tales of the tunnels, like the day when he met the renowned engineer George Stephenson. The overseer and his group of labourers were working underground when spades penetrated the earth above them. An aggrieved Verzon popped his head up through a hole to rebuke those who were putting them in danger and inadvertently scared the wits out of everyone there. Some of the working party on the surface, busy digging a stretch of the Wapping Tunnel of the Liverpool to Manchester railway, were terrified believing that they had excavated through to the very depths of hell when they saw Verzon and numerous other grimy faces emerging out of the soil.

Stephenson, who was, at this time, residing in Liverpool, in Upper Parliament Street, Toxteth, inspected Williamson's tunnels and was impressed by the quality of the workmanship. This resulted in some of the men being instantly offered jobs building the world's first inter-city rail route, an arrangement that Williamson was more than happy to sanction, since the skills his workforce had learnt would be put to good use. The pay was better and that would free up space for the philanthropist to employ more of the needy of the town. Furthermore, the rich merchant had invested in the rail scheme, and he trusted the men he bequeathed to George Stephenson to be a success for their new employer. Verzon was one of the workers who signed up with the blessing of his benefactor to Stephenson's cause and Williamson was there, on that grandiose but ultimately tragic day the 15th of September 1830, aboard a carriage pulled by the steam locomotive, *Stephenson's Rocket*. Mr Williamson subsequently enjoyed meeting the Prime Minister, the Duke of Wellington who was on another locomotive, *the Northumbria*, on the adjacent track but his day was marred when MP William Huskisson, was struck by *the Rocket* and later died.

It would be ten more years before 'The Mole of Edge Hill' departed this earth. As for Patrice Verzon, he had returned to the employ of Joseph Williamson five years earlier in 1835 after an industrial injury curtailed his service building railways, only to die in the tunnels a few years later in an industrial accident.

217

Liverpool. Present day.

"The Williamson Tunnels?" Calder reiterated.

"Yes, welcome," Tony said.

Edwin Calder glanced over to Paul and smirked.

"I've only got time to show you the Paddington section of the tunnels."

Two other men, donned in hard hats and hi-vis jackets emerged from the tunnels' entrance, covered in dirt, having spent the day excavating below ground.

"Gentlemen, if you follow them around the corner to Williamson's House, I'll fit you both out with a hi-vis and hard hat."

Ten minutes later they returned to the tunnels' entrance having been briefed on health and safety issues and what was left of Joseph Williamson's 'house', a mere ruined brick façade. They went down the steps passing another worker who was coming up and paused at a display of newspaper cuttings, articles and maps whilst the tour guide introduced them to Joseph Williamson, 'The Mole of Edge Hill'. Calder glanced again at Paul and just nodded his approval. They moved down another flight of steps after being shown earthenware extracted from the spoil and waste that had filled the tunnels years after they were dug in the early 19th century. Calder, intrigued, began to ask questions.

"How far do the tunnels go?"

"We're not exactly sure but a few miles at least in each direction according to historic reports. What we have excavated here is just the tip of the iceberg."

"Why were the tunnels dug?"

"We're not sure of the real reason but a 19th century blogger reckoned the only reason they were excavated was to give returning British soldiers some form of employment after the Napoleonic Wars. It's like one big philanthropic folly."

Paul was racking his brain to try and devise an exit strategy. Calder seemed fascinated. His interest in the history of the tunnels was genuine but only for what he might find there.

"Have you found anything of interest?"

"Come this way. I'll show you our 'finds'.

The guide, Tony, took them into a dim-lit cavernous two-storey chamber carved out of the red sandstone rock, and escorted them to an arced brick aperture in the stone wall overlooking the lower chamber. Paul glanced down from the precipice and was taken aback by the thirty foot drop. 'I wish,' he thought.

Calder had a quick eye-brow raising look too. Then his attention was drawn to an array of artefacts that had been dug out of the detritus of the tunnels. Clay pipes, broken crockery, pots and jars, broken children's toys, cutlery and other items. His attention was drawn to a delicate porcelain cup that when held up to the light revealed a portrait of King Edward VII, that was not visible otherwise.

"That's insured, that one."

"Very interesting. I'm an antiques dealer myself. Maybe we can talk business."

Tony laughed and continued his tour, bringing his visitors' attention to the craftsmanship displayed in the vaulted brick arches in the chamber. They then went down a flight of steps to the bottom of the cavern.

"The skills gained here would serve the men well. Many went on to build the Liverpool-Manchester railway, the first inter-city railway in the world, leaving more unemployed men to fill their worn shoes, giving them an opportunity also to feed their families."

At this point another worker shouted down from above.

"Tony! I'm off! Don't forget to switch the lights off at the portacabin."

"Ok, Ted. See you tomorrow."

"So, this chamber has been completely excavated? There's no other tunnels leading out of here?" Calder asked.

"There is but we haven't got permission to dig them yet. We're working on it. We know there's one at the top of the stairs where you saw those large, glazed stoneware jars."

Calder had a good look around the chamber on both levels, as did Paul, who from time to time, felt the barrel of the antique dealers gun in the small of his back, just to remind him who was in charge. They listened attentively to the tour guide as he waxed lyrical about the eccentric philanthropist Joseph Williamson for any clue about the hidden tablet.

"One anecdote called 'the Beanfest' entailed Joseph Williamson inviting some friends and other prominent guests to his mansion for dinner. Those guests entered a large room and were invited to sit at a sparsely laid wooden table with inferior crockery and cutlery that one would not expect at a supposedly lavish banquet prepared by a wealthy gentleman of that time."

"Certainly not!" Calder said.

"The feast was then presented to them. Apparently a vile mixture of bacon and beans. Many of those invited, left in high dudgeon, offended. Williamson, unperturbed, turned to those who remained and laughed. He said now I know who my friends are, please follow me upstairs where, to their amazement, was the promised lavish banquet."

"He seemed a bit of a character then, the Mole of Edge Hill," Calder stated.

Paul remained silent.

"Oh yes, indeed. If I had more time I'd tell you other recollections of him."

They trudged back up the wooden staircase.

"Any other tunnels?"

"Under Williamson's house. Our other tunnels start from there. And then there's the tunnels on Smithdown Lane but they're administered by another association."

"Can we have a look at those as well?"

"Well, Smithdown Lane will be closed. They charge for entry. It'll be open in the morning."

"What about the tunnels under the house then?"

"I'm afraid you can't see them today. This is the last tour, but I can tell you we've been making good progress there. We've just unearthed another entrance to, we reckon, another vault so maybe you can come and visit tomorrow or another day or even get involved by volunteering to help us excavate it."

Then suddenly Calder whipped out his firearm and jabbed it menacingly towards Tony who instantly freaked out.

"Shit! A gun! What the hell is going on?"

"Forget about tomorrow. We've got all night. I hope you haven't made any plans this evening, Tony."

"A-as a matter of fact I have. Royal Court. Mam I'm 'ere."

"What? Well, tough. The only fucking thing you're doing tonight is digging, with him!"

He shoved Paul towards the petrified tour guide. "Take your phones out carefully and place them on the table."

Tony glanced over at Paul.

"Do as he says."

"W-what do you hope to find here? I-I don't understand," Tony stuttered as they both put their mobiles down.

"Don't you recognise our intrepid guest here?"

Tony scrutinized Paul.

"He looks familiar but-"

Then it dawned on him who he was.

"You're from Team Quest. The ivory tablet! What? You think it's in here?" He laughed disbelievingly. Paul nodded.

"I've just found the last clue. It was a picture, of a mole."

"A mole? That's amazing! That'll really put us on the map! But, why the gun?" Tony asked.

"Because he's a greedy bastard. He doesn't want to share the artefact with the world."

"That's absurd! Besides, there's miles of tunnels down here. It'll take you forever to find it. Not in one night's digging."

"Absurd is not in the lexicon of this deranged, avaricious man. Neither is impossible."

"Enough!" Calder snarled. "Take us to the other tunnels now!"

Tony remained rooted to the spot until Calder fired at a large earthenware jug which shattered into pieces.

"Ok! No more shooting!" Tony pleaded. "I'll take you now!"

218

The three emerged from the Paddington tunnels. Tony, his hands shaking, locked up the entrance and then Calder forced the two captives at gunpoint around the corner to the other nearby site. No one was around. Tony led them to a metal hatch on the derelict land where Joseph Williamson's house once stood in Mason Street. He opened up the hatch to reveal a small ladder descending underground. They climbed down into a small chamber and Tony led them through a narrow vertical gap that had been hacked out of the sandstone. They emerged into a larger, wider chamber. He led them to the end of the vault and showed them the area they had been excavating. The spoil had been dug away to reveal an aperture which was not yet accessible.

"Right. Get those spades over there and start digging. Move!" Calder growled.

Paul and Tony grabbed a spade each and began to dig into the spoil. Tony went to get a bucket to put the mainly burnt charcoal matter in. The spoil had filled the tunnels after being dumped through shafts from street level by the residents of the former houses and business premises that no longer existed in the surrounding roads. Calder, however, stopped him and told him to just dig. They threw the detritus to one side instead.

"Do you know, Mr De Vere. You'd be dead by now if so many of my men hadn't got themselves killed. Idiots! All of them. Maybe I should have employed you instead. But I suppose we're all prone to mistakes. I regret not whipping this gun out when your colleagues were still here, Tony. There would have been four or five of you to dig for my tablet."

"The police are out there right now looking for you and Jules."

"I thought I told you not to involve the police!"

"You did but you didn't tell me not to tell anyone else. By now, your name is on every news bulletin, I would imagine."

"Why you-"

"Go ahead and shoot me."

Calder raised his pistol and scowled. He pointed it at Paul's head. Paul could see the intent in his eyes and the hatred and desperation expressed in his grimace, but then he hesitated. He knew he still needed Paul. He lowered the gun and took out his mobile.

"I don't need that bitch Johnson now though, do I?" Calder said, smirking.

He pressed the name of Dreyfuss on his phone and placed the mobile to his ear. Paul's anguish increased. His mind was racing.

"Shit! There's no signal," the antiques dealer cursed.

Paul sighed in relief.

"Listen, you do need her. She's another pair of hands. She's used to this type of work, to a degree. And you've probably got a heavy or two watching her. They could help as well."

Calder thought for one moment. He then walked up to Tony and put the barrel to his head. Tony shook with fear.

"Now Tony, is there any other way out of this chamber?"

"N-no! Just the way we came in."

"Are you sure?"

"P-p-positive!"

"Right, I'm going up top to make a call. If you two aren't here digging when I get back, I'll go straight back up that ladder and call Dreyfuss to finish off Johnson. I swear it! Capiche?"

Both captives nodded. Tony heaved a sigh of relief. Calder backed away and squeezed through the tight aperture between the sandstone walls.

"Tony, is there another way out of here?" Paul whispered.

"No."

"What's that up there?"

Paul pointed to a shaft high up on the sandstone rock 40 feet above them.

"It's a short tunnel that leads to nowhere."

"How do I get up there?"

"Down the side of that heap of spoil over there. We have an extended ladder. Calder hasn't seen it. It's well concealed."

"Well, listen I'm going up there."

"But he'll kill me."

"I think he was just bluffing. He needs you more than ever now."

"He's deluded if he thinks we're going to find the tablet in the next vault. There's miles of tunnels as I've already told him."

"Just keep digging. As far as you're concerned you tried to stop me. Ok? Sorry about this."

Paul punched him and knocked him out. Tony wilted onto the mound of spoil. Paul then found the concealed ladder, propped it against the sandstone rock and began to climb up it towards the shaft. It was a bit precarious, but he managed to haul himself into the shaft. He pushed the ladder sideways until it toppled to the ground and then began to explore the narrow tunnel. Fifty yards further up it came to a dead end. The entrance was blocked, and it was impossible for anyone to squeeze through. Suddenly he heard Calder shouting.

"Where are you? You fucking tramp!"

He heard him screaming at Tony. "Wake up! You useless fucking turd! Wake up!"

Calder slapped him but he didn't respond. He looked around and found a glass carafe of liquid. He sniffed it. He jerked his head back.

"Piss! They must piss into it when they're working," he snorted.

He poured the pungent contents over Tony's face. It had the desired effect. Tony twitched and gradually came round. Calder smashed the glass jar impulsively against the stone wall.

"Where is he? Tell me now." He started to shake the dazed tour guide violently.

523

"You said there was no other way out! Where the hell is he? You useless piece of shit!"

Tony, groggily, sat up, and fingered his tender, bruised chin tentatively.

"Ouch! He just hit me! He must have hidden in the other chamber and sneaked out when you came back down," Tony lied. "Ugh! I stink of piss!"

Calder rushed back to the narrow passageway and squeezed through the other chamber again, brandishing his pistol. He spotted a small tunnel, like a vent, and crept towards it. He put on his phone torch and shined it into the opening. There was no one there, so he cautiously climbed up on to a mound of spoil and shone the torch over the back of it.

"Damn it! He must have gone out!"

He returned to Tony and ordered him to keep digging. He paced up and down impatiently waiting for Dreyfuss to arrive. Fifteen minutes later he went back up to the entrance. Paul remained hidden in the shaft. Dreyfuss's vehicle was now outside parked by the portacabin that housed the office of the Friends of Williamson Tunnels. Dreyfuss watched as a hatch in the ground opened and Calder emerged from it. His boss signalled to him. Dreyfuss got out and opened the boot and dragged a remonstrating bound and gagged Jules out of it. He shoved her towards Calder.

"Undo her."

Dreyfuss split the cable ties binding her hands behind her back with a knife and led her at gunpoint to the hatch. She went to remove the gag from her mouth, but he placed the blade under her chin, and grinned, spitefully, shaking his head before shoving her forcefully forward.

"Get down there!"

She turned herself around and gave Dreyfuss a dirty look. Hands shaking, she grasped the top of the secured ladder and stepped on to a rung and descended. She had visited the tunnels before and suddenly it dawned on her why she was there. The final clue must have been a mole. She was unaware of Paul and Miles's fate. She feared the worst and tears welled up in her eyes. Her mascara had previously left smudged black tributaries smeared down each cheek. Calder was next to go, followed by Dreyfuss. He pushed her through to the other vault, thrust a shovel in her hands and ordered her to dig.

"Who are you?" Tony enquired.

"This is the esteemed Dr Jules Johnson," Calder explained.

"Of course, you're the archaeologist, aren't you?"

The gagged woman simply nodded, her moist eyes betraying her feelings.

"I'm Tony, one of the members of the Friends Of Williamson Tunnels."

"Enough chitchat! Get digging!"

Calder passed another spade to Dreyfuss who looked surprised.

"I've lost one. He's escaped but he won't dare contact the police."

Jules's reddened eyes opened wide. "Paul!" blurted a muffled Jules. "Is that Paul?"

"What are you saying?" Tony asked.

"She's asking if the escapee is Paul, her lover," Calder sneered.

524

Tony nodded and pointed to his face. "He chinned me. He's very much alive!"

"Not for long!" Calder spat.

Tony suddenly felt in his pockets. "The keys. They're gone! He must have returned to Paddington. His mobile's in there!"

"What? Are there any more keys to the door of those tunnels?"

"There's a set in the portacabin. In the filing cabinet," Tony admitted under duress.

"Stephane, you stay here. I'll go and check. I know where the entrance is. Any problems with these two, put a bullet through a leg. They can dig on their knees with their bare hands as far as I'm concerned."

"Right, boss."

219

Calder departed again to check the Paddington tunnels. He knew he still held the upper hand. He wanted to kill Paul, there and then, but he was still short of manpower and needed him alive for the time being. He was confident that Paul would not involve the police. Paul lay on his stomach in the shaft overlooking the chamber. He desperately wanted to call out to the woman he loved but he remained hidden. It became apparent to him that he had to act fast. He needed to attract Tony's attention to get him to lure Dreyfuss over to the side of the chamber below the shaft. Paul grabbed a stone, part of some rubble that was in the narrow passageway and threw it over to the other side of the vault. It hit the solid wall of rock making a noise.

"What was that?" Dreyfuss inquired, alerted to the noise.

The three of them looked around.

"Probably one of the ghosts of the workers who lost their lives in the tunnels when they were first dug. Or the hooded priest who's been seen floating through the chambers on many occasions. They're always playing tricks on us."

"Ghosts?" Dreyfuss replied. "A hooded priest?"

Tony glanced up at the shaft to see Paul gesticulating. He twigged that Paul wanted him somehow, to get Dreyfuss to stand underneath the shaft.

"Boss, I need to take a piss."

"You stink of piss already. No need. Have you pissed yourself? Ha! Ha!"

"No, boss. The big cheese poured a bottle of urine over me."

"Ha! Ha! Ha!"

"We use the bottle to piss in, but he's smashed it."

"Please boss, I need a pee. Can I go over there?"

Tony pointed to the side of the chamber. Paul ducked his head down.

"Ok. Be quick!"

Tony went across to the sandstone wall and stood below the shaft and peed. Suddenly he screamed. "Argh!"

"Hey, what's up, man?" Dreyfuss asked alarmed.

"My dick! I've got it caught in my zip! Argh!"

Dreyfuss just laughed. Jules cringed.

"Your day's just got worse! Ha! Ha! I've got to see this!"

The henchman, gun still in his grasp, went across to Tony. His concentration was on Tony's manhood. He chortled again. Tony furtively glanced up and saw Paul, crouched, ready to leap. The tour guide feigned injury.

"Argh! I wouldn't wish this on my worst enemy. Argh! Maybe you are my worst enemy."

"Ha! Ha! Ha! Let's have a look then. Shall I shoot it off? Ha! Ha! You better pray it's big enough or your balls will be flying off as well."

"Argh! Please help!"

Dreyfuss drew closer. Tony sank to his knees with a pained expression and indicated his organ, all with the intent of providing Paul with a better sight of his target. The Frenchman, head bowed in search of Tony's trapped foreskin, lowered his gun. Suddenly Tony threw himself to one side, the cue for Paul to leap off the ledge. He came crashing down onto Dreyfuss's barrel chest propelling him backwards before he had time to raise his weapon. He fell on the uneven bedrock. Paul landed on a mound of spoil, the blow knocking the wind out of him. The guard, dazed and shocked at the sudden assault, still managed to keep hold of his pistol. He attempted to get up raising the gun. Tony scrambled over the mound of spoil and cowered behind it, feeling helpless.

"You bastard!" Dreyfuss shouted. Paul got to his feet gingerly. Suddenly a spade slammed into the Frenchman's hand forcing him to drop the firearm.

"Argh! *Putain!*" he screamed.

He turned to see Jules holding the spade ready to hit him again. He put his arm up to parry the next blow and punched Jules on the head with his clenched fist. She fell back. Paul dived for the gun, but Dreyfuss got there first. Paul sprang up again and bravely tackled the brute. A shot rang out, but Paul had managed to divert the firearm away from him by grabbing the Frenchman's wrists. Pain seared through Dreyfuss's hand, weakened by the blow from the spade. They struggled. His adversary managed to get his finger on the trigger and in a titanic contest of strength and willpower, the Englishman prevailed, shooting Dreyfuss in the leg. He screamed again but still battled for ownership of the gun until suddenly there was a sound of a dull thud, and he sank to the floor. Tony stood over him with the spade, hands shaking. Blood oozed from the crony's fractured skull. He lay there motionless. Paul got up and rushed to Jules's side. She was groggy and the side of her head was swollen and cut. He removed the gag from her mouth.

"Jules! Are you alright?" Paul cradled her in his arms. He kissed her. She momentarily enjoyed the sensation of his lips and felt the reassuring warmth of his embrace. She nodded and smiled weakly, then grimaced as her senses refocused on her aching temple.

"Tony, take care of her."

220

Paul seized the handgun and squeezed through the gap to the entrance. He climbed the ladder and carefully eased the hatch open. He scanned the derelict yard. He detected nothing. He went to the front gate and peered both ways down the road. It was clear. He ran to the corner of the quiet side road, paused and looked right. It was still clear, so he crept up to the entrance of the tunnels and carefully tried the metal hatch. It was open. Calder was still in there. Paul ventured in and descended the steps quietly and furtively. The dim lights lit his way. He entered the vault where the artefacts were displayed and heard a noise down in the cavernous chamber below. He looked over the edge. It was Calder ripping a tarpaulin away from a workbench searching for him. Suddenly Paul heard another sound of footsteps coming down the stone steps from the entrance. He hid under the long wooden table that displayed the plethora of discovered objects and waited. A figure appeared around the corner. Paul's relief was palpable. The welcoming sight of DS Noades, holding a firearm, gave him reassurance.

"Detective Noades," he whispered.

She nervously pointed the gun in Paul's direction as soon as she heard her name being called. Paul crawled out from under the table. He had tucked his weapon into the back of his trousers. He indicated to Noades that the danger was below. She looked down over the edge and saw Calder.

"The game's up Calder! Dreyfuss is down and the police are here. You're trapped!" Paul shouted into the void.

Calder looked swiftly up to see Paul and DS Noades on the level above him, peering down from the aperture. Unexpectedly Calder began to laugh.

"Why's he laughing?" Paul asked, staring at him.

"Because of this," Noades answered.

He turned to see the detective pointing her gun at him.

"Easy De Vere. Turn around."

"What? He's responsible for all the killings! Edwin Calder! Down there!"

She relieved him of his firearm.

"Edwin!" she called. "Come up! I've got him!"

Calder climbed the staircase as fast as he could and joined them on the upper level.

"Ah, *enchanté* Maggie. It's good to know I can rely on the brotherhood of Graelians," he said as he gasped for air. "Or the sisterhood, to be precise. Did you secure the hatch?"

"As you wished. The others can't escape."

"So, you're another of these weirdos who likes to get naked. How come you know each other?" Paul remarked caustically.

528

"We met at an initiation camp a few years back in France," Calder replied. "We know each other very well after sharing the same carnal pleasures of our sex-positive group."

"That's the hump-anything-that-moves-gang, I presume," Paul retorted. "I thought you were a dyke anyway, the way you looked at Jules."

"I swing both ways, darling. Pity you and the delectable Ms Johnson aren't believers I would have fancied another *ménage à trois*."

"You'll just have to settle for Adonis over there. Why not throw a donkey into the mix as well to make up the threesome? Anyway, what's your motive?"

"I'm a Grailien, too, of course. I believe in the UFO and alien doctrine, first and foremost, but, you're right, one cannot turn a blind eye to the riches and luxuries on offer. Wealth is power. It's alluring. A vehicle for self-advancement since I have other ambitions too. Not just financial ones. I need to raise my profile in the movement if I'm to be chosen as a Rainbow Angel or even a Shining Light Angel which would give me the honour of liaising with the Elohim when they arrive on Earth."

"Let me guess. 'Liaising.' That must be a euphemism for -"

"That's enough!" Calder snapped abruptly.

But Paul persevered.

"UFO religion? You're having a laugh. More like a UFM religion. *U Fuck Me.*"

Calder menacingly raised his gun. "I said that's enough!"

"What do we do with him now?" Noades asked.

"I'd like to kill him, slowly and painfully," Calder snarled. "Perhaps auto-da-fé style. You know, my former religion, Catholicism does have its merits. Corda, yes, corda or strappado as they called it would be an ideal torture to undertake right here, right now, the victim suspended over this chasm. Funny how things pop into your mind. Cruel and horrific, I know, but times were hard in those days."

"Sounds like a good suggestion, Edwin."

"The lives of the ex-soldiers who built these tunnels would bear testimony to the hardships of that that epoch. But many of us have experienced hard times. One of my forebears spent his childhood in a workhouse, his mother a drunken whore, his father, actually, the brother of his mother, taboo subject I know, to the family's shame, allegedly a violent, good-for-nothing sailor who just apparently disappeared off the face of this Earth. Last seen in Liverpool, would you believe!"

"Fancy that. Just like Mr De Vere," Noades teased.

"At least my ancestors' pathetic, wretched lives were not in vain. They led to something positive. Me. They fuelled my interest in genealogy and history. Passions that have bequeathed me a reasonable amount of wealth and will secure me the greatest prize known to man."

"You're deluded, Calder," Paul said derisorily. "It could take months to find the stele in here."

"Or it could just be waiting to be discovered in the next chamber. Who knows? I'm sure DS Noades can concoct a story about a corpse being found on the land above the tunnels and have the area sealed off. That'll give me time to source some desperados, you know crackheads and wasters and the like, perhaps even the local

529

unemployed, to do the spade work just like the amazing Mr Joseph Williamson did all those years ago."

"That's plausible Edwin."

"Yes indeed Maggie. Do you know? I admire that man so much after hearing his story. Now, which corpse do you think we should use Maggie? De Vere's, our lovely Dr Johnson's or poor piss-stained Tony's? Of course, the other two bodies, we'll just have to bury in the tunnels. Another flash of inspiration."

"I think the other geezer. It would be crass of us not to bury the two lovers together, don't you think? After all, love is at the heart of our religion."

"You wouldn't be able to spin these lies to Armitage. She'd never believe you. Or is she in on it also?" Paul spat.

"No, she's not actually. She's on leave. Bereavement leave. Her junkie son was found floating in Birkenhead docks this morning. I needed to get her out of the way somehow, when my fellow Grailien, Edwin, called for my assistance. I pledge my loyalty to the sect above all. The architect of his demise should be with us shortly. The extra shot of heroin did the trick."

"Reinforcements! Hallelujah!" Calder shouted in celebration.

The entrance hatch could be heard opening again. A voice called out, vaguely familiar to Paul.

"Noades! Are you down there?"

"Aye!"

He heard footsteps coming down the steps. His senses were scrambled as he set eyes on someone appearing in the chamber whom he did not expect. It was Ibrahim Shaqtar. The gentleman he had met at the Lady Lever in the company of Calder.

"Ah! Ibrahim. Nice of you to make it. We've been waiting for you."

"Edwin. What's happening?" Ibrahim asked visibly shocked on seeing the firearm brandished by Calder.

More footsteps were heard. Paul's train of thought became clearer now as Richard entered, carrying a handgun.

"You! I thought the voice was familiar."

"Ah! If it's not the dirty fucking tramp!"

Richard, his mouth twisted in hate, raised his firearm threateningly and pointed it at Paul.

"Control your gorilla, Maggie."

"Richard! Behave!" she spat. "You can have him later. We need him for now."

"So, what's that worthless piece of shit doing here?"

Richard glowered menacingly. He could not resist. He suddenly launched himself forward and hit Paul with the back of his hand.

"Enough Richard!" Noades bellowed. She pushed him back.

Paul stood defiantly. He wiped the blood from his cut lip and stared down his attacker.

"I've done him a deal. Get the charges lessened or dropped completely."

"Edwin? Please tell me what the hell is going on?" Ibrahim said imploringly, his expression one of increasing concern.

Calder turned his attention to his friend. He pointed the gun at him. Alarm spread across Ibrahim's features.

"I'm sorry I had to rope you in on this Ibrahim. You're the only other person I know in Liverpool to call on. You've been very helpful so far. I'm also sorry you had to put up with that idiot Tufiq. He wasn't who he seemed, was he? Neither, for that matter, am I. We need another pair of hands to search for the ivory tablet, you see, which is hidden somewhere in this subterranean labyrinth. You still have some use to me for now."

"Edwin! You shock me. I -"

"Shut up you gullible fool!" Calder shouted viciously.

Suddenly, from a dark recess of the chamber, a cloaked, hooded figure emerged. It seemed to float, like an apparition, drifting silently towards the unsuspecting corrupt detective Noades. Paul froze. He was the first to see it. He could not believe his eyes. He felt a shiver down his spine. Before he knew how to react, Noades let out a blood-curdling scream and lurched forward, her eyes wide with terror. Her contorted face smacked sickeningly onto the hard stone floor, a pickaxe wedged in her skull. Calder, shocked and in fear, raised his gun instinctively and fired indiscriminately. The 'apparition' collapsed to the ground with an audible grunt. Paul, seizing his opportunity, leapt into action. He sprang forward and butted Richard whose attention was on the 'apparition'. He groaned in agony. Paul grabbed his arm, tripped him and slung him to the floor judo-like, snapping his wrist in the process. Then he knocked his opponent out with a vicious punch. Out the corner of his eye, he saw Ibrahim courageously tackle his former so-called friend. A shot rang out and Ibrahim slumped to the floor. Paul, having ripped the gun from Richard's grasp pointed it at Calder and fired. The chamber clicked three or four times. It was empty. Noades, he thought, must not have trusted him enough with a loaded gun. He threw the firearm at Calder, striking him on the cheek, disrupting his aim. A bullet ricocheted off the ceiling of the chamber. Paul surged forward grappling with Calder to wrestle the gun from his control. He forced the older man back towards a barrier and shoved him into it, knocking him off balance again. The plastic barrier gave way and Calder fired off the pistol again but as he attempted to place his foot on the ground, his leg extended down a hole in the stone floor. His sacrum jarred when his coccyx connected with the edge of the hole, and he grunted in pain. His left leg followed his right one through the gap in the floor and almost simultaneously his elbow and wrist then forcefully banged down hard on the stone edge of the hole and the firearm was dislodged from his grasp, clattering down onto the bedrock below from the fifty foot drop. Calder clung on desperately to the edge of the hole with both hands. He tried to get some purchase but did not have the strength to pull himself up.

"Help me, De Vere! Help me!" he beseeched. "I've got money!"

Paul had slumped to the floor, kneeling in front of him, a bullet through his gut. He held his bloodied hands to his equally blood-soaked abdomen. He watched dispassionately as Calder's fingers clawed at the stone. He gazed at the anguished, terrified countenance in front of him and smiled before collapsing.

531

"Aghhhh!" Calder screamed as he fell to his death, his crumpled body spread-eagled on the sandstone bedrock below.

The 'apparition' groaned and removed its hood slowly. Penny's swollen, bruised brow bled and hurt but not as much as the shoulder that had taken the brunt of the slug. She had fallen with the impact of the projectile and knocked herself out. She looked up, dazed. Her eyes focused on Ibrahim's lifeless body first. She then spotted some movement in his fingers. He was still alive. She noticed Paul in front of her slumped on the floor next to Noades. Penny's heart pounded like a drum, and she felt nauseous.

"Paul! Paul!" she called. "Oh God!"

She dragged herself up and went over to Paul and turned him over. He was still breathing. She looked through the gap in the stone floor and saw Calder's twisted body down below. Her bosom heaved with relief. She hauled herself up and staggered up the steps and out into the fresh air and phoned for an ambulance. She dived out in front of a passing taxi forcing it to stop, still in the bloodied black robes she wore. The driver almost wet himself with fear. She banged on the window shouting for help, beckoning them. The two shocked passengers and the driver got out and followed her cautiously into the labyrinth. On seeing the carnage, the appalled driver ran back to his car for his first aid kit whilst the others, one a nurse, attended to Paul and Ibrahim guided by Penny. They did their best to stem the flow of blood from both victim's wounds. Soon after, the place was swarming with police and paramedics. After emergency first aid, Paul and Ibrahim were stretchered off to waiting ambulances. Paul's eyes flickered momentarily, then opened. He sucked in some oxygen from the mask which covered his face. It took him a moment to come to his senses. He focused on the paramedic attending to him and heaved a sigh of relief. His conscience flooded with the traumatic events of the day like a dam bursting. He turned his head to the left and saw Penny receiving treatment on the other side of the ambulance. She had removed and discarded the hooded cape outside and sat upright, receiving a welcome whiff of oxygen also at short intervals. He was surprised to see her. He smiled weakly at her, wondering how she had been injured. As soon as she realized he was awake she fired a question at him.

"Paul, oh my God, where's Jules?"

"That's right. Ask about your friend's welfare rather than mine," Paul wheezed.

"Shut up, you big wuss. The paramedic said you'll live."

"In that case. I'll tell you."

He drew some more air into his lungs. His breathing became heavier. "She's safe," he panted. His speech became fainter. "Locked in the tunnels around the corner on Mason Street. Tell the police."

"I'm listening," DCI Armitage said, stood at the door of the ambulance.

"Detective Armitage, I thought you were on bereavement leave," he rasped.

"What? How did you know that? DS Noades was the only one I told. Officially I'm on a week's holiday."

"Noades, she had your son murdered and thrown into Birkenhead docks. I'm sorry for your loss," Penny said, grimacing from the pain in her shoulder.

532

"She what?"

"Richard Reeves forced your son to overdose. Then he dumped the body in the dock. At the behest of Noades. She did a deal with the rat bag. She wanted you out of the way for a while. I heard her confess to it. I'm sorry to tell you that, detective. She was corrupt. I heard everything. She was in with that arse-wipe Calder."

Penny sucked in more oxygen, feeling nauseous. Armitage remained in silent contemplation. Tears welled in her eyes as she fought to re-establish her professionalism. She turned as she heard someone remonstrating. It was Richard being escorted to a police van by two officers. The bereaved detective made eye contact with him, and Richard lowered his head in guilt. She glared at him until he was placed in the vehicle. Then she stopped a passing police officer.

"Officer, go down to the other tunnels in Mason Street and go and find Dr Johnson."

"She's with Tony, another hostage who's in charge of the tunnels," Paul wheezed. "Expect another dead body in there. Another of Calder's henchmen."

"Jeez, Paul, any more stiffs you haven't told us about?" Penny quipped, inadvertently forgetting Armitage's own painful loss.

"If we don't make a move, there'll be one more you can add to the body count," said the paramedic interrupting, referring to Paul.

Armitage instructed another officer to accompany the wounded duo to hospital. The ambulance set off, sirens shrilling.

533

221

Paul woke the following day after surgery. He tried to move but flinched with pain, clutching his abdomen. His bleary eyes settled on the welcome sight of Jules dozing in an armchair. After she had been notified that Miles was also dead, she wept uncontrollably. She had sat there all night and had cried herself to sleep fearing the worst for Paul, despite the positive outcome from the surgeon who operated on him.

"Jules," he called out faintly.

She opened her eyes and rushed over to him and held his hand kissing him gently. He smiled.

"How are you feeling?" she said, her reddish-purple temple and forehead showing the signs of the blow she received from Dreyfuss.

"Sore. But apart from that, fine, I think."

"What about you?"

"Apart from a lump on my head and a bit of bruising, I'm really ok."

"How's Penny?"

"In good spirits. They've patched her up. She's on the mend. Here she is now."

Penny entered, a sling on her injured arm.

"Ah, Paul. You live!"

"Just about. Penny, tell me, how did you get your injury?"

"By saving your life, you big oaf!"

"I don't understand. You weren't there. All I recall is an apparition of some sort. A mysterious figure, draped all in black, appearing out of nowhere with a pickaxe. Or was that just a dream?"

"It was me!"

"You?"

"Yes! It was me dressed in the black robes."

"What?"

"It was Penny who saved your life," Jules confirmed.

"You're not messing me around are you, you two. I know you well enough now."

"No! Penny saved your life. Aren't you going to thank her?"

"Of course. Thanks, Penny. So, how come you were in the tunnels?"

"When you contacted me and hinted that the stele was somewhere underground, I naturally thought of the Williamson Tunnels, and they fitted the timescale. I sneaked in just after a worker in a high-viz left. You were down on the bottom level of the chamber with Calder and the other guy."

"Tony," Jules said.

"That's right. I wasn't sure what was going on when I saw you with Calder. It confused me so I hid."

"So, you thought I was in on it with Calder?"

"I didn't know what to think, as I said, so I just hid. Lucky I did because when you came back up the staircase he pulled the gun on you. Then, of course, I got locked in. In the flippin' dark! I was bricking it! My phone had no signal. Neither did yours. I only had the phone torch on as a source of light. Oh my God! It's real spooky in there! I was hearing strange noises all the time."

"Go on."

"I came across a display from a movie or some drama that had been filmed in the tunnels and a creepy dummy dressed in a black cape. It freaked me out when I saw it. Then suddenly I heard the metal hatch opening. I seized a broken pickaxe for protection from the display of artefacts and I crept back to where I was hiding before. I draped the cape over me to conceal my bright clothes and I sat still amongst the display. Good job I did because it was Calder. He passed right by me. He was seething. Calling you, Paul, for everything. I was shaking so much I'm amazed he didn't notice me."

"Goodness! I don't know how you didn't wet yourself."

"Well, Jules. When you've had three kids."

"You did!" her friend laughed.

"I don't think the paramedic was too impressed when I got out of the ambulance at the hospital."

"They're used to those type of things and a lot more. Don't make me laugh. It hurts. Carry on," Paul said.

"Then when you arrived, I waited a moment to see what would happen. Then Noades showed up and again I was reassured. I became less tense and was about to reveal myself but something weird happened. I felt as if I was pinned down by some strange ethereal force and couldn't move. Then Noades turned rogue, and Calder came back up. I almost screamed as I swear to God I heard someone whispering in my ear."

"Yikes! Who or what, Penny?"

"I don't know. Like a man's voice, urging me to be strong. Then I just got this idea in my head to actually put the shroud on. I gripped the pickaxe tight. It was all like a weird dream. It was if I was mesmerized. Suddenly I felt no fear. In fact, I was very calm. Then I stole up behind Noades and hit her with the pickaxe. I don't know where the courage came from. As I said, weird! And then that horrible sod, Calder, shot me. That's all I remember before I knocked myself out."

"You'll have to tell your side of the story Paul," Jules urged.

"Another time," a doctor said entering the room with a nurse. "This man needs some rest. Visiting time's over. Besides, the police are waiting for you both outside. I've told them they'll have to wait until tomorrow to speak to Mr De Vere. There's a police guard on the door so you'll be fine."

"Ibrahim?"

"He's in intensive care. Pray for him."

Penny held out her hand to Paul. He grabbed it and squeezed it.

"Thank you Penny."

535

Jules planted a kiss on his lips affectionately. Penny's face was a picture. She was shocked. It was the first time she had seen them being intimate. Then she remembered Paul's words over the phone. 'Tell her I love her so much', which, at the time to her, seemed very odd. She stared at Jules who observed her reaction with some amusement. Then they both left the room to speak with DCI Armitage.

222

Paul sat up in bed and was watching TV footage of the Tunnels. Tony Drake was being interviewed by a reporter.

"Yes, the response has been overwhelming. Once the police have completed their enquiries the council has notified me that the Government is providing us with an army of workers to excavate the tunnels. No expense spared."

"Are you going to be involved in the process?"

"Absolutely. They are allowing my team of volunteers to be involved, given our knowledge of and expertise in the Williamson Tunnels. Dr Jules Johnson and her team will also be allowed on site, since they were responsible for solving the riddle of the great mystery bestowed upon us by the anonym who we almost certainly believe to be Mr. Joseph Williamson, the Mole Of Edge Hill."

"Let's hope the ivory tablet is located in this unique underground folly beneath the city of Liverpool."

"Indeed. Let's hope so."

One week later, the task force moved in, split between the three Williamson Tunnels sites. In the first week it was reported that three skeletons had been unearthed, located under a mound of debris in one of the freshly discovered vaults in the sprawling labyrinth of tunnels. The remains were going to be examined forthwith. During the second week of excavations, Jules, on site with Fatima and Randy and her university archaeological dig team, was notified that other tunnellers had broken into another newly found chamber, about a mile away from Paddington, extending towards Everton. Potholers brought in for the job had crawled through a narrow subterranean passage into one chamber to be met by a large, constructed brick wall and a huge carved sandstone arch above it. The following day, with Jules and her dig team present, accompanied by Paul, Penny and Edmund and the other two surviving members of Team Quest, the engineers broke through the brick wall which concealed yet another wider and larger vault which, to their surprise, revealed a huge, sturdy, bolted solid oak door at the far end. Jules was given the honour of being the first one in there, but she deigned to pass on that accolade to Paul. The door lock was breached, and Paul entered cautiously with an industrial strength light. Everyone outside waited with bated breath not knowing what to expect.

"Jules!" he called out. "It's safe to come in. My God. You've got to see this."

She followed him in tentatively and stood transfixed. There, filling the middle of the chamber was an out of character structure made of sandstone blocks. A pyramid. The pyramidion almost reaching to the ceiling of the chamber. She stood there open mouthed.

"You can all come in!" Paul shouted.

The door of the chamber creaked open, and the rest of the crew shuffled in. Everyone gasped. They all stood mesmerized. The amazed workers started to walk around the structure searching for a way in which was not apparent until one of the tunnellers noticed a square shaped stone behind the pyramid. The red dust on top of it, concealing it at first, had been disturbed by the boots of the milling workers. Two men inserted spades into the grooves and edged them around the square slab of stone. It loosened and they managed to get some leverage on it. Another two workers prised it open with their bare hands and slid the cover away revealing a set of roughly hewn stone steps. Everyone looked at Paul and so he ventured down and found himself in a small, dark subterranean passage that he could just about walk along with his six foot frame. His torch lit the way. It was only a short distance to another set of stone steps. Jules and Tony followed him with the project manager Rick, who had supervised the whole operation, in the rear. The steps, not more than six or seven led to a dead end but directly above him was another stone slab that would lead into the interior of the pyramid. Paul could not risk overdoing it with his wound so fresh, so he allowed Tony and Rick to pass him on the narrow steps to try and manoeuvre it. They could not, so Rick went back down to the other set of steps and called for assistance. Two of his engineers came along the passage with their tool kits and soon had the slab open. They courteously moved to the rear so Paul, Tony and Jules could step up first on the small set of ladders they had also requested. Paul went ahead, then Jules, then Tony. Paul helped Jules up, then held up a portable light. It illuminated the interior of the sandstone pyramid. They gasped. They walked forward a few paces to the centre of the pyramid and there, mounted on a granite pedestal, was the sought-after ivory tablet inscribed with its foreboding portend. The three stood gaping at the stele and then each other.

Jules hugged Paul carefully. He kissed her and slapped Tony on the back. Rick, the project manager came up out of the hatch with his two assistants and they high fived each other. Jules went over to the tablet and pulled out a small brush from her backpack, one she used in the field, and she gently cleared away the dust from the revered stele.

"There's dozens of people out there itching to see this. We'd best get out and let them see it otherwise we'll be here all night. Tony, you should charge a quid on the doors."

Tony laughed.

"Too right Jules. I'll stay here and make sure everyone gets a quick glimpse then I'll send them back out."

Jules moved away from the tablet, but her attention was drawn to something on the floor of the pyramid where her boots had disturbed the grains of sandstone in front of the stele. She knelt down.

"Hold it a second. I've just noticed something else."

She brushed away the dust to reveal an inscription. She read it and backed away in shock.

"No way!" she gasped. "Paul! You'd best take a look at this!"

"What's up?"

538

Paul registered the surprise on her face and looked down at the inscribed slab.

"What the -"

He carefully knelt down and brushed away more of the red dust, then read aloud the words.

"Dedicated to the memory of two courageous soldiers across the divide, Seamus O'Rourke and Pierre Cousseau. Signed, Joseph Williamson. The Mole of Edge Hill, 1829."

Paul stared at the tribute in amazement, dumb-founded.

"What's up?" Rick inquired.

"Pierre Cousseau. That's my great, great, great, great-grandfather."

"And mine too," Jules said swallowing hard. "Seamus O'Rourke."

"What?" Tony said disbelievingly. "Both. Surely not!"

Paul and Jules nodded simultaneously and left without saying a word, followed by Rick and the engineers. They filed back down the passageway and up the other set of steps to be greeted by a barrage of questions from all present.

Paul and Jules, in their reverie, ignored them all.

"Go and see for yourself," Rick said.

"Ten at a time. Just a quick peek and back. All I'll say is that, for all our sakes, it's there!"

The chamber erupted in cheers.

223

Six weeks later, Jules found herself on the edge of the Egyptian desert, on the Giza plateau staring up at the Great Pyramid of Khufu in the sweltering heat surrounded by the world's leaders and representatives of every apostolic denomination, in a show of universal solidarity. Even the Grailiens were represented, their leader, thankfully fully clothed. At her left hand side was Paul, his immediate future secured by all the lucrative media offers and contracts thrown his way, not to mention the gifts that had poured in once it was known that he had previously been homeless. Jules smiled at him then glanced admiringly at the diamond encrusted engagement ring on her finger. To her right was Penny, then Fatima, Randy, Janet the cleaner, Edmund, Tony Drake and Ibrahim Shaqtar, chosen to represent the Muslim Council of Great Britain on account of his bravery. Even Rick was there. The invited guests chatted amongst themselves whilst they waited for the ceremony to begin.

"Williamson's motives for keeping the tablet hidden away. Well, we now know his life was in danger. That's probably a good reason for keeping it hidden," Tony surmised.

"But Champollion had pretty much laid the groundwork for deciphering hieroglyphs in 1824," Randy responded in conversation with him. "So why didn't Joseph Williamson declare the stele to anyone?"

"Don't forget," Jules interrupted, "the work that Champollion and other scholars like Thomas Young did was speculative at most. Arguments, debates, and theories abounded. There were still many questions to answer. It was a slow, lingering process. Then you had the ongoing antagonism between France and Britain which impeded progress to some extent."

"You can also throw into the mix the stance of the Catholic Church," Fatima said. "The clergy was worried about the antiquity of Egyptian civilisation. They were concerned that it was possibly older than their biblical timeline which stood at approximately 6,000 years and that anything written in hieroglyphs might contradict the greatest story ever told."

"Maybe those remains found in the Tunnels played a significant part in the saga of the tablet," Penny added. "The individuals involved all seemed to die violent deaths judging by their injuries according to the post-mortem results. For some reason Joseph Williamson must have realised that the stele was perhaps a sacred, mystical artefact. Something to fear. Something to respect and perhaps protect."

"Something that evinced a powerful aura," Randy proffered. "Something that had much more worth than its monetary value. Which, of course, turned out to be true. Fate, therefore, I reckon, played a big part in his reasoning."

"That's why he had it entombed within a pyramid," Edmund stated. "A wise, intuitive man. He became its keeper. Its guardian. Speaking of pyramids."

They all held hands as the Egyptian Minister of Antiquities began his address to the legion of dignitaries and the multitude of onlookers splayed across the barren stretch of hallowed ground. Billions watched as the event was screened to every part of the world. His speech was followed by short addresses from leaders of the three main faiths, Christian, Muslim and Hindu and the Heads of State of France, Great Britain and Egypt.

The Minister paid tribute to Team Quest and read out the names of those who had perished in the search for the tablet.

"Tom Yates, Simon Kane, Lydia Longfellow, Miles Rowson."

"What about Jimmy?" Jules murmured. "We forgot about poor old Jimmy."

"And we should have remembered Viren, Stuart and Clare," Randy whispered. "Miriam too."

The survivors squeezed each other's hands as each name was heard, some of them fighting back the tears. After hearing the last short speech from the British Prime Minister, the Minister of Antiquities asked the Egyptian President to step forward again. Then he made a request for someone from Team Quest to step up on the podium. Fatima obliged, as was previously arranged, having been born in the country. She accompanied the President along a long red carpet flanked by a ceremonial guard of honour. Behind them was a beautiful purpose-built glittering gold leaf carriage pulled by six white caparisoned Arabian horses controlled by two coachmen splendidly attired in Ancient Egyptian garb. A small marble pyramid embellished with a gold leaf capstone sat atop it, carrying the sacred ivory tablet securely within it. The diminutive pyramid was being transported towards the Great Pyramid. When the procession came to a halt, soldiers of the presidential guard carefully lifted the marble and gold polyhedron shaped object off the carriage and marched it theatrically to the entrance of the Great Pyramid, in great pomp and circumstance. They disappeared into the interior of the ancient tomb followed by the President and Fatima and other dignitaries. The lines of guests waited, the chatter starting up again. Jules heard a screech. She looked up and spied a white-tailed eagle. Momentarily she and Paul were bathed in the shadow of the eagle as it soared gracefully above them. They watched it circling around in the azure blue sky. It climbed to the height of the Great Pyramid of Khufu and landed on its summit, continuing to screech. After a few moments they turned their attention to their friends again. Twenty minutes later the entourage emerged into the dazzling sunshine to great applause and cheering. Jules noticed the eagle fly away. The fate of mankind had been secured, at least, for the time being. It was time for people around the world to celebrate, but in the back of everyone's mind was the foreboding presage of a Second Coming, or perhaps, Fourth or Fifth, albeit not as everyone had envisaged, except, of course, for the Grailiens amongst them.

Steps were already in place to transform humankind's immensely damaging and uncaring footprint on planet Earth. A summit by all the world's leaders was to take place in Dubai two weeks later. People's attitudes and opinions in the weeks leading up to the return of the stele to Egypt had markedly changed. Brazil had immediately stopped its outlandish and shameful practice of burning the rainforests. Madagascar had stopped harassing its endangered orangutans and had imposed a moratorium on all its logging activities. China had banned all unregulated wet and wildlife markets. The US was committed to phasing out oil production within the next few years and had proscribed synthetic pesticides forthwith. Indonesia had started to clean its polluted waterways of plastic rubbish. The use of dredging nets was banned worldwide. The Faroe Isles, Japan, and Norway vowed to end their distasteful practice of slaughtering whales and dolphins. Even Britain's streets seemed clearer of litter. And the lakes, rivers and shores, poisoned by mindless, recurrent dumping of untreated sewage by greed-driven, callous privatized water companies, were to be restored post-haste to a pristine condition. A purge of politicians, proprietors and executives responsible for the disastrous contamination had swiftly taken place. Atonement for man's recklessness and neglect of planet Earth, with Judgement Day looming in the not so distant future, had begun in all earnest.

Epilogue

Life returned to some sort of normal for Dr Jules Pollyanna Johnson and her companions, although they all struggled to come to terms with the ultimately tragic events surrounding the quest for the stele and, like everyone else, became apprehensive about the future. Many people questioned their life choices. The Williamson Tunnels were swamped with visitors. It became the number one tourist attraction in the U.K. People were happy to pay to see them and the sandstone pyramid located within them. Fatima and Randy had taken a party of students down there one day when the tours were not operating. Jules had just returned to the new riverside apartment she shared with Paul when her mobile rang. It was Randy.

"Hi Jules. Guess what? You won't believe this. Fatima was showing the students the memorial to your ancestor and Paul's in the pyramid. One of the students opened his rucksack to grab a pen and jotter out and a flask of coffee fell out and hit the memorial slab."

"Oh dear."

"Nothing was damaged Jules, but Fatima reckoned there was a hollow underneath the stone. She sought Tony's permission to remove the slab and she was right. There was a void under it. She found something very interesting."

"Wow! What was it?"

"A gold chalice. A gold plate embossed with a cavalier on it. And a diamond encrusted necklace would you believe!"

"Good grief! Treasure?"

"Yep. We consulted Tony. He was gobsmacked, as we were. Straight away he reckoned that it was part of Prince Rupert's treasure."

"Prince Rupert?"

"The Royalist cavalry commander in the English Civil War. Apparently, he hid his treasure during the siege of Liverpool in 1644 but allegedly when he went to recover it, it had all disappeared!"

"So, are you saying that Joseph Williamson, during his excavations located Prince Rupert's treasure?"

"Yes, I'm pretty much inferring that."

"Well, there's not much of it by the sounds of it. Was there anything else in the hollow?"

"There was, but nothing of value. Well, strictly speaking I might be wrong there. We found another leather cylinder."

"No way!"

"I'm not kidding."

"Paul!" Jules screeched.

"What? I'm busy, cooking dinner!"

"Come here for a second." She placed the mobile on speakerphone. Paul arrived. "What was in the leather tube Randy?"

Paul's eyes rolled.

"An illustration, as you probably guessed. One Tony reckons will lead to the remainder or bulk of Prince Rupert's treasure that Joseph Williamson has hidden somewhere or left where he found it."

"Oh my gosh!"

"Randy, hi, it's Paul. I've only caught the tail-end of this. I presume another pursuit for Team Quest is on the cards. Go on, I also presume it's another animal illustration. Tell us then. What is it?"

"It's a -"

Merseyside People and Places

Captain Noel Godfrey Chavasse, VC and Bar, MC - doctor, British Army officer and Olympic athlete. Had undertaken further medical studies at Liverpool University after studying at Oxford. Lived in Oxford up until the age of six and resided in Liverpool thereafter. Died of wounds sustained at Passchendaele, August 1917, the most highly decorated British officer of WWI.

The Alfred Waterhouse designed Victoria Building - was built in 1892 and was formerly part of the University of Liverpool, its red brick spawning the original concept of the 'red brick university'.

Metropolitan Cathedral of Christ the King - the cavernous Edward Lutyens's designed catholic cathedral crypt was the only part of the building that was ever intended, since the original design had proved to be too costly. The planned dome's diameter would have exceeded that of St Peter's Basilica in Vatican City.

Cammell Lairds - the Sir David Attenborough research ship was constructed in the yards adding to the impressive portfolio of ships built over the years on the banks of the Mersey including Royal Navy vessels like HMS Ark Royal, the first British designed aircraft carrier and HMS Conqueror, the nuclear submarine. The passenger liner the Mauretania and David Livingstone's steam launch the Ma-Robert were also built there along with the Confederate American Civil War ship the CSS Alabama. During WWII two hundred vessels alone were built in the yards to support the war effort.

Bromborough, on the Wirral - The possible location of the highly significant Battle of Brunanburh that occurred in 937AD between the Anglo-Saxon forces of King Aethelstan and the Viking-Celtic-Norse alliance led by Celtic King Constantine and Ireland's Viking leader Anlaf Guthfrithson. The battle was instrumental in uniting Wessex and Mercia, thus creating one single and united entity - the nation of England.

Rodney Street, Liverpool - former Prime Minister William Ewart Gladstone was born at number 62. The author of The Cruel Sea, Nicholas Monsarrat was also born on the street along with poet Arthur Hugh Clough and Brian Epstein, the manager of the Beatles.

William Henry Quilliam - a Victorian white English convert to Islam, opened the first ever mosque in Britain, in 1887 on Brougham Terrace, in the city of Liverpool.

William Roscoe (1753-1831) - poet, abolitionist, banker, lawyer and Member of Parliament. Also respected as a historian, botanist, art collector and writer. Born in Liverpool.

Mother Redcaps - tavern ran by Poll Jones in the late 1700s/early 1800s. It stood on the banks of the Mersey near Egremont, Wirral.

Joseph Williamson - the Mole of Edge Hill. Born in 1769 in Barnsley, died 1840 in Liverpool. Businessman, property owner and philanthropist. Contact The Friends of Williamson's Tunnels (FoWT) for more information or The Joseph Williamson Society and Heritage Centre. www.williamsontunnels.com (There are two separate organisations for the tunnels with two separate websites.)

Fort Perch Rock - a Grade II listed sandstone fort built at the mouth of the River Mersey to protect the Port of Liverpool in the 1820s. The fort is now open after a period of closure. It houses a café and escape rooms. Information at fortperchrock.org.uk and escapethefort.co.uk

Knowsley Hall - a stately home near Liverpool. The ancestral home of the Stanley family, the Earls of Derby, which has, housed within its extensive parkland, Knowsley Safari Park. The Hall is a venue for corporate events, conferences and weddings. Information at knowsley.com

Croxteth Hall and Country Park - once the stately home of the Molyneux's, the Earls of Sefton. A venue for wedding, events, conferences and educational tours. Information at croxteth-hall.co.uk

Speke Hall - a 16th century timber framed courtyard house with gardens and woodland owned by the National Trust.
Information at spekehall@nationaltrust.org.uk

Author's Note

The Shadow of The Eagle is a self-published 'lockdown' novel, the extended hiatus from the usual daily rigours of work, providing me with the opportunity to write a story. A lengthy one at that. One which perhaps would not have been written in normal circumstances.

My interest in history and love for my home city were instrumental in placing the denouement of the story in Liverpool. Having visited the Williamson Tunnels on several occasions and heard about the construction of the labyrinth by returning Napoleonic era British soldiers it gave me the impetus to write *The Shadow of The Eagle.* I read a fabulous historical account of Napoleon's venture into Egypt: *'Napoleon In Egypt'* by Paul Strathern (Vintage Books), which gave me the historical background to the Egyptian campaign (1798-1801), seen through the eyes of fictional characters, French soldier Sergeant Pierre Cousseau, the erudite French savant Antoine Demeraux and British soldier Seamus O'Rourke.

For more information on the extraordinary life of real life character Admiral Sir Sidney Smith, I read *'A Thirst for Glory: The Life of Admiral Sir Sidney Smith'* by Tom Pocock.

Other local historical information was gleaned from the book *Recollections of Old Liverpool* by James Stonehouse or provided by Liverpool Central Library's Research Team and, of course, the internet. Thanks to all. Finally, a special thank you should be reserved for all the dedicated volunteers who have excavated and promoted the Williamson Tunnels.

Pete Davie

About the Author

Pete Davie is from Liverpool. He lives on the Wirral. Pete has written and self-published three children's story books. This is his first attempt at writing a novel.

Email: pdavie@sky.com

Printed in Great Britain
by Amazon